MORRIS AUTOMATED INFORMATION NETWORK

0 1029 0249830 6

D0463977

WITHDRAWN

FICTION   Forbath, Peter.
FORBATH
          Lord of the Kongo.

DATE			

Parsippany-Troy Hills Public Library
Parsippany Branch
292 Parsippany Road
Parsippany, N.J. 07054

NOV 26 1996   BAKER & TAYLOR

BOOKS BY PETER FORBATH

Lord of the Kongo
The Last Hero
Honorable Men
(with William Colby)
The River Congo
Seven Seasons

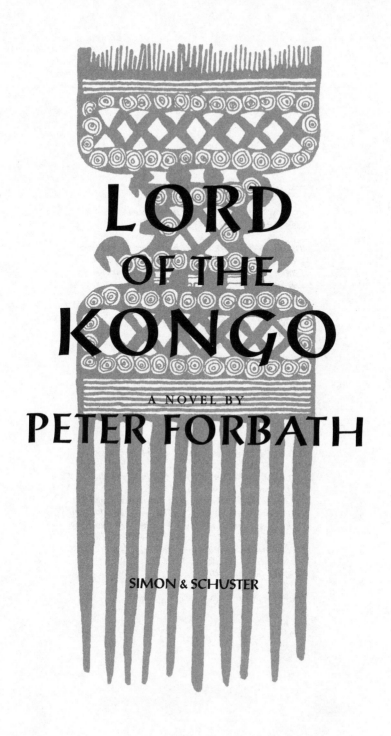

LORD
OF THE
KONGO

A NOVEL BY

PETER FORBATH

SIMON & SCHUSTER

SIMON & SCHUSTER
Rockefeller Center
1230 Avenue of the Americas
New York, NY 10020

This book is a work of fiction. Names, characters,
places, and incidents either are products of the
author's imagination or are used fictitiously. Any
resemblance to actual events or locales or persons,
living or dead, is entirely coincidental.

Copyright © 1996 by Peter Forbath
All rights reserved,
including the right of reproduction
in whole or in part in any form.
SIMON & SCHUSTER and colophon are
registered trademarks of Simon & Schuster Inc.
Designed by Edith Fowler
Manufactured in the United States of America

10   9   8   7   6   5   4   3   2   1

Library of Congress Cataloging-in-Publication Data
Forbath, Peter.
  Lord of the Kongo : a novel / by Peter Forbath.
    p.   cm.
    1. Africa—Discovery and exploration—Portuguese
—Fiction. 2. Portugal—Colonies—Africa—Fiction.
3. Kongo (African people)—Fiction. 4. Kongo King-
dom—History—Fiction. 5. Africa—Race relations
—Fiction 6. Friendship—Africa—Fiction. 7. Young
men—Africa—Fiction. I. Title.
PS3556.065L67   1996
813'.54—dc20   96-16057 CIP
ISBN 0-684-80951-6

FOR MISSY,
WHO SAW ME THROUGH THE FOREST.

Author's Note

The story told in this novel is true.
Its main characters and central
events have been taken from the
sixteenth-century chronicles of Portuguese sea captains, royal scribes
and missionary priests.

P.F.

THE KINGDOM
OF BIAFRA

Cape
Ste. Catherine

N.

The
Falls

Matadi

Mpinda
(Santo António
do Zaire)

Nzere (Zaire) R.

Mbanza Kongo
(São Salvador)

ETHIOPIAN
OCEAN

KINGDOM
of the
KONGO

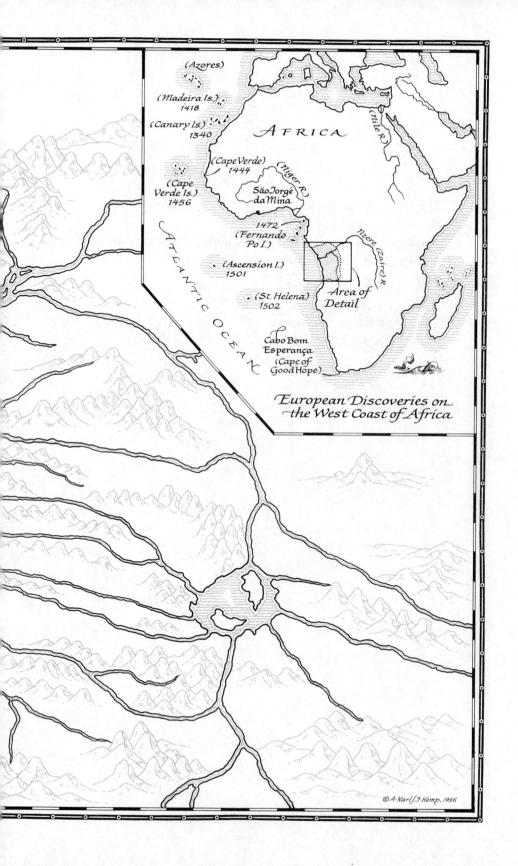

(Azores)

(Madeira Is.)
1418

(Canary Is.)
1340

AFRICA

(Cape Verde)
1444

(Niger R.)

São Jorgé
da Mina

1472
(Fernando
Po I.)

(Cape
Verde Is.)
1456

(Ascension I.)
1501

(St. Helena)
1502

Nzere (Zaire) R.

Area of
Detail

Cabo Bom
Esperança
(Cape of
Good Hope)

ATLANTIC OCEAN

(Nile R.)

European Discoveries on
the West Coast of Africa

© A. Karl / J. Kemp, 1996

There lyes of Kongo the wide-spreading Realm,
By us converted to Christ's Law;
Through which long Zaire glides with crystal stream,
A river the Ancients never saw.

> *Canto V, Stanza 13*
> *THE LUSIADS*
> *by Luis de Camões*
> *1524?–1580*

ONE

1482

I

"SAFE HAVEN to larboard." The shout came from the lookout in the crow's nest atop the *Leonor*'s mainmast. "Safe haven, safe harbor, three points to larboard."

Gil Eanes, the captain's page, a fifteen-year-old beardless boy with light blue eyes and long blond hair, carrying a tray of dirty pewter mugs and plates up the companionway from the sterncastle cabins, stopped to have a look. He couldn't see anything. The *Leonor,* a four-masted, 150-ton-burthen *caravela de armada,* beating to windward on a starboard tack, was standing very nearly two leagues offshore and making better than five knots due south under full sail. And, besides, it was midday when a hot, soupy haze, glittering harshly in the pitiless blaze of the African sun, veiled the view of the coast. He looked around to the quarterdeck. The ship's pilot, José Vizinho, a wiry Jew with windswept beard, was peering landward through a long brass spyglass.

They were then ninety-three days out of Faro (their home port in Portugal's Algarve), twenty-one days out of São Jorgé da Mina (the last European settlement on the West African coast at the time) and six days from Cape Ste. Catherine (until then the most southerly landfall ever made on that coast by a European vessel), seeking, on the orders of their king, João II, a sea route around the southern tip of Africa into the Indian Ocean. It was the twelfth of August, 1482 (according to the Julian calendar), and theirs was not the first ship to attempt this feat. For more than sixty years, ever since the Infante Dom Henriqué (who would be remembered through the ages as Prince Henry the Navigator) launched the audacious enterprise, Portuguese ships had been inching down the Atlantic coast of Africa in hope of one day finding a way around the fabled *Prassum Promontorium* and breaking into Islam's monopoly of the fabulous spice and silk trade with Calicut and Far Cathay.

"Safe haven, safe harbor, three points to larboard, southeast by south. A large bay."

The pilot Vizinho made the sighting. He lowered his spyglass and called a change of course down through the conning hatch at his feet to the helmsman at the tiller in the steerage room below the quarterdeck. Then he shouted to the bosun, who, using his pipe whistle and bellowing voice, set a gang of seamen to heaving about the heavy diagonal yard of the big lateen sail of the mizzenmast, while other hands were sent scrambling up the shrouds of the mainmast to strike the topsail. At the same time, the first mate, Nuno Gonçalves, hurried forward into the bow to uncoil the chain of the lead. This flurry of activity brought the ship's captain-general, Diogo Cão, topside.

Gil Eanes looked landward again and this time, squinting hard through the harsh, shimmering glare, he also made the sighting. During the six days from Cape Ste. Catherine, the coastline had been bounded by red-clay cliffs, and its narrow, sandy beach had sloped off so gradually into the sea from the foot of those cliffs that the offshore waters had been dangerously shoal sometimes as far as five leagues out. Here, however, the cliffs abruptly fell away and, from the now flat, low-lying coastline, two spits of land arced out into the ocean like the opposing jaws of a giant crab's claw, enclosing what appeared to be a natural, deep-water harbor at least six leagues across.

Gil looked back up to the quarterdeck. Diogo Cão, short, bigshouldered, barrel-chested, with enormously bushy black eyebrows and beard and a swarthy, pockmarked complexion, had taken the spyglass from the pilot and was studying the shore as the *Leonor* swung her head three points to larboard, course 146 degrees, and, closehauled, beating now in a side wind, made for the big bay. Suspecting that the captain-general intended to make a landfall there, Gil dashed forward into the forecastle to get rid of his tray of dirty dishes.

The pilot Vizinho shot the sun with his astrolabe, consulted his table of declinations and chalked his findings on the slate behind the compass binnacle. They were at roughly six degrees of latitude south of the equator. The mate Gonçalves, in the chains in the bow, began heaving the hundred-fathom dipsy lead. But even after closing the shore for nearly an hour (the time it took for Gil to finish his chores in the forecastle and dash back out on deck), they still were in deep water. Apparently, the sand shelving they had encountered farther north along the cliff-bound shore also ended with the cliffs. But still something wasn't quite right. The ship's bow was bucking peculiarly as if she were sailing into a seaward current, a current that seemed to grow stronger the closer she approached the inlet to the bay. And, what was more, as she approached the inlet to the bay, the ocean around her steadily changed color, taking on a darker and darker muddy brown hue.

Cão raised the spyglass to his eye again. Vizinho called another course correction down to the helmsman at the tiller. Gonçalves continued heaving the lead, still finding no bottom. Gil wiggled up on the foredeck beneath the spritsail beside Gonçalves. And from that spot, he may have been the first to see it: a clump of sod from which a tangle of blue hyacinth and green shrubbery grew, just like a miniature island except that this island was floating out toward the ship on the broad carpet of muddy brown water flowing out from the bay. But before he could call it to Gonçalves's attention, Gonçalves saw it for himself and then saw several more and shouted the news aft to the bosun, who relayed it up to Cão on the quarterdeck.

"What is it, Dom Nuno?" Gil asked.

"A river."

"A river?"

"Aye, little son, a river of very great power, of greater power than I have ever seen. Here. Give me your hand." The first mate had reeled in the lead and now let the water dripping from it form a muddy puddle in Gil's palm. "Taste it."

Gil brought his palm to his mouth.

"Well?"

"It is not salt, Dom Nuno. It is sweet."

"Aye, sweet water. River water. And what a river it must be that it pours its water this far out to sea. There, that is the river itself." Gonçalves pointed at the broad stripe of mud-colored ocean flowing out from the bay, carrying with it scores of the tiny floating islands. "That is the river pouring into the sea and bringing with it the earth of its bottom and pieces of the banks between which it has run. Look how powerful it is. Look how we must fight against it. Look how the *Leonor* butts her head against its current."

"But the bay?"

"It is not a bay, little son. It is the mouth of this powerful river." Gonçalves resumed casting the lead and taking the soundings. And then at last he hit bottom and called out, "By the mark, ninety fathoms." And then: "By the mark, eighty fathoms."

Closing an uncharted shore, with an unknown and immensely powerful river to deal with into the bargain, required very fine seamanship indeed. For who could know how the tides ran here or where the reefs and shoals might lie that could bring the *Leonor* to grief? And who could tell what winds might blow off the land to confound and confuse the sea breeze now falling off on the quarter? The point of the southerly spit of land that arced out into the ocean and formed the bottom half of the inlet emerged from the glaring haze to show itself to be a forested headland above a boulder-strewn beach on which the ocean broke in spumes of spray colored muddy yellow by the river's waters. Shortening sail to reduce speed but not enough to lose the battle against the river's always stronger current, catching a land breeze and using it to sail a while on a close reach, then jogging off, always mindful of his first mate's soundings as the ocean shallowed under him, Cão brought the *Leonor* gracefully around the headland and entered what looked like a great bay but was in fact the mouth of a great river.

In the lee of the headland, the south bank of the river's mouth sloped up from its rocky beach into a dense forest of palms and mangroves and giant ferns. It was now well on into the afternoon, the sun far to the west, and the headland cast a cool blue shadow a half-league or more out onto the water. Cão sailed into the shadow. He still had a reassuring depth of ocean beneath his keel. Gonçalves was now calling thirty fathoms, twenty-five, twenty. When he called fifteen, the *Leonor* was about a thousand yards from the bank and Cão had the helmsman swing her due east, upriver, straight into the current.

It was slow going. The *Leonor* was now sailing under only her spritsail and her much-shortened, lateen-rigged foresail—the lateen-rigged mizzen and square-rigged main course were furled—and Cão had to make judicious use of both the fast-dropping sea breeze and a freshening afternoon land breeze. They were sailing close enough along the south bank on their starboard to hear the cawing of parrots and the racketing of monkeys in the trees of the forest there and to see egrets and heron and other long-legged water birds standing among the rocks in the muddy wash at the bank's edge and also, from time to time, half-submerged crocodiles watching them pass with bulging eyes, while overhead fish eagles and gulls swooped and soared and cried. As yet, though, there was no sign of human life.

Cão continued creeping upriver for another two hours and then, with the approach of dusk and the lengthening of the shadows, he had the helmsman turn the *Leonor* toward shore—there were still nearly ten fathoms beneath her—and nose her into a backwater cove. Here he struck sail and dropped anchor. After the splash of the anchor, a soft, dusky silence fell on the ship, a silence made especially lovely by the sounds of birds singing and monkeys chattering and the rustling of the fronds of palm trees and the water slapping against the *Leonor*'s hull. All of the ship's company, some fifty men, was topside now, observing the silence, including the two Africans aboard. They were Portuguese-speaking Ashanti from the Gold Coast who had been taken aboard at São Jorgé da Mina to act as interpreters, chunky, muscular men of a startling blue-black color, their heads shaved and their cheekbones tattooed and carrying spears and buffalo-hide shields. They too peered in silence into the gathering shadows of the forest on the bank of this unknown river in this never-before-seen land. It was cooler now and much less humid in the freshening breeze blowing off the land, and great galleons of clouds were gathering in the sky, painted in the pastel shades of the setting sun.

The *ampolletta* or half-hour sand glass beside the binnacle on the quarterdeck was turned and the ship's bell rung, and the second dog watch of the afternoon was set. The reckonings that the previous watch had chalked on the slate behind the binnacle were transferred to the log and the slate wiped clean. Nuno Gonçalves went up on the quarterdeck to take his station as officer of the new watch. The ship's chaplain, Father Sebastião, an old, tonsured, gray-bearded Franciscan in a rough brown cassock and wide-brimmed hat, his rosary and crucifix wound round his waist, went up with him to give the blessing. And since the captain-general and pilot remained on the quarterdeck, the *Leonor*'s other principal officer, the master-at-arms, Fernão Tristão, who commanded the ship's contingent of halberdiers, crossbowmen, cannoneers and arquebus-armed soldiers, went up to join them. Cão had the two Ashanti interpreters come up as well.

Ordinarily, those of the crew not on this watch would now collect their supper from the bosun's mate at the cook box under the forecastle overhang (biscuit, cheese, salt pork, a clove of garlic, a tankard of Madeira wine) and retire to their favorite corners on the main deck below—only the officers had cabins with bunks in the sterncastle—to eat, to wash clothing and repair gear, to polish armor and oil armaments, to whittle or fish or simply gossip and swap yarns. But on this evening, even they remained topside on the open spar deck, clustering in the ship's waist, eager to overhear what the captain-general was saying to his officers and the Ashanti. For they were well aware that they had now voyaged farther south into the Atlantic than any European had ever voyaged before and had reached a land no European had ever seen before. Gil was among them even though he was on the next watch, the first night watch, and therefore was risking missing out on his supper as a result.

"What do you make of the situation, José?" Cão asked the pilot. "Shall we try our luck ashore? At least two hours of daylight remain to us."

Vizinho shook his head. "If any Negroes are about, my lord Captain, we do not see them only because they do not wish us to see them. They are hiding. And if they are hiding, we would never find them no matter how many hours of daylight remain to us."

"The pilot is right, my lord Captain," the master-at-arms said. "And, besides, who is to say Negroes live in this region at all?"

"Oh, Negroes live in this region, Fernão, of that you can be sure.

This is a great river, perhaps the greatest in all Creation by the look of it. And people always live on the shores of great rivers."

"That is true, my lord Captain," Vizinho said. "But it would be best to let them show themselves to us in their own good time. If we lie quietly at anchor here for a while and they see they have nothing to fear from us, their curiosity will overcome them and they will show themselves to us of their own accord. You must remember, they have never seen a ship like ours before, nor men with our white faces."

"Very well, we will wait the night through and see what morning brings. Page."

"My lord Captain."

"I will have my supper now."

"Aye, my lord."

By the time Gil finished serving the captain-general—he ate in his big cabin on the starboard side of the sterncastle, just aft of the steerage and magazine, the mast of the mizzen stepped in the center of it, with those of his officers not on watch, and, except for a few petty luxuries such as raisins and figs and jam, ate very much the same fare as his sailors—by the time Gil was done serving and clearing up after the officers, he had to go straight to the quarterdeck to report for duty on the first night watch.

This watch always began with a call of all hands to evening prayers. While Gil lit the binnacle lamp, Father Sebastião led the ship's company in reciting the Pater Noster and Credo and then in a lusty if musically ragged singing of Salve Regina. After this, the officers and men dispersed and Gil remained on the quarterdeck with the master-at-arms, Fernão Tristão, who was officer of this watch.

It was fully dark by now. The sun had dropped like a stone into the ocean on the western horizon while Gil was still in the captain-general's cabin, and when he came out, the last of its light was gone from the land and the sea and the sky. No moon had yet risen but it wouldn't have mattered if one had since the clouds that had begun gathering earlier in the evening now completely shut out the stars and sky. It was a pitch black night. It was difficult even to make out the outline of the trees on shore. And it was also a dead quiet night, except for the squawks and squeals of the birds and monkeys of the forest; the murmuring of the ship's crewmen; the creaking of her timbers; the slapping of the river against her hull as the tide came in.

The slapping of the river; Gil had trouble keeping in mind that they were anchored in the mouth of a river, not in a bay of the sea. But that it *was* a river apparently was very important. All the conversation at the captain-general's table at supper had been about that. *Rio poderoso* was how Cão had referred to it, and all had agreed that it was the largest, most powerful river any of them had ever seen.

Gil had no way of judging this but he knew that, in the more than sixty years that Portuguese vessels had been sailing down the west coast of Africa, many great rivers had been discovered—the Rio de Ouro, the Senegal and Gambia, the Volta and Benin, the Oil rivers that formed the delta of the Niger—and he knew that the captain-general, if not the others, had seen them all. So it was no small thing when the captain-general said that this river, by the size of its mouth and the strength of its current and the volume of water it discharged into the sea, might very well be the largest and most powerful in the world. And the idea clearly excited him. For who could say where such a great river came from and where it might lead? Perhaps one could sail upon it from here on the Atlantic coast of Africa clear across the continent to the Indian Ocean coast on the other side.

"Stop dreaming, boy," Fernão Tristão said. "Turn the glass. Ring the bell."

"At once, sir marshal." Gil hastened to turn the half-hour sand glass and signal that he had done so by ringing the ship's bell. All hands on watch listened for and counted the bells to know how much longer it would be before they were relieved by the second night watch, the graveyard watch. Eight bells would signal the end of the watch. Gil rang the ship's bell twice.

"Sir marshal?"

"Aye?" Tristão was a taller man than the captain-general, with a far more elegantly trimmed beard and, unlike the captain-general, who dressed as a common seaman, wore far more elegant clothes.

"Do you believe this river will take us to the Indies, sir marshal?"

"We shall see, boy. We shall see."

"How shall we see?"

"We shall sail up the river and see where it takes us. That's how we shall see."

When the watch was relieved at midnight, Gil went forward to the cook box and scrounged some hardtack, cheese and wine from the bosun's mate to make up for his missed supper and took them below to his corner on the main deck. All hands off-duty were curled up in their blankets there asleep except for the two Ashanti. They sat with their backs against the bulwarks, their knees drawn up to their chins, talking to each other softly in their own language. While Gil ate his supper, he watched them in the dim, swaying light of the oil lanterns hanging from the beams of the spar deck overhead and tried to make out what they were saying. He liked the sound of their language and had the notion that he could learn it just by listening hard enough and carefully studying the different gestures and facial expressions they made as they spoke. After a few minutes, they broke off and looked at him. He smiled. They smiled back.

"Do you know we have come into the mouth of a river, not a bay?" he asked.

They nodded.

"Do you know this river?" It probably was a stupid question. After all, these men were now hundreds of leagues from their homes in São Jorgé da Mina. But still, seeing how the captain-general and the others believed it might be the greatest river in the world, it was possible the Ashanti had at least heard of it. "Have you heard tell of it? A great and powerful river like this, you must have heard travelers tell of it."

Segou, the older of the two, replied. "No, I have never heard any traveler tell of so great and powerful a river as this."

"Nor have I," Goree, the younger Ashanti, put in.

"No, we do not know this river, little son. Nor do we know the people who live beside it. We saw them today, watching us from the forest, and we saw that they are a people very different from our people, the Ashanti people."

THE BOWSPRIT lookout on the graveyard watch was the first (apart from the two Ashanti) to see them. He raised the alarm just before the end of the watch while it was still quite dark. All hands went topside in a hurry. By the time Gil got up to the quarterdeck, José Vizinho, the officer of the graveyard watch, had gone forward into the bow, and the bowsprit lookout was gesturing excitedly upriver. Cão

and Gonçalves with the two Ashanti were on the quarterdeck looking in that direction while the master-at-arms was assembling his soldiers in the ship's waist. He was wearing a skirted vest of chainmail
under his leather surcoat, a cutlass and a steel helmet with a gracefully curved brim called a *salade,* and his soldiers were similarly armored and armed, five with crossbows, five with halberds and five
with arquebus firearms. Their threatening appearance markedly in-
creased the tense excitement among the crew, many of whom had
armed themselves with knives and marlinspikes and belaying pins
and broom handles and anything else that had come quickly to hand.
Father Sebastião stood in their midst, his eyes closed, his hands
clasped in prayer.

"Look there, my lord Captain," Gonçalves suddenly said, pointing
upriver. "They are there."

At the same moment, Vizinho shouted from the foredeck and
also pointed upriver. Several shadowy shapes, which certainly must
have been people if they weren't man-sized apes, were gathered on
the rocky bank at the eastern end of the cove in which the *Leonor*
was anchored. It was difficult to see what they looked like or even
how many there were in this last of the night's inky darkness. Those
who could be seen at all were the ones who had come right down to
the river's edge, perhaps a dozen or so, but there might be many
more in the still deeper darkness of the forested shore behind them.

"Master-at-arms."

"Aye, my lord Captain?"

"Not one of your soldiers is to take action until he hears the
command from my lips."

"It will be exactly as you wish, my lord Captain."

"Bosun. All hands to their stations."

"Aye, my lord Captain."

"Can you see them any better than I can, Nuno?"

"I don't think so," Gonçalves answered.

"And you, Segou?"

"There are eighteen with the canoes and—"

"Canoes?"

Cão and Gonçalves said this almost simultaneously and strained
even harder to see. The darkness was perceptibly thinning but actu-

ally it was sound rather than sight, the sound of soft splashing in the river, that revealed the presence of the canoes.

". . . and thirteen others on the shore," Segou went on. "In the trees, there are perhaps twenty more but they are women and children, my lord."

"Good, Segou. Very good. And those in the canoes, are they coming toward us?"

"Not yet, my lord. I do not believe they see us any better than we see them and are waiting for daylight."

"Are they armed?"

"They have bows and quivers of arrows on their backs. They will unsling them if they intend to use them."

Cão smiled at that. "And you will warn us if they do."

Segou looked at Cão and also smiled.

Gil, at this point, having kept an eye on the *ampolletta,* turned the sand glass but when he moved to ring the ship's bell, Cão put up a restraining hand. Evidently, he felt any strange sound from the ship might scare the Negroes off or provoke them to fight.

The electric tension aboard the ship was the tension of excited anticipation, not of fear. It had been a long, uneventful voyage so far, very nearly four months of the same eternal round of dreary chores, and the men were bored and restless. They wouldn't mind a good fight. Most were seasoned West Africamen and had nothing but contempt for Guinean warriors and weapons. To them, all Africans were Guineans and their bows and arrows, spears and shields simply no match for Portuguese steel and gunpowder.

"Now they come, my lord."

Segou said this just as Gil turned the sand glass for the fifth time. It was truly morning now, the sky pearly blue in the east and tinged with the first faint colors of sunrise, and the canoes gliding downriver toward the ship were easy to see.

There were six of them, abreast, dugouts, each hollowed out of a single tree trunk ten to fifteen feet long, each carrying three men. Only the man in the stern paddled; the other two sat cross-legged one behind the other, their arms folded across their bare chests, their bows and arrows slung. Eighteen men; Segou's count had been accurate. The thirteen remaining on the bank at the head of the cove were harder to see but they seemed tall and muscular and were wearing long skirts of some sort of blue velvety cloth. They too had bows and quivers of arrows slung across their backs except for one who leaned on what appeared to be a long throwing spear and wore a feathered headdress. As for the women and children Segou had mentioned, they were still out of sight in the trees.

Cão moved over to the quarterdeck's starboard rail with Gonçalves. Except for daggers in their belts, they were unarmed. The two Ashanti, with their spears and shields, stood behind them, partially blocking Gil's view. On the spar deck below, Tristão had also gone over to the starboard rail. His soldiers stood in a single rank behind him, fidgeting with their weapons and casting expectant glances up at the captain-general.

"Why do they advance no further?" Cão asked.

Segou took a step forward. And, with a quick glance at the sand glass to be sure it didn't need to be turned, so did Gil. The canoes had stopped, standing off the *Leonor*'s starboard beam a hundred yards or so, the man in the stern of each back-paddling gracefully but with terrific strength to hold his dugout against the downriver current now running out with the tide. And the two other men in each had stood up.

"Page, fetch me the spyglass."

Gil darted back to the locker beside the binnacle and used the opportunity of handing the spyglass to Cão to step right between him and Segou and so get an unobstructed view of the Negroes in the canoes. Oh, what he would have given to have the spyglass to his own eye just then. The sun had risen above the upriver horizon, lighting the great expanse of the river's mouth, lighting even the forest of its bank so everything could now be seen quite clearly, not only the men in the canoes and the men watching from the shore but also the women and children in the trees behind them.

"What are they about, my lord Captain?" Tristão called from the spar deck. "I cannot make out what they are about. They neither advance nor retreat."

"Patience, Fernão," Cão replied and turned to Segou. "What do you make of this behavior, good friend?"

"I can only say, my lord . . . they have come to look at us."

Aye, that was it, Gil realized in a flash of pure intuition; they had come to look at the sailing ship and the men aboard her, and to look at them with a burning, unimaginable intensity. For, as the pilot had said, these people had never before seen a ship like this nor men with the white faces of those aboard her. And now they saw them; for the very first time in their lives and in the lives of all their ancestors, they saw a sailing ship and men with white faces. And that was why Gil wished he had the spyglass screwed to his own eye—so he could see their expressions as they looked at something they had never seen before, as they looked at something they had never even dreamed existed before. The men standing off a hundred yards or so in the canoes were strong and young, taller than the Ashanti, slimmer and of a much lighter color, a cocoa color, a dark-honey color, with high cheekbones and slanted eyes, and, unlike the Ashanti, they did not shave their heads but wore their hair in a mass of tight black curls.

"Speak to them, Segou," Cão said. "Greet them in the name of our king."

Segou set his spear and shield aside and, cupping his hands to his mouth, shouted down to the Negroes in the canoes. Gil thought he could understand what he shouted; at least he could make out the Ashanti words of greeting (Segou and Goree had used them with him often enough) and the name of the Portuguese king, João II. The Negroes in the canoes turned to Segou when he shouted and began murmuring to each other. It seemed they hadn't seen the Ashanti until now, a black face among all the white faces. And when Goree stepped up beside Segou to shout something else, their consternation grew. But not one of the Negroes in the canoes shouted anything back.

"What did you say, Segou?" Cão asked.

"I greeted them in the name of our king and asked them the name of their king."

"And what did you say, Goree?"

"I told them that our king was a far more powerful king than their king."

Cão pulled a sour face at that. "Tell them we come in peace, Segou. Tell them we bring gifts from our king to theirs."

As Segou began shouting this message over the rail, Gonçalves suddenly realized where Gil was standing—right up there between the captain-general and Segou—and he grabbed hold of the boy's collar and shoved him back toward the binnacle. The sand had just about run out of the half-hour glass. Gil dashed to it to turn it and, because of Gonçalves's hard glare, remained beside it so again he was unable to see much of what was going on down on the water. But he could hear well enough and what he heard during the time it took for the sand to run out and he turned the glass again was that, no matter what the captain-general instructed Segou to shout down to the men in the canoes, no matter what little teasing sallies Goree piped in with on his own to the captain-general's annoyance, the men in the canoes didn't reply.

And then they simply swung their canoes about and paddled back upriver to the group on the bank at the head of the cove.

"Well, at least they don't seem to have come to fight," Cão said with a sigh of frustration.

"Dom Nuno," Gil whispered.

Gonçalves looked around.

"What are they doing now?"

Gonçalves showed Gil the back of his hand with mock ferocity and turned away. Gonçalves was Gil's special friend. A tall, lanky man with a bald head and short beard, he had taken the boy under his wing at the outset of the voyage and had taught him what he needed to know about the caravel and blue-water sailing. Perhaps remembering his own first voyage on the open ocean under lateen rigging, he had kept an eye on the boy, reining in his quick-witted enthusiasms but not reining them in enough to spoil his fun.

"Now what the devil? Have a look at that, will you," Cão said.

And Gil couldn't resist having a look and again he slipped away from the binnacle to peek between the captain-general, Gonçalves and the two Ashanti at the starboard rail.

The canoes had beached at the head of the cove and, although the paddlers in each remained where they were, the two others in each exchanged places with two of the men who had been waiting on the shore—only the one in the feathered headdress leaning on what looked like a throwing spear did not get into a canoe; maybe he was the chief—and the paddlers shoved off and the canoes came gliding downriver again toward the *Leonor.* It made absolutely perfectly good sense to Gil. Everybody wanted to get a closer look at this extraordinary apparition, this great-winged bird of a ship that had appeared in the mouth of their river with men with white faces aboard her.

"Once again, Segou. Greetings from our king."

And once again, the Ashanti shouted greetings from the king of Portugal. And once again the Negroes in the canoes murmured to each other in surprise but did not reply. And then they too, after remaining through two turnings of the half-hour sand glass, swung about and paddled upriver to the head of the cove.

"They are gone, my lord Captain," Tristão called up from the spar deck.

"Aye, Fernão, we can see that for ourselves," Cão replied with a trace of irritation.

"Will they return, do you suppose? Or should I have the soldiers stand down?"

Cão turned to Segou. "Will they?"

"I do not know, my lord."

The sun was now yardarm high and the humid heat of the day was rising rapidly. Gil took off his leather cap and wiped his brow. Some of the soldiers removed their helmets and loosened the leather straps of their armor. Most of the seamen were looking toward Cão on the quarterdeck from their stations in various parts of the ship, wondering what would happen next. The pilot, who had remained on the foredeck with the bowsprit lookout throughout the peculiar visit of the Negroes, came aft.

"My lord Captain, can I ring the bell now?" Gil asked.

"Aye, page, you can ring the bell now."

Gil struck the ship's bell seven times. One more turning of the glass and it would be the end of the first morning watch.

"Well, José, what do you make of all this?"

Vizinho, not excepting the priest, was the most learned man aboard, an accomplished mathematician, astronomer and chartmaker as well as the finest pilot in the king's fleet, and it was invariably to him that Cão turned when seeking advice. "It would not be difficult to sail farther upriver, my lord Captain," he said. "The river is deep and wide. There is more than sufficient steerageway and the land breezes can be used to advantage. And perhaps we would find more forthcoming Negroes farther upriver."

"But you don't think we should."

"No, my lord Captain. I think we should wait here a while longer."

"As do I, my lord Captain," Gonçalves said. "I think the Negroes we have seen here will return and bring others with them. I think they have gone now only to tell the rest of their people about us and will return with them."

"We do not have time to lose, Nuno. There is much to be done. We must explore this river to see where it leads, and who can say how much time we will need for that. And then we must continue our voyage south to find the way into the Indian Sea if we discover this river is not the way. And who can say how much time we will need for that."

"I understand, my lord Captain. But it would be no great loss to lose this one day. I am certain the Negroes will return this day."

II

B<small>UT THEY DIDN'T.</small> They didn't return until the following day and, by that time, the start of the second morning watch, Cão, anxious about his orders to find a sea route to the Indies, had made ready to sail. The anchors were aweigh; the foresail was unfurled and the foresail yard hoisted home; the first mate on the foredeck had uncoiled the lead chain to make the soundings; the pilot was on the quarterdeck to conn the helmsman at the tiller in the steerage room below; and the ship's longboat, roped to the bowsprit and manned by eight sweeps and the bosun's mate, was about to tow the *Leonor* out of the cove into the mainstream where she could safely make full sail to beat against the current and explore this mighty river they had found. It was then that the Negroes returned.

And they returned in force, in a flotilla of at least thirty canoes, some with only three men as on the morning before but others much larger carrying eight or ten men and one, the largest of all, perhaps thirty feet in length with a high, carved prow, carrying the man in the feathered headdress—aye, surely the chief—standing with his long throwing spear between paddlers and warriors fore and aft. Altogether there must have been more than two hundred of them.

"First mate," the bosun shouted up from the forecastle break. "The captain-general will have you untether the longboat and have her come alongside."

Gonçalves signaled that he understood, recoiled the chain of the dipsy lead and, barefoot, shinnied out on the bowsprit to untie the longboat's painter, which he flung down to the bosun's mate. No sooner had he done this than a gang in the forecastle began counter-cranking the capstan to lower the two bower anchors, and the seamen in the foremast shrouds, who just minutes before had cut the ribbons to let the foresail fall with a sharp crack, furled the sail again, while Tristão and his soldiers once again came hurrying into the ship's waist, donning helmets and armor and hefting weapons, Father Sebastião making the sign of the cross over them. All this activity caused a stir among the Negroes in the canoes, and their excited murmurings flew out across the water like a squadron of bees. And, whether because of this activity or because they had planned to do so anyway, as they had the morning before, the paddlers in the canoes halted their approach and began back-paddling to once again stand off a hundred yards or so from the ship.

Cão, carrying a small gray canvas duffle, went over to the starboard rail in the ship's waist just above where the bosun's mate had brought the ship's longboat alongside. "We shall do no more foolish shouting to them from the ship this time, Segou. This time we shall go and talk to them eye-to-eye, man-to-man. Bosun, let us have the ladder over the side."

Two seamen lowered a rope ladder to the longboat where the bosun's mate and one of the sweeps caught hold of its last rung and pulled it taut.

"Look lively, *marinheiro*," Cão called and dropped the small gray canvas duffle he was carrying into the sweep's arms. Then he said, "Come, Segou. Leave your spear and shield. We shall make friends of these savages yet." And he hoisted himself over the rail.

"Dom Diogo." This was Father Sebastião.

Cão looked back.

"You go to the Negroes in the name of our king, Dom Diogo. Allow me to accompany you in the name of our Lord."

Cão considered this for a moment. Then he said, "As you wish, padre."

"Can I go too, my lord Captain?" This was Gil.

"And in whose name would you go, page?"

Gil had no ready answer for this and, for an instant, looked around in consternation. But in the next instant he recovered his wits and blurted out, "In your name, my lord Captain. I would go in your name, as your faithful page."

"Don't play the clown, little son," Gonçalves interjected sternly. "Get yourself to the foredeck where you belong."

"A moment, Nuno." Cão was smiling genially. "Why not let him come? Why not let the boy have his first taste of Africa here where a great river has been found? Maybe he will bring us luck. Very well, faithful page, come in my name." And he went down the rope ladder into the longboat.

A few strong strokes by the eight sweeps brought the longboat to within twenty yards of the big canoe of the Negro chief and less than ten yards from the smaller canoes that had bunched in front of it protectively. And now Gil had his wish: He could clearly see the expressions on the Negroes' faces. And it was just as he had imagined it would be. They were in thrall, as if these white men had flown down to them from the stars.

Cão picked up the small gray canvas duffle he had dropped into the longboat and went up into the boat's prow. Segou went up with him. Gil and Father Sebastião followed a step behind. It was late in the morning, hot and humid, the sun shining almost directly into their eyes, and swarming clouds of tiny, fierce, stinging insects rose off the glittering surface of the river to attack the exposed patches of their skin. They didn't seem to bother the Negroes in the canoes but even Segou, from time to time, had to slap them away. Cão undid the rope of the canvas duffle and pulled out some trading truck: two hand mirrors, a few brass bracelets, several lengths of red cotton cloth.

"Very well, Segou, we begin once again. Greet the chief in the name of our king."

Gil watched the chief's face closely as Segou spoke. It was a plump, cocoa-colored, clean-shaven, grandfatherly face—the mass of tight curls showing from under his headdress of green and blue and red parrot feathers was snow-white—a good-natured face but a face now rigid with intense concentration.

"Tell him we come in peace and bring gifts from our king."

As Segou said this, Cão alternately held up the brass bracelets, the lengths of red cloth and the hand mirrors, which he tilted from side to side so as to flash and suddenly flash again the reflection of the sun. The chief's eyes and those of the other Negroes shifted to these but their expressions didn't change. They seemed neither startled nor particularly impressed by these items of European manufacture. They continued watching with silent intensity and waiting as if under a spell . . . but watching and waiting for what?

"Dom Diogo."

"Padre?"

"Allow me to speak to them. Perhaps they will respond to words of greeting from our Lord, if not from our king."

Cão let out a long sigh. "Perhaps they will. There must be something to which they will respond." And he stepped aside, allowing the priest to take his place beside Segou in the prow.

For a few minutes, Father Sebastião remained silent with his eyes closed and his hands clasped in prayer. Then he opened his eyes, undid the rosary wound around the waist of his rough, brown cassock and, with its black onyx crucifix, made the sign of the cross, a great one, reaching high and wide to encompass all the Negroes in the canoes. This interested them, this surprised them, this was something they hadn't seen before, and their eyes followed the sweeping movement of the crucifix in the priest's hand as if anticipating the magic it would produce.

"In nomine Patris, et Filii, et Spiritus Sancti . . ."

Gil did not speak Latin. It was, of course, familiar to him from church and he listened to it now in much the same way he had listened to Segou speaking in Ashanti, picking out words and phrases here and there that he had learned from his prayers as he had picked out words and phrases of Ashanti that he had learned from eavesdropping on Segou and Goree. And then something occurred to him: It was very much in this same way that the Negroes were listening to Father Sebastião, and it was in this way too that they had listened to Segou. Of course. They understood Father Sebastião's Latin no better than he did, and they no more had understood Segou's Ashanti than he had. And why should they? Just because they were Africans? But why should one suppose all Africans spoke the same language? Did all Europeans? Gil could barely understand an Andalusian or Catalan, let alone a Genoese or Fleming.

"My lord Captain, they do not understand," Gil said.

Without looking around, Cão said somewhat wearily, "I did not expect they would."

"No, my lord, I don't mean Father Sebastião. I don't mean the Latin. I mean Segou. They didn't understand Segou either. They didn't understand the Ashanti any better than the Latin. That's why they don't respond. They don't understand what we are saying to them."

"This may be true, my lord," Segou said. "What the little son says may be true."

"But the people of Benin understood you, Segou, and the Togo people and Mandingo people and also the Ibo people of Biafra."

"That is so, my lord. But those people are very much like my own people, the Ashanti people. These people are not."

Cão looked back at the Negroes in the canoes. He was still holding the brass bracelets and red cloth and small mirrors. Now he let them drop back into the canvas duffle at his feet. "Aye," he said contemplatively. "Aye, these people are not like the people we have met in Africa before. These people are not Guinean people."

THEY WENT ASHORE that afternoon, after noonday prayers and the first dog watch had been set. The dugout canoes were stilled massed on the river but the chief's canoe had returned from whence it had come, around the head of the cove, upriver.

It had departed while Cão was trying to decide how best, in the absence of a common language, to communicate with these unique Negroes. The plump, grandfatherly chief had suddenly raised his spear—except that it wasn't a spear, Gil had been able to see once they were close up, but a wooden staff elaborately carved with a coiling serpent whose head was a ball of ivory; perhaps it was the scepter of his chieftainship—he had raised this staff or scepter in what must have been a signal because instantly his paddlers had swung his canoe about and started paddling away. At the same time, though, the smaller canoes, which had formed a protective barrier in front of the chief, had pulled back and, in doing so, had opened what was unmistakably a path for the longboat to follow. There could be no doubt that the chief had expected the longboat to follow him. Indeed, he had looked back over his shoulder several times with his scepter still raised in a gesture that could be understood as nothing other than a gesture of invitation. And Cão had been sorely tempted to accept the invitation but then, weighing the dangers that might be involved, had ordered the bosun's mate to return to the *Leonor* for reinforcements.

Now the massed canoes on the river again opened a path for the longboat, as she again pushed away from the mother ship, and formed an escort on either side of her, as she set off upriver. Gil had managed to hold on to his place in the boat—Cão didn't seem to notice him one way or another and Gonçalves had given him an encouraging wink—but in addition to Segou and Father Sebastião, Tristão, in his chainmail and *salade,* and five of his soldiers, armed with arquebuses, came along this time. And this time the sweeps and bosun's mate were also armed, the first with daggers, the latter with a cutlass. And this time Cão wore shoulder armor and breastplate, a plumed helmet and double-edged sword. Only Segou and the priest and Gil had no weapons.

But it was Cão's view that the most effective weapon would have to be the canvas duffle of trading truck to which he had added what he hoped would be regarded by the Negroes as more impressive items: hawks' bells, fishhooks, German knives, kettles and pans, a necklace of bloodstone. The daggers and cutlasses and helmets and armor and, especially, the arquebus firearms, with their explosive noises and flashes of flame, were only meant for show. He had absolutely no intention of getting into a fight with these people, and he had so ordered his men. If matters turned sour, they were free to fight only to the extent of defending themselves and getting back to the longboat to effect their escape.

"Feather the sweeps, bosun's mate."

"Aye, my lord Captain."

The canoes escorting the longboat had turned toward the south bank but Cão hesitated to follow. For here the south bank had, quite abruptly, become a deep, wide, crescent-shaped cove and the forest of palms and mangroves and other vegetation, which had overhung the river, had as abruptly retreated several hundred yards inland from the water's edge, either by a quirk of nature or by the work of men, leaving a huge, red-earth clearing. And on this clearing stood a sizable village in which hundreds if not thousands of people were gathered.

The longboat was more than a hundred yards from the south bank, but even from that distance Gil could see that this village was not the helter-skelter jumble of grass-and-wattle huts of the villages he had seen at the landfalls at São Jorgé da Mina and Cape Ste. Catherine. This one was remarkably neatly made. The huts were laid out on a right-angle grid of streets enclosing on three sides (the fourth side was open to the river) a large central plaza or market square, at the center of which stood a single old, immensely tall and thick palm tree. And the huts themselves were of an admirably artful design and construction. The steep, conical roofs were made of overlapping palm fronds, creating very much the effect of European shingles and obviously serving the same purpose, each set on a circular base of closely woven basketweave with doors and windows covered by colorfully patterned mats. Except for a group of three: Taller than the others, they were enclosed by a stockade of sharpened pikes that could be entered through a heavy wooden gate. As for the people, they were much like the people Gil had already seen, the men muscular, clean-shaven, cocoa-colored, wearing long, velvety blue skirts around their waists, the women wrapped in the same material but up under their armpits so as to cover their breasts, the children stark naked except for anklets of shells and grass. The plump, white-haired, grandfatherly chief was, however, nowhere to be seen.

"Well, we are here," Cão said after several minutes surveying the village. "It seems safe enough, or at least as safe as we have any right to expect it to be."

The remark wasn't addressed to anyone in particular and no one in particular bothered to answer. Gil glanced from Cão to Tristão to Segou and then the priest. Their faces were grimly set, beaded with sweat. Swarms of insects hummed around them but they made no move to swat them away.

"Very well, bosun's mate, take us ashore."

And then the drums began.

Gil couldn't see them at first but, when the longboat reached within ten yards of the bank, the crowd gathered there moved away, some upriver to the east, some downriver to the west, some inland to where the first huts of the village stood, and, in doing so, revealed a feathered, ceremonial group at the base of the lone, tall palm tree in

the center of the market square. The drummers were among them;
the barrel-shaped drums, brightly striped in blue and red, were
gripped between their thighs and knees and beaten, in a blood-
pounding, complicated rhythm, with the heels of their palms. And
there were dancers among them, dancing to the drummers' beat,
stamping their feet on the rich red earth, swinging their hips and un-
dulating their outstretched arms with the sinewy fluidity of snakes.
These were women and Gil saw with an involuntary surge of excitement that they wore the ankle-length, blue skirts as the men wore
theirs, wrapped around their waists so their breasts were bare. And
there also were five men in the group with long, gracefully curving
instruments looped over their shoulders, great ivory horns made
from the tusks of forest beasts. They, as did the drummers and
dancers, wore headdresses of red and blue parrot feathers and dangling strings of smooth white river stones and beads of shell, and
when the longboat's prow scraped the shallows of the sloping
muddy beach, they brought the ivory horns to their lips and, bal-
looning their cheeks, emitted a sweet, prolonged note, each in a different but harmonious key.

On the first singing blast, four men raced down to the longboat,
gripped her gunwales and hauled her up on the beach with such
force that old Father Sebastião momentarily lost his balance. And
then on the second thrilling note, the villagers hurriedly formed
themselves into orderly ranks on three sides of the market square,
leaving the fourth side open to the river and the white men in the
longboat.

Cão jumped out. "Segou, come with me. You too, padre. Fernão,
deploy your soldiers in a single rank right here along the water's edge
in front of the boat. Guard it with your life. Bosun's mate, remain in
the boat with the sweeps and be ready to shove off at a moment's notice."

He said nothing about what Gil was to do, and for a moment, the
boy hesitated in confusion, his heart racing, not wanting to be left behind. But then he saw that Cão had forgotten the canvas duffle of
trading truck and he grabbed it, slung it over his shoulder and hurried
after him.

The dancers stopped dancing; the men with the ivory horns

lowered their instruments; the drummers stepped back from their drums. Cão halted a few paces from them. Gil's eyes fixed on the dancers, on their naked breasts. He felt out of breath. He couldn't take his eyes from the women until he realized one was looking back at him and he experienced a rush of panic, a sudden flush of heat in his cheeks, and quickly looked away. The way she had been looking at him must have been exactly the way he had been looking at her, with complete bewilderment and utter fascination. She was beautiful.

"The trading truck, my lord Captain."

Cão glanced around. "Ah, yes. Good for you, page. I had forgotten it." He took the canvas duffle from Gil. "Now go slowly, Segou, go very slowly this time. Use all your wit and imagination, good friend. We must make them understand us."

"Yes, my lord, I will make them understand us. I will speak with my hands as well as my voice."

"Very good, Segou. Speak also with your hands."

But there was no need. Just then, a murmuring rustled through the crowd and, as one, the Negroes looked back to the three tallest huts, which were surrounded by the piked stockade. The gate in the stockade had opened and the plump, white-haired, grandfatherly chief had stepped through.

He was carrying his serpent-carved, ivory-topped scepter but his headdress this time was white, made not of parrot feathers but of the feathers of the egret and heron and the other long-legged water birds seen along the riverbank. And he also now wore a long cape of those feathers, which was bordered at the throat and hem with red and green parrot feathers to make an astonishingly lovely garment. He was accompanied by a man nearly as old as he but much skinnier, dressed very much as he was except that he didn't carry a scepter; he held a painted gourd, probably filled with pebbles by the sound that it made. Also in the entourage were five women, modestly wrapped in the ankle-length, blue velvety cloth in the fashion of all the other women (except the dancers) but with sheets of the cloth also wrapped around their heads like turbans. The dancers and drummers and horn players moved away from the tall palm tree to make room for them.

One of the turbaned women came forward with a stool, made of wood and inlaid with ivory and shaped like an hourglass, and set it behind the chief. Adjusting his feathered robe and his long skirt, the chief sat down, his knees wide apart, his scepter across his knees, and studied the white faces in front of him for several seconds before instinctively and, of course, correctly judging Cão to be the leader of these strangers, these most alien of all the strangers he had ever encountered in his long, old life, alien in every way, in the color of their skin, in their incredible, cumbersome dress of armor and mail, in their hairiness, in the sharpness and largeness of their features, in the paleness of their eyes. *What* were they, his expression seemed to ask, not who. Then he glanced aside, swinging his head so that his feathers swayed, and another of the women of his entourage hurried forward with another wooden, ivory-inlaid, hourglass stool and set it behind Cão. Cão glanced around at it and then, after the fashion of the chief, adjusted his sword so that it would lay across his knees and sat down, his knees also wide apart. The canvas duffle rested against his leg.

And then at last, one of these people spoke.

It wasn't the chief. Perhaps in imitation of Segou speaking for the captain-general, the skinny man in the chief's entourage, the one holding the rattling gourd, spoke. He spoke quickly, sternly, with many grand gestures and at some length, and Gil instantly recognized how correct his guess had been: The language the man spoke was nothing at all like Ashanti. It was clipped, hard, sometimes hissing, sometimes humming, spoken as much from deep in the throat and by the tongue clicking against the teeth or the roof of the mouth as by lips. To Gil's ear, it was a far less pleasant language than Ashanti, harsher, stronger, more dangerous, and the face of the man speaking it seemed mean and angry and dangerous. When he finally ceased speaking, he rattled the pebble-filled gourd over the chief's head, bringing a murmur of approval from the crowd of villagers. The chief kept his eyes fixed on Cão. Cão returned the gaze as steadily.

"He is their ju-ju man, my lord," Segou said in a low voice. "Their sorcerer."

Without looking away from the chief, Cão asked, "Did you understand anything of what he said?"

"The language is very different from mine, but I believe he introduced the chief and told us many wonderful things about him."

"Did he tell us his name?"

"I am certain he did, but I cannot say what it is."

"ManiSoyo," Gil blurted out.

Cão broke his gaze with the chief and, just as he did, the chief did also, and they both looked at Gil in some surprise.

"Where did you get that idea, boy?"

Gil shrugged. "I don't know, my lord Captain, only that it seemed every time the fellow with the rattle pointed at the chief, he said that, ManiSoyo."

Cão looked back at the chief.

The chief was still looking at Gil. And he was smiling. And then he too spoke at last. He said, "ManiSoyo." And he placed the flat of his hand against his chest where the feathered cape fell open on it, and he said it again with an even broader, warmer smile. "ManiSoyo." Then he pointed at Gil with the plump index finger of his right hand.

"Well, by our dear Mother in Heaven, I've seen the devil at work today, boy. Aye, that I have." Cão too was now smiling broadly, and he gave Gil a hearty thump on the back. "Tell him your name, boy. That's why he's pointing at you."

"Gil Eanes," Gil said, pleased at the captain-general's praise, and he placed *his* hand against *his* chest and said it again. "Gil Eanes."

"Gil Eenezh," the chief repeated, grinning from ear to ear, and then crooked his finger.

"He wants you to go to him. But wait a moment." Cão bent down to the canvas duffle at his feet and, fishing about in it, pulled out the necklace of bloodstone. "Here. Take this to him. And be polite."

Gil couldn't believe this was happening. He was the center of all attention. Everyone, the captain-general, Segou, Father Sebastião, the chief ManiSoyo and all his people, the skinny mean-faced ju-ju man, the older women of the entourage, the drummers and horn players and the dancing girls, aye, especially the pretty, bare-breasted dancing girls, were looking at him with big smiles, caught up in this sudden, happy moment of communication from one side of the world to the other, a communication never before made in all history.

He took the bloodstone necklace and, in the manner of a page at the court of his liege lord, he removed his leather cap and made a deep, sweeping bow, dropping to one knee. He expected after a moment or two to be touched on the shoulder, as a *cavalheiro* or *fidalgo* would have done, by way of giving him permission to rise. But nothing happened; there was just the buzzing of many voices around him and the sound of soft, merry laughter. So he looked up. The chief was beaming at him. Apparently his bow had been understood as a gesture of courtesy and respect. He glanced round to the captain-general, who, still smiling delightedly, made an encouraging motion with his hand. So Gil turned to the chief and presented him with the bloodstone necklace. The chief took it and turned it round on his fingers, feeling the smoothness of the green chalcedony with the blood-like flecks of jasper scattered throughout the gems and then, holding the string of stones open, popped the necklace over Gil's head.

"Oh, no, it is meant for you, sir ManiSoyo," Gil exclaimed in embarrassment. "Please, sir Chief, it is a gift from my lord Captain." And he hurriedly made to remove the necklace.

But the chief stayed his hand and, smiling as brightly as before, his people tittering all around him, he gently forced Gil to keep the necklace on.

Gil again glanced back at Cão, and Cão raised his bushy eyebrows as much as to say, what is to be done, and as he didn't look displeased, Gil left the necklace around his neck. Apparently, for ManiSoyo, the necklace was a mere trinket, more appropriate to adorn a young boy than an old chief. And then he did another surprising thing: He took Gil's hand and drew the boy to his side. It was as if the chief had appropriated him because he had had the luck to guess the chief's name, as if he believed that because of that lucky guess Gil understood his language and could serve as his interpreter. And he pointed at Cão as he had pointed at Gil just moments before and spoke rapidly in his hissing, clicking, murmuring tongue. Gil didn't have the first idea what he was saying but he was prepared to take a chance at making another lucky guess.

"He is our captain-general, Diogo Cão, esquire in the household of João the Second, king of the Portuguese."

The chief looked at Gil, as little understanding Gil's language as Gil had understood his, but a warm mood had sprung up between them, a sense of playing at a game together, so the chief was just as willing to make a guess of his own. It was, however, not such a lucky guess. "King," he said, still pointing at Cão but looking at Gil. "King Porta Geeze."

Gil shook his head. He realized he had said too much. He must proceed more simply, so, also pointing his finger at the captain-general at the risk of seeming disrespectful, he said, "Diogo Cão. He is Diogo Cão."

"Deego Cum?"

Gil nodded. It was close enough. "Diogo Cão."

And the captain-general also nodded and, laying the flat of his hand against his chest, said, "Diogo Cão."

"Deego Cum," the chief said, still pointing at Cão. Then he said, "ManiSoyo." And he slapped himself on the chest.

It was a grand success. Everybody was elated, the chief above all. He would go on playing this game. Now he wanted to establish the identity of Father Sebastião, and in much the same way, the repeated pointing and chest slapping, he learned the priest's name, pronouncing it in a not-too-far-fetched version: Pader Sebastum. Then Gil realized that the skinny, mean-faced fellow who had shaken the rattle over the chief's head, the one Segou had called their sorcerer, might very well hold the equivalent status to the chief that Father Sebastião held to the captain-general and so he started up the business of pointing and chest slapping in regard to him. He turned out to be Nsaku-Soyo. The five women in the chief's entourage, however, posed something of a conundrum, because, as best Gil could make out, they all had the same name: MbunduSoyo. Were they all one family then? Soyo? But even if they were, why didn't the women have different first names?

Now, it seemed to Gil that, in all fairness, it ought to be Segou's turn to be introduced. But the chief wasn't interested in a man with a black face and, with a flick of his plump hand, he waved the Ashanti aside and pointed past him to Tristão and the soldiers guarding the longboat at the river's edge, men also with white faces. Judging the situation to be peaceful enough, Cão signaled the master-at-arms to bring up the soldiers with their firearms. Once the laborious back-and-forth of getting them all introduced was completed, the chief had his own personal bodyguard of ten warriors step forward. And here again, it transpired, they all had the same name, ending in Soyo. Did anyone else notice this peculiarity? Gil wondered. And then, in a flash of inspiration, it made sense to him.

"Soyo," he said and pointed all around, not only at the members of the chief's entourage who had been so painstakingly introduced but at all the rest, at the dancers and drummers and horn players, and at the men and women and children forming the audience along the three sides of the market square. "All Soyo. Is that not so, ManiSoyo? They are all Soyo. They are the Soyo."

"What's got into you, boy?" Cão asked. "What are you getting at?"

"They are all Soyo, my lord Captain. These people are the Soyo. They haven't been telling us their names. They have been telling us their titles. ManiSoyo. Chief of the Soyo. King of the Soyo. And Nsaku-Soyo. He is the priest of the Soyo. And the women, the MbunduSoyo, they are the queens of the Soyo . . ."

The chief was listening to Gil with keen interest without actually understanding what he was saying but divining from his gestures and the tone of his voice that what he was saying was correct, his eyes bright with amused appreciation for the boy's cleverness.

And Gil turned to him and said, "Your people are the Soyo, ManiSoyo, king of the Soyo. Our people are the Portuguese."

"Porta Geeze?"

"Aye, Portuguese." Gil pointed at Cão and Father Sebastião, at the master-at-arms and his soldiers and then at himself. "We are the Portuguese, ManiSoyo. Our people are the Portuguese."

"Porta Geeze," the chief said more definitely.

"You are the Soyo. And we are the Portuguese."

The chief smiled with satisfaction. "Soyo," he said. "Porta Geeze."

"Aye," Gil said, taking a deep breath, also satisfied at what had been accomplished, what *he* had accomplished, and looked around with immense pride.

"Very well done, boy," Cão said. "Now carry on and see what else you can learn for us. Especially about this river."

But before Gil could carry on, the ManiSoyo, obviously forgetting in the flush of this small success that they really could not understand each other's language, rattled off a long sentence in which the term Porta Geeze figured prominently and which, by its inflection, was certainly a question but which Gil could not make head or tail of, and his look of puzzlement brought the chief up short. No, they did not yet speak each other's language. The chief closed his eyes, realizing that he too must go slowly to be understood. Then he opened his eyes and pointed at the river. Gil looked where he pointed. Was he pointing at the longboat? Then he pointed downriver from whence the longboat had come. Was he pointing toward where the *Leonor* lay at anchor? Then he pointed at the sky.

All was quiet. Everyone watched this pantomime in silence. And then the chief did it again, pointing at the longboat, pointing downriver along the route the longboat had taken from the *Leonor* and then, as a final gesture, pointing at the sky. Then he took Gil's hand and looked into the boy's face, inquiring if he understood. Gil shook his head. The chief released his hand and sighed and looked at Cão.

"Porta Geeze," he said to him.

Cão nodded. "Aye, Portuguese."

"Soyo," the chief said.

Again Cão nodded and said, "Aye, Soyo."

The chief sucked in his breath and made a wide, sweeping gesture, a grand circle all around him, starting at the river directly in front of him, taking in the bank upriver, turning around on his stool to take in the huts of the village and the forest behind them and on around to the downriver bank and, finally, to the river directly in front of him where he had started. And he said, "Soyo."

"Aye, Soyo," Cão said, nodding more vigorously, and he repeated the chief's wide, sweeping gesture all around. "All this is Soyo. I understand. All this is the land of the Soyo."

"Ngete," the chief said, also nodding vigorously. And then, yet again, he pointed at the longboat, at the route the longboat had taken upriver from the *Leonor* and at the sky. And he said, "Porta Geeze?"

And it rang as clear as a bell in Gil's head. "He wants to know where we come from, my lord Captain. He shows us that this is the land of the Soyo. He wants us to show him where the land of the Portuguese lies."

"Aye," Cão replied thoughtfully. "You are right, boy. That is certainly what he wants to know. But why does he point to the sky?"

"I think he believes we have come from the sky, my lord Captain. I think he believes we have flown down from the sky in the *Leonor*. I think he believes her sails are the wings of a great bird and we have flown down to him on those great wings from a land in the sky."

Cão didn't immediately respond to this. As had the chief, he too now closed his eyes to consider the matter. And everyone watched and waited in silence for him to open his eyes. And when he did, he was smiling wryly.

"ManiSoyo," he said.

"Deego Cum," the chief replied.

"Portuguese," Cão said and pointed to Gil and Father Sebastião and Tristão and the soldiers and then himself.

"Porta Geeze," the chief agreed.

"Aye, we are Portuguese," Cão said and he twisted on his stool to look back at the river. "And we come," he said, pointing at the longboat. "We come," he said again, now pointing downriver along the route the longboat had taken from where the *Leonor* with her great winglike sails lay at anchor. "We come," he said once again and pointed at the sky. "We come from the sky."

A gasp exploded from the crowd of Soyo.

"Aye," Cão said, still pointing at the sky. "We Portuguese, we come from the sky. Our land is in the sky."

Gil was shocked. He couldn't believe Cão had said that. He looked at the priest. The priest was looking at Cão. Tristão was looking at Cão. Everyone was looking at Cão. Only Segou wasn't looking at Cão. He was looking at his feet, ashamed.

"My lord Captain—"

But there was nothing further to say. The ManiSoyo stood up from his stool. He raised his ivory-topped, serpent-carved scepter and brought it down with an explosive thud on the rich red earth. And the drums began again.

III

THEY SPENT THE NIGHT in the Soyo village—it was called Mpinda, the largest, with a population of over two thousand, of a score of Soyo villages on the river's south bank—and it was a night of great celebration, of sumptuous feasting and drumming and horn playing and thrilling, sensuous dancing, of stilt walking and acrobatics and fire eating and amazing, even frightening feats of ju-ju magic, a night in welcome and honor of the fabulous white men who had flown down to the Soyo from their land in the sky. Everyone took part, even the bosun's mate and the sweeps. The only exception was Segou. The Soyo regarded the Ashanti as some sort of pet or slave of the heaven-sent Porta Geeze and he was left outside, more or less to guard the longboat.

For his part, Cão made every effort to reciprocate the Mani-Soyo's enthusiastic hospitality. To begin with, there was the trading truck. At the first suitable occasion—after the acrobatics had finished and before a troop of warriors put on a demonstration of their incredible skill with bow and arrow—he called for quiet and opened the gray canvas duffle. But, although he withdrew each item or group of items with something of a magician's flourish to convey a sense of the unusual, the exceptional, the rare, to bestow upon each a special magnificence, whatever he brought forth was treated by the Mani-Soyo in much the same way he had treated the bloodstone necklace, with the benign amusement with which he'd regard any trinket or curio, and then he'd give it away for others to enjoy as he'd given the bloodstone necklace to Gil.

Gil could see that Cão was extremely puzzled by the old chief's indifference, if not downright contempt, for these gifts. After all, all the way down the west coast of Africa so far, tribesmen, including chiefs of the highest standing, had taken to items of European manufacture with an avidness and avariciousness that would have been pathetic if it hadn't been so laughable, and had eagerly traded hides, palm oil, ivory, gold dust and, indeed, even their own kinsmen to possess them. What then was so special about the Soyo? What made them so superior? Did they already possess items such as these? There was no evidence of that. All that could be seen was the usual African stuff, made of leaves and wood, ivory and feathers, shells and stone and bone. The one exception was the material of their skirts, almost like velvet or damask. Even so, the mirrors and knives, fishhooks and kettles and hawks' bells ought to have had some power to impress. But, apparently, not.

As a last resort, Cão had Tristão's soldiers stage a demonstration with their arquebus firearms, an invention quite new and still fairly remarkable to the Portuguese themselves. And, aye, this did evoke a sharper degree of interest, a moment of startled surprise and then a great burst of appreciative laughter and applause. But it was clear that no one had any idea what these suddenly exploding, flame-spitting, smoke-making sticks actually could do, what they actually were for. The soldiers had simply fired into the air without loading shot or ball or metal scrap. So the ManiSoyo saw the shooting as merely a novel form of fireworks and quickly countered by bringing on his most daring fire-eaters, who performed on seven-foot-tall stilts to the thundering roll of the biggest drums as if to mimic the flame and noise of the arquebuses.

Cão decided to let it go at that. It was too dark to attempt to show what the arquebuses really did, that they killed. There was too much risk of a shot going astray and, besides, it obviously didn't matter. The ManiSoyo expected nothing more remarkable of his remarkable guests, nothing more special to prove their specialness, than that they were white. That was remarkable and special enough, that and the fact that they had flown down to him from a land in the sky on the wings of that magnificent bird now floating quietly on the water a league or so downriver.

"Ask him about the river again, boy. Ask him where it comes from."

"Shouldn't we have Segou here for this, my lord Captain?" It pained Gil that the Ashanti had been left outside, like a dog. "He could manage it far better than I."

"I'm afraid we'll have to leave Segou where he is. They don't like him for some reason. That's easy enough to see. And besides, you're managing quite well enough. You've obviously got an ear for this gibberish."

They were seated on those hourglass-shaped stools on the wide veranda that circled the tallest of the three huts inside the stockade of the chief's compound. They had completed what was the third course of the feast—it had consisted of some tasty but unidentifiable freshwater fish mixed in a cereallike gruel, sharply seasoned; the first two courses had been of different kinds of very gamy meat, perhaps antelope and wild pig, also served with the spicy mash—and were now sipping a wine, which Gil had discovered was fermented from the juice extracted from the bole of the palm tree, palm wine, *malafu,* very potent, sipping it from oddly shaped gourds. In the courtyard of the compound, three steps down from the veranda, a bonfire was burning, lighting up the night and casting dancing shadows, and around it the gaily feathered drummers and horn players energetically serenaded them with music as unfamiliar and as potent as the food and wine.

"ManiSoyo."

The old chief put an arm around Gil's shoulder. *"Ngete,* Gil Eenezh."

"The river, ManiSoyo. *Nzere."* Gil had added the word for river to his slowly accumulating vocabulary.

"Ngete, Gil Eenezh. *Nzere."* The chief pointed in the general direction of the river outside the compound's stockade.

"Where does *nzere* come from, ManiSoyo? How far does it go?" Gil asked this mainly in Portuguese but with two or three of his newly acquired words mixed in and illustrated with a far-reaching gesture to the east, the direction from which the river flowed down to the sea.

The chief repeated Gil's far-reaching gesture upriver and said what must have been something like "very far," because he smiled broadly as he said it as if the greatness of the river's length was, amusingly, beyond imagining.

"How far, ManiSoyo? How many leagues?" Gil, however, instantly realized that this was a foolish way to put it. There was no reason to expect that the Soyo measured distance in leagues or, if they did, that their league would be the same as the Portuguese. The Catalan league wasn't, nor was the Genoese. And the English used another measure altogether, *milhas,* which was a third the length of a Portuguese league and half the Catalan. So he tried to put it in another way. "How many days, ManiSoyo? How many days and nights? *Lumbo? Bwilo?*" Day. Night. He had picked up these words as well, and also a rudimentary sense of their numbering system. *"Bosa? Kwali?* One? Two? Or ten? *Ikumi?"*

The ManiSoyo was full of admiration for the boy. His plump, smiling face and his bright, shrewd eyes showed just how wonderful he found it that Gil had already picked up so many words of his language and how, in using those words and a few clever gestures, the boy was able to make himself understood. And he answered him slowly, carefully counting the days and nights for him on his fingers. Twelve days and nights. And then he added another word to Gil's vocabulary. *Bwato.* And he expertly pantomimed paddling a canoe to show what *bwato* meant.

"Twelve days and nights in a canoe? I think that's what he's telling us, my lord Captain."

But before Cão could comment on this, the ManiSoyo made a thoroughly confusing gesture. He threw up his hands and wildly wiggled his fingers as if he were demonstrating an explosion of some sort, while speaking words Gil hadn't heard before.

"Something happens after those twelve days' journey upriver, my lord Captain. Something happens to the river. Something like an explosion."

Cão nodded. "Aye, something like an explosion. Turbulence is the way I'd put it. Rapids or waterfalls. Is that what happens to *zaire,* ManiSoyo?" Cão could not get the pronunciation right; it repeatedly came out *zaire* instead of *nzere.* *"Zaire* turns turbulent after twelve days' journey, becomes white water, rapids, falls?"

The ManiSoyo didn't understand.

"I'd wager that's it. After twelve days and nights in a canoe, you come to some sort of rapids or waterfalls. Twelve days and nights in a canoe. How far would that be? Say they paddle for the duration of a watch each day and again each night, making two knots. Say two leagues to the watch then, four leagues each day for twelve days. What does that make it? Forty-five, fifty leagues? The *Leonor* could do that in three days, two if the river remains anywhere as navigable as it has been so far."

No one commented on this. Cão obviously was merely thinking out loud.

And then he said, "Tell him we wish to go and see for ourselves where *zaire* explodes. Tell him we wish to go tomorrow morning and take him with us to show us the way."

MOUNTAINS REARED UP on the eastern horizon.

They were then three days and thirty leagues from Mpinda, having sailed only during the daylight hours, and throughout that time and distance, the river had remained the mighty *rio poderoso* Cão had guessed it to be on first entering its mouth, possibly the mightiest in all Creation. To be sure, it had gradually narrowed from the immense, baylike expanse of its mouth but even the many large, wooded islands that broke up its stream into various channels (each, though, as broad and as navigable as many major rivers in Europe) could not disguise its amazing size and strength. Its true north bank, occasionally glimpsed from the crow's nest, showed it to be, even at its narrowest, more than a league across. The knowledge of this, the promise it held forth, elated Cão. Perhaps, indeed, he had discovered a passageway through the heart of Africa to the Indian Ocean on the continent's eastern shore.

But then the mountains reared up on the eastern horizon.

They had first been sighted in the early hours of the day before when, still a good ten leagues away, they appeared as a hazy blue mass in the morning mist that could be mistaken for low-lying clouds. By midafternoon, they could not be mistaken for anything other than what they actually were, a massif of nearly two-thousand-foot altitude. But it was still possible then to hold out hope that they didn't block the river, that the river would soon be seen to veer around them, flowing either out of the foothills to the southeast or from the grassy flatlands to the northeast. But by this morning even that hope was gone. Cão and Vizinho, who had been charting every island and channel and reef and mudflat and cove along the way, recognized with sinking hearts that they had been sailing up what was the estuary of the river, a river that came crashing down out of those mountains to spread out and flow down to the sea across a swampy, forested maritime plain on the final leg of what must be a tremendous journey from God only knew where.

The ManiSoyo, with Gil as his interpreter, stood with Cão and Vizinho on the quarterdeck as they approached the mountains. He had been deeply disappointed on his first day aboard when he discovered that the *Leonor* wasn't going to actually fly. But he had finally consoled himself by concluding, from what he understood of Gil's explanations, that the only reason the *Leonor* never lifted off from the surface of the river was that the voyage wasn't deemed long enough for such a daring maneuver. And, besides, the sensation of speed, so breathtaking and never before experienced, of the *Leonor* making way under full sail with a spanking breeze on her quarter was thrill enough for him, a thrill very nearly the equivalent of what actually flying might have been. And from then on, he proved himself an enthusiastic and expert river pilot, pointing out the best channels to follow, the reefs to avoid, the safe anchorages for the night, and then whirling about to watch in openly innocent delight as seamen scrambled in the shrouds and hauled on the yards and trimmed the sheets to make the great-winged bird of a ship respond to the directions he gave.

As did the bodyguard of ten warriors he had brought along. They remained in the ship's waist, trying to stay out from underfoot, watching everything with awe and wonder, often leaning over the rails to let the wind and spray blow hard against their faces. It was an adventure they would tell about when they returned home, much as they would tell about a great battle they had fought or a great hunt they had made, and it would pass into the lore of the tribe as an event even greater than their greatest battle or hunt.

Around the head of the island in the lee of which they had spent their third night from Mpinda, the river's south bank, after so many leagues of dense, steaming forest and bug-infested swamps, became rocky and steep and the vegetation increasingly sparse. And the river itself, considerably narrowed to less than a third of a league across, began running much faster than before, and there were more reefs and mudflats and logjams in the stream, and the fast-running water broke over these reefs and mudflats and logjams in lively spumes of spray. The mountains themselves were still some distance to the east but it was clear that what they were seeing now was the first indication of how the river would emerge from those mountains, much narrowed and reef-strewn and running fast.

Gil looked at the ManiSoyo and the ManiSoyo threw up his hands and made those wild wiggling movements with his fingers, then pointed ahead and smiled.

"I think we are very nearly there, my lord Captain."

Cão was scanning the river through his spyglass. "Ask him which is the safest channel to follow."

As if understanding the question or simply concerned for his own safety, the ManiSoyo pointed to a stretch of relatively quiet water running closely along the increasingly higher and rockier south bank.

Under shortened sail and then with only the spritsail and fore-course unfurled, they continued upriver for another two hours—all hands topside, all hands on station—and, if there had been the slightest doubt or a last glimmering of hope that the river might yet surprise them in its course, the doubt vanished and the hope was extinguished. With every league they sailed now, the rocks and boulders of the banks piled always higher until they merged into sheer limestone cliffs, scored with jagged granite outcroppings and seamed with glittering quartz and tourmaline crystals, from which only the hardiest shrubs and trees could grow, and the banks themselves drew steadily closer together until barely two thousand yards and then one thousand yards of water separated them. And those one thousand yards and then five hundred yards of water filled with more and more reefs and mudflats over which and around which the river roiled and burst like whitecaps on the ocean, and breezes swirled off the cliff-high banks and blew down in sudden gusts out of the mountains, always more contrary and variable and unpredictable. The cause was clearly lost. *Nzere* or, as Cão persisted in mispronouncing it, *zaire,* some forty leagues from its mouth, some forty leagues up its estuary across the low-lying maritime plain, became impassable.

"*Matadi,*" the ManiSoyo said and pointed toward the south bank.

Whether this was the name of a place or the word for rock—it could have been both—a ledge of limestone jutted out over the river from the top of the hundred-foot-high cliff of the south bank. Under it, the sheer cliff of the bank curved out into the stream, forming a half-crescent cove enclosing deep, black water. Directly across from it to the north bank was now no more than three hundred yards. And up ahead beyond the overhanging ledge, the river disappeared around a sharp bend, obscured from view by the steep walls of limestone and granite that plunged into it on both sides. Gil could almost imagine the river going underground there, funneling into the mountains themselves.

"Well, José?" Cão asked the pilot, the spyglass again at his eye.

"This is the end of it for the *Leonor,* my lord," Vizinho replied. "But we might as well have a look a bit farther up in the longboat, we've come this far, so I can mark it on my chart."

"I suppose we might as well. Bosun."

"Aye, my lord Captain."

"Tell the first mate to cast the lead. We are making for that cove under the ledge."

The cove was large enough and deep enough for the *Leonor* but getting into it, because of the complexity of the winds and the prevalence of rocks, required a tow by the ship's longboat. The ManiSoyo protested this development. He spoke rapidly and intently to Gil, gesturing repeatedly toward the mountains, as the *Leonor* dropped anchor. Essentially what he was saying was that this wasn't the place where *nzere* turned wild, that this didn't truly happen until farther upstream, so why were they heaving-to here? He had great faith in the capabilities of the sailing ship and nothing Gil said could persuade him that the river was already too wild for the *Leonor* to risk trying to make further headway. After all, couldn't the *Leonor* fly?

Cão didn't pay any attention to this. He had lost interest in the

ManiSoyo. Cruelly put, the ManiSoyo was of no more use to him. He had explored the river as far as it could be explored and had discovered what he had needed to discover: that it was no passage to the Indies, that it was navigable for only some forty leagues from its mouth.

And now his mind was on other things. Even as he had the long-boat brought alongside and the ManiSoyo, still arguing the matter with Gil, climbed down the rope ladder into it, Cão's thoughts had moved on to the continuation of the voyage southward down the West African coast in search of the sea route to the Indies and to the supplies he might take on at Mpinda for that voyage: wood, fresh water, some of the fruits and meat and other food they had enjoyed at the ManiSoyo's feast, certainly some of the palm wine, perhaps also some of the remarkable velvetlike blue cloth the Soyo made to add to the ship's consignment of trading truck, and perhaps even a Soyo warrior or two to act as interpreters to this new breed of Negroes who apparently populated the African coast south of the equator. With the page so quickly catching on to the language and thus able to act as a go-between, they'd make more useful interpreters than the Ashanti.

"José, go up in the prow with the ManiSoyo and let him show you the way. Page, go forward with them."

"Aye, my lord Captain."

It surprised Gil that, instead of also coming up into the prow of the longboat, Cão sat down on a thwart amidship. His interest in the river, as in the ManiSoyo, had faded, and for the same reason. For him, this last bit of exploration was little more than a sightseeing trip to give Vizinho a chance to put one last mark of detail on his chart of the estuary before returning to the sea. Gil stood between Vizinho and the ManiSoyo as the sweeps rowed the longboat around the sharp bend where the river had disappeared.

It hadn't, of course, disappeared into a funnel in the mountains but where it had disappeared was almost as astonishing: a spectacular canyon whose sheer walls of stone, plunging down from a height of at least two hundred feet, narrowed this once mighty river to a width of less than a hundred yards. And the river came rushing out of this canyon with such force that, on its first impact, the sweeps lost their purchase and their oars flew out of the water and the longboat's prow was slammed to starboard and the boat turned broadside to the furious current.

Cão jumped to his feet. "What's the matter with you, *marin-heiros?* Are you not men? Put your backs into it. Dig into the water for your lives." He shouted this but there was no anger in his voice, only a sudden exhilaration. He was impressed by the river's fury. He remained on his feet. The river had come alive for him again.

And it was alive. Packed with boulders and rocks and logjams of giant trees torn from its banks, it poured out of the mountains in boiling stretches of white-water rapids and over ledges in splashing cascades, pounding at the longboat, bucking and pitching it like a wild horse so that Gil had to brace his knees against the gunwales to keep from being thrown over the side. But there were also calmer channels between the rough stretches and the ManiSoyo, grinning from ear to ear, clearly having the time of his life showing these white men something they had never seen before, picked out those navigable channels, pointed the way, urged them on, always farther on. Gil couldn't see how they could go much farther on. But apparently they could; apparently Soyo in their dugout canoes had gone much farther on up this racing, rampaging stream to some place up ahead that the ManiSoyo wanted them to see.

It was cool in the canyon and loud; the rushing, roiling water, crashing over the rapids and cascades and cataracts, echoed off the great slabs of limestone and granite of the canyon walls like thunder. Cão was still shouting encouragement to the sweeps, his heart in it again, as excited as the ManiSoyo, grinning as broadly as the ManiSoyo, as eager to see what the ManiSoyo so eagerly wanted them to see, but his shouting could hardly be heard over the thunder of the river.

And then, just ahead, the river was cut to half its width not only by the great blocks of the broken walls of the canyon but also by massive black boulders, and now there was only one channel to follow between those broken blocks and black boulders, and the water thundering down that channel from out between those blocks and boulders was pure boiling foam. And then the ManiSoyo pointed straight ahead at what he had brought the white men to see.

For an instant Gil had the vision of the ManiSoyo wiggling the fingers of his hand. What a weak parody, what a silly joke, what a ridiculous pantomime of what he now saw. A boiling caldron, a caldron of hell, a reach of river in a state of never-ending explosion, a volcano of water in constant eruption, a rampaging tide of such terrifying violence that no boat or ship or man could dream of living upon it for an instant, throwing up standing waves thirty or forty feet tall, as tall as any ship, as tall as any wave torn up by the most vicious storm on the Ocean Sea. Gil stared at it, heart-stopped in awe, stared up its raging surface, stared up to the head of the reach, stared up to the magnificent waterfall that created this boiling caldron: a horse-shoe-shaped ledge some forty yards across and nearly a hundred feet high over which the rampaging river fell in a single sheet of blue-silver water as thick as steel.

And there, on the south bank of the ledge of the waterfall, three men were standing. Looking up at them through the storm of spray and clouds of mist thrown up by the explosion of the river at the bottom of the falls, Gil could not properly make them out. But they were not Soyo. That much he could see. For, unlike the Soyo, they were not armed with bows and arrows. They were armed with lances of steel.

"My lord Captain, look." He couldn't be heard above the roar of the river. In order to attract Cão's attention, he would have had to tug at his sleeve but, as Cão was half a boat length aft, he tugged at the ManiSoyo instead. "Look, ManiSoyo," he shouted in the old chief's ear. "Look there, ManiSoyo." And he pointed to the three men watching them from atop the waterfall.

The ManiSoyo looked.

"Who are they, ManiSoyo?"

It was unlikely that the ManiSoyo heard the question or understood it if he had. But his wide grin of pleasure faded. His expression turned grim. And more to himself than in answer to Gil, he said, "Kongo." And he bowed his head.

IV

THE VOYAGE BACK to Mpinda, with the current in their favor, took three days. It would have taken a day less had they followed the same route downstream as they had up, but Vizinho wanted to see more of the estuary in order to improve his chart of it—he had marked the chart Zaire, thus naming the river with Cão's mispronunciation of *nzere*—so they returned by channels farther out in the stream and along stretches of the north bank. It was of course a grossly imperfect chart but, on the expanding map of the Atlantic coast of Africa that he was drawing, the most valuable portion would be the river's mouth, and he had elicited Cão's promise to spend a few days exploring it before returning to the Atlantic and resuming their voyage south.

When exactly that would be, Gil had no idea. Cão hadn't said. Given his determination to find the sea route to the Indies, it was not inconceivable that it would be right away, that he'd simply put the ManiSoyo and his bodyguard of warriors ashore on returning to Mpinda and sail on his way. But something else was working on his mind now, Gil could see. Just as his interest in the river had been reawakened, if only briefly, by the magnificent waterfall of the Caldron of Hell (it was so marked on Vizinho's chart), so the presence of the three warriors with steel lances at the top of the falls had reawakened his interest in the region. Who were they? Where did they come from? Why had the ManiSoyo bowed to them? The prospect that a more powerful and perhaps more advanced people than the Soyo, a people who knew the blacksmith's art, existed somewhere along this river Zaire had obviously given Cão pause. Perhaps he should find out more about them. Perhaps he should not rush back out to sea. Perhaps there was more to discover here than the mouth and estuary of a mighty river.

The matter was decided when they anchored once again in the wide cove in front of Mpinda. It was the twenty-second of August and it was immediately apparent that something was afoot. Instead of the huge crowd of villagers who on every other occasion had gathered to greet the white men, this time only a small group awaited them at the lone palm tree in the center of the market square. And from Cão's expression (he was studying them through the spyglass) and the ManiSoyo's expression (he didn't need a spyglass to know who they were) Gil could tell that they were not Soyo.

"Are they Kongo, ManiSoyo?" Gil asked.

The old chief nodded, then began speaking anxiously, pointing first to the longboat in tow in the *Leonor*'s stern, then to the market square. It was perfectly clear what he was saying: They must go ashore without delay. His agitation on this score was apparent: They must not keep the Kongo waiting.

Nevertheless, there was a delay while the arrangements in the longboat were made. The ManiSoyo insisted that, besides Cão and Gil, all his warriors accompany him ashore. But with these unknown and apparently fearsome Kongo awaiting them, Cão was loath to go ashore without Tristão and his soldiers. Along with the sweeps and bosun's mate, this would make for a much overloaded boat. But as the ManiSoyo wouldn't relent on having his personal bodyguard with him—apparently it was a matter of status and prestige if not actually defense—Cão finally decided to chance it with only five arquebus-armed soldiers and send back, immediately on disembarking, for Tristão and the halberdiers and crossbowmen. And furthermore, he had the sweeps and bosun's mate armed, and he armored himself in his plumed helmet, a skirted vest of chainmail and a fighting cutlass.

"Nuno, keep good watch. If the boat doesn't return immediately, if anything at all seems amiss, launch the cogs and come for us. Do you hear what I say, Fernão?"

"Aye, my lord Captain."

"We have no idea how many of these Kongo may be there. In the market square, there seem to be only a score or so. But elsewhere in the village . . . who can say? Others may be hiding." Cão climbed down the rope ladder into the longboat.

He was the last to go down. Gil was already in the boat, but he heard Cão's remark about the possible number of Kongo in the village. He looked back as the longboat shoved off. Segou and Goree were standing on the quarterdeck with Gonçalves, Tristão, Vizinho and Father Sebastião. How important the two Ashanti had seemed when they had first come aboard in São Jorgé da Mina and how useless they had become now that they had entered a world as alien to them as to the Portuguese.

There were no drums when the longboat ran up on the muddy bank this time. There was only birdsong and the buzzing of insects and the metallic humming of cicadas in the expectant silence. The ManiSoyo jumped out, hissing something in a low voice to his warriors, and they jumped out after him and, forming a phalanx behind him, followed him toward the group at the tall, lone palm tree with long-striding gaits. Cão remained in the boat's prow a moment longer, scanning the market square, then he too jumped out but kept a hand on the boat's prow while taking another long look around. Then he gave an order and the five soldiers jumped out. But, raising a hand, he kept them standing in the mud by the boat, river water lapping at their boots. Gil remained alone in the prow: the sweeps behind him, their oars shipped, twisted around to look over their shoulders.

Before the ManiSoyo and his bodyguard were halfway to the palm, three figures disengaged themselves from the group waiting there and hurried forward. Gil immediately recognized who they were: the NsakuSoyo and two of the MbunduSoyo, the ManiSoyo's wives. The NsakuSoyo wore a feathered headdress and cape and carried his pebble-filled gourd. The MbunduSoyo, wrapped in velvety blue with turbans of the same material around their heads, carried the ManiSoyo's ceremonial garb, one his feathered headdress, the other his feathered cape. They placed these on him with great care, then dropped behind the phalanx of his bodyguard, and with the

NsakuSoyo at his side, the ManiSoyo resumed advancing, although at a slower, more deliberate pace.

There were twenty of them. As best Gil could make out, they all seemed to be warriors of the type seen atop the waterfall at the Caldron of Hell, tall, muscled, strong young men of the same dark-honey or cocoa complexion as the Soyo, with high cheekbones and slightly slanted eyes, wearing the same sort of long skirt as the Soyo warriors but pale green in color and bordered in red and without bows or arrow quivers on their backs. They lounged around the bole of the palm in rather indolent poses, leaning on those lances made of steel or at least partially of steel, long, spearlike metal blades fitted into gracefully tapered shafts of dark wood. Circular shields, centered with deadly spikes like the shields of the ancient Greeks, rested against their legs. Were they also of steel or partially of steel? The sun glinted off them as if they were.

When within ten paces of them, the ManiSoyo's entourage halted. No words were exchanged. The silence was unbroken. And then the ManiSoyo dropped to his knees. Only he. The NsakuSoyo, the warriors and wives looked down at him, averting their eyes from the Kongo. He supported himself on his knees with his carved, wooden, ivory-topped staff for a moment. Then very carefully he set the staff aside and fell face forward on the red earth.

"Mother of God, he is their vassal," Cão said in a whisper.

The ManiSoyo remained prostrate for some minutes. Then, at last, the lounging Kongo warriors picked up their shields and assumed a more attentive demeanor, and one of their number stepped forward. He was shorter than the others and, at least to Gil's eyes, younger, broad-shouldered and muscular but not quite as muscularly big and bulky as the others, slimmer, lither, lighter in weight; his seemed more the physique of a boy than a full-grown man, a physique, as a matter of fact, not unlike Gil's. He was adorned, as the others were not, with bracelets of a white, shining metal—could it be polished steel or even silver?—around his wrists and biceps and ankles, and a necklace of some ferocious animal's teeth around his neck, and a broad band of silver around his head at the center of which, above the bridge of his nose, was a green stone. An emerald? He too had a lance, but no shield, and now he laid the vicious cutting edge of the lance across the back of the prostrate ManiSoyo's exposed neck.

The ManiSoyo stood up. The Kongo youth stepped back and again leaned against the bole of the palm tree, folding his arms across his chest, the lance resting in the crook of his elbow, resuming his indolent, disrespectful pose. There was nothing in the way of an exchange of greetings. The ManiSoyo simply began speaking and, as he did, the youth looked past him to the longboat and the white men and then past them out to the river to the *Leonor* anchored in the cove. What did he make of her, her sails struck, standing off under bare poles, her pennants fluttering in a light breeze, her high castles fore and aft, her round hull bobbing on the river's tide?

"Bosun's mate, return to the ship and bring the others ashore."

"Aye, my lord Captain."

"Get out of there, page."

Gil leaped out of the longboat as the soldiers pushed her off into the river and the sweeps took their first pull, their oars scraping bottom. The ManiSoyo turned around at the noise.

"Let's go to them before the old boy flies into a panic, thinking we're trying to make our escape."

"But what about the others, my lord Captain?" Gil asked.

"What others?"

"The Kongo who are hiding."

"Do you see any sign of them?"

"No, my lord Captain, but if they are hiding . . . I mean, I do not see any sign of other Soyo either."

"You are alert, page. Stay alert. But don't be too clever. You may frighten yourself unnecessarily. And, besides, we have our guns. Eh, *soldatos?*"

The soldiers grunted. They were a hardened lot, veterans of many skirmishes with Guineans on the West African coast and, in their helmets and armor and grizzly beards, looked not the least bit afraid. But there were only five of them.

"Come on then. Let's not keep these Kongo waiting."

Gil's heart was in his mouth and his mouth was dry. He didn't understand his feelings, this sudden rush of apprehension he was experiencing. He hadn't been afraid of the Soyo. Quite to the contrary;

he had pushed himself forward in order to meet them. Why then did he go forward now so reluctantly? What was it about the Kongo that made him suddenly afraid?

The Kongo youth did not change his indolent posture as the little band of white men approached. He eyed them keenly, Gil could see, but he remained leaning casually against the bole of the palm tree, his arms folded across his chest, breathing easily, showing himself to be not in the least impressed by these white, hairy, armored creatures.

He was, indeed, much younger than the others, no more than a year or two older than Gil, if even that. But his icy, disdainful, aloof bearing masked his youth. The ManiSoyo hurried back to the white men and, positioning himself between Cão and Gil, hurried them forward. The NsakuSoyo, the two wives and ten Soyo warriors stepped aside for them. The five Portuguese soldiers moved up behind them, holding their firearms at the port. Close up, the score of Kongo warriors, lances in hand, shields held low before their waists, exuded a fierceness, a menace, a savagery not sensed in the Soyo. The Mani-Soyo began speaking rapidly and anxiously to the Kongo youth, and although Gil could only guess at what he was saying, he was relieved to hear that the language he spoke was the same as that which he had been speaking all along. Evidently, the Soyo and the Kongo were kindred in language as well as in looks, if not in attitude and bearing.

"Deego Cum," the ManiSoyo said. "Gil Eenezh." And then: "Porta Geeze." And he pointed at the sky.

"He is telling him about us, my lord Captain."

"I can make that out well enough for myself, page," Cão snapped.

Gil was taken aback by the sharpness of his tone. His grizzled, pockmarked face had darkened, his bushy eyebrows had knitted together fiercely and he stared at the Kongo youth, this boy warrior, with barely restrained fury. It was the Kongo's careless, contemptuous, showily disrespectful pose that angered him.

"My lord Captain—" Gil started in a low voice.

But again Cão cut him off sharply. "Tell him to stand up. Tell him he is in the presence of a captain-general of the king's fleet."

The ManiSoyo turned to Cão at this harsh outburst.

"ManiSoyo," Gil quickly asked, hoping to stave off trouble, "who is this Kongo *muntu?*" And he pointed at the Kongo youth.

And the ManiSoyo slapped his hand down.

"What?" Gil pulled his hand away in bafflement, his heart suddenly racing.

The ManiSoyo again turned to Cão and said a word to him, a hard clack of a word—*kibiti*—spitting it out and pointing to the ground. When Cão looked at him in a mixture of anger and incomprehension, he spat out the word again—*kibiti, kibiti*—and again pointed at the ground. It was a demanding word, a commanding gesture. And when Cão still didn't respond, he grabbed Cão's shoulder and attempted to push him down. Cão instantly jerked away, throwing up an arm that knocked the ManiSoyo's hand from his shoulder.

This caused a quick stir. The Kongo warriors stepped forward, hoisting their shields, bringing their lances into play, low at their hips. Even the youth, leaning against the tree, straightened up, taking his lance in hand. The Portuguese soldiers lowered their firearms to waist level and, stepping back to get a clear field of fire, thumbed back the hammerlocks.

Heart pounding, mouth dry, Gil said, "I think he wants you to kneel, my lord Captain."

"I know damn well what he wants me to do. And he can go straight to hell if he imagines I will do it. Kneel, will I? To this savage boy with his mother's milk still on his lips? He will burn in hell before I'll kneel to him or any other savage . . . God curse you, man. I warn you now. Keep your filthy paws to yourself. Do not dare touch me again."

For the ManiSoyo had tried a second time to force Cão to his knees and, for a second time, Cão had viciously struck his hand away. Gil started saying his prayers.

But then the Kongo youth, curling his lips in disgust, taking a quick glance around at his warriors, raised his lance, grasping it just at its balance a quarter-length below the gleaming metal blade, holding it easily in his hand, and poked it forward not too aggressively, poked it forward disdainfully, poked it forward not at Cão but at the ManiSoyo, poked it at the old chief's chest, poked it so lightly that it didn't even scratch the old chief's chest but simply poked the old chief aside. Then he stood the lance on its shaft and again folded his arms across his chest. But he remained standing straight now. He did not lean back against the palm tree.

"Deego Cum," he said.

The captain-general's darkly angry face barely concealed his surprise. After a moment, he nodded, narrowing his eyes. "Aye, I'm Diogo Cão," he replied warily.

"Mbemba a Nzinga," the youth said and touched his chest. "MtuKongo." And he smiled. And it was a boy's smile, mischievous, as if all his haughty iciness had been merely a boy's playacting.

And the Kongo warriors relaxed. And the Portuguese soldiers eased down on the hammerlocks of their guns. And Gil breathed a sigh of relief.

BY THE TIME the longboat returned from the *Leonor* with the second landing party—the master-at-arms with his halberdiers and crossbowmen, Nuno Gonçalves and Father Sebastião but not Segou—Cão and the Kongo youth were seated facing each other on hourglass-shaped stools with Gil at Cão's side, doing his best to interpret what had developed into a rather lively conversation.

A few essentials had been established. The youth's name was Mbemba, son of Nzinga. He was a prince of the Kongo, MtuKongo. His father, Nzinga a Nkuwu (Nzinga, son of Nkuwu), was the ManiKongo, the king of the Kongo. And the kingdom of the Kongo encompassed a realm of as many leagues in every direction from the Zaire, *nzere,* as the mind could imagine: northward across the river for as far as a swift man could run in a hundred days; eastward from the river's mouth on the Atlantic Ocean to the waterfall of the Caldron of Hell and beyond to the top of the mountains where the river began its descent down the mountains, crashing over hundreds of cataracts and cascades each as terrible as the Caldron, out of a lake called Mpumbu; and, finally, south and southeastward from the river through the forest and into the mountains for as far as it would take a swift man to run in a *thousand* days. This realm or kingdom, which Cão calculated to be at least ten thousand square leagues with very nearly two million people (larger in both respects than Portugal itself), apparently was divided into six major fiefdoms or provinces—

Nsundi, Mbata, Mpangu, Mbamba, Mpemba and this one, Soyo—vassal principalities whose chiefs or lords, like the ManiSoyo, paid tribute and pledged fealty to the supreme sovereign of all, the ManiKongo, who ruled from his royal city, Mbanza Kongo, atop a sacred mountain some twenty days' march through the forest to the southeast.

While this information was being acquired, the villagers of Mpinda slowly reappeared. They had been hiding in their huts and even now kept their distance, clearly in reverence and fear of the Kongo prince. There were, however, no more Kongo among them, Gil noticed, and he couldn't help but think that this must be a measure of the power the Kongo wielded over their realm—and of their insolent certainty that nothing existed to challenge that power—that this boy prince would travel so lightly armed and with only twenty warriors for a bodyguard to a place where strange white creatures were said to have flown down to the kingdom from a land in the sky. And it was a further measure of this insolent sureness of omnipotence that this Mbemba never once asked about these Porta Geeze and their remarkable birdlike ship. It was as if it were beneath him to reveal an emotion as common as curiosity. Repeatedly his eyes strayed to the *Leonor* at anchor in the river and to the firearms and armor of the soldiers ranked behind Cão and to Gil standing beside Cão, to Gil's fair skin and light eyes and long, straight tawny hair—to a boy so very much a boy like himself and so very much unlike him in every way—but he always returned his attention to Cão to answer his ceaseless stream of questions as best as he understood them, never once putting a question of his own. And surely he must have had a thousand questions of his own.

The conversation broke off when the second landing party disembarked from the longboat. Tristão obviously wasn't sure of the situation and kept his soldiers, Father Sebastião and Gonçalves at the water's edge until Cão realized they were there and signaled them to come forward. The ManiSoyo, standing beside the young prince, explained who they were as they approached. Only Gonçalves was a mystery to him, and he let Gil go through the tedious business of making that introduction.

"I think we may have stumbled on something quite remarkable, Nuno," Cão said. His expression was as bright and alive as when he had first spoken of the *rio poderoso*. "A kingdom."

"A kingdom, my lord Captain?"

"Aye, or something very much like one, if this young savage here isn't merely spinning us a yarn. According to him, all the land for hundreds of leagues around, on both sides of the river and upriver into those mountains we saw, all of it compose the realm. The kingdom of Kongo, a kingdom of more than a million subjects, I'd reckon. The Soyo here certainly are subjects of it. The ManiSoyo is in fear of his life of this boy, a prince of the kingdom. He fell face down in front of him as if struck by lightning. And look at those lances, Nuno. Pure steel. Have you ever seen the like of it anywhere in Africa before? And the bracelets the boy is wearing. Silver, aren't they? And that green stone in his headband. What do you make of it? An emerald, I'd say."

"It could be, my lord Captain," Gonçalves replied slowly, apparently not entirely convinced but perfectly aware of Cão's enthusiasm and easily imagining, as Gil could, what Cão must be imagining. "And where is the king of this kingdom, my lord Captain?"

"Twenty days' march through the forest to the southeast, the boy tells me. On a mountaintop. A royal city called Mbanza Kongo. The boy has been sent to fetch us there."

"And are you thinking of going?"

"I don't know. I haven't decided. What do you think?"

"Twenty days there and twenty days back plus however many days you spend there. Nearly two months. It is a great deal of time."

"Aye, it is. But it could be quite a find, Nuno. An African kingdom of steel and silver and emeralds. Maybe even gold. What a find to bring home to João. Not only a mighty river but also a mighty kingdom."

"With respect, my lord Captain, may I remind you that you were not sent by João to find an African kingdom, nor even silver or emeralds or gold. You were sent to find the way to the Indies."

"I know."

"Two months is a great deal of time to lose, my lord Captain. Especially as we have no sure idea how much farther we may yet have to sail before we come to the Indian Sea. It is nearly four months already that we have been under way and there is still the voyage home to consider."

"I know, Nuno. I said, I know."

Throughout this exchange, the Kongo youth watched the two

white men closely, and when Cão broke off and removed his helmet
and ran a hand through his hair, he turned to Gil to learn what had
been said. Gil had no idea how to translate it and decided that it
didn't really matter anyway, so he pretended not to notice the young
prince's inquiring look. Evidently annoyed at being ignored, the
Kongo prince suddenly stood up from his stool.

"Mbanza Kongo," he said and pointed with his lance to the
southeast, the direction through the forest behind Mpinda where the
ManiKongo's royal city was located and where, presumably, the
ManiKongo was waiting to meet the white men from the sky.

"My lord Captain, he wishes us to go—"

"Aye, page, I understood that," Cão interrupted testily. "It wasn't
all that difficult to understand. Nuno."

"Aye, my lord Captain?"

"It is a damn hard thing to do, Nuno, to simply sail away and
never know what we might have found."

"Aye, my lord Captain."

"A kingdom, Nuno. A mighty kingdom on the shores of a mighty
river. Can we simply sail away and never know?"

"Perhaps one of us could go."

"Eh?"

"Or a few of us, while the rest of us sail on to the Indian Sea.
Whoever goes could be fetched up again on the voyage home."

"Aye, Nuno, perhaps that's the solution. But which one of us?
Not you nor I nor the pilot. We must sail the *Leonor.*"

"Allow it to be me, Dom Diogo." This was Father Sebastião. "Allow me to be the one to go."

"You, padre?"

"It is my place to go. It is my place and my duty to bring the
word of our Lord to a mighty kingdom like this. And I am not required for the voyage to the Indian Sea."

"Forty days, my lord Captain, and add another twenty for the
stay," Gonçalves said. "Sixty days. Make it two months exactly. Surely
in two months we can sail to the Prassum Promontorium and return
here to fetch the padre on the voyage home. It cannot take us much
longer than that. In any event, we are not outfitted for a voyage much
longer than that. Even reckoning so, it will be very nearly a year before we see the roads of the Tagus again."

"But he cannot go alone."

"I will not be alone, Dom Diogo. God will be with me."

"Aye, good padre, God will be with you, but still . . . You must have attendants. We can spare some soldiers for the padre, can't we, Fernão?"

Tristão hesitated.

"Two soldiers at the very least. Two halberdiers as his body-guard."

"As you wish, my lord Captain."

"And also the page."

"Me, my lord Captain?" Gil nearly jumped out of his boots.

"Aye, you, my faithful page. You have made friends with these people. And you speak their language as the good padre does not."

"But I don't really, my lord Captain. I barely understand—"

"Every day you speak it better. I hear it myself. By the time you reach his royal city, you will speak it well enough to speak to the Kongo king."

V

I WON'T GO, DOM NUNO. I tell you, I won't. They will kill me."

"Be still, little son. The matter is settled. And no one will kill you."

"They will. I know they will. They don't want me. They want the captain-general. You saw what a fuss the MtuKongo, Mbemba, made when he finally understood that the captain-general was not going, that only Father Sebastião and I were going, and the two halberdiers. He wouldn't have it. He said his father would receive only the captain-general, no one of a lesser rank, certainly not a ship's boy, not even a priest. He is a king and he will receive only a king. They think the captain-general is our king."

"Aye, that was all true enough but only until he learned that you were the son of our king, the son of the captain-general and thus a prince as he is a prince. Then he relented quickly enough, did he not?"

Gil and Gonçalves were in the magazine in the *Leonor*'s stern-castle, rummaging through the stores to find suitable clothing and armor and weapons and adornments to masquerade the page as a prince.

That had been Gil's last hope of avoiding the journey to Mbanza Kongo: that the ManiKongo would not receive him. But then Cão had hit on the idea of representing Gil as his son and as such Mbemba's equal and arguing that, if it was no insult to send Mbemba, the ManiKongo's son, to the captain-general, how could it be a sign of disrespect to send the captain-general's son to the ManiKongo? And the young Kongo prince, Mbemba, had rather taken to the idea that this strange, fair-haired, light-eyed boy of very nearly his own age was a prince like himself and a prince of a realm so distant and different that no one had ever dreamed that it existed and, as such, a realm possibly as powerful as his own.

"And why in God's name would you imagine they would kill you anyway?" Gonçalves went on, pulling out of a slop chest an embroidered black velvet surcoat that he judged would fit the boy. "Has any one of these people so much as lifted a hand in anger or hostility against us? They hold us in awe, little son. They believe us creatures heaven-sent. Of course they won't kill you."

"But I don't *want* to go, Dom Nuno. It's all right for the padre and the soldiers. Their business is on the land, to convert the heathen or fight them. But I am *marinheiro*. My business is on the sea. I want to sail with you and make my name on this voyage of discovery to the Indies."

"You will make your name just as well by discovering an African kingdom. Do you think João will not well reward you for bringing home the story of this kingdom? Do you think he will not be greatly pleased to hear of a kingdom of silver and gold and precious stones that you have found?"

"The padre could do as well."

"The padre does not speak the language, and the story he will bring home will be for the pope, not the king. Now hold still and try on this surcoat. It is handsome enough for a prince."

When they went topside, Gil was wearing the embroidered surcoat over a skirted vest of chainmail with a breastplate hammered with the royal coat-of-arms, a *salade* Gonçalves had polished up and affixed with a peacock's plume, puffed-out, knee-length leather pantaloons, knee-high black wool stockings striped in silver thread and a short stabbing sword, scabbarded and hanging from a wide, silver-buckled leather belt. Only his boots were his own. Cão was waiting on the quarterdeck with Vizinho.

"What say you, my lord Captain?" Gonçalves asked proudly, shoving Gil forward to show off the costume.

Cão raised his bushy eyebrows in admiration. "Well done, Nuno.

He is handsome enough to actually be my son. Eh, José?"

"This is no longer a mere page, my lord Captain," the pilot replied, smiling. "This surely must be a prince."

"My lord Captain—" Gil started.

But Cão raised his hand. "I will listen to no further word of complaint from you about why or whether you will or will not go, boy. I have already commanded you to go."

"I have no further word of complaint, my lord Captain. I see that my fate is sealed. But I have a request."

"And what is that?"

"I would have Segou come with me."

"Segou?"

"With respect, my lord Captain, you overestimate my facility in the language of these people. Segou speaks and understands it far better than I. In moments of confusion or trouble, I would be able to turn to him."

"That may be, but you see that these people despise him."

"The Soyo do. Perhaps the Kongo will not. But, in any case, they need have nothing to do with him. I would keep him by my side so that I can turn to him when the need arises. And the Soyo and the Kongo can make of that whatever they wish."

Cão looked around. The pilot was at the compass binnacle, and the priest and master-at-arms were in the ship's waist with the two halberdiers who had been selected to make the journey to Mbanza Kongo, but neither Segou nor Goree were anywhere to be seen. They probably were below decks, sulking. Segou's pride had been mortally wounded by the way the Soyo had treated him and the younger Ashanti commiserated with him.

"And he would be of help in other ways. He is at home in country such as this. He is familiar with forests such as these. It is true that we have been treated well by these people so far but who can say what may yet transpire before you return to fetch us home. Two months is a long time and we may yet have to fend for ourselves in these forests."

Cão pursed his lips. "Very well, page. What you say is fair. Segou will accompany you. The bosun will roust him. Is there anything else?"

Gil shook his head. "No, my lord Captain, there is nothing else."

"Your sea chest is in the longboat, little son," Gonçalves said. "Come along."

"Take good care of yourself, Gil," the pilot called from the binnacle.

"I will, Dom José. And think of me as you chart the coast and give my name to some cove or little island along the way."

Vizinho smiled and raised his hand. "Go with God," he said as Gil turned away.

"You do not bid me farewell, page?"

Gil looked back at Cão.

"Oh, now, boy, do not be so angry with me. I send you on a grand adventure. You will thank me for it when I bring you home and present you to João."

Gil shrugged and followed Gonçalves down to the spar deck where Father Sebastião and the two halberdiers were waiting to board the longboat. Looking neither to the left nor right, Gil went straight to the rail to vault it and start down the rope ladder into the longboat. But Father Sebastião detained him.

"Gil Eanes," he said, and then to the two halberdiers. "Vasco Dias. Dinis Gomes. We undertake a solemn mission in the name of our king and our God. Let us invoke the aid of the Virgin Mary and ask for her benediction for our journey."

When the prayer was completed, Gil again started over the rail, but again he was detained, this time by Gonçalves.

"Don't forget this, little son," he said and held out the bloodstone necklace. "It's your lucky charm."

Gil took the necklace and put it around his neck. And then he threw his arms around Gonçalves and hugged him.

This was the twenty-sixth of August, a date Gil fixed firmly in his mind. For it was from this date that he would begin his count of the sixty days until the *Leonor* returned to fetch him home.

THEY DID NOT set off for Mbanza Kongo until after the *Leonor* had sailed. This wasn't Gil's idea. It was Mbemba's. As far as Gil was concerned, he would just as soon have been well on the way before then, partly because he was in a hurry—the sooner he got there, the sooner he'd be back—and partly because the sight of the *Leonor* weighing anchor and making sail only added to his feelings of loneliness and loss, the loneliness of being abandoned by his shipmates to the company of savages, the loss of the chance to participate in what could be the most important ocean voyage ever undertaken.

But, even though Mbemba too was in a hurry, it was precisely in order to see the *Leonor* weigh anchor and make sail that the young Kongo prince delayed their departure. Despite his posturing of indifference, despite his refusal to show himself in any way impressed or amazed by the white men and their things and ask any questions about them, the truth of course was that he was burning with a boy's curiosity about them. Seeing the *Leonor* riding at anchor under bare poles was one thing. Seeing her sails unfurl with a sharp crack and catch the wind and billow forth, seeing her rush out into the river with a startling surge of uncanny speed, her pennants flying, her prow churning up spumes of spray as if indeed she were a giant waterbird making her run across the river's glistening, glassy surface before taking flight, well, that was quite something else. Gil saw it in his eyes. His pose remained that of calculated nonchalance, but it was there in his shining, disbelieving eyes, the recognition that he was seeing something truly marvelous, something beyond the ken of even his great Kongo kingdom.

A caravan of some two hundred souls had been assembled for the journey to Mbanza Kongo. It was formed in three parts. In the advance were two or three score Soyo warriors, hunters, trackers and beaters plus a band of trumpeters and drummers and fetishers, the last shaking rattles and beating on sticks, whether to alert the countryside to the caravan's progress or drive the evil spirits of the forest away, Gil had no idea. In the rear were a hundred or more Soyo porters and women, carrying on their heads a monumental tonnage of rolled mats and baskets and bundles and jars and clay pots containing God only knew what—provisions for the journey, tribute to the ManiKongo?—as well as the sea chests, duffles and other baggage of Gil, Father Sebastião, Segou and the two halberdiers. In between was the princely contingent of Mbemba's bodyguard of twenty Kongo warriors armed with their shields and lances, plus sixteen Soyo litter bearers, four bearers to a litter, each of the four litters made of wonderfully supple, tanned hide stitched to two long iron-wood poles. The litters were for Mbemba, Gil, Father Sebastião and the NsakuSoyo.

The NsakuSoyo was coming along. Gil hadn't expected that. Maybe it was simply as a courtesy to Father Sebastião, since the understanding was that the two were of equivalent rank, as Gil and Mbemba were supposed to be of equivalent rank. But it could have been to keep an eye on the Franciscan priest. Gil was aware that the ju-ju man had watched, with undisguised disapproval, Father Sebastião's fumbling attempts to instruct the Soyo in the Faith or at least interest them in various sacerdotal articles of the Church. So he might have insinuated himself into the caravan to protect his people from the influence of this alien religion. But, whichever the case, Gil wasn't happy to find him waiting by a litter when the caravan prepared to get under way. The skinny man's mean face gave him a chill.

And there was another cause for unease. This had to do with Segou. Mbemba and the Kongo warriors hadn't seen the Ashanti until now, and it turned out that they held him in as much contempt as did the Soyo. They wouldn't have him in their company; if he had to come along, they wanted him relegated to the rear of the caravan with the porters and the women. But Gil held his ground. Segou was his friend. Segou would march at his side or neither of them would march at all. Mbemba didn't believe this, but he relented to the extent of allowing the Ashanti to remain with Gil under the condition that he give up his spear and shield. Segou protested, knowing that to go unarmed meant he would be regarded as a slave, but finally acquiesced because of Gil's promises and special pleading. It was, however, not a good beginning.

And there was yet another problem: Who actually was in command of this little band of white men, this deputation from the captain-general to the king of the Kongo? Cão had not bothered to make it clear. As far as Mbemba was concerned, Gil of course was, and Father Sebastião was perfectly willing to have it that way. He couldn't imagine how any conflict could arise; his mission to the Kongo was of an entirely different character from Gil's and undertaken in the name of an entirely different authority. But the two halberdiers—Vasco Dias and Dinis Gomes—were another matter. They

both were men in their thirties, chosen by the master-at-arms just because they were among the oldest and hardest and most brutishly
fearless of his soldiers. As far as they were concerned, the savages
could believe whatever they wished about Gil—that he was the captain-general's son, that he was a prince—they knew he was nothing
but a ship's boy and they'd be damned if they'd take orders from him.
But as there was no difference in rank between them, or much difference in age or experience, they'd be damned if they'd take orders
from each other either.

The first day's march from Mpinda was eastward along the riverbank, the drummers, trumpeters and fetishers leading the way and
raising a terrific celebratory or warning din. Mbemba and Gil, Father
Sebastião and the NsakuSoyo were meant to follow in the litters but
the idea of being carried made Gil acutely uncomfortable. No one
had carried him anywhere since he had been a babe in his mother's
arms, and when Father Sebastião insisted on walking in order to pursue his ministry among the porters and women and other common
folk, Gil used that as an excuse to eschew the litter as well. And when
he did, so did Mbemba, apparently considering it improper to travel
with his head higher than that of his white counterpart. And when
he got down from the litter, so did the NsakuSoyo, not daring to have
his head higher than the MtuKongo's. He got down with a certain ill
grace and fell into step beside Father Sebastião.

It wasn't particularly difficult going. Mbemba set an easy, am-
bling pace and the path was wide and well-cleared and well-trodden,
with the river on the left and shaded by the palms and mangroves
and giant ferns of the forest on the right. Swarms of butterflies
swirled up from the path in clouds of brilliant colors as they advanced; spiderwebs, wet with the morning dew, glittered like silver
threads when struck by the sun rising and passing overhead; parrots
and macaws, woodpeckers and crows and finches and tiny hum-
mingbirds, singing and trilling and endlessly calling to each other, flit-
ted in and out of the trees while brown and black and red and
dog-faced monkeys leaped and crashed through the branches and
vines, squawking and screeching in annoyance or panic as the caravan passed. Occasionally a small animal, too swift for Gil to identify—
a hare, a wild pig, a rodent, a civet cat—scampered across the path,

and occasionally there'd be a village along the way whose inhabitants would come out to pay their respects to the young Kongo prince and ogle the remarkable white men he was taking to meet their king.

Mbemba walked beside Gil. Gil wasn't quite sure what to make of him. He wanted to like him and he was likable enough when he let his guard down and allowed his youthfulness to show. But he was unpredictable in this. His mischievous, boyish smiles came and went quickly and, as if suddenly remembering his high station and regal role, he'd assume an aloof, superior, haughty air, insolently full of his own self-esteem.

Segou followed a few steps behind them, never out of hailing distance, humiliated by his status, apprehensive of the Kongo warriors who walked on all sides of him, regarding him with undisguised scorn. The two halberdiers were far more relaxed; ever contemptuous of Guineans, they sauntered along with their heavy axe-headed pikes balanced easily on their shoulders, gossiping, arguing, joking, spinning each other boastful yarns. They were meant to be Father Sebastião's bodyguard but, in their ceaseless, mindless talk, they soon lost track of him. He had fallen to the rear to walk among the porters and women. It annoyed Gil that they so blatantly ignored their duty to the old Franciscan but he was too timid of them to say anything about it. The few times he looked back to check on the priest himself, the priest was either reading aloud in Latin from his breviary or singing hymns or passing around his rosary and crucifix for the fascinated Soyo to admire. The NsakuSoyo, scowling, stuck as close to him as Segou stuck to Gil. But he didn't seem to notice. He seemed content. He was doing the work that God and the Franciscan father provincial had sent him to do and the worst that could happen to him would be to suffer martyrdom in their names.

The day came up as hot and sticky as usual but now doubly uncomfortable for Gil in his unaccustomed mock prince's costume. He eyed Mbemba and the Kongo warriors, half-naked in their long skirts, with envy. Was it really necessary for him to wear this burdensome outfit? Would he diminish himself in Mbemba's eyes and thus endanger himself if he replaced the plumed helmet with his leather cap and removed the breast-plated vest of chainmail altogether? He could tolerate the leather pantaloons and embroidered surcoat (although

8

God knew how much cooler he'd be in his baggy seaman's trousers and loose serge blouse), and he actually rather liked wearing the short, scabbarded stabbing sword—it gave him a certain swagger—but how could he go on for twenty days in this stifling climate wearing all this steel? He couldn't. He'd just have to chance it. He'd remain costumed as a prince for the first day's march and he'd costume himself again as a prince when they reached Mbanza Kongo, but starting the next day, he decided, he'd dress in a fashion that would allow him to make the journey in a semblance of comfort.

They spent the first night of the march at a Soyo village about five leagues east from Mpinda. Once the headman had prostrated himself at the feet of the Kongo prince and the Kongo prince had laid his lance across his exposed neck, a fine feast was served and there was drumming and horn-playing, dancing and stilt-walking, fire-eating and magic tricks, after which the travelers retired to huts that had been prepared for them. Only Segou was ignored, in this as in every other respect. He was expected to sleep outside Gil's hut as he had been expected to feed off Gil's scraps from the feast. Gil chose not to make an issue of it but, when the village seemed sound asleep, he fetched Segou inside.

The next morning Gil repacked his sea chest and stepped outside the hut wearing, of his princely costume, only his short sword and bloodstone necklace. He looked around for Mbemba to see how Mbemba would react to this change. It was still dark, the air still fresh and cool and damp with dew, the birds just awakening with song, but the caravan was already assembled and Mbemba was busying himself with it and didn't notice Gil. Father Sebastião, bareheaded and wearing a white stole over his cassock, and the two halberdiers, without their pikes or helmets, came over from their huts. Segou was still inside Gil's, uncertain about coming out.

"Have you eaten, padre?" Gil asked. He wasn't altogether certain how closely in touch the old Franciscan, in his spiritual preoccupations, was with practical matters such as these. "You know there'll be no breakfast." Nor a midday meal either, he might have added. They had learned that much about these people, that they ate only once in the day, in the evening, and then well enough to carry them to the next evening, so the captain-general had arranged to have a supply of biscuits, salt pork, salt fish and wine from the ship's provisions sent along with their sea chests and baggage. Gil had shared biscuits and wine with Segou before he had dressed. "And you, Gomes? Dias? Have you eaten?"

"They have eaten," Father Sebastião answered for them with a sigh. "They have eaten meat. They forgot today is a fast day. And you, my son, did you also forget?"

Gil had but as he had only eaten the biscuit, he was able to answer honestly enough, "No, padre, I only had some hardtack and wine."

"That is good, my son. We must not forget these things, especially here among these poor heathen. We must set them an example. And now we will say matins. We mustn't forget our prayers either. *Dominus vobiscum . . .*"

Segou came out of the hut when Father Sebastião began reading the morning office. He wasn't Christian but he joined the kneeling group anyway, feeling safer close to the white men. It was the first time the priest had conducted a prayer service in view of the Negroes, and the scene of the kneeling men in the first glimmering light of the dawn, the soft chanting of their voices as birds awakened singing, the graceful strokes of the sign of the cross Father Sebastião made and the men repeated, attracted their attention. Mbemba and the NsakuSoyo came over. When Father Sebastião concluded the brief service and closed his breviary and recited the Trinity, again making the sign of the cross, and Gil and the halberdiers crossed themselves and stood up, Gil turned to Mbemba, expecting him to make some comment about Gil's changed costume.

But he didn't. He did something else. He made the sign of the cross. It was a swift flash of a gesture and, when it was completed, Mbemba smiled his boyish, mischievous smile. Gil took a quick look around. Apparently no one else had seen it. Father Sebastião had removed his stole, kissed it and was now carefully folding it away while the NsakuSoyo watched him suspiciously. The two halberdiers had gone to fetch their pikes and helmets while Segou ducked back into Gil's hut to be out of the way. Gil looked at Mbemba again. With a flicker of the smile still playing on his lips, Mbemba made the sign again.

"*Ngete,* Mbemba," Gil said encouragingly. And he made the sign of the cross himself. "This is the cross of our Lord Jesus in Heaven."

"*Nzambi Mpungu?*"

"*Nzambi Mpungu?*" Gil shook his head. "I do not understand."
He said this in Kongo. They were words—I do not understand—with
which, from so much repetition, he was by now all too familiar. "What
is *Nzambi Mpungu?*"

Mbemba looked away to consider the matter. Then, still smiling,
he held out his arms, palms up, and rolled his eyes heavenward in
reverence or, perhaps, only in mock reverence.

But it thrilled Gil. "Aye, Mbemba. *Ngete.* That's it," he said in a
rush of excitement. "The Lord in Heaven. *Nzambi Mpungu.* Padre."

Father Sebastião looked around.

The NsakuSoyo also looked around.

"Mbemba—"

"*Ve,*" Mbemba snapped harshly. "No." His playful smile faded. His
expression turned severe.

"What is it, my son?" Father Sebastião asked.

Gil hesitated. He didn't like the NsakuSoyo, with his mean, suspicious face, watching, listening. And, apparently, neither did Mbemba. He glared at Gil. His face was again a mask of princely hauteur.
Gil realized he had made a mistake. He should never have called to
Father Sebastião. Mbemba had meant his show of interest, his inquiry
into this ritual of the white men, to be a matter just between them,
the two youths, the two boy princes. With a final glare of disgust, he
went back to where the caravan was assembled waiting to start the
day's march.

"What did you want to say about Mbemba, my son?" Father Sebastião asked, coming over.

"It wasn't anything, padre. I thought . . . but I was mistaken."

"What did you think?"

"I thought he made the sign of the cross."

"The sign of the cross? Who? Mbemba? O Holy Mother. O
Blessed Virgin. This is a miracle, my son. The good Lord has looked
down on me with favor and has already rewarded my poor efforts. I
must go to him. His soul is stirring."

"No, padre. Please. Don't go to him. I was mistaken. It wasn't
that at all."

"What was it then?"

"Just a signal. Just a signal to start the day's march."

That evening when, once again, the caravan halted for food and rest at a Soyo village on the riverbank, Father Sebastião summoned Gil and the halberdiers (Segou joined them for his own, eminently practical reasons) to vespers. He had decided that, given the circumstances of the march (no halt was ever called once it got under way), it was permissible to forgo the other canonical hours but that, no matter what the circumstances, the morning and evening devotions would be faithfully offered.

The Soyo of the village and of the caravan gathered around to witness what to them was a mysteriously novel entertainment. The NsakuSoyo too, of course, was there, all suspicion and mean-eyed watchfulness. But this time Mbemba and his warriors were nowhere to be seen. Gil wasn't surprised. All during the day's march, Mbemba had held himself aloof, responding to Gil's attempts at conversation (and attempts to apologize for his blunder that morning) curtly. Gil didn't take it badly. He suspected Mbemba was as annoyed with himself for having revealed his curiosity in the white men's ways as he was at Gil for having betrayed his curiosity to Father Sebastião and the NsakuSoyo, and was probably off somewhere now with his warriors brooding about it.

Father Sebastião, however, hesitated to begin without him. He had set his heart on the Kongo prince, Gil knew. Time and again during the day's march, he had called Gil to his side to question him on the probability of Mbemba's having or not having made the sign of the cross that morning. He wanted to believe that he had, for he felt that if he could arouse the mystery of the Faith in the youth's soul, if he could touch the youth's heart and mind with the Gospel of the Savior, if he could bring a prince of these people to the Church, the people would follow and he would convert a kingdom.

He had donned a white linen alb over his cassock and a white silk sleeveless vestment, embroidered with a cross of gold thread, over the alb, and his gold-embroidered stole over the vestment and had had the halberdiers set two sea chests one on top of the other to serve as an altar and had it covered with a white silk altar cloth and had the monstrance and chalice and missal and two lighted candles placed on it and had it situated at the very center of the village's market square—for he wanted to make of this service a glory, a marvel, a wonder to behold, an unforgettable experience for all the poor benighted heathen gathered in the market square but, above all, for the Kongo prince.

He proceeded slowly, drawing out the readings and hymns, pausing when turning the pages of the missal as if he had lost his place, hoping that Mbemba, given enough time, might yet appear.

The Soyo watched him in rapt, silent attention and when at last he was done, he turned to them with a blank expression as if not aware of their presence, he was that disappointed that Mbemba had failed to appear. But then he recalled himself. After all, these plain people too were the lost souls he had come to save; they too were as much in need of the Word and Grace of God as was the Kongo prince. And, with a sudden kind smile creasing his gaunt, mottled face, he made the sign of the cross over them as well and, still wearing his vestments, went toward them, extending his hands.

The NsakuSoyo was instantly at his side, shouting at the Soyo, waving them angrily away. They dispersed; they fled the priest's approach as if in a panic. Cooking fires were started. Bundles were snatched up. Huts were cleared out and made ready for the visitors. In a moment, Father Sebastião stood alone in the market square with the NsakuSoyo. The NsakuSoyo grinned a mirthless grin as Father Sebastião began removing his vestments. Gil went down to the river.

Dugout canoes were drawn up on the sloping, muddy bank. Men had been out in them fishing with lines and nets and wicker traps when the caravan had arrived at dusk, and a few were now pushing out again for some night fishing, carrying burning brands to light their way. A trunk of some hardwood tree, twenty feet or so long, felled somewhere in the forest and dragged down to the water's edge, lay among the canoes. It was the makings of a new dugout; work had already begun on it, the hollowing out with axe and fire. He sat down on it. It would be a while before the nightly feast was ready, and Mbemba, wherever he had gone off to with his warriors, would surely return by then. And then would be soon enough for Gil to go back as well.

He removed his leather cap and ran his fingers through his long,

straight, tawny hair, combing out the greasy knots, and, with his elbows on his knees, rested his chin in his hands. The canoes gliding
out on the river, the men standing while paddling with graceful
strokes, became spots of flickering orange, the flames of the brands
they carried, in the deepening blue of the coming night, and clouds
rolled in from the east, shutting out the few stars that had winked on
in the deepening blue of the darkening sky. There had been clouds
every night since they had come upon this river Zaire but it had not
yet rained. The trilling of the birds of the forest slackened and the
whirring of the cicadas rose into a single, steady, prolonged note of
metallic song and the mosquitoes came up from the marshy shore in
dark puffs like smoke.

"Gil Eenezh."

Gil looked round. "Mbemba. *Keba bota.*" He started to get up
from the tree trunk.

But Mbemba put a hand on his shoulder and sat down beside
him, resting his lance against the tree trunk. He was no longer wearing his silver bracelets and anklets, nor his necklace of animal teeth,
nor the emerald-studded, silver headband. It had been his response to
Gil's change of costume; he too had diminished his princely appearance, possibly for the same reason he had chosen to walk when Gil
had refused to be carried in the litter, so as not to seem to put himself
above the white prince. Gil wanted to believe it was a gesture of
friendship. Nevertheless, his warriors were with him with their
lances and shields, forming a loose circle around him, guarding him.

"The Soyo fish," Gil said in Kongo, pointing to the flickering orange lights of the canoes on the river.

"Yes, they fish."

"What do they fish?"

"Many fish. Small fish. Large fish. One fish, very large." Mbemba
stretched out his arms to indicate the size, a good two yards. "Fish like
mchento, a woman." And he traced the voluptuous curves of a
woman with his hands.

"A woman?" Gil shook his head and smiled. "No, Mbemba, not a
woman."

"Yes, Gil Eenezh, a woman." Mbemba also smiled. "A woman
from here to here." He ran his hands from his head down around his

shoulders and torso to his hips. "Then a fish to there." He indicated his legs and feet.

"*Sereia?*" Gil said in Portuguese. "A mermaid?"

"Mermaid?"

"We say mermaid for a fish half-woman, a woman half-fish."

"You have mermaid too?"

"People say so. Diogo Cão and Nuno Gonçalves say so. But I myself have never seen one."

"And they fish for mermaid too?"

"Oh, yes, they always fish for mermaids," Gil said, smiling more broadly, thinking how nearly every sailor he had ever known had sworn that, at one time or another, he had spotted a mermaid on a voyage.

"From bird?"

"Eh? What's that? From bird?"

"They fish for mermaid from bird?"

It took Gil a moment to remember that Mbemba, that all these people, thought of the *Leonor,* the great sail-winged ship, as a bird. "Yes, from *bwato,*" he answered, using the Kongo for boat rather than bird. "They fish for mermaid from boat."

"No. Not from boat. From bird."

Gil didn't answer right away. He wasn't sure just how seriously Mbemba was insisting on the distinction between bird and boat. But finally he said, "Yes, they fish for mermaid from bird."

"In sky?"

Now Gil was in trouble. "In sky?" he repeated, not because he didn't understand the word for sky but in order to gain time.

"They fish for mermaid from bird in the sky?" Mbemba pointed overhead.

There couldn't be any doubt. A boat was on the river. A bird was in the sky. Mbemba was very deliberately making the distinction between a boat and a bird. Why? What was he getting at? His mischievous smile was full of the same sort of amused mockery as his smile had been when he had made the sign of the cross that morning. Was it meant to disguise his curiosity, make light of his interest in these things of the white men? Or was he making fun of Gil, making fun of the idea of white men fishing for mermaids from a bird in the sky?

"With *Nzambi Mpungu* in the sky?"

And then Gil understood. *Nzambi Mpungu*, the Kongo for heaven, the Kongo for God. What Mbemba was getting at, what he was asking Gil in this roundabout, mischievous way, what he was pressing Gil to say quite unequivocally, was that the white men, these Porta Geeze, had, in their great sail-winged bird, flown down from Heaven, had come from God.

And he didn't believe it. The ManiSoyo had believed it. The NsakuSoyo had believed it. Everyone had believed it. But this Kongo youth didn't believe it. Gil could see he didn't in his laughing eyes, his mocking smile. No, he didn't for a moment believe that they had flown down from Heaven, that they had come from God. He was only testing to see if Gil would say they had, if Gil would lie. Gil looked away.

Mbemba stood up. The sudden movement caused Gil to look back.

"You do not come from *Nzambi Mpungu*, Gil Eenezh," the Kongo prince said, no longer smiling. "You do not come from the sky."

Gil said nothing. He did not know what to say. Even if he had, his mouth had suddenly gone dry.

"I know this, Gil Eenezh. I know this here, in my head. I know this here, in my heart. But what I do not know is where you do come from in your great bird-winged boat."

Gil licked his lips. The game was up. It would be stupid to lie. "I will tell you, Mbemba," he said.

"Yes, you will tell me."

"I come from very far."

"I know this."

"The ocean, Mbemba? The sea? Where the river runs? Where the river ends? The sea?"

"Yes, the sea."

"I come from the sea."

"Oh, the sea. Not the sky. Now you come from the sea."

Gil sighed and ran a hand over his face, rubbed his eyes.

"Slowly, Gil Eenezh. Tell me slowly."

Gil uncovered his eyes. "Not *from* the sea, Mbemba. From the other side of the sea. I come from the sea's other shore."

Mbemba shook his head. "No, Gil Eenezh, you do not come from the sea's other shore. The sea is forever. The sea does not have another shore."

"It does, Mbemba." Gil stood up. How could he explain this? How could he make Mbemba understand? "The river, Mbemba? *Nzere?*"

"Yes, Gil Eenezh. The river. *Nzere.*"

"The river has another shore, does it not?" Gil pointed at the river. Its opposite bank could not be seen in the gathering darkness but he judged that to be an advantage. "There, there," he said, "there across the river, we cannot see it, but there is the river's other shore, is it not?"

Mbemba half-turned to the river and looked out at the flickering spots of flame of the fishing canoes on the dark water, then turned back to Gil.

"Here is this shore of the river, Mbemba," Gil said. "And there is the other shore, even though we cannot see it."

Watching Gil closely, Mbemba nodded. "Yes, there is the river's other shore, even though we cannot see it."

"And so the sea also has another shore, Mbemba. Here is this shore of the sea. And there, far across the sea, even though we cannot see it, there is the sea's other shore."

Mbemba continued watching Gil closely. The Kongo warriors were also watching him. They probably could hear what he was saying. They certainly could see the gestures he was making. Did they understand any better than Mbemba? Did Mbemba understand at all?

"There is where I come from, Mbemba, there, far across the sea, from the sea's other shore."

"From the sea's other shore," Mbemba repeated, but more to himself than to Gil. It was a fantastic concept for him, Gil could see, a tremendous leap of faith, a staggering reach of the imagination. "The sea has another shore as the river has another shore?"

"Yes, Mbemba. And there is the land of the Portuguese, there on the sea's other shore, as here is the land of the Kongo, here on this shore."

"And there is where you come from, there from the land of the Porta Geeze on the sea's other shore?"

"Yes, Mbemba. Now you understand."

"No, Gil Eenezh, I do not understand. But you will tell me. Slowly you will tell me. Slowly you will tell me all of these things of the Porta Geeze. And then I will understand."

VI

D URING THE NEXT FEW DAYS, the path the caravan followed veered away from the river, east by south, but on the fifth and sixth days it veered back so that by the seventh day from Mpinda the river was once again no more distant on the left than it had been at the start (although narrower now, running faster, more broken by reefs and rocks), and the path continued along the bank for a few more days, although now ascending so that each day it was always higher above the river than it had been at the start. And then on the tenth day, some forty leagues east of Mpinda and, by Gil's rough estimate, no more than a day from Matadi—that mammoth ledge of limestone jutting out over the river where the *Leonor* had anchored when the longboat had gone to explore the Caldron of Hell—on the tenth day, the caravan came to a fork in the road. One branch continued east along the river's always higher and rockier embankment, probably all the way to Matadi. The other branch angled southeast by east into the forest on the right. It was this branch that the caravan took, leaving the river behind.

"Segou."

The Ashanti quickly came up the two or three paces he lagged behind Gil and Mbemba.

"We must remember this change in the road, Segou. I do not have materials with which to draw a map so we must remember it in our mind."

"I will remember it in my mind, Gil. On the tenth day of the march from Mpinda we turned away from the river and went into the forest."

"Good, Segou. We must remember all the changes in the road in this way. Because we cannot say if a day will come when we must follow this road by ourselves."

"I know this, Gil. I will have the map in my mind when that day comes."

Mbemba, walking on Gil's right and a half-step ahead, had cocked his head slightly as if to listen to this exchange. Gil wondered if he had understood any of it, if he was slowly acquiring a command of Portuguese as Gil was of Kongo. Although circumstances didn't favor it—little Portuguese was spoken in his hearing and he never asked for translations as Gil constantly did—it couldn't be ruled out. He was quick and clever and forever on the alert and, although he might feel that, for his dignity's sake, he must mask it with mockery and ridicule, revealing it only in the most roundabout ways, his appetite for knowledge of these Porta Geeze and their land on the other shore of the sea was as keen as his lance.

"We speak of the change in the way we go, Mbemba. We see we now go away from *nzere*. Do we return to *nzere* later?"

"No. Mbanza Kongo is away from *nzere*. Mbanza Kongo is . . . there." Mbemba indicated the road leading into the forest with his lance.

"Mbanza Kongo is in the forest?"

"No. Mbanza Kongo is on the mountain. We go through the forest to come to the mountain. The forest hides and guards the mountain."

Gil nodded.

"There is also forest in the land of the Porta Geeze?"

"Oh, yes, there is forest in the land of the Portuguese. But no forest such as this."

They entered the forest as if entering an underworld. With the Zaire no longer on the left but vanishing ever farther behind; with no longer even a glimpse of its shining sheet of sun-struck, steel-gray water to recall an open land and sea and sky stretching away from horizon to horizon; with mangroves and palms, iroko and baobab and mahogany and bamboo now growing on both sides of the road and their overhanging branches and leaves and vines and shrouds of moss twisting and tangling into an unbroken canopy of vegetation a hundred feet, two hundred feet overhead, utterly shutting out the sky; a hot, sweltering, insect-infested, aqueous gloom closed down around the caravan as the water of the sea closes down around a sinking ship.

They had entered a realm of perpetual dark. Not even a vagrant beam of sunlight penetrated here. And it was quieter here. Gil, sweat soaking through his shirt and trickling down his thighs, could no longer hear the trumpeters and drummers and fetishers in the advance of the caravan (perhaps they had fallen silent in the forest), and the sounds and songs and calls of the birds and monkeys and the unseen, unknown animals in the trees were sporadic, fleeting, fugitive, of a different character and purpose; they were the sounds and songs and calls of alarm, startling in their suddenness, unpredictable in their location, echoing eerily in the long, brooding silences between them. But the road itself remained wide and smooth and well cared for. It was truly a royal road, a road to a royal city. Gil couldn't help but marvel at this, couldn't help but wonder at the incredible labor involved in building and maintaining such a road. How rich and powerful the king who could build and maintain such a road in this rioting mass of otherwise utterly impenetrable vegetation.

About two leagues into the forest from the fork in the road, they came to a river. It was little more than a stream in comparison to the mighty Zaire but still a good hundred yards wide, flowing from the northeast to the southwest, doubtless flowing to the Zaire. The bridge that spanned it was yet another example of the immense effort that went into maintaining this royal way, a sturdy structure of vines and bamboo and split logs, anchored by gateways of towering poles on each bank and slung across the fast-running water without need for additional supports yet swaying only slightly under the impact of the hundreds of pairs of feet that crossed it. On the other side was a village. It was only a few yards back in the woods but, because of a barricade of dense brush around it, Gil wouldn't have noticed it except that the caravan turned off here to spend the night. This surprised him. He hadn't realized it was that late in the day. In the unvarying, fetid dusk of the forest, where the passage of the sun across the sky couldn't be seen, it was impossible to judge the time of day.

The village was of a very different design and architecture from the Soyo villages along the Zaire's embankment with their open vistas on that great river. This was a forest village, a huddle of low, small, beehive-shaped dwellings made of bent bamboo plastered with mud and arranged in no discernible order in a painfully hacked-out clearing beneath the close-crowded, mammoth trees with no vista of any kind. And the people of the village were as poor and primitive as their surroundings. Although obviously akin to the Kongo and Soyo in their honey-colored complexion, high cheekbones and slanted eyes and, as Gil later learned, in their language as well, they were smaller, wirier, more timid and wary. Dressed in skirts of shredded leaves or loincloths of monkey skin or a material made from beaten bark, by and large unadorned except for an occasional parrot feather or a necklace of monkey teeth, armed with blowpipes of poison darts, they awaited the arrival of the caravan clustered at the entryways of their huts with a pathetic servility, staring at the white men in a kind of horrified disbelief.

"Who are they, Mbemba?"

"Mbata. The forest is the land of the Mbata."

The chief came forward—a wrinkled wretch distinguished from the others by a headdress of basketweave with a monkey's tail dangling from it down his back and the skull of a monkey hanging from a leather thong on his chest—and prostrated himself before Mbemba. Mbemba took no notice of him. He looked around the village with his iciest princely scowl. Then he said something to the Nsaku-Soyo, who, in turn, spoke angrily to the prostrate chief. The chief raised his head from the dirt to reply.

"What did he say?" Father Sebastião asked.

Gil shook his head and turned to Segou.

"There will be no feast tonight," Segou said. "The hunting failed."

Mbemba looked around at this whispering. Then, without laying his lance across the chief's neck, he made a tour of the huts, peering into some with undisguised disgust, kicking at the walls of others to see how soundly they were built, selecting a few he found suitable enough for himself and his party. His warriors followed him, speaking

harshly to the Mbata, poking them aside with their lances, shoving
them away from their huts with their shields, and then the caravan's
porters dispersed through the village to find places to lay down their
loads. At their approach, the Mbata, already in apprehensive retreat
from the warriors, cleared out of the village altogether and disappeared into the surrounding trees, abandoning the village to the caravan. All the Mbata except their chief. As Mbemba had not given him
permission to rise by touching him with the lance, he remained face-
down on the ground in the center of the village clearing.

They ate from the caravan's own provisions that night, the Portuguese supplementing the fare with their own salt meat, hardtack
and wine. And there was no entertainment of any kind that night either. Even Father Sebastião, affected by the airless, dismal gloom that
had engulfed them upon entering the forest, limited himself to a brief
vesper service and retired to the hut the NsakuSoyo had picked out
for him. Gil, however, stayed up a while longer, sitting *à la turc* on the
spongy earth of the forest floor with his back against the caked mud
wall of the hut that Mbemba had picked out for him.

He removed his shirt and used it to wipe off the film of sweat
that coated his body. Not even night brought relief from the awful
heat and suffocating humidity of the forest. No sooner had he dried
himself than the sweat began to prickle and run again. His shirt stank
of it and so did he. He thought of the small river they had crossed. He
would have liked to have a swim in it and wash his clothes. But even
though it wasn't far, he decided against it. It wasn't because he didn't
think he could find his way there and back. After all, there was the
road. The road would lead him to the river and back. No, it was the
dark, the extraordinary dark of the forest, a dark he had never before
experienced, a dark so tangible it seemed it could be cut and would
bleed sweat. He did not fancy wandering about in that dark.

He replaced his shirt—as soon as he had taken it off, a swarm of
insects had attacked his exposed flesh—and picked up a twig. He
traced a line with it in the damp earth. That was another concern he
had about the dark of the forest, the difficulty of determining direction and the passage of time when neither the sun nor the stars
could be seen beneath its dense canopy. The line he traced represented the river Zaire and the road along its bank, roughly west to

east, from Mpinda, where he scratched a cross, to the fork in the road (another cross) and beyond it to where he guessed Matadi to be. At the fork, he traced another line, representing the branch of the road that angled southeast by east into the forest. But from that point on, without the east-west bearing of the Zaire by which to orient himself, without any sure means of knowing the hour of the day upon reaching landmarks such as the small river and the bridge and this village, he knew that the map he drew would become always more inaccurate. Already he could not be certain where exactly to mark the small river and the bridge and this village. Even so, he must do this. Each night he must draw, as best as he could, a map like this of the journey so far and commit it to memory. For any map, no matter how inaccurate, would be better than no map at all in finding the way back through this forest.

He looked up. Mbemba had come out of his hut. Evidently the softer, boyish side of his nature had gotten the better of him and he had decided that the prostrate Mbata chief had suffered sufficient humiliation. He went over to him and then, just to prove he still was the imperious prince, he gave the poor wretch a swift kick in the ribs. The fellow jumped up and ran off into the forest. Mbemba watched him go, then came over to Gil. He did not have his lance with him and was wearing only a breechclout. Immediately, however, his warriors appeared out of the darkness, wearing their long skirts, carrying their steel lances and shields.

"I sleep, Gil Eenezh. You do not sleep."

"Soon I will also sleep, Mbemba."

"What do you do that you do not sleep?" Mbemba squatted on his heels beside Gil. "What is this that you make?" He pointed at the lines and crosses Gil had traced in the dirt.

"A map." Gil said this in Portuguese, *um mapa,* not knowing the word in Kongo, if there even were such a word.

"A map?"

"Yes, a map. Look. Here, this is *nzere.*" With the twig, Gil retraced the line he had drawn to represent the great river and then he scratched the word alongside it, taking a guess how it was spelled: Enzary. "And here, this is Mpinda." He pointed at the cross he had made to mark the village at the start of the line and wrote its name, spelling it as it sounded to his ear. "And here is where the road by the river turned into the forest. And this is the bridge that crossed over the little river. And here is this village of the Mbata." He scratched the letters Embatta next to the cross that marked the village. "This is a map. It shows the road we march and the villages and other places we pass on the road. It shows us the way we go."

Squatting on his heels, his hands hanging loosely between his knees, Mbemba studied the lines and crosses and letters Gil had scratched in the damp forest floor. Then, with a flick of a finger, he asked, "What is this?"

"*Nzere,*" Gil replied.

"No. This is *nzere.*" Mbemba ran his finger along the line representing the river. "I ask, what is *this?*" He pointed at the letters Gil had written beside the line: Enzary.

"*Nzere,*" Gil said again, not immediately recognizing the confusion he was causing.

"You say this is *nzere* and you say this is *nzere?* They cannot both be *nzere.*"

"You are right, Mbemba. I say this badly. I say it again. This long straight line from here to here, this is *nzere* itself. But these many little lines pushed together here, they make the word *nzere* . . ."

But even as he was saying this, Gil knew he had made a stupid mistake. It wasn't the concept of the map that confused Mbemba. Given a bit more time and repetition, he would grasp the concept easily enough. After all, it was merely a drawing, a representation of a tangible reality, and these people made drawings, representations of tangible realities, all the time. But the words and names Gil had scratched on the map had introduced Mbemba to a baffling idea. He should never have bothered to write them down. They were of no importance anyway. Gil bent over and began rubbing out Enzary.

But Mbemba grabbed his wrist. "Why do you take this away? I ask you what it is. Tell me what it is. And also, what this is. And what this is."

Gil sighed. How could he tell him? He could think of no other way to tell him. So he told him in the same way. "This is the word for *nzere.* And this is the word for Mpinda. And this is the word for Mbata. This is how we write the words we speak. Do you not write the words you speak?"

"Write?"

Gil of course had said *escrever*. "This is how we draw the words we speak. We write them. It is *escrita*, writing. Do you not draw the words you speak? Do you not write them? Do you not have writing?"

Mbemba looked at Gil with a princely frown of annoyance that Gil knew enough by now to know was a frown to conceal his inability to comprehend what he was hearing, to hide the fact that this concept of writing was totally alien to him, beyond the reach of all his experience.

Gil shook his head despairingly. He couldn't explain writing any better than he had. He did not in fact understand it himself any better than he had explained it. He was only just barely literate himself. His ability to write and read was self-taught and, as such, shaky and limited at best. Only someone who was fluent in it, who had learned it properly and used it regularly would have a chance of explaining it to Mbemba any better than he had. Not a ship's boy or a common mariner or a soldier but a captain-general, a pilot, a priest . . .

"Father Sebastião. He can tell you what writing is."

"Let us go to Pader Sebastum then."

"Now? No, Mbemba. Now he sleeps. Tomorrow we will go to him."

"No. We go to him now." Mbemba stood up. "Pader Sebastum."

Mbemba's sudden shout in the silence of the forest dark stirred a number of people awake. Segou peered out of the low entryway of Gil's hut. The two halberdiers stepped out of theirs. The Kongo warriors, not understanding why their prince had shouted, drew closer.

"Pader Sebastum, I will speak to you."

Father Sebastião poked his head out of his hut, looked around perplexed, then crawled out on his hands and knees and stood up. He was wearing a long linen shirt, not his cassock, in an attempt to find some relief from the airless, oppressive heat.

"Pader Sebastum, tell me what Gil Eenezh draws in the earth there."

"What is he saying, my son? Is something wrong?"

"No, padre. It is only that I was trying to explain writing to him." "Writing?"

The NsakuSoyo had also come out of his hut as had most of the Soyo porters and women.

"Aye. I was showing him a map I had drawn of the journey so far and wrote the names of some of the places on it. Mpinda. Nzere. Mbata. I think he got the idea of the map all right but the names, the writing, I don't know how to explain that to him. I don't think these people have writing, padre."

"You ask Pader Sebastum to tell me what is writing, Gil Eenezh?" Mbemba interrupted impatiently.

"Yes, Mbemba, I ask him. I thought you could explain it to him better than I can, padre."

"He wants to understand writing?"

"Aye."

"O dear Jesus. O dear Mary and Joseph. I knew the dear Lord was opening his heart to us ever since that day he made the sign of the cross. This is wonderful news, my son. We have touched his soul. We have awakened his spirit. Yes, of course he must understand writing. We must teach him the word." Father Sebastião ducked back into his hut and, after only the briefest moment, reappeared with his breviary, his gaunt, mottled old face alight with the happiness of a boy. "Writing, Mbemba. Here are the words of writing, the words of our Lord and Savior Jesus Christ." He opened the breviary at random and thrust the closely printed pages toward Mbemba.

This startled the Kongo youth. It wasn't at all what he was expecting. "What does he do, Gil Eenezh? You say he will tell me what is writing."

"He does tell you. Look at what he shows you. This is writing too."

Not understanding what the two youths were saying, Father Sebastião chose this moment to begin reading from the breviary. *"De profundis clamavi ad te, Dominum . . ."*

Mbemba turned to him. Gil noticed the NsakuSoyo take a step closer. So did the Kongo warriors. The two halberdiers came over. Segou decided to come out of the hut. Gil only vaguely recognized what the padre was reading, but whatever it was, he couldn't see the sense in it. This was no time for prayer. And least of all in Latin, for Heaven's sake.

"I don't think this is what's wanted, padre."

"Patience, my son. These are the words of God. His soul thirsts for these words. That is why he wants to understand writing, to understand the words of God." The priest resumed the prayer.

Gil looked at Mbemba. To his surprise and relief, Mbemba was watching the priest intently, watching his eyes move back and forth across and down the page while his lips formed the words of the prayer.

"He speaks the words of the writing," Gil ventured hopefully.

Mbemba glanced at him and then back to Father Sebastião. He had seen Father Sebastião read before, from the breviary, from the missal. That wasn't the novelty. No, what was new, what held his attention now was the idea that this looking into the breviary while at the same time speaking words was somehow connected, that the words being spoken were somehow related to the lines and dots and other markings at which Father Sebastião was looking on the breviary's page. Could he make the connection, Gil wondered; would he realize the relationship between the written words and those spoken? In his place, Gil wondered, would he himself have been able to make the connection, realize the relationship? For seeing it through Mbemba's eyes, Gil recognized what a truly astounding idea it was.

"Pader Sebastum?"

The priest looked up from the breviary.

"This is writing, Pader Sebastum?"

"What does he say, my son?"

"He asks you if this is writing."

"Yes, Mbemba, this is writing. These are the words of God. Here, take it. See it for yourself." And the priest stretched out his hand, meaning to give the breviary to Mbemba.

And his hand was knocked aside and the breviary was sent flying. The NsakuSoyo had done this and then stepped between Mbemba and the priest and began shouting at the Kongo youth.

"What is it? What has happened?" Father Sebastião cried out and went scrambling after his prayer book.

Mbemba glared at the NsakuSoyo. But the NsakuSoyo wasn't intimidated. He continued shouting at the Kongo youth, hectoring him, scolding him, chastising him as if he were a child. Apparently as ju-ju man, as sorcerer, as a maker of magic and medicine, he had the standing, the status, the exceptional right to speak so harshly even to a prince.

"What is the trouble, my son?" Father Sebastião asked, returning hastily with the breviary.

And the NsakuSoyo whirled toward him. And all the disapproval and dislike and, yes, fear of the white priest that the ju-ju man had been feeling and barely restraining from the very start erupted. And he struck Father Sebastião across the face. He couldn't have been much younger than the priest but he certainly was far stronger. The blow knocked Father Sebastião to the ground.

"You heathen dog. You turd." This was one of the halberdiers, Vasco Dias, the more pious of the two or the more superstitious. He bolted forward.

"No, Dias. Don't. Mbemba." Gil rushed to Father Sebastião's side, glancing back over his shoulder at Mbemba, expecting to see Mbemba take some action against the NsakuSoyo.

"I'm all right, my son. I'm all right. It's nothing," Father Sebastião said, struggling to his feet.

"Rest a moment, padre."

"No, no, it's all right. Just give me a hand." With Gil's help, Father Sebastião stood up and put his hand to his mouth and looked at his hand to see if there was any blood on it. There wasn't. "Why did he do that?"

"I don't know." Gil looked at Mbemba.

Mbemba had taken no action against the NsakuSoyo. The Nsaku-Soyo was still shouting at him. He wasn't listening but he wasn't talking back either. He wasn't doing anything. Why wasn't he? He was a prince. Father Sebastião was in his charge. Why didn't he punish the NsakuSoyo for his shocking behavior? Why didn't he at least protest it? Was the NsakuSoyo too powerful? Or was Mbemba too young and inexperienced? And what had triggered the NsakuSoyo's outburst of such rage after all this time anyway? Was it that, in Mbemba's interest in listening to the priest read from the breviary, he had sensed a threat greater than the interest the porters and women had shown in the rosary and crucifix? Or was it the breviary itself, the writing in the breviary, the magic of the writing in the breviary that had frightened him into so violently coming to the defense of his own faith?

"I will speak to him," Father Sebastião said.

"No, padre, please, let us leave it as it is for now."

"But it is only some foolish misunderstanding, my son. We must make it right. We must not lose this God-given opportunity. Don't you see? We have Mbemba's soul in our hands." And the priest started toward Mbemba and the ju-ju man again.

And again the ju-ju man whirled toward him.

"No," Gil cried out, and flung himself between the ju-ju man and the priest.

And so the ju-ju man's forearm slammed into Gil's face instead of the priest's and Gil went hurtling back against the priest and together they fell backward to the ground, Gil on top of the priest, the priest's head hitting the ground with a sickening thud.

"Dog turd."

"Watch yourself, Dias."

Dias had again taken a step forward but caught himself when Gomes shouted at him. Gomes hadn't moved at all. The Kongo warriors had turned to them, their lances and shields poised. And the two halberdiers were unarmed and unarmored.

So, in this fleeting, explosive instant, it was Segou who acted. It was Segou who leaped forward. It was Segou, although also unarmed and unarmored, who sought to come to the aid of Gil and the priest. What had he thought in that fleeting, explosive instant? Had he thought to protect Gil and the priest from further attack by the ju-ju man? Or had his hatred of the Kongo and the Soyo for their despicable treatment of him launched his impulsive, senseless, courageous act?

A lance immediately skewered him through the stomach.

"Mother Mary," Gil screamed.

Segou doubled over, clutching at the shaft of the lance. Then he straightened up in wide-eyed surprise and released the shaft of the lance. Then, as if in slow motion, he fell on his back. The gleaming, steel blade of the lance, red with blood, protruded from his back just below his waist and was driven into the ground by the hammer blow of his own dead weight hitting the ground. The warrior who had made the killing thrust with the lance released its shaft as it was pulled from his grip by Segou's fall. Segou was pinned to the ground. He was alive. Again he clutched the shaft of the lance that stuck out of his stomach. And he began thrashing his feet. The warrior stepped on his chest and slowly eased out the lance, slicing Segou's hands.

Blood spurted from his hands. Blood spurted from his stomach. Blood spurted from his mouth.

"Mother Mary, Mother of God." Gil dashed to Segou, dropping to his knees at the Ashanti's side. "Segou. Oh, my God. Segou."

Segou looked at Gil. "Little son," he said. Then he closed his eyes. His hands fell away from his stomach. And his feet stopped thrashing.

"Segou. Segou."

Segou did not reply.

"He's dead," Gil said in stunned disbelief. "They killed him." The boy looked up, looked around. "They've killed Segou."

"Stupid savage, what did he think he was doing?" the halberdier Dinis Gomes said.

"What? What did you say?"

Gomes didn't repeat it. Dias pushed him away.

"He's dead," Gil said again more loudly, his unbelieving horror rising. "They've killed him. They've killed Segou."

The Kongo warriors were standing around with their lances and shields still poised, the lance of the one who had killed Segou dripping Segou's blood. And the Soyo porters and women were standing around, and the NsakuSoyo was standing around, and the halberdiers were standing around, and Mbemba was standing around, looking down at Segou, looking down at the dead Ashanti without any particular pity. For all of them, he had been merely a Guinean, merely a slave, a dog.

"Padre, Segou is dead. They've killed Segou, padre."

And it was only then that Gil realized that Father Sebastião was not among those standing around. He wasn't standing at all. He was still lying on the ground. He was still lying flat on his back on the ground, like Segou.

"Padre? Oh, my God, padre." Gil jumped up and now raced over to Father Sebastião and dropped to his knees beside *him*. "Father Sebastião. Please. Dear God, please."

The old Franciscan opened his eyes. "My head," he said and raised his head and put a hand on the bald pate of his tonsure and, when he took his hand away this time, there was blood on his hand. "I knocked my head," he said in bewilderment. "I think I knocked myself unconscious."

"Can you get up?"

Father Sebastião pushed himself up into a sitting position, resting on his elbows, the blood from the wound on his head trickling down the back of his neck. "In a moment, my son. I think I knocked myself unconscious when I fell."

"Segou is dead, padre."

"Segou?"

"They killed him, padre."

"Who killed him?"

"The Kongo killed him. They ran him through."

"Why?"

"Why? I don't know why. What does it matter why?" The hysteria in Gil was mounting; tears were welling up in his eyes. "He is dead, padre. Don't you understand? He tried to come to our aid and they ran him through and killed him."

"Where is he now?"

"Where is he now? Where would he be? He is where they killed him." Gil looked back to where Segou lay on the ground. Flies were already swarming around the face; hard, shiny black bugs were already crawling in the gore spilling from his stomach. "Oh, cover him over, can't you?" Gil shouted hysterically at Gomes and Dias. "Find something with which to cover him over, for pity's sake."

But neither of the halberdiers took notice. They were watching the Kongo warriors, paralyzed by the sight of their poised lances, paralyzed by the memory of the lance's swift killing power, slicing through the Ashanti's flesh and gristle and bone as easily as through hot butter.

But then Mbemba said something and the Kongo warriors lowered their lances and shields and melted back into the village's darkness, and the Soyo porters and women dispersed, and the NsakuSoyo, with a look of grim satisfaction, returned to his hut. Only Mbemba remained for a moment longer, looking at Gil with no expression at all, and then he too went back into his hut, leaving the four white men alone in the center of the village clearing with the corpse of the killed Ashanti.

FATHER SEBASTIÃO now traveled in a litter. It was only to be until he recovered from the knock on his head, he insisted. Each night he was sure that the following day he'd be able to walk again. But what, in his gentle optimism, he tried to dismiss as a minor, unfortunate accident (refusing to dwell on how it had actually come about or to place any blame for it) was in fact a severe injury. The bleeding stopped, the swelling receded and the cut itself healed so that, after a few days, he no longer required bandages. But something more serious than the bleeding and swelling and cut had happened to his head. He was always dizzy. He suffered terrible headaches. His vision was impaired. His nose often bled. He had difficulty conducting matins and evensong.

So Vasco Dias assisted him. It surprised Gil. He had expected that, because of Father Sebastião's pain and confusion, the ritual of morning and evening prayers would become increasingly fitful and gradually cease altogether. But neither Dias nor Gomes would allow this. The killing of Segou had shaken their confidence far more than they would have cared to admit. It would be foolhardy, in such suddenly uncertain circumstances, to neglect to seek God's benediction and pray for His protection.

"How are you feeling, padre?"

"Much better, my son. Oh, yes, much better. I'll be on my feet tomorrow, you'll see." Father Sebastião said this with his eyes squeezed shut as if by doing so he could squeeze out the pain in his head caused by the jouncing of the litter. His wide-brimmed hat rested on his chest over his hands, which clutched his rosary. Dried blood crusted his nostrils. "Yes, by tomorrow I'll be ready to begin Mbemba's instruction."

"Mbemba's instruction?"

"I will teach him God's words. He still wishes to understand the writing, does he not?"

"Aye, padre," Gil replied, not at all sure it was so.

"Oh, it is a glorious triumph. *Deo gratias.*" Father Sebastião opened his eyes. "We have captured a soul, my son. We have saved a soul from eternal damnation. We shall make a great ceremony of his baptism."

"Aye, padre. But don't excite yourself. You must rest."

A few paces ahead of the priest's litter, Gomes and Dias walked side by side. They stuck close to the priest now, walking guard on his litter during the day, alternating a watch on his hut at night, fearful of being bereft of God's grace if he died. And they were always in full armor now and kept their halberds close to hand. Gil also wore his chainmail and helmet now as well as his sword. Having seen how easily the steel lance had sliced through Segou, no one of them was really sure just how effectively the chainmail and breastplates would deflect a similar thrust. But no one of them was taking any chances in this regard either.

The march became steadily more arduous. Apart from the enervating, sweltering heat and the claustrophobic, dispiriting gloom of the forest, which would have been punishment enough, the road, although broad and still well-cleared, started to climb and wind. Gil realized the road was now climbing into the southern foothills of the mountain range that crossed (and blocked) the Zaire, and its twistings and windings were meant to minimize the steepest of the ascents into those mountains. Gil was glad that Father Sebastião was being carried. Even unhurt, the old Franciscan would have had a rough time of it on this road.

At midmorning of the fourth or fifth day after Segou had been killed, the fourteenth or fifteenth day since leaving Mpinda (Gil knew he had lost count of at least one day since entering the forest), at midmorning of that day, he saw Mbemba waiting by the side of the road some fifty yards ahead. The road there wound around and under the overhanging ledge of a boulder, and Mbemba and his warriors were squatting on top of the boulder. When the halberdiers, Father Sebastião's litter and Gil came into view, Mbemba jumped down to the road. Gomes and Dias swung their halberds off their shoulders and, looking up at the warriors still squatting atop the boulder (they formed what very much appeared to be an ambuscade), halted. Father Sebastião's litter bearers and Gil also halted. The NsakuSoyo came up alongside, signaling the Soyo porters and women behind him to halt. Mbemba came back to Father Sebastião's litter and looked in. The old Franciscan wasn't aware of this. His eyes were closed. He probably wasn't even aware that the litter had halted.

"He is hurt very bad," Gil said. "The NsakuSoyo hurt him very bad."

Mbemba ignored this. He didn't need to be told this. He knew it perfectly well. He shouted to the Soyo porters. Immediately, the bearers of the three other litters, those meant for Gil and the NsakuSoyo and himself, came running up.

"You go in the litter now, Gil Eenezh," Mbemba said. "I go in the litter now also."

Gil glanced at the NsakuSoyo. Mbemba had said nothing about his going in the litter but Gil knew this wasn't meant as punishment for what he had done to Father Sebastião. The NsakuSoyo didn't need to be told to go in the litter. According to protocol, he could go in the litter if Mbemba went in the litter.

"No, Mbemba, I do not go in the litter."

Gil actually would have been glad to be carried now but, out of vindictiveness, he wanted to keep the NsakuSoyo from traveling in the litter. For, according to that protocol, if Gil did not travel in the litter, Mbemba would not travel in the litter either and the hateful ju-ju man would just have to go on walking too. It was Gil's only way, childish and self-defeating though it might be, of punishing the NsakuSoyo for what he had done to Father Sebastião and Segou. And he derived a measure of satisfaction seeing the ju-ju man's expression turn sour when he said it.

"No, Mbemba, I do not go in the litter."

"Hear me, Gil Eenezh. The road grows hard during these days now. There, around the big rock, the road grows very hard for you. You go in the litter for these days."

"No, you go in the litter for these days. You go in the litter where the road grows hard for *you*. I am strong enough for the road no matter how hard it grows. I do not go in the litter."

Mbemba shook his head and said with some irritation, "You will see, the road is as hard as I say it is." And he fell into step beside Gil as the march resumed.

The road ahead indeed was hard, steeply rising and winding to the east and vanishing into the forest there, then reappearing at a much higher elevation and switching back into the forest to the west. Between the lower and higher stretches of the road was a deep, wide ravine, not quite as densely overgrown with trees and bush as the forest on either side but filled with mammoth rocks and great slabs of broken granite. Although he could not see it, Gil suspected a sizable river ran through the ravine.

"I am sorry for Pader Sebastum, Gil Eenezh," Mbemba said after a few moments.

Without looking at him, Gil said, "And Segou, Mbemba? Are you also sorry for Segou?"

"Your slave?"

"He was not my slave. He was my friend."

"How was he your friend? Did he come from your land on the other shore of the sea?"

"No. Still he was my friend."

"I do not understand this."

Gil halted for a moment. "You do not come from my land on the other shore of the sea, do you?"

"No."

"And are you my friend?"

The question clearly startled Mbemba. He stared at Gil for a long moment. Then he smiled, a pleased boy's smile. "Yes, Gil Eenezh, I am your friend."

"Yes, Mbemba, you are my friend," Gil said, although not smiling himself. "And so Segou was my friend." He resumed walking. "But Segou was a good friend and you are a bad friend."

VII

FATHER SEBASTIÃO died on what Gil calculated to be the seventeenth day after leaving Mpinda (although it could have been the sixteenth or even the eighteenth; he had now lost at least two days in his count but wasn't sure in which direction), seven days (or six or eight) after he had been injured and Segou had been killed. It came as an appalling shock. Neither Gil nor the halberdiers had realized just how severely he had been hurt, that his skull had been fractured.

It was Dias who found him dead in his hut that morning. He had gone in to fetch him for matins and what he found was, indeed, so shockingly unexpected that he came out again saying only that Father Sebastião seemed so badly done in that he couldn't be awakened. It was Gomes who had the presence of mind to lay his ear on the old Franciscan's chest and pronounce him dead.

This was at what would prove to be the last Mbata village of the forest. The caravan was already assembled in the first dim light of the dawn filtering through the cathedral of surrounding trees, and Mbemba and the NsakuSoyo were waiting for the white men to get on with the brief devotion they held each morning before starting the day's march. Gil followed Gomes into the hut and also laid his ear on the priest's chest. Then, kneeling by his side, he studied the old man's face. The face was not peaceful; it was twisted in a rictus of pain and, although Gil did not say it aloud, a terrible suspicion passed through his mind, that the old man had not died of his head injury but had been killed during the night on the orders of the NsakuSoyo. He came out of the hut trembling.

"Father Sebastião is dead." He said this to Mbemba.

Mbemba did not immediately respond, clearly stunned by the news. The NsakuSoyo, however, quickly turned away.

"Do you hear what I say, Mbemba? Father Sebastião is dead." Gil's trembling voice rose an octave.

"No, Pader Sebastum is not dead," Mbemba finally replied and went toward the hut.

Dias and Gomes stood in front of the low entryway, blocking it with their crossed halberds.

"He is not dead," Mbemba said again with angry force and glared at the two halberdiers.

They did not move out of his way. The anxiety that their priest's death had stirred in them, their horrified recognition that the kindly old Franciscan would no longer be there to lead them in prayer, hear their confessions, intercede with God in their behalf, seemed to have given them a courage they hadn't exhibited before—or had paralyzed them with fear.

"Let him by," Gil said in Portuguese. "Let him see for himself."

Dias and Gomes pulled back their axe-headed pikes and Gil followed Mbemba into the hut. Mbemba dropped to his knees by the old man's head and stared at the gaunt, ashen, agony-twisted face. Then he slipped a hand under the head and raised it and, with his other hand, began rubbing the old man's cheek, pinching the skin, squeezing the nostrils, plucking at the eyelids.

"Stop that. He is dead. Leave him in peace."

"No, he is not dead. I say he is not dead." Mbemba stood up. He knew perfectly well the priest was dead but he did not want to believe it. It seemed almost as much of a shock to him as it was to Gil and the halberdiers. "He only sleeps. The NsakuSoyo will awaken him with his magic." He ducked out of the hut.

"No." Gil dashed out after him.

But Mbemba had already called to the NsakuSoyo and the ju-ju man, with his rattle, was coming to the hut.

"Keep him away. Do you hear me, Mbemba? Keep that devil's witch away. He will not touch Father Sebastião. I will not allow it."

And in a rush of hysterical rage, Gil drew his sword. "He is the one who killed Father Sebastião. If he dares touch him again, I will kill him. Do you hear me, Mbemba? If he dares put his hands on Father Sebastião again, I will kill him as he killed Father Sebastião and Segou."

Fortunately, in his wild agitation, Gil said all this in Portuguese so only the halberdiers understood him.

"Do you mean that, boy?" Gomes hissed. "Because if you mean that, boy, be prepared to die."

"Let us all be prepared to die," Gil answered and extended his sword so that it pointed straight at the NsakuSoyo's chest. "Not a step closer, you sorcerer, you devil's witch. Not a step closer, you turd of a dog." And he lunged with the sword, sending the NsakuSoyo scuttling back.

"*Kyrie, eleison. Christe, eleison.* Lord have mercy. Christ have mercy. I am ready to die," Dias sang out and swung down his heavy axe-headed pike.

But Mbemba jumped between Gil and the NsakuSoyo, taking the point of Gil's sword on his own chest. "Do not do this, Gil Eenezh. The NsakuSoyo will not touch Pader Sebastum if that is your wish."

"That is my wish."

"It will be as you wish."

Gil lowered the sword but did not scabbard it. His heart was pounding against the wall of his chest like a hammer. The sweat was streaming down his face like a river. The sword hanging from his hand trembled against the side of his leg. Dias and Gomes held their halberds poised, also trembling, also streaming sweat, also breathing hard.

"You're mad, boy," Gomes said in a hoarse whisper but not without admiration.

Gil took no notice of this. He kept his eyes fixed on the Nsaku-Soyo. The ju-ju man had recovered from his momentary fright and was speaking angrily to Mbemba. Mbemba said something to him and turned away, and this provoked him to an even angrier outburst. Quite clearly he was complaining about Gil's threatening move and Mbemba's failure to do anything about it. When Segou had made a similar move, Mbemba had had his warriors cut the Ashanti down without hesitation or remorse. Why not Gil, then? His move had been even more threatening than the Ashanti's. Again Mbemba replied curtly without turning around. And that infuriated the ju-ju man even more and he grabbed Mbemba's arm. And now Mbemba did turn around. And he shoved the NsakuSoyo away.

A horrified gasp burst from the Soyo at the sight of their priest so rudely manhandled.

"You have caused trouble enough, NsakuSoyo," Mbemba snapped. "My father, the king, sent me to fetch to him the white men who have flown down to us from their land in the sky. One is already dead. There will not be another."

The NsakuSoyo didn't answer this. His expression closed down into a clenched, hate-filled watchfulness. Mbemba would pay for this, it seemed to say. Mbemba would pay for having chosen the white men's side against him, a sorcerer of the kingdom; Mbemba would pay for such apostasy.

They buried Father Sebastião in the hut in which he had died. There had been a dispute about where to bury him. Their concern had been that, once the caravan departed and the Mbata returned to reclaim their village, the Mbata would desecrate the grave. Gomes was convinced the Mbata were cannibals—he was convinced all "Guineans" were cannibals—and they'd dig up the poor padre and eat him. But that possibility existed no matter where they buried him, unless of course they did not mark the grave. But Dias had insisted that they had to mark the grave; not to do so would be a sacrilege. It was Mbemba who settled the matter. He had hovered around the three white men during the preparation of the corpse, intensely curious to see what white men did to prepare one of their priests for the journey to *Nzambi Mpungu,* and slowly came to understand their concern.

"Let him sleep in the house, Gil Eenezh," he said. "Let him sleep there as he is."

Gil and the halberdiers had dressed the priest in his vestments and had placed his rosary and crucifix between his clasped hands. Kneeling around him under the hut's low roof, they looked up at Mbemba standing at the entryway.

"We will close the house around him with earth and he will not be disturbed. I will say this to the Mbata. I will say to them that this is now a sacred place and it must never be disturbed."

Gil translated this for Dias and Gomes.

"It would be like a mausoleum," Dias ventured uncertainly.

"That would be all right, wouldn't it?"

"We could place a cross outside in front."

"Aye, that would do it," Gomes said, doubtless thinking of the labor that would be saved by not having to go to the trouble of digging a hole in the ground. "Aye, that would do it all right, as long as he warns them damn heathen to keep away from the place."

"The Mbata will not disturb him, Mbemba?" Gil asked. "You say this to me?"

"Yes, Gil Eenezh, I say this to you. The Mbata will not disturb him. He will sleep in peace."

"He promises the Mbata won't bother the hut."

"Then I say it's all right. Eh, Dias?"

Dias nodded slowly. "Aye, but we must say a prayer first."

"You say it."

"I can't read. You can, boy." Dias fished out Father Sebastião's breviary from the sea chest that contained the priest's sacerdotal articles and handed it to Gil. "You read the prayer."

"I can't read Latin," Gil said, taking the breviary and opening it at random. "I couldn't even find the prayer for the dead."

"But we must have a prayer. He was denied the last rites. He must at least have a prayer."

Gil thumbed through the breviary, searching for a paragraph, a sentence, a phrase that looked familiar. *"Deus qui inter apostolicos sacerdos familum tuum . . ."* His voice trailed off and he continued turning the pages. Then he said, "The Pater Noster. That would be all right, don't you think? This is it here. I think I can read it."

"Read it then."

They all removed their helmets and Gil began reading from the breviary. *"Pater noster, qui es in caelis . . ."*

He was aware that Mbemba was watching him. The young Kongo prince was watching him exactly as he had watched Father Sebastião when *he* had read from the breviary, watching his eyes move across each line on the page and then down to the next line, trying intently to make the connection between this and the words Gil was speaking.

"... *sed libera nos a malo,*" Gil concluded and looked at the halberdiers.

"That was fine," Gomes said.

"In nomine Patris, et Filii, et Spiritus Sancti."

"Amen." They all crossed themselves and stood up, putting their helmets back on.

"What should we do with these?" Gil asked, indicating the sea chest of sacerdotal articles.

"Leave them here," Gomes said. "We'll bury them with him."

"Won't we have any use for them?"

"What use? You mean as trading truck?"

"No. For prayers or something. What do you think, Dias?"

"I don't think we have any right to make use of them in that way. Only a priest can."

"Well then, I say let's leave them here by his side," Gomes said.

"It would be fitting," Dias agreed vaguely.

They went out of the hut, Gil still holding the breviary. It was absentmindedness. Had he thought of it, he would have left it to be buried with the priest. But his mind was on other things.

"We close the house of Pader Sebastum now, Gil Eenezh?" Mbemba asked.

"Yes."

Mbemba shouted to the Soyo porters. They had remained assembled in the caravan all this time waiting for the march to get under way, their loads and bundles and baggage at their feet. Several came forward on Mbemba's command.

"They will close the house," Mbemba said.

Gil nodded. It was light, as light as it would ever become in the sea-green gloom of the forest; it must already be midmorning. The NsakuSoyo was seated in front of his hut, watching what was going on with a distant stare. The drummers, trumpeters and fetishers, who would lead the way out of the village when the march resumed, and many of the Soyo women had gathered around him. They hadn't gotten over their shock at seeing him so irreverently treated, and Gil wondered if he could incite them to avenge his humiliation.

"Where are you two going?"

Dias and Gomes, carrying their halberds, had started out of the village into the forest.

"To cut wood for the padre's cross," Gomes said.

Gil watched the pair disappear into the dense brush. They were talking to each other in low, agitated voices. He turned back. The Soyo porters had begun packing the damp, red earth of the forest floor into the entryway of the priest's hut. The Kongo warriors were standing around watching them; evidently they didn't do this kind of work. The NsakuSoyo remained seated with his adherents around him.

"Gil Eenezh?"

Gil turned to Mbemba.

"What words did you speak when you spoke the writing of Pader Sebastum?" Mbemba asked.

It took Gil a moment to understand that Mbemba was referring to the prayer he had read from Father Sebastião's breviary. And it was only then that he realized he still had the breviary in his hand. "I spoke the words of *Nzambi Mpungu.*"

"The writing is the words of *Nzambi Mpungu?*"

"Not all writing is the words of *Nzambi Mpungu* but this writing is. This writing is how *Nzambi Mpungu* speaks to us. And how we speak to Him."

Mbemba frowned at this. Clearly here was yet another concept beyond his experience and thus almost impossible to comprehend. "This writing must be very strong magic then."

"It is very strong magic. It is the strongest magic, stronger than the magic of the NsakuSoyo or any ju-ju man."

Mbemba's frown deepened. Apparently, he felt he should not allow Gil to say such a thing, that for him even to listen to it was blasphemy, and Gil expected him to respond with some sort of protest. But he didn't. What he said, he said so softly Gil at first did not believe he heard him correctly.

"Will you let me have this writing, Gil Eenezh?" was what he said, glancing toward the NsakuSoyo, keeping his voice low so as not to be overheard. "Will you give me this strong magic that is the word *Nzambi Mpungu* speaks?"

Gil also glanced over to the NsakuSoyo and thought: Father Sebastião might yet triumph over that hateful man; his death, instead of being a stupid meaningless accident, might yet prove to be a martyrdom of sorts. And he gave the breviary to the young Kongo prince. And this time no one knocked it from his hand.

THEY EMERGED FROM THE FOREST the following day. It came as a surprise, abrupt and utterly unforeseen. One moment, they were struggling up a steep incline in the fetid, claustrophobic gloom of the trees and the next, on reaching the top of the incline, they were stepping out of the trees into bright sunlight under a brilliant blue, overarching, cloudless sky, a rush of fresh air filling their lungs and a grand vista opening in every direction as far as their eyes could see: rolling hills and valleys, lush meadows and glades covered in tall yellow elephant grass and flowering groves of acacia and eucalyptus and bushes of mimosa and tamarind, criss-crossed by sparkling rivers and streams, abounding in great herds of wild game and great flocks of wild fowl, a breathtakingly beautiful country, a thousand, perhaps two thousand feet above the level of the sea. It was the country of Nsundi, the principal province or fiefdom of the Kongo kingdom.

The road, still wide and clear, continued to climb on emerging from the forest, now generally east by south, but much more gently and, because of the freshness of the air and openness of the landscape, much more easily. And as it climbed into the bright rolling hills and wound its way over the meadows and through the valleys and across the fast-running streams, people gathered along its verges to watch the caravan pass by.

They were the Nsundi, a tall, strong, handsome and haughty people, dressed in skirts and robes of that unusual velvetlike cloth and in tunics and capes of beautifully tanned hides and spotted fur, wearing headdresses of feathers and ivory and jewellike beads, adorned with bracelets and anklets and necklaces of what surely must be silver and precious stones, and armed with steel. And their villages were larger and more impressive than not only those of the Mbata in the forest but also those of the Soyo down at the coast, fortified by high, sturdy stockades with heavy, carved gates and tall watch towers. And the dwellings within, set in orderly fashion around not a single market square but several, were constructed of timbers, rectangular in shape, their roofs, of closely woven thatch, canted and gabled with verandas at the front and back under the overhanging eaves. And the reception the caravan received at these villages was also different, neither abject as in Mbata nor boisterously festive as in Soyo but calm, correct and severely dignified. The Nsundi chiefs and headmen did not prostrate themselves at Mbemba's feet but approached him directly and clasped his shoulders by way of greeting, and although the three white men in helmets and chainmail must have astounded them as much as they had the Soyo and Mbata, they masked their wonder with polite indifference and arranged no special feasts or entertainments in their honor and gave them a single dwelling to share.

"Two or three more days," Gil said.

"What's two or three more days, boy?" Gomes asked.

"Until we reach Mbanza Kongo."

"Two or three more days, eh? Well . . . I don't know."

"What do you mean you don't know?"

Gomes shrugged.

"Aye, Gomes, answer the boy. What do you mean you don't know?" Dias said.

"Well, what I don't know is why in blazes we should keep on to Mbanza Kongo."

"Because the captain-general commanded us to go there," Gil said. "To meet the Kongo king and greet him in João's name and see what sort of place it is and bring back—"

"We'll bring back nothing from there," Gomes snapped. "We'll die there."

Gil and Dias looked at each other.

"Sure we'll die there," Gomes went on, his voice rising. "What makes you think we won't? They killed the Guinean, didn't they? They killed the padre. What makes you think they won't kill us as well?"

"So, what are you saying?" asked Dias. "Speak your mind. What do you propose we do if not go on to Mbanza Kongo?"

"Go back. To the Zaire."

"On our own? Just the three of us?"

"Aye."

"But how could we do that? How would we find the way? How

could we carry our sea chests and provisions? What would we eat?"

"And what would we say to the captain-general when the *Leonor* returns for us?" Gil put in.

"We could think of something to say. We could agree among ourselves what to say."

"You mean make something up? Lie?"

Gomes shrugged and looked away.

"Like that we were attacked on the road and they killed Segou and Father Sebastião and we ran away to save our lives?"

Gomes looked back at Gil and said with enthusiasm, "Aye, boy, like that. It ain't so far from the truth. Something like that is going to happen, you can be sure of it."

"He's right," Dias said. "Something like that is going to happen. I feel it in my bones."

The three fell silent. Then Dias asked, "You really think we could make it back on our own?"

"Sure I do. We'll just keep falling farther and farther back and then we'll slip away. Eh, boy? What do you say?"

Gil took a moment to reply. Then he said, "I don't think they'll kill us. They killed Segou because he attacked the ju-ju man and they never liked him anyway. And the padre was an accident. The ju-ju man didn't mean to kill him. He just wanted to keep him away from Mbemba. And you saw what happened when I drew my sword on him. They didn't kill me."

"That's true, Gomes," Dias said.

"That's because they think he's a prince, you fool. And they ain't going to kill a prince so easily. But they don't think you're a prince, Dias. And they don't think I'm a prince. Now do they?"

Dias didn't reply.

"You may think you're safe enough, boy. The prince. The captain-general's son. And maybe you are. And maybe you're not. You can take your chances if you want. But me and Dias . . ."

Ever since Father Sebastião died, Gil and the two halberdiers had stuck close together during the marches. But the next day, Gomes and Dias marched several paces behind Gil, out of earshot. Gil was in no doubt why. They didn't want him to hear what they were talking about. They were talking about running away.

Gil truly believed that, whatever else might happen in Mbanza
Kongo, the Kongo wouldn't kill them, that in the last resort Mbemba
would protect them as he had protected Gil against the NsakuSoyo.
But, even if he were wrong about this, Gil also truly believed that
they'd never be able to get back through the forest to the Zaire on
their own. Even so, if Gomes and Dias decided to go back, he would
go back with them. The prospect of arriving in Mbanza Kongo all
alone, the only white man in a savage kingdom, frightened him far
more than the perils of going back through the forest with the halberdiers did. So he continually looked for them during the march
and, when they lagged too far behind, he'd stop to let them catch up.

In this open, gently rolling, bright yellow grassland, unlike in the
forest, it was possible to see far ahead, the road winding up and down
and around the hills, the trumpeters and drummers and fetishers well
in the advance marching on the winding road, the palisaded villages
back in the hills and along the road, the people of the villages gathering along the sides of the road and, beyond that, on the distant horizon still several leagues away, a mountain rising out of the highest of
the yellow hills into the crystalline blue sky where eagles and hawks
soared in lazy circles like sentinels of heaven.

"There is Mbanza Kongo," Mbemba said.

"There, on the mountain?"

"Yes, that is the mountain of Mbanza Kongo."

As they advanced toward it down the long sloping bosom of a
meadow, Gil realized that it wasn't actually a mountain but rather a
high tableland thrust up from the lower-lying country by a sheer,
rugged escarpment of jagged rock and red earth. At its base, a sizable
river ran. This was the Lelunda, and on its near bank stood the largest
village encountered so far. It was called Mpangala, and the road ran
directly to the front gate of its stockade.

Gomes and Dias came up alongside Gil and Mbemba when they
first became aware of Mpangala and the river Lelunda and the mountain or tableland rising up from the Lelunda's opposite bank. And
then they began lagging always farther and farther behind. It was
now or never for them, Gil knew; if they were going to desert, they
would have to do so before they crossed the Lelunda and began the
climb up the mountain.

And then Gil heard music from far down the road, blowing up to him on the fresh breeze that blew across this lovely, open land. Either the drummers and trumpeters and fetishers had started up again after all the days of silence in the forest or they had been playing their instruments all along, beating their drums, blowing their horns, shaking their rattles, banging their sticks, but now Gil was drawing close enough to them to hear them. For they, in the lead, had reached Mpangala's front gate and had halted. In an hour or less, Gil himself would reach the gate. He looked back yet again. And this time the two halberdiers were nowhere in sight.

"We stop, Mbemba. My soldiers." Gil pointed back.

Mbemba looked back.

"I do not see my soldiers," Gil said and stopped. "We must wait for them."

Mbemba continued a step or two and then, with a sigh of annoyance, also stopped. "We cannot wait for them here," he said and returned the few steps to Gil's side and took him firmly by the arm. "We will wait for them in Mpangala."

A huge crowd of villagers—hundreds, possibly thousands—were gathered on either side of Mpangala's front gate. The gate stood open. The NsakuSoyo and his musicians and fetishers had already passed through and waited in the first of a series of market squares as Gil and Mbemba, flanked by Mbemba's warriors, entered, the musicians and fetishers drumming and trumpeting and rattling and banging with great ceremonial fervor. Some distance beyond the NsakuSoyo, the chief of Mpangala, with his headmen and ju-ju men and wives and bodyguard standing around him, sat on a stool at the base of a giant fig tree. When Mbemba and Gil reached the NsakuSoyo, the NsakuSoyo fell into step beside them and the musicians and fetishers gathered behind them and they all advanced toward the seated Mpangala chief.

He stood up and grasped Mbemba's shoulders and spoke a few words of greeting to him. Mbemba replied, grasping the chief's shoulders in return, and as he did this, Gil took another quick look back. If Gomes and Dias had come as far as Mpangala, Gil couldn't tell because of the crowd of people pushing through the gate on the heels of the Soyo porters and women of the caravan. If they were there, they were lost in the crush of that crowd.

"Gil Eenezh."

Gil turned around. The musicians and fetishers had fallen silent. Mbemba was introducing Gil to the Mpangala chieftain.

"Gil Eenezh, prince of the Porta Geeze, the white strangers who have flown down to us on the wings of a great bird from their land in the sky."

From their land in the sky? Gil looked at Mbemba with a start. He knew Gil didn't come from a land in the sky. He knew he came from a land on the other shore of the sea. Gil had admitted that to him days before. But he was keeping it a secret. Why? To protect Gil by allowing him to remain cloaked in the awe that the idea evoked? As a token of their friendship?

"Mpanzu a Nzinga." Mbemba was now introducing the Mpangala chieftain. "ManiNsundi. MtuKongo."

Gil understood the title ManiNsundi: the paramount chief or lord of Nsundi, the province or fiefdom through which they had been passing since leaving the forest of the Mbata. But MtuKongo? That meant he was a prince of the Kongo as Mbemba was a prince of the Kongo. Did he hold that title as lord of the kingdom's principal fiefdom? Or was he a prince of the blood as his name seemed to suggest?

"Mpanzu a Nzinga?" Gil repeated inquiringly. "Mpanzu, the son of Nzinga?"

"Yes."

"As you are Mbemba a Nzinga? Mbemba, son of Nzinga?"

"Nzinga a Nkuwu, the ManiKongo, is our father. Mpanzu is my brother."

Gil took a closer look at the Mpangala chieftain. He was considerably older than Mbemba, at least twenty years older, and much bigger, taller and broader, although not in a particularly muscular way, rather flabby, in fact, with quite a paunch and softer features and bulging, rheumy eyes. If they were brothers, Gil thought, they could only be half-brothers; the lithe, handsome Mbemba surely had a different mother. Mpanzu was dressed in a long skirt and long cape of the velvety material, sky-blue in color and embroidered with white zigzag patterns at the edges, and was adorned in a profusion of necklaces and bracelets of silver and ivory, cowrie shells and animal teeth, wore a headdress of eagle feathers and antelope horns and carried a short, silver-inlaid ivory baton.

"Why have you come to us, Gil Eenezh?" he asked in a soft, gravelly voice. "Why have you flown down to us from your land in the sky, prince of the Porta Geeze?"

"Why, MtuKongo?"

"Surely you have come to us for a reason, Gil Eenezh. Surely there is a purpose in your coming. I ask, what is that reason? I ask, what is your purpose?"

"To bring greetings to your king from my king, MtuKongo. To bring greetings and gifts to the ManiKongo as tokens of the Portuguese king's esteem."

Mpanzu cocked his head as if less than entirely convinced by this answer. But he said, "Let us go then to the ManiKongo, Gil Eenezh, so you can bring him your king's greetings and gifts. He awaits you."

Gil realized that Mpanzu was now in charge of the journey to Mbanza Kongo, that Mbemba had relinquished command to the elder brother, the ranking prince. But it wasn't until Mpanzu had led them through the several interconnected market squares of the large village and they had come to a gate in the stockade on the other side that Gil understood what Mpanzu had in mind. The gate was a river gate; it opened on to the Lelunda River and a fleet of canoes was drawn up on the river's bank, prepared to ferry the caravan across. They were going to go straight on. It wasn't yet noon and apparently the ascent of the escarpment to the plateau of the tableland above could be accomplished before nightfall.

"No, Mbemba. Stop. You said we will stop in Mpangala to wait for my soldiers."

There was a terrific confusion of activity on the riverside of the village, hundreds of people swarming on the riverbank, hundreds surging through the river gate down to the riverbank, hundreds pushing and jostling their way back into the village. The Soyo porters and women were wading into the water to load the canoes with their bundles and baskets and baggage but it was clear that they weren't going on, that the journey for them ended here. Nsundi porters and women from Mpangala were taking their place, boarding the canoes, and some of the canoes were already shoving off, while warriors from the village, and musicians and fetishers and hunters and trackers, the ManiNsundi's people replacing the ManiSoyo's, were climbing into other canoes and also shoving off. In all the confusion, Gil found himself being rushed down to the river's edge against his will, slipping and sliding in the mud of the bank, in danger of losing sight even of Mbemba in the busy crush.

"I do not see my soldiers, Mbemba. We must wait until they come. You said we will wait in Mpangala until my soldiers come."

"What is the trouble?" Mpanzu asked, looking around with some impatience.

"His soldiers, Mpanzu," Mbemba said. "He has two soldiers who accompany him."

"Where are these soldiers? Why are they not with him? What sort of soldiers are not always at the side of their prince?"

"Lazy soldiers. Worthless soldiers," Mbemba replied.

"If they are such lazy, worthless soldiers," Mpanzu asked, "why has he not killed them?"

"He is a gentle prince."

"Hah," Mpanzu snorted. "He is like you."

Mbemba accepted the taunt with a younger brother's wry smile and said, "He wishes to wait for them here."

"No. He will wait for them there." Mpanzu pointed to the river's opposite bank and then waded into the water to board the largest of the canoes drawn up on the near shore.

"Come, Gil Eenezh," Mbemba said, taking Gil's arm and directing him to that canoe. "There will be time for your soldiers to come before we begin to climb the mountain of Mbanza Kongo."

To Gil's dismay, the NsakuSoyo was in the canoe. Of all the Soyo, he was the only one going on. Perhaps it was his mission to tell the ManiKongo of the arrival of the *Leonor* and of all that had transpired with the white men before Mbemba had come to Mpinda. Or perhaps he was going along to speak his mind about the white strangers.

They made rapid headway crossing the river. Although it was more than a thousand yards wide, the canoe was huge, at least sixty feet long, and had ten paddlers standing along each side who drove them through the water at a startling speed. The canoes that had shoved off before them passed them on their way back so that, when they ran up on the opposite bank, a bustling crowd was already there, warriors and fetishers and trackers and hunters and porters and women sorting through the bundles and baskets and baggage, making up the new caravan, the caravan that would ascend the escarpment to Mbanza Kongo.

Gil was the last to go ashore, lingering in the canoe's stern, trying to spot the halberdiers at Mpangala's river gate, and when he did finally go ashore, he remained at the river's edge, looking across, ignoring the bustling activity of the assembling caravan. He knew by now that he wouldn't see what he wanted to see. He knew by now that Gomes and Dias had run away. But he refused to acknowledge it. He could not begin to consider the idea of being altogether alone; he couldn't begin to imagine the loneliness of being the only white man in this black, savage land.

"Gil Eenezh."

Gil looked away from the river. Mbemba had donned his princely adornments, the necklaces and bracelets and anklets of silver, the silver headband with the green, emeraldlike stone. In addition, like his half-brother Mpanzu, he was wearing a cape, a tunic of soft hide and a headdress of feather and horn. Two porters from Mpangala stood behind him. They had brought over Gil's sea chest.

"We go to the king," Mbemba said and indicated the sea chest.

Gil understood. He kneeled beside the sea chest and opened it.

"I help you?" Mbemba asked.

Gil shook his head. A prince should have a retainer to help him but he had none. So slowly, automatically, as if in a daze or a trance, he changed into his princely costume by himself. Mpanzu and the NsakuSoyo came over.

"We go," Mpanzu said to Mbemba.

Mbemba looked at Gil questioningly and Gil looked back across the river.

"They do not come." It was the NsakuSoyo who said this. "The worthless soldiers do not come."

Gil turned to him in fury. "Why do you say this, sorcerer? You do not know this."

"I do know this," the NsakuSoyo replied with his mean smile. "I see this with my own eyes."

"What do you see with your own eyes?"

"I see them go back to the forest."

Oh, God. Oh, dear God. Looking at the hateful ju-ju man, Gil knew this was true.

"We go now, Gil Eenezh?" Mbemba asked.

Gil nodded. Mpanzu and the NsakuSoyo turned away. Litter bearers came up and Gil watched Mpanzu and the NsakuSoyo get into their litters. The bearers of two other litters stood waiting.

"We go now to the king," Mbemba said.

Again Gil nodded and took one final look back across the river. Then he got into his litter and was hoisted shoulder-high by the four bearers.

VIII

MBANZA KONGO was a city of more than thirty thousand people and more than five thousand buildings, spread out over more than three thousand hectares on the bright-yellow grassland plateau of the mountaintop in a sprawling confusion of twisting streets, broad avenues, bustling market squares, flowering gardens and wooded parks, a royal city even by the standards of Europe at the time, certainly a royal city to Gil's eyes. No stockade enclosed it; its commanding location on the highest ground of the surrounding country apparently was defense enough, the red-clay cliffs of the escarpment plunging hundreds of feet down to the valley of the Lelunda on the north, west and south, the plateau sloping off through thousands of acres of cultivated fields and pastureland into a forest on the east.

It was from the east, up that slope, out of that forest and through those fields that the caravan from Mpangala approached the city at dusk of the same day it had started up the mountain (the sixteenth of September by Gil's uncertain reckoning) and what seemed to be virtually every one of the city's inhabitants was out to meet it, lining the streets, jamming the squares, standing on the rooftops, clambering out on the branches of the trees in the parks, competing for a view of the white prince who was said to have flown down to them from a land in the sky.

Sitting upright in his litter, crossing and recrossing his legs in an effort to assume a dignified posture, holding on to the litter's poles to steady himself against the bearers' jouncing gait, holding on to his plumed helmet to keep it from jouncing off his head, Gil was uneasily aware of the thousands of eyes fixed on him, the thousands of fingers pointing at him. Mbemba was carried beside him, legs *à la turc*, torso erect, arms folded across his chest, his lance in the crook of one arm, having no trouble maintaining a severely princely composure, the feathers of his headdress fluttering in the sweet breeze blowing across this lovely open savanna highland. Mpanzu preceded them, the NsakuSoyo followed behind, scores of warriors formed an escort on both sides of them, and the drummers and trumpeters and dancing fetishers accompanying them played a thrilling music in impassioned celebration of their arrival in the city of the Kongo king.

Once they passed through the outlying fields and entered the precincts of the city itself, Gil became disoriented. With its jumble of buildings of every size and shape and use, with its maze of streets leading in and out of countless squares and parks, with its masses of people, it would be a city easy to get lost in under any circumstances. But, in addition, the caravan followed a confusingly circuitous route, winding to the north and south, east and west and all around again, as if to put Gil, like an extraordinary bounty of war or treasure of peace, on display in every quarter.

Then they came to a river and halted. This was the Luezi, a tributary of the Lelunda. Flowing in a sinuous arc from north to southwest and spilling over the escarpment there in a sparkling cascade, it hived off about a third of the city into a separate and distinct district. Gil immediately recognized what it was: the district of the king and his court. The buildings over there, located close to the edge of the plateau and with a spectacular view out over the escarpment to the rolling countryside below, were larger, more imposing and complex in design, made of boards and timbers and elaborately woven thatch with peaked roofs and porticoes and breezeways and flowering arbors, and enclosed in a palisade that further set them apart from the plebeian districts of the city. Three broad avenues, lined with fig and palm trees, radiated from three gates in the palisade, each flanked by watch towers, and terminated at three bridges that crossed the Luezi.

It was at the middle bridge that the litters were set down and

Gil got out, massaging a cramp in his thigh, and looked around with
a boy's curiosity and a boy's trepidation. It was fast coming evening
now. A fingernail sliver of moon had risen and stars were winking on
in the deep-blue, cloudless sky, and the air was fresh and clear and
there even was a pleasant chill. They were well up out of the suffocating heat and humidity of the forest here, well up out of the
mosquito-infested swamps of the Zaire's maritime plain. It was no
wonder the Kongo kings had chosen this place for the royal city of
their realm. It was a beautiful and healthy place.

A sizable body of men waited at the foot of the middle bridge.
Most were warriors but a handful were obviously dignitaries of some
kind, probably courtiers of the king. Mbemba and Mpanzu went over
to them, but when Gil started to follow, the NsakuSoyo hissed at him.
He glanced at the hateful ju-ju man, made a fierce face at him and
went on. But then Mbemba signaled him to remain where he was. He
looked around. The members of the caravan from Mpangala, the
porters and women and litter bearers, were picking up their loads
and dispersing back through the crooked, crowded street that had
brought them to the bank of the Luezi. Where were they going?
Among the bundles and baggage and baskets they were carrying
away were his sea chest and duffle.

"Mbemba." Gil started toward the bridge again.

And again the NsakuSoyo made a hissing sound and Mbemba
looked around and raised his lance to indicate that Gil should stay
back. But Gil went on.

"Where do they go, Mbemba?" he asked, gesturing at the caravan's porters. "They take away my things."

With a glance at Mpanzu, Mbemba hurried back to intercept Gil.
"You stay here, Gil Eenezh," he said sternly, taking Gil's arm and turning him away from the bridge.

"But my things."

"Do not fear for your things. They take them to your house."

"My house?"

"There, that is your house. Your things will be safe in your house."

Gil looked at the building. It was a small dwelling fronting the
river's quay, next to what Gil thought might be a forge. It had a veranda in front, on which a few women and children stood.

"You stay in your house with your things until my father is ready to receive you."

"And you, Mbemba? You will stay with me?"

"No. I must go to my father. He awaits me. I will return for you when he is ready to receive you."

As Mbemba rejoined Mpanzu, the others moved out of their way and the two princes started across the bridge. The others fell in behind them and, when they did, the NsakuSoyo darted after them. Gil understood what was happening. They were going to the Mani-Kongo to tell him about Gil. He would want to be prepared for the astonishment of the white stranger.

By the time they reached the other side of the Luezi and passed through the middle gate in the palisade, it was dark. The sky was awash with stars, the crescent moon stood directly overhead and fires were being lit throughout the city. Gil decided to have a closer look at his house.

Two older women, four younger ones, a girl, two little boys clutching the legs of one of the older women and an infant in a sling on the back of the other older woman, waving its tiny hands, were on the veranda. The little boys were naked but the women were modestly dressed, wrapped up under their armpits in plain brown cloth of the sort made from beaten bark, with turbans of the same material around their heads.

The girl, however, wore a dress or kanga of that peculiar velvetlike material, pale green in color and bordered in red, and she didn't wear a turban, revealing a small, shapely head of close-cropped hair, tightly braided in an intricate pattern of criss-crossing rows; several strings of polished stones and colorful cowrie shells hung around her neck. She stood slightly behind the woman with the baby and, while the others stared down at Gil with undisguised fascination, she pretended not to pay any attention to him, busying herself playing with the baby instead. She was a pretty little thing—smooth dark-honey skin, high forehead and sharp cheekbones, slanted lustrous brown eyes with long lashes like a doe's, swollen moist lips, small ears, a pointed chin, and a figure just budding into young womanhood. She probably wasn't more than thirteen or fourteen.

Adjusting the silver-buckled belt from which his short, scab-barded sword hung, then gripping the hilt (less because he felt he had anything to fear from these women and children than to give himself something of a swagger in front of them), Gil went up on the veranda. *"Keba bota,"* he said.

"Keba bota," they replied. *"Keba bota. Keba bota,"* they said, one after another, even the little boys but not the girl, and moved out of his way to allow him to enter the house, one of the little boys pulling aside a woven raffia mat that covered the entryway.

The room he entered, under a beamed roof of thatch, opened at the back on to another veranda and the step down from that veranda led to a fenced-in yard where a cooking fire was burning. The four younger women went out to the fire. Two brought back a kettle of steaming, savory food, a platter of fruits and legumes, and a gourd of palm wine; the two others returned with burning brands with which to light palm-oil lamps hanging from the roof beams. Gil looked around. He couldn't tell whether this was the only room in the house but he fervently hoped it wasn't because he couldn't see any of his things in it.

It was sparsely furnished: A few big decorated clay pots and painted gourds lined its walls; some diamond-patterned woven mats covered its windows and were scattered on the floor boards; and an hourglass-shaped stool stood at its center. The woman with the baby on her back gestured Gil toward it. Throughout the journey from Mpinda, he had had supper with people he knew, Mbemba, Father Sebastião, Segou, Gomes, Dias, during the final days only with Gomes and Dias but at least with them. Now he would have his supper alone. Was it to be like this from now on? He removed his helmet, un-buckled his sword, got out of his surcoat, unfastened the straps of his breastplate, and piled them all neatly beside the stool, then sat down on the stool in his vest of chainmail.

The women and little boys watched him do this with rapt at-tention. So did the pretty girl in the green-and-red kanga. She had re-mained in the entryway on the front veranda, partially hiding herself behind the mat that hung over it. Gil looked at her but she was too quick for him and looked away before he could catch her eye. He turned to the steaming kettle. It contained a brownish porridge with

pieces of chicken in it, and peas and nuts and mushrooms. He was familiar with this sort of food by now and knew it was good and was
hungry for it. He crossed himself, absently touching the bloodstone
beads at his throat and muttering a Hail Mary. Then he fingered out a
sticky lump of the porridge and hopped it around on his palm for a
moment to cool it before popping it into his mouth. It was very spicy
(apparently the Kongo had no taste for sweets) but he had gotten
used to that and rather liked it. Then he picked up the gourd of palm
wine and drank a long, bracing draught, thinking it might not be an
entirely bad idea to get a little bit drunk, and then looked at the girl
in the entryway again. And this time he was quick enough and did
catch her eye, and smiled at her.

Instantly, she let go of the hanging mat she hid behind and ran
away.

"Eh? What's the trouble?" Gil stood up. "Why does she run away?
Where does she go?"

"She is wanted at home," the woman with the baby answered.

"Where is her home?" But before the woman could answer, Gil
strode to the entryway, pushed aside the hanging mat and stepped
out on the veranda.

He didn't see her right away, and then he did. She was running
across the middle bridge, running toward the middle gate in the palisade through which Mbemba and Mpanzu and the NsakuSoyo had
passed on their way to the king. So her home was in the royal district. And Gil suddenly remembered that the color and design of her
dress or kanga, the pale green bordered in red, were the same as Mbemba's kanga and those of the warriors of his bodyguard. Was she a
member of Mbemba's family then, of his entourage? Was she his serving girl, his concubine, his wife? The gate in the palisade opened and
she ran through. When it closed again, Gil went back into the house.

"Who is she, *mchento?*" he asked the woman with the baby.

"Nimi a Nzinga."

Gil's eyebrows shot up. "Nimi a Nzinga? As Mbemba is Mbemba
a Nzinga?"

"Yes," the woman replied, smiling at Gil's quickness at making
the connection.

"She is a princess?" Gil said this in Portuguese. He did not know the word in Kongo. He had not yet met a Kongo princess. The woman of course did not understand him. He tried again. "She is a child of Nzinga a Nkuwu?"

"Yes," the woman said. "She is a daughter of ManiKongo. She is NtinuKongo."

"NtinuKongo," Gil repeated. Princess of the Kongo. He sat down on the stool again and took another long drink of the palm wine. Nimi a Nzinga, NtinuKongo. She was either Mbemba's sister or his half-sister, depending on who her mother was. A pretty little thing.

MBEMBA DID NOT RETURN that night. But, although his absence quickened Gil's simmering unease, Gil had as yet nothing concrete to be afraid of. To the contrary, he was treated with respect and a genuine friendliness and was very well looked after into the bargain. The two older women with their children (the infant and the two little boys) and the four younger women (but not, alas, the pretty Kongo princess) remained as his servants at the house. And the house did have another room, and his sea chest and duffle were in it and, as Gomes and Dias had not attempted to take theirs with them in their flight back down to the coast, so were their sea chests and duffles, as well as the boxes and crates of the ship's provisions.

This other room was his sleeping quarters. (The women and children lived in separate, smaller dwellings in the yard at back.) Besides a collection of pots and gourds, another hourglass-shaped stool, the sea chests and crates, it contained a palliasse of woven mats, velvety coverlets and a wooden headrest, laid out as a bed under a window that opened on to the front veranda and provided a view of the Luezi and the royal district on the other side. When he went into this room after supper the first night, the two older women followed him in with kettles of hot and cold water, lengths of cloth, sponges and pumice stones. He took off his boots and chainmail vest and waited for them to leave before undressing any further to bathe.

But they didn't leave, and neither did the four younger women and the two little boys. Apparently they wanted him to undress in front of them, curious to see what he looked like under his clothes, curious to know whether this white prince from the sky was physically formed any differently than their own men and boys and whether the whiteness of his skin would wash off when he washed and reveal skin as dark as theirs. With nervous amusement, he ordered them away. But after he had stripped naked and was sponging the dirt of the many days on the road from his body, he discovered that one of the younger women had sneaked back and was watching him from the entryway. He turned to her all of a sudden and showed himself to her brazenly, thinking that this would send her skittering away in embarrassment. But she was unembarrassed and calmly continued watching him and even inched into the room a bit. And he was the one who became embarrassed and turned away and put on his shirt. But he didn't order her to leave.

He went to the window and looked out to the royal district. He still thought then that there was a chance Mbemba would return for him that night and wondered whether he ought to dress up in his princely costume again. But the gates in the palisade across the river remained resolutely shut and all he could see over there in the night were the hundreds of points of light of the fires burning within the royal enclosure. He turned back to the room. The young woman was now sitting, cross-legged, just inside the entryway, leaning against its frame, her kanga hiked up above her knees, its fold under her armpit slightly loosened, watching him impassively with slightly parted lips. He was not so young or so dumb as not to know why she was there, but he still didn't say anything to her. He lay down on the palliasse with his back to her. He didn't close his eyes. He was wide awake. He felt her presence, heard her soft breathing as clearly and keenly as he felt the chill in the air and heard the humming of the cicadas and the hooting of owls in the night outside. Was it up to him to say something? He wouldn't dare. So he waited, his heart thumping, holding his breath. And, of course, after a while, she lay down beside him, letting her kanga fall away.

He asked her her name.

She didn't reply. With a sudden, silent ferocity, she pulled him on top of her and wrapped her surprisingly strong legs around his waist and her surprisingly strong arms around his neck and, with her soft, heavy breasts flattened against his chest, filled his mouth with her tongue to stop him from asking the question again.

He twisted his face away, feeling the slow, deliberate movements of her hips drawing him into her, and tried again. "Tell me your name," he demanded with a certain urgency. "I wish to know your name."

But she grabbed at his long hair and pulled him down and caught his lower lip between her small, sharp teeth and bit into it painfully, the movements of her hips becoming quicker, her grip on him always more fierce. Giggling foolishly, he had to fight to free himself, tasting blood in his mouth from his bitten lip, smelling the musky scent of her body.

"Why won't you tell me your name?"

He realized what she was doing. She was hurrying him. She had been sent to him to perform this duty and wanted it over with as quickly as possible. And she knew how to hurry him, with the movements of her hips, with the thrust of her belly, with the grip of her thighs, tearing at his long hair, nipping at the flesh of his throat with her small, sharp teeth. He clenched his fists to hold himself back.

"Say your name. For God's sake, say it."

"Nimi."

"What?"

"Nimi. Nimi a Nzinga." And thrusting up at him, now filling his mouth with the nipple of one breast to silence him, she scored her fingernails across his back.

And he was young and strong and full of life and could not hold himself back.

She pushed him away.

He rolled on his side and closed his eyes, holding his breath. Then he released his breath and gulped at the cold night air and opened his eyes and looked at her in the cold moonlight, in the cold starlight. She was lying on her back, her breasts heaving, one hand between her legs, absently stroking the fluid on her thigh.

"Why did you say your name is Nimi a Nzinga?"

She turned her head toward him.

"Nimi a Nzinga is NtinuKongo."

She sat up. "You should sleep with Ntinu. You are Mtu," she said lackadaisically. "You should sleep with a princess. You are a prince."

"But what really is your name?"

"It is of no importance."

"It is of importance to me."

She shrugged and fished around on the palliasse until she found her kanga. Then she stood up and neatly wrapped it around herself, up under her armpits, over her breasts.

"Where are you going? Don't go. Stay. I wish you to say. I command you to stay."

He didn't say this seriously. He wasn't really commanding her. He was just fooling. He wanted to make her smile. But she didn't smile. She took his command seriously and removed her kanga and lay down on the palliasse beside him. There was a sad calm about her, the dutiful resignation of a serving woman sent to perform a service for a prince.

"You don't have to stay if you don't want to."

"I stay."

"But do you want to?"

"Yes, Gil Eenezh, I want to." She moved closer to him and tangled her legs with his and put an arm around his waist and rested her head on his chest. But she didn't smile.

He lay on his back, an arm around her shoulder, peering down his nose at the top of her head. Her hair was close-cropped (he supposed all the women, under their turbans, wore their hair close-cropped), but it wasn't braided into criss-crossing rows like the princess Nimi's. Odd that, in the heat of the moment, she had called herself Nimi. Was it because she thought the idea that he was making love to a princess would further arouse him, further hurry him and so get it over with more quickly? Or because, in that moment, she wished she were a princess?

"I won't tell anybody."

"Uh?"

He realized she had dozed off and he had awakened her. "I will keep it secret if you tell me your name."

She turned her face against his chest. "Sleep, Gil Eenezh," she murmured. "We sleep now."

But he didn't sleep. He listened to her breathing, felt her warm breath on his chest. She wasn't happy to be there. She didn't want to be his friend. He fingered the beads of the string of bloodstones around his neck and thought of Dom Nuno and Dom José and the captain-general. He wasn't happy to be here either. He wanted a friend. Where was Mbemba?

She sat up.

"What is it?"

"Ssh. Listen."

He couldn't hear anything other than the usual sounds of the night, the owls hooting, the hum of cicadas. "What?"

She was wide awake, head cocked, hands pressed against the palliasse beneath her, ready to spring up. And then she did spring up and dashed to the window. He dashed after her.

"It's Mbemba," he said with a great rush of relief. "At last he's returning for me."

"No," she said and dashed away from the window.

The middle gate of the royal enclosure had swung open and a procession of torch bearers was emerging, making for the middle bridge. In their train, a man was being carried in a litter. Another man walked beside it and more torch bearers followed him. Gil couldn't make out who either man was but surely one of them must be Mbemba, returning to take him to the king.

"Who is it then, if not Mbemba?" he asked, turning back into the room. "Mpanzu?"

"No." She was putting on her kanga.

"Who then?"

"Lukeni a Wene."

"Who?"

"The NgangaKongo."

"I don't know who . . . where are you going?"

She had dashed out of the room. He dashed after her.

"Wait. I command you." He was serious now. He fairly shrieked the command.

She stopped on the back veranda. She was in a panic and her panic infected him. She clutched her kanga—she hadn't taken the time to properly fold it and it was in danger of falling off—and stared at the front entryway in horrified expectation of what or who would appear on the veranda there. The procession from the royal enclosure had not yet reached the bridge but now he heard drumming.

There were drummers in the procession. Their beat was slow, low, ominous. What time was it? The moon, the crescent moon, had set. It must be after midnight.

"Who is Lukeni a Wene? Who is the NgangaKongo?"

"He who makes the stars shine and the sun rise and the dead walk."

A sorcerer? A priest? The ju-ju man of the Kongo? Was the title here Nganga, not Nsaku? "Nsaku?" he asked. "NsakuKongo?"

"Greater than Nsaku. Stronger, more dangerous, more wonderful."

NgangaKongo, the highest priest of the Kongo. "He comes here?"

"He comes for you."

The procession of torches was now crossing the bridge. The drumming was louder. Involuntarily, he shivered in the cold night. Then he remembered he was naked.

"You stay here. I command you to stay here," he said and dashed back into the other room to get dressed.

He didn't know why he wanted her to stay. He only knew he didn't want to be alone. He wanted someone with him, even this terrified young woman. But, actually, he had very little hope that she would stay, so in dread of the NgangaKongo was she, and sure enough, when he was dressed—in his shirt and pantaloons; he didn't think he had time to get into his armor—and returned to the main room, buckling on his sword, she was gone. He went out on the back veranda. The fenced-in yard was deserted, the dwellings of the women dark, the mats over the windows and entryways pulled down. He hurried back through the main room of the house to the front veranda. Despite the noise of the drumming and the blazing light of the torches, the quay along the river was as deserted as the backyard, and the houses along the quay were as dark and silent as the houses in the backyard. Everyone was hiding from the Nganga-Kongo. He gripped the hilt of his sword and assumed a brave and defiant stance, shivering in the cold, the wind ruffling his long hair, and watched the priestly procession cross the bridge and come down the quay.

The torch bearers were warriors; bows and quivers of arrows were slung on their backs, unsheathed knives hung from their waists. They wore crimson kangas embroidered with yellow sunbursts, and the flames of their torches, whipping furiously in the wind, emitted a sweet odor much like incense. The drummers wore dark, shiny leather breechclouts and headdresses of red and yellow parrot feathers, and their faces and chests were painted a ghostly white, their drums swinging from their hips in cadence with their steps. And there were fetishers among them, also painted white, rattling pebble-filled gourds, striking sticks together, banging small hammers against horseshoe-shaped iron gongs in time to the drumming's steady, hypnotic beat. They approached with a slow, stately, swaying stride, the bearers of the litter deliberately swaying the litter like a pendulum, the man walking beside the litter swaying with the litter as if in a trance. And as they neared the house, chanting began, a deep, somber, moaning chant that could just as easily have been the Latin chanting of the Mass, no less reverential was it, no less holy in sound.

The warriors, holding their incense-burning torches at chest level with both their hands like votive candles, lined the quay in front of the house. The drummers and fetishers, chanting their mysterious orisons, playing their reverential music, formed a semicircle beneath the veranda as if forming the chancel of a church. The bearers of the litter and the man walking beside it stepped into that chancel. By the wildly dancing light of the wind-whipped flames of the torches, Gil instantly recognized the man standing beside the litter, and his heart jumped. It was the NsakuSoyo, wearing his ceremonial headdress and cape of feathers, a painted, pebble-filled gourd in one hand, a knife in the other. As the bearers set the litter down, the mean-faced ju-ju man kneeled beside it. The drumming stopped. The chanting stopped. Except for the rushing noise of the torch flames beating in the wind, all was silent. Then a gong was struck and the man in the litter stepped out.

Lukeni a Wene, the NgangaKongo. The high priest of the Kongo, the pope of these people. Gil shrank back. He was horrible. Gil could understand why the young woman had run away from him. He was a hunchback dwarf of an indeterminate, an ancient age, completely hairless. And emphasizing this grotesque hairlessness, his entire body was painted white and, although he actually wore a loincloth, it was as white as his body so he seemed naked. Black leather pouches hung around his neck but otherwise he was unadorned and his hands were empty. He looked up at Gil through the black holes in the white paint on his face as if through the eyeholes of a white mask. His lips were black.

"Gil Eenezh."

His voice was shrill, high-pitched, a weird power in it. And the gaze of his eyes through the black holes of the painted white mask was steady and penetrating. Be careful. Keep your wits. He can cast a spell.

"Yes, I am Gil Eanes, Lukeni a Wene."

"You know who I am?"

"I have been told who you are."

"Who am I?"

"The NgangaKongo."

"Yes, I am NgangaKongo, great sorcerer of the kingdom, first at the nostrils of the universe, he who makes the stars shine and the sun rise and the rain fall and the dead walk again on this land. I am the priest of the king of this kingdom, who consults me in all things. Do you fear me?"

"I honor you, Lukeni a Wene. I honor and esteem you as I honor and esteem the priest of my king."

"You answer well, Gil Eenezh. He answers well, NsakuSoyo. Perhaps it is not as you say."

The ju-ju man from Mpinda, who had remained on his knees until now, stood up. "It is as I say, NgangaKongo," he said. "You shall see."

"Yes, I shall see. Come to me, Gil Eenezh."

Gil glanced around. Then, hesitatingly, he stepped down from the veranda.

"Come closer."

Gil did not want to look into the black eyes of the grotesque hunchback dwarf. He did not know what sorcery lurked in their steady, penetrating gaze. He went closer to the sorcerer with downcast eyes. The half-circle of drummers and fetishers tightened around him. The NsakuSoyo moved over to the sorcerer's side.

"Closer, Gil Eenezh. Closer."

Although he was still a few steps from him, Gil could smell the sorcerer's breath, the smell of a perfume like the smell of the incense wafting around him from the votive torches, the smell of church. "I await Mbemba a Nzinga, the MtuKongo, Lukeni a Wene. Have you come in his place to take me to the king?"

"No, Gil Eenezh, the king is not yet ready to receive you."

"He is still not ready to receive me? When will he be ready to receive me?"

"When I have brought him a lock of your hair."

"What?"

"Cut a lock of his hair, NsakuSoyo."

"What? No. Stay away from me, NsakuSoyo." Gil's hand went for his sword. "I warn you, NsakuSoyo, do not come a step nearer to me."

The hateful ju-ju man had started toward Gil, raising the knife he held in one hand, but, remembering the incident on the road, remembering Gil's murderous lunge at him with the sword, he stopped and backed away.

"What do you fear, Gil Eenezh?" the NgangaKongo said. "I thought you did not fear me. I thought you had only honor and esteem for me as the priest of my king."

"I have honor and esteem for you, Lukeni a Wene. But I have no honor or esteem for him. He killed Father Sebastião, who was *my* priest. He killed Segou, who was my friend."

"An evil priest. A slave, not a friend."

"Be silent, NsakuSoyo. Give the knife to me."

Silenced, the ju-ju man placed the knife on the palm of the NgangaKongo's outstretched hand.

"You say you honor and esteem me, Gil Eenezh, as the priest of my king."

"Yes, Lukeni a Wene, I do."

"Then you will allow me to cut a lock from your hair to take to my king."

Gil sucked in his breath. "Yes, Lukeni a Wene, I will."

"Come closer then."

A gong was struck, a single, somber note reverberating in the silence. And the low, somber chanting began again, in celebration of the ritual that was about to occur. Because the sorcerer was so short—he barely came up to Gil's chest—Gil was obliged to bow his head to him as if to a priest about to bestow a blessing. This priest, however, grasped a handful of Gil's long blond hair and, clearly sur-

prised to find it so silky and soft, ran his fingers through it, stroking it
for a moment. Then he sliced off a small sheaf and closed his hand
around it, and the chanting rose an octave in celebration of what had
been done. What had been done? Gil didn't know what had been
done. But he knew that the ritual that had occurred, the sorcery that
had been performed, was for these people what the ritual and faith
of the Church was for him.

"Now we shall see, Gil Eenezh."

"What shall you see, Lukeni a Wene?"

"Who you are and what you intend. Now we shall see why you
have come to our land from your land in the sky."

"How shall you see this, Lukeni a Wene?"

"From this lock of your hair." The sorcerer opened his hand. "Because this is a fragment of yourself, Gil Eenezh. Because this is a piece
of your being."

IX

He fell ill. He knew what it was: the sorcery of the NgangaKongo. He dreamed it that night, a simple but frightening dream, and then dreamed it over and over and over again, night after night.

A fire was burning in the night. It was a small fire, built of glossy leaves that produced a green smoke and a sweet smell. The hairless, hunchback dwarf, high priest of the Kongo, naked and whitened with lime and wearing a monstrous wooden mask, also whitened with lime, sat cross-legged before the fire, holding his upturned, cupped palms over the flames. The strands of tawny hair he had cut from Gil's head, those fragments of Gil's being, those pieces of himself, lay in the cup of the upturned palms. The fetishers, also naked and whitened with lime, stood behind him, peering over his shoulder into the upturned palms. There were others there as well, standing behind the fetishers, but Gil couldn't see them clearly; the small fire didn't cast its eerie, green light that far into the blackness of the cold night.

"*Nzambi Mpungu,*" the great sorcerer shrilled and offered up his cupped hands. "*Nzambi Mpungu,* I send this to you."

And the holy music of the fetishers began, the shaking of rattles, the banging of sticks, the thumping of drums, the ringing of gongs, and their pious, somber chanting. And the NgangaKongo overturned his palms and the strands of hair fell into the flames and caught fire and flew up to the sky in a shower of crackling sparks. And Gil began to burn with a feverish heat. The sorcerer had set him on fire.

He tried to awaken himself from this dream but couldn't. He tried to call out in the night but his words choked in his throat. And then the crackling sparks died and the feverish heat subsided and he felt the shivering cold of the wind in the night.

His eyes were open. It was still night. Was it the same night or the next night or the one after that? His face was being mopped with a cool, damp cloth smelling of vinegar. It was the young woman, the nameless woman, who mopped his face, so it couldn't be the same night. She had run away that night. He turned his face away from her cold cloth because he was freezing again, and pulled up his knees and clasped his hands between his knees and huddled down against the freezing wind.

"Nimi, the night is cold."

She crawled into the palliasse beside him. She wasn't Nimi, of course. She wasn't the Kongo princess. She only had said her name was Nimi in order to excite him. She wrapped her arms around his shoulders and tangled her legs with his and drew him to her breasts to warm him in the cold night.

But the NgangaKongo had no pity; the terrible sorcerer set fire to him again. And he burned with a terrible fever again. She must feel him burning. She must be burning with him. Her hair too must have caught on fire.

"*Nzambi Mpungu*, I send this to you."

"Why does he do this?"

"Ssh."

"*Nzambi Mpungu*, I send this fragment of the white stranger to you. I send you this piece of his being. From this, *Nzambi Mpungu*, tell me who he is and why he has come. From this, tell me whether he brings good or evil to our kingdom. From this, O *Nzambi Mpungu*, tell me whether we should welcome him or drive him away."

"What?" Gil tried to sit up.

"Ssh, Gil Eenezh. Ssh. Ssh." She held him more closely to her breasts.

Was she in the dream? Did she hear what he heard? Did she see what he saw? The NgangaKongo tossed the last of the strands of hair into the fire and, in the blaze of this final shower of sparks, Gil was able to see the others standing behind the fetishers. Mbemba was among them, and Mpanzu, and the NsakuSoyo. They came forward and sat cross-legged around the fire and, each in his turn, spoke to the NgangaKongo at length. Gil couldn't hear what they said. But he could see from the expressions on their faces and the gestures they made that they spoke with fervor and in dispute. Were they speaking about him? Were they disputing whether he should be welcomed or driven away?

"What do they say? I cannot hear what they say."

"Ssh, Gil Eenezh. Ssh." She cradled his head against her breasts. "Sleep, Gil Eenezh. Sleep."

No, she was not in the dream. She did not see the shower of sparks whirl up into the black velvet of the sky and die there among the stars. She did not see the NgangaKongo stand up and walk into the fire. She did not see him stamp out the flames with his bare feet and, in stamping them out, stamp out the dream.

He woke up. It was daylight. Nimi a Nzinga was standing at the low entryway to the room. He was sure she was the real Nimi, the Kongo princess—the pale green kanga bordered in red, the braids criss-crossing her head, the slanted, lustrous eyes—but then his view of her was blocked by the young, nameless woman bending over him. She held a gourd to his lips and, with her other hand, raised his head so he could drink from it. He expected it to be *malafu,* the palm wine, but it was something creamy and bitter, probably goat's milk. He took the gourd from her and drank thirstily, hungrily. When he had drained it off, she took the gourd away and, in doing this, moved out of his line of sight so he saw the princess Nimi again.

"*Keba bota,* NtinuKongo."

She didn't reply but at least she didn't run away. The serving woman blocked his view again, handing him a bowl of porridge, then sat back on her heels and looked back and forth between Gil and the girl as if curious to see what would transpire between them. Gil held the bowl to his lips, looking at the girl over its rim, and ate the porridge with a sharp appetite. It was a good sign, his hunger, his thirst, a sign of restored health. He set the bowl aside and looked around. From the quality of the light in the room, he judged it was early morning. He started to stand up but, just in time, remembered he was naked under the coverlets of his palliasse.

"I wish to dress, *mchento.*" He said this for the girl's benefit; he doubted that, as a princess, she would be as brazen about this sort of thing as the serving women. "Will you fetch my clothes?"

"Do you wish also to bathe?"

"Yes. I wish also to bathe."

"I will fetch the bath water."

"*Ntondesi.* Thank you."

The girl stepped back from the room's entryway to let the serving woman pass and, for a moment, both of them were out of sight in the other room. He heard them speak together softly, giggle together conspiratorially, then the girl reappeared. He remained sitting on the palliasse with the coverlets drawn up to his waist, trapped there by the girl's presence and his own shyness.

"You are Nimi a Nzinga?"

She nodded.

"You are the sister of Mbemba a Nzinga, daughter of the king?"

She nodded again.

"I am Gil Eanes."

"I know this," she said. Her voice was small and sweet and, as she spoke, she furrowed her brow and pouted her lips, as if restraining a mischievous smile. "Everybody knows this."

"I wait for Mbemba to take me to your father. Does everybody also know this?"

"*Ngete,* everybody also knows this."

"And does everybody also know why he has not yet come for me in all this time?"

"Oh, he has come for you, Gil Eenezh. He has come for you many times. But each time he has come for you, you were sleeping so deeply no one could wake you."

So that was it. Gil heaved a sigh of relief. There was nothing to the dream after all; the cause of the delay was his illness, not a dispute over whether to receive him. "I was sick," he said, feeling much better. "And are you now no longer sick?"

"No. Now I am well. Now I am very well."

"This is good because Mbemba comes for you again today."

"Today? Then I must hurry. I must be ready for him when he comes. Where is the woman with the bath water, what is her name? Where are my clothes?"

"Her name is Nimi."

"What?"

"Did you not ask to know her name?"

"Her name is Nimi, like yours?"

"Yes. And your clothes are there." She pointed at Gil's sea chest. "Shall I fetch them for you?"

How odd that the serving woman's name should turn out really to be Nimi after all. "Yes, fetch them for me."

"I cannot fetch them for you. I am NtinuKongo and I do not fetch anything for anybody." And she smiled a bright, teasing smile, clearly delighted with herself for having played this trick on him.

He laughed at her sudden spirited show of sassiness and decided to play a trick on her in his turn. "Then I must fetch them for myself, mustn't I?" he said and made as if to turn back the coverlets from his naked loins and get up.

"Yes, you must," she replied, watching him.

And he hesitated. She was watching him with such innocent intensity, was waiting for him to uncover himself with such unguarded anticipation, that he blushed. Apparently she was just as curious about him physically as the serving women had been, and just as unashamed about it.

"Go away, Nimi," he said, grinning. "You are just a little girl."

"I am not so little."

"Little enough. Go away now and let me dress."

After she left, Gil went to the window. He had been mistaken about the time of day; it was much later in the morning than he had judged. The dimness of the light was the result of an unbroken, slate-gray overcast of clouds. He hadn't seen clouds like this before. There had been clouds down at the coast but only much later in the day, rolling in from the east at dusk, and up here on the plateau the sky had been crystal clear both night and day. Perhaps during the time he was sick, the season had changed. It was now very nearly the end of September or maybe even the beginning of October; perhaps this was the start of a season of rain.

While he was looking out the window, waiting for his serving woman, the other Nimi, to bring his bath water, the middle gate in the royal enclosure across the Luezi swung open. He didn't wait to see who would emerge. He was sure it was Mbemba. Giving up any thought of bathing, he quickly dressed in his princely costume, then began rummaging through the crates and boxes of the ship's provisions.

The captain-general had sent along a chest of trading truck that Gil was to present as gifts to the Kongo king. But having seen the arts and crafts of the Kongo, Gil knew the stuff would be dismissed as little more than amusing trinkets at best. But maybe there was something else, something a bit special, a bit odd, a bit out of the way. Not the lengths of cloth, certainly, not the hawks' bells or fishhooks, not even the mirrors or knives or pots and pans. The Kongo had such as these in abundance. He pushed them aside. There must be something better. He wanted to have something better to present. They were suspicious of him. He wanted to allay their suspicions. Then he remembered Father Sebastião's breviary and Mbemba's fascination with it and the NsakuSoyo's fear of it. Aye, that was the thing, the one thing the Kongo didn't have: writing.

"The MtuKongo comes, Gil Eenezh." Nimi a Nzinga, the NtinuKongo, was once again standing in the room's entryway.

Gil nodded and followed her out through the entryway into the main room. All the serving women, the baby and the two little boys were there, lined up in a formal row. Their expressions were serious; he was going across the river to meet the king. He looked at his young woman, the other Nimi, who had slept with him all these nights, and smiled at her. To his surprise and delight, she smiled back. Was this her way of saying goodbye and, just possibly, good riddance?

He went out on the front veranda. The princess Nimi went with him but only as far as the entryway. Mbemba with a bodyguard of his warriors was coming down the quay.

"I am happy to see you standing here, Gil Eenezh."

"I am happy to have you see me standing here, Mbemba. I am sorry I was not standing here the many times you came for me before."

"You were sick."

"Yes, I was sick. I was burning. I dreamed that I was thrown into the flames of a fire."

"That is a strange dream to dream."

"Yes, it is a strange dream. Do you think it is also a true dream?"

"All dreams are true."

"But I do not know the end of this dream, Mbemba. I did not dream it to the end."

"This is its end, Gil Eenezh. You have awakened and I have come to take you to my father. I have come to take you to the king."

Mbemba stepped up on the veranda and gripped Gil's shoulders in the Kongo way of greeting. It was the first time he had done this and it gave Gil a thrill of pleasure, a rush of confidence and relief.

"Who is that?"

"Who?"

"Is that Nimi? Is that you, Nimi? Come out here."

Gil turned around. Mbemba had spotted his sister lurking in the house's front entryway.

"Come out here, girl," he said sharply. "Come out here at once."

Nimi stepped out on the veranda and struck a childish pose, one bare foot on top of the other, hands clasped behind her back. But her lustrous brown eyes were sparkling mischievously. She obviously wasn't afraid of her brother.

"What are you doing here? Are you a serving girl in this house?"

"No."

"Then why are you here?"

"I visit my friend."

"What friend do you have in this house?"

"Gil Eenezh."

Gil was as shocked as Mbemba by this insolent declaration. He looked at Nimi and then at her brother. Both were staring at him, the girl with a bright, teasing smile, Mbemba with a smoldering suspicion.

"How is he your friend? You have never seen him before."

"I have."

"When?"

"When you first brought him to this house. And every day afterward."

"I did not know this, Mbemba," Gil put in hastily. "I did not know she was here. I was sick." It was obvious that Mbemba was furious, livid with suspicion that something clandestine, illicit, might have occurred between his sister and Gil. "Did I, Nimi? Tell Mbemba I did not know you were here."

"He did not know I was here. He was sick. He slept."

"Then why did you come here?"

"To see him."

"To see him sleep?"

"Yes, to see him sleep," Nimi replied impudently.

Mbemba shook his head. He wasn't much mollified; his suspicion was still very much alive. "You had no business doing that," he said testily. "You have no business being here now. I will see that you are beaten for it. Now go away from here. Go back to your own house."

"I will go back with you and Gil Eenezh."

"Do you want me to have you beaten right now?"

"You cannot have me beaten. I am NtinuKongo." She said this as she had said it to Gil earlier, as if she had only recently realized the privileges her title conferred—perhaps she was an especially beloved of the ManiKongo's daughters—and unclasped her hands from behind her back and placed them defiantly on her hips.

Again Mbemba shook his head in exasperation but he was not quite so angry anymore. Although he refused to show it, he obviously was amused by the girl's impudence. Perhaps she was an especially beloved of his sisters. "You are a terrible girl, Nimi," he said with a sigh. "You make me seem a fool in front of Gil Eenezh. You know I would not have you beaten in front of him."

"You would not have me beaten in any case, Mbemba," Nimi said, coming over to him and taking his hand. "You are a gentle prince."

"Do not be too sure of it, terrible girl," he said, pushing her away.

She hopped down happily from the veranda and joined the ranks of Mbemba's bodyguard. They bowed to her and moved away respectfully but she immediately began chattering to them and a few of them laughed at whatever she said.

"Are you ready to meet my father, Gil Eenezh?"

"I have gifts to bring to him from Diogo Cão."

"That is kind and proper of Deego Cum."

"They are nothing wonderful in themselves but they are sent by him to your father as tokens of his esteem."

"As such, they will be received by my father as wonderful." Mbemba called to the warriors on the quay and two, handing off their lances and shields, went into the house to fetch the chest of trading truck.

"Do you remember Father Sebastião's breviary, Mbemba?"

Mbemba cocked his head in puzzlement. "Pader Sebastum?"

"Yes, his breviary."

"I do not understand what you ask, Gil Eenezh."

"The breviary. The book of writing. The *escrita.*"

"The *escrita?* The writing? Yes, the writing through which *Nzambi Mpungu* speaks."

"You still have it?"

"Yes."

"It is very precious, Mbemba. It is very strong magic. It is the strong magic of the Portuguese."

"I know this."

"It is stronger magic than the magic of the NsakuSoyo, stronger even than the magic of NgangaKongo."

Mbemba didn't reply to this. He narrowed his eyes, not willing to agree to such blasphemy.

"Will you show it to your father, Mbemba? Will you give it to him as a gift from the Portuguese?"

WARRIORS, ARMED WITH BOWS and arrows, and trumpeters, with gracefully curved ivory horns looped over their shoulders, stood on the watch towers on either side of the middle gate in the palisade that enclosed the royal district. And when the gate was swung open by warriors below, these armed with shields and steel lances, the trumpeters above gave out a screaming blast on their horns.

Directly ahead, no more than thirty paces down a narrow path from the gate, was a second gate in yet another palisade, this one too with watch towers on either side of it. Nimi dashed toward it but when she reached it, she turned left and disappeared. Gil and Mbe-

mba, with Mbemba's bodyguard in their train, followed at a more
measured, dignified pace. When they came to the second gate, they
stopped. Gil took a quick look to the left. He couldn't see where
Nimi had gone. The path in that direction seemed to dead-end at the
wall of the outer palisade. He looked up at the sky. The slate-gray
overcast was steadily darkening. Rain surely was on the way. Indeed,
there already were distant flashes of sheet lightning, distant rumbles
of thunder.

"Wait here, Gil Eenezh, until this gate is opened for you," Mbemba said.

"Where do you go?"

"I must make myself ready to meet the king."

"You will return before this gate is opened for me?"

"No, I will be with the king when this gate is opened for you."

Mbemba continued down the path to the left, which Nimi had
taken, and disappeared as thoroughly and confusingly as she had. Gil
looked around. Mbemba's warriors had formed themselves into ranks
on either side of him, except for the two carrying the chest of trading truck; they came up to stand directly behind him. Gil reset his helmet on his head, smoothed down the front of his surcoat and, with
his hand on the hilt of his sword, faced the gate. There was a sharper
flash of lightning, a closer crack of thunder. Then, after several more
minutes, the trumpeters in the watch towers beside this gate emitted
their heralding blast. And the gate was swung open and Gil saw the
cantonment of the king.

It was smaller than he had imagined but still quite grand
enough. The inner palisade did not entirely enclose it; it was open on
the west so there was a fine vista out over the escarpment to the
rolling grasslands below. And there, practically at the very edge of the
plateau, stood the largest and handsomest of the many large and
handsome buildings in the cantonment; surely the palace of the king.

It had three peaked roofs of thatch, each with a great sunburst
pattern woven into it, and wide verandas all the way around supported by heavy, carved timbers. It was set in an arbor of flowering
trees and the path to it from the gate was amazingly and beautifully
tiled with thousands of colored stones. Phalanxes of warriors, armed
with lances and shields, wearing yellow and red parrot feathers in

their hair and bright crimson kangas embroidered with yellow sunbursts (doubtless the colors and design of the king) lined the path.
Behind the warriors, hundreds of people were crowded on the verandas of the scores of other buildings in the cantonment, staring in
keen anticipation at the open gate.

Gil wasn't sure whether he should wait for some sort of signal
before entering but when, after several minutes, none was forthcoming, he stepped through the gate. The trumpeters in the watch towers blasted another powerful note and, from somewhere up ahead,
trumpeters answered with a blast of their own, and unseen drummers started up a throbbing, excited beat. A soft drizzle of rain started
blowing on the wind out of the west, off the yellow hills below the
plateau, and the lightning and thunder were closer and more fre-
quent.

A congregation of men stood on the palace's front veranda. Cer-
emonially dressed in headdresses of feathers and antelope horn, in
capes of feathers and velvet cloth, they obviously were members of
the court, some princes in their own right, some lords of provinces,
some captains of the king's legions, some ministers of the king's
council, the equivalent of the princes and counts and dukes and captains and *fidalgos* at the court of King João. When Gil reached the
foot of the veranda, they moved aside, revealing a cloth-covered entryway.

The drumming and trumpeting stopped. Gil looked back. The
gate was now shut and the king's warriors had formed a semicircle
in front of the palace to hold back the people crowding closer to see
the young white prince who had flown down to them from the sky.

"*Keba bota,*" Gil said to the courtiers on the veranda. "I am Gil
Eanes and I bring greetings to the king of the Kongo from the king of
the Portuguese."

No one responded to this, but the crimson hanging, spangled
with yellow sunbursts, was drawn aside. And just then there was a
terrific bolt of lightning and a startling crack of thunder and the sky
broke open. Gil hastily hopped up under the eave of the veranda out
of the sudden crash of rain.

The room he entered was long and narrow and dark except at
the far end. There, fifty or sixty paces ahead on a raised platform, fires

of glowing charcoal burned in two large clay pots. Between the fire pots stood a throne and, in the throne, sat Nzinga a Nkuwu, the ManiKongo. The throne was cut from a single block of ebony with a high back, inlaid with ivory and carved into a lion's head, with wide armrests fluted into lion's paws, and draped haphazardly with tanned hides, the spotted fur of a leopard and lengths of crimson cloth embroidered with yellow sunbursts. It was a large throne but the ManiKongo barely fitted into it.

He was huge. Gil fairly gasped out loud at his astonishing size. And it was all fat, great slabs of flabby flesh hanging in thick folds from his chin and arms and thighs and breasts (aye, in their fleshiness, they were almost womanly breasts), overflowing his belly. And all this startling flesh was on repulsive display because he was half-naked. He wore a pillbox hat of woven raffia, embroidered with his sunburst insignia, but his torso was covered only by the golden fur of a lion, the beast's tail still attached and tossed over his shoulder, and his loins were covered only by a short, crimson kilt, also bearing his crest of yellow suns. Although his head was of a normal size, set on that incredible mound of flesh it seemed tiny, and there was something peculiar about the way he held it, the chin tilted up, his eyes peering down from under heavy lids over a bulbous nose. His massive arms were stretched out on the armrests, an ivory staff inlaid with spirals of silver and studded with chips of green stone lay across his glutinous thighs, and his swollen, grossly veined bare feet rested on a small footstool draped in leopard fur.

And there, at his feet, sat Lukeni a Wene, the NgangaKongo, priest of the king, great sorcerer of the kingdom.

The two MtuKongo stood on either side of the ManiKongo, the slim, boyish Mbemba a Nzinga on his father's left, the big, beefy Mpanzu a Nzinga, lord of Nsundi, on his father's right as befitting the eldest and heir. Both were dressed in beautiful capes and skirts of velvet, both wore headdresses of blue and white egret feathers encircling pairs of kudu horns, both were adorned with bracelets and necklaces of silver and ivory and glittering green and yellow stones. A step behind Mpanzu, and so not as well-lit by the glowing coals in the clay pots, was the NsakuSoyo, watching Gil's entry into the throne room with obvious hostility. Behind the throne, a rank of ser-

vants, wearing the crimson kangas with yellow sunbursts of the
ManiKongo's household, held palm fronds woven into a fringed para-
sol over the ManiKongo's head.

Hesitatingly, Gil started down the long, narrow room. As he
neared the throne, he tried to catch Mbemba's eye. He had no idea
what was expected of him and hoped Mbemba would give him a signal of some kind. But Mbemba's expression was severe and aloof and
utterly unhelpful in this regard. Well, he wasn't going to grovel, that
was certain; he wasn't going to prostrate himself. He remembered
how angrily the captain-general had resisted when the ManiSoyo had
tried to get him to kneel in front of Mbemba; he certainly wasn't going to behave with any less dignity than the captain-general. But still,
here was a monarch of a great kingdom and he deserved the respect
and deference Gil would pay to any foreign monarch of any great
kingdom. So, when he was but a few paces from the elevated platform on which the throne stood, Gil, clutching the hilt of his sword
with one hand, removed his helmet with the other and, sweeping it
across in front of him, its plume brushing the floor, dropped to one
knee.

"Meu senhor," he said in Portuguese. "My lord."

He held the bow, eyes lowered, listening to the terrific downpour of rain pounding on the thatch of the peaked roof. Again there
was a bright flash of lightning, a tremendous crack of thunder. He
raised his eyes and found himself looking straight into the black holes
of the mesmerizing eyes of the terrible white mask that was the face
of the NgangaKongo, sitting at the ManiKongo's feet.

He looked away with a start of fright, looked up at the Mani-
Kongo. The ManiKongo, his chin tilted up in that peculiar way, looked
down from under his heavy, half-lowered lids, but he wasn't looking
down at Gil. He was looking down somewhere to Gil's left. Behind Gil,
the two warriors with the chest of trading truck had prostrated themselves. But the ManiKongo wasn't looking at them either. Who was he
looking at? Mpanzu placed an arm across the back of the throne and,
leaning over, whispered in his father's ear. The ManiKongo shifted his
oddly cocked head so that he looked down somewhat more directly at
Gil. And Gil realized what the matter was: The ManiKongo's eyes were
clouded over, milky white. The ManiKongo was blind.

"This is Gil Eenezh, my father, the white prince who has come to us from a land in the sky." It was Mpanzu, the crown prince, who made the introduction. "This is Nzinga a Nkuwu, Gil Eenezh, the ManiKongo, *ntotila nekongo, ngangula a kongo.*"

"Keba bota, meu senhor," Gil said, and stood up. He had rehearsed a little speech and launched into it now. "I thank you for receiving me in your house this day, ManiKongo. I have been eagerly waiting for this day so as to bring greetings to you from my king, João the Second of the Portuguese, and to present gifts to you as tokens of his esteem. He has instructed me—"

"But he is just a boy," the ManiKongo interrupted, shifting his massive bulk forward in the throne and tilting his chin up even higher to peer down at Gil with his clouded eyes. "Such a young voice, so sweet. How many years do you have, white prince from the sky?"

Gil hadn't expected anything like this. His rehearsed speech flew out of his head. "I have nearly sixteen years, my lord."

"Sixteen years. Just like my son." The ManiKongo groped with his left hand toward Mbemba. "You too have sixteen years, do you not, my son?"

Mbemba took his hand. "Yes, Father."

"Sixteen years. A young prince. Come to me, young prince from the sky."

Stepping gingerly around the NgangaKongo, who turned to watch him, Gil went up onto the platform.

"Give me your hand, Gil Eenezh." And, for a moment, the ManiKongo held both Gil's and Mbemba's hands. "Yes, the strong hands of the young. But yours is white, they tell me."

"Yes, ManiKongo."

"Each part of you is white, they tell me."

"Yes, ManiKongo."

The ManiKongo released Gil's and Mbemba's hands and eased his bulk back into the throne. "As white as the NgangaKongo?"

Startled, Gil looked at the hairless, hunchback dwarf, whitened all over with lime. Had he whitened himself like that in mimicry of Gil? Did Gil look like that to these people? Was the ugly painted white mask of a face meant to represent the face of a white man?

"But your whiteness never washes off, they tell me."

"No, ManiKongo. My skin is white. The whiteness never washes off."

"That is what they tell me." The ManiKongo heaved a sigh and slumped into his throne, as if the effort of sitting forward and holding up his head and interesting himself in Gil had been very tiring for so fat a man.

So they waited for him to regain his strength, while the rain beat on the roof and thunder rumbled outside. And after a few minutes of rest, the ManiKongo raised his head again.

"My father," Mpanzu said, placing an arm across the back of the throne again and leaning over to whisper in the ManiKongo's ear. "Gil Eenezh wishes to present the gifts he brings from his king. Will you have him present them now?"

"Yes, have him present them now."

But it wasn't the ManiKongo who said this. It was the Nsaku-Soyo, standing behind Mpanzu in the shadows beyond the light of the glowing coals. He stepped forward now into the firelight and Gil tensed at the sight of his mean face, knowing he wanted to cause whatever trouble he could.

"Yes, have him present them now, ManiKongo. Have him show you how wonderful they are."

"Who speaks?"

"I speak, ManiKongo, the NsakuSoyo."

"Speak, NsakuSoyo."

"I have seen these gifts from the white king in the sky, ManiKongo. I have seen them when they were presented to the ManiSoyo in Mpinda. I have seen how wonderful they are." His voice dripped with sarcasm. "Have him present them to you so you too may see how wonderful are these worthless trinkets brought from a land in the sky."

"They are but tokens, ManiKongo," Gil hurriedly put in.

But Mbemba cut him off. "They are not but tokens, Father," he said. "They are far more than mere tokens. I too have seen them, Father, and they are wonderful. And here is the first of them and the most wonderful of them all." He turned back the hem of his cape.

And Gil's heart jumped. For under the cape, tucked in the waist of Mbemba's kanga, was Father Sebastião's breviary, the small, black-leather-bound book embossed with a golden cross.

"No," the NsakuSoyo gasped on seeing it and whirled around. "NgangaKongo," he hissed. "He has brought it here, just as I had feared."

The hunchback dwarf stood up slowly and squinted at the book in Mbemba's hand with his piercing, black gaze.

"What is it?" the ManiKongo asked, tilting his head higher.

"Evil," the NsakuSoyo said. "Do not touch it, ManiKongo. It is evil magic." And he reached for the breviary, tried to take it from Mbemba's hand.

But Mbemba pulled his hand away. "Yes, it is magic, Father, but it is not evil magic. It is good magic. It is the magic of the Porta Geeze, the wonderful magic of their kingdom in the sky. It is *escrita*, Father." He used the Portuguese word. There was no word for it in Kongo. "It is writing."

"What is *escrita*, my son?" the ManiKongo asked. "What is writing? Here, give it into my hand so I may know what it is."

Mbemba placed the breviary in the ManiKongo's big, fleshy palm.

"I warn you, ManiKongo," the NsakuSoyo said. "Do not take this thing. There is terrible evil in it. I warn you, Nzinga a Nkuwu. Have it thrown into the fire before its evil poisons our kingdom."

"What evil do you warn me against, NsakuSoyo? What evil is there in this to poison our kingdom?" The ManiKongo brought the breviary up to his unseeing eyes. "I cannot tell what it is. I have never held its like before." His fingers explored the small book, discovered how to open and close it, ruffled its pages. "Is it a box? But what sort of box is it that opens in this way? And what sort of leaves are these that it contains but do not fall out?"

"It is writing, Father."

"Again you say this, my son. But what is writing?"

"It is what we have never known, Father. It is the drawing of words that are spoken. It is the drawing of speaking. This writing, Father, this writing you have in your hand is the drawing the white men have made of the words *Nzambi Mpungu* has spoken. It is the drawing of *Nzambi Mpungu* speaking."

"This is not true, MtuKongo," the NsakuSoyo snapped furiously.

"It is true," Mbemba retorted as angrily. "I have seen this with my own eyes, Father. I have seen *Nzambi Mpungu* speak to the white men in this writing."

"No, MtuKongo," the NsakuSoyo interrupted, almost hysterical now at Mbemba's blasphemous persistence in challenging his religious authority on a matter pertaining to *Nzambi Mpungu,* on a matter pertaining to God. "The white men have deceived you, Mbemba a Nzinga. You are young and easily deceived by the cunning of these strangers. What you have seen with your own eyes is not *Nzambi Mpungu* speaking in this writing but evil speaking."

Still fingering the breviary, still trying to discern by touch what this most alien of devices could be, the ManiKongo turned to his right. "And you, my son Mpanzu," he said, "you who are my eldest and closest to my throne, what have you seen with your own eyes?"

Gil, wide-eyed and tense, had looked back and forth from Mbemba to the NsakuSoyo to the ManiKongo during this dispute. Now he looked at Mpanzu. This, of course, was the dream he had dreamed. Mbemba believed he brought good. The hateful ju-ju man from Mpinda believed he brought evil. What did Mpanzu believe? And then it would be the NgangaKongo's turn to say. And, finally, the ManiKongo's.

Mpanzu, however, affected a neutrality bordering on indifference. "I have seen nothing of any of this with my own eyes, my father," he answered laconically. "I have seen nothing of even this *escrita* before now."

"Then see it now, my son." The ManiKongo passed the breviary to the big, beefy prince. "See it now with your own eyes and tell me what you see."

Mpanzu took the small book and turned it over in his hands with mild curiosity, feeling the embossed cross, examining how the pages were bound into the spine. Then he opened it at random and stared at one of the pages. "These black signs and symbols," he asked with a certain scornful skepticism, "this is writing, Gil Eenezh?"

"Yes."

Mpanzu studied the page. Then after another few moments of consideration, he asked, "This writing is *Nzambi Mpungu* speaking?"

"It is as Mbemba says. Writing is the drawing of words that are spoken. This writing is the drawing of the words *Nzambi Mpungu* has spoken."

Mpanzu thumbed through several pages of the breviary, then said, "Let us hear the words *Nzambi Mpungu* has spoken, Gil Eenezh." He handed the breviary to Gil. "Let us hear *Nzambi Mpungu* speak."

Father Sebastião should be here, Gil thought. The poor padre had prayed for just such an opportunity as this, had suffered martyrdom for just such a chance as this. He would have gloried in the moment, reading the words of God to a heathen king and his princes. This was priest's work, not anything a half-literate ship's boy was capable of doing. He was already far beyond his depth in simply having tried to explain writing. He looked at Mbemba haplessly. Mbemba nodded at him encouragingly. He put his helmet back on and opened the book. By chance, he opened it to the Sanctus. He stared at it for a moment and realized that, knowing enough of it from memory, he actually could read it if he read it carefully. It gave him a surge of confidence.

"*In nomine Patris, et Filii, et Spiritus Sancti,*" he said and made the sign of the cross.

"No," the NsakuSoyo cried out. "Do not allow this, ManiKongo. This is the evil. This is the evil by which your son was bewitched."

Gil ignored him and proceeded to read from the breviary. "*Sanctus, Sanctus, Sanctus Dominus Deus Sabaoth. Pleni sunt caeli et terra gloria tua . . .*"

And he heard Mbemba say softly, "Watch his eyes, Mpanzu. Watch how they move across the line of the writing from one end to the other and then down to the next line of the writing and move across it and then the next. He is speaking the writing, Mpanzu. He sees the writing and speaks what he sees."

"*Hosanna in excelsis,*" Gil concluded and looked up.

Mpanzu was staring at him with knit brows.

"Did you see, Mpanzu?" Mbemba asked.

The big, beefy prince nodded. "Yes, I saw."

"What did you see, my son?" the blind ManiKongo asked, again shifting forward cumbersomely in his throne.

"He speaks the writing, my father. It is as Mbemba says. The writing is the drawing of the words he speaks."

"And is there evil in this, my son?"

"I do not know, my father. How can I know? It is not in my power to know that which has never before been known. We must ask the NgangaKongo."

"You are wise, my son. Yes, the NgangaKongo will decide whether there is evil in this gift. Give the writing to the Nganga-Kongo, Gil Eenezh. Take the writing into your hands, Lukeni a Wene, and tell me if there is evil in this gift the young white prince brings to us from his land in the sky."

"I will tell you, Nzinga a Nkuwu." The hunchback dwarf stepped forward. "I will tell you if there is evil in this gift of writing."

The high priest of the king, the great sorcerer of the Kongo, he who was first at the nostrils of the universe, he who made the stars shine and the sun rise and the rain fall and the dead walk again, he had remained aloof during the dispute, patiently awaiting this moment when his ultimate authority would be acknowledged and he would be asked to decide. A small, satisfied smile played on his black lips as he took the breviary from Gil. A grotesque creature, a frightening figure, but one with the power and influence of a pope over a king. Did Gil have reason to fear him? What did he know? What had he discovered from the lock of hair he had taken from Gil's head? Had he discovered that Gil did not come from the sky? He held the breviary in his cupped, upturned palms as he had held Gil's hair in the dream, and closed his eyes.

And the low, holy chanting began, the reverential music of the fetishers. Gil looked around in surprise. All those in the throne room, the courtiers and warriors along the walls, had begun chanting. Even Mbemba and Mpanzu and the NsakuSoyo and, yes, even the ManiKongo had begun chanting, and had closed their eyes. A shiver rattled Gil's bones. They all seemed to have fallen into a trance. There was a terrible crack of thunder and the rain beat down over their heads like hail. Gil stepped back. The sorcerer opened his eyes.

"Tell me, Lukeni a Wene, shall we accept this gift of writing the young white prince has brought to us from the sky? Or is there evil in it?"

"There is evil in it, ManiKongo. We shall not accept it. We shall throw it into the fire before it poisons our kingdom."

"No." This was Mbemba. "No, Father, this is not true. Writing is not a gift of evil—"

"Be silent, my son. The NgangaKongo speaks. Speak, Lukeni a Wene. What is the evil in the writing that will poison our kingdom?"

"The evil, Nzinga a Nkuwu, is like the writing itself. The evil is that which we have never before known."

"Speak plainly, NgangaKongo. Tell me what this evil is that we have never before known."

"First, the theft of our souls, ManiKongo. And then the theft of our bodies."

X

"WHY ARE YOU HERE? You shouldn't be here."

"I can be here. I can be anywhere. I am NtinuKongo."

Gil shook his head. He couldn't help smiling at her cheekiness but her presence made him nervous. "Mbemba will be angry," he said. "He will be angry at you and he will also be angry at me."

"No, he will not be angry. How can he be angry when he has sent me to you himself?"

This was late the next day and it was still raining. They were in a small house in the royal district to which Gil had been escorted—and to which he had been confined ever since by the relentless downpour—after the audience with the ManiKongo had ended the night before.

It had ended oddly and uncertainly, as far as Gil was concerned. Having made his ominous pronouncement about the nature of the breviary's evil, the NgangaKongo, looking to the ManiKongo for his agreement, had repeated his intention of throwing this dangerous gift into the fire. But the ManiKongo had not given his agreement; as if exhausted by the dispute and disappointed by the outcome, the fat, blind king had once again slumped back into his throne and said nothing. And before Mpanzu could answer in his father's place, the wives of the king had all of a sudden entered the throne room with a retinue of princesses and ladies-in-waiting and, in the ensuing commotion—a rearranging of courtiers along the walls, a whispering of greetings and bowings and scrapings—Gil lost sight of the breviary. He thought at first that the NgangaKongo had indeed thrown it onto the glowing coals of one of the clay fire pots, despite not having received either the ManiKongo's or Mpanzu's permission, because it suddenly vanished from the sorcerer's hands. But in the next moment he realized, from the way the sorcerer suddenly looked around in consternation, that someone had snatched it from him.

Of the ManiKongo's several wives who had entered, two went directly to his side, and Gil at once recognized who they were. One, more than a decade the younger, small and delicate, obviously was Mbemba's mother. The other, big-boned with a darker complexion and heavy buttocks, fifty years old or more, almost certainly was Mpanzu's. They both wore the crimson kangas with the yellow sunbursts of the ManiKongo's household and, besides turbans of the same colors and design, were adorned, indeed heavily burdened, by an astonishing profusion of jewelry of silver and brass, ivory and precious stones. The younger of the two, Mbemba's mother, immediately kneeled next to the ManiKongo's throne in a show of concern over his evident fatigue, and in response to whatever she murmured to him, he took her small face in his big hands and smiled at her. The older queen, her black eyes flashing in the firelight, first paused to have a good, searching look at Gil, then she also bent down to her husband. She surely was the principal wife and reigning queen, the MbandaKongo, mother of the firstborn and heir, ruler of the royal household. But from the tender way the old ManiKongo held her face and smiled at her, it was easy to see that the younger, the shapelier, the prettier, this bride of his late years, was his favorite.

And then the audience abruptly ended. The ManiKongo was too tired to carry on. It was the MbandaKongo who decided this. On her whispered instruction, Mpanzu raised his arm and suddenly there was a flurry of movement as the lords and ladies of the court rushed forward. Gil was pushed aside and what ensued was at once both remarkable and bizarre.

Women as well as men, queens and princesses as well as captains and counts, competed to lift the mammoth ManiKongo bodily out of his throne. They grappled for parts of him, for a hold on his arms or legs, for a place under his armpits or thighs, for a grip around his massive belly or flabby breasts, and those who could not find some flesh of his to grasp prostrated themselves beneath his feet. A litter was brought forward by eight giant warriors and, amid much harsh gasping and groaning, this mountain of a man was lifted onto it and carried out through an entryway behind the throne, his court crowding out after him into some other room of the palace.

For a moment, Gil thought Mbemba would stay behind. He was the last to reach the entryway and he hesitated there and looked back at Gil, but then he too passed through and let the crimson velvet hanging with the yellow sunburst emblems fall behind him, leaving Gil alone with the warriors of the king's guard. They escorted him to his new house in the royal district through the pouring rain.

Nimi was waiting for him in the new house, not Princess Nimi, the other Nimi from his other house on the other side of the Luezi, but he didn't at first realize this. There were several other women waiting in the new house to serve him and he was soaked to the skin and in a hurry to get out of his clothes and, besides, the place was poorly lit and the rain was smashing down and lightning flashed and thunder cracked and his mind was in a whirl. What had happened at the audience, what had been decided? He really didn't know what he would tell the captain-general about what had happened when the *Leonor* returned to fetch him home. He had been received by the ManiKongo. He could tell him that. But *how* had he been received? the captain-general would want to know. Had he been received with favor? Had his overture from King João been reciprocated? Were the Portuguese welcome in the kingdom? He didn't know; he really didn't know.

It wasn't until he went to sleep in his new house that night that he realized that the other Nimi was there. She came to him in the darkness of the storming night and, without a word, with her dutiful resignation, slipped under the coverlets of his palliasse. He was astonished and pleased. He knew, though, that she hadn't come to him of her own free will, that she couldn't possibly have crossed the bridge and passed through the palisades into the royal district on her own. Someone had sent her, just as someone had sent his sea chest and duffle, and the sea chests and duffles of the halberdiers, and the crates and boxes of the ship's provisions, from the other house on the other side of the river. He had found them waiting for him in this new house, and now he found her waiting for him as well. Who had sent her? Who thought her as much his possession as the sea chests and duffles and boxes of provisions? He didn't ask her; he knew enough by now to simply accept her, as he accepted all the other services he was provided. So he made love to her and then let her leave when she wanted to leave and lay awake listening to the drumming of the rain on the roof.

It didn't let up. It seemed it never would let up. Gil watched it throughout the following day, falling in blinding, steel-gray sheets, forming into rivers and lakes and swamps, flooding the land.

His house was located on the south side of the cantonment, near the wall of the inner palisade, among a number of similar houses which intervened between his house and the ManiKongo's palace to the west so that he couldn't see what, if anything, was going on there. He would have gone out to have a look but the relentless rain, the thunder, the lightning, the darkness, the thick clouds rolling low over the swamped land, the swirling winds, deterred him. So he remained on the veranda, watching the rain. And then he saw Nimi, Nimi a Nzinga, the Kongo princess, running toward his house through the pouring rain.

"Why are you here? You shouldn't be here."

"I can be here. I can be anywhere. I am NtinuKongo," she answered, hopping up on the veranda under the shelter of its eave.

"Mbemba will be angry. He will be angry at you and he will also be angry at me."

"No, he will not be angry. How can he be angry when he has sent me to you himself?"

"Mbemba sent you to me? No, Nimi, I do not believe you."

"He did," she said sharply, turning to him with bright eyes. "You must not say you do not believe me. I am NtinuKongo."

Gil shook his head. He couldn't help smiling at her cheekiness but her presence in his house made him nervous. "Why did he send you to me?"

"To bring you to the Mbanda Lwa."

"The Mbanda Lwa?"

"She is our mother, the second queen of the kingdom. Come. I will take you to her."

The house of the Mbanda Lwa was not far but, despite dashing
through the curtains of rain and making great leaps over swampy
puddles and ducking under the eaves of buildings along the way, Gil
was pretty well soaked by the time he and Nimi got there. Located in
the garden of the ManiKongo's palace, lushly arbored by flowering
bushes and trees near the edge of the plateau, it was a rambling structure, much smaller than the palace with only one peaked roof but
with several wings as if it had been built in stages over the years. Warriors, armed with lances and shields and wearing the king's colors,
stood guard all the way around the veranda of its central wing. Mbemba stood with them at the main entryway, wearing only his kanga.

"Go inside," he said. "Quickly, Gil Eenezh, go inside."

His uncharacteristic edginess as he rushed Gil into the house, as
if worried Gil would be seen, set off alarms in Gil. Seen by whom?
Who was about in this infernal thunderstorm to see him? He glanced
back and realized that, of course, the warriors standing guard on the
veranda of the ManiKongo's palace could see him. Was he being
taken to the Mbanda Lwa without the ManiKongo's knowledge?

"This way, Gil Eenezh," Mbemba said impatiently. "This way."

The Mbanda Lwa was waiting for them in a room in the farthest
back corner of the building. She was seated cross-legged on a cush-
ion of mats and folded cloths and, like Mbemba, was plainly dressed,
wearing a black-and-white-striped kanga, her head uncovered, revealing closely cropped hair, braided much as Nimi's, and a necklace of
white and black stones and shells. Her hands were clasped in her lap,
casually holding a length of crimson cloth that trailed across her
knees, the only regal touch about her. The room was as plainly furnished as she was dressed. And no one else was there. The mats on
the windows along the room's west wall were rolled up, and on a
pleasanter day at this hour, sunlight would be streaming in but, as it
was, the room was dismally gray and dim. It was light enough, however, for Gil to see that Nimi had inherited her mother's eyes, slanted
and doelike, and her golden brown complexion. The Mbanda Lwa
was a beautiful woman just becoming old and with all the ripe ele-
gance of a woman of that uncertain age.

"Gil Eenezh, Mother," Mbemba said.

"Minha senhora." Gil began to make a sweeping bow.

But before he could complete it, Mbemba sat down cross-legged on his mother's right and Nimi plopped down on her left. Apparently, no formality needed to be observed with this queen, or at least not under these circumstances. But what were these circumstances?

"Sit down, Gil Eenezh," the Mbanda Lwa said. "Move away, Nimi. Don't you see you are in the way? Sit down here by my side, white prince who comes to us from a land on the other shore of the sea."

Gil's heart jumped at those words and he looked at Mbemba.

"I have told my mother your secret, Gil Eenezh. It is a secret she will keep. Sit down at her side as she asks."

Gil sat down, while Nimi scrambled around to sit on the other side of him. He didn't know what to think. Why had Mbemba confided to his mother that he came, not from the sky, but from the other shore of the sea? Why had he confided it to her and to no one else? Why did he treat it as a secret at all, for that matter, and as a secret worth keeping from all the others besides? He glanced around the room uneasily, sharply aware that there wasn't even one serving woman in attendance nor even one bodyguard, sharply aware also of how oddly he had been brought here—Nimi coming for him instead of Mbemba although Mbemba had been angry to find them alone together before, Mbemba hurrying him into the house before anyone could see him although everyone had already seen him—sharply aware of the informality of the occasion, the barrenness of the room, surely a little used room at the back of the house. Was a conspiracy brewing here in which he, unwitting, was being included?

"Do not be concerned, Gil Eenezh," the Mbanda Lwa said and, unclasping her hands, placed one reassuringly on his knee. "It is as my son says. I will keep your secret as well as he has."

"*Ntondesi, minha senhora,*" Gil said, and because she had unclasped her hands, he saw that a small, black, boxlike object was lying in her lap, partially covered by the crimson cloth.

"For us it is as wonderful that you have come to us from a land on the other shore of the sea, having never known the sea had another shore, as it would be if you truly had come to us from a land in the sky."

"That pleases me, my lady."

"But for others in this kingdom, it would not be as wonderful."

"Which others, my lady?"

"Mpanzu. Lukeni a Wene. The Mbanda Vunda."

"The Mbanda Vunda?"

"The mother of Mpanzu. The first queen of the kingdom."

"And also the ManiKongo, my lady, the king of the kingdom?"

"Yes, perhaps also Nzinga a Nkuwu, the king of the kingdom. They know the sky because they see the sky and therefore that you come from the sky is wonderful for them. But they do not know the sea has another shore because they cannot see that shore and therefore they do not know that the magic you bring from the land on the other shore of the sea is as wonderful as any you would bring from a land in the sky. But my son Mbemba and I know it is as wonderful." And saying this, the young queen uncovered the small, black, boxlike object lying under the crimson cloth in her lap.

It was the breviary. So Mbemba was the one who had snatched it from the NgangaKongo before the sorcerer could throw it into the fire. And he had given it to his mother.

"Show me how to make use of this magic that you have brought from your land on the other shore of the sea, Gil Eenezh."

"I do not understand, my lady."

"This magic you have put into our hands, Gil Eenezh," she said, opening the breviary at random and resting her hand on the pages as if on a sacred talisman. "You have told my son this magic is stronger than the magic of the NsakuSoyo."

"Yes."

"Stronger also than the magic of the NgangaKongo."

"Yes."

"I wish to make use of this magic."

"But it is this that I do not understand, my lady. In what way do you wish to make use of it?"

"I wish to make use of it against the magic of the NsakuSoyo. I wish to make use of it against the magic of the NgangaKongo. I wish to make use of it on behalf of my son."

Gil looked at Mbemba. Mbemba was watching him intently. Now Gil was beginning to get an inkling of the conspiracy that was brewing here, the conspiracy into which he was being drawn.

"Show me how to make use of this magic," the queen said again.

Gil looked back at her, the second if more beloved queen, the queen whose son was not heir to the throne. "I do not know how to show you this, my lady," he said. "I do not know how to make use of it in this way."

"You do not know, Gil Eenezh, or you will not say?"

"No, my lady, I would say if I knew. But I do not know. Only a priest of my people would know how to make use of the writing in this way."

Mbemba leaned forward. His unexpected movement gave Gil a start. He understood only too well now what was afoot and he didn't like it a bit. But Mbemba was only reaching for the breviary. He took it from his mother's hand.

"Then show us how to speak the writing, Gil Eenezh," he said. "Show us how to speak it as you speak it. Show us that if nothing more and it will be magic enough."

HE HAD LOST HIS WAY returning to the house. Nimi hadn't accompanied him—she was long asleep by then—and Mbemba had shown him out of the Mbanda Lwa's house through a series of rooms different from those through which he had entered, which had disoriented him right from the start, and then there was the rain and the darkness and the confusion of shapes and shadows caused by the sudden flashes of lightning and the similarity of the other houses around his house, and he wasn't paying close attention to where he was going anyway. His mind was still caught up in the effort he had made to teach Mbemba and his mother how to read, and to read a language that not only they but he himself didn't understand. It was ridiculous. It was impossible. But Mbemba and his mother had refused to accept that. They had kept him at it until the darkest hour before the dawn. They were determined to learn how to speak the writing in the breviary.

For the Mbanda Lwa, Gil had realized, to speak the writing was to possess a magic stronger than the magic of the NsakuSoyo and the NgangaKongo, strong enough to overthrow the prescribed order of things in the kingdom and, when the time came, when the king died, to put her son instead of Mpanzu on the throne. For Mbemba, the matter was more complicated. To be sure, he too was ambitious for himself and believed that the ability to read and write would give him a special power by which to further his ambitions. But somehow this young, bright African prince had divined that there were more and better uses to be made of writing than this narrow and practical use. For him, writing was a tangible talisman of the mysterious world beyond the farthest horizons of his Kongo kingdom, of that world across a sea no one had known had another shore, of that wider, unknown world which he now wanted to know, although for what purpose exactly he himself didn't seem yet able to say. In either case, though, this was a dangerous game they were playing and Gil wanted no part of it. He didn't fancy the idea of being drawn into a contest between the old queen and the young, between the heir apparent and the pretender, between the known world and the unknown. He was but a ship's boy with his own ambitions. It was time for him to go.

Which was his house? Sheltering under the eave of one house, wiping away the rain that cascaded down his face from the brim of his helmet, he looked across a veritable river at another. No one was about. No fires or lanterns were burning. There was no sound except the sound of thunder and the splashing of the rain. Was that his house? The mats over the windows were not lowered. Would Nimi and the other serving women have forgotten to lower them? But if that wasn't his house, if others were living in it, they certainly would not have forgotten to lower the mats against the rain. It must be his house. Putting his hand on his helmet to hold it on, he leaped across the intervening river of rainwater and up onto the house's front veranda.

He immediately stopped. Something was amiss. He grasped the hilt of his sword and listened. Thunder rumbled, there was a flash of lightning and a crack of thunder, the rain pelted down. He backed down the step of the veranda into the downpour and drew his sword and looked around. Seeing nothing, hearing nothing unusual, getting drenched, he slowly advanced up onto the veranda again, holding the short, double-edged stabbing sword in front of him. With its point, he moved aside the mat covering the front entryway. It was pitch-dark inside. He waited a minute for his eyes to adjust to the darkness, then stepped in.

The house had been ransacked. The sight of the wild disorder had the impact of a physical blow. He actually jumped back, his heart suddenly racing, and whirled around, swinging the sword, slicing at the empty air. When he realized what he was doing, he forced himself to stop, forced himself to look around. The palliasse had been pulled apart; his sea chest and duffle, and the sea chests and duffles of the halberdiers, had been opened and their contents scattered; the crates of the ship's provisions had been broken open and dumped.

Who had done this? What were they looking for? Whoever they were, whatever they were after, they seemed to have been in a terrific hurry, as if they hadn't been sure when he'd return. Perhaps his return had surprised them. Perhaps they were still about. He made a slow tour of the house, nervously poking his sword into the dark corners. Nothing seemed to be missing. He kneeled beside his sea chest, taking off his helmet but holding firmly on to his sword.

And then he was jumped.

"Nimi. Mbemba."

He was suffocating. He couldn't see. Some sort of sack had been pulled over his head. He was thrown on his back and a rope was being tied around his neck to secure the sack, and simultaneously his wrists and ankles were being tied together to secure his flailing arms and kicking legs. Then a pole was run under his tied ankles and tied wrists and he was lifted by it. He could picture it in his mind's eye: He was hanging from the pole upside down by his tied ankles and tied wrists like a trussed pig, like a calf being taken to the slaughterhouse. He tried to raise his head but he couldn't hold it up and it fell back, the blood rushing into it, and banged on the floor. And then the pole was lifted high enough so that his head cleared the floor and he was being carried, swinging back and forth by his ankles and wrists. His helmet and sword were gone.

He was carried out of the house. He felt the painful jolts of the two steps down from the veranda and then the smash of the drenching sheets of rain. He had to contain his panic. But he couldn't contain his panic. His heart was exploding. He couldn't breathe. He was drowning in the rain. Would Mbemba know he was being kidnapped? Could he do anything about it even if he knew? Gil began to pray wildly. Snatches of the prayers he had been reading from the breviary to Mbemba and the Mbanda Lwa such a short time before came rushing into his head.

Where were they taking him? He must pay attention. After the two steps down from the veranda into the pouring rain, he felt, from the swing of his hanging body, that they turned left, to the south. That was away from the ManiKongo's palace, away from the house of the Mbanda Lwa, toward the wall of the inner palisade. He must picture this in his mind's eye; he must try to follow the direction in which they carried him in his mind's eye.

Perhaps he fainted. The rain plastered the sack against his face, sealing his nose, his mouth, his eyes. His arms pulled out of their sockets. The skin of his wrists was being rubbed raw at every jolting step. His feet twisted in his boots. The edges of the breastplate cut into his stomach and neck. The empty scabbard dragged along the ground. Perhaps he fainted again. He had no idea where he was being carried. He had no idea how long he was carried. Then, suddenly, he was dropped to the ground.

The splash into a cold rain puddle shocked him back to consciousness. The pole was pulled out from under his wrists and ankles. His ankles were untied. He was grabbed under the armpits and yanked to his feet, and his wrists were untied. He immediately began plucking at the sack, plucking it out of his mouth and nose and eyes, then began grappling at the rope that tied it around his neck. His hands were seized and wrenched up his back and his surcoat was ripped in two and torn from his arms. Then someone began fumbling at the buckles of the straps that fastened the breastplate to his chainmail vest. The buckles proved too complicated and the straps were cut. A knife had come into play. The breastplate was tossed aside. And then the knife was used on the chainmail vest.

And then he realized what was going on: He was being stripped of his clothes. After the chainmail was removed, his shirt was torn off and, when his boots proved recalcitrant, they were cut away and his stockings were ripped to shreds. Then several hands went at his pantaloons. The knife was used to cut the leather thongs of its flies. But this was not yet enough. The codpiece was cut away as well. And then they released him and backed away.

He was entirely naked except for the sack over his head and the bloodstone beads around his neck. Instinctively, he clasped his hands over his loins and felt himself shrivel up under them. The rain was falling steadily but much more lightly and there was only an occasional rumble of distant thunder. He stood ankle-deep in the marshy puddle. He was cold, he was frightened but he was also humiliated; he felt like the worst kind of fool standing with his hands covering his private parts like a girl. He was a strong boy, well-muscled by his years at sea. If this was his end—and what a useless end, what an unlooked-for end; he should have found his end in the sea and not on a pointless errand to a savage king—but if this was the end God meant for him, he would face it like a man. *In nomine Patris, et Filii, et Spiritus Sancti.* He took his hands away from his loins and made the sign of the cross.

"First you will steal our souls, Gil Eenezh, and then you will steal our bodies."

Gil looked blindly from inside the sack in the direction from which these words came, words shrilled in the high-pitched voice of the NgangaKongo. He could picture the hairless, hunchback dwarf and he shivered in the cold rain.

"First you will steal our souls, Gil Eenezh, and then you will steal our bodies."

"Why do you say this, Lukeni a Wene? I have come in peace and friendship, bringing greetings and gifts from my king."

"Gifts of evil, Gil Eenezh. Gifts of the evil *escrita.*"

"The writing is not evil. Why do you say the writing is evil?"

"Nzambi Mpungu tells me the writing is evil."

A murmur rose up from the others there. They believed him, of course. Why shouldn't they? They had no less reason to believe him, the sorcerer and priest of their lifetime, than Gil had to believe Father Sebastião and all the other priests of his lifetime. They had no less reason to trust in the sorcery and ritual of the NgangaKongo than Gil had to trust in the faith and ritual of the Church. What was remarkable was that Mbemba was willing to consider exchanging his belief and trust in the one for the other.

"Yes, the writing is evil, the evil that will steal our bodies and our souls."

"Where is this evil, Gil Eenezh?" This was a different voice, a hoarse growl of a voice.

Gil turned toward it. "Mpanzu?"

"I have searched for it among your possessions but cannot find it."

So that was why the house had been ransacked; they were looking for the breviary. "I do not have it, Mpanzu. The NgangaKongo has it. I gave it to him at the request of the ManiKongo."

No one replied to this. Not being able to see, Gil did not understand the silence. What were they doing?

"The NgangaKongo has the writing," he said again with a rising urgency, worried by the silence. "Does he say he does not have it? But I gave it into his hand. You saw this with your own eyes, Mpanzu."

And then his arms were grabbed again. And someone stepped directly in front of him and he felt the point of a knife push against the base of his throat, where his heart was pounding.

"I do not have the writing," he screamed.

"Who has the writing if you do not have it?" Mpanzu asked. It was he who held the knife against Gil's throat.

"I do not know. I brought it as a gift from my king to your father and he told me to give it to the NgangaKongo. I do not know what became of it after that."

"Mbemba has the writing."

This was yet another voice. It was a woman's voice. Was it the voice of the Mbanda Vunda, the reigning queen, Mpanzu's mother?

"Mbemba and the Mbanda Lwa," she said, drawing closer. "They have the writing. Is this not so, Gil Eenezh? They have the writing to work its magic against us."

Her voice was steady, calm, assured. She knew. But did he dare concede it? Wouldn't he be implicating himself if he conceded that he knew Mbemba and the Mbanda Lwa had the breviary? Wouldn't he be admitting he knew of the conspiracy they were hatching? So he said again, desperately, "I do not know, my lady. I do not know who has the writing."

And the knife point pressed harder into his flesh.

"No, Mpanzu. Please."

"Mbemba has the writing. Is that not so, Gil Eenezh?"

"Yes."

Mpanzu sliced upward with the knife.

Bless me, Father, for I have sinned . . .

Gil's heart stopped. His bowels gave way. His world went black.

But he didn't fall. He didn't fall because those holding his arms didn't allow him to fall. But why didn't he feel the pain? Why didn't he feel the hot blood gushing from his throat? Was he already dead?

No, he wasn't dead. Mpanzu hadn't cut his throat. He had merely cut the rope that secured the sack over Gil's head. And then his arms were released. Merciful Father . . . He didn't move. He didn't dare move. He waited. Oh, Holy Mother . . . He waited for what would happen next. But nothing happened next. He felt the excrement running down the back of his legs. They could see this; they all could see this shameful sign of his cowardice and fear. But no one remarked on it. No one remarked on anything. He kept on waiting, not daring to move.

"Mpanzu," he said in a small voice after a while. "Mpanzu?" Wasn't he there? Wasn't anyone there? Slowly, sure that at any moment someone would stop him, he removed the sack from his head.

No one was there. He didn't know where. It was a forest. The rain came down in a steady drizzle and there was no moon or stars in the sky.

XI

HE REMAINED PARALYZED with fright for an immeasurable length of time, quailing in his humiliating nakedness, mortified by his cowardly behavior. For an immeasurable length of time, he didn't believe he was alone; he believed they must still be there in the forest, hiding in the darkness of the trees. When morning came, dismally chill and wet but no longer really raining, and he saw no sign of them in the swirling mist, he decided it was safe at least to sit down. He sat down against the bole of a palm tree, drawing his knees up to his chin and hugging himself like the lost boy he was, and surveyed the ground: a glade in a forest with a few lichen-spotted boulders and a lightning-split tree trunk sprouting fungus, awash from the days of torrential rain, but a glade in what forest he had absolutely no idea. As the morning advanced, though, and he emerged enough from his numbed state to follow the progress of the dull pewter disc of the sun across the heavily overcast sky, he was able at least to establish the compass rose. He sat facing north; west was on his left, east on his right, south behind him.

The sack that had covered his head was half-sunken in the ooze of mud not far from his feet. The length of rope that had secured it around his neck lay beside it, and floating in a nearby puddle were the lengths of rope that had been used to tie his wrists and ankles. But not the least rag or remnant of his clothes was anywhere about, not the vest of chainmail or breastplate, not the torn surcoat or shirt or stockings, not his boots or pantaloons or codpiece. They had all been carried away. Perhaps they too had been considered things of evil to be burned in a cleansing fire. Staring dumbly at the sack for the longest time, it slowly dawned on him that he could use it to cover his shameful nakedness. Again checking around to reassure himself he really was alone, he fished it out of the mud, washed it off in a puddle and split its seams with a jagged stone. He could wrap it around his waist as a kilt or pull it between his legs as a breechclout. He tried it both ways. Neither was particularly satisfactory but at least as a breechclout he felt his manhood protected. He knotted the lengths of rope together to make a belt.

What he had to try to do now was get back down to the Zaire, and get back down there in time to meet the *Leonor* when she returned to fetch him home. He did not know how much time he had before the *Leonor* would return. The arrangement had been for the *Leonor* to return in sixty days. Considering the days he had lost count of on the road, he probably had to figure the journey to Mbanza Kongo had taken at least twenty days. And figuring he had lost count of another five or six days while he was sick, he probably had been here about ten days. That meant that, if he wasn't too wildly off in his count, he had no more than thirty days to find his way down to the coast. Traveling alone in this miserable weather, not knowing the country, foraging for food without tools or weapons, unable to count on anyone's help—to the contrary, having been branded as the bearer of evil and cast out of the kingdom to die, he'd have to stay clear of everyone along the way—he would need every minute of every hour of every one of those thirty days. So he'd better get going. But which way should he go?

As best he'd been able to judge, he had been carried out of the royal district to the south. So he had to take that as his starting point, that he was now somewhere to the south of Mbanza Kongo. At the outset, then, he should travel north until he reached the outskirts of the city and, orienting himself by that, veer to the east in hope of finding the road that led down from the plateau to the Lelunda River. What he would do once he got down from the plateau, how he would cross the Lelunda and the hilly grasslands of Nsundi, how he would survive in the forest of the Mbata (had the halberdiers, Gomes and Dias, managed it?), he would worry about then. This was enough to worry about now.

To the north then. But to the north how? To the north he faced a wall of forest, a tangle of undergrowth, a cage of intertwined vines and branches smoking in the mist. There was no path or trail out of the glade to the north and he didn't have the means—his sword was long gone—to cut his way out. He walked around the glade, sloshing through the mud and puddles, and found a game trail leading to the west. This must be the path by which he had been carried into the glade. Perhaps it curved to the north farther on. He'd just have to try it and see. There was no other way to go.

And then the rain came again. He smelled, heard it, saw it coming a good hour in advance—the fast darkening of the silvery light, the sheet lightning, the thunder, the cold wind blowing out of the west—and it stopped him. He had been under way a few hours by then but had gotten nowhere in particular, not even another glade. The game trail hadn't curved to the north or, where it had, it had always curved back so that his progress had been generally westward. But there was no sign of the edge of the plateau or the cliffs of the escarpment; there was no sign even of the end of the forest. He huddled down into the spongy moss between the protruding roots of a giant mangrove tree, deciding to wait out the rain there, and heaped clods of the moss on his lap and legs in a sorry attempt to blanket himself against the cold downpour.

He woke up, toppled over on his side. He sat up in a hurry. The rain had stopped and the sky was vaguely brightening in the east. What had startled him awake? He looked up into the branches over his head; water drained off the leaves into his face. He looked down the game trail to the west and east; the storm had flooded it into an ankle-deep stream. He looked behind him into the forest to the north. That was it, some kind of noise in that direction, a murmuring, voices, human voices. The game trail finally did curve north here and there were people on it. He couldn't see them because of the dense tangle of the forest's foliage but, once they came around the curve, they would see him. Who were they? Hunters in this part of the forest by chance? Or warriors sent back to see what had become of him? It didn't matter which. He mustn't be seen.

He scuttled around to the other side of the mangrove tree and crouched in the undergrowth there. But he saw instantly that the mess he had made at the tree's base, tearing up the moss to make a blanket for himself, would give his presence away. He scuttled back to patch it up, realized he couldn't and decided to try to get as far away as he could. The branches and vines of the forest snatched at him, scratched and slashed his bare legs and naked torso, tripped him up. After only some twenty paces or so, he crouched in a rain puddle behind a black boulder and held his breath.

A man appeared out of the trees around the curve in the trail. He wore a spotted leopardskin breechclout and plain leather tunic, stained black by the rain, and carried a steel lance; a cane bow and leather quiver of arrows were slung over his shoulder. He paused for only a moment, then went straight to the mangrove tree where Gil had slept. He kneeled to examine the torn-up moss, then looked north into the forest straight at Gil.

It was Mbemba.

Two other men came round the curve in the trail. They were members of Mbemba's bodyguard, wearing kangas of his design and colors. And then the girl Nimi and the woman Nimi also came out of the trees, the woman carrying a basket on her head. Gil stood up.

"Mbemba."

"There he is," the princess Nimi cried out and began hopping up and down on one foot. "We have found him, Mbemba. I told you we would find him."

Mbemba broke into a bright, boyish grin. "I have been searching for you, Gil Eenezh."

"You have found me," Gil said, making his way out of the woods, also grinning.

"I say thanks to *Nzambi Mpungu* that I have found you still alive."

"I also say thanks to *Nzambi Mpungu*. But I also say thanks to you. I know what risk you take in helping me, Mbemba, and I thank you for your friendship and courage." Gil grasped Mbemba's shoulders in a heartfelt greeting.

"I knew we would find you," the girl Nimi said, still hopping up and down. "I told Mbemba we would find you. Are you well, Gil Eenezh?"

Gil laughed. "Now I am well. Now that I see you, NtinuKongo, I am well. *Keba bota,* Nimi."

"*Keba bota,*" the other Nimi said, but she neither smiled nor looked at him. She set her basket down on a bit of high ground, out of the slosh of rainwater, and began unpacking it.

Gil winced at her indifference and turned back to Mbemba. "I do not understand why this was done to me, Mbemba. Does your father know of it? Did he agree to it?"

Mbemba nodded, watching the woman Nimi pull a spotted breechclout and a stitched leather tunic much like his own from the basket.

"So he also believes the writing is evil."

"Yes. Here, *mchento,* let me have those." Mbemba took the breechclout and tunic from the woman. "Take off that foolish sack you wear, Gil Eenezh, and put these on."

"But why does he believe it?" Gil asked, taking the clothes.

"Why shouldn't he believe it? It is what the NgangaKongo says. Why shouldn't he believe what the NgangaKongo says? He is the great sorcerer of the kingdom, the high priest of the king. Doesn't your king believe what his high priest says?"

"Yes, but why then do you not also believe what he says?"

Mbemba didn't reply to this.

And so his sassy little sister replied for him. "It is because he knows what the NgangaKongo doesn't know. It is because he knows you do not come from the sky."

"Is that why, Mbemba?"

"We must go, Gil Eenezh. We cannot remain here. I will show you the way back down to the sea."

They did not go the way they had originally come. They went down from the plateau to the south, not the east, down the cliffside of the escarpment through an abandoned quarry where iron ore had been mined, then across the Lelunda River to the west, not the north, and they kept going to the west, far to the west, following game trails and narrow footpaths, not the broad royal road, up and down the rolling hills of the yellow grasslands of Nsundi, skirting the villages along the way, before at last circling to the north and descending into the dark, steaming, claustrophobic forest of the Mbata.

The princess Nimi accompanied them only as far as the forest of the Mbata. She wanted to go on—for her, this was all just a lark—and made a dreadful fuss when Mbemba told her she had to go back. It was late in the day when they reached the forest, raining lightly but steadily. The two warriors had gone into the forest to hunt. The other Nimi had gotten a small fire started—despite the eternal wetness, she cleverly managed this feat at every camp—and was building shelters of leaves and branches for the night. Gil had sat down on a rock by the fire and was examining his feet. He didn't like the look of them. He wasn't used to going barefoot such distances in such rough country. He washed them in a puddle; they were bruised and bloody. The woman Nimi saw what he was doing and, without looking up at him, kneeled in front of him and took his feet in her hands. First she rubbed blades of the yellow grass across the worst of the cuts, causing them to sting fiercely, then plastered his soles with cool mud.

"But I will never see him again."

Gil looked up from his feet.

"Will I?" the girl Nimi was protesting to her brother.

Mbemba shrugged. He also was at work building shelters for the night.

"He will never return to us from his land in the sky, will he?" the girl persisted. She really wasn't clear where Gil came from, the sky or the sea's other shore. Each equally remote, both were the same to her. "Will you, Gil Eenezh?"

At this, Mbemba left off his work and looked at Gil, obviously as interested as his sister in what Gil would answer.

Gil hesitated. Then he said softly, "No, Nimi, I don't think I will."

"You see, Mbemba, it is as I say. I will never see him again. So you must let me stay, at least for this one last night. I will start home tomorrow."

"No, you will start home as soon as the warriors return from the hunt to take you home."

"No, I will stay. You cannot make me go. I am NtinuKongo."

"Do you want to see how I can make you go, NtinuKongo?" Mbemba said, standing up suddenly.

And as suddenly Nimi scurried over to Gil and flung an arm around his neck. "He is my friend and I will never see him again," she cried out. "Let me stay with him for just this one last night."

"Let her stay, Mbemba," Gil said. "It is already late. She could not travel far before darkness comes anyway."

"This is not a matter on which you may speak, Gil Eenezh," Mbemba snapped angrily. "You return to your land on the other shore of the sea, never to return to us in this land. So you may not speak on a matter concerning those of us in this land."

"I am sorry, Mbemba," Gil said, taken aback by the Kongo youth's sudden anger. What had caused it? "I have spoken out of turn."

"Yes, you have spoken out of turn. What happens in this land no longer concerns you now that you return to your own land."

"I will always remember this land, Mbemba."

"Yes, you will always remember this land," Mbemba said, more quietly but not much mollified. "Make yourself ready, Nimi. I see the warriors return. I will send one home with you."

Catching sight of the two warriors coming out of the forest— they had killed a small bushbuck and were carrying it on a pole between them—seeing them approach, Nimi cried out, "No, I'm not going. I'm not. I'm not." And she threw her other arm around Gil's neck, practically toppling him off the rock on which he sat.

At this, the other Nimi let go of Gil's feet and moved away, as if expecting trouble.

"Nimi, please," Gil said, trying to untangle the girl's arms while peering apprehensively at Mbemba over her shoulder. "You must do what your brother says."

"No. I will stay with you. You are my friend. Are you not my friend?"

"Yes, Nimi, I am your friend, but—"

"Then I will stay with you." And she clutched his neck even more tightly and, in doing this, did in fact topple him off the rock and, clinging to him, toppled on top of him.

"Stop this foolishness," Mbemba shouted, striding over threateningly but actually restraining a smile at the ridiculousness of the accident. "Stop this foolishness at once, you silly girl." And he grabbed Nimi under her armpits, yanked her off Gil and set her on her feet like a sack of flour.

And she ran away. And, instantly, Mbemba ran after her and, in three long strides, caught up with her and tackled her and they both went rolling over in the tall, wet, yellow grass. Gil scrambled to his feet, but he immediately realized that what they were doing they must have done a thousand times before because once they started rolling in the grass they just kept on rolling, over and over, brother and sister, clinging to each other, wrestling with each other, and when they finally came up, they came up laughing, spattered with mud.

"You are a horrible girl, Nimi, a horrible, horrible girl."

"I can stay. Can't I, Mbemba? Can't I?"

Mbemba walked back to the fire, knocking the mud off his arms and tunic. "Just for this one night. Tomorrow you go home."

"Yes, tomorrow I go home. But tonight I stay."

Mbemba dressed out the bushbuck and they ate it half-raw, barely singed, because the fire of wet brush and twigs was so small, along with some wild roots the woman Nimi had foraged. The girl Nimi ate with a hearty appetite, chattering away merrily, teasing her brother about getting her way with him, and then she made another silly fuss when he told her to go to sleep.

Gil left them quarreling and crawled under the shelter the woman Nimi had built for him and had another look at his feet. After a bit, Mbemba and his sister stopped arguing and went into their separate shelters, and then the only sounds were the rain pattering on the leaves of the lean-to shelter and the distant rumble of thunder and the peeping of tree frogs. Gil took off his breechclout and leather tunic (both were sodden) and lay down on the bed of leaves and branches the woman had made and covered himself with a dry kanga she had unpacked for him from her basket. He hoped she would come to him but didn't expect her. She hadn't come to him any night during the march so far. Apparently, this time this was not one of the services Mbemba had brought her along to perform.

"Who's there?" Gil suddenly said.

"Ssh."

He pushed up on an elbow. "Nimi?"

"Yes."

But it wasn't the serving woman Nimi. It was the princess Nimi.

"Oh, my God, what are you doing here? No, no, don't come in. You mustn't come in. Go away."

"Ssh. You will wake Mbemba."

"My God, Nimi, he will kill us. He will kill both of us."

She scampered into the shelter on all fours and clamped a hand over his mouth. "He won't know, if you keep still. Nimi is watching out for us."

"Are you crazy?" he said, peeling her fingers away from his mouth. "I am going to call to him if you don't go away. I am serious, Nimi. I am going to call to him right now."

"He will kill us if you do that. He will kill both of us."

"That's what I said."

"So you must not call to him then." She was giggling as she snuggled against his naked body under the kanga.

"Nimi, stop that. Don't do that. What do you want? Why have you come?"

"To have you make a baby in me."

"What?"

"Ssh. Ssh. You must not wake Mbemba."

"Nimi, no." He took hold of her wrists, tried to push her away, but she was as slippery as an eel. Her kanga had come undone and his hands brushed against her blossoming breasts, got caught between the thighs of her wriggling legs. "We cannot do this, Nimi. We must not do this. It is crazy. I am going away. I will never return."

"I know, and that is why we must do it now. My mother told me we must do it before you go away."

"Your mother? The Mbanda Lwa?"

"She told me I must have you make a baby in me so we can have a life in our land from your land in the sky even after you have gone away."

"She told you that?"

"Yes, she told me you will leave a life in me that will have the magic of your land in the sky."

"Did she also tell Mbemba that?"

"No. She will tell him after you have gone away and the life you have left in me is growing."

"He will kill you then, Nimi. He will kill you and the baby then."

"No, he will not kill anyone because he will also want the baby you will have left in me. He will also want the magic of the baby from your land in the sky."

"No, this is crazy. The Mbanda Lwa is crazy. You are only a little girl."

"But I know how to do it. The Mbanda Lwa told me what to do and what you will do. Only we must not wake Mbemba." She squirmed out of her kanga and threw an arm across his chest. "Come on top of me, Gil Eenezh. I am not afraid. I want you to make this magical baby in me. Will it also be white?"

THEY WENT DOWN through the forest of the Mbata far to the west—Gil and Mbemba, the woman Nimi and one warrior—so far to the west that, when they at last emerged from the forest gloom, they were west of Mpinda, high up on the rocky headland of the southern point of the inlet to the huge, baylike mouth of the Zaire with a clear view out to sea. And the first thing Gil saw out on the storm-swept, white-capped, steel-gray sea was the billowing white sails of the *Leonor.* He gave out a yelp of relief and delight. He hadn't been late for the rendezvous; he was in time to be fetched home.

"How happy you are to leave us, Gil Eenezh," Mbemba said.

"I am happy to return to my family and friends, Mbemba."

"Yes, I understand. You have been treated badly by my family and friends. And I am sorry for this. Perhaps if you had been treated well you would have stayed with us for a longer time and other white men would have come to us and stayed with us for a time as well."

"You would wish this, Mbemba? Shall I tell my king that this is what you would wish?"

"Yes, Gil Eenezh, tell your king that I would wish that white men would come to our land from their land on the other shore of the sea and stay with us for a time so that we could learn the writing and the other wonderful magic of their land."

"But this is not what Mpanzu would wish, nor the Mbanda Vunda, nor the NgangaKongo, nor even the ManiKongo."

"No, this is not what they would wish."

"And this I must also tell to my king."

"Yes, this you must also tell to your king." The young Kongo prince looked away. *"Mchento,* let me have that."

The woman brought over her basket and Mbemba squatted on his heels beside it. While he rummaged through it, Gil took another look out to sea. Because of the distance and the swirling sheets of rain, he couldn't judge the *Leonor*'s headway. Wandering from tack to tack under shortened sails, rolling and pitching in the flashing waves, the wind and weather hard against her, she might not be able to enter the river's mouth until the storm let up.

"Here, Gil Eenezh."

Gil looked back at Mbemba.

"The writing." Mbemba had fished Father Sebastião's breviary out of the basket.

"You still have it?" Gil asked in surprise. "They did not take it from you and burn it?"

"No, I saved it to return to you."

"But it is yours, Mbemba. Father Sebastião meant for you to have it."

"It is mine to keep?"

"Yes, surely."

"*Ntondesi.* I will keep it then and somehow I will learn to speak it as you tried to show me."

They scrambled down from the rocky headland through the palms and mangroves and giant ferns that forested the Zaire's bank, staying clear of the roads and paths that led to Mpinda and the other Soyo villages along the bank just as they had stayed clear of the roads and paths leading to the villages of the Nsundi and Mbata. It was a rough scramble down, Mbemba and his warrior slashing at the undergrowth with their lances to clear a way, and it took over an hour to reach the narrow, boulder-strewn beach of the river's south bank where the waters of the ocean and the waters of the river met, where the ocean's surf crashed yellow-brown with the river's mud.

The rain was falling with renewed force. Spidery filaments of lightning streaked across the pewter sky. Thunder cracked like distant cannon. The sea was high, spumes of spray flying off the wind-lashed waves. Gil stepped out from under the cover of the palms and mangroves and waded knee-deep into the river, bracing himself against the pull and punch of the fast-running waves, in order to get a view of the *Leonor.* She had come about. He wished he had a spy-glass. She seemed now to be tacking on a starboard reach to the north, away from the inlet. With a glass, he might be able to see how

her sheets were trimmed and so judge when she could be expected
to come about again. He waded back to the beach.

"Am I to wait for them here, Mbemba?"

"Yes. It would not be wise for you to go to Mpinda."

"But that is where they expect to find me."

"I will go to Mpinda and make an arrangement with the Mani-
Soyo so they will know where to find you."

"You would not endanger yourself by doing that?"

"No, my mother is of the ManiSoyo's house. She is a Soyo
princess as well as a Kongo queen. So the ManiSoyo will do as I tell
him and no one will be the wiser until after you have gone."

"And after I have gone? Will there be trouble for you then?"

Mbemba grasped Gil by his shoulders. "You worry about me, Gil
Eenezh, and I thank you for it," he said. "But you need not worry
about me. I am the beloved of my father. I am safe from harm as long
as my father lives."

"Then may your father live a very long time."

Gil watched Mbemba disappear into the forest along the Zaire's
south bank, upriver east toward Mpinda. The warrior followed a step
behind him; it would be unseemly for a prince of the Kongo to appear in a village without at least one bodyguard.

The woman immediately set about building a shelter. She was
extremely quick and clever at it, working without tools of any sort,
pulling up saplings, twisting vines and branches together, interweav-
ing them with palm fronds. She was extremely quick and clever at all
this sort of work, getting a fire going even in the rain, preparing and
cooking a variety of foods even from the wilds of the forest, healing
bruises, making love. Had she learned these arts in order to be a servant in the court of the king or to be a good wife to a farmer or
herdsman, smithy or warrior among the common people in the royal
city? How little he knew about her. He couldn't even really be sure of
her name. But what he could be sure of was that she could never
have expected to find herself serving him, a white prince from the
sky. What twist of fate had cast her in that role? How had she come
to be the one sent to him that first night in Mbanza Kongo? Whatever
the twist of fate, however she had chanced to be the one, she didn't
like it, that much was abundantly clear. She did what she was told,

performed her duties well but was only waiting for the day he'd be gone and she could return to whatever her life had been before he had so suddenly come into it, truly as if fallen from the sky.

The wind had dropped, the rain had slackened, the tide was running in but the *Leonor* had not come about. She was still sailing north. If she continued on this tack, in another hour or less, from his vantage point, he would lose sight of her behind the red-clay cliffs that bound the coast north of the northern headland of the inlet to the river's mouth.

He waded farther downriver toward where it emptied into the ocean. But this wasn't smart. The long lines of breakers roaring inshore, spume whipping from the curling caps, were too fierce. He could easily lose his footing and be sucked under and drowned. He scrambled back to the bank, then climbed over the jagged black boulders along the narrow beach to the outermost point of the inlet's southern promontory. He was utterly exposed to the full fury of the beastly weather here, the outrushing river and the inrushing ocean exploding beneath his feet, but at least he could keep the *Leonor* in sight. She seemed to be sailing only under her forecourse now; even her mizzen seemed furled. It didn't make sense. Without her mizzen, she couldn't tack to come about. But she must come about. She couldn't just keep sailing north.

"Gil Eenezh. Gil Eenezh."

He glanced over his shoulder. The woman Nimi was climbing over the slippery boulders toward him. He couldn't tell how long she had been calling to him. Even now her voice was blown away by the wind. She was gesturing upriver. He looked where she gestured. A dugout canoe was coming downriver. He clambered down from his exposed, rocky perch. Mbemba was standing in the canoe's prow. His warrior was standing behind him. A Soyo from Mpinda was seated in the stern, paddling. Gil glanced around to the *Leonor.* She was just reaching the cliffs far north up the coast.

"Your soldiers, Gil Eenezh." Mbemba jumped out of the canoe. "The two soldiers who accompanied you but ran away before reaching Mbanza Kongo . . ."

"Yes, the halberdiers, Gomes and Dias."

"They said you were killed."

"What?"

"They said Pader Sebastum was killed and your slave Segou was killed. And they also said you were killed."

"To whom did they say this? Did they say this to you? Are they there in Mpinda? I never believed they would manage to make their way back through the forest."

"They managed to make their way back through the forest but they are not in Mpinda."

"Where are they then?"

"They went away, Gil Eenezh. They went away to their land on the other shore of the sea."

"I don't understand you, Mbemba. How did they go away to their land on the other shore of the sea?"

"In the great bird-winged ship. She has already come. And now she is already gone."

Gil whirled around to look out to sea. The *Leonor* was just passing behind the cliffs.

"No, Mbemba. There is some mistake. You said they told you I had been killed. You said they told you Father Sebastião and Segou had been killed. How could they tell you that if they are gone?"

"No, Gil Eenezh, I have not spoken clearly. They did not tell *me* that."

"Then who did they tell?"

"Deego Cum."

"Diogo Cão?"

"Deego Cum was already here. The great bird-winged ship was already here. Deego Cum came in the great bird-winged ship to Mpinda and your soldiers told him you had been killed and Pader Sebastum and your slave Segou had been killed. So he took them on the ship and they went away, back to their land on the other shore of the sea."

"No, Mbemba. No."

"I am sorry, Gil Eenezh."

Again Gil turned to look out to sea. The *Leonor* was gone. She had disappeared behind the cliffs, sailing north to Portugal. He had been left behind, stranded in this savage kingdom in Africa. Mbemba put an arm around his shoulders. He shrugged it off. He was not yet sixteen years old. He began to cry.

TWO
1492

Here the river flows into the sea. How calm was the sea, an azure sheet of mottled glass shading into the deepest blue, the river painting a broad, muddy stripe far out on its rippling surface under the scarlet-stained pearl-blue of the dawning sky. Long-tailed white gulls, screaming, their wings tipped black, circled in mated pairs over the sea; hornbills and parrots, yellow-beaked and riotous in color, squawked from the emerald green of the palms and mangroves along the river's shore. Listening, he sat quietly in the sail-rigged canoe, letting the tiller drift, his head bowed in fatigue, the prow of the odd craft nudging gently, on the gentle swell of the tide, against the black boulders of the beach. In a moment, the sun would appear above the rocky headland, here where the river flows into the sea.

He had been to Cape Ste. Catherine again, a voyage of more than a hundred leagues. He had been to Cape Ste. Catherine perhaps for the hundredth time and, for the hundredth time, had failed to get any farther north. The trick was to stand out on a bold tack into mid-ocean, leaving behind all sight of land in order to avoid the currents and winds beating against him along the coast, and pick up the favoring westerlies far out at sea that would carry him to the settlement at São Jorgé da Mina where he would find Portuguese men and ships to take him home. But he did not have the vessel or crew, the instruments or charts to attempt such a perilous enterprise, nor perhaps the courage either. And so each time, perhaps a hundred times over the years, the winds and currents had driven him back. But perhaps not the next time. Perhaps the next time he would have the courage. It was madness, he knew—he might very well be mad after all these years of a wasted, shipwreck life—but it was a necessary madness. The obsessive hope of one day sailing away, the endless planning and work it involved—designing and building always handier sailing craft, charting the stars in every season, and the tides and winds—was what gave purpose to his forlorn existence and kept him alive.

He looked up. The sun had risen, and squinting landward into its hot orange light, he saw children on top of the rocky headland, staring down at him, Soyo children, probably from Mpinda, mostly boys. He stood up and they ran away. They were afraid of him but endlessly fascinated by his forbidding strangeness. He had grown big and tall and extremely strong. His long, tawny mane of hair was streaked blond by the sun, and his full beard was only a shade darker, his eyes as blue as the sea. Bare chest scarred by the claws of a civet cat, broad shoulders twice broken on the hunt, powerful arms thickly veined, the string of bloodstones, many times restrung, tight around his throat, wearing loose, knee-length trousers of tanned hide, belted with thongs from which hung a leather scabbard containing an ivory-handled knife, he was a creature out of a sorcerer's tale, a figure of myth, the evil white prince who had fallen from the sky, forever trying to fly away home. One of the Soyo boys, more daring than the others, crept back and threw a stone at him. It fell short and bounced off the boulders into the water. He turned away and looked out to the distant line of the horizon between the pale-blue sky and deep-blue sea.

For years, he had kept watch on that horizon, sure that one day he would see the billowing sails of a caravel appear upon it, making for the mouth of the Zaire, not to fetch him home, of course—he was believed dead and, in any case, of little account—but to follow up the *Leonor*'s discovery of this great river and to establish trade with the kingdom on its bank. But none had ever appeared. Perhaps the *Leonor* had never reached Lisbon to tell of the Zaire and the

Kongo kingdom, foundering on her homebound voyage. Or perhaps the *Leonor* had discovered the ocean passage round the bottom of Africa and the ships that sailed from Portugal now sailed directly for the rich trade of the Indies. Whichever the case, it didn't matter any longer. Long ago, he had resigned himself to the idea that if he ever were to get home again, he would have to stand out on that bold tack into midocean, there beyond the line of the distant horizon, far out of sight of land, and catch the westerlies that would carry him home.

He furled the sail, coiled the standing rigging and lifted the mast out of its step amidship and laid them in the canoe's bottom. Then he removed the tiller and offset rudder from the gudgeons in the stern and placed them beside the mast and rope and sail. And then he picked up his paddle, pushed off from the boulders on the beach and paddled into the mouth of the river.

He lived on an island in the mouth of the river. It was one of the larger islands in that great baylike expanse, densely wooded and, except for small game and wild cats, monkeys, birds and gray bats, snakes and crocodiles and swarms of butterflies, uninhabited. From its eastern, upriver end, the Soyo village of Mpinda on the Zaire's south bank could be seen; from the western end, there was a clear view out to the sea. Coming now from the sea, he paddled toward the western end where he made his home, in sight of the sea.

Situated in a clearing he had cleared himself near a freshwater spring, it consisted of a main house, built along European lines but with a roof shingled in palm leaves and walls of limed mud, and four smaller structures: a storehouse, cookhouse, granary and workshop. Behind the main house was a kraal for pigs and goats, a coop for fowls, and a garden of yams and plantains, onions and taro and greens. In front of the main house, at the water's edge, he had built a landing stage where a dugout canoe and another sailing craft, this one double-hulled with a square-rigged mainsail and a lateen mizzen (one of his more ambitious ventures, which had proved impossible to handle alone in rough weather and high seas), were drawn up on the marshy, muddy shore. He eased the craft he was in between these two, shipped his paddle and jumped out. He had been gone for

nearly a month this time and didn't know what he would find. He
never knew what he would find when he returned from one of his
voyages.

"*Mchento.*" He went up on the front veranda of his house and
looked in. "*Mchento.*" He came down from the veranda and walked
around back.

He had a boar and two pregnant sows in the kraal, a billy goat
and a nanny with a suckling kid. They seemed well cared for, slop in
their trough. And the vegetable garden was recently hoed; hens and
half-grown chicks pecked busily between the rows. She must be
around somewhere. Leaning wearily on the kraal fence, he let his
hands dangle so the pigs and goats could lick the dried salt of the
ocean from his fingers.

He had gone ashore at Cape St. Catherine and had spent three
days there, repairing rigging, resetting sail, hunting and foraging extra
food and taking on fresh water. But no sooner had he pushed out to
sea again than a squall had blown up and capsized him. He had very
nearly lost his life, had very nearly lost his boat and had lost very
nearly all his equipment and supplies. The hull, as always, was the
problem. Over the years, he had experimented with a variety of sails
and masts and riggings and, actually, any one of them would have
been good enough, but the round-bottomed hull of a dugout canoe,
or even of two lashed together, was just too prone to capsizing in
open water. But as much as he had tried, he had never succeeded in
laying the keel for a flatter, wider-beamed hull that didn't leak like a
sieve, so he had had to stick with the dugout design. But he knew
that if he were ever to get away in that sort of hull, he would have to
have at least one other hand aboard as movable ballast to fight
against its tendency to heel. Just one other. He could get away, he was
sure, if he could only find one other willing to get away with him. But
there was no other willing to get away with him in all this savage
land.

"So, you have come back again."

He turned around.

She was old. Each time he saw her after a time away, he was
struck anew by how very quickly she had grown old, how very
quickly she had shriveled up in their exile. She wore her kanga

around her waist like a man, allowing him to see how her once-full breasts had collapsed into ugly, empty sacs, and grimaced at him so he could see how many of her teeth were missing. It was his fault— she had been taken from her people in Mbanza Kongo and made an outcast on this island because of him—but he had no pity on her; he didn't sleep with her anymore. As much as she resented him, so he resented her. She was barren. Actually, it was precisely because she could have no children that she had been given to him in the first place all those years ago, but, senselessly, he blamed her for it anyway. Had she borne him even one son or daughter, the child would be nearly ten now and capable of serving as the needed other hand for the voyage to São Jorgé da Mina. But perhaps he did have a child; perhaps the other Nimi, the princess Nimi, had borne him a son or daughter. He didn't know, nor did he ever expect to know.

"Yes, I have come back again, *mchento*, and I am hungry."

"This new little bird also would not fly you home?"

She was referring to the sail-rigged canoe. She persisted in pretending that she believed the sailing craft he kept building so obsessively were little birds, ducklings of the great sail-winged caravel *Leonor*, in which he hoped to fly back to his land in the sky. She knew better, of course; she knew by now that he didn't come from the sky, and her persistence in this pretense was just another means of taunting him.

"I say I am hungry. I have not eaten in many days. Will you fetch something for me or must I beat you?"

She shrugged and went into the house.

After he had eaten, he went to sleep and slept away the rest of the day, exhausted from the voyage and dreamless. He got up at dusk, washed in the spring behind the house, dressed in a kanga—only on his voyages, when he was attempting to reach the Portuguese settlement at São Jorgé da Mina, did he wear trousers and other semblance of European clothing, as he didn't want to appear before the white men there looking like a savage—and pushed off into the river in his unrigged dugout.

He was going fishing. They were out of fresh fish and meat; the woman did not fish or hunt when he was away. He paddled along the

northern shore of his island to its eastern end from where he could
see Mpinda on the Zaire's south bank. Fishing canoes were also pushing out from there, carrying torches to light their way in the gathering twilight. He kept his distance from them. It would cause trouble
if he didn't. He was forbidden to go among them for any reason. He
paddled farther upriver and cast his net wide in a graceful arc, then
let the canoe drift downstream on the current and outgoing tide,
trawling the net. He did this several times but had no luck. So, after a
while, he let the canoe drift back to the eastern end of his island and
dropped a line over the side in the European fashion and sprawled in
the canoe's bottom and stared across Mpinda. The cooking fires burning there; the people hurrying about among the tall, conical huts; the
muted sound of drumming from inside the stockade of the Mani-
Soyo's compound, celebrating a feast or ritual unknown to him—it all
might as well have been a world away. He had never been back to
Mpinda in all these years, didn't know whether the grandfatherly
ManiSoyo still lived, whether the hateful NsakuSoyo had died. And it
didn't matter a whit to him.

A cracking noise, steps in the underbrush of the forest behind
him. He rolled onto his stomach in the bottom of the canoe, then,
tossing his long hair out of his eyes, peered over the gunwale. A
bushbuck had come out of the forest to drink in the river, a young
animal, the antlers still mossy green. He had a cane bow, strung with
a fine leather thong, and a sheaf of iron-tipped arrows, feathered
with gull wings, in the bottom of the canoe, as well as his ivory-
handled knife. Ducking down, he fitted an arrow to the bowstring,
touched the bloodstones at his throat for luck, then got on his
knees. He was upwind of the buck. It raised its head, looked around
alertly but didn't see him and lowered its head to the water again,
switching its white tail. He drew back on the bow. It was an easy
kill; he could put the arrow between the buck's forelegs, straight
into the heart. He should make it quickly, though, before others of
the herd came out of the forest and caught his scent. But it was too
easy.

Releasing the tension on the bowstring, he slipped back down
into the canoe's bottom, unknotted his kanga and let it fall away, removed his knife from its scabbard and grasped it between his teeth

and, first checking around for crocodiles, slipped over the side of the canoe into the river, as naked and silent as a snake.

The river was only waist-deep here, the bottom slimy, water bugs skittering away in every direction across its black surface. He dropped to his knees so that he was neck-deep in the water, took hold of the gunwale and, hidden behind the canoe, floated it toward the bushbuck. He stayed upwind of the animal and, when he was about ten yards from it, stood up just enough to peer over the canoe. The buck had raised its head again and was staring directly at the canoe, snuffling its wet muzzle, still not sure what to make of what it saw. He let go of the gunwale, sucked in a lungful of air and dove. With two powerful strokes, his hair streaming over his shoulders, the knife between his teeth, he swam under the canoe and came bursting out of the water in the shallows of the bank with a murderous cry.

Birds exploded from the trees in a shrieking panic, monkeys scattered hysterically through the branches. The buck, turning to run in sudden desperation, skittered in the slippery mud of the bank. He leaped on its back like a lion. He was bigger and heavier than the young animal and its spindly legs buckled under the walloping impact of his weight. Jerking its head around wildly, it slammed a prong of its antlers against his cheek, drawing blood. But he hung on, locking a powerful arm around the long, smooth neck, and the buck went down, rolling on its side, kicking. Going down with it, one leg trapped under it, he took the knife from his mouth and plunged it into the animal's neck. Blood spurted into his face, gushed hot over his hand. He pushed the knife in deeper, twisted it and sliced across the throat. The buck looked at him sorrowfully, its big, brown eyes glazing over. In a few minutes it was dead.

Why had he done this? Why hadn't he simply shot the arrow? What was this fury in him to kill with his own hands? Christ, have mercy. It was at times like these that he really believed he had gone mad.

"THE MTUKONGO COMES. Wake up. Do you not hear me? I say the MtuKongo comes." She was shaking his shoulder.

He slapped her hand away. "Leave off, woman. I hear you." He swung his legs over the side of the bunk and sat there, rubbing the sleep out of his eyes.

This was his bedroom in the main house. The bunk, like a captain's bunk in a caravel's sterncastle, was built along the room's north wall with a window, a port, at its foot in the west wall so that he could see out to the ocean while lying down. A mattress of grass and two pillows of gull feathers lay on it, and lengths of cloth and tanned hides covered it. There was a table by the low window and a chair with a leather seat and leather backrest where he often ate (also while looking out the window to the sea) and wrote, using parchment and the quills of waterbirds and a purple ink of berry juice (which, however, faded to invisibility with time), and made his useless calculations of the winds and tides and drew his useless charts of the sea and sky. Animal skins were scattered on the packed-mud floor—there was no sense laying boards; the rains and humidity rotted them, the driver ants and termites devoured them and rats found the space underneath them a comfortable place to nest—and lanterns, burning palm oil, hung from the lime-washed roof beams. His bow and a leather quiver of arrows hung from pegs on the south wall by the door across from the bunk, a shield and iron lance leaned against the wall beside them, and a crucifix he had carved with a bleeding Jesus hung on the wall over the head of the bunk. Under the bunk, he had a chest for his clothes.

"He comes from Mpinda. He will soon be here."

"*Ngete, mchento. Keba,*" he snapped with irritation. "I hear you. Now leave me be."

Nevertheless, she lingered in the doorway to make sure he did not go back to sleep. She was dressed properly this morning, her kanga covering her breasts, and she wore a string of seashells around her neck. The visit of the MtuKongo excited her; she would seize the rare occasion to petition once again for her release from this exile. It would do her no good, but her pathetic hope that one day she would be released was as obsessive as his pathetic hope that one day he would sail away home.

"Have you prepared food?"

"The MtuKongo does not eat at this hour."

"No, but I do. Prepare food."

After she left for the cookhouse, he kneeled beside the bunk, clasped his hands beneath his chin and closed his eyes. He didn't actually pray. It was only a habit left over from all those years when, on waking, he had prayed for a ship to come and save him from this wasted life. Then he put on his kanga, strapped on his knife and went out of the house barefoot. Although long before he had made boots for himself, he had gotten used to going barefoot. The woman brought him a bowl of taro porridge and a cup of goat's milk, and after having had his breakfast, he walked along the island's south beach, eastward, upriver toward Mpinda, absently kicking stones.

There were war canoes in the cove in front of Mpinda, a fleet of about fifty big craft with high-curved prows decorated with black eyes or white lightning bolts or the heads of serpents and beasts. Each had ten standing paddlers on a side and carried about forty warriors, a formidable army of more than two thousand fighting men, going off to some war.

He had seen armies like this pass this way before, and while he never learned exactly what their various wars were about—he had learned very little about life in the Kongo in his exile—he had learned that war was a commonplace in this land. Indeed, not unlike the European kingdoms of the time, the Kongo kingdom was a creation of war. The provinces and fiefdoms, the tribes and clans and vassal states that formed it had all once been independent nations in their own right. And although the wars of conquest that had forged them into a single realm and forced the submission of their chiefs and lords to the throne of the supreme sovereign in Mbanza Kongo had been fought in a time before living memory, in the time of the first ManiKongo, the mythic Blacksmith King who had brought the civilizing art of iron making to the people, they, no less than the feudal principalities of European kingdoms, jealously guarded a large measure of autonomy and bristled with sectarian pride. Their allegiance to the ManiKongo could never be taken entirely for granted; they were not unknown to rebel. The last time he had seen a war fleet like this on the Zaire, the rebels had been the Bateke, a vassal people on the northern bank of the upper river, above Matadi, beyond the cataracts of the Caldron of Hell. Perhaps they were the troublemakers again.

He fingered out the last of the porridge, drank off the last of the goat's milk and handed the bowl and cup to the woman, then squatted at the water's edge and washed his hands, peering across the river at Mpinda into the rising sun. The largest of the war canoes, with rampant lions painted on both sides of its prow, had detached itself from the rest of the fleet in the cove and was coming downriver toward the island. There was only one warrior in it, standing amidship between the rows of standing paddlers, wearing a pale green kanga bordered in red, a headdress of egret feathers and antelope horn and a necklace of lion's teeth. While still some yards away, he jumped out of the canoe and waded ashore.

"*In nomine Patris, et Filii, et Spiritus Sancti,* Gil," he called out, making the sign of the cross and grinning broadly.

Gil stood up. "Mbemba," he said.

The Kongo prince grasped Gil by the shoulders and gave him a vigorous shake. He wasn't quite as tall as Gil but he too had grown big and strong and imposing during these years and, except for an ugly scar across his left cheek—a lance wound suffered in some battle—was strikingly handsome. "*Deo gratias,*" he said, still smiling widely. "I am happy to see that you are still with us."

Gil shook his head. He was angry at Mbemba—he was always angry at him—but he couldn't help smiling whenever he saw his handsome, good-natured face and heard him proudly show off his prayer-book Latin. "For my part, Mbemba, I am not happy to be still with you."

Mbemba chose to ignore Gil's bitter tone and turned to the woman. "And you, *mchento,* have you taken care of my friend since I was last here?"

"It is not necessary, MtuKongo. He takes care of himself. He does not need me for anything. Ask him yourself. I could return to my people in Mbanza Kongo and—"

"What? You mean to start that lamentation again? Do not. I will not listen to it."

"But, MtuKongo, please . . ." She grabbed Mbemba's hand and brought it to her lips. "Please, it has been so many years. If I could see my people just once again. You must not leave me here to die without ever seeing my people just once again . . ."

"Will you not stop this? Stop it at once." In jerking his hand away from the woman's lips, the Kongo prince accidentally struck her chin and she stumbled backward in surprise, tripped and fell. He glared down at her. "Your place is here, *mchento,* and here you will stay."

"Oh, let her go, Mbemba," Gil said. "Let her go back to Mbanza Kongo. It does not matter to me."

"You hear him, MtuKongo?" She scrambled to her feet. "He says so himself. It does not matter to him."

"But it matters to me. He must have a woman. He cannot stay here without a woman. It would not be natural."

"Send him another woman then. Send him a younger woman, a more beautiful woman."

"No other woman, no other person is permitted to come here. You know that yourself. Now leave us."

Tears welling up in her eyes, she went back to the house. Neither of the men watched her go.

"Why have you brought this great force of warriors here, Mbemba?" Gil asked. "What is the trouble? Is it the Bateke again?"

"Yes."

"But I thought you killed their chief the last time and took hundreds of his warriors as slaves."

"I did. But now they have a new chief."

"And he also will not pay tribute to your father?"

"No, so I suppose I must kill him as well and enslave *his* warriors."

"Take me with you. I will help you kill him."

Mbemba pulled a sour face.

"Oh, never mind."

"Gil, you know . . ."

"Yes, I know."

"It is forbidden for you to leave this island."

"I said, I know."

"I am sorry."

"Yes, you are sorry."

"Do not be so angry, Gil. I have brought many valuable goods for you."

"*Ntondesi,*" Gil said and turned away.

Mbemba signaled to the paddlers in the big war canoe, now drawn up on the beach, and they began unloading baskets and bundles and jars and kettles from it. Gil didn't bother to watch. He knew well enough what Mbemba had brought—tools, weapons, rope, earthenware, cloth, hides, palm oil and wine, that sort of thing, valuable goods indeed. Mbemba always brought such things on his periodic visits to the island and Gil was grateful for them. They made his life easier, allowed him to concentrate his energies on his obsessive, improbable efforts to escape. Even so, he turned away now with ill grace and walked westward, sullenly, down the beach toward the ocean. Mbemba fell in step beside him.

Mbemba's visits had long since stopped being a secret; everyone knew of them and no one objected to them anymore. For, with the passage of the years and the failure of the other white men to return, Gil had come to be perceived always less and less as a threat, always more and more as a hapless freak of nature, an astonishing curiosity of the gods. Exiled to the closely circumscribed world of the island and river and open sea, bereft of allies of his own kind, he was considered incapable of causing any real harm. And Mbemba's continuing friendship with him was discounted as nothing more than a sign of the gentle prince's good heart.

"Is this a new boat? I do not think I have seen it before."

They had come round to the western end of the island where the sail-rigged canoe was drawn up on the landing stage between the double-hulled craft and the dugout.

"Have you tried it on the ocean yet?"

Gil nodded.

"How did it fare?"

"Why do you ask me that? Am I not still here? Do you think I would still be here if this boat had fared any better than the others?"

Mbemba sighed—he had heard this many times before—and looked round at the paddlers bringing the supplies ashore. The woman had come out of the house to supervise them.

"None of these boats will ever succeed as long as I must sail them alone. If I had another, just one other . . . even that woman there. I could teach her what to do. I could teach her to be my mate. But she will not hear of it. No. She would be glad enough if I sailed away and never returned, but she will not help me. Everyone would be glad enough if I sailed away and never returned, but no one will help me. Not even you, Mbemba."

Mbemba looked back, fingering the scar on his cheek. It reddened angrily when he became upset.

"You could command her to sail with me. You could command *someone* to sail with me. You are MtuKongo. You could sail with me yourself."

"Gil . . ."

"I could teach you, Mbemba. It is not difficult. Let me show you. Come here. I will put up the mast. We can go out right now. You will see how easy it is. In a few days, you will know everything you must know in order to be my mate and together we will sail to the land on the other shore of the sea."

"Stop it, Gil. That is enough of such foolishness."

"What? You do not want to sail with me to the land on the other shore of the sea? But I thought you wanted to learn the magic of the white men there."

"That was long ago."

"Yes, that was long ago," Gil replied, calming down. "That was very long ago. That was too long ago. There is no need for you to learn the magic of the white men anymore." He stepped into the sailboat and sat down on the thwart astern and stared glumly out to sea.

Mbemba watched him for a few moments, then looked round for his paddlers again. They had finished offloading the supplies. "I must go, Gil," he said.

"No." Gil turned around quickly. "Do not go. You have only just come. Stay awhile with me. The Bateke chief can wait to die."

"I must go before the sun is high."

"Yes, all right, but there still is time. Sit with me here and let us speak together for a while."

"You will not try to trick me and sail this boat out on the ocean once I am in it?"

"No, no." Gil smiled. "Forgive me for all that foolishness. Sometimes I do not know what I say. I am too much alone. I have a worm in my head."

"I understand." Mbemba removed his headdress and stepped

into the boat and sat on the thwart beside Gil, putting the headdress down in the boat's bottom between his feet.

"Tell me a little of the world, Mbemba. I know so little of what happens anywhere, even just a league from this cursed island. Tell me, how is your father?"

"He is well."

"Truly?"

"Well enough. Anyway, he is still alive."

"I am glad for that. That one time he received me—I often think of it—he treated me with kindness. Does he ever ask after me anymore?"

"No. I do not think he remembers you anymore. He remembers very little now. Mpanzu rules in his place more and more."

"But your mother, the Mbanda Lwa, she still remembers me."

"Oh, yes, she still remembers you."

"But not with kindness."

"She expected too much of you, Gil."

"Yes, she expected far too much of me . . . and of the magic of the writing. Does she still ask you to teach her how to speak the writing of the breviary?"

"Not for a very long time now."

"No, it has been a very long time now since she believed the writing was a wonderful magic. I cannot blame her."

"Her mind is on other things."

"What other things?"

Mbemba shrugged. "She is an ambitious woman, and will find herself in trouble for it one day."

"She still hopes to push you ahead of Mpanzu when that day comes?"

"You must never say that to anyone, Gil."

"To whom would I say it? To the birds in the trees? To the fish in the sea?"

Mbemba smiled. "She is Soyo, you know, of the ManiSoyo's house, and as proud and ambitious as only the Soyo can be. So she believes that it should be a son of Soyo blood, her son, who should take the Kongo throne when the ManiKongo dies, not Mpanzu, the rightful heir, who is of Nsundi blood."

"But you do not believe that?"

"No. I have no such ambitions. I am content with my place."

"Does Mpanzu know this?"

"Would he permit me to command the armies of the kingdom if he did not know this? Would he trust me to lead these warriors into battle against the Bateke now if he did not know this?"

"And his mother, the Mbanda Vunda? And the NgangaKongo?"

"They trust me. They all trust me. Why should they not trust me? I have never done anything to betray their trust. It is only the Mbanda Lwa they do not trust. Only the ManiKongo's special love for her protects her. But when he dies, she will find herself in serious trouble if she persists in her ambitions."

"So you will never be king."

"No."

"The gentle prince will never be king and so there will never be anyone to help me sail away."

Mbemba did not reply to this and Gil looked back out to sea.

"I have to go now, Gil."

"Yes."

Mbemba picked up his headdress and stood up.

Gil stood up with him. "She must be very beautiful now," he said.

"Who?"

"Nimi."

"Nimi?"

"Not this Nimi. Your sister Nimi, the NtinuKongo."

Mbemba's scar flared and he gave Gil a hard look, then put on his headdress and stepped out of the canoe.

"*Is* she very beautiful now, Mbemba? She was so very pretty as a girl, she must be very beautiful now, a grown woman. Is she a wife? Does she have many children?"

He asked this while walking beside Mbemba up the beach toward the war canoe. He didn't expect Mbemba to reply. Mbemba never replied to his questions about Nimi. She was a forbidden subject, and he asked his questions about her partly to vex Mbemba, to express his dissatisfaction with his friend for failing to help him get away, but also because he wanted the answers. He brooded over

her a great deal in his loneliness, the sassy little thing who had
come to him so long ago to make a magical baby inside of her. He
had spun a great romance about her during these endless, empty
years, embroidering a silly fairy tale out of that one awkward night.
What had become of her? Had he made a baby inside of her? And,
if he had, what had become of the child, half-white, in this Negro
kingdom?

"Does she ever speak of me?"

Mbemba stepped into the war canoe and said something to the
paddlers before turning back to Gil on the beach. *"Dominus vobiscum,* Gil Eenezh."

"You do not answer me."

"No."

"Perhaps the next time."

Mbemba shrugged.

"When will the next time be?"

"I will pass this way again on my return from the Bateke, if I
have not been killed."

"And if I am still here."

"Yes, and if you are still here. I wish you luck, Gil. God be with
you."

"And also with you."

Mbemba barked a command and the paddlers pushed off into
the river and, with long, graceful strokes, returned to Mpinda. In the
next few minutes, the war canoes in the cove assembled into ten files
of five and, with Mbemba's canoe in the lead, headed upriver, a formidable fighting force setting off to wreak terrible havoc on an enemy, to kill a chief and take many slaves.

Gil watched until the last of them disappeared around a bend,
then turned back to the ocean. Once again he was alone. His woman
was standing on the veranda of the house, looking at him somberly,
but he had nothing to say to her; she might as well have not been
there. He walked back down the beach to the landing stage and got
into the newest of his sailboats again.

Perhaps the thing to do was build an outrigger. A much smaller
dugout, serving as the outrigger-float, attached to a much larger main
hull might offset the main hull's tendency to heel in rough seas. It

shouldn't be too difficult to build. He ran his fingers through his long hair, combing it back out of his face, and looked out to sea, out to the distant line of the horizon, the line beyond which he must sail if he were ever to get home to Portugal again.

II

THE SKY WAS OVERCAST. Each day now for the last few weeks, it had grown more darkly overcast. Clouds rolled in on the southeast trades, dimming the sun to a pewter disc, veiling the moon and stars in ghostly shrouds, wetting the bush with a heavy dew, coloring the river and ocean steel-gray. By Gil's calculation, it was the twelfth of October, 1492. The season of rain was on the way.

His new sailboat, the outrigger, was ready. Bamboo spars attached the outrigger float to the main hull's weather side. The raked mast carried an oversize lateen sail laced to an oblique yard. Its halyard and sheet were rigged so that they could be handled from the float those times he'd have to crawl out there to keep the boat from capsizing. And the tiller in the main hull's stern was fitted with an extra-long hiking stick so he'd also be able to steer from out there when necessary. Actually, it looked pretty good, lying half-in and half-out of the river on the landing stage in front of his house, good enough to name. Maybe he'd name it the *Princess Nimi*. He sat back on his heels and looked up at the darkly overcast sky.

That was the next problem, the weather. Should he use the remaining weeks until the rains came to test the boat and make whatever adjustments the trials suggested, then wait out the rains and set sail for São Jorgé da Mina in February? But if he did that, he would sail straight into the rainy season north of the equator. On the other hand, if he sailed right away, he might, with luck, reach the equator

just before the rains came south of the line and just after they ended
north of the line. Of the two, the latter was probably the better gam-
ble. It was more important to have good weather north of the equator, where he'd be standing out on that bold tack into midocean in
search of the westerlies, far out of sight of land, than during the voyage along the coast to the equator where, if the weather turned
against him, he could always run for shore. And, besides, what was
the sense in waiting? There was nothing to wait for. Mbemba had
come and gone and probably wouldn't come again until the Bateke
caused more trouble. And there was no sense waiting for that. Mbemba couldn't do anything for him. But still, he should take the boat
out for at least one trial run first.

He pushed her off from the muddy bank, sat down on the
thwart astern and paddled out toward the river's outlet on the ocean.
A brisk, damp wind was blowing southeast to northwest, and when
he reached the rocky headland of the outlet's south point, he shipped
the paddle and hoisted the sail. It fluttered for a moment in confusion, then snapped full in the wind. Holding the sheet with one hand,
he pulled starboard on the tiller with the other, and as the boat began
running north before the wind, he looked up at the billowing sail and
thought that, before he really set off, he would paint an insignia on it,
a cross of some kind, so he'd be recognized at sea as a Christian.

He sailed the four or five leagues across the width of the river's
mouth to the north point of its outlet, easing the sail all the way out,
watching the outrigger-float skip along the water's choppy, gray surface, feeling the speed and balance of the craft. At the north point, he
trimmed sail, jibed onto a beam reach and sailed out into the ocean.
Along the ocean beach here were the red-clay cliffs behind which he
had seen the *Leonor* disappear so many years ago. He stood off from
them and continued running north. The boat handled well. But this
wasn't yet a true test of her worth. All his boats had handled well sailing north to the equator with the wind aft or on the quarter. The true
test would come only when, once north of the equator, he'd have to
beat against the wind while searching for the westerlies. Actually, he
could simulate those conditions by sailing well away from the coast
here, coming about and beating windward close-hauled.

He looked up at the sky. The sun, pale and luminous and swimming in the streaming clouds of the overcast, stood almost directly overhead. He had all the afternoon in which to try this and no worry about losing anything of value (except his life) if he capsized while trying it since he had taken only his knife, bow and a quiver of arrows aboard. So he reached out to sea, north by west, his long hair flying in the wind, screaming gulls circling overhead, the cliffs of the coastline sinking beneath the eastern horizon behind him.

Now he had to be careful; he mustn't lose his bearings, sailing by dead reckoning. Oh, what he would have given for a compass. He fixed the position of the wan sun, estimating its elevation above the hazy western horizon by handspans. He splashed water on his face in order to feel more keenly the direction of the wind blowing against his cheek. He kept watch on the changing size of the waves, short and choppy and running inshore. Even so, he lost his nerve after a few minutes and turned north again to get one more look at the coastline.

He knew that coastline like the back of his hand, having sailed along it so many times over the years. There was the big rock he called Seal Rock because he had once seen seals sunning on it. And there was Lion's Cove where he had seen a pride of lion swimming in the sandy shallows. And there was Shipwreck Beach where he had been blown ashore in a ferocious storm and stranded for four days. And that was Waterfall Bay where a beautiful cascade crashed down from the cliffs into a wide pool of surprisingly deep water. All right, he had his bearings fresh in mind, he knew exactly where he was. He pushed the tiller to larboard and eased out the sail. The bow of the craft swung through the compass rose from north to west and stood straight out into the ocean again.

And then he saw it. He saw it almost right away but didn't believe what he saw because of the clumps of low-lying clouds on the western horizon. It must be only another clump of low-lying clouds. His heart began racing, though. He cleated the sheet and stood up. Oh, what he would have given for a spyglass now. He ducked under the yard and went forward into the bow, tossing his head so that the wind blew his hair out of his eyes. But was it just another clump of low-lying clouds? Oh, Lord Jesus, no: Those weren't clouds. Those were sails. They must be sails, hulling up from under the curve of the horizon. What else could they be? A great-winged bird? His heart jumped into this throat. Aye, a great-winged bird flying down from the sky. He started to laugh. But then his boat, its tiller untended, began yawing. He scrambled aft, roped the tiller, then hurried forward again and peered out across the choppy, steel-gray sheet of the sea. They *were* sails. They couldn't be anything but sails. He couldn't see what kind of sails or how many or what type of ship carried them. But they were sails, all right; they were sails, by God.

"Ahoy. *Amigos,* ahoy. Men of God, ahoy."

It was ridiculous, of course. How far away was the ship? A league, at least. They couldn't possibly hear him; they probably couldn't even see him. But he didn't care. He went on shouting anyway, shouting his heart out, waving his arms.

But finally reality struck. He couldn't tell in which direction the ship was sailing (or how fast), but he wasn't so sanguine as to imagine she was sailing to the Zaire. More likely, she was sailing either to or from the Indies. He had long suspected that the ocean passage around Africa had been found—very possibly by Diogo Cão himself—and that ships had been regularly plying the route well offshore all these years. He had never seen one because he had never had the courage to sail far enough out to sea nor the luck to sail out at just the right time, when one was passing. But he had now; he had had both the courage and the incredible luck. He mustn't let her get away. He would never have such luck again. He scrambled back to the helm. He would sail northwest with the wind on his quarter in order to make the fastest headway possible and see, after a league or so, if he could tell which way she was headed.

And after a league or so, he could. She was headed south, outbound for the Indies. He was going in the wrong direction. He came about, hurriedly, clumsily, shipping water, and beat close-hauled to the southwest. He was now nearly two leagues offshore. The ship was another league farther out. He was a league upwind of her. On his present course, he would cross her bow if he were sailing as fast as she was. He gripped the tiller so fiercely his arm went numb. The sheet, coiled around his fist, was rubbing the flesh of his palm raw. He slipped off the thwart and stretched out low in the boat's bottom to cut wind resistance, and urged the craft on with every fiber and muscle of his being.

She was a three-masted caravel, perhaps of one hundred tons

burthen. And she was flying the Portuguese colors. But what was
even more heartening was that she seemed to be sailing, not due
south, but south by east. If this were not an illusion of the winds and
clouds and sea, she would cross his bow and not the other way
around. He adjusted his course south by west and tied the tiller, made
more sail and cleated the sheet, then took off his kanga, went forward
of the mast and began waving it like a madman.

She was carrying guns: four lombard cannon aimed through
ports on the main deck larboard, three swivel falconets attached to
the larboard bulwarks of the spar deck with probably the same con-
figuration starboard. He could see several seamen on the spar deck, a
lookout in the crow's nest atop the mainmast, an officer of the watch
by the compass binnacle on the quarterdeck, a mate leaning against
the bowsprit on the forecastle deck, peering forward through a spyglass. It was on the mate that he concentrated all his attention, directed all his efforts, willing him to look around with the glass and
see the wildly flapping kanga.

Her name was the *Beatriz*. He had just made out the gold let-
tering on her larboard bow when the mate turned the spyglass toward him. He was now only a few hundred yards away, but the mate
swept the glass right past him and looked aft.

"*Marinheiro,* ahoy. *Companheiro de* Beatriz, *acqui.*"

"*Acola. Olhar acola.*"

Gil looked up in surprise.

It was the lookout in the crow's nest, not the mate on the forecastle deck, who had spotted him. "There, look there, two points to
larboard. Who is it?"

The lookout's shouts alerted the mate and he swung his glass
back to Gil. The seamen on the spar deck ran over to the larboard
rail, gawking and gesturing, and the officer of the watch hurried
down from the quarterdeck into the ship's waist. Satisfied that he had
been seen, Gil put his kanga back on, scrambled back to the helm and
steered south by east, parallel to the ship. He was still a hundred
yards or so off her larboard beam but he didn't dare get any closer,
fearful of her wash.

The mate dashed down from the forecastle deck and chased the
gawking seamen back to their duties, then handed the spyglass to the

officer of the watch, possibly the pilot or master-at-arms. Another officer—the captain?—now came topside, took the glass and, in his turn, peered long and hard at the tall, muscular, half-naked, blond-bearded creature in the curious outrigger sailing alongside his ship. Then he shouted to the mate, who sent seamen clambering up the shrouds of the mainmast and foremast. They were heaving to. Gil jumped up and struck his own sail. Soldiers, armed with arquebuses and crossbows, appeared along the larboard rail, but they didn't worry him. No one was going to shoot him; he wasn't going to die, not now, not after all these years. He was rescued. He was saved. He picked up his paddle and, as the ship slowed, paddled toward her with a wild man's enthusiasm and a savage's skill.

"Who are you?"

The captain and the pilot or master-at-arms, the mate and now also a priest were peering down at him over the larboard rail. The mate, tall and lanky, with a close-cropped gray beard and almost completely bald, was the one who was shouting down to him.

"Stand off and tell us who you are."

"Throw me a ladder so I can come aboard."

"Ask him if he speaks Portuguese."

"What?"

"Do you speak Portuguese?"

And Gil suddenly realized he hadn't been speaking Portuguese; he had been speaking Kongo. "Aye, I speak Portuguese. Of course I speak Portuguese. I am Portuguese. From the Villa Real in Tras-os-Montes."

"What does he say?" This was the captain, questioning the mate. "Do you understand what he says?"

"He says he is Portuguese, from the Tras-os-Montes."

"Do you believe him?"

"For the love of God, look at me. Can't you see I am Portuguese? I am late of the king's ship *Leonor.*"

"What is that you say? Of the *Leonor?* That cannot be. I know all who sailed aboard the *Leonor,* having sailed aboard her myself. What is your name?"

"Gil Eanes."

"Gil Eanes?"

And in the moment the mate repeated his name, Gil recognized who he was. He also had sailed on the *Leonor.* "Nuno Gonçalves? Is that you, Dom Nuno? Of course it's you. Don't you recognize me? It's me, Gil Eanes."

"Gil Eanes? But how can it be you? You are dead."

"No, I am not dead. Look here. Look at what I wear. Don't you remember these bloodstones?"

"Gil. Is it really you, Gil? Oh, Holy Mother, I cannot believe it."

"Who is he?"

"Gil Eanes. He was page to Diogo Cão, master of the *Leonor* when she first sailed to these waters. We believed him killed by the Negroes of the kingdom on the *rio poderoso* we discovered there. Throw him a ladder."

A rope ladder was dropped over the side. Gil grabbed it and started scrambling up. But then he stopped abruptly and took a good look at the faces peering down at him, the first white faces he had seen in ten years. They shocked him. They seemed so very ugly and filthy and strange, mottled pink and gray and yellow, covered with matted greasy hair, features too big and sharp, teeth broken and black, eyes bloodshot and rheumy, some gouged out, showing shriveled sockets or hidden behind patches. Is this what white men looked like? Is this what he looked like? He didn't remember it so. He dropped back into his boat and strapped on his knife and slung his bow and the quiver of arrows over his shoulder and then tied his boat to the bottom rung of the ladder so it wouldn't float away. Why did he do this? He would never again need the knife or bow and arrows or outrigger. He was going home to Portugal, perhaps the long way around via the Indies but home to Portugal at last.

Nuno Gonçalves smothered him in a bear hug as soon as he set foot on board, then pushed him away and held him at arm's length, grinning at him from ear to ear.

"Dom Nuno."

"I don't believe this, Gil. How can I be expected to believe this? It's a miracle. Oh, Holy Mother of God, is it really you, little son, come back from the dead? Look at you. A wild man of the forest. Where is the boy I knew? This man before me frightens me." But far from being frightened, Gonçalves embraced him again. "Oh, what a story you must have to tell, little son. Oh, what adventures you must have survived to be here to tell it."

"Gonçalves."

"Oh, pardon me, my lord Captain, I forget myself . . . Gil, allow me to present our captain-general, the discoverer of the Cabo Bom Esperança, Bartolomeu Dias de Novais."

He was a short man with a big belly and spindly legs, watery eyes and a sorrowful expression. His hair and beard were completely white but he really wasn't very old; his hair and beard must have turned white from some terrible fright. He was elegantly dressed, wearing an embroidered velvet surcoat and matching pantaloons, white lace at the wrist and knees, a stiff white ruff collar around the neck, a polished steel helmet on his head, a ceremonial sword at his side. The discoverer of the Cape of Good Hope, the promontory at the bottom of Africa where the Atlantic and Indian oceans met. Gil, half-naked in his kanga, looking like some blond savage out of the African forest, didn't know how to greet him. Should he drop to a knee? Kiss his ring? He couldn't remember the correct form and only nodded. Dias nodded back, seeming less displeased than perplexed. Soldiers and seamen gathered around, gaping at Gil with vulgar curiosity.

To Gil, still unaccustomed to the look of these white men, the ship's master-at-arms, Tomé Rodrigues, whom Gonçalves introduced next, seemed the roughest of the rough lot, trucked out in chainmail and shoulder armor, a red bandanna around his head, a brass ring in one ear, a leather patch over one eye, his black beard greasy and unkempt, his long hair braided into a tarred pigtail, an unsheathed cutlass in his hand. And the pilot, Antão Paiva, seemed as much the ugly brigand in soiled trousers and blouse, a dirk in his belt, and was probably suffering from the flux besides by the look of his greenish pallor and the stink of his breath.

The ship's chaplain, however, was of an entirely different class. As tall as Gil but far more delicately built and not much more than a few years older, twenty-nine or thirty, but with startlingly scarlet lips, his name was Rui de Sousa. He was a canon from the college of Santo Eloi, dressed in a well-fitted, buttoned, black cassock and wide-brimmed black velvet hat, a black onyx rosary with a silver crucifix

hanging down his narrow chest and a neat black moustache and goatee framing the lower portion of his chalky, sharp-featured, foxlike
face.

"Are you Christian, my son?" he asked after Gonçalves had introduced them, and grasped both of Gil's hands while his eyes roamed
disapprovingly over Gil's half-naked torso.

"Of course I'm Christian, padre."

"And have you kept the faith?"

Vaguely irritated by the question, Gil withdrew his hands. "As
best I could, a castaway."

"When you are ready, I will hear your confession."

Gil didn't respond to this, although a few rude ways of responding to it crossed his mind.

"Now tell us your story, Gil. Tell us the whole of it." Gonçalves
again threw an arm around Gil. "What an amazing story it must be,
what a remarkable adventure. I can't say you look any the worse for
it, though. How big and ferocious you have grown. He was just a snip
of a boy when I last saw him, my lord Captain. I can't get over it. Returned from the dead. It *is* a miracle, isn't it, padre?"

"We will not know until we hear his story," the priest replied.

Gil told his story at the captain's table in the big cabin in the
ship's sterncastle, Gonçalves sitting on the bench next to him, the
captain-general at the head of the table in a sea chair, the priest across
from him on the bench on that side. The pilot and master-at-arms had
remained topside, making sail, resuming the outbound voyage to the
Indies.

"And what became of this Bemba?" the priest asked.

"Mbemba."

"Mbemba. What became of him? Was he killed?"

Gil shook his head.

When he first began telling the story, Gonçalves had frequently
interrupted to fill in events from his point of view, how the *Leonor*
had returned to the Zaire and found the two halberdiers waiting at
Mpinda, how they had reported Gil and Father Sebastião killed and so
on. But once Gil was well-launched on the tale, he fell silent and listened with admiring attention. The captain-general, Bartolomeu Dias,
also listened in silence but not anywhere nearly as attentively. There

was something curiously apathetic about him, those sad eyes, that distracted expression, as if the fright that had turned his hair white still hung heavy on him. He let the young, pale, sharp-featured priest conduct the interview as if the priest and not he were in command.

"I would have thought they would have killed him for helping you. Why didn't they, do you suppose?"

"He is the beloved of his father, the king."

"They have feelings like that?"

"Perdão?"

"These Negroes, they have feelings like filial love?"

"They have very much the same feelings we have, padre."

"Do they? How interesting." The priest smiled a slight but startlingly scarlet smile. Then he turned to Gonçalves. "Well, Dom Nuno, I believe it is as you say."

"What is, padre?"

"That the survival of your friend is a miracle. How wonderful are the ways of the Lord. He has preserved your friend through all these years . . . He has saved you, Senhor Eanes, not only for your own sake but also in order to assist us in the work He has sent us to do."

"What work is that?"

"The evangelization of the kingdom of the Kongo."

"The kingdom of the Kongo? What have you to do with the kingdom of the Kongo? You are bound for the Indies. Aren't you? Nuno. My lord Captain. Aren't you bound for the Indies?"

"The Indies?" Dias sat forward in his sea chair with a start, suddenly alert. "How could we be bound for the Indies? The way to the Indies hasn't been found. They said I should have found it. They said Cão before me should have found it. Poor Cão. At least I was spared his fate. But I would have found it, had João given me another chance. But no, he has given the chance to da Gama."

"Dom Bartolomeu, you speak ill of His Majesty."

"Do I, Father de Sousa? Aye, I suppose I do. But I have a quarrel with him. He should have given me a second chance."

"He has given you a second chance. This is your second chance."

"Is it? Aye, I suppose it is. And if I fail in this too, then I surely will go the way of poor Cão."

"You will not fail in it. None of us will fail in it. It is God's will.

Did He not give us this miracle of Senhor Eanes's survival as a sign we would not fail?"

"Perhaps, Father de Sousa. Perhaps." Dias slumped back in his sea chair.

What was the matter with him? And what did he mean by going the way of Cão? What had happened to Diogo Cão?

"No, we are not bound for the Indies, Senhor Eanes. We are bound for the Kongo to save the souls of the Negroes there and to trade for the riches of their kingdom.

"IT'S MADNESS, NUNO. I tell you, they won't let us come ashore. They'll slaughter us if we try."

"That may be, Gil, but what's to be done? We sail on the orders of King João."

They were alone in the magazine of the *Beatriz*'s forecastle, and as so many years before aboard the *Leonor,* Gonçalves was rummaging through lockers and slop chests for suitable clothing for Gil to wear. He could not go about half-naked like a savage forever.

"But King João doesn't know what I know, Nuno. Dias can have me presented at court when we get home and I'll explain it to him. He'll understand. And, besides, he's more concerned about the success of Vasco da Gama's voyage than this one. You said so yourself."

"Even so, Dias won't turn back. He's in fear of his life. He counts himself lucky he didn't suffer Cão's fate when he failed to push on to the Indies after rounding the Cape of Good Hope. But even if he could be talked into turning back, Father de Sousa would never let him. He's an ambitious priest, that one. He sees this as his chance to make a name for himself in Rome. Here, try this on."

Gil took the blue serge blouse Gonçalves held out to him but didn't put it on. He looked up at the oil lamp, swinging with the roll of the ship from an overhead beam. The ship was making four or five knots, south by east. In a few hours, before nightfall, she would reach the mouth of the Zaire. He had to stop her. He couldn't go back to the Kongo. Not with a ship of white men. They would blame him. They would say that all his years of trying to fly away in his little birds had only been to bring back another ship of white men. And they would kill him. They would kill all of them. But how could he convince Dias of this?

Gonçalves had explained Dias's fear. When the *Leonor* had re-turned to Lisbon all those years before (it had been 1484) without finding the sea route to the Indies—she had sailed only another three hundred leagues down the Atlantic coast from the Zaire's mouth be-fore turning back—King João's displeasure had been so great that he had had Cão imprisoned. Whether, as grim rumor had it, he also had had Cão put to death, no one really knew. Gonçalves doubted it; he believed Cão still languished in a dungeon in the palace at Sintra. But one thing was certain; Cão had never been heard of again.

Because of the difficulties Cão had encountered—the increas-ingly powerful adverse winds and currents the farther south he had sailed—João had briefly considered the possibility, proposed by a cer-tain Christovão Colom, a Genoese sea captain then living in Lisbon, of reaching the Indies by sailing not southward down the West African coast but due west across the Atlantic. In the end, though, João had rejected the scheme as fanciful—Colom had then taken his *Empresa de las Indias* to the monarchs of the Spains—and selected Dias to do what Cão had failed to do. And, in 1488, Dias had very nearly done it. He rounded the *Prassum Promontorium* at the bot-tom of Africa—which he named Cabo Tormentoso, Cape of Storms, but which João later renamed Cabo Bom Esperança, Cape of Good Hope—and sailed another fifty leagues up the other side. But when it came to standing out across the Indian Ocean, his crew had threat-ened mutiny. His ship was leaky, her rigging in shreds, provisions were low and there was an awfully long way to go to get home again. So Dias had turned back.

His reception on his return had been only barely warmer than Cão's. In recognition of his feat of rounding Africa and reaching the Indian Ocean—the first European to do so since ancient times, if even then—he escaped arrest and imprisonment but fell into dark disfavor nevertheless and Vasco da Gama was chosen to complete the voyage to the Indies in his stead. In hope of redeeming himself, Dias had petitioned for the command of the *Beatriz* to explore the *rio poderoso* Cão had found and establish a trading settlement in the kingdom on its shore. How well da Gama had succeeded, Gonçalves could not say—the *Beatriz* had sailed before da Gama's fleet had been outfitted—but Dias was convinced that his very life depended on how well *he* succeeded.

"He would rather die in glory on the banks of the Zaire, Gil, than in disgrace in the dungeons of Sintra."

"And he will too. And so will you, Nuno. And so will we all."

The ship's bell just then was struck eight times.

"This is my watch, Gil," Gonçalves said. "Stand it with me. You know this coast. If I remember anything of it from the last time, we should arrive on soundings during this watch."

"Haven't you heard a word I've said, Nuno? We cannot sail into the Zaire. We'll be massacred if we do. We must turn back. You must help me convince Dias of that."

"He can't be convinced. He must at least make an attempt to go ashore. His honor demands it. Then, if the situation is as dangerous as you say—"

"What do you mean, *if* it is as dangerous as I say. Don't you believe me?"

"Of course I believe you, but . . ."

"But what?"

"Well, you must admit we were treated decently enough by the Negroes the last time."

"It is different now, I tell you. They believe we bring evil. They believe we come to steal their bodies and their souls. They won't treat us decently this time. They will kill us this time."

"Dias will just have to see that for himself. And Father de Sousa too. Now come topside and stand the watch with me."

"You don't believe me. You think I am just saying this because I don't want to go back there, because I want to go home."

And maybe it was so. Maybe he was exaggerating the danger because he did not want ever to go back to the Kongo again; because after all these years, he wanted so badly to go home at last. Wearing the blue serge blouse Gonçalves had found for him and a pair of trousers cut from Dieppe canvas but still barefoot, his knife still strapped around his waist, his bow and quiver still slung over his shoulder, he followed Gonçalves up to the quarterdeck. Whispering seamen and soldiers backed away from him. What a sight he made for them, half Portuguese seaman, half Kongo savage. The pale disc of the sun now stood less than two handspans above the cloudy western horizon.

Dias, Father de Sousa and the pilot Paiva were on the quarter-deck. Father de Sousa had just completed blessing the new watch, and Dias and Paiva had resumed poring over a chart spread out on the pilot's table beside the binnacle. Gil recognized the chart: It was the chart of the Zaire's mouth and estuary that the pilot of the *Leonor,* José Vizinho, had drawn ten years before.

"You must be very familiar with the tides and currents of the river Zaire, Senhor Eanes," Dias said, looking up from the chart. "And the shoals and winds."

"I am, my lord Captain."

"Then I would count it as a favor if you would take the helm when we arrive on soundings."

"No, my lord Captain, I will not do that."

"Gil."

"No, Nuno, I will not pilot us into certain disaster."

"Why certain disaster, *senhor?*" Dias asked. "Why do you keep in-sisting it must be certain disaster? I am well armed. I have cannon and falconets aboard. I have a company of soldiers who are veterans of the Guinea trade and no strangers to Negro wars. You have been too long away, I fear, *senhor,* and have forgotten the worth of Por-tuguese steel and gunpowder and fighting men."

"No, my lord Captain, I have not forgotten. But I know they would be of little use against the Kongo."

"Why? Look here. Look at Cão's chart. It shows the river's estu-ary to be completely navigable for some forty leagues from the sea. Is that not correct?"

"It is."

"So I can sail up the river to this large village or town marked here . . . what is it? . . . Mpinda."

"You can."

"Very well then, if the Negroes are as unfriendly as you say and resist our coming ashore, I can simply stand off here in front of Mpinda and bring my cannon and falconets to bear until their resis-tance is broken or they are driven off."

"And what do you suppose you will accomplish by that?"

"Eh?"

"I will tell you what you will accomplish. You will kill a lot of people but you will also raise tens of thousands more against you. And what will you do then? Do you think you will be able to do the king's work of establishing a settlement to trade with these Negroes then? Do you think the padre will be able to do God's work of instructing them in the Faith then?"

"He is right, Dom Bartolomeu," Father de Sousa said. "I am afraid he is right. We will not be able to do what we have come here to do by force."

"So what do you propose we do?"

"I think we should ask that of Senhor Eanes. What do you propose we do, my son?"

"What I have proposed all along, padre. Turn back. Return to Portugal. I will explain to the king—"

"No, we will not turn back. We will not return to Portugal. We will not be so easily defeated. Do not even think of it. Think of something else."

"What?"

"Surely after living so long among these Negroes, you can think of something else."

"I cannot."

"What about Mbemba, this prince of the Kongo, this beloved of his father the Kongo king, this friend who you once taught to read? What about him, my son?"

III

THE *BEATRIZ,* UNDER BARE POLES, rode at anchor in the small cove Gil called Waterfall Bay, hidden in the lee of the cliffs of the coastline, some two leagues north of the north point of the inlet to the Zaire. Gil had piloted her there. He had stripped out of his borrowed seaman's garb and again wore only his kanga, the knife at his waist, the bow and arrows on his back. His outrigger had been brought alongside and the ship's ladder lowered to it. Night had fallen. A half-moon, newly risen, raced through the streaming clouds of the overcast. There were no stars.

"I have your word, my lord Captain? You will not stir from here until I return?"

"You have my word, *senhor.*"

"This is safe haven, my lord Captain. There is all the sweet water you can want from those falls. There is plenty of firewood on the beach and plenty of fish in the sea. And you will see that at dusk small game come down to the pool beneath the falls to drink if you are in want of fresh meat. So there is no reason for you to stir from here until I return."

"And when do you suppose that will be?"

"I cannot say. Considering the folly Father de Sousa has persuaded me to attempt, I may never return. My advice to you is to wait for me until the moon is new and if I have not returned by then, make sail for Portugal. Do not come into the Zaire. For if I have not returned by then, you can be sure I have been taken and, if I have been taken, you can be sure the Kongo know you are here and will be waiting for you in their tens of thousands on the banks of Zaire."

"How will they know?"

"I will have told them," Gil replied dryly. "I am not reckless when a knife is held at my throat."

Dias looked at Father de Sousa.

"Will you not let me confess you before you go, my son?" the priest said.

"I have nothing to confess, padre."

Father de Sousa smiled his thin, startlingly scarlet smile. "The Lord be with you then, my son."

"And also with you, padre."

"Let me come with you, Gil."

"No, Nuno. The best service you can perform for me is to make sure the *Beatriz* remains here. For if she shows herself to the Kongo before I return, I will surely be killed."

"Why do you insult me by saying that, *senhor?*" Dias broke in peevishly. "Have I not given you my word?"

"You have, my lord Captain, but I notice Father de Sousa has not." And with that, Gil vaulted the larboard rail with the agility of a big cat and swung down the rope ladder into his outrigger.

He paddled out of the small cove into the ocean, hoisted sail and, with the wind shifting from the southeast, headed off it on a close reach southwest by south. The light of the cloud-shrouded, waxing moon was not much to sail by but it was enough. His vision was sharp; all his senses were sharp, sharpened by his years in a dangerous wilderness. He could see the rocks along the shore that would imperil him, the high surf breaking on the cliff-bound beach, the sandy shoals. He could taste the salt on the drizzly mist and smell the honey of the bougainvillea that grew around the tidal lagoons. He could feel the neap tide running out beneath the hull of his boat and the pull of the northerly current, and hear lion growl and jackal laugh on shore and sense the endless emptiness out to sea. He was at ease on this ocean along this coast and had time to think.

The idea, Father de Sousa's idea, was to get a message to Mbemba. Gil's initial reaction to that had been to play the priest for a fool.

He would return to the Zaire, lay low for a while, then sail back to the *Beatriz* and tell them Mbemba had rejected their overture and again urge them to turn back for Portugal and take him home at last. But he knew a schoolboy's trick like that wouldn't work. Gonçalves was right. Neither the priest nor the captain-general, one out of ambition, the other from fear, would turn back before making an attempt to go ashore, even by main force if necessary, to plant the king's standard and raise the cross of the Church. And a war would ensue and the *Beatriz* would be destroyed and he would never get home to Portugal anyway. So he had to consider the priest's idea in earnest: Get a message to Mbemba that white men had come again.

When he rounded the headland of the north point of the Zaire's mouth, the moon was down and the sky and water and land were pitch-dark. He furled sail, coiled the rigging, unstepped the mast and paddled by feel and smell and sound toward his island. It was amazing how well he managed in the darkness, how familiar he had become with these waters, this land, this sky. It was his home; it was more his home now than Portugal. He had grown to manhood here. Here, in this land of the Kongo, he had become the man he was. What sort of man would that be in Portugal?

All was quiet on the island. Even the tree frogs and cicadas and owls fell silent as he splashed ashore. He waited until they had resumed their soft night music and listened for any unusual sound, his usual precaution. There was none and he started toward the house.

Why hadn't he confessed to the priest? By the precepts of the Faith, he had sinned in a million ways offensive to God. He should have taken the opportunity to confess and hear once again those words that, as a boy, had given him such comfort: *Ego te absolvo.* But there was something about this priest. He did not like this ambitious priest. But there was more to it than that. There were the sins themselves. They did not seem so terrible to him. Maybe the priest was right to ask if he were Catholic. Maybe he wasn't Catholic anymore. Maybe he had become a heathen of this river and sea, of this sky and forest, of this Kongo.

He went into the house and looked into the woman's room. She was asleep, curled up on her palliasse, her back to him. While he stood in the low entryway, she awakened—he could tell by the

change in her breathing—but she didn't turn to him. She pretended
to still sleep.

"Nimi."

Had he, as usual, addressed her simply as woman, *mchento,* she
probably would have gone on pretending to sleep. But his use of her
name startled her and she sat up. "What?"

He didn't say anything for a long moment.

"What is it?" she asked again with rising annoyance. But as he
went on looking at her without replying, her eyes widened and her
annoyance abated. She realized something extraordinary had happened. "What has happened?" she asked.

He stepped into the room and squatted on his heels beside her
palliasse. And in a surprisingly tender gesture, he grasped her shoulders.

She shivered under his touch. "What has happened? What do
you want?"

"I want your help."

"To do what?"

"If you help me, Nimi, I make this promise to you. You will be set
free, free of me, free of this cursed island, free to return to your own
people. But if you do not help me, if you betray me, I make *this*
promise to you." He slid his big hands down the slope of her shoulders and, still as tenderly as the lover he once had been, encircled her
throat with his fingers. "I will kill you."

She didn't move; her breath came a bit more quickly but she
wasn't afraid. She looked at him boldly. No, she was afraid neither of
him nor of dying, resigned as ever to her fate. "What do you want me
to help you do?"

He removed his hands from her neck and sat back on his heels.
"To go to Mbanza Kongo. To find Mbemba and speak to him."

"Why?"

"As I said, to set us free. To set us both free, of each other and of
this cursed place."

"How will that set us free? You have spoken to Mbemba many
times before and he has never agreed to set us free before."

"It will be different this time."

"Why will it be different?"

How much did he dare tell her, this woman who blamed him for her life? How far could he trust her, this woman whom he had treated so long with such loveless scorn?

"What has happened to make it different?"

"It is a secret. It is a secret no one but Mbemba must ever hear."

She waited for him to go on, her toothless mouth drawn into a hard line, her leathery face set as hard as a nut.

"You know the great-winged boat that brought me here? . . ."

She nodded.

"It has come again. It has come to take me home to my land on the other shore of the sea. And once I am gone, so then you too will be free to go to your home."

She didn't say anything to this.

"But you know what Mpanzu would do if he hears of it. You know what his mother, the Mbanda Vunda, and what the Nganga-Kongo would do if they hear of it."

She nodded again.

"Then you know why it is a secret."

"Yes."

"So? Will you help me get to Mbanza Kongo to speak to Mbemba?"

"When do you wish to go?"

"Now. This very night."

She asked him nothing more. She got up, put on her kanga and fetched a basket of things for the journey.

They crossed the river to the mainland in his fishing canoe. He sank the canoe with stones in a marshy backwater of the river's south bank where he hoped the Soyo boys from Mpinda would not find it and he would, when they returned this way, and set off for Mbanza Kongo not by the royal road east of Mpinda—that would be madness—but up through the forest of the Mbata from the ocean coast on the west.

He kept a sharp watch on her. She followed him compliantly enough but he did not wholly trust her. He knew only too well her feelings for him. But it wasn't so much during the journey to Mbanza Kongo that he had to worry that she might betray him. During the journey, she was in as much danger as he. She had no more right than he to leave the island of their exile and, if caught, would suffer for it as much as he. But once in Mbanza Kongo, she would be among her own people and she would have less to fear. And therein lay his dilemma. For it was precisely because she would be among her own people in Mbanza Kongo that he needed her—his only hope of getting word to Mbemba was with the help of her people—but it was also precisely then, when she would be among her own people, that she would have the best chance to betray him.

"Ssh."

"What is it?"

"Hunters pass. Ssh."

He ducked back into the hut. She remained standing outside holding a basket of mushrooms on her hip. Hiding behind her in the hut, he watched as the hunters walked by in single file along a game trail not a hundred feet away in the woods. They had been to an elephant trap somewhere near and had had success. Two of them carried the great, yellowed tusks of a full-grown bull, the others huge chunks of bloody meat, swarming with flies. They glanced at her as they passed. They thought nothing of seeing a woman gathering mushrooms in these woods a few leagues to the southwest of Mbanza Kongo, and passed on.

"Will he come?" Gil asked when they were gone.

"No. He will send for you."

"Send for me? To the royal district?"

"Yes."

"No, that is too dangerous. Why can't he just come here? It would be safer."

"I don't know. I wasn't told."

"What were you told? Put the basket down and tell me everything you were told."

They had come to Mbanza Kongo from the west, climbing up to the plateau of the royal mountain through the abandoned iron-ore quarries in its escarpment, and had made camp here in the same woods where he had been left to die so many years before. The house on the quay of the Luezi River, where he had stayed while waiting for Mbemba to take him to the ManiKongo ten years before, where Nimi had first come to him, the house of her sisters and mother and aunt and the baby and two little boys (though they wouldn't be babies and little boys anymore and the mother and aunt might be dead), that house was about four leagues northeast of this campsite. And as soon as they had finished making camp and building the small hut here, she had gone there. That was five days ago and he had awaited her return with much apprehension.

He trusted her considerably more now than at the outset. He had reason to. During their journey through the forest of the Mbata and across the open, hilly grasslands of the Nsundi, she had proved a resourceful accomplice. She had done the hunting as well as the foraging. She had found the hiding places. She was the one who had stolen the canoe in which they had crossed the Lelunda River at the base of the escarpment and then had had the presence of mind to float it far downstream so they'd be harder to follow when it was discovered missing. And she was the one who had remembered the way up though the old iron-ore quarries to these woods on the plateau. She understood both the peril and the promise in what she was doing and seemed willing to risk the one for the other. Even so, he had awaited her return from the house of her family these five days with growing apprehension.

Anything could have gone wrong. Even if she hadn't betrayed him, someone might have betrayed her. Since she herself could not cross the bridges over the Luezi to the royal district nor pass on her own through the palisades of the royal enclosure to get word to Mbemba, she had to find someone who could and, by that alone, might arouse suspicion. Her plan was to enlist the help of her older sister. When last she had seen her, ten years before, that sister was a wife of a warrior in Mbemba's bodyguard. But the sister might no longer be the warrior's wife or the warrior might no longer be a member of the prince's bodyguard or, even if nothing had changed in either respect, neither might agree to get involved in such a treasonous enterprise. The other possibility was the aunt. Actually, the house belonged to the aunt, and the reason it had been chosen originally as the place for Gil to wait when Mbemba first brought him to Mbanza Kongo was that the aunt was a serving woman in the house of Mbemba's mother, the Mbanda Lwa. But whether the aunt was still alive, whether she still served the second queen and whether she'd risk her neck for her niece's sake if she were still both, there was no way of knowing after so many years.

"I was told he would send for you."

"Who told you? Your sister?"

"No, my aunt."

"She went to Mbemba?"

"No, she went to the Mbanda Lwa."

"Oh, no."

"What?"

"I am not sure that was wise. What did she say to the Mbanda Lwa?"

"That you wished to speak to Mbemba."

"Only that? She did not say anything about the great-winged boat?"

"She does not know anything about the great-winged boat. I did not tell her anything about it. I did not tell anyone. You said it is a secret that only Mbemba can know."

"That's right. You did right. And then? Go on. What did the Mbanda Lwa say when your aunt told her I wish to speak to Mbemba?"

"That Mbemba would send for you."

"The Mbanda Lwa said that? Not Mbemba?"

"My aunt did not speak to Mbemba. She only spoke to the Mbanda Lwa."

Gil looked out the low entryway of the hut. The moon, glowing fuzzily behind the overcast, was nearly full. The *Beatriz* would wait for him until it was new again. "When was this?" he asked after a moment.

"Three days past."

"Already three days past and Mbemba still has not sent for me?"

"He will not send for you here."

"No?"

"He does not know you are here. He does not know where you are. No one does. This too I have kept secret."

"You watch over me well, Nimi."

"He will send for you at the house of my family. My aunt told the Mbanda Lwa to have him send for you there. I will be there. If those who are sent for you are truly from Mbemba, I will bring them here. If not . . ." Her voice trailed off.

"You also doubt the Mbanda Lwa?"

She shrugged. "I will return to the house of my family now."

"I will go with you."

"No, you will not be safe there. In this, I also doubt my family," she said and ducked out of the hut and slipped off into the misty moonlight of the woods.

He watched her go. Aye, he trusted her but he knew that, if the Mbanda Lwa betrayed them, she could no more protect him than she could protect herself. No matter what her vow or how great her courage, she would be forced to reveal his hiding place. And he wanted to be prepared for that. So he gave her a few minutes' head start and then followed her.

The moon was down when they reached the outskirts of the city, where the woods ended and the cultivated fields and the first houses began, and he hurried to close the distance between them as they passed through a field of head-high grain, afraid of losing sight of her in the moonless dark. But then she made straight for the Luezi River. He couldn't follow her there. There were warriors on the quay, guarding the bridges that crossed the river to the royal district. He let her go and retreated into the woods to consider the situation.

What he had hoped to accomplish by following her to her house was to get a good look at whoever was sent for him there, and get that look before she brought them to the camp in the woods, willingly or by force, so he would have time to make his escape if he saw that they hadn't been sent by Mbemba. Well, maybe he didn't actually have to be at her house to get that look. Chances were that, having gone this way, she would return this way, so maybe he could get that look in enough time if he just waited for her here.

And he did. It was only a few hours later when they appeared, Nimi in the lead, two men walking side by side a step behind her. They could be warriors, tall, slim, young, but they didn't seem armed. One carried a long pole of the sort used for poling fishing canoes in shallow water; the other had a cloth of beaten bark draped over his shoulders that might be a fishing seine. Were they fishermen then? Nimi carried her basket on her head as before.

She walked quickly, the two youths hurrying to keep up. Gil took this as a good sign. She seemed eager to get to the camp in the woods; she didn't appear to be going there against her will. And the fact that she had returned so soon also was a good sign. If these men weren't from Mbemba, it surely would have taken them longer than this to force her to lead them to the hiding place.

He circled through the trees, keeping a sharp watch on them. The men were wearing pale green kangas bordered in red. They must be Mbemba's warriors, although they looked surprisingly young. He lost sight of them for a few minutes when they entered the field of head-high millet and sorghum grass. Where they emerged into view again, the trees of the woods began.

Nimi stopped there and looked back, obviously checking to see if they were being followed. The two youths also looked back. Nimi said something to them. They listened attentively, as if she were their mother. She pointed in one direction, then another. They looked where she pointed. Then the one with the long pole started into the woods on his own. Nimi let him get some distance ahead, then sent the one with the fishing seine after him. Another good sign. They would never walk off and leave her if they were taking her by force.

"Nimi."

She jumped.

"Here."

"Gil Eenezh?"

"Yes."

"You frightened me," she said as he grasped her arm and pulled her back into the trees.

"Is it all right?"

"I think so."

"They come from Mbemba?"

"That is what they say. They wear the colors of his household."

"But you are not sure? You do not recognize them?"

"How would I recognize them? They are boys. They were but little children when I was sent away with you. They say they are my cousins."

"Your cousins?"

"Do you remember the two little boys who were in the house of my aunt when you stayed there? That is who they say they are. They say they were sent by Mbemba because he believed you would recognize them from before and therefore trust them."

"Wasn't your aunt at her house to say whether they were her sons?"

"No."

"Where was she?"

"With the Mbanda Lwa."

Gil peered through the trees after the two youths. The first one, with the pole, had already disappeared into the darkness of the woods. The other, with the cloth draped over his shoulders, kept glancing back. "Where have you sent them?"

"To the clearing at the head of the trail. I told them to go there and wait for me. I wanted to see if they would obey me."

"They seem to."

"Yes. I think they are who they say they are. I would not have brought them to you if I did not think so."

"I know that, Nimi," Gil said and, pulling his knife out of its scabbard, stepped out of the trees. *"Mbakala,"* he called softly. "Boy."

The youth with the cloth, glancing back anyway, saw him right away and froze in his tracks. Gil went up to him fast, holding the knife low and, when he reached him, immediately slammed him in the chest with the flat of his hand. It was a hard blow but, more to the point, so unexpected that the youth was knocked flat on his back. Gil was on him in an instant.

"Gil Eenezh," Nimi cried out. "What do you do?"

"Get his brother, Nimi. Bring him back here," Gil said, dropping one knee square in the middle of the youth's chest and laying the knife blade across his throat. "Speak the truth, *mbakala.* Speak only the truth if you value your life."

"I will, Gil Eenezh."

"Are you from the household of the MtuKongo, Mbemba a Nzinga?"

"I am, Gil Eenezh."

He was terrified, his eyes bright with fear, sweat pouring down his face. Gil could well imagine what the poor devil was thinking: The evil white prince who had fallen from the sky, the terrible creature of the sorcerer's tales, had got hold of him and would now steal his soul. Gil looked up and saw Nimi bringing back the other youth. He too stared at Gil as if being brought face to face with the demon of all his worst nightmares.

"Have you ever seen me before, boy?" Gil snapped at him.

"I have, Gil Eenezh."

"What was I wearing when you saw me before?"

"Iron and steel," the youth replied quickly. "A headdress of iron, a tunic of steel."

Gil eased off the chest of the fallen youth and sat back on his heels. It was possible they were who they said. It even made a certain sly sense to have sent them. Mpanzu would not have known to send them, nor the Mbanda Vunda or the NgangaKongo. "You have come to take me to the royal district?"

"We have, Gil Eenezh."

"How do you propose to do it?"

"They will carry you there as a corpse," Nimi said.

She took the long pole from the one youth, picked up the cloth of beaten bark the other had brought. The cloth was to be the bier. Gil was to be sewn into it—Nimi had the needle and thread in her basket—and then he would be hung, by the head and feet, from the pole, and the two youths would carry the pole across the Luezi.

"No one will interfere," she said. "No one interferes with the dead of the household of a prince."

"And you?"

"I will wait for you at our camp in the woods."

"How long will you wait?"

"Until you come and set me free."

IV

MY LADY . . ."

"You have grown into a strong man from the boy I once saw, Gil Eenezh. Come closer. Let me look at you."

"My lady, with respect, I was told I would be brought to the MtuKongo, your son, Mbemba a Nzinga, not to you, the Mbanda Lwa."

"And you shall, Gil Eenezh, you shall."

"When?"

"As soon as he returns."

"He is not here? He does not know I have come to Mbanza Kongo to speak to him?"

"No, but he returns soon and will be told as soon as he returns."

"Then it was you who sent those boys to me, and sent them falsely, giving them Mbemba's colors to wear."

"A small deception, forgive me, but when my serving woman told me you were in Mbanza Kongo I thought it best you await Mbemba's return here with me, where you are in less danger, than in the woods, where you could be discovered at any moment."

He did not believe this, any of it—neither that she tricked him into coming to her in order to protect him nor that Mbemba was not in Mbanza Kongo—but he only said, "It was kind of you to be concerned for my safety, my lady."

"Yes, it *was* kind of me, so there is no need for you to look so anxious. No harm will come to you here. You and I, we have the same enemies, Gil Eenezh. Sit down."

He sat down, cross-legged, on the pile of mats she indicated, opposite the pile of mats she sat on, her heels tucked under her, lounging against cushions at her back. She was, of course, ten years older than when he last saw her, thicker in the waist, flabbier in the bosom, fleshier under her chin, but still a striking woman with her small-featured face and honey-dark complexion, her long-lashed, large eyes studying him with keen intelligence. She wore three skirts, the first to her ankles, the next to her knees, the topmost a mere apron, each in a different shade of velvety brown. Her head was wrapped in a turban of the lightest shade of that brown; her loose blouse, beaded with cowries, was of the darkest shade. Although this certainly wasn't her most regal attire, it was far grander than what she had worn the last time she had received him in this room.

It was the same room, the hideaway room at the back of her palace, the room of her schemes and conspiracies, and just as empty now as it had been then. The two youths who had brought him here in their false colors had departed in haste as soon as they had cut the stitches of the bark cloth into which Nimi had sewn him. The only other person present was an old serving woman standing in the shadows beyond the light of a single palm-oil lamp. Was she Nimi's aunt, the mother of the two youths who had brought him here? If so, his presence in Mbanza Kongo might still be known only to a very few.

"I am glad you have come, Gil Eenezh. You have done a very stupid thing in coming but, even so, it pleases me."

"Why, my lady?"

"Because I have often wondered what the men of your people look like. I did not see them when they were here. I saw only you and you were then only a boy. Now I see you as a man. I was told of the hair your men grow on their faces and I thought, oh, how very ugly that must be. But now I see it on your face and do not find it so very ugly." She leaned forward a bit and delicately brushed his beard with the back of her hand. "No, it is not so very ugly. It is as soft and yellow as the lion's mane." She laughed lightly saying that and leaned back against her cushions. "Yes, I am pleased you have come, Gil Eenezh, so that at last I can see for myself what a man looks like with hair on his face. But that is not why you have come, to show me that."

"No, my lady."

"No, you have come to speak to my son, but to speak to him about what? It must be a matter of great importance that you have risked your life to do so."

"It is."

"What is it, I wonder?"

He cocked his head noncommittally.

"You will not say? No, of course not. I did not expect you would when I sent for you. I knew I would have to guess it for myself."

There was a seductiveness about her, the way she leaned forward to touch him, the way she leaned back languorously against her cushions, her feet tucked girlishly under her, the way she now laughed at him teasingly with her eyes. But there was a cunning in her seductiveness. She wanted to find out why he had come to Mbanza Kongo in order to see if it might be of any use to the schemes and conspiracies that endlessly brewed in her restless soul.

"Yes, I knew I would have to guess it for myself. Shall I?"

"As you wish."

"The white men have come again from their land on the other shore of the sea."

Gil tried not to show his shock when she said this, but his heart skipped a beat. How could she know? Nimi had sworn no one had been told. She couldn't know. She could only be guessing. But it was a cunning woman's guess.

"Have I guessed correctly? Is that why you have come to Mbanza Kongo at the risk of your life? To tell Mbemba that the white men have come again? This too would please me, if it were so."

"So you would see the hair *they* have grown on *their* faces?"

"That," she replied, again laughing lightly, "and also to learn how to use their magic."

"To learn how to use their magic? You still think of that? After all this time?"

"Why not? It is strong magic, is it not? Did you not once tell me it is a stronger magic than the magic of the NsakuSoyo, than that of even the NgangaKongo?"

"I did, my lady, but I did not think you believed me since I was unable to show you how to make use of it."

"But how could you show me? Did you not also tell me that only a priest of your people could show me? And you are not a priest of your people, Gil Eenezh."

"No, I am not a priest of my people, my lady."

"So I have often thought that, if the white men were ever to come again, a priest might come with them who could show me how to use this strong magic."

"For Mbemba's sake? To use to push him ahead of Mpanzu?"

Again she laughed that throaty, trilling laugh and said, "Yes, for Mbemba's sake. To use to push him ahead of Mpanzu."

"And would that also please Mbemba?"

"Mbemba never speaks of the white men anymore, and also forbids me ever to speak of them. He is afraid of the trouble it could cause after his father, the ManiKongo, dies."

"But you are not afraid."

"No, I am not afraid."

"I see you are not. I see you are a woman not easily made afraid. But even so, I am surprised you still have the white men's magic in your mind after all this time. I am surprised you have not long before this forgotten about it."

"But how could I have forgotten about it when I have kept close to me a remembrance of it, the gift I arranged to have you leave me before you were sent away?"

"What gift do you speak of, my lady? The breviary?"

"The breviary?"

"The writing."

"No, I do not speak of the writing. That gift you left with Mbemba."

"What gift then?"

"You do not know?"

"No."

"No, of course you do not know. How could you know? Who was there to tell you? Only Mbemba and he would never tell you."

"Tell me what?"

"*Mchento.*" She signaled to the serving woman standing in the shadows. "Bring them to us, *mchento.* They wait outside."

"Who waits outside?" Gil sprang to his feet. "Who does she bring to us?"

"Why do you worry yourself so? Have I not said, we have the same enemies, you and I? You have nothing to fear from me, Gil Eenezh. Sit down."

But he remained standing. And, after a few moments, the serving woman returned with two others.

"Nimi," the Mbanda Lwa said.

Nimi? Had she also tricked Nimi into coming here from the camp in the woods?

"Come to us, Nimi."

But it wasn't Nimi who stepped out of the shadows into the lamplight. It wasn't an old woman, a haggard woman, a woman made old before her time. It was a young woman, a beautiful woman, a woman to stop the breath in a man so many years without a woman: long in the legs, narrow at the waist, full in the bosom and hips, wide at the shoulder, wrapped tightly in a kanga of pale green, bordered in red, a single strand of river pearls around her slender neck. Lord Jesus, of course, she was the other Nimi, the NtinuKongo, the princess of whom he made a fairy tale throughout his shipwreck years. How old was she now, twenty-three, twenty-four? A woman at the moment of her fullest flowering, in her ripest, most desirable bloom. Her skin was as smooth and clear as dark amber, her hair close-cropped but no longer braided like a girl's, her lips puffed and pouted as if stung by bees, her cheekbones high and planed, slanting her lustrous brown eyes, her jaw as firm as if carved from dark wood, her flat nostrils flared. She looked at Gil with a quiet gravity, showing no trace of the lively, mischievous girl she once had been. But he could see her pulse beating fast in the hollow of her throat beneath her pearls. His heart suddenly was also beating fast.

"Gil Eenezh."

"Nimi a Nzinga."

"Do you recognize me, Gil Eenezh?"

"How could I? You were but a child when last I saw you."

"But you remember me."

"Of course I remember you. How beautiful you have become."

She smiled slightly but it was a joyless smile.

"And do you recognize me?"

"No. You did not have hair on your face when last I saw you."

"But you remember me."

"How could I not remember you? Are you not the father of my son?"

So enthralled had he been by the sight of this comely young princess that he hadn't taken notice of the other person who had come into the room with the old serving woman: a small boy, still standing in the shadows, holding the old serving woman's hand. Now Nimi turned to him and took his hand from the old serving woman's and brought him into the lamplight and kneeled beside him, putting an arm around his shoulders.

Ten years old . . . no, ten years minus the nine months she had carried him after that night at the edge of the forest in the rain. Will he be white? she had asked then. He wasn't white. His skin was as dark as the skin of her arm around his shoulders. But his hair was long and soft and tawny blond and his eyes were blue.

"The gift my mother arranged to have you leave behind when you were sent away," Nimi said, hugging the boy close. "The magical life she had you make inside of me as a remembrance of the magic of your people on the other shore of the sea. Your son, Gil Eenezh."

Gil also got down on his knees and looked into the boy's light blue eyes, his own eyes. From what little he knew of little boys, this little boy, wearing only a breechclout, seemed strong and healthy and finely formed but, like his mother, unnaturally grave. "What is your name, *mbakala?*"

The boy nestled deeper into his mother's arm, half-turning away from the big hairy white man kneeling in front of him, knitting his brows.

"Kimpasi," his mother answered for him.

"Does he know who I am?"

"He does."

"Come to me, Kimpasi."

"Go to your father, *mbakala.*"

She removed her arm from the boy's shoulder and he stepped forward without further prodding, frowning seriously. Gil grasped his shoulders in the way the men of the Kongo did in greeting one another and held him at arm's length, studying the wonderful confusion of this little *mestiço*'s light and dark coloring, soft and sharp features, earnest and innocent expression, and was as wonderfully confused himself. A son, a son by this beautiful Negro princess, a son of the Kongo and Portugal, his son. What did it mean? Suddenly, everything seemed changed by it. Suddenly, the long loneliness of his exile no longer seemed quite so empty nor the lost years of his life quite so wasted. He had a son. He pulled the boy into his arms, tears glazing his eyes, and realized that the boy had also begun to quietly cry.

"He should never have been born."

"Oh, no, Nimi, do not say that. How can you say that?"

"Because he suffers so. He suffers the sins of his father."

"What do you mean?"

"Like you, Gil Eenezh, he is considered an evil in this land and must live his life in exile, hated and feared by all around him.

"Oh, *mbakala,* poor *mbakala.*"

The boy twisted out of Gil's embrace and returned to his mother's, rubbing his eyes with clenched fists.

"And you, Nimi? Is it the same for you, his mother?"

"I too am hidden away in this house, Gil Eenezh, my birthright taken from me, and live a life of disgrace for having lain with the evil white prince who fell from the sky, for having borne his evil son."

"I am sorry, Nimi. I am so very sorry. Do you blame me for it?"

"No, I blame my mother who sent me to you when I was a stupid child and could not know what my fate would be."

Gil looked at the Mbanda Lwa. The woman seemed unperturbed; she must have heard this accusation countless times.

"Have you come to take us away from our disgrace and suffering, Gil Eenezh? I have often dreamed you would come one day and take us away."

"Where would he take you, foolish girl?" the Mbanda Lwa interjected. "To his island in *nzere?* Do you suppose your life would be any better there? Do you suppose your suffering would be any less?"

Nimi didn't answer. Enfolding her son in her arms, she rested her cheek against his long, soft hair and tears also sprang into her eyes. How hard it must have been for her who, as a girl, had so often proudly proclaimed her title as NtinuKongo and had so gleefully delighted in its privileges to have grown to womanhood an outcast in the kingdom where she once had reigned.

"No, you and Kimpasi will remain here with me until Gil Eenezh has a better place to take you."

"Will that ever be?"

"It will be when the white men come again."

"But will they ever come again?"

"They came once. They will come again." The Mbanda Lwa turned to Gil. "Perhaps they already have."

Gil looked away from her.

"Have they, Gil Eenezh? Have they come again?"

Gil stood up. "Where is Mbemba, my lady? I am here to speak with him."

"Yes, you are here to speak with him. *Mchento,* send for the MtuKongo. Tell him Gil Eenezh is here to speak with him. Tell him Gil Eenezh has brought him remarkable news."

"No."

"You *must* go to them, Mbemba. I will go with you. We must not make the same error twice. There will not be a third time."

"Not another word, Mother. I will not listen to another word about this from you. You will keep yourself out of it entirely. I will only speak with Gil Eenezh about this."

"Their magic is strong, my son. Their magic is wonderful. You have known that since you were a boy. You were the first to know it. We must not let the chance to acquire it slip through our fingers a second time."

"Do you not hear me? You have nothing to say in this. Nothing. I know you. You wish only to turn it into another of your intrigues."

Gil had never seen Mbemba like this. His anger was enormous, directed as much at his mother for her meddling as at Gil for having violated his exile and come to Mbanza Kongo. The scar across his cheek flared with his anger. But there was more to it than anger. The news Gil had brought had utterly unnerved him. His fascination with the white men, his curiosity about their world beyond the farthest horizons, his desire to know it for its own sake as well as for its magic, which had dulled and died in him in the course of all these years, had been resurrected by Gil's news. And he didn't want it to be. It tore at him. It disrupted his life. It disordered his sense of duty. It confused him about where his loyalties lay.

"Who knows about this?" he asked.

"Only those in this room," the Mbanda Lwa answered, not so easily shut up.

"And my serving woman," Gil added.

"Where is she?"

"At a camp in the woods to the south of the city."

"I ask this of Gil Eenezh, Mother. Will you allow him just once to answer for himself."

"Very well, but you waste precious time with these useless questions."

"I will be the judge of that. I will be the judge of everything that is done in this matter."

"There is no need to worry about the woman, Mbemba. She will not speak of it to anyone. She understands it must be kept secret."

"So no one else knows? Only we know?"

"Yes."

"*Keba.* Now tell me, how many have come this time?"

"As before. A single ship, the captain-general and his crew."

"Deego Cum?"

"No, another captain-general this time."

"And also a priest," the Mbanda Lwa put in.

"Yes, and also a priest."

"How many is that?"

"Forty seamen. Twenty soldiers. The priest and the ship's officers. Seventy men, no more."

Mbemba looked around the room, the confusion and indecision in his expression painful to see. They were all standing about in postures of extreme agitation, casting shadows of angular excitement in the flickering lamplight, except the boy Kimpasi. He had fallen asleep on the Mbanda Lwa's cushions, his long blond hair fallen across his pretty face.

"What is he doing here?" Mbemba suddenly snapped at Nimi. "Take him to his room." His anger included Nimi and the boy, perhaps especially Nimi and the boy. That Gil now knew what he had kept

from him so long upset his sense of the orderly, settled course his life
had taken in the years since the white men departed as much as did
the news of their return. "He shouldn't be here. It is late. Why is he
here anyway?"

"Why else than to meet his father," Nimi snapped back.

"Whose idea was that?"

"It was mine," the Mbanda Lwa said.

"No, it was mine," Nimi interrupted tartly. "When I learned that
Gil Eenezh had come to Mbanza Kongo, I decided it was time he saw
the son he had fathered and I saw again the father of the son I bore.
It has been ten years, Mbemba. Do you not think that is time
enough?"

"*Keba.* You have seen him and he has seen the boy. Now take
the boy away. This does not concern you."

"How does it not concern me? What else is there to concern
me? I have lived my life a despised woman just because of this. I have
had no other life than that of the mother of the son of the white man
who fell from the sky. And now white men have fallen from the sky
again. And you say it does not concern me. Of course it concerns me.
And it also concerns the boy."

Her spirited impudence as a girl had been transmuted, by her
years of isolation and disgrace, into a somber, steely grit, and she was
as little afraid of her brother now as she had ever been. And her
brother, perhaps affected by her long years of unhappiness, could no
more resist her now than he ever could. He shook his head in exasperation and turned back to Gil.

"Where are they now?" he asked.

"Aboard their ship, the *Beatriz,* in a well-hidden cove north of
nzere. I told them to remain their while I came here to see if permission would be granted for them to enter the kingdom."

"Go back and tell them permission will be granted," the Mbanda
Lwa broke in again.

"How many times must I tell you to keep yourself out of this? Of
course permission will not be granted. Who will grant it?"

"Your father, Nzinga a Nkuwu, the ManiKongo. He will grant it."

"You see, it is just as I say. You should keep yourself out of this.
You only speak foolishness when you do not. My father will not grant

them permission. He is old and blind and will not rule on this at all. He will allow Mpanzu to rule on this, and the Mbanda Vunda and the NgangaKongo, as he did before. And they will rule against the white men, as they did before."

"We must not allow that. We must go to him and convince him to welcome the white men. We should have done it when the white men first came. You were still a boy but I should have done it. And I will do it now, even if you will not. I will not wait another ten years for the white men to come again, even if you will."

"You will do nothing of the sort. I forbid you to do anything at all." Mbemba fingered the inflamed scar on his cheek for a moment, then added in a quieter, more thoughtful tone, "And, besides, we could never convince him to overrule Mpanzu, his appointed heir, or the Mbanda Vunda, his first queen, or Lukeni a Wene, the high priest of his kingdom. We'd be the worst kinds of fools to think we could ever convince him to rule against the natural order of his realm."

"We could, Mbemba. I know we could."

"No, Mother, we could not. But even if we could, I would not wish to."

"What?"

"He is my father. He is the king. Yes, the white men's magic is wonderful, but my allegiance is to my father, the king, and to the natural order of his realm. I will do nothing in violation of that." Mbemba said this with a measure of regret—clearly, the appeal of that wider world that the Portuguese symbolized for him was still alive in his heart—but he was a faithful son, a loyal prince, and knew where his duty lay. "Tell them that, Gil. Go back to the white men and tell them they are no more welcome now than they were before."

"I have already told them that."

"And?"

"They do not listen to me, Mbemba. They have come this time to stay, as they did not before, and will not depart merely because I tell them they are not welcome. They must be shown they are not welcome."

"How?"

"I warned them that, if they sailed into *nzere,* an army of ten thousand would oppose them."

"You want a war with them, Gil? You cannot want a war with them. They are your own people."

"No, I do not want a war with them."

"They would be destroyed in a war."

"I know that. But I don't think there need be a war. They are not madmen, Mbemba. If, when they sailed into *nzere,* they found an army of ten thousand waiting to oppose them, they would see that what I say is so and would depart without a war."

"And you would depart with them?"

"It is my hope. It is my plan."

"Yes, at last you would be able to fly away home as you have always hoped and planned."

"And take us with you."

This was Nimi. Gil turned to her. She had sat down beside Kimpasi and taken his head into her lap. And Gil was struck anew by how this mother and son made up for all the wasted years of his manhood, how they filled the void of all the lost years of his life. They were his family. He had no other. No one awaited his return in Portugal. No one there even knew he was alive.

"You must not leave us behind now that you have a better place to take us, Gil Eenezh. You must help us escape from our exile as you escape from yours."

"Would your brother and mother allow it?"

"It is not for them to allow. We will go with you whether they allow it or not."

"Oh, I allow it, girl," the Mbanda Lwa said. "Go with him. Let at least one of our house acquire the white men's magic."

Gil looked at Mbemba.

"She has suffered much," Mbemba said. "They both have. Take them with you if you think you can give them a better life than this."

"Any life will be better than this," Nimi said. "Kimpasi, wake up. We are going on a journey, *mbakala,* a wonderful journey, to the land on the other shore of the sea." She pulled the boy to his feet and hurried out of the room.

"Come, Gil," Mbemba said once Nimi and Kimpasi were gone.

"Where do you go?" the Mbanda Lwa asked.

"To show the white men they are not welcome here."

"Do not do this. Please, my son. Go to them first before you decide what to do."

"I do not have to go to them first to decide what to do. My allegiance is not first to them."

"Then I will go to them."

"I warn you, Mother. I warn you for the last time. You will not go to them. You will not go anywhere. You will stay here and, once and for all, put your foolish schemes aside."

It was late morning when Gil and Mbemba stepped onto the front veranda of the Mbanda Lwa's palace, a gloomy gray morning with a damp fog swirling in the wind. A bodyguard of Mbemba's warriors in their pale green kangas bordered in red waited on the veranda. They looked at Gil in surprise but said nothing. Warriors of the Mbanda Lwa also were on the veranda and, down from the veranda, under the acacia and flowering jacaranda that lined the stone-tiled streets of this innermost courtyard of the royal district, were warriors of the ManiKongo in their crimson kangas embroidered with yellow sunbursts, and of Mpanzu in their sky-blue kangas decorated with white lightning bolts. They too were astonished to see the white men here in the very heart of the kingdom from which he had been banished but also made no move against him. He was safe with Mbemba.

"Go to the white men," Mbemba said, "and tell them once again that they are not welcome here. Then I will go to them with an army of ten thousand, as you suggest, to show them that what you say is so."

"Keba."

"No one will know of this. Not my father. Not my brother. Not his mother. Not the NgangaKongo. For if they knew, the army *they* would send against the white men would not just be for show. And the white men would be killed and their ship destroyed and you would not be able to fly away with my sister and your son."

"I thank you for this, Mbemba."

"You know what I think of your people, Gil. You know I do not think they bring evil. You know I think they bring good. You know I would welcome them if I were king."

"Yes, I know."

"So I do not want them destroyed, not only for your sake and

Nimi's and Kimpasi's, but also because I do not want to make enemies of them. For who can say, they may come again in another time, in a time when they will be welcome."

"But not in ou   me, Mbemba, not in yours and mine. For you never will be king."

"No, not in our time, Gil, for I never will be king."

V

Thunder rumbled faintly in the distance; there was a pale flash of sheet lightning; a misty drizzle blew in from the sea and racing in the ragged clouds of the midnight sky was a crescent moon. In less than a week, the moon would again be new and, if Gil hadn't returned by then, the *Beatriz* would weigh anchor and make sail for the Zaire. He had to hurry; he wanted to detain the ship long enough so that Mbemba's army of ten thousand would be waiting in the mouth of the Zaire when she did.

His fishing canoe was undisturbed. No one had found it sunken in the marshy backwater of the Zaire's south bank downriver from Mpinda where he had left it nearly six weeks before. He could make out its dark outline just below the river's murky surface. The trouble, though, was that a crocodile had chosen it as a convenient place to lie in wait for prey. Gil flung a rock at the creature but didn't wait to see what effect that had. He knew it wouldn't have any effect—it was just an expression of his annoyance—and he went back into the bushes where he had hidden the canoe's paddles. He had his knife but didn't want to waste time wrestling and killing a crocodile. So, with one of the paddles, he waded into the river knee-deep, circled around so as to come at the crocodile head-on and gave it a terrific whack on the snout.

With lightning reflex, the reptile thrashed, its wicked tail slashing through the water like a running shark. But Gil was ready for that. He

neatly leaped out of the way, and delivered another resounding crack
to its head and eyes with the paddle. Again the dangerous tail
slashed, but this time the irritated creature also snapped, scissoring
open its murderous jaw. And that was what Gil was waiting for. He
jammed the paddle down the crocodile's gullet, lodging it between
the terrible rows of teeth, then let go and back-paddled hastily out
into the river. And that pretty much was that. In time, the crocodile
would manage to work the paddle out but, vulnerable now, it wasn't
going to undertake the task here, where Gil could further torment it.
It slithered off the canoe, submerged and swam downriver. When it
crawled up on the muddy bank a few hundred yards away and began
slamming the paddle petulantly against the trunk of a mangrove, Gil
dove to the sunken canoe and began unloading the stones from it.
Then, while the princess Nimi and the serving woman Nimi and the
boy Kimpasi watched from the water's edge, he hauled the canoe up
on shore and dumped the water from it.

"Where is she, Gil Eenezh?" the princess Nimi asked.

"Who?"

"The *Beatriz*. I do not see her."

"She waits for us farther up the coast where Mpanzu and the
others cannot find her," Gil said as he refloated the canoe.

"Who is she, the *Beatriz?*" Kimpasi asked.

"The great bird-winged boat I have been telling you about,
mbakala," Nimi said. "We go to her now and will fly away with her
and it will be just like flying on the wings of a great bird. You will
see."

"Fly away with her to the land on the other shore of the sea?"

"You know of the land on the other shore of the sea, Kimpasi?"
Gil asked. "Your mother has told you of it?"

"No, my great-mother, the Mbanda Lwa. She has told me of it
many times."

Of course, the Mbanda Lwa. She would have told him of it repeatedly, endlessly. She would have filled the boy's head with fanciful
tales of a magical land on the other shore of the sea, wanting him to
know who he was, wanting him to believe he was exceptional.

"Why do we fly away there?"

"Because it is a better place for us than here, *mbakala*," Nimi said and got down on her knees beside the boy. "We will not be out-casts there. We will not be treated like demons there."

The boy knitted his brow in that precociously serious way he had.

"You will be happy there, Kimpasi, I promise you," Nimi went on, putting an arm around his waist. "You will not always be alone there as you are here. You will have friends to play with there. No one will tease you or chase you or run away from you because all the lit-tle boys there have eyes as blue as yours and hair as yellow. Look at your father. Look at his eyes and hair. Everyone in his land on the other shore of the sea has eyes and hair like that. Isn't that so, Gil Eenezh?"

Gil hesitated. Was there any point complicating matters trying to explain the many races of Portugal or the reception a little *mestiço* boy could expect from the Portuguese? No, there was no point, at least not yet. So he just nodded.

"There, *mbakala,* you see."

The boy continued frowning with an uncertain disquiet. Unlike his mother, he was not leaving the only home he had ever known, no matter how much he had suffered there, with careless abandon.

"You don't have to decide this now, Kimpasi," Gil said to him. "You can decide it later. There is time."

"Why is there time?" Nimi asked.

"Because we cannot go to the *Beatriz* in this little canoe. We must first go to my island in the river to fetch a boat I have built that can take us out on the ocean. And also we must wait for daylight."

"It is settled then, *mbakala.* First we will go to Gil Eenezh's is-land for his other boat. Then we will wait for daylight. And then you will decide if you want to fly away on the wings of the *Beatriz* to a land where you can be happy, where we both can be happy at last."

Gil steadied the canoe as Nimi lifted the boy into it. Then he reached out his hand to the other Nimi, his serving woman. She grasped it but didn't get into the canoe.

"It is time for us to say farewell, Gil Eenezh," she said. "You return now to your home on the other shore of the sea and I return to mine in Mbanza Kongo. After all these years, we are finally free of each other, as you promised we would be."

"Yes, that is what I promised you would be." Gil, however, kept
hold of her hand, not quite ready to let her go. "You have been good
to me all these years, *mchento*," he said after a long moment, "and I
want to thank you for it."

The woman smiled her toothless smile, her leathery face creasing into a thousand wrinkles.

"I am sorry for the terrible life I brought on you and ask you to
forgive me for it."

"I forgive you for it."

He released her hand and gently pushed her away. "Go then,
mchento. Go to your home. Go with God."

"And you also, Gil Eenezh. *Dominus vobiscum.*"

She said this so softly that, by the time he realized what she had
said and could express his surprise at her use of the Latin—she had
been paying closer attention all these years than he had thought—
she had vanished into the mangroves and palms that forested the
riverbank. He looked after her for a moment, then shoved the canoe
off into the river and jumped in, kneeling in the stern.

"Will you be sorry she is gone?" the princess Nimi asked, standing in the prow with Kimpasi. "Will you be sorry you will now only
have me?"

Gil grinned at this beautiful young woman and said, "No, Nimi, I
will not be sorry." He picked up his other paddle and dipped it into
the river. "Come here and sit with me. You too, Kimpasi. Come and sit
with your father."

Nimi sat down in front of him, cross-legged, facing forward, but
the boy shook his head and remained standing in the prow looking
out across the river he had never seen before, looking toward a future none of them could imagine. The distant rumbles of thunder, the
faint flashes of lightning in the black night came more frequently
now, and the wet, salty wind blowing in from the ocean rippled the
river's black surface.

"And you, Nimi?" Gil asked as his strong strokes drove the canoe
swiftly away from the riverbank. "Will you be sorry you came with
me?"

"No, I also will not be sorry." She looked around at him, her big
brown eyes shining. "I have waited a very long time for this day, Gil

Eenezh. I have waited a very long time for you to come and take me away from Mbanza Kongo. I have waited a very long time for you to take me to a land where I can be a princess again."

The way she said this, the trill in her voice, the shine in her eyes, reminded Gil again of the childishly haughty way she used to proclaim herself NtinuKongo. How much the title had meant to her. How much she must regret its loss. How much she must long to regain it.

"I *will* be a princess in your land on the other shore of the sea, won't I? You are a prince in that land and I am the mother of your son so I must be a princess there too, mustn't I?"

Gil hesitated at this as he had hesitated at her hopeful suggestion that Kimpasi would be welcomed by the Portuguese as one of their own.

"My mother says I will."

Again her mother, again the Mbanda Lwa. All that woman's misconceptions would have to be corrected, all her falsehoods and fanciful fables would have to be put right, not only about Kimpasi but also and especially about himself, about who he really was, a common seaman, not a prince, and about the life that awaited them in Portugal. And corrected and put right soon, before they boarded the *Beatriz*. He thought of the ship's officers and priest and her rough and ugly crew. He thought of what their reaction would be when he returned not alone but with an African woman and their *mestiço* son. And he thought he must prepare Nimi and the boy for that. But he didn't have the heart to do it yet. So, as before, he didn't actually answer her, only nodded noncommittally.

And, as before, it seemed to satisfy her and, looking forward again to see where they were going, she pushed herself back a bit so that her buttocks touched his knees and the small of her back pressed against his thighs. Did she realize that even this slight contact with her young and desirable body would feel wonderful to him, so long without a young and desirable woman, would thrill and excite him? Of course she did. But he didn't mistake it for an expression of desire on her part. She could have no such feelings for him yet. She knew him hardly at all. No, she was a woman fleeing a hateful past for a hopeful future, and he was little more to her just now than the in-

strument of her flight, and this tentative display of her sensuality little more than encouragement for him in that role, her rescuer, her
white prince.

"Nimi, listen to me."

"I listen to you, Gil Eenezh."

"Do not say Gil Eanes to me anymore. Say only Gil, as I say only
Nimi to you, not Nimi a Nzinga."

"That is what Mbemba says to you, only Gil."

"Because he is my friend, as you must now be my friend." He
stopped paddling and put an arm around her waist and drew her
even closer, wanting to feel her beautiful body even more fully
against his. "Will you be my friend?"

"I will be your friend, Gil. And also your wife, and your princess
too."

Kimpasi, in the prow, looked around at them, frowning. Then he
pointed out across the river and asked, "Is that your island, Gil
Eenezh?"

Gil looked over Nimi's head. They were more than halfway
across the river's channel, approaching the island at its western end.
"Yes, and there . . . can you see it? . . . that is my house."

This interested Nimi and she disentangled herself from Gil's embrace and went up into the prow beside the boy. "Where is your
house?"

"There, at the end of the island, looking out to the sea," he said
and resumed paddling.

"I see it. Do you see it, *mbakala?* There, just at the edge of the
trees. Oh, it is a nice house, isn't it?"

The boy didn't reply. He probably didn't think it was a nice
house at all, compared to those he knew in the royal district in
Mbanza Kongo. Nimi probably didn't think it was so nice either but
was willing to pretend.

Gil swung the canoe to the west, toward the ocean, then came
about so as to run up on the landing stage in front of the house.

And as he did so, Kimpasi asked, pointing at the outrigger
beached there, "Is that the boat that will take us out to the ocean, Gil
Eenezh? That one, with the pole standing in the middle and the little
boat stuck to its side?"

"Good for you, Kimpasi," Gil said, gliding the canoe alongside the outrigger. "What a clever boy you are to have known that right away."

"Why can we go out on the ocean in that one and not in this one?"

"You do not have to paddle that one." Gil shipped his paddle and jumped out of the canoe. "It is a sailing boat. Do you want me to show you how it works?"

"Yes."

As Gil began shoving the canoe up on the landing stage, Nimi also jumped out. She didn't think to help him, as the other Nimi would have—she probably hadn't been required to do any sort of work like this in all her life—and ran to the house.

"Show me," Kimpasi said, clambering into the outrigger where he began rummaging in the gear. "What is this? And this?" He tugged at the rigging, fooled with the sail cloth, swung the rudder back and forth.

"Be careful, Kimpasi. Do not break anything. I will show you." But Gil didn't immediately get into the outrigger with the boy. Once he had the canoe beached, he stood beside it looking at the house, wondering what Nimi was doing inside.

"But here is a paddle. Look, I have found a paddle. So you *do* have to use a paddle with this boat too."

"That is only for when the sail is not hoisted." Gil got into the outrigger. "This is the sail. When it is hoisted, you do not have to paddle because the wind blows in it and pulls the boat. Let us hoist the sail. But first we must put this stick in this hole. Here, you do it."

By the time Nimi came out of the house again, Gil had run up the lateen-rigged sail and it was flapping and fluttering in the wind, much to Kimpasi's delight, and he was showing the boy how to maneuver its sheet.

"Listen to the noise it makes," the boy was saying excitedly. "Beat. Beat. Beat. Just like the wings of a bird beating in the wind."

"That is just exactly what it is like, Kimpasi. And that is just exactly how it works too. You will see when we take it out on the ocean. Now, do you want to see my house?"

"All right."

Nimi came down from the veranda as they approached. "It is

time to go to sleep," she said. "Oh, I am so tired. It is so late it is almost morning. Are you tired too, *mbakala?*"

"No, I am hungry."

"Yes, we all are hungry," Gil said. "I will prepare some food."

"I have already done so," Nimi said.

"You have been to the cookhouse in back?"

"And to the kraal and workshop and granary and garden. I have looked at everything."

"And?"

"It is nice, Gil. It is all very nice. And, anyway, we will not have to stay here very long. By daylight, we will be on our way to the land on the other shore of the sea where I will be *ntinu* again."

She took Kimpasi's hand and started up the steps of the veranda, then looked back and extended her other hand to Gil and they went into the house together, this odd little family between two worlds.

THE RAIN CAME an hour before dawn. A crack of thunder and then the sudden clatter of rain on the roof woke him. He hadn't been sleeping deeply, had been sleeping hardly at all, too excited to sleep. He sat up and looked at Nimi. She was sound asleep. Unlike Gil, the excitement of the quickly changing circumstances of her life had exhausted her.

They were in the other Nimi's room. Kimpasi was in Gil's. The boy had been so taken with the bunk and Gil's other things there— the sea chest, writing desk and chair, the crucifix on the wall—that he had refused to sleep anywhere else. Gil was happy to let him. It brought him a small step closer to Gil's world, that alien world with which he must now quickly become familiar. Nimi had taken the palliasse in the other Nimi's room and Gil had made up a second palliasse beside it, and they had lain down together with little fuss or awkwardness directly after they had eaten.

He had been mistaken about her. She was not the spoiled child he had supposed, not the sheltered princess for whom everything all her life had been done by servants. Apparently, after her fall from grace, she had had to learn how to do for herself. She had prepared a fine meal for the three of them over a cooking fire she had built herself in the yard behind the house, using provisions she had found in the storehouse and granary, and vegetables she had picked from the garden. She had even milked the nanny goat in the kraal so Kimpasi would have milk instead of *malafu* to drink. And then she had boiled a kettle of water and given the boy a bath before tucking him into Gil's bunk, and had brought a second kettle of water into the other Nimi's room so she and Gil also could wash before lying down together.

Her body was as magnificent as he had imagined it would be, and in the soft orange glow of the palm-oil lamp hanging from the roof beam, she had allowed him to watch her without coyness or false modesty while she sponged herself over the kettle. He already was naked, having washed first, and watched her from the palliasse, propped up on an elbow. He hadn't taken anything for granted then, so he had tried not to let himself become aroused by the sight of her nude. But this had proved impossible.

She had pretended not to be aware of his arousal, pretended to a matter-of-factness in the mundane business of washing, but every movement she made was keenly aware and knowingly seductive: her full breasts rising and falling as she reached over her wide shoulders to scrub her back, the muscles of her buttocks tightening and relaxing as she ran the sponge up and down her long legs, her slender neck arching as she threw back her head and squeezed the sponge so that the water cascaded from it over her nipples and across her belly and gathered in a twinkling pool in the black triangle between her thighs, her amber-dark skin glistening silkily as she sponged the water away, touching herself as he wished to touch her, caressing herself as he wished to caress her, her face turning in and out of the lamp light, her expression studiedly indifferent and, in its very indifference, unbearably alluring, biting her lower lip.

When she was done, she wrapped herself in a clean kanga, which had disappointed him, and snuffed out the lamp. With the sky blanketed by clouds and the moon almost gone, the dark had been immediate and complete, and she vanished into it. Then, in the momentary flickering light of a flash of sheet lightning, he saw her again, stretched out beside him on her palliasse, the kanga fallen open on her thighs. He turned to her, his cheek still resting on his hand propped on his elbow, and waited the few moments it took for his eyes to become accustomed to the dark. She was looking up at him, her swollen lips moist and slightly parted. He made no move. He wanted to be sure. And then she undid the kanga and let it fall away entirely and turned her face from him in a gesture of abandonment. But he still did nothing, enduring the mounting pressure of his desire, enjoying the thrilling tension that he knew would now soon be eased. With puzzlement and a trace of anger at this flirtatious delay, she turned back to him, reached up and took a handful of his beard and tugged him down to her. And he did not resist any longer. He slid one arm under her shoulders and the other between her legs and, in this way, lifted her from the palliasse and took her into his mouth, wanting to devour her.

Later she said to him, "For this too have I waited a very long time, Gil."

Still on top of her, he hugged her more closely, tangling his legs with hers, feeling the stickiness between their bellies.

"In all these years, I have been with no other man."

"I am glad."

She waited a moment, then gently pushed him off her and rubbed her eyes. "It was not natural," she said huskily and turned on her side, her back to him. "But no other man would have me. The NgangaKongo said I was a witch."

Gil got up on his elbow again and looked at the back of her head, the nape of her neck, the sinuous curve of her spine, the apple shape of her buttocks, her long, strong legs, and felt desire mounting in his loins again. But she was drifting off into sleep, her breathing deep and heavy. So he let her be and thought again about what lay ahead of them, the ugliness they surely would encounter on boarding the *Beatriz,* the difficulties they surely would face making a home in Portugal. But he didn't care. She was beautiful. She was a princess. She was the mother of his son. And he was as much a man of her kingdom as of his own. Who better to have for his woman, his wife, than a beautiful princess of a kingdom in which he had grown to manhood and fathered a son?

"Will we return someday, Gil?"

It surprised him that she was still awake. "Return here, Nimi, to the Kongo?"

"Yes."

"Why would we ever return here? Why would we ever want to return here? Haven't we both suffered enough here?"

"I mean when I am a princess again. When you have made me a princess again." She slurred her words drowsily. "I would rather be a princess here among my own people than in your land on the other shore of the sea."

"Nimi." He put a hand on her shoulder. "Listen to me, Nimi. There is much I must tell you about my land on the other shore of the sea . . ."

But she hadn't listened to him. She had taken his hand and, holding it trustingly, had fallen soundly asleep.

And she was now still sleeping soundly, although thunder rumbled and lightning flashed and rain drummed on the palm-frond shingles of the roof. She seemed very young in her sleep, younger even than her twenty-three years, young and innocent and naive, doubtless dreaming now the foolish dreams with which her mother had filled her head. He would have to disabuse her of the foolishness. He would have to tell her plainly what the future held in store. He would have to disentangle her from her mother's schemes and dreams.

He got up, wrapped on a kanga and went out of the room to look in on Kimpasi. The boy too was sleeping soundly—what were his dreams?—but no longer on Gil's bunk. Obviously the novelty of it had given way to the strange discomforts of the grass mattress and feather pillows, and he was sleeping on the floor, frowning, his long blond hair all over his face, his hands clenched into little fists. He was a pretty lad once you got used to the confusion of his coloring, the odd mixture of his features, and he had his father's build. He would grow up into a strong man and perhaps a quick and clever one too and, in his own peculiar way, handsome as well, and maybe put to sea as his father had. In a few years, he would be old enough to ship out as a *grumete* or page. And why not? It was a good calling for someone with such a muddled pedigree; men of every breed and stripe sailed aboard the ships of the West African trade. But he would have to be a Catholic.

That hadn't occurred to Gil before, and it occurred to him now with a shock. Lord Jesus, of course, the boy must be baptized. As it was, he had lived on the brink of damnation for very nearly ten years. Did Gil really believe this? Perhaps no longer with quite such fervent assurance as he once had but certainly enough not to be willing to take chances with the soul of his son. As soon as they went aboard the *Beatriz*, he would have Father de Sousa baptize the boy and give him a Christian name. And Nimi? Aye, and Nimi too. She must be christened and then married to him properly, in the Faith.

The boy stirred in his sleep and opened his eyes. Clearly he did not remember where he was. He looked at Gil blankly and then, in such a lovely, unguarded way, smiled. "Gil Eenezh," he said. "I was dreaming about you."

"Were you, *mbakala?*" Gil went into the room and squatted beside the boy. "What were you dreaming?"

The boy furrowed his brow. "I do not remember," he said and sat up. "Is it daylight yet? Can we go out on the ocean in the sailing boat yet?"

"Soon. Let's go and make it ready."

"I will do it. I know how to do it. You showed me how." The boy scrambled to his feet.

He was nude and thought nothing of it; he probably was used to going around nude. But, by Portuguese standards, he was too old for that. It wouldn't do.

"Where is your kanga, Kimpasi? Or would you like to wear one of mine?"

"One of yours."

Gil pulled the chest out from under the bunk and sorted through it until he found one of his best kangas. He folded it in half so it wouldn't be too long for the boy, then took the boy's hand, drew him close and wrapped the kanga around his waist, and kept him close for a moment, looking into his light blue eyes. Such bright eyes. Aye, he would grow up quick and clever and strong. What Christian name should he be given?

"And that. Can I also wear that?"

"What?"

The boy pointed at the string of bloodstones around Gil's neck.

"Yes, Kimpasi," Gil said with a pleased smile. "You can also wear this." He took off the necklace and reclasped it around Kimpasi's

neck, from where it hung down almost to the boy's belly. Gil patted
the smooth, round belly and said, "There. It looks very nice."

"*Ntondesi,* Gil Eenezh."

"Listen, Kimpasi. Will you do something for me?"

"What?"

"Call me *pai.*"

"What is that?"

"It is the word for father in the language of my land, the land on
the other shore of the sea. Portugal."

"Portugal?"

"Yes, that is the name of the land I come from and *pai* is the way
we say father in that land. Will you call me that?"

The boy frowned.

"I *am* your father. You know that, don't you?"

The boy nodded and looked half-away.

"Well, you think about it. I would very much like to have you call
me father. Will you think about it?"

"Yes."

"Now let us go and make the sailing boat ready."

They went out on to the veranda together and then Kimpasi
darted ahead, ran down to the landing stage and climbed into the outrigger. The rain was slackening. In this season, it would rain several
times during the day and night and, often, quite heavily but never for
very long each time. By daybreak, it would have let up entirely, not to
resume again until after noon. The thunder and lightning had already
ceased. Gil followed the boy to the outrigger.

And the boy jumped out of it. "Mother," he called.

Gil looked around. Nimi had come out of the house.

"Where are you going, Mother?"

She didn't hear him. She came down from the veranda, turned
away from the sea and hurried upriver, along the island's south
beach, toward its eastern end. Something had awakened her from her
sound sleep.

"Where is she going?"

"I don't know," Gil said and took hold of Kimpasi's hand.

A festival of some kind was going on across the river in Mpinda.
A huge bonfire was burning in the middle of the Soyo village's main

market square and stilt walkers, clad in body suits of woven raffia and
wearing wooden masks of various fabulous beasts, were dancing
around it to the music of kudu horns and drums. And a fleet of canoes was drawn up on the beach with Soyo warriors, feathered and
armed, in them, making ready to shove off. Nimi was staring across at
this with her hands on her hips.

"What is it?" Gil asked, hurrying up to her with Kimpasi in tow.

"The Soyo are celebrating the visit of a Kongo queen."

"A Kongo queen? Which Kongo queen?"

"My mother, the Mbanda Lwa."

"The Mbanda Lwa is in Mpinda?" Gil looked across the river.

"She has been following us, Gil. No matter that Mbemba forbade
her, she is following us to the white men. She is not content to see
them depart. She fears that, if they depart, they will never come again
and their magic will be lost to her forever."

"But how can she hope to keep them from departing when
everyone in the kingdom and now even Mbemba himself wishes
them to depart?"

"She is Soyo, Gil. Did you know that?"

"Yes."

"She is a daughter of the house of the ManiSoyo. She is Ntinu-
Soyo as well as MbandaKongo. So she can call on the Soyo for help to
keep the white men from departing."

VI

"His mother?"

"Aye, his mother. The Mbanda Lwa."

"But what about him? Where is he? Isn't he coming?"

"Oh, he's coming all right, my lord Captain," Gil replied. "With an army of ten thousand, as I warned you he would."

"Ten thousand?" This was the ship's one-eyed master-at-arms, Tomé Rodrigues. "Surely you exaggerate, *senhor.*"

"I do not exaggerate, sir marshal. He is assembling ten thousand warriors in the mouth of the Zaire, making ready to kill us all if we should be so mad as to dare enter his kingdom."

Father de Sousa intervened. "This Mbanda Lwa, Senhor Eanes," he said with keen interest. "Being his mother, she must be the Kongo queen."

"She is *a* Kongo queen, padre. His father, the king, has other wives."

They were gathered around Gil on the *Beatriz*'s quarterdeck, not only Dias and Rodrigues and Father de Sousa but also Nuno Gonçalves and the sickly, foul-smelling pilot, Antão Paiva, all eager to hear what word he had brought back from Mbanza Kongo. It was late afternoon and it had stopped raining, but by the look of the darkly lowering sky, it was sure to start again before nightfall.

"So take my advice, my lord Captain," Gil went on. "Make sail for Portugal. It is the wisest course, the only course. For if you go on, certain death awaits us. And neither God's work nor the king's work can be done by dead men."

"And what say you, Dom Tomé?"

Rodrigues shook his head. "I find it hard to believe that this Mbemba could assemble an army of ten thousand, my lord Captain. In all my years in the West African trade, I have never seen an army of Guineans in such numbers. But even if Senhor Eanes does not exaggerate, I say, sail on. We have nothing to fear no matter how many of these Guineans come against us. They are no match for our guns."

"How many can you kill with the first volley of your guns, sir marshal?"

"Eh?"

"A hundred? A few hundred? A thousand perhaps? But then you will have to recharge and by then the remaining thousands will have swarmed aboard the ship. And that will be the end of us, and the ship."

"Is he right?" Dias asked with rising concern.

But before Rodrigues could answer, Father de Sousa again interrupted, pursuing his own thoughts. "This Kongo queen, Senhor Eanes, the Mbanda Lwa, why has she come?"

Gil had been afraid of this. As soon as he had discovered that the Mbanda Lwa had followed him, he had been afraid that Father de Sousa, if not the others, would see it as an opportunity to be seized, a reason to be encouraged, a development undermining the threat posed by Mbemba's ten thousand.

"What does she want?"

"To see your beards."

The priest arched a sharp eyebrow. "What do you mean by that, *senhor?*"

"Only that she is an inquisitive woman, padre. Other than myself, she has never seen white men. She did not see those of the *Leonor* because they never went to Mbanza Kongo. So when she heard that another ship of white men had come, she decided to see them for herself before they were killed or driven away. The men of the Kongo do not have beards."

"I see." The priest's thin, scarlet lips curled into a mirthless smile. "Well then, let us show her our beards."

"What foolishness is this, Father de Sousa?" Dias protested. "We have more important matters to consider than a woman curious about our beards. We have an army of ten thousand Guinean warriors to consider."

"This woman is a queen, Dom Bartolomeu. Let us consider her first and those ten thousand warriors only afterward. For who can say? As a queen, she may have influence over those ten thousand. Eh, Senhor Eanes?" Again the priest smiled his startlingly scarlet smile and walked over to the ship's larboard rail.

The *Beatriz* still rode at anchor under bare poles in the lee of the cliffs of Waterfall Bay where Gil had left her six weeks before. But now a large hut, made of bent bamboo and roofed with palm fronds and enclosed by a low palisade, stood among the flowering trees on the bank of the pool formed by the waterfall. The Mbanda Lwa had had the hut built before allowing Gil to announce her presence to the white men so as to have a place in which to receive them with appropriate ceremony. Members of her entourage, who had accompanied her from Mpinda, stood at the gate of the hut's palisade.

"Which one is she?" Father de Sousa asked, squinting landward over the rail through the misty drizzle.

"She does not show herself. She is in the hut."

"Who are those who do show themselves?"

"The men are warriors of her bodyguard, the women her servants."

"And that young woman who has come down to the water's edge, is she too a servant?"

"No, she is her daughter."

"Mbemba's sister?" The priest's interest sharpened.

"Aye, his sister. Nimi a Nzinga, NtinuKongo."

"NtinuKongo?"

"Princess of the Kongo."

"So a Kongo princess as well as a Kongo queen has come to see our beards. And the lad holding the Kongo princess's hand?"

Dias and Gonçalves, Rodrigues and Paiva, also had come over to the rail. Gil wondered if any of them could make out Kimpasi's *mestiço* coloring. Probably not at this distance, in this stormy afternoon's darkness. He could hardly make it out himself.

"He is her son."

"And who is his father?"

"I am."

At that there was a snort of harsh, derisive laughter. Gil looked around.

"By Jesus, *senhor,* I congratulate you." It was Rodrigues who said this, chortling with a nasty glee. "You haven't held anything back, have you? You've gone savage all the way." The one-eyed, pigtailed brigand nudged Paiva, causing him to also start sniggering. "Aye, by Jesus, all the way. Right down to your very cock."

Gonçalves, seeing the look that crossed Gil's face, snapped, "Don't start anything, Rodrigues."

"What am I starting? I ain't starting anything. It's Senhor Eanes who seems to have started something. A family of mongrel whelps." Rodrigues laughed out loud at his own wit. "How many more half-breed bastards have you sired on the savage beauties of this kingdom, *senhor?*"

"I'm warning you, Rodrigues," Gonçalves said.

Rodrigues shrugged and rolled his one good eye leeringly. Paiva went on snickering.

"Pay them no mind, Gil."

But this, of course, was just the sort of thing Gil had expected, and he decided he'd best deal with it on the spot, while Nimi and Kimpasi weren't present to be humiliated by it. So he said with a forced calm, "My lord Captain, is this man important to you?"

"Which man, *senhor?*" The question startled Dias; he wasn't quite following the drift of things, still caught up in worry about Mbemba's army. "The master-at-arms? Of course he's important to me. He commands the company of soldiers and gunners aboard my ship."

"Then you wouldn't gladly see his throat cut?"

"What's that?" Rodrigues's nasty grin turned sour; his ugly face went black. "You threaten me, *senhor?*" His hand went to his cutlass.

But Gil was on him like a cat, his ivory-handled knife out of its scabbard in a flash. By the time Rodrigues drew the cutlass, Gil was behind him, grabbing his tarred pigtail, pulling his head back, jamming a knee into the small of this back, laying the blade of his knife across his throat. Seeing this, Paiva emitted a yelp of alarm and leaped out of the way.

"What's he doing?" Dias cried out. "My God, the man's gone mad. Gonçalves, do something."

But there was nothing Gonçalves could do. Gil had Rodrigues in a death grip, head yanked back by the pigtail, body bent back over his knee, throat bared to his knife blade. And then he took a swipe with the knife blade. It was a swift and light swipe but the blade was murderously keen and instantly a thread-thin line of blood droplets sprang up along the tautly stretched skin of Rodrigues's throat. Feeling the sting, Rodrigues dropped his cutlass and clutched at Gil's wrist with both hands. But Gil was too strong for him. Kicking the cutlass away, he twisted the knife so that its point stabbed at the hollow at the base of Rodrigues's throat, again drawing droplets of bright blood.

"Gil, no. Don't."

"Stay away, Nuno."

Under the pressure of the knife point at his throat, under the pressure of the knee in his back, Rodrigues's legs slid out from under him and he sat down with a jarring thud, his legs splaying out in front of him. Gil went down on his knees behind him, still pulling back his head, still sticking the knife point into his throat.

"I won't have this," Dias was shouting. "I won't have this sort of thing on my ship."

"Then you had best order this man to keep his filthy mouth shut."

"Calm yourself, *senhor.*" This was Father de Sousa. "You allow yourself to be aroused too easily."

"I never again want to hear any such foul comments about my son and his mother, padre. I never again want to hear any such obscene laughter behind their backs."

"You misunderstood Dom Tomé. He meant no disrespect."

"Didn't he?" Gil looked down at Rodrigues, splayed helplessly on the deck in Gil's iron grip. "Didn't you, sir marshal?"

Rodrigues had closed his one eye. He opened it now, glistening with hatred and fear. "Leave off, man," he growled. "By Jesus, leave off. You're killing me." Sweat streamed down his face, smearing the blood on his neck.

"You don't answer me, sir marshal. Did you mean any disrespect?" Gil moved the knife point from Rodrigues's neck to his mouth. "I want you to answer me." And he pushed the knife point between the man's lips.

"For God's sake, Dom Tomé, answer him," Father de Sousa cried out. "Beg his pardon."

"I beg your pardon," Rodrigues whispered, trying to keep the blade from slicing his lips.

In a gesture of utter disdain, using his enormous strength, Gil flung Rodrigues away like a rag doll, and looked at Paiva. The pilot was visibly trembling.

"This is an outrage, an intolerable outrage."

"It's settled now, Dom Bartolomeu," the priest said. "Senhor Eanes was momentarily aroused, feeling himself insulted. But he is calm now."

"I don't care if he's calm now. Rodrigues is an officer of my ship. If you ever try anything like that again, *senhor,* I'll have you clapped in irons."

"I'm not a member of your ship's company. I'm not under your command."

"Everybody aboard this ship is under my command, *senhor.*"

Gil stood up and walked back to the rail and looked landward to where Nimi and Kimpasi were standing on the beach. He could imagine the wonder with which they were looking back out at the greatwinged boat riding at anchor in the hidden cove, the great-winged boat that would fly them away to a magical land on the other shore of the sea. He probably hadn't done them any good with his outburst. They probably would still suffer indignities when he brought them aboard. And he had made a mortal enemy of Rodrigues into the bargain.

Gonçalves came over and put a hand on his shoulder. "Don't fret, little son," he said softly. "No one will give your boy and the woman any more trouble. I'll see to that."

"*Ntondesi.*"

"*Ntondesi?*"

"Thank you."

"That's Kongo talk, is it?"

"Aye."

"Do your boy and the woman speak any Portuguese?"

"No."

"Well, we'll teach them soon enough. We'll make Christians of them in a hurry."

"Aye, Nuno, that's what I want. I want to make Christians of them in a hurry. Do you hear that, padre? I want you to baptize them."

"Is that why you brought them here? Not to see our beards?"

"Aye, that's why I brought them here. Will you baptize them?"

"Of course. It will be a great joy and privilege. That's why the Lord sent me. To save the souls of all the poor heathens in this benighted land and show them the path to eternal life. Your boy and his mother will be the first of my many triumphs for Jesus in the Kongo. And the Mbanda Lwa? Will she be the second?"

"She didn't come here to be baptized."

"No, *she* came here to see our beards."

"That's right."

"Well, then, let us show her our beards."

HAVING GONE AHEAD in his outrigger, Gil was waiting on the beach with Nimi and Kimpasi when the longboat pushed off from the *Beatriz* the next morning in a light but steadily falling rain. Dias, Father de Sousa and Rodrigues were in the longboat along with eight seamen manning the sweeps and ten soldiers armed with crossbows or arquebuses and armored in helmets and chainmail.

Gil would have been happier to see Gonçalves in the boat instead of Rodrigues but, as mate, he had been left behind in command of the caravel. Rodrigues, in shoulder and leg armor as well as chainmail, wearing a battered helmet over his red bandanna, his cutlass drawn, stood in the prow of the longboat, scowling at the approaching shoreline as if looking for trouble. Dias sat on a thwart amidship, huddled under a piece of canvas to protect his fine clothing from the rain. Father de Sousa stood in the boat's stern beside the helmsman, his delicate hands clutching the silver crucifix of his rosary, gazing forward with an expectant smile, the rain draining off the wide brim of his canonical hat.

"I don't like them," Nimi said when they were near enough to see. "They are ugly and make me afraid."

"Do not be afraid of them, Nimi. They are no uglier than me." Gil put an arm around her shoulder. "You are not afraid of them, are you, Kimpasi?"

The boy shook his head bravely but his brows knitted into a severe frown. If he was not afraid, he certainly was abashed by this, his first sight of a gang of hairy, armored white men.

"Come, *mbakala,* let us help them bring their boat ashore."

Gil took Kimpasi's hand and started wading into the bay, meaning to grab hold of the longboat's prow and pull it up on the beach. But no sooner had the boat scraped bottom than Rodrigues leaped out, barking a command, and instantly the soldiers on board also leaped out and came splashing ashore. And this unexpected burst of apparently threatening activity was enough to shake Kimpasi's brave resolve and he let go of Gil's hand and ran back to his mother.

"What are you doing, Rodrigues?" Gil shouted. "There's no need for this."

Rodrigues ignored him and, in the next moment, he had his soldiers lined up along the beach, those with the arquebuses kneeling and aiming at the Mbanda Lwa's hut, the crossbowmen standing behind them, fitting arrows to their bows. Seeing this, the warriors of the Mbanda Lwa's bodyguard at the gate of her hut's low palisade raised their shields and lances. The serving women there scurried back inside the palisade. Nimi dragged Kimpasi farther away from the water's edge.

"I tell you there's no need for this sort of thing, Rodrigues."

"I'm not so stupid as to walk into a trap, *senhor.*"

"Trap? What trap? There's no trap."

"How do I know how many more of these savages are out of sight, back there in those trees?"

"Oh, Jesus. My lord Captain, call off this dog of yours."

Dias had stood up in the longboat, still holding the canvas over his head against the rain. He looked around uncertainly.

"Padre, this fool will cause unnecessary problems with his hostile display."

"It is only a precaution, Senhor Eanes." Father de Sousa hoisted the skirts of his cassock as he waded primly ashore.

"We don't need this sort of precaution, padre. The Mbanda Lwa has only these few warriors here."

"Are you sure?"

"Of course I am sure."

"Well, if you are sure . . . Dom Tomé, have your soldiers stand down."

"They will stand just where they are, padre. You may trust this man, but I don't. I don't trust him any more than I trust these savages."

"Well, at least have them put up their weapons, for God's sake," Gil said in exasperation. "Because if one of them loses his nerve and fires, I will not answer for the trouble it will bring down on our heads."

"Do what he says, Dom Tomé."

"You are making a mistake, padre."

Gil looked around at the warriors guarding the Mbanda Lwa's gate. Obviously, they didn't like the sight of the white soldiers lined up on the beach. But Gil knew he wasn't going to be able to get the soldiers withdrawn entirely. Not only Rodrigues but Father de Sousa and Dias were just too nervous about this, their first landing on an unknown African shore. And, Gil thought ruefully, perhaps his own warnings had affected the Portuguese more than he had realized.

"Introduce us to the princess Nimi a Nzinga, *senhor*," Father de Sousa said. "And also the boy. What is his name?"

"Kimpasi."

"I should like to meet them, my first converts."

Gil gave Rodrigues a hard, warning look, then called to Nimi. But she pretended not to hear him and backed still farther away, tugging Kimpasi along with her. And when Gil started toward her, the priest following at his heels, she turned and dashed to safety behind the hut's palisade with the serving women, dragging the boy after her.

"Rodrigues has frightened her with his manly show of arms," Gil said with disgust and went to the hut.

As he approached, the warriors at the gate came even more tensely alert. If Rodrigues regarded him as one of them, a savage, the warriors resolutely saw him as a white man, a demon fallen from the sky who had been condemned to exile by their high priest, and they watched him suspiciously as he passed through the gate, trusting him as little as Rodrigues trusted him, allowing him passage only because it was the whim of the queen they served.

"Have they gone away?" Nimi asked as soon as Gil came through the gate.

"You know very well they have not gone away," Gil answered with some irritation. "You know why they are here. Your mother wants to meet them."

"Even so, I wish they would go away. They are so ugly. And why did they rush at us from their boat? I thought they wanted to kill us."

"It was a mistake."

"They frightened Kimpasi."

"I know." Gil squatted on his heels in front of the boy. "It was a mistake, *mbakala*. They meant no harm. You mustn't be afraid of them. They are not as bad as all that."

"I am not afraid of them," Kimpasi said.

"Good for you. You'll see, in time, you'll get used to them." Gil stood up. "We must all get used to them, Nimi," he said with great severity. "Because before long, we will be living among them. They will be our people."

"Have you told them I am NtinuKongo?"

"Of course I told them." Gil cupped her chin in his big hand. "And they will treat you with honor and respect, do not worry, and not only because you are NtinuKongo but also because you will soon be baptized."

"What is that?"

"A rite that will make you one of their Faith. Now go to your mother and tell her I bring the white men to her," Gil said and went back out the gate.

Although they had lowered their weapons, the Portuguese soldiers were very much on their guard, fidgeting with their firearms and crossbows, eyeing the warriors at the gate from under the dripping brims of their helmets. Rodrigues paced up and down in front of them, slapping his cutlass against his leg. Dias no longer held the canvas over his head but wore it wrapped around his shoulders like a cape, looking miserable in the rain. Father de Sousa had walked over to the pool formed by the waterfall and was kneeling on its bank under the flowering trees, praying, his clasped hands holding his rosary, his eyes turned up to the top of the cliff where the waterfall burst over a limestone ledge at the start of its thundering descent.

"How beautiful this place is, Senhor Eanes," he said when Gil came over. "It is a paradise, lacking only God. But we shall make up for that lack. We shall bring God to this paradise and He will bestow His blessing on it and its beauty will be all the greater for that."

Looking up where Father de Sousa looked, seeing it for a moment with the priest's eyes, Gil also was struck by the stunning beauty of the white, foaming cascade plunging down the side of the cliff through the shimmering gray curtain of rain into the crystal pool below, set like a jewel among the emerald green and red of the flowering trees. But the priest was mistaken about it in one respect: God *was* there, the Kongo god, *Nzambi Mpungu*. The Catholic God could not make a more beautiful place of it than *Nzambi Mpungu* already had.

"Come, padre. We must not keep the Mbanda Lwa waiting."

Circular in plan, the bent bamboo of its structure forming a domed roof, lighted by the soft orange glow of palm-oil lamps, the Mbanda Lwa's hut was high enough to stand in. Serving women stood in it at the back, holding platters of food and drink. Nimi stood between them, holding Kimpasi's hand. And the Mbanda Lwa stood in front of them among a profusion of cushions and woven mats and folded cloths.

She was regally attired. Apart from her several skirts of crimson and gold and her crimson blouse embroidered with the golden sunbursts of the ManiKongo's crest, she wore a cape of red and yellow parrot feathers and a headdress of similar feathers set in an ivory crown. Ivory bracelets filigreed in silver adorned her arms from her wrists to her elbows, and necklaces of brass set with pearls covered her breastbone from her bosom to her chin, and bronze earrings worked into the form of flying birds with ruby-red stones for eyes weighted her lobes. But what immediately caught Gil's attention, as he entered with Dias and Father de Sousa (Rodrigues remained outside with his soldiers in order to keep watch on the Soyo warriors), was the small, black-leather-bound book with a gold cross embossed on its cover that she held in her hands.

Father Sebastião's breviary. On seeing it, Gil knew that he would not be able to keep lying about her reason for wanting to meet the white men much longer.

"Invite them to be seated, Gil Eenezh," she said and sat down herself, crossed-legged, among the cushions and mats, and dropped the breviary into her lap.

Nimi sat down next to her, pulling Kimpasi, still standing, close to her side and keeping an arm protectively around his waist. And then, when Gil and Dias and Father de Sousa were settled on their cushions and mats, the Mbanda Lwa signaled to the serving women and one brought forward a platter of painted wooden cups. The Mbanda Lwa took the first and had the others handed around.

"It's *malafu*," Gil said. "Palm wine."

"Shall we offer a toast?" Father de Sousa asked. "Or will she?"

"I don't know."

The Mbanda Lwa held her cup in both hands just under her chin and, with her head slightly cocked, studied the white men with such intent interest that it seemed, indeed, as if she had had them come to her only in order to see their beards. Her large brown eyes went back and forth between the priest and the captain-general, taking in the sharp differences: Dias's white hair and beard and watery eyes, his flushed complexion, embroidered surcoat and other finery; the priest's stark marble skin, black moustache and goatee, his tightly fitted black cassock, the silver crucifix hanging on his chest.

"Is he the priest of your people, Gil Eenezh?" she asked after several minutes of this silent scrutiny, indicating, with a slight thrust of her chin, Father de Sousa.

"He is, my lady," Gil replied, thinking it clever of her to guess it straight away. After all, why shouldn't she have thought the Portuguese priest would be the older, white-haired man dressed in velvet and lace and not the younger, more austere in appearance?

"How is he called?"

"Rui de Sousa. To show our respect, we address him as Father. Padre de Sousa."

"Pader de Sooza."

"What does she say to me, *senhor?*"

"She doesn't say anything to you, padre. She only asked your name."

"Mbanda Lwa," Father de Sousa said and, raising his cup, bowed his head to her respectfully.

She bowed her head in response, her eyes glittering in the light of the oil lamps, a small pretty smile playing on her lips. "And the other, Gil Eenezh? Who is he?"

"Master of the *Beatriz,* my lady. Bartolomeu Dias de Novais."

This was too much of a mouthful for the Kongo queen.

"We address him as Lord Captain, my lady. *Senhor Capitão.*"

"Senor Captan."

Hearing this, Dias also raised his cup but then went on to take a long drink from it. "I must say, very nice stuff," he said with a smack of his lips. "Just the thing to warm the bones on a miserable day like this."

Although she evidently hadn't planned to do so, the Mbanda Lwa also took a drink of the palm wine, no doubt not wanting to expose Dias's rudeness. And when she drank, so did Nimi, and then Gil and Father de Sousa as well. As he drank, Gil's eyes wandered to the breviary in the Mbanda Lwa's lap. He wondered if Father de Sousa had yet noticed it. Probably not. There was too much else to notice. At the back of the hut where the serving women stood were bundles and baskets, very likely gifts the Mbanda Lwa had brought from Mbanza Kongo for the white men. They had not yet been opened but Gil could guess what they contained: lengths of the beautiful velvetlike cloth the Kongo made, dyed in many colors and woven into many patterns; the finest iron and steel weapons and tools of the skilled Kongo smiths; jewelry of silver and ivory, studded with precious gems; artifacts and fetishes and statuettes cast in bronze or carved from wood or stone; jars of palm oil and wine, tanned hides and the pelts of leopards and lions. They couldn't help but make a strong impression on Dias and the priest, as she of course intended them to make; they couldn't help but whet the white men's appetite for establishing a trading settlement in a kingdom with such goods.

"She is a very handsome woman," Father de Sousa said. "Such a truly refined and intelligent face. Not in the least bit savage."

"Does that surprise you?"

Father de Sousa shrugged. "They are all very handsome, especially the girl. She really is quite beautiful, Senhor Eanes. I understand how she tempted you in your loneliness. And your boy is altogether charming with those blue eyes and blond hair. Don't you think them a fine-looking race of people, Dom Bartolomeu?"

"What I think is that we ought to get on with this, Father de Sousa," Dias replied testily. "We have shown her our beards. Now what?"

"Food has been prepared," Gil answered. "I expect she will invite us to eat. And she also has brought gifts, so she probably will want to present them before going on with anything further."

Dias shook his head in annoyance and drank off the rest of his palm wine. Seeing this, the Mbanda Lwa signaled the serving woman to refill his cup. In stepping forward with an earthenware pitcher of the *malafu*, the serving woman got between Gil and the Mbanda Lwa and blocked his view of her for a moment. And it was then that he heard this:

"*Agnus Dei, qui tollis peccata mundi, miserere nobis.*"

He couldn't believe it. It wasn't Father de Sousa. It was a woman who had spoken the Latin words. And then the serving woman, having refilled Dias's cup, stepped away and Gil saw that the Mbanda Lwa had taken the breviary up from her lap and had opened it. She was now, however, looking at Father de Sousa with bright eyes. Father de Sousa was looking back at her in amazement. It was obvious that he, like Gil, could not believe what he had heard. And then she lowered her eyes to the open page of the breviary and spoke again.

"*Agnus Dei, qui tollis peccata mundi, miserere nobis.*" She was actually reading from the breviary page. It was no trick of memory. She had learned to read the Latin, if not what it meant. "*Agnus Dei, qui tollis peccata mundi, dona nobis pacem.*"

"My lady. Oh, my lady," Father de Sousa cried out and got up on his knees. "Oh, how wonderful this is, my lady. How glorious. God has found you and taken hold of your heart. Our Lord Jesus, the Lamb of God, has whispered to you and seized your soul. Glory be to God in the highest. *Te Deum laudamus.*" He made the sign of the cross.

Not understanding what he was saying, never having seen the sign of the cross made, the Mbanda Lwa drew back in some alarm.

"Padre . . ."

"This is more than I had any right to expect. Oh, dear God, here in this beautiful wilderness, here in this savage paradise, I have heard a heathen queen pray to the Lamb of God."

"She does not understand the words, padre. Surely you can see that. She has learned to read them but without understanding what they mean."

"That may be so. But she *has* learned to read them. And that means that she has wanted to understand them. And that is a first step, a great and miraculous first step in her yearning to come to the Lord." Still on his knees, Father de Sousa extended a hand to the Mbanda Lwa and again she flinched away from him. "Let us pray together, my lady."

"You are frightening her, padre."

"I do not wish to frighten her. No, no, of course not. *Desculpe me, minha senhora.*"

"What does he say, Gil Eenezh?"

"He begs your pardon, my lady. He became very excited when he heard you speak the writing. I must say, I myself became very excited when I heard it. I did not know you had learned how to speak the writing."

"Yes, I have learned how to speak the writing, Gil Eenezh. And now I will learn how to make use of its magic."

"My lady?"

"You have always told me that only a priest of your people could teach me how to make use of the strong magic of the white men's writing. And now here at last is a priest of your people. Tell him that I wish to learn how to make use of this strong and wonderful magic you have brought to us from your land on the other shore of the sea."

Gil did not say anything. He did not know what to say. He realized only too well what would happen if he translated this for Father de Sousa. Father de Sousa would seize on it; he would see in it exactly what Gil did not want him to see in it: a chance, through this Kongo queen, to gain a foothold in the Kongo kingdom.

"Why do you not speak, Gil Eenezh? Why do you not tell Pader de Sooza what I wish?"

"What is she saying, my son?"

"Has the cat got your tongue, *senhor?*" Dias put in, losing patience with Gil's long, indecisive silence. "What is the woman saying?"

"She is a foolish woman, my lord Captain."

"I thought we decided that she is a refined and intelligent woman."

"She believes the breviary is magic."

"Oh?"

"They do not have writing here in the Kongo, so they believe the writing in the breviary, the only writing they have ever seen, is magical. They believe the writing in the breviary is how God speaks to us and how we speak to God."

"How did they come to believe that?" Father de Sousa asked.

"I told them it was so."

"And it *is* so, my son. You have not deceived them. The hymns and psalms and lessons of the Divine Office are how we speak to God. And the readings from the Scripture and Gospels are the words of God speaking to us."

"Aye, but she has made more of it than that, padre."

The Mbanda Lwa was watching Gil intently.

"She believes that in this, in our speaking to God through the writing in the breviary and in God's speaking to us through it, we possess a strong and wonderful magic, a magic so strong and wonderful that it can overcome all the magic of all the priests and sorcerers of her kingdom."

"And she believes this also because you told her it was so?"

Gil nodded.

"And it *is* so. Of course it is. The magic of our prayers, the magic of the word of our Lord, is a stronger and more wonderful magic than any magic anywhere."

"Aye, but now she wants to learn how to use this magic."

"Use it?"

"She wants you to teach her how to use it, padre. I told her only a priest of my people could teach her how to use it."

"Use it in what way? Use it to what purpose?"

"In her own way. To her own purpose."

"I see." Father de Sousa sat back on his heels and raised the silver crucifix of his rosary to his lips and kissed it. *"Gloria in excelsis Deo,"* he muttered softly. "I thank you, O my Lord Jesus, for granting me this sacred opportunity. I will not fail you in it."

The Mbanda Lwa was now watching the priest. She knew that Gil had transmitted her request to him.

"Tell her, my son, tell her there is only one way she can learn how to use the magic of the breviary."

"And what way is that?"

"She must become Catholic. She must receive the sacrament of baptism."

Gil had expected this. In converting a Kongo queen, Father de Sousa believed he would be taking the first step toward converting her kingdom. And she would eagerly agree to the conversion, believing that by doing so she would acquire a magic by which to make Mbemba king.

VII

BEFORE ANYTHING ELSE, there is the question of their Christian names. We must settle that first."

Gil was now sitting next to Nimi and had taken Kimpasi on his lap.

"For the Mbanda Lwa," Father de Sousa went on, "I suggest Leonor."

"After the Portuguese queen?"

"Do you not think it appropriate?"

"The Mbanda Lwa is not the first queen of the Kongo, padre, as is Leonor of Portugal."

"No, but she will be the first *Catholic* queen of the Kongo."

Gil didn't say anything to that.

"And by the same token, I suggest the name Beatriz for her daughter."

"Who is Beatriz?"

"Daughter of João and Leonor. The duchess of Viseu. Our ship is named for her."

"I see."

"As for your boy, well, I leave that to you."

"Name him for our monarchs' son Affonso."

"Oh, no, *senhor,* we must reserve that name for Mbemba."

"For Mbemba?"

"He is the son of the Kongo king and so must bear the name of the son of the king of Portugal."

"What nonsense is that, padre? Mbemba has no need for a Christian name. He is not going to be baptized. Nothing could be further from his thoughts. He is bringing an army of thousands against us. How could you imagine he'd ever think of converting?"

"I am not quite so ready to give up hope on that, Senhor Eanes. I have a great and abiding faith. The Lord has already surprised us with His blessings. First He kept you alive. Then He sent your woman and boy here to be saved. And now the Mbanda Lwa too awaits the sacrament. The ways of the Lord are wondrous indeed. He may yet send Mbemba to us as well."

"Not in a thousand years."

"God has a thousand years, Senhor Eanes. Let us leave it in His hands. Now, what Christian name do you want for the boy?"

Gil considered this for a few moments. Then he said, "It is my hope he will grow up to be a seaman. So let him bear the name of the Navigator, the greatest of our seamen, the Infante Dom Henriqué."

"Very well. Henriqué it will be."

The longboat had been sent back to the *Beatriz* to fetch the sea chest containing Father de Sousa's vestments and other sacerdotal articles, and he now opened its heavy, iron-bound lid and began rummaging through it. The Mbanda Lwa, Nimi and Kimpasi watched with acute interest as he pulled his white-linen alb on over his black cassock, draped his gold-embroidered stole around his neck, then set up a sort of altar on the chest itself: altar cloth, missal, silver candlesticks, a silver pitcher of holy water. Rodrigues was now present: He had come in from the rain to participate in the meal the Mbanda Lwa had had served and to share in the gifts she had brought. Both he and Dias were dozing fitfully, in the soporific glow of the candles and lamps, from having overindulged in the palm wine.

"Dom Bartolomeu. Dom Tomé. We are ready to begin."

"About time," Dias said, jerking his head up with a start. "Is there any more of that *malafu* available?"

"I am sure there is. But let us wait to drink it in celebration of the souls we are now about to harvest for Christ." Father de Sousa opened the missal. "Senhor Eanes, will you stand sponsor for these children?"

"Yes."

"What names do you give them to be known by our Lord?"

"Leonor. Beatriz. Henriqué."

"And what do you ask of God's Church for them?"

Gil didn't know the response, so Father de Sousa prompted him in a low voice.

"Faith. The grace of Christ. Entrance into the Church. Eternal life," Gil repeated after him.

It lasted barely a half-hour. Father de Sousa read from the Gospel according to Matthew. Then came the prayer of the faithful: "By the mystery of your death and resurrection, bathe these children in light, give them the new life of baptism and welcome them into Your Holy Church . . ."

Dias and Rodrigues joined in the response: "Lord, hear our prayer . . ."

And then the invocation of the saints: "Holy Mary, Mother of God, Saint John the Baptist, Saint Joseph, Saint Peter and Saint Paul, pray for us . . ." And then the prayer of exorcism: "Almighty and ever-living God, You sent Your only Son into the world to cast out the power of Satan, to rescue man from the kingdom of darkness and bring him into the splendor of Your kingdom of light. We pray for these children: Set them free from sin, make them the temples of Your glory, and send Your Holy Spirit to dwell in them. We ask this through Christ our Lord . . ."

Father de Sousa's voice was soft but full of vibrant emotion. There was no trace of cynicism in it. He seemed truly to believe in the words he spoke, in the sacrament he performed, in his mission to save these benighted souls. And the effect of his belief was powerful, recalling Gil to the long-ago mysteries of his own childhood. How doubly powerful the effect must be on the Mbanda Lwa and Nimi and Kimpasi, he thought, and he glanced at their faces, lighted by the orange glow of the oil lamps and the flickering candles in the silver candlesticks, their eyes bright with wonder in that light, listening without understanding the strange, sonorous words of the priest, and even the brigand Rodrigues and the befuddled Dias were carried along by the mesmerizing sound and the mystical feeling it evoked, and they intoned the responses reverentially.

"Blessed be God."

Father de Sousa leafed through the pages of the missal, stared for a moment in silence at a new page, then closed his eyes as if gathering his strength. When he opened them again, Gil saw that a film of tears had formed over his eyes. With one hand resting flat on the missal page, he lifted the pitcher of holy water with the other and looked directly at Gil with those glistening eyes.

"Do you believe in God, the Father almighty, creator of heaven and earth?"

Again Gil wasn't sure whether it was his role to respond, but Father de Sousa nodded at him, so he said, "I do."

"Do you believe in Jesus Christ, His only son, our Lord, who was born of the Virgin Mary, who was crucified, died and was buried, and who rose from the dead and is now seated at the right hand of the Father?"

"I do."

"Do you believe in the Holy Spirit, the holy Catholic Church, the communion of saints, the forgiveness of sins, the resurrection of the body and life everlasting?"

"I do."

"This is our faith. This is the faith of the Church. We are proud to profess it, in Christ Jesus our Lord."

"Amen," Gil said.

"Amen," said Dias and Rodrigues.

"Have them kneel, my son."

Gil got on his knees, lifting Kimpasi off his lap and setting him on his knees as well. The Mbanda Lwa and Nimi followed his example.

"Leonor."

"He speaks to me, Gil Eenezh?" the Mbanda Lwa asked.

"Yes."

Father de Sousa set the missal aside and held the pitcher of holy water over her head. "Leonor, I baptize you in the name of the Father . . ."

The unexpected splash of water startled her and she flinched involuntarily. But she made no move to wipe the water away; she allowed it to trickle down her forehead onto her cheeks. And in the next instant her expression of surprise gave way to a smile of excitement. This was sorcery and she recognized it as such and was not disappointed.

"... and of the Son ..."

And she received the second sprinkling with a kind of delight, her smile wider, her eyes bright, imagining the sorcery working in the droplets on her face.

"... and of the Holy Spirit."

She closed her eyes and bowed her head as if knowing what to expect—perhaps there was a rite of this sort in the Kongo religion as well—and Father de Sousa placed his hand on her head.

"This is the fountain of life, water made holy by the suffering of Christ, washing all the world. Leonor, you who have been washed in this water now have the hope of the kingdom of Heaven."

When Father de Sousa removed his hand, the Mbanda Lwa opened her eyes and looked at Gil. "Is it done, Gil Eenezh? Am I now Catholic?"

"I am not sure, my lady."

"Beatriz."

"It is your turn, Nimi."

Nimi winced each of the three times Father de Sousa sprinkled her. And Kimpasi began giggling when his turn came and was giggling still when Father de Sousa completed the rite and set the pitcher beside the missal on the sea chest and sat back on his heels and closed his eyes. After a moment, though, Kimpasi stopped giggling and frowned at Father de Sousa. The priest suddenly looked exhausted, his ordinarily pale complexion seeming even more waxen in the lamplight, his breathing slow and deep.

"Are you all right, padre?" Gil asked.

Father de Sousa opened his eyes. "Oh, yes, I am quite all right. This has been a most joyous experience for me, Senhor Eanes, bringing these souls to Christ."

"Have you any doubts about it?"

"Why do you ask that? Of course I have no doubts about it."

"Then they are baptized?"

"Well, there is the ritual of clothing them in white. And the anointment with the chrism. But that isn't strictly necessary. Yes, they are baptized. Let us pray." Father de Sousa picked up the missal again. "Our Father, who art in Heaven ..."

Hearing these words and recognizing them, the Mbanda Lwa

picked up the breviary, which she kept on her lap throughout, and opened it to the appropriate page. *"Pater noster, qui es in caelis: sanctificetur nomen tuum . . ."*

Father de Sousa broke off his own recitation, allowing her to go on alone.

". . . adveniat regnum tuum: fiat voluntas tuà, sicut in caelo, et in terra." She looked up from the breviary, momentarily surprised at the silence around her, all eyes fixed on her. Then, with a proud smile, she went on to the end. *"Panem nostrum quotidianum da nobis hodie: et dimitte nobis debita nostra, sicut et nos dimittimus debitoribus nostris; et ne nos inducas in tentationem; sed libera nos a malo."*

"O dear Lord, O Blessed Virgin, I thank you for this moment." Father de Sousa made the sign of the cross. "You ask me if I have any doubts, Senhor Eanes. How can I have any doubts when I have witnessed this?"

Gil himself was not sure what to make of it. The Mbanda Lwa, in her glorious headdress of ivory and feathers, her beautiful jewelry sparkling in the candlelight, looked radiant. Perhaps something miraculous had indeed happened. "They are baptized then," he said in Portuguese. And then in Kongo, "It is done, my lady."

"I am Catholic?"

"Yes, my lady, you are a Catholic."

"And so I now possess the magic of the writing?"

With a sigh, Gil replied, "As well as any Catholic, my lady, yes, you now possess the magic of the writing."

"Then let us go to Mpinda."

"To Mpinda?"

"The ManiSoyo awaits us there. I told him I would return there with the white men."

"You told him about the white men? He knows they have come again?"

"Yes."

"Who else knows? Does the NsakuSoyo know?"

"Yes, he knows. All the Soyo know."

"Dear Jesus," Gil groaned. But he should have expected this of her. He should have known that this endlessly scheming woman would not keep the secret. And now the secret would spread and soon everyone in the kingdom would know that the white men had come again.

"I told the ManiSoyo I would follow you to the white men and meet their priest. I told him I would learn from their priest how to use their magic and then would return to Mpinda with them and show him and all the Soyo how wonderful that magic is."

"What is she saying?" Father de Sousa asked.

But before Gil could reply, Nimi spoke up. "I will not go to Mpinda," she said with sudden heat. "You can go, Mother. You can go and show the ManiSoyo whatever you wish. But Kimpasi and I will not go with you. We will never go back to that land where we have been hated and feared. We have fled that land with Gil Eenezh for a land where we will be treated with honor and respect and where I will be a princess again."

"But you can be a princess again in your own land now, girl," the Mbanda Lwa said. "Would you not prefer that? Would you not rather be a princess again among your own people than among these white men?"

"Why do you say that to her?" Gil broke in angrily. "How can she be a princess again among her own people?"

"But surely you see how. Surely you realize that, once I show the ManiSoyo how wonderful is the magic I have acquired from the white men, he will want to acquire it for himself."

"He said that?"

"Yes. He said that, if I can show him that the white men's magic is truly wonderful, he would welcome them to Mpinda. He would give them a place there and stand with them there against those who would drive them away."

"That would be rebellion, my lady."

The Mbanda Lwa smiled. "Yes, it would be rebellion. And with the white men and their wonderful magic at his side, it would be a rebellion in which he would be triumphant."

"And I would be a princess among my own people again?"

"You are a daughter of the ManiSoyo's house through me. You are the mother of a son of the white men by Gil Eenezh. With the ManiSoyo and the white men together triumphant over the very ones who made an outcast of you, what do you think, girl? Of course you would be a princess in your own kingdom again."

"Is this so, Gil?" Nimi asked. Clearly, the idea appealed to her.

"For it to be so, the ManiSoyo would have to join forces with the white men in a war against his own king. Do you think he would?"

"If the magic of the white men is strong enough. And you yourself said it is. You yourself said it is stronger than the magic of the NsakuSoyo, than even that of the NgangaKongo."

"What are you talking about, *senhor?*" Father de Sousa again demanded. "Would you be so good as to tell us what you are talking about."

"I'm afraid you've gotten more than you bargained for, padre."

"What more than I bargained for, *senhor?*"

"The Mbanda Lwa wants to go to Mpinda now. She believes that, having been baptized, she can perform amazing feats of magic. I warned you about this, padre. That was the only reason she agreed to receive the sacrament. She thinks she now can call on God to perform a miracle that will convince the people of Mpinda to welcome you."

Father de Sousa looked at Dias and then at Rodrigues, and for a moment the three men looked at each other in silence.

Then Father de Sousa said, "I am not sure why you think this is more than we bargained for, Senhor Eanes. On the contrary, it strikes me rather as exactly what we had hoped to accomplish."

"Padre, you did not hear what I said. She believes you have given her the power to perform miracles by baptizing her."

"Perhaps I have."

"Padre, please. I am willing to respect your faith but even your faith cannot go so far as that. We have allowed this woman to delude herself. She possesses no magic. She can perform no miracles. We know that even if she doesn't. To go with her to Mpinda is to invite catastrophe. She will not be able to convince the people there to welcome us. Because she has no magic to show them."

"I think we should leave that in God's hands, Senhor Eanes."

"Or in the hands of our gunners," Rodrigues put in.

"What?"

"If what we need is a miracle, Senhor Eanes, if what we want is a feat of magic that will convince these savages to welcome us, I can think of nothing quite so effective as a demonstration of the fire-power of our cannon and falconets."

"You are mistaken," Gil retorted hotly. "These people won't be impressed by that. We tried it once. Ask Nuno Gonçalves. He was there. Diogo Cão had his soldiers fire their arquebuses when we first came to Mpinda, but the people there shrugged it off as if it were nothing but harmless fireworks."

"I find that hard to believe. Everywhere else up and down the African coast, in my experience, the savages have dropped on their faces in terror when they saw shot and shell, ball and grape, explode in the countryside and tear through flesh and bone. Why should these savages be any different?"

Gil didn't reply. He remembered that Diogo Cão had not let his soldiers load shot or shell. The ManiSoyo and his people had not seen what the firearms were actually designed to do. Had they actually witnessed the destructive power of the guns, they might have been just as impressed—and terrified—as Negroes elsewhere along the coast. It might have seemed to them an incredible feat of magic, a miracle of awesome incomprehensibility, a gift perhaps even worth rebelling against their king to acquire.

"Maybe Dom Diogo was too gentle in his demonstration of the power of his guns," Rodrigues went on. "Did he have anyone killed?"

"Of course he didn't have anyone killed. Dom Diogo didn't come here with the idea of killing anyone."

"Well, there you have it. That explains it. I promise you, if a few of these savages had been killed, the rest would have been properly impressed."

"Padre, are you going to listen to this sort of talk? You can't pos-sibly agree that the way for the Mbanda Lwa to demonstrate to these people the magic of the Faith is by killing them."

"No, of course not. But still . . . Perhaps it wouldn't be necessary to kill anyone. Perhaps it would be enough just to have the cannon and falconets fire. If they've never seen its like before it might seem a miracle to them. It might seem like the thunder and lightning of God."

"I don't believe this, padre. You are willing to use the sacrament in this way? You are willing to let the Mbanda Lwa's baptism be turned into a trick as cheap as this?"

"If it is a trick, Senhor Eanes, it is not a cheap trick. No trick is cheap when it is played in the service of God and His Church."

VIII

Hundreds of war canoes jammed the estuary of the Zaire.

They couldn't at first be seen. Rain was pounding down on the river in blinding sheets through which very little could be seen, thunder cracking overhead, jagged bolts of lightning streaking across the steel-gray sky, as the *Beatriz* groped her way out of the storm-swept ocean into the protected, baylike expanse of the river's mouth, sailing on the wind under only her forecourse and mizzen, the wind singing in her rigging and shrouds. Squinting through the downpour, Gil, on the quarterdeck, searched for landmarks in the intermittent blue-white light of the lightning bolts while shouting bearings to the pilot Paiva between the deafening cracks of thunder. Nimi, Kimpasi and the Mbanda Lwa (none of her serving women and warriors were with her; Dias hadn't allowed them on board), accustomed to the violence of the storms in this season and thrilled by the strange sensation of the ship's bounding motion, were also on the quarterdeck. So was Gonçalves, as officer of the watch. Dias and Father de Sousa, however, had retreated down to the steerage with the helmsman when the rains came.

"We're arriving on soundings now, pilot."

Paiva relayed this down to the helmsman through the conning hatch at his feet.

"I'll go forward and cast the lead," Gonçalves said and started down from the quarterdeck.

"No, Nuno, wait. What's that?"

"What?"

Gil wiped the rain from his face, slicking back his drenched hair, and peered forward intently. They had cleared the cliff-bound coast north of the river and had rounded the northern headland of the inlet to the river's mouth; his home, the island of his exile, was about a thousand yards to larboard and the ship was making for the Zaire's south bank, slapping hard against the chop running out with the tide.

"I can't see a damn thing in this blow," Gonçalves said, coming back to the binnacle.

"Look there."

After staring hard in the direction Gil pointed, eastward up the channel between the island to larboard and the boulder-strewn beach dead ahead, Gonçalves shook his head hopelessly.

"Do *you* see them, Nimi?"

"*Bwato,*" Nimi answered, shielding her eyes with her hand. "Many *bwato,* Gil. More than I have ever seen."

"My lord Captain," Gil called down through the conning hatch. "You'd best come topside."

"What *bwato,* girl?" the Mbanda Lwa asked.

"There," Nimi said, now also pointing. "Look how many there are."

"I see them," Kimpasi piped in. "They are everywhere."

"What are they saying, Gil? What do they see?"

"Canoes, Nuno. Hundreds of canoes."

Dias and Father de Sousa came up from the sterncastle, hunching against the wind and the rain.

"Let me have your glass, my lord Captain."

"Is something wrong, *senhor?*"

Gil didn't answer, taking Dias's spyglass and screwing it to his eye.

Gonçalves answered for him. "There are canoes on the river, my lord Captain. Hundreds of them."

"Those are the *bwato* of the ManiSoyo, Gil Eenezh," the Mbanda Lwa said, having spotted the canoes herself.

Gil glanced at her doubtfully, then resumed scrutinizing the canoes through the spyglass. They were of various sizes but all were war canoes. He had seen their like enough times not to be mistaken about it. Their high, curved prows were decorated with paintings of serpents and ferocious beasts, the larger ones carrying as many as forty warriors besides armed paddlers, the smaller ones no less than ten. They were about half a league away but in their extraordinary numbers, dozens abreast, dozens deep, stretching upriver hundreds of yards and the hundreds of yards from island to bank, they completely blocked the channel through which Gil had intended to steer the *Beatriz* to Mpinda.

Now one of the largest, with four smaller ones as an escort, emerged in the lead of the flotilla, rampant lions painted on both sides of its prow. Gil adjusted the spyglass's eyepiece to focus on it: Ten paddlers stood along each gunwale, stroking with long paddles topped with ivory balls; thirty feathered warriors stood in six ranks of five amidship armed with lances and shields; and standing in the prow, also armed with a lance and wearing a headdress of feathers and horn, was Mbemba, looking up at the tall sailing ship with a grim expression, the scar across his cheek livid with anger or excitement.

"The ManiSoyo has sent them to welcome us to Mpinda, Gil Eenezh," the Mbanda Lwa was going on. "He awaits us there, eager to witness the magic I promised to perform for him."

"No, my lady, those are not the ManiSoyo's canoes. They have not been sent to welcome us. Those are the canoes of your son Mbemba. He has brought them to drive us away."

Seeing that Dias and Father de Sousa had joined Gil and Gonçalves at the binnacle, Rodrigues, who had been in the ship's waist with his soldiers and gunners, now also came up to the quarterdeck. "What's the trouble?" he asked.

"Senhor Eanes says there are hundreds of canoes on the river," Dias replied. "Let me have my glass, *senhor.*"

Rodrigues looked around, trying to spot the canoes through the driving curtains of rain, with as little success as the others.

"Holy Mother of Christ," Dias gasped after a few moments of peering through the spyglass Gil had handed him. "Have a look at this, Dom Tomé." He passed the glass to Rodrigues.

It was a formidable sight, especially for anyone who hadn't seen its like before: the hundreds of war canoes, the thousands of warriors in them, decked out in feathers, decorated in war paint, brandishing lances and shields, bows and arrows, axes and clubs, all massing in a seemingly impenetrable barrier across the river's mouth, the rain beating down on them, thunder cracking around them, lightning flashing over their heads, the river beneath them black and deep, the shoreline behind them a black wall of trees, fortifying a savage kingdom. Aye, a most formidable sight, surely formidable enough to give any reasonable man pause, to frighten even Dias and Rodrigues and Father de Sousa off, as Mbemba had vowed to do.

"Who are they?" Rodrigues asked, lowering the spyglass.

"The army of ten thousand I warned you about. You doubted Mbemba could assemble so many. Do you doubt it now?"

Rodrigues didn't reply and resumed scanning the river through the spyglass with a measure of awe.

"We can't go on, my lord Captain," Gil said. "You can see that for yourself. It's just as I warned you it would be. We must turn back before we're all killed."

"No." Rodrigues telescoped the spyglass shut with an angry slap of his hand. "We don't have to turn back. No, by Christ, not while we have the queen Leonor aboard."

"What do you mean?" Dias asked, glancing at the Mbanda Lwa.

"I mean that this is the perfect moment for her to demonstrate the magic she has acquired by her baptism, my lord Captain," Rodrigues answered with sharp sarcasm. "The magic of our guns. Let me have them fired."

"You're mistaken, Dom Tomé," Father de Sousa said. "This is not the perfect moment for that."

"Why not? I assure you, padre, one salvo from our larboard cannon and these savages will scatter out of our way like rabbits."

"That may be, but how will they know the salvo is the thunder and lightning of God?"

"Eh?"

"We don't want to scatter them out of our way like rabbits, Dom Tomé. We want to win them over to our side. That's the whole point of the trick. Not to make war but to make friends. So we must arrange it so that they see the cannonade as God's thunder and lightning, so that they see the thunder and lightning as a magic they too, like their Catholic queen, can learn to call down from the heavens by receiving the sacrament."

"And how do we do that?"

"By getting Mbemba on board. By having him witness for himself Queen Leonor perform this magic." Father de Sousa turned to Gil. "You must get Mbemba to come on board, *senhor.*"

Gil looked back out to Mbemba's big canoe. It was now only a few hundred yards upriver from the *Beatriz,* approaching slowly but steadily under the powerful strokes of its twenty paddlers, the four smaller canoes in escort following closely in its wake. And the hundreds of other canoes behind them were now also on the move, advancing down the river's estuary toward the river's mouth.

"Get him to come on board, *senhor.* Tell him his mother is on board."

"He knows that. He's been to Mpinda. The ManiSoyo must have told him she followed me to the ship."

"Tell him she wants to show him the magic she has acquired by her baptism."

"He must already know that too. The ManiSoyo must also have told him that."

"You can't be sure. Make sure. Call to him. Go to him."

"You can't let him go to him, padre," Rodrigues interrupted. "You can't trust him. He'll give the trick away if he goes to him."

"You don't have to worry about that, Rodrigues. Because I'm not going to him. I don't have to. He's coming to us."

Although Mbemba's canoe was still a good hundred yards away, there could be no doubt that, in its steady, relentless advance, it was making for the ship. And the massive flotilla, also advancing steadily through the pouring rain, was fanning out from the Zaire's estuary into the wide expanse of the river's mouth.

"He *is* coming to us," Father de Sousa exclaimed. *"Deo gratias.* This is just what we want. Dom Tomé, make the cannon ready to fire."

"My lord Captain?" Rodrigues wasn't taking his orders from the priest.

"Aye, Dom Tomé, make the cannon ready to fire," Dias agreed anxiously.

"No one's to be hurt, my lord Captain," Gil said with a sudden rush of concern as Rodrigues started down to the gunports on the main deck. "You hear that, Rodrigues? You're not to fire on those canoes. You're not to fire on anyone."

Rodrigues, however, just kept on going.

"Where is Queen Leonor's breviary?" Father de Sousa asked with rising excitement. "Mbemba must see her praying from it when the guns fire."

"Pader de Sooza speaks to me, Gil Eenezh?"

"Explain it to her, Senhor Eanes. She can read the Pater Noster or the Agnus Dei. It doesn't matter which. God will hear her whichever prayer she reads and answer her by bringing down His thunder and lightning."

Gil looked from the priest to the Mbanda Lwa, then out to the river again. Mbemba's canoe had nearly reached the ship. "Nuno, throw him a ladder."

Gonçalves bounded down from the quarterdeck.

"Senhor Eanes. Explain it to her. Explain that that's the magic she's acquired."

"You explain it to her, padre. It's your trick and it's a cheap trick and I don't want any part in it."

Father de Sousa's face went ashen and he also looked out to the river again and saw Mbemba's canoe and the four smaller ones in escort nudge up against the ship's larboard beam just forward of where Gonçalves was having the rope ladder lowered. "Paiva, go to my cabin and fetch my breviary," he shouted at the pilot, then turned back to Gil. "I *will* explain it to her, *senhor.* It won't be so difficult to explain. Hurry, Paiva."

As the pilot dashed down to the priest's cabin in the sterncastle, Rodrigues suddenly reappeared on the spar deck. "My lord Captain," he shouted. "Those savages are surrounding the ship.

It was true. The canoes of the flotilla, fanning out into the river's mouth, were encircling the *Beatriz,* closing her off from the ocean, hemming her in against the river's south bank.

"They're getting under the guns. The guns won't be of any use if we allow that. We must make for open water, my lord Captain, before it's too late."

But it was already too late. Warriors from Mbemba's canoe were coming up the rope ladder. With their shields slung over their left shoulders and their lances gripped in their left hands, they came up swiftly and easily two by two, side by side.

"Oh, no," Rodrigues barked. "We're not going to have that. You mustn't let those savages come on board, my lord Captain."

"It's just his bodyguard, my lord Captain," Gil countered. "He's a prince and must have a bodyguard with him."

"Bodyguard be damned." Rodrigues began shouting orders to his soldiers and gunners.

They snapped into formation along the spar deck, helmeted and suited in armor and chainmail, wielding crossbows, arquebuses and halberds. The gunners on the ship's bulwarks swiveled the falconets around. Every seaman aboard was armed with a cutlass or knife or marlinspike. Below on the main deck, the cannoneers were charging and loading their weapons.

"Call them off, my lord Captain. There isn't going to be any trouble."

But before Dias could take a hand in this, the first two of Mbemba's warriors came over the rail, and Dias involuntarily backed away from them. They were big, powerful men, swinging their shields from their shoulders, hefting their lances to shoulder height, their faces and torsos painted green and red. Within seconds, two more followed them, and then two more and two more. In all, ten came over the rail and formed a phalanx along the bulwark in the ship's waist.

And then Mbemba himself came over the rail.

The first of him that was seen were the horns and feathers of his headdress, then his handsome face, made all the more striking by the savage scar from the corner of his left eye to the left corner of his mouth, his eyes narrowed against the driving rain and slanted by his high cheekbones, his full mouth unsmiling, a string of lion's teeth around his neck. When his torso appeared above the rail, shining like polished amber in the rain, all his immense strength was immediately apparent in the cut and bulk of the hard muscles of his chest and shoulders. He vaulted the rail like a cat and, leaning on his lance lightly, looked around with quiet authority.

"My God," Father de Sousa said in a low voice. "What a magnificent creature."

Mbemba looked at him and then at Dias, as they both came down from the quarterdeck, and then at Gonçalves and Rodrigues and the soldiers and gunners ranked behind Rodrigues, and then at the seamen at station in the ship's shrouds and rigging, taking them all in with a quiet menace, a dangerous calm, a magnificent creature indeed, revealing no emotion at what he saw. And then his eyes went beyond the men and scanned the whole of the ship from stem to stern, and Gil remembered he had never been on a caravel. He had seen the *Leonor* riding at anchor in front of Mpinda all those years ago but had been too boyishly proud then to accept Diogo Cão's invitation to go aboard. What did he think of what he now saw? Was he as impressed, as amazed, as intrigued, as he had expected to be? In this too, he concealed his feelings and turned to the Mbanda Lwa.

She was still standing on the quarterdeck with Nimi and Kimpasi. She looked a bit uneasy but put on a brave face and smiled at her son.

"Why did you disobey me, Mother?" Mbemba asked her softly, as if not wanting the others to overhear him, as if speaking to her privately. "Why did you come to the white men when I told you it was forbidden?"

"There was good reason and when you hear the reason you will be glad I came . . ." she started to answer defiantly. But she didn't finish the thought. All of a sudden, her smile vanished and a look of surprise replaced it, and then a look of fright.

Not understanding why she hadn't completed her thought, Nimi completed it for her. "She has learned how to use the magic of the writing, Mbemba," she said. "She has become Catholic and now knows how to use the writing's magic."

"Keep still!"

"I will not keep still. You must let her show you this magic. It will make you king."

"She is your woman, Gil. Keep her still."

"Nimi." Gil started over to her.

"Throw her in the river."

Gil spun around. Two of Mbemba's warriors had stepped forward and were coming up to the quarterdeck. For an instant, Gil thought they were coming up for Nimi and he placed himself in front of her, going for his knife. But they were not coming for Nimi. They were coming for the Mbanda Lwa. And the Mbanda Lwa turned to run.

The two warriors seized her.

"Throw her in the river," Mbemba said again.

She was a small woman and it took only one of the warriors. He grabbed her about the waist, lifted her to the rail and dropped her over the side. Tumbling once head over heels, she hit the water on her back with a resounding smack and sank like a stone.

"YOU BRUTE," Nimi was screaming as her mother resurfaced and, gasping wildly, began thrashing about in the rain-hammered river. "You brute. You fool."

Warriors in one of Mbemba's escorting canoes fished the woman out and the canoe immediately turned and set off upriver, taking her back to Mpinda. She huddled in the canoe's bottom, putting her hands on her head; although her humiliation must have been enormous, she didn't seem to have been injured by her fall. Frightened by the violence done his grandmother and by his mother's screams, Kimpasi started crying.

"You are a brute, Mbemba, and a fool besides."

"Stay out of this, Nimi." Gil grabbed her arm to keep her from rushing at her brother.

She struggled to free herself. "He could be king," she wailed, tears of fury and frustration springing into her eyes. "The white men's magic could make him king and I would be the sister of the king and a princess in my own land again."

"I said, stay out of this." Gil gave her an angry shake. They were at cross-purposes; they had been at cross-purposes ever since the Mbanda Lwa had revealed her scheme for forging an alliance between the Soyo and the Portuguese. "Your son is crying. Attend to him."

Startled by his tone—Gil had never yet spoken to her in this way—Nimi went to Kimpasi and embraced him, whispering words of consolation in his ear. But she continued to glare at her brother nevertheless.

Mbemba paid her no mind. He had turned to look out toward the river's south bank. Emerging from the forest there, gathering on the beach among the black boulders pounded by the storm-driven surf, were Soyo warriors, a hundred or so, in their dark-blue kangas, armed with their arrows and long bows. Gil only just now noticed them himself. Were they part of Mbemba's plan to scare off the *Beatriz?* Gil looked at Mbemba inquiringly. Mbemba looked away.

"Nunyo Gonzalvez," he said.

Gonçalves started at the sound of his name.

"You remember him, Mbemba?"

"Was he not with Deego Cum when the Porta Geeze first came to us?"

"He was."

"I remember him standing at Deego Cum's right hand."

"He remembers you, Nuno."

"Mbemba a Nzinga." Gonçalves bobbed his head in what was meant to be a respectful bow.

"Go home, Nunyo Gonzalvez," Mbemba said to him in his strong calm voice. "Return to your land on the other shore of the sea. You are not welcome here."

Had he mistaken Gonçalves for the captain-general, thinking that, as mate, he had succeeded to the absent Diogo Cão's command? Or did he address him simply because he was a familiar face among this lot of ugly strangers?

"If you are in want of food for your voyage home, we will provide it. If you need cloths or tools, wine or water, for your journey to your land on the other shore of the sea, these too will be given to you. But go on that journey, Nunyo Gonzalvez. Resume your voyage. Return to that unknown world from which you have come or we will destroy you to save ourselves from the evil you bring from there."

Gonçalves did not reply when Gil translated this. It wasn't his place to reply. He turned to the captain-general and the priest.

And the priest immediately embarked on a speech. "What evil, Mbemba a Nzinga? We do not bring evil. Tell him that, Senhor Eanes. Tell him we do not come here with evil in our hearts but in peace and friendship, to teach the ways of our world, to learn the ways of his, to trade, and to preach the word of the one and only God."

Gil cut him off with exasperation. "I've already told him that, padre. Don't you think that's what I told him when I was in Mbanza Kongo? Dear Jesus, how many times do you expect me to tell him that before you'll finally get it through your head that his mind's made up? He wants us to go."

"Then tell him we'll go."

"What?"

This was Rodrigues. "It's the way out of this trap he's got us in. His canoes have cut us off from the ocean. They've gotten under our guns. But if we say we'll go, he'll call them off. He'll give us safe passage and we'll be able to make for open water. And then, by Christ, we can come about with our cannon blazing."

"No."

"But don't you see, padre? We can't play your trick anymore. We don't have the queen Leonor on board anymore. The cunning savage, he got rid of her. We've no other choice."

"We've got to have another choice. We'll never accomplish what we've come to accomplish by force." Father de Sousa clasped his hands. "O heavenly Father, help me make him understand we mean no harm. Help me make him see that, by welcoming us to his land, by joining his world to ours, he would perform an act that would be heroic in Your eyes. He would civilize his kingdom. He would save the souls of his people from eternal damnation. As was done with the Ashanti people at São Jorgé da Mina . . . yes, São Jorgé da Mina. That's it, Senhor Eanes. That's the example to hold up to him. Tell him about the Ashanti people at São Jorgé da Mina, *senhor.*"

"What should I tell him about them?"

"Tell him how our settlement there brought them great good. Tell him how our trade enriched them, how our Church elevated them, how our weapons armed them against their enemies, how our ships opened the world to them . . ."

Mbemba didn't know who the Ashanti were (Gil reminded him that Segou had been Ashanti) or where São Jorgé da Mina was (Gil described it as beyond the Kongo's farthest northern horizon), but the notion that the Portuguese had visited some other African land and had been welcomed by some other African people was new to him; it piqued his curiosity and, as he had always wanted that for his own land and people, aroused a tremor of envy in him. His hard-set expression softened, and still leaning on his lance, he once again let his eyes roam about the *Beatriz,* seeing aboard her precisely those wonders unknown to the Kongo—the ship herself, her winglike sails, her intricate rigging and machinery, the compass binnacle, the weapons and armor of her soldiers and crew, the cannon—that Gil was now telling him the white men had brought to this other African land, to these other African people.

"And also the writing?"

"The writing?"

"Did the Porta Geeze also bring the writing to these Ashanti people?"

"Like your mother, Mbemba, many of these Ashanti people have become Catholic."

"And the words these Ashanti people speak, have they now also been made into writing?"

Gil cocked his head, not sure what Mbemba was asking.

"Has writing been made of the words these Ashanti people speak, Gil? Can writing be made of the words any people speak? Can the Porta Geeze make writing of the words my people speak?"

"I don't know."

"That would be the most wonderful magic of all."

Of course it would. Of all that the white men had to offer, of all Europe's arts and crafts and Christianity's spiritual glories, writing was the one skill, the single concept, the Kongo most conspicuously lacked. They had their own God and priests, rites and rituals; they had no need for the Church's. Nor could Portugal provide them with anything more manifestly useful for their daily lives than the works of their own weavers and blacksmiths, farmers and herdsmen, hunters and fishermen, builders and carvers of wood and stone. But writing, a written language, that surely would revolutionize their civilization as no other invention of European technology or idea in Christian theology could, and it was a measure of Mbemba's singularity that he recognized this.

"Ask your priest if writing can be made of the words the Kongo people speak."

"He wants to know if Kongo can be made into a written language, padre."

Father de Sousa's pale, foxlike face lit up in amazement. "My God," he exclaimed. "What an extraordinary creature he is. He is not to be gotten at with magic tricks. He is not to be impressed by the thunder of our guns. But writing, a written language . . . how extraordinary that this is what would excite his imagination, a Negro heathen of the forest . . ."

"Well, can it or can't it, padre?"

"It can. I'm sure it can. It wouldn't be easy. It would take an immense effort. But it could be done. Given enough time."

How much time? Mbemba wanted to know.

"How can I answer that? I don't think it has ever been done before, putting a savage language into writing. My God, imagine what would be involved. You'd have to compile a vocabulary, contrive a grammar. You'd have to invent an alphabet to represent the pronunciation of their words. It could take months, years, even just to make a start. But it would be worth it. Dear Lord, what a magnificent accomplishment it would be. We could teach it to everyone. We could translate the Gospel into it. . . . Tell him that, Senhor Eanes. Tell him that, if he welcomes us to his land, if he allows us to build a church and trading settlement here, we will bring the magic of a written language to his kingdom."

"Ask him what sort of settlement he speaks of," Mbemba said.

"Why should I ask him that? What difference does it make?"

"Ask him if the settlement could be built on your island in the river."

"What are you thinking, Mbemba? You can't be thinking you could keep secret such a settlement."

"I tell you to ask him, Gil."

But Gil didn't get a chance because just then Rodrigues again broke in.

"What's going on now? Over there. Look over there." The master-at-arms was pointing to the south bank where the Soyo warriors had been gathering. "What are those savages up to?"

The Soyo were launching canoes. Mbemba went over to the ship's rail and, to Gil's surprise, seemed as puzzled by this development as everyone else.

"The ManiSoyo," Mbemba said.

Going over to the rail himself, Gil asked, "Why does he come?"

Mbemba shook his head.

"You did not ask him to come?"

"No."

"MtuKongo," the ManiSoyo called up to the ship from his canoe. "Do you hear me, MtuKongo?"

"I hear you, ManiSoyo."

"You have been betrayed, MtuKongo. The NsakuSoyo has betrayed you. He has sent word to Mbanza Kongo that the white men have come again."

Mbemba winced as if physically hit.

"I am sorry for this, MtuKongo. I did not know of it. The Nsaku-Soyo sent word to Mbanza Kongo without allowing me to know."

"When did he send it?"

"As soon as he learned from the Mbanda Lwa that the white men had come again."

"So word that the white men have come again must soon reach Mbanza Kongo."

"It already has. The NsakuSoyo's runners were quick. Your brother, Mpanzu a Nzinga, has already heard it."

Mbemba squeezed his eyes shut.

"And hearing it, you know what he will believe. He will believe you have rebelled against the king. He will believe that, in keeping secret the return of the white men, in coming to them here in secret with this great army, you intend to make league with them against the kingdom. And so he will come here with an army even greater than yours to defeat your rebellion and drive the white men away."

"Do you know this, ManiSoyo? Do you know he is coming here with an army greater than mine?"

"I know this, MtuKongo."

Mbemba closed his eyes again. His plan was wrecked; his strategy to scare off the Portuguese without a war was in shambles.

"Shall we fear this, MtuKongo?"

"Why do you ask that?"

"Because the Mbanda Lwa says we need not fear it. She says she has acquired the strong magic of the white men. She says she now has the power to speak to the white men's God and call down His thunder and lightning so there is nothing to fear, no matter how great Mpanzu's army."

"The Mbanda Lwa," Mbemba said bitterly. "All would have gone well, no one would have known the white men had come again, if only she had kept herself out of this, as I ordered her to do."

"But is it so, MtuKongo? Has the Mbanda Lwa acquired so strong a magic? For if she has, then I also will not fear the coming of Mpanzu's army."

"What are they talking about?"

Gil turned away from the rail. "Mpanzu is on the way here, my lord Captain, with an army even greater than this one."

"Mpanzu? Mbemba's brother?"

"Aye. He has discovered we are here and he is coming with an army twice the size of Mbemba's to drive us away. And he won't be as reasonable about it as Mbemba has been, I can tell you. He won't bother to come and talk to us. He won't offer us provisions for our voyage home. He will attack us straight away with all his force if we don't depart before he gets here."

"When will he get here?" Rodrigues asked.

"Just a moment, Dom Tomé," Father de Sousa interrupted. "Just a moment, just a moment. There is something here I don't understand. What do you mean Mpanzu *discovered* we are here, Senhor Eanes? Didn't he know we were here? Didn't Mbemba tell him?"

Gil wanted to bite his tongue. He realized he had said too much.

Father de Sousa's thin, scarlet lips twisted into a knowing smile. "So, he did not tell him. He kept our presence here a secret from him. Evidently, he does not share Mpanzu's opinion of us."

"Only in that he was willing to give us a chance Mpanzu wouldn't," Gil shot back. "A chance to get away from here with our skins. But he will drive us away as surely as Mpanzu will if we don't take this chance he's given us."

"I don't think Mpanzu is quite as sure of that as you seem to be, Senhor Eanes. Otherwise why would he come here with an army of his own?"

Gil didn't reply.

"Who else, besides Mbemba, doesn't share Mpanzu's opinion of us, I wonder?" the priest went on. "Queen Leonor. We know she doesn't. Perhaps the ManiSoyo doesn't either—or wouldn't if Queen Leonor demonstrated her powerful magic for him. . . . If only we could get her back on board."

Gil turned away from him in disgust.

"What will you do when Mpanzu comes, MtuKongo?" the Mani-Soyo was asking with mounting urgency. "Will you fight him? The Mbanda Lwa says that, now that she possesses the white men's strong magic, you should fight him and we, the Soyo, should fight beside you to take the Kongo throne for you, a prince through whose veins flows Soyo blood."

"Do not repeat the foolishness of the Mbanda Lwa, ManiSoyo," Mbemba replied angrily. "Of course I will not fight Mpanzu. Nor will you. We are not in rebellion against our king. We do not seek the Kongo throne."

"Then what will you do?"

Mbemba looked back over his shoulder and once again let his eyes roam over the ship. And all the confusion and indecision that had disordered his expression when he first heard that the Portuguese had returned disordered his expression now. All his mixed emotions about the white men showed in his expression. Their very nearness, the very nearness of their wonderful things, tore at his loyalties again.

"Will you drive the white men away before Mpanzu comes? Is that what you will do, MtuKongo?"

Mbemba turned back to the river. "No, ManiSoyo, I will not drive the white men away before Mpanzu comes. I will go to him. I will meet him on his way here and will ask him to see the white men with his own eyes. He has never seen them with his own eyes. So I will go to him and ask him to come to the white men in peace and see them with his own eyes."

"No, Mbemba," Gil broke in. He didn't want Mbemba to waver in his decision to scare off the *Beatriz;* he didn't want him to do anything to keep the ship from turning back for Portugal. "Do not do this."

"I must."

"Why? For the sake of the writing?"

"It can be said that way."

"It seems of such great value to you?"

"It is a thing we have never imagined for ourselves, Gil. It is a thing of which we have never even dreamed. It is a thing of a world unknown to us. In this, yes, it seems of great value to me. For, by it, we can know what we have never known, imagine what we have never imagined, dream what not even the wisest of our sorcerers has ever dreamed, a world larger than our own world, the world on the other shore of the sea. We should know that world, Gil. We should become part of it. The task of doing that somehow has fallen to me."

"This is what you will say to Mpanzu when you meet him on his way here?"

"He is not a bad man, Gil. He is only mistaken. Soon my father will die and he will be our king. He will be a greater king if I can persuade him to know the larger world and become part of it."

IX

Gil . . . wake up, little son."

Gil rolled onto his back and opened his eyes and saw Gonçalves leaning over the bunk.

This was in a small sterncastle cabin, across the passageway from the captain's, that Father de Sousa had had prepared for the Mbanda Lwa and Nimi and Kimpasi when they had first come aboard the *Beatriz* in Waterfall Bay and that contained their belongings. Nimi, with the boy clutched tightly in her arms, was asleep on the deckboards in the middle of the cabin. Mother and son had started out together in the cabin's other bunk, but unused to its strange comforts, had abandoned it during the course of the night. A guttering oil lantern, swinging with the roll of the ship, hung from an overhead beam, casting a dim orange light.

"What is it, Nuno?"

"The queen is here."

"What?" Gil sat up, fully awake with a start.

"Queen Leonor, she has come out to the ship. She is asking for you."

"Did you let her come aboard?"

"No."

"You mustn't let her come aboard. You know what would happen if she came on board."

"Aye, I know."

"Where is she?"

"In a canoe lying off our starboard beam."

Gil looked at Nimi. Thank God, she was still sleeping. He didn't want her to awaken. He didn't want her to know the Mbanda Lwa was there. He was sure she would try to intervene on her mother's behalf if she did.

"All right, Nuno, I'm coming but don't wake anyone else. No one else must know."

He kicked away the rough woolen blanket that covered him, put on his kanga, belted on his ivory-handled knife and followed Gonçalves out of the cabin. It was almost daybreak. The storm had abated during the night and much of the overcast had blown out to sea and the stars that had winked on in the sky upriver were already fading in the pearly gray light of the coming dawn.

"Is this your watch, Nuno?"

"No."

"Whose is it?"

"Paiva's."

Gil looked round at the pilot lounging against the compass binnacle on the quarterdeck. "Why are you up, then?"

"I couldn't sleep."

Gil turned back to Gonçalves. In the faint light, he could see the worry etched in the leathery creases of the balding mate's good-natured face.

"Trouble's coming, little son. I feel it in my bones."

"I feel it too, Nuno. I shouldn't have gone to sleep either."

"We'll take turns not sleeping from now on."

"Aye, that's what we'll do," Gil said with a smile, glad to have someone near he could count on as a friend, and went with him to the starboard rail in the ship's waist.

The *Beatriz,* her sails struck, was now riding at anchor in the cove in front of Mpinda. While Mbemba had still been on board, she had sailed here the previous evening, Gil conning the helmsman during the voyage in the then still pouring rain. Then Mbemba had disembarked and had set off with a bodyguard of his warriors to meet Mpanzu. His flotilla of war canoes, having accompanied the *Beatriz* up the river's estuary to Mpinda, had formed a cordon across Mpinda's cove, trapping her there as surely as they had trapped her in the river's mouth. But there had been another development during the night while Gil had slept: War canoes were now lined up along the riverbank in front of Mpinda as well. They weren't Mbemba's canoes, though. They were the ManiSoyo's. And one of them had come out to the ship. Only because he knew from Gonçalves that she was there was Gil able to detect, in the poor light of the false dawn, the Mbanda Lwa standing in it among a bodyguard of Soyo warriors.

"My lady," Gil called down to her.

"Is that Gil Eenezh?"

"It is, my lady. What is it that you wish?"

"Throw down the rope steps, Gil Eenezh, so I can come up on the boat."

"I cannot do that, my lady. It is forbidden."

"Who forbids it?"

"You know very well who forbids it. Your son, the MtuKongo, forbids it."

There was a moment of silence while she considered this. Then she said in a louder, more imperious tone, "Throw down the steps, Gil Eenezh. I am Catholic and wish to speak to my priest."

This wasn't smart. In the quiet darkness, their voices carried. Paiva, on the quarterdeck, would hear them and wonder what was going on and come over. And he would alert the others. And nothing would suit the others better than to get the Mbanda Lwa back on the ship.

"Help me lower the ladder over the side, Nuno."

"You're letting her come on board?"

"No, I'm going down to her."

The ManiSoyo was in the canoe with the Mbanda Lwa. It surprised Gil but he realized it shouldn't have. It explained why the Mbanda Lwa had come out to the *Beatriz* once she was sure Mbemba was gone. He hopped from the bottom rung of the ladder into the canoe.

"ManiSoyo."

The old chieftain only nodded in response. He had aged well, plump, white-haired, wearing a beautiful robe of heron feathers,

heron feathers in his hair, a kindly grandfatherly figure, very much as
Gil remembered him from so long ago. If the NsakuSoyo had been
Gil's first enemy in this land, the ManiSoyo had been his first friend.
And he didn't seem hostile even now, merely reserved, as if yet un-
decided what side to take in this competition of hopes and ambitions. Kneeling in the canoes lined up along the beach of his village
behind him were thousands of his warriors, facing the thousands of
Mbemba's warriors in the canoes on the river. They might have been
poised to fight each other but they also might yet be induced to
make common cause.

"Tell Pader de Sooza I am here, Gil Eenezh. Tell him Queen
Leonor, who he himself made the first Catholic queen of the Kongo,
wishes to speak to him."

"What is it that you wish to speak to him about?"

"I have asked the Mbanda Lwa to fulfill her promise to me, Gil
Eenezh," the ManiSoyo said. "I have asked her to show me the magic
she claims now to possess."

"Why must you speak to Padre de Sousa in order to show the
magic to the ManiSoyo, my lady? As you say, Padre de Sousa has made
you Catholic and, by this, put the magic into your own hands."

"I too have asked this, Gil Eenezh," the ManiSoyo said. "But the
Mbanda Lwa says she cannot perform the magic without the proper
fetish."

"What fetish?"

"The writing, Gil Eenezh," the Mbanda Lwa said.

"The breviary?"

"I must speak the incantation of the writing in order to call to
the Catholic God to bring down His thunder and lightning. But I no
longer have the writing with me."

It made sense; certainly to the ManiSoyo it must seem a perfectly
sensible explanation. No magic could be performed without the
proper fetish and, because of her unceremonious departure from the
ship the day before, the fetish, the breviary, was still with her other
things in the small sterncastle cabin.

"I wish Pader de Sooza to give me the writing so I can show its
magic to the ManiSoyo."

"He will not give you the writing, my lady. He will not receive you at all. He has agreed to wait here until Mbemba returns from his meeting with Mpanzu. He has agreed this is a matter for the two brothers to decide."

"Mbemba may not return for many days."

"Padre de Sousa is willing to wait those many days. And so should you. And you as well, ManiSoyo."

With a shrug, as if relieved of the burden of deciding whose side to take, at least for the time being, the old chieftain went aft into the stern of the canoe.

"Who can say what will happen in those many days, Gil Eenezh," the Mbanda Lwa persisted.

"No one can say, my lady."

"Mbemba might never return. Mpanzu might not allow him to return."

"Or Mpanzu will return with him, as he seeks to have him do."

"Come, Daughter."

The Mbanda Lwa glanced around at the old chief as he sat down on the stern thwart and gave an order to his paddlers. They immediately dipped into the water and began turning the canoe away from the ship. Reluctantly, the Mbanda Lwa went aft to take a seat beside him and Gil grabbed hold of the ship's ladder and, hanging on it, pushed the canoe off with his foot to speed it on its way.

He remained hanging on the ladder for several minutes, watching the canoe paddle to shore, but he knew this wasn't the end of it. The Mbanda Lwa wouldn't so easily give up her attempt to enlist the ManiSoyo to her cause. She would come out to the ship again, and again, and, sooner or later, Father de Sousa and the others would see her and, no matter what Gil said or did, they would eagerly invite her on board and the guns would be fired—to what effect he did not dare imagine. He looked up at the sky. Dawn was beginning to break but a heavy cover of dark storm clouds was rolling in from the sea again. The rains weren't over; they would come again later in the day. He scrambled halfway up the ladder.

"Nuno."

Gonçalves was peering over the rail down at him.

"Nuno, listen, you were right. There's going to be trouble."

"What did she say?"

"She wants to get hold of the breviary. She thinks she needs it to demonstrate the magic for the ManiSoyo. I managed to forestall her for now but she'll try again. And the next time we won't be so lucky. The padre or the captain-general or Rodrigues will be up and they'll have her come on board, and there's nothing I'll be able to do to stop them."

"You could refuse to translate for them."

"It wouldn't do any good. The padre would figure out soon enough what she wants."

"What can we do?"

"Warn Mbemba. Because once she gets on board and the guns are fired, there's a fair chance the ManiSoyo will go over to her side. And Mbemba has to know this. We can't let him come back here not knowing it."

"But how can we let him know?"

"He's only had a few hours' head start and I've a pretty good idea where he's gone. Mpanzu is coming down the royal road from Mbanza Kongo with his army so Mbemba must be going up that road to meet him. I've traveled that road. I think I can catch up with him before he meets Mpanzu. Anyway I've got to try."

"What do you want me to do?"

"Anything you can to keep the Mbanda Lwa off the ship. And also, watch after Nimi and Kimpasi for me."

"Aye, don't worry about them. I'll watch after them for you."

"*Ntondesi.*"

Gonçalves smiled, knowing the word. Gil glanced around. Pink pastel daylight was washing up in the eastern sky. He had better get going; he had to make use of whatever darkness was left.

"Don't tell anyone where I've gone, Nuno."

"I don't know where you've gone, little son."

Gil scrambled back down the ladder—he didn't want to dive off it and risk alerting Paiva by the splash—and slipped into the river as silently as he could. Holding on to the ladder's bottom rung, he looked at Mbemba's war canoes blocking the cove, then at the Soyo canoes lined up along the shore. Chances were they couldn't see him, a speck in the water in the night's last darkness. But he didn't want to take the chance. He had to get clear of them.

Clinging close to the ship's hull, he worked his way along her starboard beam to the stern, rounded it, submerged and pushed off the hull with his feet. He swam underwater as far as his breath could carry him westward, downriver toward the ocean, in the opposite direction from that in which he would have to go to catch up with Mbemba. But it would be stupid to swim in that direction, eastward, upriver. He would waste too much strength fighting the current and the outgoing tide. No, he'd best get clear of the canoes downriver, go ashore there well west of Mpinda and then cut south into the forest, the way he had gone to Mbanza Kongo with his serving woman. He wouldn't go all the way this time, of course. Once far enough south of Mpinda, he would turn eastward and strike back toward the royal road.

The first time he came up for air, he removed his knife from its scabbard and clasped it between his teeth, thinking of the crocodiles he might encounter going ashore.

AFTER VERY NEARLY twenty-four hours of hard traveling, Gil caught up with Mbemba at a small Soyo village on the bank of the Zaire, some fifteen leagues upriver from Mpinda. But he caught up with him too late. Mpanzu and his army were already there.

Dawn was again breaking. It had stormed on and off during the previous day and night and now a light rain was steadily falling. And in this lightly falling rain, thunder rumbling in the distance, lightning occasionally flashing overhead, the thousands of warriors of Mpanzu's army were assembling in the village's market square and along the riverside road, and the hundreds of his war canoes were assembling on the river, making ready to resume their journey to Mpinda with the break of dawn. Mbemba stood with his brother at the river's edge while all around them drummers drummed and kudu horns blared and fetishers shook their rattles and banged their iron gongs and danced and pranced in a war-hot frenzy.

Making his way out of the forest from the south, Gil crouched in the thick, rain-sodden bush about a hundred yards west of the village and surveyed this martial scene. How long before had the brothers met? he wondered. Had Mbemba yet had a chance to argue his case on behalf of the Portuguese? What had been Mpanzu's response if he

had? From this distance, Gil couldn't make out the expression on either of their faces, nor even if they were on good enough terms to be
speaking to each other. From the look of the preparations taking
place, though, it seemed that at least no open hostilities had broken
out between the two, that Mpanzu wasn't treating Mbemba as a traitor to the throne for having kept the return of the Portuguese a secret. His warriors seemed to be mingling peacefully with the
bodyguard Mbemba had brought with him.

The drumming ceased. One by one, the kudu horns fell silent.
Sensing something unusual was happening, the fetishers stopped
dancing and turned around and drew back as Gil appeared out of the
forest. And then Gil suddenly realized that, among the fetishers, shaking a rattle of his own, was the NsakuSoyo. The unexpected sight of
the skinny, mean-faced ju-ju man sent a shiver through him and he
thought: The NsakuSoyo would always be wherever there was trouble. Giving him barely a passing glance, Gil went on to the river's
edge where Mpanzu and Mbemba were standing.

He hadn't laid eyes on Mpanzu in all the ten years of his exile.
Remembered as a dangerous figure, an implacable foe, big and beefy,
taller and broader than Mbemba with bulging, goiterous eyes, he had
grown bigger and beefier and more dangerous-seeming during these
years. Like Mbemba, he was stripped for war, wearing only a kanga in
the colors of his house, a lion's-teeth necklace and a headdress of eagle feathers and water buffalo horn, leaning on a lance. He watched
Gil approach stone-faced, his protruding yellow eyes showing neither
surprise nor anger nor any other emotion, a blank, deathly calm in
them. Mbemba, however, showed both, anger and surprise, his scar
flaring.

"Gil Eenezh," Mpanzu said when Gil reached the river. He spoke
gravely, his voice deep and hoarse but as empty of expression as his
eyes. "White prince from the sky."

"Mpanzu a Nzinga," Gil responded, trying to match Mpanzu's
calm although his heart was beating wildly. "Crown prince of the
Kongo."

"Beware, MtuKongo," the NsakuSoyo said. "Surely he has not
come here alone."

"Have you come here alone, Gil Eenezh?"

"I have come here alone but under your brother's protection, MtuKongo."

Mpanzu looked at Mbemba.

Mbemba's annoyance with Gil was plain to see but he said, nonetheless, "Yes, Mpanzu, he has come here under my protection."

"Of course he is under Mbemba's protection, MtuKongo," the NsakuSoyo said with rising agitation. "They are in this together. They are in this with the Mbanda Lwa. Beware, MtuKongo, for they mean to steal your throne."

Mpanzu ignored this. "And why have you come here alone under my brother's protection?"

"I bring you a message from my people, the Portuguese."

"And what message is that? Is it that they have agreed to fly back to their land in the sky, as my brother tells me he commanded them to do?"

"I did not tell you they had yet agreed to that, Mpanzu," Mbemba interrupted. "I told you I had not yet asked them to agree to it until you have had a chance to see them with your own eyes."

"Yes, you told me that. But I thought they might have come to their senses since you left them and have agreed to fly away home in order to save themselves from the destruction I will inflict upon them if they do not, and that is the message they have sent Gil Eenezh to bring to me. Is that the message they have sent you to bring to me, Gil Eenezh?"

"No, MtuKongo."

"What is it then?"

"They have asked me to tell you that they wish to speak to you and explain to you why they have come—"

Mpanzu cut him off calmly, without bluster or threat but with an unarguable authority. He might not be as quick or far-seeing as Mbemba but he was a steady, stolid man, utterly sure of himself and of his beliefs. "I already know why they have come, Gil Eenezh. The NgangaKongo told me why, when they first came."

"The NgangaKongo never saw them," Mbemba again broke in. "He never saw them with his own eyes. Nor did you. Nor did our father. But now you have a chance to see them with your own eyes and decide for yourself whether they bring evil, as the NgangaKongo warns, or whether they bring good, as I believe."

"And if I decide they bring evil after I have seen them, will they agree to fly back to their land in the sky?"

"It doesn't matter whether they agree or not," Mbemba replied with a quiet assurance of his own. "If that is what you decide after you have seen them, after you have spoken to them, after you have witnessed the magic they perform, I will drive them away whether they agree or not, as I have sworn to you I will."

Mpanzu studied his brother for a long moment, then turned to the NsakuSoyo.

"Do not believe him, Mpanzu," Mbemba said hurriedly before the ju-ju man could say a word, knowing what he would say. "Do not believe the lies he tells. I am loyal to you and our father. I do not share my mother's ambition. I condemn her for it. Do with her what you will. Do with me what you will. I am in your hands. And I will deliver her into your hands as well. But first take this chance and go to the Porta Geeze and see them once with your own eyes."

Mpanzu nodded with a slow, ponderous thoughtfulness. How different he was from what Gil had imagined him to be. Not an unreasoning savage but a quiet, deliberative man, true to his priest, his king and his kingdom, as the heir to a throne should be, caring only for the world he always had known, concerned only that no evil be brought to it from a world unknown.

"Come with me, Gil Eenezh," he said after several moments of reflection and began wading out to one of his canoes on the river.

"Where do we go, MtuKongo?" Gil asked, following him.

"To your people, the Porta Geeze."

"To make war on them? To drive them away?"

"No, to see them with my own eyes, as my brother wishes."

Mpanzu got into the largest of the canoes, both sides of its high prow decorated with paintings of crocodiles, ten paddlers standing along each gunwale, thirty warriors kneeling in ranks of five in its bottom, a drummer and trumpeter seated in its stern. The NsakuSoyo got in after him and, on Mpanzu's signal, so did Gil. Mbemba, however, did not. With a sinking heart, Gil watched him get into another canoe, and wondered if and when he'd get an opportunity to tell him what his mother was scheming.

Gil had never before been in the midst of a war party like this, and at first, it seemed to him a chaos of savagery, the thousands of warriors assembling along the muddy bank, the hundreds of canoes assembling on the rain-beaten river, the head-cracking noise as the drummers and trumpeters resumed their frenzied music and the fetishers resumed banging their gongs and shaking their rattles. But the Kongo was a kingdom forged by war out of rival tribes and clans and feudal principalities, a kingdom well-experienced in and disciplined by war, and soon, even to Gil's eyes, an order emerged from the chaos. The warriors on land and the canoes on the river formed into distinct units very much like platoons and squadrons, each with its own captains, each with its own band of fetishers, each responding smartly to the commands signaled by the drums and kudu horns and iron gongs.

Those on land moved out first, the fetishers leading the way westward down the royal road toward Mpinda, the warriors following them at a slow trot. At that pace, they would reach Mpinda well before nightfall. The canoes, however, would get there much before them. For as soon as the platoons of warriors had started down the road, the drummers and trumpeters in the canoes gave the signal, and the squadrons on the river also started for Mpinda, traveling swiftly on the downstream current.

The canoe Mbemba was in, with an escort of four canoes carrying the bodyguard of warriors he had brought with him, went into the lead. The hundreds of canoes behind them formed into squadrons of fifteen abreast, spanning the river from the south bank to the banks of the islands well out in the stream. Mpanzu's crocodile canoe took up a position in the center of the tenth squadron behind Mbemba's, a commanding position from where he could survey his entire fleet, and behind it came at least ten squadrons more. It made for an astounding force and, adding in the warriors on land, a seemingly invincible one. No wonder Mpanzu had acceded to Mbemba's request to judge the Portuguese for himself. There must seem to him little risk in satisfying Mbemba on this—and doubtless also satisfying what must surely be his own curiosity to at least once see the white men for himself—for, once he had done so, he couldn't imagine having any trouble driving them away with a force such as this, if that was what he decided to do. But he wasn't reckoning with the guns. How could he? Never having seen them fired, having no idea what they were, he couldn't even begin to guess what havoc they could wreak against even so formidable a force as this.

X

SWINGING LAZILY on her anchors in the current and the tide, the
Beatriz, her pennants fluttering in the squally wind, was pointing almost directly at the river's south bank, her starboard beam facing
east, upriver, when Mpanzu's fleet, coming downriver, reached the
cove in front of Mpinda later that morning. The ship was still trapped
in the cove by the cordon formed by Mbemba's war canoes, and the
Soyo canoes were still drawn up on the bank in front of the village.
The rain had stopped but the sky remained heavily overcast, so there
was an oppressive humidity to the day, and swarms of mosquitoes
arose from the river's steely gray surface to add to Gil's discomfort.

He had gone up into the prow of Mpanzu's crocodile canoe—
the NsakuSoyo was seated among the thirty kneeling warriors in its
middle and Mpanzu stood in the stern with the drummer and trumpeter in order to keep an eye on Mbemba's canoe and the four of his
bodyguard, all still well in the lead of the following squadrons. He
was anxious to see what Mbemba would do now that they were in
sight of the *Beatriz.* Would he make straight for the ship to let Father
de Sousa and the others know that Mpanzu was coming in peace? Or
would he wait for Mpanzu's canoe to catch up so Gil could translate
for them?

And that was when he saw it: four pinpoint flashes of bright,
white light along the ship's starboard beam.

There was no sound for several eerie seconds, but even before he heard the distant thud of the explosions and saw the black smoke billow out over the water, he knew what it was. The *Beatriz*'s four starboard cannon had fired through the gunports on her main deck, and after several seconds more of an unreal silence, four towering geysers of water erupted from the river's surface in an uneven row.

Instinctively, Gil flinched.

"What is that?" Mpanzu asked.

The sight was so strange, so extraordinary, so utterly unimaginable that Mpanzu wasn't frightened by it. His husky voice asked the question calmly, expressing only an amazed curiosity. Gil looked round at him, then back at the ship. Was this the Mbanda Lwa's demonstration, for the ManiSoyo's benefit, of the magic powers she had acquired by her baptism? Or had she already demonstrated that, and was this something worse? The first volley had seemed carefully aimed, falling harmlessly behind Mbemba and his escorting canoes and in front of the first squadron of Mpanzu's fleet, and that was a reason to be hopeful.

But then the cannon fired again. And what hope Gil harbored was blasted away. Rodrigues was just finding the range. The ball and shot of two of the cannon, flying over Mbemba's canoes, smashed into the river so close to the first squadron of following canoes that the waves they threw up swamped and capsized several. The third cannon scored a direct hit on three canoes bunched close together on the squadron's north flank, and the fourth cleared the squadron entirely to blow apart two in the next squadron.

Rodrigues was shooting to kill. And he was killing. Twenty, thirty, maybe fifty of Mpanzu's warriors must have been killed in that second cannonade, cut to pieces by scraps of flying metal, chain and grape, broken by ball and shot, rocks and stones, blown into the river and drowned. And if there was any doubt about Rodrigues's intentions, while the cannon were being reloaded, the three swivel falconets mounted on the starboard rail of the spar deck opened up.

Gil flung himself face down in the bottom of the canoe. Kudu horns shrieked. Drums began beating a frenzied tattoo. There was a howling all around him. The NsakuSoyo was screaming. Mpanzu was shouting. Gil couldn't tell whether they were shouting and screaming at him or had been hit. But then he felt the canoe swerve sharply to larboard, toward the river's south bank, breaking off its approach to the *Beatriz.*

He looked up just as the third cannonade erupted and saw its ball and shot and grape strike straight into the fourth and fifth squadrons of Mpanzu's fleet. And now the falconets were also beginning to find the range, adding to the terrible turmoil and destruction. Even so, despite this unimaginable fusillade, despite this incomprehensible barrage of unearthly thunder and lightning and hellish black smoke, the Kongo warriors did not scatter like rabbits as Rodrigues had predicted. They did not turn tail and run, did not succumb to panic and flee. With an amazing discipline, the hundreds of canoes still afloat, responding to the commands of the drums and kudu horns, maintained their ranks and also veered to the south, away from the *Beatriz,* toward Mpinda.

Except for Mbemba's and the canoes of his bodyguard. Racing ahead, they had by now gotten close enough to the *Beatriz* to be safely under her cannon. But they were now also close enough to be in danger of being hit by the fire of the falconets and the much shorter-ranged arquebuses of the soldiers lining the starboard rail. Watching aghast from a crouch behind the high, crocodile-head prow of Mpanzu's canoe, his heart pounding in his throat, Gil expected to see them hit, expected to see Mbemba cut down.

But they weren't hit; Mbemba wasn't cut down. Neither the gunners on the falconets nor the arquebus-armed soldiers were firing on them. And then it struck Gil that the canoes of Mbemba's flotilla, those cordoning off Mpinda's cove, were not being fired on either. The four cannon on the ship's larboard beam and the three falconets mounted on her larboard rail, which were aimed at those canoes and could easily have blown them out of the water, were not being brought into play. Only Mpanzu and his warriors were being fired on.

This must be the work of the Mbanda Lwa. She must be the one directing the firing, wanting not only to astound the ManiSoyo by it and so bring him over to her side but also to kill Mpanzu with it and so clear the way for her son to take the Kongo throne. In a rising panic, Gil looked aft again.

The NsakuSoyo was cowering in the bottom of the canoe, holding his head in his hands. Mpanzu, however, remained standing in the canoe's stern, unflinching despite the violence erupting all around him. Sensing Gil's eyes on him, he looked around and said something. Gil couldn't hear what he said. He had spoken in that quiet, thoughtful way of his, astonishingly showing no fear, his manner and bearing collected and dignified. Perhaps he still did not realize what the guns were capable of; perhaps he still was not ready to accept the evidence of his own eyes. But then the cannon fired again and this volley struck close enough to his own canoe that the impact of the waves they caused knocked him off his feet. He immediately got up on his knees and, when he spoke this time, he spoke loudly enough, a terrible anger at last infusing his words, for Gil to hear him.

"Is this the magic Mbemba wished me to see, Gil Eenezh? Is this the good he believes the Porta Geeze bring to our kingdom?"

"No, MtuKongo. This is his mother's work. This is the work of the Mbanda Lwa. Mbemba did not know of it."

"Did not know of it? How could he not know of it?" the Nsaku-Soyo shouted wildly. "Is he not his mother's son? It is as I have warned you, MtuKongo. He is in this together with her. Of course he knew of it. Look at him there, safely out of harm's way."

The fourth cannonade had scored more direct hits and the river was littered with the shattered shards of sunken canoes and the broken bodies of killed warriors. But beyond this carnage, Mbemba's canoe was now directly alongside the *Beatriz,* indeed safely out of harm's way. Mbemba was in its prow, waving frantically, shouting up at the figures on the spar deck.

"He is trying to stop it. You can see that, MtuKongo. This is not his work. This is his mother's work and he is trying to stop it."

But again the cannon fired and more canoes were hit or swamped and more warriors were injured or killed or drowned, and Mpanzu's once calm, thoughtful, dignified face twisted into a mask of fleshy fury, his bulging yellow eyes full of wrath. Clearly, he believed Mbemba had betrayed him. How could he believe otherwise? Clearly, he believed Mbemba had led him into this deadly ambuscade. And this too was what the Mbanda Lwa had wanted.

And then something still more terrible happened: The Soyo canoes, beached in front of Mpinda, now pushed out into the river and the warriors in them, armed with long bows, let go a flight of arrows at Mpanzu's canoes, running hard for shore.

"Oh, Jesus," Gil gasped. "Oh, dear Lord Jesus." The ManiSoyo, the kindly old Soyo chief, had been won over by the thunder and lightning of the guns. The war had started. The Mbanda Lwa had succeeded in starting the war. Gil hesitated for only a moment. He mustn't get caught on the wrong side of this war. He had to get back to the *Beatriz*. He had to get back to Nimi and Kimpasi. He dove into the river.

Two of Mpanzu's warriors dove in after him.

THERE WAS NO GETTING OUT of range of the guns, no matter how hard they ran for shore. The cannon had the range to bombard the shore. And the bombardment now was virtually continuous. In the silvery gray half-light of the lowering rain clouds, the rapid fire of blinding flashes and deafening blasts, black smoke billowing out over the river, truly must have seemed to Mpanzu's warriors like God's thunder and lightning. A dozen, a score, perhaps thirty of their canoes had been hit and sunk, another score capsized; hundreds of warriors were dead or dying in the water, hundreds more were broken and bleeding in the canoes still afloat. And now they faced the Soyo canoes racing out from Mpinda to prevent them from gaining the shore.

What could the ManiSoyo be thinking, sending his canoes out into this hellish bombardment? Didn't he realize that the shot and ball and grape would make no distinction between his and Mpanzu's canoes once he engaged them at close quarters? Probably not, Gil thought. Dragged back into Mpanzu's canoe by the two warriors and held captive there with a lance at his throat, he watched helplessly as the canoes raced out from the shore.

But then the bombardment suddenly stopped. Had the guns jammed? It wasn't likely that all four would jam at once. Gil twisted away from the lance at his throat to look back at the *Beatriz* and saw Mbemba boarding her. Was he responsible for stopping the bombardment? Or had Rodrigues ordered the cease-fire in order to spare the Soyo? For the battle with the Soyo had been joined. It was hand-to-hand battle. Without the intervention of the white men's guns, it was battle of the kind traditionally fought in the Kongo, with bows and arrows, lances and shields, clubs and axes and battering rams, amid a terrific din of shrieking horns and beating drums and clanging gongs and the hair-raising howls of men.

Canoes clashed. Warriors leaped from one to another, wielding their weapons. Arrows swarmed through the storm-thick air like maddened hornets, humming viciously, biting into flesh. Originally, Mpanzu's force had considerably outnumbered the Soyo and would easily have overwhelmed them. But with his ranks drastically diminished and blasted into chaotic disarray by the cannon, the Soyo proved a match for him.

An arrow killed the warrior holding the lance at Gil's throat, piercing him clean through from spine to belly, and he fell on top of Gil, spitting blood in his face. Gil grabbed the lance and scuttled backward on his buttocks. But the NsakuSoyo, crouching amidship, jumped on him, screaming hysterically. Gil, half his age and twice as strong, easily threw him off. Even so, he couldn't get out of the canoe. Canoes were packed all around Mpanzu's canoe, forming a bulwark to protect their prince. Only here and there did Soyo manage to penetrate it, and the murderous fury with which they were repelled was awful to see. Limbs were severed by axes, throats cut by lances, chests caved in by battering rams, faces destroyed by clubs. One Soyo was decapitated in the act of drawing his bowstring, his head plunging into the river like a cannonball, and yet for several horrifying seconds he remained standing, still drawing the bow, blood spouting from between his empty shoulders, before beginning a crazily jittery dance, dropping the bow and falling into the river as if diving after his head.

Gil had no idea how long the battle lasted. It probably wasn't much more than a half-hour, one turning of the sand glass, but it seemed to him to go on forever in its terrible violence, its relentless bloodletting. Then it abruptly broke off.

The Soyo canoes backed away; Mpanzu's canoes backed away. They had fought each other to a standstill, which, in practical terms, represented a Soyo victory since they had prevented Mpanzu from gaining the shore. The drums took up a slower beat, the kudu horns and iron gongs fell silent. A swath of river about a hundred yards wide, red with the blood of corpses, lay between the opposing forces. Would Rodrigues resume the bombardment now? Gil wondered. With the two fleets no longer so closely engaged, he could fire on Mpanzu's without worrying too much about killing Soyo. There was no way of knowing. For after only a minute or two, Mpanzu raised his lance and his kudu horn player blared forth a shrieking note of command and all the kudu horns echoed it and the drummers started up another frenzied beat and the gongs began clanging and the fetishers howling and the paddlers dug hard into the water and again Mpanzu's canoes were racing for shore. Gil scrambled to his knees, hefted the lance he had taken from his guard and braced himself for the shuddering impact with the Soyo.

In the first battle to reach the shore, Mpanzu's canoe had stayed well back in the middle of his fleet, guarded on all sides by his canoes, so Gil had been kept out of the worst of it. But on this attack, Mpanzu, doubtless made reckless by his anger and frustration over his warriors' failure to break through the Soyo, ordered his canoe into the lead, exposing Gil to the full fury of the fight.

Two Soyo canoes slammed up alongside Mpanzu's and the warriors in them leaped out. One came straight at Gil brandishing an axe. Gil thrust at him with the lance, caught him in the groin, felt the lance slice in with horrifying ease, then get stopped by bone. The Soyo fell backward. Gil jumped up and tried to pull the lance out but it was stuck on innards. He twisted it viciously, castrating the man. The man was still alive, screaming.

There was screaming on all sides. Then the kudu horns began screaming, not a single note this time but two, one higher than the other, each repeated quickly in a trilling trumpet call. It was a special command. And then Gil realized that the first platoons of Mpanzu's land army had reached Mpinda.

That broke the back of the Soyo resistance. The Soyo could not stand against the massive numbers of Mpanzu's warriors charging into Mpinda down the royal road from the east. The villagers began running every which way, into the forest, into the river. And then the Soyo warriors also began running, first those on land, trying to reform in a better place from which to fight, then those in the canoes on the river.

A hut in Mpinda burst into flames. Then another. Mpanzu's warriors, swarming into Mpinda, were setting the village on fire. The Soyo on land fled into the forest to the west. The Soyo in the canoes fled downstream toward the ocean. Mpanzu's warriors gave chase. But Mpanzu called off the pursuit. Within minutes of the arrival of his land army, Mpanzu's canoe reached the shore, and he leaped out shouting, and his horn player blasted forth a new command and the canoes chasing the Soyo downriver and the warriors chasing them in the forest rushed back to Mpinda.

Mpanzu's canoe was swung around to face out into the river, and Gil jumped out and splashed ashore, leaving his lance stuck in the corpse in its bottom. All of Mpanzu's surviving canoes, as they ran up on the beach, were also swung around to face out into the river, and the warriors rushing back into the village assembled behind them, massing into a human fortress in front of Mpinda. Mpanzu, ankle-deep in the river and shouting commands to the captains of his platoons and squadrons, no longer regarded the Soyo as the great danger. The great danger was now the *Beatriz* and her cannon, and Mbemba and the war flotilla he had blocking Mpinda's cove. Believing Mbemba had lured him here to kill him, Mpanzu expected his brother now to attack him under the cover of the Portuguese guns and do the job the Soyo had left undone.

All of Mpinda was now in flames. Even the tall huts in the Mani-Soyo's compound were on fire. Bodies, twisted grotesquely, were strewn across the village's market square, hacked to pieces, clubbed to death, skewered by arrows, covered with flies, the stink of them mixing with the acrid stink of the black smoke of the burning huts. Not all of the living had succeeded in fleeing. Hundreds of villagers and scores of Soyo warriors had been captured and were being herded into their chieftain's burning compound. Gil had the horrifying notion they were going to be thrown into the flames as punishment for their rebellion. But he didn't have a chance to dwell on it because just then, out of the milling mass of warriors, the ManiSoyo was brought forward.

It shocked him. He hadn't thought the old chief was in Mpinda; he had thought he was aboard the *Beatriz* with the Mbanda Lwa. He looked terrible. His face and torso were caked with dried mud; his white, woolly hair was caked with dried blood. Warriors surrounded him and one prodded him forward with the point of a lance. When he came within a few paces of Mpanzu, he prostrated himself. Mpanzu glanced round at him, then looked back out on the river, loath to be distracted from the work of deploying his army and fleet to stand off the attack he expected from his half-brother.

"Tell him I had no part in this, ManiSoyo," the NsakuSoyo cried out. He had survived the fight by cowering in the bottom of Mpanzu's canoe and jumped out of it now and dashed over to the defeated old chieftain. "Tell the MtuKongo how I counseled against this treachery. Tell him how I always remained loyal to the king." When the ManiSoyo did not reply to this, the ju-ju man dashed over to Mpanzu. "I was always against the white men, MtuKongo. Wasn't I the one who sent word to you that they had come again? Wasn't I the one who warned you not to trust Mbemba?" He was pleading for his life; he was Soyo and feared he would be punished along with all the Soyo for their rebellion. "Wasn't I the one—"

Mpanzu whirled on him. "Stand away from me, NsakuSoyo."

Instantly two warriors grabbed the ju-ju man and pulled him back, and then, of his own accord, he dropped to his knees and prostrated himself. "Please, MtuKongo," he whimpered, his face in the mud.

He was going to die, Gil realized; both he and the ManiSoyo were going to die. And Gil himself also was going to die. Mpanzu surely considered him as treacherous in this as either of them, as treacherous as Mbemba and the Mbanda Lwa.

"Why does he delay?" Mpanzu asked, turning back to the river. "Why does he hesitate? Has he no courage?" He asked this quietly, more of himself than of anyone, expecting no answer.

But Gil, anxious about his fate, answered. "He will not attack you, MtuKongo. He does not want to fight you. If he wanted to fight you, he would have attacked you long before this. He would have attacked you when your back was to him and you were fighting the Soyo."

Mpanzu did not acknowledge the logic of this. He did not want to acknowledge it. For ten years now, he had lived with suspicions about Mbemba's fancy for the white men, about the Mbanda Lwa's schemes for her son, and what had happened today had confirmed him in these suspicions. His large, goiterous eyes stared out on the river, bulging with the fury of these suspicions.

But just now there was no suspicious activity to be seen on the river. The guns of the *Beatriz* remained dumb; the canoes of Mbemba's flotilla remained in their place. The broken bodies and broken canoes of the battles were being carried down to the ocean on the river's swift current, and the rain was near; the storm clouds lowering over the water gleamed a sinister yellow.

"You are mistaken about him, MtuKongo," Gil went on. "I know how bad this must seem in your eyes, but he did not betray you. He himself was betrayed. His mother betrayed him as surely as she betrayed you. He is not in this treachery with her. He did not fight against you when he had the chance. Is this not so?"

"It is so," Mpanzu replied without looking at Gil. "But it is also so that he did not fight *with* me when he had the chance."

Gil sighed. Aye, that also was so. It was what he most lamented about Mbemba, his wavering between the Portuguese and his own people, his hope of mediating between the two worlds, of bringing them together, of somehow having the best of both. And this was where it had got him, in neither world, with the worst of each.

"If he was not in this treachery with his mother, as you say, if he did not intend to lead me into this trap she had set for me, why did he not fight with me when he saw that she had betrayed me? Why did he not order his warriors to attack the Porta Geeze when he saw the Porta Geeze attack me? There are enough of them. They are well enough armed. Why doesn't he order them to attack the Porta Geeze now, if he is as blameless as you say?"

"Because he still hopes to make peace between you and them."

"Peace? Is this how peace is made in your land in the sky, Gil Eenezh?"

Gil winced at the sarcastic fury in Mpanzu's voice.

Mpanzu turned to the prostrate Soyo chieftain. "Is this also your explanation for what you have done, ManiSoyo? Is this why you turds of the Mbanda Lwa's house rebelled against your king? To make peace with the white men?"

"We must make peace with them, MtuKongo," the old chieftain replied in a strangled voice. "Their magic is strong. We cannot stand against it. You have seen for yourself how strong their magic is."

"Not strong enough to have saved you, ManiSoyo," Mpanzu shot back with scorn.

"No, not strong enough for that, MtuKongo," the ManiSoyo conceded mournfully. "But that is because I am not Catholic. That power is given only to those who have been made Catholic by the priest of their magic. The Pader de Sooza. Those he makes Catholic acquire the power of his God's magic. Those who become Catholic, the magic saves."

"He comes," the NsakuSoyo suddenly called out. "Look, MtuKongo. Mbemba now comes against you."

Simultaneously, Mpanzu and Gil whirled round. Mbemba was climbing down the ship's ladder into his canoe. The four canoes of his bodyguard were forming into a phalanx in front of him, facing the shore. And ten, fifteen, twenty canoes of his war flotilla were paddling out of the cordon that blocked the cove to assemble in two squadrons behind him. Dear Jesus, no, it couldn't be what it seemed; Mbemba couldn't be launching his fleet against Mpanzu. Gil couldn't have been so wrong about him. But then Gil saw someone else climbing down the ship's ladder. A woman. He recognized her just as she jumped from the ladder's bottom rung into Mbemba's canoe.

"The Mbanda Lwa," the NsakuSoyo cried out again. "She comes with him. Beware, MtuKongo. She possesses the white men's magic and seeks your throne."

Mpanzu barked a command. The kudu horns blared, the drums started up an urgent beat, the paddlers in Mpanzu's canoes pushed out into the river and his warriors on the bank surged forward.

"No, MtuKongo," Gil shouted above the din. "He brings her to you to make peace. He wants you to know this was her doing, not his."

Mpanzu glanced at Gil, then went into the river himself. His canoe was waiting for him, but he didn't get into it. He stood beside it, knee-deep in the water, one hand resting on its high, crocodile-head prow, and watched Mbemba's canoes approach. They approached slowly, warily, the four close together forming a screen in front of Mbemba's, the twenty in two squadrons close behind it.

And then Mbemba began shouting. He was still too far away to hear. Gil looked around. No one was paying any attention to him, and he fleetingly thought that this might be his chance to escape. But escape to where? To the west, downriver? The bulk of the Soyo army was in the forest to the west, the bulk of their canoes downriver, and he couldn't be sure whether they would treat him as a friend or a foe. Upriver then, to the east. But the bulk of Mpanzu's army was there, still coming down the royal road to Mpinda, and he knew how they would treat him. He was as much caught in between as Mbemba was.

The Mbanda Lwa moved up into the prow of Mbemba's canoe, just behind her son, smiling with much self-assurance, obviously pleased with the treachery she had wrought. Her hands were clasped in front of her, holding a book. The breviary. She must have recovered it from the sterncastle cabin so that she could convincingly perform her magic for the ManiSoyo, so that she would be seen to be the instrument of the bombardment of Mpanzu's fleet.

Gil's mind began racing. Something odd was afoot.

"Mpanzu, I will speak to you," Mbemba was shouting. "I will explain this treachery to you and ask your forgiveness for it."

"Come closer, Mbemba," Mpanzu shouted back and hopped into his canoe. "I cannot hear what you say."

This wasn't true. Mpanzu was urging him to come closer only in order to get his hands on him. But Mbemba wasn't stupid. He understood what his brother believed about him, what his mother had so cunningly contrived to have Mpanzu believe about him, and while still some two hundred yards offshore, he ordered his canoes to halt their approach. Mpanzu's canoes inched farther out into the river and his warriors also moved forward, wading deeper into the water. The forces of the two Kongo princes faced each other with weapons poised, nerves high-strung. Behind Mbemba, the *Beatriz* rode at anchor with her guns doubtless primed. Behind Mpanzu, Mpinda was in flames, thick with the stench of smoke and death. In this situation, the slightest miscalculation could set off the fighting again. The rain was nearer, blowing in from the sea.

"I say, I ask for your forgiveness for this treachery, Mpanzu. I say, I wish to explain to you that it was not my doing."

"Whose doing was it?"

Mbemba turned to his mother and pulled her up beside him. "It was her doing, Mpanzu. It was the doing of the Mbanda Lwa." Then he said something to her in a quiet voice that, indeed, could not be heard on shore.

She stepped in front of him, smiling her pleased smile, the breviary clasped in her hand. Clearly, she felt empowered by the holy book and was not in the least bit afraid.

"Is it as Mbemba says?" Mpanzu shouted to her. "Is this treachery your doing, Mbanda Lwa?"

"Address me as Queen Leonor, Mpanzu a Nzinga."

"What?" Mpanzu, of course, had never heard the name or title before.

"I am Leonor, first Catholic queen of the Kongo. I have been made so by the priest of the white men, the Pader de Sooza."

Mbemba grabbed her arm with fury.

She shook him off, unfazed. "Yes, it is as Mbemba says, Mpanzu. This is my doing. I am the one who called down the thunder and lightning of the white men's God against you. I am Catholic and possess this strong magic and can call it down against you whenever I wish." She raised her hands, holding up the breviary for Mpanzu to see.

"It is the writing, MtuKongo," the NsakuSoyo shouted and came running into the river. "Beware of it. It is the fetish by which they invoke their terrible magic."

Mpanzu turned to him. "Why do you always tell me what I already know, NsakuSoyo?" he growled. And then: "Kill him."

Instantly, two warriors seized the ju-ju man. He had only a moment in which to scream. Then he was run through by a lance. His screams throttled in his throat and turned into an ugly gurgle. It was exactly the way Segou had died, pinned to the ground by a lance, his legs and arms flailing horribly, then stiffening grotesquely and falling still. Mpanzu turned away. The Mbanda Lwa was still calling to him.

"Your day is at an end, Mpanzu. You must submit to this strong magic I possess and stand aside for my son."

Enraged by what she was saying, Mbemba grabbed her arm again and shoved her sprawling into the stern of the canoe. She sat there, clutching the breviary to her bosom, still smiling.

"Is this how you ask my forgiveness for this treachery, Mbemba?" Mpanzu shouted. "By telling me to submit?"

"No, Mpanzu—"

"Because I will not submit. I will not submit to this magic of the Porta Geeze. I will not submit to this evil they bring to our land."

"I do not ask that of you, Mpanzu."

"What do you ask of me, then?"

"Only what I asked of you before my mother worked her treachery against us. See the Porta Geeze with your own eyes. Judge them for yourself. They wish to make peace with you. They used their magic against you only because of the Mbanda Lwa's lies. And now they are sorry for it and wish to tell you so."

Mpanzu looked around as if he were considering this. But Gil could see he wasn't. He was looking around only to appraise the deployment of his army and fleet, to measure his chances against Mbemba's forces and the Portuguese guns. His bravery in this was impressive and tragic to see. For although he fully comprehended now the awful destructive power of the guns, he was nonetheless ready to fight them to keep the Portuguese from his kingdom. He looked back at Mbemba.

"The Mbanda Lwa must be punished, Mbemba."

Mbemba didn't reply to this.

"If this treachery was her doing only, if you and the Porta Geeze had no part in it, if it was the work of her lies, then give her over to me to be punished for it."

Mbemba looked round to his mother. She stood up.

"Give her over to me to be punished as proof that you had no part in her treachery."

Mbemba thought this over for a few moments. Then he said, "Send one of your canoes for her, Mpanzu."

Mpanzu gestured with his lance and one of his canoes started paddling out into the river.

"No," the Mbanda Lwa screamed. "If you give me over to him, he will kill me."

And just then there was a bolt of lightning and a crack of thunder. Mpanzu looked up. Mbemba looked up. Everyone looked up.

Even Gil looked up at the heavily overcast sky. It was just the storm drawing closer but, with the memory of the cannonading so fresh in everyone's mind, with the warriors on neither side really able to distinguish between the thunder and lightning of the guns and the thunder and lightning of the sky, all tensed to expect the worst.

And then Gil cried out, his heart jumping into his mouth, "Mbemba. Don't let her do that."

Mbemba whirled around. His mother had scampered back into the stern of the canoe and, facing toward the *Beatriz*, had opened the breviary. It was a signal, Gil had realized in a flash. Father de Sousa or Dias or Rodrigues must be watching her through a spyglass. They must have arranged it in advance. If matters didn't proceed to her liking, she was to pray from the breviary and God would answer her prayer with His terrible magic.

And the cannon fired.

The first volley overshot its target. The ball and grape smashed into the forest behind Mpinda, tearing off branches, breaking tree trunks, bringing down a shower of leaves, sending monkeys and birds scattering in squawking, chattering panic. Gil instinctively dropped to his knees beside Mpanzu's canoe and hunkered against it for protection. But to his amazement, the canoe began to move. The paddlers were pushing out into the river. Standing in its prow, Mpanzu was pointing at Mbemba with his lance and shouting, and his kudu horns were blaring and his drummers were drumming and the fetishers were banging their gongs and howling.

They were going on the attack. It was madness; they should be fleeing, not attacking into the mouths of the cannon. It was heroic madness. They had seen what the cannon could do; they believed it was the thunder and lightning of the white men's God, and still they were willing to go on the attack, still they were willing to lay down their lives fighting the white men who had brought this evil to their kingdom from that unknown kingdom in the sky.

Mbemba had jumped on the Mbanda Lwa, torn the breviary from her and thrown it into the river. But it was too late. And he knew it was too late. He turned around to see Mpanzu's fleet coming toward him. He pushed his mother aside and stood up, gesturing frantically at Mpanzu, waving him off, making a last, desperate appeal to his brother, still hoping to make peace between him and the Portuguese. Oh, the folly of it, the tragic folly.

Mpanzu's bowmen on the shore let go a volley of arrows and Mbemba was hit. He fell backward, his head landing in his mother's lap.

Gil jumped up and started to run. But the cannon fired again. And a cannonball dealt him a shattering blow to his side.

XI

THE SMALL HUT of mud and wattle didn't have windows, its low entryway was sealed with earth and he could hear rats skittering around in its dank, dark corners.

This was somewhere in the royal district of Mbanza Kongo but, not being able to see out, he couldn't be sure exactly where, and wracked with pain, didn't much care. Two or three ribs in his left side had been cracked and one might have punctured a lung. His wrists were bound behind his back, and a noose around his neck was tied to a post driven into the hut's mud floor, fettering him in a position in which he could do little to ease his pain. And he was starving. He couldn't remember the last time he had eaten. It was several days now since he had been put into this hut—he could count the days only imperfectly by the change in the light that filtered through the chinks in the hut's roof—and he had not been given anything to eat here. And he couldn't remember having eaten during the journey here from Mpinda.

He had collapsed on the first day of that journey. The four warriors who had brought him to Mbanza Kongo had set off at a killingly swift pace and he couldn't keep up. Each step jarred his shattered side, and he stumbled and fell and cried out in anguish and, coughing, spit blood. The warriors hated and feared him and would have gladly left him to die where he fell but didn't dare. He was needed alive. Mpanzu had ordered them to keep him alive, believing that, as a Catholic, he could, with the proper fetish, not only call down the thunder and lightning of the white men's God but stop it as well. So they made a litter and carried him.

This was an improvement, marginally. At least he didn't have to expend any effort of his own, but the pain caused by the warriors' jolting gait was no less than if he had been walking himself, and he became feverish. Perhaps the warriors had offered him food, but the fever nauseated him and he couldn't eat. He lay face down on the litter, trying to shield himself from the driving rain, and drifted in and out of consciousness during the weeks of hard travel through the forest of the Mbata and across the rolling grasslands of the Nsundi and up the escarpment of Mbanza Kongo's royal mountain, and was unconscious when he was put into this hut.

The rats awakened him. Was one scratching at the mud packed in the entryway, trying to get out? He squinted into the gloom. He could hear something scratching and scraping at the mud in the entryway but couldn't see any rats. And then, after a moment, it was more than just scratching and scraping. The mud was being shoveled away. The sealed entry was being opened. When it was broken through, a gust of fresh wind blew into the dark hut and he saw that it was a black, moonless, overcast night outside but no longer raining.

"Gil Eenezh."

"Who is that?"

"Nimi."

"Nimi?" He repeated the name with a surge of startled disbelief. But then: "Oh, Nimi. *Mchento.*"

It was the other Nimi, his old serving woman. Was she a prisoner too? She pushed a basket through the entryway, then followed it on her elbows and knees. Those who had broken open the hut for her remained outside.

"Untie me, *mchento.*"

She shook her head and began unpacking her basket.

"Nimi, please. I am badly hurt and in great pain."

"Forgive me, Gil Eenezh, it is forbidden. But they have given me food and drink for you. They are anxious that you do not die."

She had produced a gourd and a cup from her basket and now filled the cup from the gourd and, lifting his head with one hand, held the cup to his lips with the other. It was *malafu* and he drank it so thirstily that much of it splashed down his chin into his overgrown beard. Then she took out of the basket a bowl of cold posho and fed this to him with her fingers.

"Now show me where you have been hurt."

"In my side. I think some bones may be broken and also I am coughing blood."

"Lie back."

He lay down as best he could but didn't actually rest his head on the ground because the noose strangled him whenever he put his head too far back. She ran her fingers down his ribs, feeling his injuries more than seeing them in the dark.

"Be careful," he said, wincing under her touch.

She turned back to her basket. She had some sweet-smelling salve in there, and as she began applying it to his side with a clean cloth, he tried to remember what had happened after he had been brought down by the cannonball on Mpinda's beach.

Mpanzu's warriors had continued fighting through five or six more volleys from the *Beatriz*'s cannon. But then Rodrigues found the range and the cannon fire became so accurate and the slaughter so vast that, by the time Mbemba's canoes, seeing their prince hit and dashing forward to his rescue, and Mpanzu's canoes, rushing out into the cove on the attack, had engaged at close quarters and Rodrigues had stopped the bombardment in order to spare Mbemba's men, Mpanzu's warriors were hopelessly outnumbered and they at last broke and ran. They overran Gil and he was taken captive. He didn't remember how he had been captured. All he remembered was that, in the furor and tumult, fire and noise of the disorderly retreat, his wrists had been tied and he had been dragged by a rope around his neck into the forest behind Mpinda.

The Soyo had attacked them as they had retreated into the forest. It was a harrying attack, meant mainly to keep them retreating. And then the rain had started again and, in the downpour, the Soyo had broken off their attack. But it was clear that they intended to continue in their rebellion; it was clear that they believed their wisest course now was to throw in with the white men and their terrible magic. Would the other peoples of the Kongo follow their example once they too saw the terrible magic of the white men? And they would see it. Rodrigues surely would arrange to have the *Beatriz*'s guns brought ashore.

"Do you know what is happening, Nimi? Have you heard how the fighting progresses?"

"Only a very little," she answered without looking up from cleaning his wounds.

"Have you heard anything of the NtinuKongo or of my son?"

She shook her head.

"Do you know if they have been hurt?"

"I am sorry, Gil Eenezh, I do not know."

"Mbemba was hurt. I saw him go down under a shower of arrows. Is he dead?"

"I have not heard."

"What have you heard?"

"Only that the white men are coming to Mbanza Kongo and, as they come, they bring down thunder and lightning, destroying all in their path."

"Where are they now?"

"On the royal road, halfway through the forest of the Mbata."

"Do the Mbata fight against them?"

"How can the Mbata fight against them? The thunder and lightning sets fire to their homes and lays waste their villages. No, the Mbata do not fight against them. Most flee from them but many surrender to their terrible magic and become Catholic and fight with them. As the Mbanda Lwa has done. As the ManiSoyo has done. As Mbemba has done."

"Mbemba? Is that what you heard? They say Mbemba has become Catholic?"

"It is what they say."

"It is what the Mbanda Lwa would want them to say, but I am sure it is not true."

She shrugged and turned back to her basket. She had completed cleaning his wounds and now pulled out a length of kanga cloth and wrapped it tightly around his ribs. "Now eat some more," she said and raised his head again and brought the bowl of posho to his lips again.

"Enough, woman," a voice called into the hut from the dark outside, a shrill, high-pitched voice. "Come here."

Gil recognized the voice. "Lukeni a Wene?" he asked. "Nganga-
Kongo, is that you who speaks?"

Nimi scrambled over to the hut's entryway on his shrill command.

"Give this to Gil Eenezh, woman."

She turned back to Gil, holding what appeared to be a small
box.

"What is it, NgangaKongo?"

"The fetish, Gil Eenezh. The fetish with which you will stop the
thunder and lightning of your Catholic God."

Gil squinted hard at the box in Nimi's hands. It was the size and
shape of a small book. "Is it writing, NgangaKongo?" he asked, in-
credulous.

"Yes, it is writing, Gil Eenezh."

"Let me have it, Nimi." In his astonishment that the Nganga-
Kongo had a book—what book could it be?—he forgot his wrists
were tied and reached for it eagerly, and the sudden, aborted movement caused a jolt of white-hot pain to his shattered side and a spasm
of blood-flecked coughing. When the pain subsided and he recovered
his breath, he said peevishly, "What do you expect me to do with this
writing, NgangaKongo, when I am bound like a pig? Have me un-
bound."

"Unbind him, woman."

Nimi pulled a knife from her basket—Gil noted this; it might
come in handy one day to know she had a knife in her basket—and
cut the thongs that bound his wrists. With his hands free, he slipped
the noose from his neck and took the book.

It wasn't a book. It was only a remarkable imitation of a book, a
brilliantly accurate copy of the only book the NgangaKongo had ever
seen. Like Father Sebastião's breviary, it had covers of black leather,
the front cover embossed with a gold cross, and the pages, expertly
stitched between them, were sheets of a very fine cloth, a hundred
perhaps. He opened it at random, almost expecting to see hymns and
prayers in Latin script written on the pages, so beautifully was it
made.

"Speak the writing, Gil Eenezh, and tell your God to stop the
thunder and lightning that kills our people."

"I cannot see the writing to speak it in this dark, NgangaKongo."

"Here, woman."

A lighted oil lamp was passed through to Nimi. Gil closed his eyes against the sudden, unaccustomed brightness, then looked down at the pages opened in his hands. And he began shaking his head at the travesty he saw there. Oh, dear Jesus. It was laughable, and he would have laughed if it weren't also somehow so heart-breakingly pathetic in its yearning, mistaken aspiration. This wasn't Latin script. This wasn't writing of any kind. This was a fantasy of writing, the scribbling of an innocent child. Mimicking the words and sentences he had seen in the breviary, the NgangaKongo had neatly inscribed these pages with sentences and paragraphs of stars and crosses, dots and squiggles, circles and exes, arrows and squares, a gibberish of meaningless symbols that revealed how wholly incomprehensible the very idea of writing was to a people who had no use for it and so had never invented it for themselves. Truly, for them, it was only a fetish, a fetish of an alien sorcery.

"Now speak the writing, Gil Eenezh," the NgangaKongo said again in his eerie, high-pitched voice from the dark outside. "Speak the writing and stop the evil of your God's magic."

"I cannot speak this writing, NgangaKongo. I do not know how to speak this writing. I have never seen such writing before."

The NgangaKongo did not reply to this.

"Do you hear what I say, NgangaKongo? This is not writing with which I can speak to my God."

"He has gone," Nimi said.

"Gone? Where has he gone?"

"To see if you have stopped the thunder and lightning that kills our people."

"No, NgangaKongo, wait." Gil dashed to the hut's entryway.

And was kicked in the face.

He didn't see who did it. He didn't even get a chance to see outside, so swift and sudden was the blow. He fell back, wrenching his side, and the combination of the blow and the renewed searing pain in his side caused him to lose his senses. He couldn't have been unconscious very long, but when he came to, he found himself once again alone in the dark. Nimi was gone, the lamp was gone and the entryway was again sealed with mud. He might have dreamed the whole episode except that the NgangaKongo's "book" lay beside him and he was still untied. He picked it up. It was, he realized, the instrument of his survival, his chance of getting out of here alive.

The hut was broken open again the following morning, letting fresh air and bright sunlight in. Bright sunlight? It astonished him. Could the season of the rains be over? Could this already be the beginning of the year's first dry season? Could so many months have passed since the Portuguese had come again? Ten warriors, wearing kangas in the colors and design of the royal house, stood outside the hut. The NgangaKongo was not with them.

"The ManiKongo sends for you, Gil Eenezh," one of the warriors said.

Gil ducked out through the hut's low entryway and looked around. The air was translucent, the sky brilliantly blue and spotted with puffs of sparkling white clouds. A score of small, windowless mud-and-wattle huts like his were clustered around a clearing still awash with rain puddles, glittering in the bright sunlight. Their entryways, as his had been, were sealed with packed earth, and a stockade of bamboo stakes encircled them. Were people sealed inside them as he had been in his? Although there was no sign or sound of them, he was certain there were. Because it occurred to him what this was: a prison. Who, he wondered, were the other prisoners? Was Nimi?

The warriors marched him across the clearing to a gate in the stockade. When the gate was swung open and he stepped through, he recognized where he was. Directly ahead was the palace of the ManiKongo with its three peaked roofs of thatch, its columned verandas, set in a lush garden of frangipani and bougainvillea, flamboyants and flowering trees. As he was led to its front veranda, he remembered the first time he had been brought here so long ago: The emissary of the king of Portugal to the king of the Kongo, wearing velvet and chainmail and a plumed helmet, armed with a sword and bearing gifts, and an assembly of the Kongo's nobility had awaited him on the veranda. Now he was a prisoner, half-naked and half-starved and almost certainly facing death, and no one at all was on the veranda waiting for him. Prodded forward by a warrior's lance, he went up onto the veranda. The embroidered crimson cloth that covered the main entryway was pulled aside.

As that first time, at the end of the long, narrow audience room which he entered from the veranda, Nzinga a Nkuwu, the ManiKongo, sat on his throne on a raised platform, grotesquely fat and blind, a pillbox hat of basketweave on his oddly small head, the golden fur of a lion and the spotted skin of a leopard thrown over his massive shoulders. His high priest, the wizened, hunchback dwarf, also as the first time, was seated at his feet. And his first queen, the Mbanda Vunda, Mpanzu's mother, bigger and blacker than Gil remembered her, her skin much aged and wrinkled, stood at his right, one arm resting on the carved lion's head on the backrest of the throne. Servants held palm fronds as a canopy over the king's head. Warriors lined both walls of the long, narrow room. But there were no nobles of the ManiKongo's court. Gil started toward the throne, wondering whether the king had been abandoned by his courtiers or his courtiers had taken the field against the Portuguese.

"Is that Gil Eenezh?" the ManiKongo asked when Gil was about halfway to him.

Gil stopped, surprised by the whispery gentleness of the huge man's deep voice, then remembered that it had been as soft and kind the first time as well. Should he prostrate himself before him as an appeal to this kindness? He hadn't that first time but the circumstances were dangerously different now.

"Is that Gil Eenezh, the white prince who came to us from a land in the sky?" the ManiKongo asked again, cocking his head in order to peer down at Gil from under the heavy lids of his clouded, unseeing eyes.

"It is, my lord."

"Come closer."

As Gil resumed his approach to the throne, the Mbanda Vunda leaned over her husband and whispered in his ear. The NgangaKongo looked round to hear what she was saying. Then both the priest and the queen turned back to Gil, their eyes hard, their expressions severe. He stopped again and decided not to prostrate himself. No gesture like that or of any sort would help him with these two.

"I am told that the thunder and lightning of your God has not stopped, Gil Eenezh. Although the rains have ended and the skies have cleared, I am told your God still sends down His thunder and lightning to kill my people."

Was this what the Mbanda Vunda had whispered in his ear? Was he merely repeating what she told him to say? Very likely, in his blindness and immobilizing grossness, he no longer truly ruled his kingdom. Mbemba had said that Mpanzu ruled for him more and more. Perhaps in Mpanzu's absence, the Mbanda Vunda and the Nganga-Kongo were the true rulers here.

"Why is this, Gil Eenezh?" the ManiKongo went on. "Tell me why, after all these ages in which we have lived in contentment without them, without even knowing of them, the white men have come to us from their land in the sky and called on their God to kill us with His thunder and lightning. In what way have we offended them? In what way have we offended their God?"

"You have offended them in no way, my lord. And in no way have you offended their God. This that has happened was never meant to happen. This that has happened, happened by mistake. Mbemba—"

"Do not speak of Mbemba to the ManiKongo, Gil Eenezh," the Mbanda Vunda interrupted sharply. "Do not speak his name or that of his mother, the Mbanda Lwa. They have rebelled against the ManiKongo and are his enemies and must not be spoken of before him."

"No, Gil Eenezh, they must not be spoken of before me," the ManiKongo said in his gentle, whispery voice. "They have rebelled against me and are now my enemies. And for this evil too I can thank the white men. They have stolen the souls of my youngest son and of my youngest queen and made them my enemies."

"As long ago I foretold they would," the NgangaKongo said.

"Yes, Lukeni a Wene, as long ago you foretold they would," the ManiKongo said and reached out his hand.

The NgangaKongo took his hand. "But we will recapture their souls, Nzinga a Nkuwu. We will recapture all the souls the white men have stolen from us. This too I have foretold."

"Yes, this too you have foretold, Lukeni a Wene," the ManiKongo said and released the priest's hand and let his chin drop on his chest, and the weariness of the movement bespoke a great sorrow.

"Where is the fetish? Bring the fetish to me."

The fetish, the book of writing the NgangaKongo had crafted. Gil had forgotten about it, had left it in the prison hut. But one of the warriors who had come for him had fetched it and now hurriedly brought it forward. The NgangaKongo took it from him and stepped down from the throne's platform.

"Here, Gil Eenezh."

Taking the "book," Gil looked at the ManiKongo. He had slumped back in his throne and held his head in his hand in a posture of hopeless resignation, almost as if he were crying. Perhaps he was crying, crying for the stolen souls of his beloved youngest son and beloved youngest queen.

"Now you will speak the writing of the fetish, Gil Eenezh," the NgangaKongo said. "You did not speak it when it was given to you before. We waited with patience for you to speak it and stop the thunder and lightning. But the thunder and lightning go on. Although the rains have ended and the skies have cleared, the thunder and lightning still kills our people. We will wait no longer. You will speak the writing to your God and stop His killing now."

The threat in his words, shrill and high-pitched and spoken as an incantation, was unmistakable. But what was he threatening? Clearly, he still believed Gil had the power to silence the guns, so the threat could not yet be Gil's death. Dead, Gil could not silence the guns.

And then there was a stirring in the room. The embroidered cloth hanging behind the throne, which, Gil remembered from the last time, covered the entryway into another room of the palace, parted. And a woman was pushed through, a serving woman, *his* serving woman, the other Nimi. A warrior pushed her through roughly and she fell to her knees and prostrated herself in front of the throne. She *was* a prisoner. Of course she was. Because she had left her exile with Gil to bring word of the white men's return to Mbemba in secret, she was as much implicated in the treachery against the king as he was, as Mbemba and the Mbanda Lwa were.

"What do you want of her? Why have you brought her here?"

"Tell him, woman."

She raised her head and glanced around with frightened eyes. The warrior who had brought her in stood over her with his lance.

"Speak the writing, Gil Eenezh, and stop the thunder and lightning that kills our people."

The plaintiveness of her plea was sickening to hear. She was in fear of her life. She expected to be killed. And she would be killed. That was the threat, and it was real. He had seen how quickly and remorselessly these people killed. He wanted to protest that this imitation writing in his hands was no kind of writing, that no prayer to his God or any god could be spoken from it. But they wouldn't believe him and they would kill her. They would kill her in front of his eyes. And they would kill him too—because there would no longer be any reason to keep him alive. He opened the "book" and stared at the meaningless writing of its pages.

"Please, Gil Eenezh. Do not delay."

The warrior standing over her head had placed the blade of his lance across the back of her neck.

"Do not touch her. Stand away from her. I will speak the writing to my God but stand away from her. She has nothing to do with this."

The NgangaKongo made a gesture and the warrior withdrew his lance. Nimi, however, remained prostrate, trembling, not daring to move. It was disgusting. The poor, dear woman who had so faithfully cared for him all these years although he had destroyed her life. Would God forgive him? Would God forgive any of the Portuguese who, in coming to this kingdom, had destroyed so many of these people's lives?

"Speak the writing, Gil Eenezh."

"I will speak it, but I will not speak it here. It would do no good to speak it here."

"Where will it do good to speak it?"

"Where my God will hear me speak it. Where He is. With the Portuguese. Take me to them."

THEY HAD EMERGED from the forest of the Mbata into the grassland of the Nsundi and were marching down the royal road toward Mpangala. From where he stood, hundreds of feet above them on the cliffs of the escarpment, Gil had a spectacular view: the black line of the wall of the forest on the horizon far to the north; the yellow hills of the highland savanna rolling away from it to the south, east and west;

the broad, brown-red stripe of the royal road snaking through this grassland to the stockaded town of Mpangala on the banks of the Lelunda River; the river itself winding round the base of the escarpment's cliffs. The NgangaKongo and the Mbanda Vunda stood with him, looking down on the scene, among a bodyguard of the ManiKongo's warriors.

The Portuguese were still a few hours' march from Mpangala. As far as Gil could see, no army was in the field to oppose them. Almost certainly, Mpanzu had retreated into Mpangala, had gathered what remained of his forces behind the town's stockades. What slowed the Portuguese was their difficulty in moving the guns. Mounted on wheeled caissons and accompanied by carts of gunpowder and wagons of provisions, five of the lombard cannon (apparently the others had been left with the falconets aboard the *Beatriz*) were being trundled slowly up and down the steep hills of the road by teams of gunners and seamen. In front of them marched the soldiers armed with arquebuses, their armor and helmets glistening in the bright sunlight, pennants of the Church and flags of the Portuguese king snapping in the fresh breeze of this highland blowing over their heads. Behind them came the ship's halberdiers and crossbowmen, with their own flags flying, and a fighting contingent of seamen, veterans of the Guinea wars, armed with cutlasses and knives, one of whom carried a tall wooden cross. And following them, in a disorderly column stretching a league or more back up on the road, were thousands of warriors with lances and shields, axes and clubs, long bows and arrows. From this distance, Gil could not make out who these warriors were. Surely most were Mbemba's. But many must be Soyo, given the ManiSoyo's rebellion, and, according to Nimi, Mbata were among them as well.

Several litters were being carried midway in the column. The captain-general and Father de Sousa probably traveled in them. Rodrigues, though, almost certainly was one of those armored figures marching under the colors with the guns and soldiers. And Gonçalves? Had he been left behind in command of the *Beatriz* or was he with them? Gil hoped he was. The Mbanda Lwa surely was— she wouldn't miss out on this triumph of her ambitions—doubtless also traveling in one of the litters, and Mbemba too, if he were

wounded but still alive. And Nimi and Kimpasi? The Mbanda Lwa
would have insisted on bringing them along as her blood-link to the
Portuguese, the boy probably walking beside his mother's litter, fascinated by the guns.

"Are you close enough now to the Porta Geeze for their God to
hear you, Gil Eenezh?" the NgangaKongo asked.

"No," Gil replied.

"Then let us go closer."

They resumed their descent of the escarpment. The road they
followed switched around the cliffs so, for a time, the grassland below
couldn't be seen. When it came back into view, about two hours later,
they were only a hundred feet or so above it and could now see
down into Mpangala. Although smaller than Mbanza Kongo, it was
still a considerable town, with hundreds of well-made buildings of
timber and thatch, set around a series of interconnected market
squares, and housing a population numbering in the several thousands. The royal road passed directly through it from the main gate in
the stockade on the north to the south gate, a river gate, which
opened onto the banks of the Lelunda.

A hushed air of watchful alarm hung over the place. Whatever
activity would normally be taking place at this time of day had
ceased. All the women and children were out of sight. Warriors were
massed on the walls of the stockades and in the lookout towers at
the gates. Gil had seen these people fight on the river; he had never
yet seen them fight on land and couldn't imagine how, arrayed like
this within the fortifications of the town, they expected to beat off an
army with guns.

That army had now reached within a half-league of Mpangala. At
the pace of its advance, its cannon, if not yet the arquebuses, would
be in range of the town in less than an hour. Gil hurried the descent
of the escarpment, once more losing sight of the battleground below
as the road again switched back around the cliffs.

Gnarled trees, growing out of the side of the cliffs, overhung the
road. Monkeys scampered in the branches; parrots squawked in the
leaves; swarms of butterflies swirled in the beams of sunlight that
struck through this foliage. When they came around again, Gil saw
that the Portuguese-led column had halted, the litters had been set

down, the five cannon were being emplaced side by side across the road and barrels of gunpowder were being unloaded from the wheeled carts. The figure directing this deployment, now much more clearly seen, was Rodrigues, in chainmail and shoulder armor, a red bandanna under his helmet, waving his cutlass. The soldiers armed with the arquebuses and the halberdiers and crossbowmen fell back on his command—they were still well out of range—and Mbemba's warriors and the Soyo and the Mbata spread out into the grassland on either side of the road. Seeing the disciplined way they did this, Gil realized they had done it before. Probably all the resistance they had confronted in their march up from the Zaire, they had confronted in this way. The sounds of drums and trumpets and the clanging of iron gongs blew up on the breeze.

"I must go closer, NgangaKongo."

"No, Gil Eenezh, this is close enough. Your God can hear you from here. He is not deaf."

And just as the NgangaKongo gave Gil the "book," the cannon fired.

All heads turned. No one here, not the NgangaKongo or the Mbanda Vunda or the ManiKongo's warriors, had seen the cannon fire before. Although distant, the detonations were sharp and clear in the crystalline air, truly very much like distant thunderclaps, and the bright white flashes at the cannon mouths, wreathed in black smoke, could easily be mistaken for flashes of lightning by those who had never seen cannon before, and the explosions of earth and stone and clumps of grass that occurred moments afterward surely must have seemed to them like the wrath of God. For how could there be thunder and lightning when the sky was cloudless and blue?

The five explosions occurred well short of Mpangala's north stockade. Rodrigues did not yet have the range. Even so, the phenomenon caused wild consternation in the town. For there too were men and women who, although they had heard by now horrible stories of it, had not yet seen this terrible magic with their own eyes. And started running.

"Speak the writing," the NgangaKongo commanded in his shrill voice. "Speak the writing now and stop this thunder and lightning."

Mpanzu's warriors still stood bravely at the town's north stockade with their weapons poised, their bows feathered and drawn. But someone had thrown open the gate in the south stockade, the river gate, and people were rushing through it down to the Lelunda. Canoes were beached on the bank there and panicked fights broke out for possession of them. One pushed out into the river so overloaded with scrambling women and children and old men that it capsized. One got away from those trying to get into it and, empty, floated downstream. Two made it across to the opposite bank. Two others headed upriver and disappeared around the foot of the cliffs. Several people ran into the river without canoes and began swimming for their lives. And then the cannon fired again.

One misfired, another fell short but three had the range. The ball and shot and chain of one smashed into the north stockade, breaking away a large chunk. The other two cleared the stockade and their grape and shrapnel and stone crashed down on the warriors behind it.

There was screaming. Gil thought it was the screaming of the townspeople under bombardment, and it probably was partly that. But it also was the screaming of the NgangaKongo, clutching his arm and screaming in his ear. And it also was the screaming of the warriors in the Portuguese-led column, Mbemba's warriors and the Soyo and Mbata.

Raising a howling ululation, brandishing their lances and shields, bows and arrows, axes and clubs, they had begun advancing on Mpangala at a quick trot. A vast horde of humanity flowing across the grassland, they passed the emplaced cannon, and as they passed, the Portuguese soldiers fell in with them, waving their weapons and banners, howling themselves, charging the town. And then there was a third cannonade and a whole section of the north stockade was blown apart.

"Kill him." This was the Mbanda Vunda shouting in a rage. "Kill him now." She rushed over to the NgangaKongo, who was still clutching at Gil's arm. "Don't you see, Lukeni a Wene? It is he who is calling down the thunder and lightning."

Suddenly a warrior was coming at Gil with a lowered lance, its vicious steel blade glinting in the sun.

"Keep him away from me." Gil wrenched free of the Nganga-

Kongo's grasp, the sorcerer's nails scoring the flesh of his arm. "It is not I who calls down the thunder and lightning, Mbanda Vunda, but it is I who can stop it."

"Stop it then."

Gil dropped to his knees. *"Pater noster, qui es in caelis . . ."*

He was gambling and praying that the cannon would cease firing now that the Portuguese soldiers and their warrior allies were charging Mpangala. Because by the time the cannon could be reloaded for a fourth volley, the soldiers and warriors would be so close to the walls of the town that Rodrigues would risk hitting them if he fired again. So he must hold his fire, as he had held it when the Soyo had engaged Mpanzu's fleet on the Zaire, as he had held it when Mbemba's warriors came ashore at Mpinda.

". . . santificetur nomen tuum . . ."

Gil glanced up from the "book." The advancing army was within a few hundred feet of Mpangala and the cannon hadn't fired again. And now they couldn't fire again, not with the soldiers and warriors that close. "You see, Mbanda Vunda. You see, NgangaKongo. I have stopped the thunder and lightning. My God has heard me and no longer sends down the thunder and lightning."

The Mbanda Vunda and the NgangaKongo were staring down at Mpangala. Gil couldn't tell whether they believed his claim or even cared. For it didn't matter now, seeing what was happening in the town below. Mpanzu's warriors were retreating in the face of the onslaught of the Portuguese-led column and in fear of further bombardments, retreating from the shattered walls of the north stockade, retreating through the streets and squares of the town to the river gate, retreating across the Lelunda.

The attacking army entered Mpangala, the warriors and soldiers and seamen streaming through the gaps in the broken north stockade, still howling and brandishing their weapons but meeting no resistance. Bumping and lurching as they were manhandled down the road, the cannon and supply carts and wagons followed them in. Rodrigues ran beside them. And there was Dias, wearing a full suit of armor. And behind him came Father de Sousa, walking beside the seamen who carried the tall wooden cross.

The townspeople who had not managed to flee cowered away

from this conquering host. But when Father de Sousa came among them in his stark black cassock and wide-brimmed black hat, they surged forward with a morbid curiosity, somehow divining that here was the priest of the terrible magic that had conquered them. He made the sign of the cross, smiling triumphantly, and to Gil's amazement and disgust, they prostrated themselves before him as he passed.

XII

THEY MET WITH the ManiKongo; day after day on returning to
Mbanza Kongo, the NgangaKongo and the Mbanda Vunda and various
nobles of his court met in council with the immense, blind king, de-
bating courses of action, arguing strategies, offering invocations to
the gods, lamenting their fate, as they prepared for their final stand
against the white men.

Gil wasn't included in these meetings, but he wasn't shut away
again in the prison compound either. They believed he had silenced
the guns at Mpangala and treated him with a certain measure of awe.
He was given quarters of his own in the palace, Nimi was restored to
him as his serving woman, and although always under the watchful
eyes of guards—after all, he would be called on to work his magic
again and so mustn't be afforded any opportunity to escape—he was
allowed considerable freedom of movement within the royal district,
which he took advantage of to learn the news and hear the rumors
of the war.

Eight days after subduing Mpangala, the Portuguese crossed
the Lelunda River and began the ascent of the escarpment to
Mbanza Kongo. It was an arduous and dangerous enterprise. Canoes and rafts had to be built to ferry the men and guns across the
Lelunda; harnesses and hoists had to be devised to haul the caissons and wagons up the escarpment's steep, winding road; and the
column came under constant attack by the remnants of Mpanzu's

army throughout the climb. Admittedly, these never actually threat-
ened to halt the column's implacable advance, but they took a toll
nonetheless in the lives of men and the loss of time. The reckoning
in Mbanza Kongo was that it would take the Portuguese until the
next full moon to reach the top of the plateau because of these difficulties.

And now the moon was again full.

Gil heard the bombardment like distant thunder in a dream. But
he knew that, in this season, there could be no thunder, and he
wasn't dreaming. He was lying wide awake on his palliasse in his
room in the ManiKongo's palace. He jumped up, wrapped on his
kanga and dashed out onto the palace's front veranda. Day was just
breaking, the air still crisp from the cold of the night before.

The courtyard in front of the palace was aswarm with warriors,
milling about in wild agitation under the flamboyants and bougainvillea and flowering trees of the courtyard's garden, drums drumming,
trumpets blaring, fetishers banging their iron gongs. Mpanzu, big and
beefy, wearing a fighting headdress of feathers and horn, armed with
a great oval shield decorated with the yellow sunburst insignia of the
royal house and wielding a lance as tall as he, was at the center of the
tumult, shouting commands to the captains of his warriors, deploying
his guard.

Gil hadn't seen him since Mpinda, and the sight of him now was
a shock. He had been grotesquely wounded either in the battle on
the bank of the Zaire or in some subsequent battle during the retreat
up from the coast through the forests and the grasslands. His right
ear was missing and that side of his face, a pulpy mass of festering
flesh, was horribly burned. It might have been burned in the fires
caused by the cannonades or deliberately burned to cauterize the
wound that had taken the ear but, whichever was the case, the mutilation produced an ugly grimace, permanently revealing a row of
missing teeth. And he was utterly exhausted; the lids of his bulging
yellow eyes drooped and twitched. Seeing Gil come out onto the
palace's veranda, he went over to him. A warrior of his bodyguard
came with him.

"I am told you stopped the thunder and lightning at Mpangala,
Gil Eenezh," he said in his husky, quiet voice, made quieter and more

hoarse by his fatigue. He gestured to the warrior. "I am told you stopped the white men's magic with this."

Gil didn't reply. The warrior had handed Mpanzu the Nganga-Kongo's "book."

"Well, it is time for you to stop it again."

Gil followed Mpanzu through the gate of the inner palisade that enclosed the royal district and up onto the watch tower at the gate of the outer palisade.

The outlying districts of Mbanza Kongo were in flames. Dwellings, kraals, shops, warehouses and market stalls had been set alight by the bombardment of the Portuguese guns. But the bombardment itself, that distant thunder, no longer could be heard. That part of the city had already fallen and, as Gil and Mpanzu watched from the watch tower in stunned silence, the conquering host was surging through the streets and alleys, parks and squares of the sprawling plebeian districts toward the opposite bank of the Luezi River.

And what a host it was, numbering in the tens of thousands, as if all the warriors of the kingdom had risen in revolt against their king. Gil hadn't expected that, couldn't believe it. He had known, of course, that Mbemba's thousands had joined the Portuguese, and that thousands of Soyo and Mbata had also made common cause with them. But now it was clear that, in their march across the grasslands, the Portuguese had also gathered thousands of Nsundi to their side by the terrible magic of their guns.

The cannon were being emplaced along the quay of the Luezi's opposite bank. The gunpowder carts and supply wagons were being drawn up beside them. The arquebus-armed soldiers, the halberdiers and crossbowmen, the contingent of seamen armed with cutlasses and knives, were mustering behind them, their pennants flying, the towering wooden cross of Christ planted in their midst. And everywhere as far as the eye could see were the thousands and thousands of rebel warriors, buildings burning all around them, people fleeing from them on every side. Gil looked at Mpanzu. The ugly grimace of his mutilated face was drawn back into a bitter, despairing snarl.

In the improving light of the dawn, Gil could see Rodrigues walking down the line of the emplaced cannon, checking charges and fuses, waving his cutlass. Dias, still in a full suit of armor, followed him. Father de Sousa stood by the towering cross. The Mbanda Lwa stood beside him. They were talking to each other or, at least, making broad gestures at each other. What further disastrous misinformation were they imparting to each other in this way, lacking a common language? And then a litter was brought over and set down beside the Mbanda Lwa. The man lying in it pushed up on his elbows and stared across the Luezi toward the palisades of the royal district, unnoticed by either the priest or the queen. Gil immediately recognized who he was: Mbemba, wounded but still alive.

Gil's eyes darted to the others gathered around the guns, searching for Nimi and Kimpasi. He saw Gonçalves. So Gonçalves hadn't been left behind in command of the *Beatriz* (Paiva probably had). He jumped out of one of the supply wagons. He probably was in charge of the supplies. And then Gil saw what else he was in charge of. Turning back to the wagon, he held out his arms and Kimpasi jumped into them. Then he helped Nimi down as well. Dear, good friend, he had kept his promise. He had kept close watch on Nimi and Kimpasi through all this. Gil wanted to shout across to them. But Mpanzu grabbed his shoulder.

"Take this, Gil Eenezh," he growled. "Take the fetish and stop the thunder and lightning of your God with it."

Gil took the NgangaKongo's "book" and opened it slowly, stalling for time. He could not play the same trick here that he had played at Mpangala. For here Rodrigues would not need to send his soldiers and warriors to engage Mpanzu's at close quarters. He could keep them safely out of the line of fire on the Luezi's opposite bank and bombard the royal district from there until it was reduced to ruin.

"Can you stop the thunder and lightning, Gil Eenezh, or not?" Mpanzu demanded as Gil continued to delay.

"What would it matter, MtuKongo?" Gil finally answered. "Even if I stopped the thunder and lightning, you could not defeat an army as mighty as this which you see standing against you now."

"I could, if the thunder and lightning were brought down upon them."

This startled Gil. He hadn't thought of this.

"Call to your God to bring the thunder and lightning down

upon them, and then they will not be able to defeat me."

"But that cannot be done, MtuKongo. You cannot expect the white men's God to bring His thunder and lightning down upon His own people."

Mpanzu studied Gil for a long moment with his beastly snarl. Then he said, "So this fetish is of no worth. It is a worthless fetish."

"It is a false fetish, MtuKongo. Surely you have known that all along. Surely you have known the NgangaKongo could not make a true fetish of a god he does not worship."

Mpanzu nodded slowly, ponderously. "Yes, I have known that all along. Give it to me. Give me this worthless fetish."

Gil handed it over and Mpanzu flung it with disdain from the watch tower into the Luezi. It floated for a few moments, then overturned and sank. They both watched this happen. Then Mpanzu looked up, looked around at his own forces drawn up on this side of the river, then looked across the river at the forces drawn up with the Portuguese, outnumbering his a hundred to one.

"The war is at an end, MtuKongo," Gil said quietly. "It is time to make peace with the white men."

"What are the terms of their peace?"

Gil didn't answer this because he didn't know the answer.

"Go to them, Gil Eenezh. Go to these white men from the sky, go to these Porta Geeze and ask them what are the terms of their peace."

"Alone, MtuKongo? You would allow me to go to them alone? You are not afraid I will run away?"

"No, Gil Eenezh. I am not afraid you will run away. I believe you want to make this peace. Am I wrong?"

"No, MtuKongo, you are not wrong. I want to make this peace and will not run away."

"I will await your return in the palace of my father. Come to me there at this time tomorrow and tell me the terms of the white men's peace."

Gil's appearance on the middle bridge caused a stir of excitement on the other side. The soldiers and gunners and seamen began pointing at him and shouting. Dias and Father de Sousa hurried forward to meet him. But Kimpasi broke free of them all and dashed to

the bridge and, even before Gil stepped off it, flung himself at his father. Gil hoisted him up in his arms.

"Are you dead, *pai?* Everybody says you are dead."

"Of course I am not dead, Kimpasi. Do I look dead?" And carrying the boy in his arms, Gil went to Nimi.

She hung back, watching him approach, her big brown eyes
wide with surprise.

"Do you also believe I am dead, Nimi?"

"I see you are not, Gil. And I am glad for it." And she threw her
arms around him and said, "You are alive and we have won the war
and I am a princess in my own land again."

Gonçalves thumped him on the back. "That's twice you've returned from the dead, little son."

"Thank you, Nuno. Thank you for everything."

Gonçalves shrugged and stepped aside as Dias and Father de
Sousa pressed closer, wanting to put in a word of their own. But Gil
looked past them at Mbemba, propped up in the litter beside the
Mbanda Lwa. He set Kimpasi back on his feet and went over to the
litter and kneeled beside it.

"Mbemba."

"Affonso."

Gil looked around.

Father de Sousa had followed him over. "He is Affonso now, Senhor Eanes," the priest said, a satisfied smile curling his thin scarlet
lips. "Prince Affonso of the Kongo. He has accepted the sacrament of
baptism."

"Is that true, Mbemba?"

Mbemba looked at Gil blankly, his eyes unfocused. He was
clearly having difficulty holding himself up on his elbows. Gil put an
arm around his shoulders. He was as light as a feather. His face was
drawn, his cheeks hollow, his eyes sunk in deep, dark sockets, and his
naked torso was covered with at least a half-dozen wounds. Healing
now, ugly puckered scabs, they were the wounds he had received
from the arrows that had cut him down on the Zaire. It was a miracle
he was alive.

"It is Gil, Mbemba. Don't you recognize me?"

"I recognize you, Gil," Mbemba replied in a whispery voice and essayed a small smile. "We have both survived this unnecessary war."

"Yes, we have both survived this unnecessary war."

"We have out God to thank for it."

Gil glanced up at Father de Sousa and the Mbanda Lwa. The priest was smiling contentedly, not understanding what was being said.

"He died, Gil Eenezh," the Mbanda Lwa said. "He was killed by Mpanzu's arrows but then the Catholic God brought him back to life."

"Who told you that?"

"Pader de Sooza told me that."

"Yes, I expect he did." Gil turned back to Mbemba. "So it is true, Mbemba. You have become Catholic."

"Yes, it is true, Gil. I have become Catholic."

Gil hesitated for a moment, an unaccountable anger choking in his throat. "But why, Mbemba? Why have you become Catholic?"

Mbemba seemed puzzled by the question. His eyes drifted out of focus again. Then he said, "To bring the writing to my people, Gil. To bring that magic and all the magic of the unknown world on the other shore of the sea to my people."

In his anger, Gil wanted to argue with him about this. But he realized that Mbemba hadn't really answered his question, had only recalled something from his memory, had answered by reflex. He wasn't in his right senses; he probably hadn't been since the arrows cut him down. In his weakened state and half-insensible, he had been used, and was still being used, by Father de Sousa and the Mbanda Lwa.

"Lie back, Mbemba. Rest awhile." Gil eased Mbemba back down on the litter. "This unnecessary war is over now. Soon we will go to your father and make the peace."

"What's going on, my lord Captain?" This was Rodrigues, coming over from the guns. "Do I start the bombardment now or have these savages decided to surrender?"

"Senhor Eanes?" Dias asked in his typically uncertain way.

"There is no need for any more bombardments, my lord Captain. These people are willing to make peace. They have sent me to ask what terms you offer."

"Terms, *senhor?* What do you mean terms?" Rodrigues barked. "There are no terms, *senhor.* Either they surrender or we will blast them into their graves."

"Hold your tongue, Rodrigues." Gonçalves quickly got between Gil and the master-at-arms. "This is none of your business. This is for the captain-general to decide."

"Dom Nuno is right, Dom Tomé," Father de Sousa said. "Dom Bartolomeu will decide this matter. Go stand by the cannon. Make ready to fire them. But let us all pray to our dear Lord Jesus Christ that we will not have to do so, that we have come to the end of the killing at last."

"You do not have to pray to the dear Lord Jesus Christ for that, padre," Gil said sharply. "I tell you, these people are willing to make peace. Offer them reasonable terms and there will be no need for any more of your killing."

Father de Sousa's satisfied smile stiffened. "And what would you deem reasonable terms, Senhor Eanes?"

Gil looked at Dias. "My lord Captain, you were sent on this voyage by King João to establish a trading settlement here."

"Aye."

"And you, padre, you were sent here to preach the Word of God and harvest souls for the Church."

Smiling his thin, scarlet smile, Father de Sousa nodded.

"Offer those terms then, my lord Captain. I am sure they would be willing to make peace on those terms. I am sure the ManiKongo, in order to put an end to this killing of his people, would be willing to grant permission for the establishment of a trading settlement here in Mbanza Kongo and also one down at the coast at Mpinda. And for a church and mission to be built there and here as well."

"That sounds fair to me. Does it to you, Father de Sousa?"

"No, Dom Bartolomeu, it doesn't. There has to be one thing more."

"And what is that, padre?" Gil asked.

"In light of the baptism of Queen Leonor, in light of the baptism of Prince Affonso, in light of the thousands of Kongo people who have flocked to the cross and asked to be baptized in the course of this terrible war, I am afraid we must include as one of our terms for

peace the baptism of the ManiKongo. A Catholic king must now sit
on the Kongo throne."

Gil began shaking his head, the anger in him welling up uncon-
trollably. "I cannot believe I hear such hypocrisy spoken by a priest of
my Church."

"Be careful what you say, Senhor Eanes."

"You know perfectly well why the Mbanda Lwa accepted the
sacrament of baptism. You know perfectly well why Mbemba accepted it. You know perfectly well why all those people, terrified by
our guns, have asked for it. It has nothing to do with our Faith, padre.
They know nothing of our Faith. To pretend otherwise is hypocrisy."

"That is not for you to judge, Senhor Eanes. I am the priest. I
have the ear of God. And I say to you that the baptism of the
ManiKongo is part and parcel of the terms we offer to him for making the peace."

"He will never accept it."

"Let him tell us that, Senhor Eanes. Go to him and present these
terms to him and let him tell us that he is willing to allow the killing
of his people to continue rather than accept them."

THE MANIKONGO WAS DEAD.

The Mbanda Vunda had killed him, and his massive corpse, covered in crimson cloth with a single yellow sunburst embroidered on
it, now lay in state on the raised platform at the foot of the throne.
Mpanzu, his eldest son and heir, sat on the throne under a canopy of
palm fronds. By killing the father, the mother had made the son the
king of the Kongo, taking upon herself the awful responsibility of
judging him better fit to rule the kingdom in these sorely troubled
times than her blind old husband. In a magnificent headdress of
heron and egret feathers, wrapped in the crimson-and-yellow kanga
of the royal house, resplendent in jewelry of silver and ivory, pearls
and precious stones, she stood at Mpanzu's right, a hand firmly grasping his shoulder, bracing him. The hunchback dwarf, Lukeni a Wene,
high priest of the kingdom, stood at his left, his wizened body covered with gray ash. And those nobles of the court still loyal to the
crown lined the walls of the long, narrow audience room, decked out
in horns and feathers and velvet robes.

Gil stood among them. In the flickering shadows cast by the coal fires burning in the tall clay pots on either side of the throne, he was almost lost from sight and, for the moment, forgotten. All eyes were fixed on the entryway to the room, awaiting the appearance there of the Portuguese coming to make the peace. Trumpet blasts from the watch towers at each subsequent gate heralded their approach through the palisades enclosing the royal district, guarding the palace of the king.

Gil looked again at the corpse. Although the killing must have taken place several days before, no putrefaction yet marred the face. The fat, ugly, blind old face seemed in a deep worried sleep. Gil was glad he was dead. He was glad that the ManiKongo had escaped the cruel choice the Portuguese presented. But he was not as sure as the Mbanda Vunda at least pretended to be that Mpanzu, as king, was any more capable than his father of saving the Kongo from the Portuguese. He sat with a regal stiffness on the throne, wearing the pillbox crown of woven raffia, a short crimson kilt embroidered with the sunburst crest, leopard skins and lion furs draped over his shoulders, the royal scepter of silver-embossed ivory and emerald-green stones lying across his lap, and the ferociousness of the snarl of his mutilations in the half-light of the glowing coals enhanced the impression that here was a younger, stronger, more masterly king, an undaunted foe. But how could he be expected to choose any differently than his father when the guns of the Portuguese were emplaced and primed to reduce this final redoubt of his kingdom to a flaming ruin?

There was a terrific blast of the trumpets from the watch towers of the innermost gate, and the drumming began, a steady, monotonous, mournful beat. Gil looked back to the room's entryway. The warriors on the veranda outside had pulled aside the velvet hanging that covered it. For a moment, the frame of the entryway remained empty. Then two Portuguese soldiers stepped into view, indeed like alien creatures fallen from the sky in their helmets and chainmail and shoulder armor and bristling beards, armed with arquebuses. Two others followed them and then the captain-general, even more alien than the soldiers in a full suit of armor, adorned at the collar and sleeves with ruffs and lace, carrying the visored helmet in one hand like a grotesque second head, clasping the jeweled haft of a ceremo-nial sword with the other.

Two more pairs of arquebus-armed soldiers followed him, and then Father de Sousa, like a wraith all in black except for the polished silver of the crucifix hanging down his chest, his hands folded pi-ously before him, grasping his breviary. Behind him came two sea-men carrying between them a sea chest that Gil recognized as the one that contained the priest's baptismal tools. And then came four Kongo warriors, wearing kangas of pale green bordered in red and carrying between them Mbemba in his litter. The Mbanda Lwa walked beside it, dressed in as much dazzling jewelry and feathered finery as the Mbanda Vunda.

They entered the audience room slowly, consciously or uncon-sciously walking in step to the slow, measured beat of the drums. When they were halfway down the long, narrow room, Gil stepped out of the shadows, stepped in front of them, and they halted.

"Senhor Eanes," Father de Sousa said and came up to stand be-side Dias.

The Mbanda Lwa also came up, and on her signal, the four litter bearers brought Mbemba forward as well and set him down beside her. The eight soldiers deployed around them, fidgeting with the matchlocks of their weapons, eyeing the loyal Kongo along the walls.

"Will you be so good as to act as our intermediary, Senhor Eanes, and make the introductions according to the protocol of this court."

Gil turned to the throne, but before he could begin the pro-ceedings there was sudden commotion. He looked around.

It was Mbemba; he was struggling to get out of his litter. He was pathetically feeble, and his mother was trying to restrain him, but he pushed her aside impatiently, and with the help of two of his bearers, his arms over their shoulders, stumbling in his eagerness, he went to the corpse of his father. He knew he was dead. They all did. Gil had reported it, had explained what the Mbanda Vunda had done and why. But apparently it was only on actually seeing the body lying there that the half-insensible Mbemba truly grasped the reality of it.

He went up on the throne platform and, shrugging off the assis-tance of the bearers, dropped to his knees beside the corpse. He stared at the old face, worried in death, then slowly lowered his own

face to the old face and placed his cheek against its cheek and, drap-
ing an arm across the body, lay down across it. All eyes were on him.
No one stirred. And in the silence, Gil could hear his quiet sobbing.
Then the Mbanda Lwa went forward and grasped his shoulders and
pulled him off the body. He sat back on his heels and looked up at
the throne, looked into the ferocious snarl of his half-brother seated
there.

"I am sorry, Mpanzu," he said in a rasping whisper. "I am sorry for
this."

"You are sorry for the death of our father?"

"Yes, I am sorry for the death of our father."

"I believe you are sorry for that, Mbemba. You were his best
loved." Mpanzu's voice dropped to a husky growl. "And you broke his
heart. You went to the white men against his wishes and gave them
your soul."

With his eyes not quite focused and glazed over with a film of
tears, it was unclear whether Mbemba, in his dazed condition, understood Mpanzu's quiet condemnation. In any case, he didn't argue
with it. And again a long silence filled the room.

Father de Sousa broke the silence. "Can we go on, Senhor Eanes?
Will you present us to the Kongo king in the name of the king of Portugal."

"There is no need to present you, padre. The Kongo king knows
who you are. He knows only too well who you are."

Father de Sousa smiled his thin, tight smile. "And I suppose he
also knows why we are here?"

"He does."

"Then we can dispense with the protocol usual at a royal court
in these circumstances? Very well. Let him tell us straight away how
he responds to the peace terms we have offered."

"The Portuguese await your answer to the terms they have offered for making the peace, ManiKongo. Will you give them your answer now?"

Mpanzu's snarl flickered slightly in the semblance of a smile
hearing Gil use his new regal title. Then he said, "Yes, I will give them
my answer now."

"Accept the terms, Mpanzu," Mbemba interjected softly, still kneeling at the side of his father's body, still looking up, half-dazed, at his half-brother on the throne.

Like the Mbanda Vunda with her hand on her son's shoulder, the Mbanda Lwa, standing behind Mbemba, placed her hand on his.

"Accept the terms, Mpanzu," Mbemba pleaded, "and put an end at last to this unnecessary war."

"I will put an end to this unnecessary war, Mbemba," Mpanzu replied. "But I will not accept the terms." And then to Gil: "Tell them that, Gil Eenezh. Tell them I will not become Catholic. Tell them this ManiKongo will not give them his soul."

"But then the war will go on, Mpanzu," Mbemba said.

"No, Mbemba, the war will not go on. I will end the war but also keep my soul."

"I do not understand."

"You do not? But your mother does. You understand, do you not, Mbanda Lwa?"

"I do."

"*You* will be the ManiKongo, Mbemba," Mpanzu said, his voice dropping again to a husky growl. "You have given your soul to the white men so you can be their king. You can be their Catholic king."

"Senhor Eanes, would you be good enough to let us know what is being said?" Father de Sousa interrupted querulously.

Gil didn't answer him, too astonished by what was now transpiring.

Mpanzu stood up and his mother removed her hand from his shoulder and moved away from the throne. Clearly, this had been agreed on in advance. No one was surprised. There was no unusual stirring among the nobles in the room. They watched what was happening in a submissive silence. Even the NgangaKongo made no protest. Perhaps there was some trick in this that Gil could not fathom.

"Come, Mbemba," Mpanzu said and, holding the scepter in one hand, reached out with the other toward his kneeling brother. "Come, take the throne of our father and be the king for the Porta Geeze."

Mbemba shook his head in confusion.

"Go, Mbemba. Take the throne, my son," the Mbanda Lwa said

excitedly and grasped him under his arms, trying to lift him from his knees. "Help him up. Help him take the throne."

The two litter bearers, who had helped Mbemba to his father's side, now helped him to his feet. Mpanzu grasped his hand and guided him to the throne. Gil glanced around, suddenly anxious. Were they going to kill Mbemba? Was that the trick? Were they going to kill him as soon as he was the ManiKongo?

"Sit down, Mbemba. Sit down in our father's place."

In his feebleness, Mbemba flopped into the throne. His confusion was pathetic. He looked around with unfocused eyes.

"Here, ManiKongo." Mpanzu handed Mbemba the royal scepter. "Here, my lord." He removed the pillbox crown of woven raffia from his head and placed it on Mbemba's, his voice that low, husky growl.

Father de Sousa no longer interrupted. He no longer asked to know what was going on. He and Dias and the Portuguese soldiers could see for themselves what was going on and watched in the same amazement as Gil. After giving Mbemba the royal scepter to hold, after placing the royal crown on his head, Mpanzu took the lion furs and leopard skins from his shoulders and draped them around Mbemba's. Mbemba slumped back into the throne, looking up at Mpanzu. His eyes seemed to clear. Perhaps only now did he fully realize what was being done. The Mbanda Lwa came over to his right side, where the Mbanda Vunda had been standing and was standing no more, and placed her hand on his shoulder, as the Mbanda Vunda had placed hers on Mpanzu's, bracing him.

"Now you are the ManiKongo, Mbemba a Nzinga," Mpanzu said. "Now you are the king of the Kongo, the Catholic king of the Porta Geeze, and this unnecessary war is put to an end."

"I do not want this, Mpanzu," Mbemba said. "It is not what I ever wanted."

"It may not be what you wanted, Mbemba. But it is what the Porta Geeze want."

"And what your mother wants." This was the Mbanda Vunda. "It is what she has schemed for all her life. It is why she started this unnecessary war. It is the fulfillment of her ambition."

"Go away, lady," the Mbanda Lwa said. "Your place is no longer here."

"No," the Mbanda Vunda said. "My place is no longer beside the throne of this kingdom." And she stepped down from the platform and went to stand among the nobles of the court.

Then Mpanzu also stepped down. The NgangaKongo remained a moment longer.

"Lukeni a Wene?" Mbemba turned to him.

"Listen to me, Mbemba a Nzinga," the hunchback dwarf said in his piercing, high-pitched voice. "Listen to what I foretell. You will be the last king of the Kongo. In your reign, the kingdom will be destroyed. The white men, who have made you king by the magic of their God's thunder and lightning, will destroy the kingdom first by stealing its soul and then by stealing its body."

Then he too stepped down from the platform. But he did not go to stand with the others along the walls of the room. He walked up the long, narrow room toward its entryway. He stopped when he reached Dias and Father de Sousa and glared at them but said nothing and continued on his way, passing out through the entry onto the palace's front veranda and disappearing from view.

"*Alleluia, alleluia. Te Deum laudamus,*" Father de Sousa exclaimed. "We praise Thee, O God, for answering our prayers. A Catholic king sits on the throne of the Kongo. The killing has ended and our Lord Jesus Christ now reigns in this once-benighted land."

He hurried forward and stepped up on the platform and stood before Mbemba.

"King Affonso," he cried out in triumph, "first Catholic king of the Kongo. *Dei gratia. Deo gratias.* By the grace of God. Thanks be to God."

He removed the crucifix from around his neck and placed it around Mbemba's, then turned to face the nobles.

"*In nomine Patris, et Filii, et Spiritus Sancti,*" he intoned, making the sign of the cross to the right and to the left, bestowing his blessing on all present.

And at this there was a stirring in the room. Gil looked around quickly, thinking whatever trick had been planned was now to be played. But he saw no trick that he could fathom. All he saw was that slowly, one by one, led by Mpanzu and the Mbanda Vunda, the nobles of the court of the ManiKongo were filing out of the room. He looked back at Mbemba.

Mbemba was pushing himself up out of the throne, trying to stand. Believing he wanted to make a pronouncement as the new king, Father de Sousa and the Mbanda Lwa were helping him. But to their consternation, he shook himself free of their help and again dropped to his knees beside his father's body and, sobbing, fell forward across it.

THREE
1502

I

LORD, YOU ARE HOLY INDEED, the fountain of all holiness. Let Your Spirit descend upon these gifts to make them holy so that they may become for us the body and blood of Your son, Jesus Christ."

Rui de Sousa, consecrated bishop of the Kongo eight years before by Pope Alexander VI in recognition of the remarkable evangelization of the African kingdom, had, on this first Sunday after Epiphany, 1502—the Baptism of the Lord—chosen to celebrate the Eucharist himself. Wearing white and green vestments, his deacon standing beside him, two assisting priests holding his miter and staff, the sweet smoke from the silver censers swirling around him, he kneeled before the linen-draped stone altar in the apse, picked up the host from the silver paten and, extending it with both hands toward the life-size image of the crucified Christ that hung in the central vault of the ambulatory, chanted the familiar words.

"Before He was given up to death, a death He freely accepted, He took bread and gave You thanks. He broke the bread, gave it to His disciples and said: 'Take this, all of you, and eat it. This is my body which will be given up for you.'"

The cathedral was hushed, the worshipers straining to see the mystery taking place behind the chancel screen. King Affonso and his queen Inez kneeled in front of their thrones in the chancel. Gil Eanes kneeled in the first row of stalls on the left side of the choir with the princess Beatriz, the dowager queen Leonor and other members of the royal court. Kneeling in the stalls on the right side were the members of the Portuguese colony, shopkeepers, artisans, traders, soldiers and the master-at-arms Tomé Rodrigues. Out in the nave, the pews were filled to capacity, nearly two hundred Negro faces upturned in rapt fascination.

"When the supper was ended, He took the cup. Again He gave You thanks and praise, then gave the cup to His disciples and said: 'Take this, all of you, and drink from it. This is the cup of my blood, the blood of the new and everlasting covenant. It will be shed for you so that your sins may be forgiven. Do this in memory of me.'"

Bishop de Sousa raised the silver-and-gold chalice, one hand under the stem, and held it above his head for what seemed an interminable length of time, trembling slightly in the breathless silence of the awed and wondering congregation. Then he spoke again. "Let us proclaim the mystery of faith."

And the silence washed away and the cathedral rang with song. "Christ has died, Christ is risen, Christ will come again."

The cathedral was dedicated to the Holy Savior and the kingdom's royal city was now known by its name, São Salvador. It was an imposing structure, certainly by the standards of old Mbanza Kongo, constructed of granite blocks with bell towers flanking its decorated portal, a baked-tile roof covering a colonnaded nave, stained-glass windows illuminating the transepts, gold-leaf paintings of the stations of the cross lining its aisles. It had been built in the third year of Affonso's reign—as a fitting seat for the vicar of what was then Rome's first and, for the next three hundred years, only African see—by craftsmen sent from Lisbon by João II.

The Portuguese monarch had greeted the astonishing news of Mbemba's conversion and coronation, brought home to him by a triumphant Bartolomeu Dias in the European winter of 1493, with immense enthusiasm and had eagerly dispatched follow-up expeditions to develop trade with and propagate the Faith in this first black Catholic kingdom. In every dry season for the next few years, his caravels and storeships had sailed up the Zaire's estuary, bringing goods of European manufacture to barter for the ivory and timber, hides and furs, peppers and palm oil of the Kongo forests, as well as men to reinforce the small Portuguese settlement Dias had left behind in Rodrigues's and de Sousa's charge.

The cathedral of São Salvador was built and a Portuguese quarter of shops, taverns, barracks and cloisters sprang up around it. The palisades enclosing the royal district were torn down and replaced by an ironstone parapet, mounted with cannon and mortars. Baptisms were performed in the thousands by a growing community of Franciscan priests, who also started work on the creation of a written Kongo language. Schools were established for the sons of the nobles of the ManiKongo's court, some of whom, including Gil's son, were sent to Lisbon to continue their education at the College of Santo Eloi. And the population of São Salvador doubled as people from all over the kingdom flocked to this thriving center of new trade and learning. And Mpinda too was transformed during these years of João's enthusiasm, into a flourishing seaport—gateway to Europe and the wider world—with the construction of piers for the oceangoing ships, warehouses for the cargoes they brought and a stone fortress along the riverfront to protect the traffic from pirates and privateers, and was now known as Santo Antonio do Zaire for the church that had been built there honoring that saint.

But then João's enthusiasm ebbed and the development of this unprecedented relationship between a European and an African kingdom ceased. The reason: the discovery of the long-sought sea route to the Indies. Following in the wake of Dias's aborted voyage to the Cape of Good Hope in 1487, Vasco da Gama finally accomplished the feat in 1497, and the trade in silks and spices, which burgeoned soon afterward, proved far more profitable for the Portuguese king than the Kongo trade. So always fewer of his ships called at the port of Santo Antonio and trade with the kingdom correspondingly decreased. And as trade decreased, the ranks of the Portuguese colony thinned. And with fewer soldiers, artisans and priests, no new churches were built, baptisms languished, the schools fell into disrepair, the word of the Gospel was not spread much beyond São Salvador (and even there the converted quickly lapsed in their piety) and the work on devising a written Kongo language was left incomplete.

This had been a sore disappointment for Affonso. Having committed the atrocious act of rebelling against his father and usurping his brother's throne, he had expected to have far more to show for it than this, had hoped miracles would come of it to assuage the guilt of

what he had done. Even so, he had no real cause for complaint. For if
there had been no miracles, it was equally true that the doom the
NgangaKongo had foretold had also not come of his welcoming the
white men to the kingdom. The old sorcerer had died some years before under uncertain circumstances and his dire prophecy had died
with him. Mpanzu and the Mbanda Vunda had been banished into exile beyond the kingdom's frontier and were heard of only in frag-
mentary rumors. And the peoples of the two kingdoms, black and
white, lived together in an untroubled harmony of mutual benefit and
respect.

"This is the Lamb of God who takes away the sins of the world.
Happy are those who are called to His supper."

Princess Beatriz nudged Gil.

Startled from his thoughts, Gil joined her in the response. "Lord,
I am not worthy to receive You, but only say the word and I shall be
healed."

Bishop de Sousa broke the host, placed a piece in the chalice,
ate the rest and drank the wine. Then he came forward into the chancel with the deacon and assisting priests. Affonso and Inez stood up
and went to him to meet Christ in the Eucharist. Both were dressed
in the style of Portuguese royalty. Affonso wore a five-pointed gold
crown (a gift from João), a crimson tabard emblazoned with the yellow sunburst crest of the ManiKongo's house and a short ceremonial
rapier of the finest Toledo steel (another gift from his brother
monarch). Inez wore a silver tiara, a pale-rose silken gown whose am-
ple skirts trailed behind her, and veils of lace. When they had received
the host and drunk the wine and returned to kneel in prayer in front
of their thrones, the assisting priests went down into the nave and
Queen Leonor stood up. Beatriz nudged Gil again.

He shook his head. "You go, Nimi. I haven't been confessed."

She made a face and followed her mother to Bishop de Sousa.
They too wore silken gowns and veils of lace. Also dressed in the European fashion and bearing such titles of European royalty as duke
and earl and count, the other members of Affonso's court went after
them. Then Tomé Rodrigues, in shoulder armor and chainmail, a black
patch over one eye, his big beard specked with gray, led the members
of the Portuguese colony to the deacon. Most of the people lining
the aisles of the nave to receive communion from the assisting

priests wore the usual dress of the Kongo, but some had added scraps of Portuguese clothing, a leather surcoat here, a pair of serge trousers there, linen blouses, cloaks with hoods, even boots. These were mainly merchants who had prospered in the Portuguese trade or servants who had found work in the Portuguese quarter or devoted subjects of Affonso who showed their devotion by imitating his Europeanization.

"The body of Christ."

"Amen."

"The body of Christ."

"Amen."

Still kneeling, Gil rested his forehead on his clasped hands. He didn't pray. He rarely prayed, rarely sought absolution, rarely received communion. This was less because he had lost his faith entirely by now than that he despised Rui de Sousa, and had remained behind in the Kongo with him and Rodrigues after Dias had sailed only most grudgingly. Disgusted with the hypocrisy and force of arms by which the priest and master-at-arms had engineered Christianity's victory in the kingdom, he had had every intention of returning to Portugal aboard the *Beatriz* and, through Nuno Gonçalves's good offices, had even gotten Dias to agree to sign him on as a member of the crew on condition his wages be taken in payment for Nimi's and Kimpasi's passage. And neither the priest nor the master-at-arms, who both regarded him as a troublesome presence, had raised any objections.

It was Affonso who had raised the objections. Still terribly weak then from the wounds he had suffered in the war with Mpanzu, still pathetically confused by its unexpected and unwanted outcome, he had begged Gil to stay, had forbidden him to leave, had argued plaintively during those turbulent weeks after his coronation and before the *Beatriz* sailed that he had to have his Portuguese friend by his side as adviser and confidant in the strange and uncertain future that now lay ahead of him. But as much as he had been touched by this, as much pity and sympathy as he had felt for the reluctant king—Affonso's future would indeed be a strange and uncertain one—Gil would have resisted his pleas and threats and arguments and have sailed for Lisbon if it hadn't been for Nimi. Nimi, the princess Beatriz; she too had begged him to stay.

He had seen it coming, of course; he had seen it coming since the day of her baptism. The promise her mother had made her that day had been kept. Those who had cast her out of the kingdom had been cast out themselves, and as sister of the new king and daughter of the dowager queen, she had been restored as a princess of the highest rank among her own people. What reason was there for her to flee to Portugal now? What more than this could she expect in the land on the other shore of the sea? Gil had no good answer for her. There was no good answer—what indeed could she expect in Portugal, a Negro woman with a *mestiço* son fathered by a common seaman?—so he hadn't answered her and had gone on making the preparations for their departure. But then, at the last possible moment, on the very morning they were to start down to the coast—the caravan with which they were to make the journey was already assembled in the courtyard in front of the ManiKongo's palace—she had announced that neither she nor their son would depart with him.

This hadn't surprised him either. He had also seen this coming. He had hoped it might be otherwise but he had been only too well aware that her feelings for him had been born of her need—her need for his help to escape—and were hardly profound. They had been too little together, had come to know each other not nearly well enough during the months of war and separation, for her to have developed any deeper, stronger feelings for him than need. And now that she no longer needed him, she could allow him to depart with no great care or heartache or sense of loss.

But he needed her. He needed her and the boy. He had grown to manhood in their land and had no family other than them.

He had looked out at the men assembling in the caravan under the flowering trees of the ManiKongo's courtyard. In less than a month, they would reach Mpinda and board the *Beatriz*. And in less than four months after that, the *Beatriz* would cross the Tagus bar and anchor in the Lisbon roads. And after that? What would become of him after that, the marooned seaman long given up for dead and forgotten, returning home after all these years? Perhaps, at first, much would be made of him. Perhaps he'd be presented at João's court and feted for his role in the evangelization of the heathen kingdom. But then? The best he could hope for then was to resume his career at sea, his experiences in the Kongo perhaps proving valuable enough to some ship's master to win him a pilot's berth aboard a merchant-man trading to Africa. And who would be his family then?

"You will not be a prince in the land on the other shore of the sea," Nimi had said to him that morning. "But here you will. Here you will be the white man who stands closest to the throne."

"Why should that matter to you?" he had asked.

"Because I will be your wife," she had answered. "The Pader de Sooza will make me your wife. And then I will be the wife of the white man who stands closest to the throne."

She slipped back into the choir stall now and kneeled in prayer beside him, her eyes piously closed, delicately munching on her wafer. Although thicker in the waist and heavier in the bosom, she was still a very beautiful woman, with her high, chiseled cheekbones and slanted, luminous eyes and dark-honey complexion. The new order in the kingdom suited her. After all those years isolated and despised for bearing the half-white child of the evil white prince from the sky, she had blossomed in her high position at her brother's court, shamelessly enjoying and flaunting her privileged station, eagerly adopting the European fashions, practicing her Catholicism with ardent ostentation, adamantly insisting on her Christian name, becoming more "Portuguese" than the Portuguese. It was as if she had had to get her own back for all those years of disgrace and humiliation. If so, she had, and with a vengeance, and Gil was glad for her and, he had to admit, glad for himself as well. For he too had lived a richer, more comfortable and privileged life as a courtier of the Kongo king than any he could have dreamed of as a seaman in Portugal. Still, there was a discontent in him, a restlessness; he mistrusted the future.

"May almighty God bless you and cause His countenance to shine upon you. *In nomine Patris, et Filii, et Spiritus Sancti.*"

"Amen."

"The Mass is ended. Go in peace."

Bishop de Sousa made the sign of the cross, then turned away rather abruptly and went over to Affonso. The king stood and the prelate spoke to him with some agitation in a low voice. Gil watched this from across the chancel.

De Sousa had not aged well in the African climate; he had lost most of his hair, his moustache and goatee had gone white, his complexion had taken on a sickly cast and was stretched over his sharp, foxlike features like yellow parchment, and his always delicate physique seemed now merely skin and bones under his loose-fitting vestments from the repeated bouts of fever he had suffered. Affonso towered over him, broad-shouldered and muscular, still very much a warrior figure even in his European clothes. But he too showed the toll taken by the years; he too had much gray in his hair, and his expression was drawn and somber, reflecting his sovereign responsibilities and his many disappointments, and that old scar across his cheek was slightly livid. De Sousa was speaking to him either in Latin or Portuguese—he had never really learned Kongo, and Affonso spoke both European languages well—and whatever he was saying evidently annoyed Affonso, by the look of the scar. Inez, the queen, stood to the side, understanding neither language, and waited patiently for the conversation to be done. But then the bishop put a hand on the king's arm and the two men walked back through the apse toward the door that led from the ambulatory to the vicarage, and Inez, gathering up her skirts, flounced across the chancel to Beatriz in the choir stall.

They were great friends, Beatriz and Inez. It was part of Beatriz's importance in the kingdom that she was the queen's closest friend, even though Inez was very much younger. She was not yet twenty. She was a Soyo princess, NtinuSoyo, the grand-niece of the old Mani-Soyo. Affonso had taken her as a child-bride six years before at the urging of his mother, the dowager queen Leonor, who conceived of the marriage as a further means of consolidating Soyo control on the Kongo throne. She was a rather homely girl, short-legged and dumpy, but good-natured and guileless.

"*Keba bota,* Gil Eenezh."

"Dona Inez."

"What shall we do today, Beatriz? It is a beautiful day."

"It is our Lord's day. We must do something in His glory. Are you coming, Gil?"

"In a moment."

Gil was looking back toward the ambulatory. So was Leonor,

with a puzzled frown. The deacon had scurried after Affonso and Bishop de Sousa and all three had stopped at the door to the vicarage and were talking animatedly. Then, with a shrug of irritation, Affonso passed through the door and the bishop and deacon hurried after him. What was going on? Gil wondered. He glanced at Leonor and their eyes met.

She was an old woman now by the standards of the time and place but nonetheless retained an undeniable attractiveness, a shadow of her daughter's beauty, and carried herself with a regal authority and grace. She was no friend of Gil's; she was well aware of his opinion of her relentless ambition and of his refusal to forgive the treachery she had practiced to fulfill it. But she was just as well aware of his role as her son's most trusted adviser and treated him with a cautious respect. She raised her eyebrows now as if inviting him to explain what Bishop de Sousa and the deacon wanted of Affonso. But as he didn't know and would not have volunteered the information even if he did, he only bowed and, with a polite sweep of the hand, indicated that it was, of course, her place to precede him from the choir down into the nave. Inez and Beatriz had already gone down. Leonor smiled wryly and followed them, Gil a step behind her. Then the courtiers and colonists, who had waited patiently in the choir stalls for their turn, formed up two by two for the procession up the nave's central aisle and out of the cathedral's cool, stained-glass light into the bright sunlight of the warm Sabbath morning.

The cathedral was located outside the ironstone, gun-mounted parapet that walled off São Salvador's royal district, and an expansive plaza paved with flagstones stretched from its portal down to the banks of the Luezi River. The city's Portuguese colony at this time numbered something less than one hundred, counting the soldiers and priests, and most of the traders and shopkeepers, artisans and soldiers—and also not a few of the priests—had taken wives and concubines from among the Kongo women and fathered families with them so that, among the many children running around the plaza, there were dozens of little *mestiço* girls and boys. One of the girls was Gil's and Beatriz's, a seven-year-old by the name of Tereza with the wiry brown hair, cropped short, and lovely soft features of her mother and her father's light blue eyes. She came rushing up to him as he emerged from the cathedral a step behind Leonor, tackled his leg, kissed her grandmother, then dashed off after two little Negro boys who were the twin sons, Diogo and João, of Affonso and Inez.

Inez and Beatriz just then were engaged in some inconsequential gossip with Tomé Rodrigues but, when Gil approached, the master-at-arms bowed stiffly and walked away. Their relationship hadn't improved much in these ten years, and this was mainly Gil's fault. He generally kept himself aloof from the Portuguese; since Nuno Gonçalves's departure, he had made no effort to find a friend of his own race, preferring to identify himself (to himself as much as to the Portuguese) solely as a liege man of the ManiKongo, and they in turn treated him with the deference that the role commanded while, behind his back, they complained and made mean-spirited jokes about him.

"Where are the children?" Beatriz asked.

"I just saw them." Gil turned to look for his daughter and the little twin princes and saw the deacon anxiously making his way through the crowded plaza toward him.

He was an older man, older than his bishop, in his late fifties, but a relatively recent arrival to São Salvador. His predecessor had died of snakebite more than six years before, but because of the much diminished traffic from Portugal, he hadn't gotten there until three years ago. Despite his age, he was full of canonical zeal and considered this missionary posting a grand opportunity to do God's work. A Franciscan who had served as an examiner for the Inquisition then in full flower in Portugal—the Jews had been expelled from the kingdom at the time of Vasco da Gama's voyage, three years after their expulsion from the Spains—he had thought to bring its methods to the Kongo. He was constantly deploring the lack of rigor with which the Kongo Catholics observed the Faith and their heretical readiness to fall back on fetishes and fetishers in times of personal crises. Thickly bearded and beetle-browed, he wore a white soutane and sandals, his bare head tonsured. When he caught Gil's eye, he waved at him urgently, pushing people out of his way.

"Father Duarte."

"His Majesty sends for you, *senhor.* He asks that you join him and His Grace in the vicarage at once."

"Nimi," Beatriz was calling. "Where is that woman? Oh, there you are. Find the children, *mchento*. We are taking them for a bath in the Luezi."

"They are playing just over there, my lady." This was the other Nimi, the old companion of Gil's exile. She was still Nimi, never having been baptized, and a member of Gil's household, perhaps the most trusted of the large retinue of servants and warriors and retainers who had gathered around him during these years. "Tereza, come here," she called. "And bring the boys with you."

"Senhor Eanes, please, His Majesty is waiting."

"I'm coming, padre. Nimi, Mbemba has sent for me. You go on. I will catch you up when I can."

"Has he not also sent for me, Father Duarte?" Leonor asked.

"Why no, Dona Leonor."

"Are you sure?"

"He only asked me to fetch Senhor Eanes."

"Why? What has happened?"

The deacon looked to Gil for help. Clearly he wasn't meant to discuss whatever had happened with her or anyone. But the woman intimidated him, as she did almost everyone.

"I am sure Mbemba will tell you all about it later, my lady," Gil said.

"I am sure he will."

THE SITTING ROOM OF THE VICARAGE was handsomely appointed with furniture and artifacts imported from Europe and with paintings and tapestries by European artists. There was no Kongo work in the room; Bishop de Sousa had no eye or taste for it. When Gil and the deacon entered, he had just sat down in a high-backed chair behind a large oak table that served as a desk and, with his elbows on the table, rested his head in his hands. He had changed out of his vestments and was wearing a black cassock, black biretta and silver crucifix, and looked thoroughly vexed. Affonso sat opposite him in a similar chair, also obviously annoyed. A young priest, short and fat and tonsured, stood behind the bishop's chair. Gil didn't recognize him and it was only after he had stepped into the room, directly from the bright sunlight of the plaza, and his eyes had become accustomed to the dimness, that he noticed that the fellow's soutane was torn and caked with dried mud, and that his face was bruised and swollen and caked with dried blood.

"Who is this man? What has happened to him?"

"Father José," Bishop de Sousa replied and stood up behind the table. "He is our missionary in Mpangala."

"He looks as if he has been in a fight."

"He has been in a fight," Father Duarte said. "With the heathen Nsundi in Mpangala, trying to prevent them from participating in an act of devil worship."

"Please, Father Duarte. Allow me to do the talking here."

"I am sorry, Your Grace."

But sitting back down at the desk and again resting his head wearily in his hands, Bishop de Sousa didn't do any talking for a few minutes. Then he said very softly, "He must be killed, Your Majesty. How many times have I advised you of that? He is a threat to your throne and must be killed."

Gil looked at Affonso inquiringly.

"He speaks of Mpanzu," Affonso said.

This startled Gil. "Mpanzu? Who even knows where he is?"

"We know, Senhor Eanes," the deacon broke in again. "He has returned from exile and is stirring up rebellion against the throne."

"Father Duarte!"

"I am sorry, Your Grace."

"Father José, tell Senhor Eanes what happened."

The fat young priest came around from behind the bishop's chair hesitantly. "Well you see, Senhor Eanes, as I told His Grace, I did not know he was there. He must have come to Mpangala during the night while I was sleeping."

"Mpanzu?"

"Yes. As I say, he must have come under the cover of darkness, while I slept. With his mother. Well, not exactly with her. She is dead, you see. With her corpse, I mean."

"The Mbanda Vunda is dead? Did you know this, Mbemba?"

"Of course I knew it," Affonso replied testily. "I do not need a priest to tell me what is happening in my kingdom. She died some weeks ago and Mpanzu brought her to Mpangala to bury her. As is proper for a son, he brought her bones home to rest with her Nsundi ancestors."

Gil looked at de Sousa. He had leaned back in his chair and now, with an elbow on the armrest, held his head in his hand in that position.

"Go on, Father José," he said.

"Well, I didn't know she was there either. I mean I didn't know her corpse was there. He must have brought it to Mpangala during the night while I was sleeping, you see."

"Yes, padre, I see. It is perfectly understandable. You could not have known either Mpanzu or the corpse of his mother was there because you were sleeping. But then you woke up. And then what?"

"Well, there was this terrific commotion going on. Actually that was what woke me up. Horns blaring, drums beating. It wasn't yet daybreak. It was still quite dark. But when I went outside, I saw that all of Mpangala was awake. All the Nsundi were gathering in the main market square for some sort of ceremony."

"The funeral," Affonso said with exasperation. "The Mbanda Vunda's funeral. The funeral of a Nsundi queen. And this priest took it upon himself to intervene."

"It was my duty, Your Majesty. It was a heathen ceremony, an offense to our Lord, and I am a priest of our Lord. Oh, you should have seen it, Senhor Eanes. It was filthy, the work of Satan. The women were all naked except for little aprons, writhing obscenely to the beat of the drums. And the sorcerers, *sorcerers,* Senhor Eanes, painted and naked too except for feathers, agents of the Evil One, shaking their rattles, screaming foul incantations, dancing like devils. It was filthy, I tell you. I had to try and stop it."

"And quite right you were too," Father Duarte put in excitedly again. "How could you stand by and watch such unclean doings? I would have done the same, of that you can be sure."

Gil ignored the deacon. "And that was when you were beaten?"

"I couldn't believe it, Senhor Eanes. They all turned on me. I went to them peacefully. I meant to speak to them reasonably. I wanted to show them the error of their ways. But they turned on me. All of them, Senhor Eanes. Even men and women who have attended my Masses. Even men and women who I had baptized myself, who I have confessed, who have received communion from my hand. Yes, even *Catholic* men and women, Senhor Eanes. They all turned on me with sticks and clubs."

"He might have been martyred."

"I was prepared to be martyred, Father Duarte. I would have been happy to be martyred defending the Faith. But they threw me into the Lelunda like so much offal and returned to their heathen ceremony. It went on all day. I watched it from the other side of the river. Satan ruled in that place and there was nothing I could do about it. So I came here. I do not think I can ever go back there, Your Grace." The young priest turned to his bishop. "I do not think the Nsundi . . ." But all of a sudden he lost control of himself and began sobbing.

"Do not worry yourself, my son." Bishop de Sousa stood up and came around the table and patted Father José's hunched shoulders. "You will go back to Mpangala. We will see to that. Won't we, Your Majesty?"

Affonso remained seated. "Father José made a very stupid mistake, Bishop," he said laconically. "He should never have interfered with the burial of a Nsundi queen by her son. They were not of his flock. They were not Catholic. They had long before this refused baptism. Mpanzu had every right to bury his mother according to the old traditions and beliefs. No, I think it best you send another priest to Mpangala."

"That is not the issue, Your Majesty. That is not what we are discussing here. It does not matter which priest I send to Mpangala. What matters is that a priest, any priest, was attacked there. Why do you refuse to recognize the seriousness of that? Why do you refuse to see that this attack on Father José was not only an attack on the authority of the Church in the kingdom but also an attack on your authority as the sovereign of the Church in the kingdom?"

"You are making far too much of this, Bishop."

"I am not. Please, listen to what I say."

"I do not need to listen to what you say. I already know what you will say."

"What will I say?"

"What you always say. That Mpanzu is my enemy."

"Do not be so blithe about it. He *is* your enemy. He has always been your enemy, your most dangerous enemy. You sit on the throne he considers rightly his. You have taken the Faith of a people he believes bring evil to this land. And you are Soyo while he is Nsundi."

"So I am to fear that he has returned from exile now—now after all these years—in order to take back the throne, in order to drive the white men from the kingdom, in order to restore Nsundi rule over it."

"Exactly so, Your Majesty. This attack on Father José should be proof enough for you. He used the pretext of his mother's funeral to incite the Nsundi against their priest. What is to prevent him from next finding a pretext to incite them against their king?"

"So he must be killed."

"Yes, Your Majesty. So he must be killed."

Affonso slowly shook his head. "No, Bishop, I will not kill my brother. How can you even suggest it? Am I not my brother's keeper?"

Bishop de Sousa flushed at the quiet rebuke.

"Are we not taught that it was for just such a crime that the Lord cursed Cain and set a mark on his forehead and cast him out into the wilderness?"

Bishop de Sousa did not reply to this. He went back around the table and sat down, once again taking his head in his hand.

Affonso's easy familiarity with Scripture did not surprise the prelate or Gil. His ability to quote from either testament, his sure knowledge of the words of God, his understanding of the precepts of the Faith, were well-known and admired. In the years since his baptism and coronation, he had set himself the task of learning all that could be learned of Christianity, not merely in its ritual and miraculous aspects but also in its finest metaphysical detail. Whether this meant he was a convinced Catholic, that he believed the Holy Roman Church possessed Eternal Truth, Gil never really was sure and, indeed, had reason to doubt. But what Gil did not doubt was that Affonso had recognized, almost from the beginning, that all that he wished for his kingdom from the land on the other shore of the sea, all those inventions and attributes of European civilization that he so admired and desired, such as firearms and sailing ships and, above all, writing, for which he had defied his father and usurped his brother's throne, were embodied in and indistinguishable from Christianity and that to obtain them for his people, to make the Kongo part of the wider world, he must himself be Christian.

"But you are right to be mistrustful of the Nsundi, Bishop," he said now.

Bishop de Sousa straightened behind his desk.

"I realize well enough that their loyalty to the throne is not as unconditional as I would want. But we have only King João to thank for that."

"King João? Why King João?"

"Because he has abandoned us, Bishop. How long is it since any of his ships has called at Santo Antonio? More than two years. Nearly three."

"But I have explained why that is, Your Majesty."

"Yes, Bishop, you have explained why that is. The India trade. He has abandoned us for the India trade, so we no longer can expect his ships to call at Santo Antonio with the goods we need and the men we need to build the churches and schools we need to spread the Faith and strengthen the throne."

De Sousa sighed. "You know I have always agreed with you in this complaint, Your Majesty. You know how many times I have written to Lisbon petitioning for more priests and teachers, traders and soldiers. You know I have warned King João time and again that all the progress we have made for the Church and Portugal here in the Kongo will come to naught if he fails us in this."

"And he has failed us in this."

"I admit that, Your Majesty. He has failed us in this. So we are obliged to manage our affairs in our own way."

"And that is how I propose to manage this affair with the Nsundi, Bishop. In our own way. In the way the Kongo have always managed such affairs."

"How is that?"

"Not by killing Mpanzu," Affonso said and stood up. "No, not by killing him, not after all these years." He went over to a small, roseate stained-glass window that looked out on the cathedral plaza and watched the men and women and children, black, white and brown, milling about happily in the bright sunlight there.

No one said anything. De Sousa remained seated, waiting for Affonso to go on, uncertain what he would say. Gil, however, had a fair idea. He knew that Affonso had long been concerned with the questionable loyalty of the Nsundi, that Leonor had frequently offered advice and warnings about it.

"No, killing Mpanzu would not improve the situation in the least, Bishop." Affonso turned back from the window. "It would only make the situation worse. Mpanzu is still a great man to the Nsundi. He is still the ManiNsundi, their lord and prince. Killing him would only increase their enmity, further weaken their loyalty. It might even incite the very rebellion you fear. What we must do is precisely the opposite of that. We must draw them closer to the throne, not drive them farther away. We must give them a larger role in the kingdom, not set them farther apart."

"And how do you propose to do that?"

"By taking a Nsundi princess for my queen."

"*Perdão?*"

"Mpanzu's youngest daughter. She lives quietly in Mpangala and is regarded with great respect by the Nsundi. I will marry her, and as a queen of the Kongo, she will bring her people's respect to me. It is what my father would have done. It is what all the ManiKongos have done through the ages to insure the loyalty of their subject peoples."

"But you cannot marry her. You are already married. You already have a wife and queen."

"I will have two."

"That is out of the question."

"And three or four if necessary to secure my throne and the peace of the kingdom, as my father did before me and all the ManiKongos did before him."

"But you are not a ManiKongo as your father was before you or as were all the ManiKongos before him. You are Catholic. You are the first Catholic ManiKongo and as such are forbidden to have more than one wife."

"It would be heresy."

"Please, Father Duarte."

"It must be said in plain language, Your Grace. What His Majesty proposes would be heresy, the rankest blasphemy, a sin for which he would be damned to burn in hell for all eternity. And, besides, what sort of example would it set for the people of the kingdom? Their own king committing such an iniquity? Do we not have trouble enough keeping them faithful to their duties and obligations? Do we not have to constantly fight their lax observance, their inclination to idol worship and witchcraft? And then to have their own king—"

"Yes, Father Duarte, that is all true. It *is* all true, Your Majesty. It would make a mockery of the Faith. It would destroy the Church. I could not permit it. I would not permit it. I would never marry you to another woman."

"Then I would have to find a priest who would."

"No Catholic priest would perform such an iniquitous ceremony."

"I was not thinking of a Catholic priest, Bishop," Affonso said and returned to his chair. "I was thinking of a priest of the Nsundi."

"A ju-ju man?"

"Under the circumstances, that might be best in any case. If I married one of their princesses in the old way, that might give the Nsundi an even stronger reason to swear allegiance to me."

"If you dared do such a thing, you would be cast out of the Church. I personally would excommunicate you."

Affonso sat down in his chair.

"Do you understand what that means, Your Majesty? You would be condemned to darkness. You would never see the light of Heaven. You would no longer be Catholic."

"And you, Bishop, would no longer have a Catholic king on the Kongo throne."

II

I SUPPOSE this was your idea, my lady."

"I may have been the first to suggest it, Senhor Eenezh, but now it is the king's idea. Why? Do you disapprove?"

"I am not so fine a Catholic as you, my lady. If you see no offense to the Faith in it, why should I?"

"But I see offense to the Faith in it," Beatriz said. "It is a mortal sin. No man may have more than one wife. Marriage is one of the seven sacraments. Bishop de Sousa says—"

"Bishop de Sousa no longer opposes the marriage, Beatriz," Queen Leonor interrupted with quiet assurance.

"He doesn't?" Gil raised an eyebrow. "I find that hard to believe."

"Nonetheless, it is so. He and I had a long talk. Actually we have had several long talks in the last few days, and he has come to understand how important this marriage is to the peace of the kingdom and the security of the throne and that it would be far better for him to have it take place in the Church than out of it, since it will take place in any case."

"He is a practical man, the bishop."

"And he conceded, after some discussion, that there are, after all, provisions in Church doctrine that accommodate a special circumstance like this."

They were in the main room of Gil's house in São Salvador's royal district, a large, sprawling, old-fashioned structure of Kongo design. Though it had been copied in many other matters, the European style had not been copied in architecture. The stone dwellings of the Portuguese quarter, crowded on top of each other along narrow alleyways, struck the Kongo as far too cramped and dark and airless. Affonso had moved into the old ManiKongo's palace unaltered, and Gil's big house, directly across from it in the royal gardens, was built along the same lines, with peaked roofs of thatch, a multitude of interconnecting rooms and columned verandas all around. Its only European touch was the chapel Beatriz had insisted on having added on at the back.

"Did he happen to mention which provision in Church doctrine he had in mind, my lady?"

"He spoke of annulment."

"Ah yes, of course. Annulment."

"What is annulment?" Beatriz wanted to know.

"It is a complicated and mysterious process, Nimi, by which the Church can discover that two people who are married are not married after all and never were."

"Which two people?"

"In this case, I imagine Bishop de Sousa is thinking of Affonso and Inez."

"But how can that be? They have been married for years. Bishop de Sousa married them himself. They have sons and daughters."

"I said it was a mysterious process, another of the great mysteries of the Faith."

"But what about Inez? What will happen to her?"

"Nothing will happen to her," Leonor said. "She will remain a wife and queen of Affonso, exactly as she would have in the old days when the ManiKongos took as many wives and queens as they deemed necessary to hold the kingdom together. The annulment will only be a gesture to Bishop de Sousa so that he can in good conscience marry Affonso to the NtinuNsundi in the Church."

"Is that what Bishop de Sousa told you, my lady?"

"No, *senhor,* it was what I told him. Just as my husband took both the Mbanda Vunda and myself as wives, so Affonso must have both Soyo and Nsundi queens to insure the peace of the kingdom."

"And he agreed to that?"

"As I say, *senhor,* we have had many long talks, and he came to understand that he must either agree to it or be obliged to excommunicate the Kongo's first Catholic king."

"And he is a practical man."

Leonor smiled, pleased to show off this latest example of her political skill.

"But who is this NtinuNsundi, Mother?" Beatriz asked.

"Her name is Mfidi. Mfidi a Mpanzu."

"Mfidi a Mpanzu? She has no Christian name? She is not baptized?"

"How could she be baptized? Be sensible, girl. She is Mpanzu's daughter."

"Well, she cannot be married in the Church if she is not baptized."

"No, but Bishop de Sousa is seeing to that. He has sent Father Duarte to Mpangala with Father José to begin her instruction. And he has also begun his own examinations to determine the grounds for the annulment of Affonso's marriage to Inez."

"Then Affonso's marriage to Mfidi is not particularly imminent," Gil said. He wore a kanga and was barefoot, as was his custom when at home, and was clean-shaven. He had shaved his beard many years before to distinguish himself from the other white men, and wore his long, blond hair tied in a queue. "As I am sure Bishop de Sousa explained, an annulment can take a very long time, sometimes years."

"In this case it will not take years. Bishop de Sousa assures me that he will complete his examinations by the time Mfidi is ready to be baptized."

"Months then?"

"Perhaps two or three months. Affonso will be able to marry Mfidi before the rains come."

"What is she like? Is she tall or short, fat or slim?"

Gil felt a pang of sympathy for Beatriz, hearing the anxious tremor in her voice as she asked this. Undoubtedly, she opposed her brother's polygamous marriage genuinely for religious reasons; of all the Kongo Catholics, she was among the most authentically devout, regarding the Faith as the instrument of her restoration and power. But she also had practical matters to consider. Her importance and position at her brother's court could be considerably diminished by the enthronement of a second queen.

"Is she pretty or ugly, young or old? Who is her mother?"

"She is young. She is the youngest daughter of Mpanzu's youngest wife," Leonor answered. "She is nearly as young as Inez was when Affonso married her—"

"What is it, *mchento?*"

The other Nimi had come into the room. "The two boys of your guard for whom you have been waiting, Gil Eenezh," she said. "They have returned. They are in the garden."

"You will excuse me, my lady."

The dowager queen nodded absently and continued telling her daughter about Mfidi as Gil went out onto the veranda.

It was another brilliantly sunny day. This was the long, dry season of cloudless blue skies, gentle breezes, crystalline air, warm days and cold nights here on the high plateau above the Nsundi grasslands. The jacaranda and acacia, the flamboyants and flame trees in the garden outside the house were in full flower and birds were singing merrily in their branches. Two big, strong men (not boys at all) were squatting on their heels in the red dust under one of the flame trees.

They stood up when Gil and Nimi came down from the veranda. Like Gil, they were barefoot and wore kangas, and they also had parrot feathers in their hair like Kongo warriors of old—not a stitch of European clothing on them—but they were armed with arquebuses instead of lances and shields and held them with a confident familiarity. They were Nimi's cousins, the sons of her mother's sister, the brothers who Gil had met as small boys (and still thought of as boys) that day twenty years before when Mbemba first brought him to their mother's house on the Luezi quay in Mbanza Kongo. And because of this history, they were, like Nimi, among the most trusted of his retainers, the first in his bodyguard. He had stood godfather for them when they were baptized and had given them the Christian names of another good friend: the older was Nuno, the younger Gonçalo.

"Have you seen him, *mbakala?*" Gil asked, going over to them.

"We have, my lord," the older brother, Nuno, replied.

"How did he seem?"

The brothers glanced at each other uncertainly. Gil squatted on his haunches by a frangipani bush and indicated that they should do the same. Nimi remained standing several paces away, watching that they weren't disturbed.

"Did he seem well?"

"He is fat and old, my lord," Gonçalo, the younger, said. Actually he was the quicker of the two and, although he always deferred to his older brother, he would take the lead whenever Nuno seemed at a loss. "And his face is even uglier than I remember. But otherwise he seemed well."

Gil nodded, trying to imagine how Mpanzu must look now, how grotesque his mutilated face, missing an ear, must have become as he had aged and grown as fat as his father. He had no bad feelings for the old prince, lord of the Nsundi. Indeed, he remembered him with a certain nostalgia, the ponderously thoughtful, straightforward man who was an enemy only because he had sought to defend his king-dom against an evil he believed the white men would bring to it from the sky and who had been utterly dignified and uncomplaining in defeat. "Was it in Mpangala that you saw him?"

"No, my lord, he is no longer in Mpangala." This was Nuno again, surer of himself with matters of fact than with opinions and judg-ments. "He departed when the soldiers of the captain Rodrigues came."

"There are Portuguese soldiers in Mpangala?"

"Three halberdiers and three with firearms. The captain Ro-drigues brought them in escort of the deacon and the young priest José."

"It is said that the young priest José feared returning to Mpan-gala without them," Gonçalo put in. "It is said he feared the Nsundi would fall on him again when he began the instruction of the Ntinu-Nsundi."

"I see." Gil brushed away a bee. Bees were buzzing all around, drawn by the sweet perfume of the frangipani blooms. "So Mpanzu departed when the soldiers came."

"Not at once, my lord," Gonçalo continued. "It is said that he in-tended to remain in Mpangala and there were many Nsundi who were ready to hide him there. He only departed when the captain Rodrigues and the white soldiers began searching and burning the houses where they believed he was hiding."

"Searching and burning houses? That dog Rodrigues. Who gave him leave to do that?"

Neither brother commented. Both were well aware of their liege lord's feelings about the master-at-arms.

"And after Mpanzu departed, I suppose Rodrigues and the soldiers tried to hunt him down," Gil said, thinking sympathetically of the fat, old, exiled ManiNsundi alone and on the run in his own land.

"They did, my lord."

"But they didn't find him."

Nuno gave a snort of derisive laughter. "How could they find him? They are so clumsy in their helmets and armor. And they have never learned the ways of our grasslands and forests. No, my lord, they didn't find him."

"But you found him."

Nuno shrugged modestly and smiled at his brother.

"Where did you find him? Is it far from Mpangala? Does he now return to his exile beyond the kingdom's frontiers?"

"No, my lord. He traveled for only seven days from Mpangala, east along the Lelunda River. A small village of Nsundi fisherfolk on the river's bank took him in and gave him shelter."

"It is said that he plans to return to Mpangala once the soldiers of the captain Rodrigues leave," Gonçalo added.

"I see," Gil said again and again brushed away a bee, then let his hands hang between his knees and absently fingered the red dust between his bare feet. "So he must already know what is intended for his daughter Mfidi. He must already have heard that the ManiKongo means to take her for his wife."

"Yes, my lord, he has heard," Nuno said. "Everyone in Mpangala has heard. The news of it traveled swiftly from São Salvador. But if there had been any question, the coming of the Fathers Duarte and José to instruct Mfidi in the Faith answered the question."

"And that is why Mpanzu plans to return to Mpangala after the soldiers leave," Gonçalo said. "To prevent Mfidi's marriage to the ManiKongo."

Gil nodded and picked up a handful of the warm dust and let it trickle slowly through his fingers. He had expected this. He had realized, almost as soon as he had heard of Affonso's intention (surely put into his head by his mother), that Mpanzu would not stand idly by and let one of his daughters be used to consolidate his Catholic half-brother's hold on the Kongo throne.

"And how does he plan to prevent Mfidi's marriage to the ManiKongo, *mbakala?* Have you also learned that?"

The brothers looked at each other. Then Nuno said, "He plans to seize her and carry her off or kill her before she can be baptized or married."

"It is said she will not be baptized or married until the rains come, my lord, if even by then," Gonçalo elaborated. "It is said that the deacon and the bishop agree that her instruction in the Faith must take at least that long. So Mpanzu has time in which to carry out his plan."

"Yes, he has time," Gil mused. "The bishop is certainly in no hurry to marry her to the ManiKongo. He may not dare refuse to perform the ceremony outright, but he surely will delay it as long as he can. But what about the Nsundi? Will they not oppose Mpanzu in his plan? Will they not prevent his daughter from being carried off or killed by him? Surely they must be pleased that a princess of their house is to become a queen of the Kongo. After all, it is to please them in just this way that the ManiKongo decided to marry her."

"What you say is true of many of the Nsundi, my lord," Gonçalo answered. "Many of the Nsundi believe it is an honor that the ManiKongo has chosen one of their own for his queen. Many of the Nsundi, my lord, but not all. There are Nsundi who believe that not just the queen but the king himself should be one of their own. And those who believe that have guns."

"What?"

"Mpanzu has gathered an army around him, my lord," Nuno said. "An army with guns."

"But how did they get them?"

"How, my lord? Why, they made them."

Of course they had made them. Why couldn't they have made them? They were excellent blacksmiths, skilled carvers of wood.

They had worked the iron ore and copper that abounded in their kingdom and carved the wood of their forests since the beginning of their civilization. And the guns of the Portuguese had been around long enough by now for them to have figured out their mechanisms and how to reproduce them. Of course they could make guns. But no matter what their skills and ingenuity, there was one thing they couldn't make.

"And the powder, Nuno? How did they get the powder for the guns? They could not make the gunpowder."

"No, my lord, they could not make the gunpowder. But they could trade for it. And when they could not trade for it, they could steal it."

Idly sifting the dry red dust between his fingers, Gil considered this. Then he asked, "How large is this army of gunmen that Mpanzu has gathered around him?"

"We do not know, my lord. In the fishing village on the Lelunda where Mpanzu hides, we saw two hundred. But it is said there are hundreds more, perhaps thousands more, in the hills and grasslands and forests of Nsundi, who also consider Mpanzu the rightful ManiKongo."

Gil looked up into the bright blue, cloudless sky. His image of Mpanzu had to be changed. The old ManiNsundi was not the pathetic creature he had imagined. For ten years now, he had been quietly gathering an army of gunmen around him. It probably wasn't an army that could actually challenge Affonso's rule, but it might be one able to spirit Mfidi away before Affonso could marry her. Perhaps Bishop de Sousa was correct to an extent; perhaps Mpanzu was a greater threat than Affonso or, for that matter, Gil himself had realized. Perhaps, for ten years now, Mpanzu had only been biding his time.

"You have done well, *mbakala*," Gil said. "You have served your king well."

The brothers beamed.

"You must not speak of this to anyone."

"You have no need to tell us that, my lord."

"You must not speak of it even in the confessional."

"The priests shall not hear of it from us, my lord. Not even Bishop de Sousa himself shall hear of it from us."

"Good." Gil clapped the brothers on their shoulders. "Stay close. We have more work to do in service to our king."

"We will stay close, my lord."

Caisson-mounted lombard cannon were emplaced on each side of the steps leading up to the front veranda of the ManiKongo's palace, each manned by a gun crew of three Portuguese soldiers. They were essentially a ceremonial guard with little practical to do and had long since removed their helmets and gotten down on their knees in the red dust to throw dice. They stopped their game when Gil approached. He didn't bother to greet them but went straight to one of the barrels of gunpowder that stood, with the pyramids of black cannonballs, behind the guns. How long had it been since anyone had had occasion to look into it? In the peace that reigned in the kingdom, there had been no reason to fire the cannon in years, so it probably had been that long since anyone had checked the barrel's contents. If there were men also in São Salvador who regarded Mpanzu as the rightful Kongo king, the powder in this barrel might very well have been stolen or traded away by now, with no one the wiser.

"*Faça favor, cabo.* Open this."

The corporal of the guard came forward and tried to pry open the barrel's lid with his fingers. But it was sealed tight by time and weather. So he drew his cutlass and sliced around its circumference until he could pop it off with the flat of his blade. Then he stepped back and looked at Gil questioningly.

Gil put his hand in the barrel. It was full to the brim. He was relieved to discover that. Even so, he scooped out a handful of its contents. And his relief quickly turned into alarm. For what he had scooped out was not gunpowder but a handful of sand.

He looked around. The warriors on the palace's front veranda—every fifth one armed with an arquebus and thus entitled to rations of gunpowder—were carefully selected members of the king's personal household guard and almost certainly trustworthy. But all sorts of people passed through the royal compound daily. Anyone among them might be disloyal. These Portuguese soldiers, passing the time engrossed in the toss of their dice, certainly weren't alert enough to keep the gunpowder from finding its way into the wrong hands. Indeed, for the right price, they might themselves be willing to trade it away.

"Is anything wrong, *senhor?*" the corporal asked.

Gil shook his head and went round to the back of the palace.

The courtyard back there, another lush garden in full and fragrant bloom, stretched all the way to the edge of the plateau and gave out on a breathtaking view over the cliffs of the escarpment to the rolling hills of the Nsundi grasslands below. Affonso and Inez were seated cross-legged on mats near the plateau's edge while their children—the twin boys (dual heirs to the throne), two older girls and an infant boy—ran around them in a game of tag. Warriors were on guard here as well, and servants and a handful of courtiers, both men and women in European dress, waited in attendance at a discreet distance. The king and queen, however, were barefoot and wore plain kangas. A book lay open across their laps.

Gil recognized the book. It was the book, immensely precious, in which Affonso painstakingly inscribed Kongo words. This was his great passion, his undying obsession, to which he devoted almost all his spare time: the creation of a written language for the Kongo. When the priests, too few now to take time for it from their battles against the influence of the ju-ju men, left the work undone, he had taken up the task himself. He had gotten so far as to assemble the rather extensive vocabulary inscribed in this book, having invented an alphabet and spelling by which to render the Kongo language's pronunciations, and although he was still at a loss as to how to formulate a grammar, he used the vocabulary to teach his wife and children how to read and write. That was what he was doing with Inez now, and she was paying attention only fitfully.

"My lady," Gil said as he approached them. "Your Majesty."

Inez jumped up, obviously delighted at any interruption that would put an end to her studies. "Oh, Gil Eenezh, have you heard the news? There is going to be a new queen."

"Yes, my lady, I have heard."

"Father Duarte is in Mpangala instructing her in the Faith right now. She will be ready to receive the sacrament before the rains come and then Affonso will marry her."

Gil looked at Affonso. He smiled and also stood up. Clearly Inez

presented no obstacle to his second marriage. He hadn't expected
her to. She was a true child of the Kongo. For her, as for so many of
the kingdom's converts, Christianity was little more than a novel entertainment, a marvelous sorcery, a colorful ceremony of astonishing
rituals and thrilling mysteries. For her, as for so many of the new
Catholics, it was the old religion, the religion of *Nzambi Mpungu*
with its ghosts and fetishes, spirits and diviners, that was still the true
religion, and *Nzambi Mpungu* was still the true God, a belief bred
deep in the blood and bones at birth and not easily expunged, not
even by a decade of Christianity. That her husband intended to take a
second wife did not in the least violate this inborn belief; to the contrary, it was utterly in keeping with everything she believed. She had
always expected to be one of many wives as her mother had been
and *her* mother before her. She was the first wife and queen, and the
coronation of a second was an excitement for her. It meant she
would now have a partner with whom to share her queenly duties
and wifely intimacies. Obviously, the matter of the annulment meant
nothing to her, as it meant nothing to anyone except the priests.

"Of course she will have a palace of her own," she was saying
now cheerfully, "but I think it should be right here, between this one
and yours across the garden. And then all three of us can always be
together like sisters, Inez and Beatriz and Mfidi . . . no, not Mfidi. She
will have a Christian name too. What will her Christian name be, Affonso?"

"That will be for Bishop de Sousa to decide," Affonso replied.
And then: "You wish to speak with me, Gil?"

"I do."

Gil walked closer to the edge of the plateau and looked down
the face of the cliffs to the Lelunda River snaking around the base of
the escarpment. Ten leagues upriver to the northeast was Mpangala.
Twenty leagues or so farther eastward along the river's bank was the
Nsundi fishing village where Mpanzu was hiding.

"What do you wish to say to me?" Affonso asked, following Gil
to the plateau's edge.

"Mpanzu means to prevent your marriage to Mfidi."

"That sounds very much like something Bishop de Sousa would
say to me."

Gil looked around. "Do not confuse me with Bishop de Sousa because my skin is also white. Two of my best men have spied this out."

"Nuno and Gonçalo?"

"Yes."

"Gil, you know I have no hatred in my heart for Mpanzu. You
know I do not see him as my enemy. I am sorry for him. I am sorry
for what I did to him. I am sorry for it every day of my life. I often believe I was wrong to do what I did, that it served no good purpose at
all, and pray to God for forgiveness for having done it."

"I know that."

"All the power of the kingdom that rightfully was his, I took
from him and made him an exile in his own land. Because of me, he
is alone and powerless. How can I see him as my enemy when he is
alone and powerless? He can do me no harm."

"I too believed that, Mbemba. But we both were mistaken. He is
no longer alone and powerless. He has gathered an army of Nsundi
around him. And they have armed themselves with guns."

"This is what Nuno and Gonçalo tell you?"

"Yes. I sent them to Mpangala and they tracked Mpanzu to a fishing village seven days' journey from there and spied this out."

"Go on."

"It is not yet a great army. I do not think it numbers more than a
few hundred, perhaps a thousand. But it is great enough to cause serious mischief."

"Like preventing my marriage to Mfidi."

"Yes."

"And what else?"

"I do not know. Perhaps Mpanzu believes that, in time, he can increase the size of his army to the point where he could attack you
with it. Perhaps he believes that, by preventing your marriage to
Mfidi, he will show a strength that will encourage more Nsundi to
gather around him. Perhaps . . . but whatever else he may be planning, we know from Nuno and Gonçalo that at the very least he
plans to seize Mfidi and carry her off, maybe even kill her, to keep
you from marrying her."

"So what do you advise me to do?"

"Do you trust me?"

"Do you doubt that I do?"

"No."

"I trust you."

"Then let me be the only one to know what is done."

"*Keba.* But there is one thing."

"What is that?"

"Whatever is done, Mpanzu must not be harmed. I forbid it. I have already done him too much harm."

MPANGALA WAS DARK except for the sentry fires at its river gate, specks of flickering yellow light reflected in the fast-running black waters of the Lelunda. The moon was down and the velvet-black dome of the sky was awash with stars as Mpangala slept in these final hours of the night, except for the sentries at the river gate. Gil squatted on his heels on the bank opposite them, looking across the Lelunda to the Nsundi town, tree frogs croaking soothingly around him, cicadas humming their lulling, metallic hum. A hundred yards or so to his right, eastward upriver, a small herd of gazelle had come to the river to drink. A hundred yards or so behind him, to the south, the red-clay cliffs of the escarpment reared up into the star-filled sky. To his left, westward, the Lelunda made a sharp bend and disappeared from view around the cliffs.

Mpangala, like its name, hadn't been changed by the coming of the white men. In their first burst of enthusiasm, the Portuguese had concentrated their civilizing efforts, for obvious reasons, on the seaport at Mpinda and the royal capital of Mbanza Kongo. Mpangala and the other important towns of the kingdom were to receive the benefits of European Christianity in a second stage of development. But with the opening of the sea route to the Indies, that second stage had never occurred. To be sure, from time to time over the years, missionaries had taken up residence in Mpangala in an attempt to convert the inhabitants (the young Father José was only the latest), but the town still had no church by which to be named; no ironstone wall had replaced the wooden stockade that enclosed it; no cannon or mortars guarded its gates; no Portuguese traders or tradesmen had settled in its precincts; and the chieftain who ruled it was Catholic in name only.

"My lord."

Gil swiveled on his heels and peered upriver. The gazelle had scattered. A canoe was gliding downriver. The soft splash of its paddle had scattered them.

"Nuno?"

"Yes, my lord."

Gil stood up and waded ankle-deep into the water. Nuno was standing in the prow of the canoe, leaning on his arquebus. Gonçalo was seated in the stern, paddling, his arquebus across his knees. Gil was armed only with his ivory-handled knife. He grabbed hold of the canoe and pulled it up on the bank.

"Is Mpanzu still in the fishing village?"

"He is, my lord."

"Has he any more warriors with him now?"

"No, my lord. The number is the same as before. Two hundred. Twenty with guns. But there is a great and important fetish in the village now. It must have been brought there after we went away the last time."

"What kind of fetish?"

"We don't know, my lord. We only know that it is so great and important that it has a house of its own."

"Is it a war fetish?"

"We do not think so, my lord. Mpanzu makes no preparations for war. He waits quietly in the fishing village, waiting for the captain Rodrigues and the white soldiers to depart Mpangala."

It took only a few minutes to cross the Lelunda. The sentries at the river gate, squatting around their fires, stood up and came down to the water's edge, young Nsundi warriors armed with lances and shields. They might have been surprised to see Gil—he rarely came to Mpangala—but they recognized him at once and helped beach the canoe.

"I go to the captain Rodrigues," Gil said, jumping out of the canoe. "Where does he stay?"

"In the house of the white priest José," one of the sentries replied. "On the main market square."

Two halberdiers were in the main market square. Evidently, they were meant to be on guard at Father José's house on the east side of the square but, in the course of a long, uneventful night, they had wandered over to the well at the center of the square, had removed their helmets and laid their halberds aside and were now dozing at the base of a large, ancient baobab tree that shaded the well. They didn't stir when Gil and the brothers came up to them. Gil didn't disturb them. He looked around to get his bearings in the darkness.

From here, he could see the north gate; warriors doubtless were on sentry duty outside it. There were warriors also on the verandas of the buildings on the west side of the square because those buildings, enclosed by a palisade, composed the compound of the chief of Mpangala. One of those buildings was the dwelling of Mfidi a Mpanzu and her mother, Mpanzu's youngest wife. The deacon, Father Duarte, probably was staying with them there, and not at Father José's across the square, in order to more closely supervise the girl's religious instruction. Which one it was, Gil didn't know. He hadn't bothered to follow the intricate maneuverings for power among the remnants of the Nsundi hierarchy after Mpanzu's defeat and banishment. What he did know, though, was that the new Mpangala chief was the eldest brother of Mpanzu's youngest wife—and thus Mfidi's maternal uncle—who had converted to Christianity, taken the name Bernardo and sworn allegiance to Affonso.

"Soldatos!"

Both soldiers awoke simultaneously and scrambled to their feet, grabbing for their helmets and halberds. In the faint starlight, they didn't immediately recognize Gil; in kanga and barefoot, he seemed to them just another Kongo savage, and they lowered their axe-headed pikes at him menacingly.

"Is the master-at-arms no longer in Mpangala?" Gil snapped, slapping one of the halberds away. "Is that why you no longer need stand guard on his quarters?"

They recognized him then, and one blustered, "Oh, holy Mother of God, we did not see it was you, *senhor.*"

"How could you see anything, you lazy dogs? Your eyes were closed."

"No, *senhor,* it was only—"

"Return to your posts before the master-at-arms wakes and has you flogged."

"At once, *senhor.*"

They scurried back across the square and took up their posts on the veranda of Father José's house.

"Which is the house of the NtinuNsundi, Nuno?"

"That one over there, my lord."

Nuno indicated Mfidi's dwelling with a thrust of his chin, understanding he should not be too obvious about it with the Portuguese soldiers watching. It was a small house with a single peaked roof behind the triple-roofed dwelling of the chief. Three warriors stood on its veranda, eyeing Gil and the brothers.

"Wait here for my signal as we planned."

Nodding, Nuno and Gonçalo went around to the north side of the baobab tree and squatted beside the well. Gonçalo drew up the goatskin and both had a drink from it. Gil looked up at the sky. It was still a good two hours until first light. He walked over to Father José's house. The halberdiers on the veranda came to attention. Gil ignored them and went around to the cookhouse in the back. The cookhouse was empty; the embers in the firepit in front of it were cold. The small huts of the priest's servants were shuttered and dark. The only sounds back here were those of livestock shuffling in the kraal.

And then there was a shout, a sudden full-throated cry.

It caught Gil completely by surprise. He spun around, his hand going to the haft of his knife. There was a second shout. It came from the north gate. Gil dashed back around the priest's house. Nuno and Gonçalo jumped up at the well. The two halberdiers bolted down from the veranda. A third shout came as the warriors at the north gate swung it open. The halberdiers ran toward it, themselves crying out an alarm that brought the four other Portuguese soldiers of Rodrigues's contingent scrambling out of their quarters in the priest's house. Then Rodrigues himself appeared on the veranda, half-dressed, in stockinged feet, buckling on his cutlass, looking around in confusion. He didn't see Gil. When he saw that the north gate was open, he hurried to it after his soldiers. A moment later, Father José came out of the house, pulling on his cassock, and ran after Rodrigues.

Gil looked across the square to the chief's compound. Among the crowd of people there awakened by the commotion was Father

Duarte. Mfidi was almost certainly one of the girls in the crowd milling around the deacon. With admirable discipline, Nuno and Gonçalo had remained by the well under the baobab tree, waiting for Gil to signal them. He signaled them now and, as they made their way through the crowd in the chief's compound, he went over to the north gate to see for himself what was going on.

"What are you doing here, *senhor?*" Rodrigues asked, turning around in surprise as Gil approached.

Gil didn't reply, looking out the gate. A lone runner was coming down the royal road toward Mpangala at a fast trot, brandishing a long bow over his head and shouting. He was a Soyo warrior; the long bow, the quiver of arrows on his back, his dark-blue kanga, identified him as such.

"Boats," he was shouting. "Great, bird-winged boats coming to *nzere.*"

"Can you make out what he is saying, Senhor Eanes?"

Gil looked around. It was Father Duarte. He looked past the deacon back to the chief's compound, trying to see if Nuno and Gonçalo had gotten hold of Mfidi. He couldn't. The excited crowd that had gathered in front of the gate blocked his view.

"Boats, he is saying," Father José suddenly exclaimed. "He is saying boats, sailing boats are coming to the Zaire."

"I don't believe that," Rodrigues said.

Gil stepped through the gate and went up the road to meet the runner. Rodrigues and the two priests hurried after him. The runner slowed to a walk, breathing heavily.

"Boats," he said more quietly. "Many great, bird-winged boats of the Porta Geeze are coming to *nzere,* my lord."

"How many?" Gil asked, putting his hand on the runner's shoulder and bringing him to a halt.

"Five, my lord," the Soyo said, glad to stop and catch his breath. "Their great white wings were seen six days ago along the ocean shore. It is said they will reach Santo Antonio within four or five days if the weather holds, the first such boats to call at the port in more than two years."

III

ONE WAS A *CARAVELA DE ARMADA,* four-masted, of two-hundred-tons burthen, more than eighty feet from stem to stern, armed with twenty main-deck guns, clearly the flagship of this altogether unexpected fleet. Three were smaller, three-masted *caravelas redonda* of around one hundred tons each, carrying culverins and lombard cannon. And the fifth was an unarmed pinnace, a two-masted vessel (both masts lateen-rigged), serving as the expedition's storeship. They made an astonishing sight, crowding the cove in front of Santo Antonio do Zaire. Never before had so many ships called at the port at one time. When Gil first saw them, from the vanguard of the royal caravan coming down the riverside road from São Salvador, they were riding at anchor under bare poles some two hundred yards offshore, their flags and ensigns snapping in a stiff early morning breeze blowing in from the sea. Evidently, they had made port several days before. What was odd, though, was that, as far as Gil could see, none of their officers or crew had yet disembarked nor had any of their cargo been brought ashore.

Gil was on foot. He had traveled in a litter during most of the two weeks' journey from São Salvador but had dismounted when in sight of Santo Antonio and had gone ahead, eager to learn why, after so many years of neglect, the Portuguese king had dispatched a fleet of such remarkable size and apparent richness to the Kongo now. Affonso, as required by protocol, was still being carried and so was

Bishop de Sousa. Rodrigues, however, had also gotten down and, while the rest of the caravan turned into the riverside town's main market square, he followed Gil to the water's edge to get a closer look at the peculiarly quiet ships bobbing at anchor on the Zaire's fast-running current and outgoing tide. A soldier from the Santo Antonio fortress, in chainmail and helmet, a cutlass at his side, a spyglass in his hand, came running over and saluted.

"What's the trouble here, *cabo?*" Rodrigues asked. "Why has no one yet come ashore from those ships?"

"I cannot answer that, sir marshal. When they first dropped anchor, we went out to them as we always do but they warned us off. They fired their cannon to warn us off."

"Fired their cannon, did they? Let me have that." Rodrigues took the spyglass, fixed it to his one good eye and began scanning the fleet on the river.

Gil looked around. The nobles of the ManiSoyo's court, decked out in their finest Portuguese garments, were gathered in the shade of the huge, lone palm tree that stood in the middle of the town's main market square, awaiting the arrival of the royal caravan. When the litters were set down and Affonso and Bishop de Sousa got out, also wearing ceremonial garb, kudu horns blared forth a thrilling chord of greeting, dancers began dancing to the excited beating of drums and the ManiSoyo stepped forward. Under the new order of the realm, he was no longer obliged to prostrate himself abjectly at the feet of the ManiKongo and bare his neck to the royal lance. Instead, in the European fashion, he dropped to one knee and took the king's hand and kissed it, then turned to the bishop and repeated the gesture of homage and fealty.

He was not the ManiSoyo of old. The old, white-haired, grandfatherly ManiSoyo had died peacefully in his sleep many years before, content with the role he had played in bringing the white men's magic to the kingdom. This ManiSoyo was a grandnephew (cousin to Inez), a small, rather effete man some years younger than Affonso (and Gil), perhaps not yet thirty, but credited with a sharp intelligence not unlike that of his blood kin, the dowager queen Leonor. Because of his granduncle's early alliance with the Portuguese and because too of his importance as the lord of Santo Antonio, the gateway through which all European commerce passed, he had prospered under the new regime. And for this, if no other reason, he was a devoted Catholic, baptized Jorgé, and a sworn enemy of all the enemies of the Portuguese.

"Holy Mother of God."

Gil turned back to Rodrigues. "What is it?"

Rodrigues lowered the spyglass. "Plague," he said.

"What?"

"There is plague aboard those ships, *senhor.* That's why no one has come ashore. See for yourself." Rodrigues handed the spyglass to Gil. "They must wait for it to burn itself out before they can come ashore."

Gil looked through the glass at the flagship. Atop her mainmast, above the royal ensign, the black flag of plague was flying in the morning sunlight. He had never experienced plague himself but had heard stories told of the dreaded black death that periodically swept Europe in those years, how it could be brought aboard a ship by a seaman who didn't know he was infected (or knew but didn't say), how it would suddenly reveal itself once the ship was far out to sea, sweeping through the crew, randomly killing some, randomly sparing others, but always finally crippling the ship. That was what must have happened here, Gil thought. The plague must have revealed itself only after these ships had sailed too far from Lisbon to turn back, indeed after they had sailed too far beyond São Jorgé da Mina to call in there. Perhaps these ships hadn't been bound for the Kongo at all. Perhaps this was a fleet of Indiamen bound for the Spice Isles and Far Cathay who had discovered the plague aboard only after they had sailed well beyond São Jorgé da Mina and had altered course for the Kongo only because Santo Antonio was the nearest port of call. That would explain why this expedition had come here now when none of such size and richness had ever come here before.

"How long does it take for it to burn itself out?" Gil asked, lowering the spyglass.

"It's always different. Sometimes all must die before it dies. Sometimes only a few."

The drumming and horn playing in the market square ceased. The formalities of the welcoming ceremony had been completed and

Affonso, Bishop de Sousa and the ManiSoyo came down to the water's edge.

"Dom Jorgé," Gil said, bowing politely.

"I was just telling His Majesty that these ships do not let us approach, Senhor Eenezh." The ManiSoyo had a dainty little voice to go along with his dainty little figure. "I cannot imagine why. We were so pleased to see so many come to us after all this time and hurried out to welcome them. But they did not let us get near. What can the reason be? Can you say, *senhor?*"

Gil glanced at Rodrigues. He had moved a few steps away and was conferring with the bishop in low tones.

"There is a sickness aboard the ships, Dom Jorgé," Gil said. "They did not let you get near so as to prevent you from being poisoned by it."

"What sort of sickness?"

"The Portuguese call it *peste.*" But since that word was meaningless in Kongo, Gil added, "Black death."

"Black death?" Jorgé repeated and shivered extravagantly.

"How do you know this?" Affonso asked.

"They are flying flags to signal us of it." Gil handed the spyglass to Affonso. "Do you see the black flags atop the mainmasts? They signal us that the black death is aboard. Once it has burned itself out, they will haul down the flags and only then come ashore."

"But they are coming ashore now." Affonso returned the glass to Gil.

The longboat of the fleet's flagship had been brought alongside her starboard beam and men were climbing down into it from the spar deck. Some were seamen, carrying sweeps to man the longboat. Some were soldiers, their armor glinting in the sun. One was a priest, his white soutane flapping in the wind. Two others were ship's officers, wearing plumed helmets. One of these officers seemed to be having trouble getting down the rope ladder and was being helped by the priest.

"Sir marshal." Gil passed the glass to Rodrigues and pointed out to the river. "Can the plague have already burned itself out?"

Rodrigues brought the glass to his eye. But it wasn't needed. The longboat, pulling for shore, could now be seen plainly without it. One of the officers stood in its bow wearing shoulder armor as well as the plumed helmet and leaning on a sword. Six seamen, three to a side, were manning the sweeps, and two soldiers sat on the thwart between each pair of oarsmen, firearms across their knees. The other officer was seated on the stern thwart, the priest kneeling behind him. Indeed, that officer seemed to be lying back in the priest's arms. Also wearing a plumed helmet but no other armor, he was wrapped in a gray blanket. The priest's head was lowered so that his wide-brimmed hat shaded the officer's face from the sun. As the boat neared shore, the officer in the bow jumped out. He was a scrawny, toothless man with an unkempt black beard and darting dark eyes. He glanced back to check on the other officer, lying in the priest's arms, then looked around at the men on the beach. He obviously recognized Bishop de Sousa and Rodrigues by their attire, but his glittering eyes nevertheless fixed on Affonso. Bigger than the others, stronger, more stalwart in bearing, striking in his crimson tabard, Affonso made the more imposing appearance.

"Dom Affonso? ManiKongo?"

"Yes," Affonso replied. "And you, *senhor?*"

The man removed his helmet, made a sweeping bow and dropped to one knee. "Your Majesty, I am Alvaro Lopes, second-in-command of this fleet, sent to you by your brother monarch, Manoel the Fortunate, king of the Portuguese."

"Manoel the Fortunate? Is João the Second no longer king of the Portuguese?"

"No, Your Majesty." Lopes replaced his helmet and stood up. "It is my sad duty to tell you that João is dead."

"But who is this Manoel the Fortunate?"

"Cousin to João."

"Cousin to João? How is it that his son, the Infante Affonso for whom I am named, did not succeed to his father's throne?"

Lopes looked at Bishop de Sousa, then said, "Things of this sort happen, Your Majesty. I am sure His Grace will understand. It is not for me, a simple ship's captain, to attempt to explain the sort of things that happen at the court at Sintra."

The bishop nodded. He did understand. And so did Gil: intrigue at the Portuguese court, a politics whose details could not be appreciated half a world away.

"Was the succession peaceful, Dom Alvaro?" Bishop de Sousa asked.

"There was no bloodshed, if that is what you ask, Your Grace. To the best of my knowledge, the Infante Affonso still lives. More than that I cannot say."

"Let us leave it at that, then. It is enough for us to know that a new king sits on the throne of Portugal. It is enough for us to know that it is Manoel the Fortunate, long may he reign, who we must thank for sending this uncommonly grand expedition to us."

"But has he sent it to us, Dom Alvaro?" Gil asked.

Lopes turned to him. "Gil Eanes?"

"Aye."

"Ah, Senhor Eanes, I am happy to meet you. Much is spoken of you in Lisbon."

"Much good, I hope."

"Com certeza."

"Are your ships not Indiamen, Dom Alvaro? Were you not bound for the Indies and called in here only because of the plague you have aboard?"

"Oh, no, Senhor Eanes. It is true we have plague aboard, but we were always bound for the Kongo. These ships were outfitted at enormous expense by King Manoel expressly for the Kongo."

"Then King Manoel must take a greater interest in the Kongo than ever did João. For João never sent us so many ships as these."

"He does, *senhor.* His interest in the Kongo is very great."

"Why is that? Is the Indies trade no longer as rich as it once was?"

"The Indies trade remains a source of much wealth for the crown. But King Manoel believes that much wealth can also be had in the Kongo."

"What wealth? What wealth does King Manoel believe can be had in the Kongo that has not already been had?"

"Why do you ask this, Gil?" Affonso interrupted. He spoke in Kongo so Lopes would not understand. "Do you harbor suspicions against this man and his ships?"

Gil thought for a moment about the suspicions he did harbor, but they amounted to very little even to himself. After all, why couldn't a new king have a different range of interests than the old?

Why couldn't Manoel value the palm oil and timber, ivory and hides of the Kongo as highly as João had valued the silks and spices of the Indies? So he shook his head.

"You say you are second in command of this fleet, Dom Alvaro," Affonso said, again speaking in Portuguese. "Who is its captain-general?"

"Simão da Silva, knight of the Order of Christ. He is there in the longboat, Your Majesty. He regrets he cannot present himself to you properly, but he is dying. The black death is taking him quickly."

All eyes turned to the officer lying in the priest's arms. White-haired and white-bearded, he clearly had once been a big man but had been pitifully wasted away by his illness. Even from this distance, the ugly lumps and boils of plague could be seen on his face, grotesquely distorting and discoloring it. The priest was wiping this awful face with a cloth he repeatedly dipped in the river.

"He delayed coming ashore until now, Your Majesty, in the hope that he might yet recover and be able to present himself to you properly. But this morning it became plain he would not survive another day so he ordered me to bring him to you at once. He urgently desires an audience so that, as his last act, he may personally convey to you greetings from the new king of Portugal and his pledge of a renewed and strengthened alliance as signified by this valuable expedition he has sent to you. Will you go to him?"

"I do not think that would be wise, Your Majesty," Bishop de Sousa said. "The man is very sick. You run the risk of catching his sickness."

"Does the priest with him also have the sickness, Dom Alvaro?" Affonso asked.

Lopes glanced around at the priest tending to the captain-general. "No, Your Majesty, he is as healthy as I am."

"And yet he does not seem to fear catching the sickness."

"Father Henriqué is a courageous young man, Your Majesty."

"Then I can be at least as courageous as he," Affonso said and went to the longboat.

"My lord Captain, His Majesty is here," Lopes said softly. "Wake up, my lord Captain, the Kongo king has come to grant the audience you seek."

Simão da Silva opened his eyes with an effort painful to see and looked up in a daze, almost surely unseeing. "Your Majesty . . . Dom Affonso, ManiKongo . . ." His voice was a barely audible whisper, painful to hear. "I thank God for allowing me to live long enough to greet you in the name of my king. . . . Does he understand me, Alvaro? Is anyone here to translate for him? Should I speak in Latin? Would Latin be better?"

"Speak in either Portuguese or Latin, Dom Simão," Affonso said. "I will understand you in either case."

"Oh, yes, of course. I was told in Lisbon that you are a man of much learning and speak both Portuguese and Latin fluently. *Dei gratia.*" Da Silva tried to push himself up into a sitting position, and the effort caused greasy beads of sweat to break out on his forehead. "Your Majesty . . . I thank God for allowing me to live long enough to . . . to present to you with my own hand this *regimento* from your brother, Manoel of Portugal. This *regimento . . .* where is the *regimento,* padre? I must present it to the ManiKongo with my own hand."

"Do not excite yourself, Dom Simão," the priest said. "The *regimento* is just here."

A scroll of vellum parchment, tied with a purple ribbon and sealed in red wax with the royal coat of arms, lay on the blanket across da Silva's lap. The priest picked it up and gently slipped it between da Silva's fingers.

"Your Majesty, this *regimento,* which I present to you with my own hand, as charged by my king . . ." Da Silva paused to catch his breath, then closed his eyes; his fingers curled tightly around the scroll as if fighting off a wave of pain. "Your Majesty, this *regimento* heralds a renewed and strengthened alliance between our kingdoms . . ." But then his fingers uncurled and the scroll rolled out of his hand and he slumped back into the priest's arms.

Affonso glanced at Lopes.

"My lord Captain."

Da Silva whispered something.

"What do you say, my lord Captain?"

"In manus tuas, Domine, commendo spiritum meum."

"He is dying," the priest said quietly. "Confess your sins, Dom

Simão. Say an act of contrition for your soul's sake. There is no time
to lose." And when da Silva didn't respond, the priest spoke the
prayer for him. "O my God, I am heartily sorry for having offended
Thee . . ."

Affonso, Gil and Lopes watched as the priest performed the last
rites, speaking quickly, repeatedly making the sign of the cross and
then bending down and kissing the man's disfigured cheek. He had
long blond hair; it fell to his shoulders from beneath his hat. And
when he bent down to kiss da Silva's cheek, the hair fell across da
Silva's agonized face.

"Is he dead, padre?" Lopes asked.

"He is dead, Dom Alvaro. *Requiescat in pace.*" Father Henriqué
straightened up and removed his hat, and with the cloth he had used
to mop da Silva's face, now mopped his own.

And Gil saw his face. It was a *mestiço* face. "Kimpasi? My God, is
that you, Kimpasi?"

Father Henriqué smiled a small, sad smile. "Yes, *pai,* it is me,
come home from Portugal."

And Gil thought, what omen is this, his son returning to the land
of his birth aboard this plague fleet? The youth wore a string of
bloodstones around his neck.

KIMPASI, FATHER HENRIQUÉ, was very young for a priest, not yet
twenty—perhaps special dispensation had been given because of his
curious heritage—tall, slim, clean-shaven and, in the delightful confusion of his coloring and features, unconventionally handsome. But
there was none of the gaiety of youth in him. He had been a grave
and solemn boy, and his years in Lisbon—he had been sent to the
College of Santo Eloi when he was fourteen—seemed to have turned
him into an even more serious and somber and melancholy man. It
dismayed Gil. Actually he had had no idea his son had been studying
for the priesthood in Lisbon; he had expected him to return to the
Kongo an accomplished navigator (like the prince for whom he had
been named) or pilot or mapmaker, in any case schooled in a profes-
sion fitting him out for a career at sea. But he had no chance to question him about this or anything else. For during the next few days,
Henriqué was occupied helping prepare da Silva's corpse, assisting

the bishop at the funeral Mass and conducting the burial service in the graveyard of the church of Santo Antonio do Zaire. Then he returned to the ships of the fleet to resume his vocation among its company, comforting the dying, hearing their confessions, performing their last rites, burying them at sea. It could be weeks, if not months, before the plague ran its course and those who had survived could begin offloading cargo and Henriqué would be free to come ashore again.

Alvaro Lopes, however, had remained on shore. With Simão da Silva's death, he had succeeded to the command of the expedition as well as to a title that no one, until the day after the funeral, had realized da Silva also had held: that of Portuguese ambassador to the kingdom of the Kongo. It was an astonishing title. There never had been any such anywhere in Africa before and, when Lopes revealed it, it brought a gasp of amazement and created yet another puzzlement.

"Ambassador, Dom Alvaro?" Bishop de Sousa repeated. "You are to serve as King Manoel's ambassador to the ManiKongo's court?"

"Yes, Your Grace," the scrawny, unkempt, toothless sea captain answered with ill-concealed satisfaction. "And as governor of his Portuguese colony here as well."

"Ambassador and governor as well." The prelate smiled his thin, scarlet, mirthless smile, evidently calculating how this would affect his own role in the kingdom. "I must say, that is quite an honor King Manoel has bestowed. And not only on you, Dom Alvaro, but also on us. It is a measure of the importance with which he regards our small colony."

"It is, Your Grace. As I have said, he has high hopes for his Kongo colony."

This was in the reception hall of the Santo Antonio fortress. It was a high-vaulted room, its narrow embrasures letting in very little of the day's bright sunlight, furnished with high-backed chairs and a large banquet table; religious paintings and tapestries and full suits of armor hung on its stone walls. Besides Lopes and de Sousa, Affonso and the ManiSoyo, Jorgé, sat in the chairs around the table. Although there was also a chair for Gil, he stood behind Affonso's. As for Rodrigues, he came and went, busying himself inspecting the Santo Antonio garrison. At the moment, he wasn't there.

"I remain puzzled about these high hopes that King Manoel has for his Kongo colony, Dom Alvaro," Gil said now. "What can they be that they require the presence here of an ambassador and governor after all these years?"

"It is all explained in King Manoel's *regimento, senhor.*" Lopes was in possession of the vellum scroll that da Silva had let fall on dying. He produced it now from inside his leather jerkin and, with a dirty thumbnail, began slicing the wax of its royal seal. "Perhaps now is the time to read it."

"Dom Alvaro."

"Your Majesty?"

"That *regimento* was sent to me by King Manoel, was it not?"

"It was, Your Majesty."

"Then if you would be so kind as to let me have it." Affonso extended his hand across the table.

"Yes, of course, Your Majesty. I only thought to save you the bother of reading it."

"I can read, Dom Alvaro."

"Yes, of course." Lopes put the scroll in Affonso's hand.

Affonso broke the seal and unrolled the scroll and, holding it at arm's length, began reading aloud, as if to demonstrate his ability to Lopes: "Most powerful and excellent king of the Kongo, Dom Affonso my brother, greetings. We send to you Simão da Silva, nobleman of our house, a person whom we most trust. We beg you to listen to him and trust him with faith and belief in everything he says for he speaks in our name . . ." But then he fell silent and continued reading it to himself. He read for several minutes, then handed it over his shoulder to Gil.

"You understand, Your Majesty, that wherever King Manoel mentions Simão da Silva, may God rest his soul, my name must now unfortunately be substituted," Lopes said.

Affonso acknowledged this with a barely perceptible nod and pushed away from the table to turn and look at Gil.

Gil had little experience with royal communications and regal decrees and it took him a few moments to orient himself with this one. After a long introductory paragraph, written in elegant flourishes of flattering prose—"We are informed, most powerful and excellent

ManiKongo, that your Christian life is such that you appear not as a man but as an angel sent to convert your kingdom . . ." etc., etc.—the document, this *regimento,* was cast in the form of three sets of instructions to Simão da Silva (and now presumably to his successor Alvaro Lopes). The first set detailed the men and supplies the Portuguese king was sending to the Kongo aboard the plague-ridden ships, now lying at anchor in the river outside, for the purpose of reinvigorating the long-lapsed evangelization of the kingdom and strengthening its moribund alliance with the Portuguese crown. The second set dealt with the behavior da Silva (and now Lopes) was to demand of the settlers in what would now be a considerably enlarged Portuguese colony, empowering him as governor to arrest, punish and, if necessary, expel those who did not lead exemplary lives. The final set was the shortest but held Gil's attention the longest.

"This expedition," Manoel had written, "has cost us much. It would be unreasonable to send its ships home with empty holds. Although our principal wish is to serve God and the pleasure of the ManiKongo, nonetheless you [meaning da Silva and now Lopes] should make him [Affonso] understand, speaking in our name, with what goods he should fill the holds of our ships to repay us for our philanthropy."

There was no mention of what goods Manoel had in mind, no mention of how much of what merchandise he would regard as fair repayment for the cost of the expedition. This was to be decided by another officer of the fleet, a man by the name of Fernão de Mello. This de Mello would make a careful survey of the Kongo's wealth and then choose that which he judged would constitute reasonable compensation for the expedition's costs. But why was it necessary to make a survey of the Kongo's wealth? Surely, after all these years, the Portuguese were well familiar with the Kongo's wealth. And it was precisely in this that Gil's vague, unformed suspicions lay.

"Do you not find that the *regimento* answers your questions as to King Manoel's hopes for the Kongo, Senhor Eanes?"

"Not entirely."

"What still puzzles you?"

"Who is Fernão de Mello, for example."

"Donatário of São Jorgé da Mina. He has not been able to come ashore yet since he too has been stricken by the plague. But in his case, *Deo gratias,* there is every expectation he will recover."

"But there is no gold in the Kongo."

"Gold? Why do you speak of gold, *senbor?"*

"Because the gold dust of the rivers of the Ashanti country is the most valuable traffic and trade of São Jorgé da Mina. So I assume that, in sending its *donatário* here, King Manoel must hope that gold dust can also be found in the rivers of the Kongo."

"Perhaps that is so, *senbor."*

"But I tell you there is no gold in the Kongo. If there were, it would have been found long before this."

"Fernão de Mello is expert at finding gold, Senhor Eanes."

"And if he doesn't find any here, as I am sure he will not?"

"Then it will be for him to say what other goods should fill the holds of the king's ships to repay their costs. Does that not seem fair to you, Your Majesty?"

Affonso studied Gil for a long moment, as if trying to discern what he was thinking. Then he turned to Lopes. "If there is gold to be found in our kingdom, Dom Alvaro, we will be glad to have it found. So this Fernão de Mello is welcome to search for it wherever he wishes and we will assist him in every way. But the Kongo has many other riches and, if no gold is found, we will fill the holds of the king's ships so abundantly with those that Manoel will be just as well pleased. For this is our wish above all, Dom Alvaro, to please our brother Manoel. We are exceedingly grateful for this expedition he has sent us. We have long yearned for an expedition such as this in order to resume building churches and schools in our kingdom, in order to resume educating our sons and instructing our people in the Faith, in order to resume work on the creation of a written language, in order to resume bringing the Kongo closer to the kingdoms on the other shore of the sea. Therefore you can rest assured, Dom Alvaro, that we will repay Manoel for his generosity by filling his ships with whatever riches, be it gold or anything else, will most please him."

"Graciously said, Your Majesty."

Affonso again looked around at Gil.

Gil made no comment. He simply returned the *regimento* to Affonso and, speaking in Kongo, said, "I am sure you will understand if I take my leave of you now, Mbemba. I am anxious to see Kimpasi. It has been too many years."

"Of course. Embrace the boy for me and tell him I eagerly wait to hear of his adventures in Lisbon."

Gil hired a canoe from a Soyo fisherman and paddled out to the flagship of the plague fleet. He couldn't be sure Henriqué was on the flagship; the young priest's duties probably took him from ship to ship, but the seamen of the flagship were likely to know aboard which one he was that particular day.

"Stand off, *senhor.* Do not come closer. We have plague aboard."

The man shouting this, at the starboard rail in the ship's waist, was tall and lanky and almost entirely bald. And for an instant, Gil thought he recognized him.

"Is that you, Nuno?"

"What's that you say? Please, *senhor,* stand off. Do not come any closer. We have plague aboard."

Going closer nonetheless, Gil saw that the man was not his old friend. "I know you have plague aboard. I am looking for Father Henriqué. Is he on this ship?"

"Aye, he is on this ship. What do you want of him?"

"Fetch him for me. Tell him Gil Eanes is here."

"You are Gil Eanes? *Marinheiro.* Fetch the padre. Tell him Senhor Eanes is here."

A ladder was lowered.

"You should not come aboard, Senhor Eanes. There is still much sickness about."

"You look healthy enough to me."

"I am, *senhor.* Thanks be to God, I have been spared so far."

"You are not mate of this vessel, are you?"

"No. Bosun. We have all heard of you, Senhor Eanes. You must not catch this God-cursed sickness. It will be my neck if you do, for letting you come on board."

"Is Nuno Gonçalves mate of this vessel, by any chance?"

"He *was* our mate, *senhor.* But he died of the plague ten days before we reached this port and was buried at sea."

"*Pai.*"

Gil turned around. Henriqué was hurrying toward him up the companionway from the sterncastle cabins. He was bareheaded, his blond hair blowing in the wind, his white soutane flecked with spots of dried blood, a black rosary around his waist, the string of bloodstones around his neck.

"Kimpasi."

Father and son stopped a few paces from each other in a moment of awkward emotion. Soldiers and seamen began gathering around. Did they know the relationship between them? Did they know that their courageous young *mestiço* priest was Gil's son? With a paternal gentleness, Gil touched the bloodstones around Henriqué's neck.

"You still wear these?"

"I do," Henriqué said with a small, sad smile.

"I am glad," Gil said, then grasped his son's shoulders in the traditional Kongo way of greeting, held him at arm's length for a moment, then pulled him into an embrace.

A murmur of surprise and pleasure rippled through the watching crewmen.

"You shouldn't be here, *pai*. The plague is still very strong among us. Each day another dies of it."

"Everyone tells me that. But I couldn't wait to speak with you and hear of your experiences in Portugal. I didn't know you had decided to study for the priesthood. I expect your mother will be pleased, but I rather imagined a career at sea for you."

Henriqué didn't reply to this. He smiled that wan, sad smile of his and lowered his eyes. What was the matter with him? What was this melancholy in him? Gil glanced at the crewmen.

"Is there somewhere we can be alone, Kimpasi? Do you have your own cabin aboard?"

"Yes, but it is being used as an infirmary. There are many sick and dying in it. Let us go up on the forecastle deck. We can be alone there."

It was a pleasant spot, the forecastle deck, looking out on the thickly wooded islands in the broad, powerful river flowing down to the sea, exposed to the cool, refreshing wind blowing in from the sea, gulls and fish eagles circling overhead. Gil took a seat on the capstan; Henriqué sat down on the coil of anchor rope.

"I am glad you still call me Kimpasi, *pai*," the young priest said in his faintly doleful way. "No one calls me that. You are the only one."

"Am I?"

"Yes. From the day of my baptism, even mother always called me Henriqué. Do you still call her Nimi?"

"Yes."

"And the king? Do you still call him Mbemba?"

"I do."

"You never believed in our baptisms, did you, *pai?*"

Gil shrugged.

"I knew that. Even as a little boy, I knew you had lost your faith."

"Why do you say that? I haven't lost my faith."

"You do not have to protest to me, *pai*. I do not speak to you as a priest. I understand why you lost your faith. Because of the war against Mpanzu. Because of the role Bishop de Sousa played in the war. Isn't that so?"

Again Gil shrugged, perturbed by the humorless solemnity, the earnest mournfulness, with which his son spoke.

"I also had no faith for those reasons, *pai*. Growing up, I also did not believe in this God that Bishop de Sousa had brought to us from the land on the other shore of the sea."

"Then why did you become a priest?"

"It wasn't my idea at first. It was grandmother's. Queen Leonor's. Or do you still call her the Mbanda Lwa? She told me it was the way to acquire great magical powers and I was very young and easily impressed by the idea of acquiring great magical powers. And mother encouraged me too. I knew they were saying this behind your back, *pai,* and I didn't like that and made up my mind that I wouldn't do it. But when I arrived in Lisbon . . ."

"Yes?"

Henriqué hesitated. Then he said, not defiantly but quietly, with a sorrowful sincerity, "I discovered my faith in Lisbon, *pai*. I found our Lord Jesus Christ at the College. I was called to His service there."

Gil sighed. What could he say to that? How could he argue with such a confession? "That is a fine thing, Kimpasi."

"It is. A blessed and joyous thing."

"Why then aren't you joyful? You seem so sad to me. Is it because of this black death all around you? Were you happier before this voyage?"

Henriqué looked away, looked out to the river flowing down to the sea, turned his face into the wind blowing in from the sea, and said something that was blown away by the wind.

"I didn't hear what you said, Kimpasi."

The young priest looked back. "Do you know that there is a new world, *pai?*"

What foolishness was this? A new world? A new Jerusalem perhaps? Had his son become some sort of zealot? Had the canons at the College of Santo Eloi addled his brain with some sort of religious fanaticism?

"Have you not heard that a new world has been discovered, *pai?* Has news of it not reached the Kongo yet?"

"What new world, Kimpasi?"

"It is called Brasil. Pero Alvares Cabral discovered it nearly two years ago. He was in command of a fleet of Indiamen. But he was blown off course in a storm in the middle of the Atlantic and sighted a mountain at seventeen degrees of latitude south of the equator. At first he thought it was just an uncharted island, but when he closed the shore to investigate, he saw it wasn't an island at all but a great land mass, a mainland, an unknown continent, a new world. Some say he wasn't the first to discover it. A Genoese sea captain by the name of Christovão Colom, in the service of the monarchs of the Spains, sailing west across the Atlantic in search of a sea route to the Indies by that way five years before da Gama, reached a large group of islands in very much the same longitude as this Brasil, but many hundreds of leagues to the north of it. He claimed these were islands lying off the coast of the Indies and named them the West Indies. But there are many who now say that they aren't the Indies at all but a part of the same continent as Brasil."

Gil listened to this with much admiration for his son's knowledge.

"It has caused tremendous dispute, *pai.* Evidently this new world is very rich. They say there are great quantities of gold in its mountains and rivers, far more than anything found in the Ashanti

country around São Jorgé da Mina or anywhere else in Africa or the
Indies. But to whom does it belong? King Manoel naturally claims it
for Portugal because of Cabral. But Isabel and Ferdinand of the Spains
claim it for themselves because of Colom. Pope Alexander has had to
intervene to settle the claims."

"And how has he settled them?"

"He issued a Papal Bull of Demarcation, *Inter caetera,* which
draws a line from north to south across the Atlantic about four hundred leagues west of the Azores and Cape Verde Islands, and granted
all the lands and seas lying east of the line to Portugal and all the
lands and seas lying west of it to the Spains. A treaty was signed at
Tordesillas by the monarchs of Portugal and the Spains accepting
this."

"You are going too quickly for me, Kimpasi. I cannot visualize
this without a map. Surely the Kongo and, indeed, all of Africa must
lie east of this line and so belong to Portugal. But what of this Brasil?"

"King Manoel, of course, says it too lies east of the line. But no
one can be certain. No one can say exactly where the line passes
through this new world because there are no good maps of it. The
mapmakers for the Spains put it in one place, the Portuguese in another, according to which best suits their interests. The only way any
of this new world will truly belong to one or the other is by the establishment of settlements there. So a furious competition has begun
between Portugal and the Spains to establish settlements there. There
is a terrific need for men for this because, it is said, the people of this
new world cannot be employed to do it."

"Why not?"

"They live wild. They are a wild people and, it is said, they die
when they are employed to do this sort of work. So men must be
brought there to do it."

"This is all quite extraordinary, Kimpasi. No, we have had no
news of it here in the Kongo. But tell me, why does the discovery of
this new world make you so sad?"

"Because of this terrific need for men. This terrific need to bring
thousands and thousands of men to build the settlements in this new
world."

"Yes?"

"What makes me sad is who these men are."

"Who are they?"

Henriqué didn't answer. He suddenly looked away. Gil turned around. A man was coming up on the forecastle deck from the ship's waist. He was exceptionally tall, wearing a gray cloak with its hood pulled over his head, obscuring his face. Whoever he was, Henriqué obviously hadn't wanted him to overhear their conversation.

"Senhor Eanes?"

"Aye." Gil stood up.

"I was told you were aboard and was anxious to meet you. I am Fernão de Mello, *donatário* of São Jorgé da Mina."

"Dom Fernão. I also was told you were aboard and was anxious to meet you."

"I am greatly in your debt, *senhor.*"

"Why is that?"

"Because of your son. He has looked after me throughout my illness and pulled me back from the jaws of death with his courage, patience and faith."

"I had heard you had been stricken by the plague."

"I am almost recovered now, thanks to Father Henriqué."

The man pulled back the hood of his cloak. His pallor was a ghostly gray; his face was long and gaunt with hollowed-out cheeks and deep-set eyes; his black beard and hair were extremely close-cut, but there were no traces of the plague's boils and lumps on him.

"It will be just a matter of weeks before I am completely recovered and, more important, not much longer than that before this plague will have run its course and we can begin disembarking our men and bringing our cargo ashore."

IV

Fᴇʀɴ̃ᴀᴏ ᴅᴇ Mello, it quickly became clear, and not Alvaro Lopes, was the true commander of King Manoel's fleet. Simão da Silva, as a knight of the Order of Christ, had outranked him and, had he lived, doubtless would have had the final say in things. But once the plague had run its course and the black flags were hauled down and the landing of men and cargo from the five ships began, Lopes, despite the titles he had inherited from da Silva, was seen to defer to the *donatário* of São Jorgé da Mina at every turn. Apparently, that title, *donatário*, proprietor-general, outranked even those of king's ambassador and colonial governor.

This was three weeks after the fleet's arrival, two days before the start of Lent. Only 408 of its original complement of 633 passengers and crew had survived the black death but, even so, it was an extraordinary number. In one fell swoop, the Portuguese population in the Kongo was nearly tripled. But what was even more astonishing was the tonnage and value of the cargo they brought ashore. It took ten days to empty the holds of the ships; the warehouses of the Santo Antonio fortress were packed to the rafters; crates and bales, kegs and barrels piled up on the piers. There were guns and gunpowder, armor and armaments. There were missals and Bibles and furnishings for churches and mission schools. There were spyglasses and compasses, sextants and surveyor's tools. There were wheeled carts and hoists, tackles and pulleys and loads of building materials. There were

food plants and fruit trees—sugar cane, guava, lemon, lime and orange—unknown to the Kongo and now to be transplanted there.
And overseeing it all was the uncommonly tall, wraithlike figure of
the *donatário* in his long gray hooded cloak, with the scrawny, toothless Lopes scurrying beside him, nervously responding to his every
command.

Gil watched them with a profound disquiet, a deep unease. This
invasion of Europeans, this influx of European manufacture would, he
feared, overwhelm the Kongo and utterly transform it. Enough goods
and settlers were being landed to vastly expand the Portuguese settlements in São Salvador and Santo Antonio, to build churches and
man garrisons in the other main towns, and to establish plantations
of outlandish crops everywhere else in the kingdom. The Kongo
would be remade into a counterfeit Portugal, and he did not like it. After twenty years, he no longer considered himself Portuguese; Portugal was but a dim memory for him. After twenty years, he had grown
irretrievably into the fabric of Kongo life; he did not want his long-
lost Portugal brought home to him now. But apart from his personal
dissatisfaction, there were also his suspicions, made all the keener by
what he had learned from his son. Why was King Manoel investing so
heavily in the Kongo now when João had ignored it for so long? What
was the connection between that and the discovery of this new
world of Brasil? Surely the timing could not be mere happenstance.

"Is it not everything we have always dreamed of, Gil?" Affonso
said.

They were standing on the fortress's ramparts, looking down
into its market court into which culverins and carts, hoists and boxes
were being hauled for lack of any other place to store them.

"Look at those guns. Look at those extraordinary mechanisms.
Look at the books. Look at all that treasure. It is everything we have
ever dreamed of. Now we will truly be a part of the wider world.
Now we will finally have a written language of our own." Affonso
smiled with bright and innocent delight. "I knew this day would
someday come, Gil. It is why I defied my father and took the throne
from Mpanzu. Mpanzu would never have allowed this. He would
never have stopped fighting to keep the wider world from us."

Gil made no comment. Affonso had been in a state of mounting elation and excitement ever since learning of the Portuguese expedition, and his elation and excitement were near bursting now, seeing the richness of its cargo. He seemed young again; the years of disappointment had fallen away from him, and Gil did not have the heart to spoil his pleasure with unformed, unfounded suspicions.

"What is the matter?" Affonso finally noticed Gil's sulky silence. "What troubles you?"

"Do you remember Nuno Gonçalves, Mbemba?"

"Of course I remember him. He was mate to both Diogo Cão and Bartolomeu Dias."

"And also to Simão da Silva aboard the flagship of this fleet. But the plague took him. He was buried at sea."

"I am sorry to hear that. He was a good friend to you."

"Maybe my last friend in Portugal."

"I am sorry," Affonso said again.

But he waited. He knew Gil well enough to know that Gonçalves's death, as sad a loss as it might be, did not account for Gil's mood. So he waited for him to go on.

And after a few moments, he did go on. He said, "You are ManiKongo, Mbemba. You must never forget that."

Affonso cocked his head, taken aback by this superfluous observation.

"Much will change in the kingdom now. All this . . ." Gil pointed down into the market court of the fortress and then out to the piers. "All this will change the kingdom in ways we cannot foresee. But you must never forget you are king. No matter how much is changed, you must never forget it is you who rules here. You will be given advice on how to rule by de Mello and Lopes. In the *regimento,* King Manoel charges you to listen to their advice. But you must not let them rule your kingdom by the advice they give you. You must not let them make you a king in name only."

"Is that what you believe they intend?"

"I do not know. I tell you that truthfully, Mbemba. I do not know what they intend. But I do not understand why, after so many years, they have come now with so much treasure and so much force. I do not understand what they hope to get in return for it and it worries me. Perhaps I have grown stupid about my own people, having lived so long away from them. Perhaps they only intend that which you yourself most desire, to make the Kongo part of the wider world. But I consider it my duty to you to tell you of my worries and put you on your guard."

"Yes, that is your duty to me, Gil, and I thank you for always having performed it well." Affonso again looked down into the fortress's market court. And then he said, "But now put your worries aside, Gil, and rejoice with me in the arrival of this treasure-laden fleet. It is a great thing for me. It has erased the doubts I have had about what I have done. It has lifted from my shoulders the guilt I have long suffered for defying my father and taking my brother's throne. It is my vindication, Gil, and I thank God for it."

"HAVE YOU COME HOME to stay?" Tereza asked, crawling into her brother's lap. "Or will you go away forever again?"

"I have come home to stay, little monkey," Henriqué replied with his sad smile and wrapped the little girl in his arms.

"This is exactly what I had hoped for," Leonor said. "A priest in our own family."

"Have you decided what you will do?" Gil asked.

"Bishop de Sousa has offered to take me on as his secretary at the vicarage, *pai*."

"Oh, that is wonderful, Henriqué," Beatriz said. "I was afraid His Grace was going to send you on his crusade and it again would be years before we had you near."

"What crusade?" Gil asked.

"His Grace has spoken of nothing else since King Manoel's ships arrived, Gil. He says that now that he has so many more priests, he will be able to launch a great crusade to baptize all the people of the kingdom and I was afraid Henriqué would be one of the priests sent to some far-off mission in the countryside. I am so glad he will be here at the cathedral where we can see him every day."

"Will you, Kimpasi?" Have you accepted the bishop's offer?"

"I'd rather not." Henriqué ran a hand wearily through his long hair. "I'd much rather serve in a mission somewhere in the countryside. I have some ideas of my own about how best to bring the Faith to our people."

They were in the main room of Gil's house, celebrating Henriqué's homecoming. A grand meal had been served and now platters of fruit and cups of palm wine were being handed around.

Father and son had arrived in São Salvador just that morning, having traveled from Santo Antonio with the first caravan of goods and men to be dispatched to the royal capital from the plague fleet. News of the plague fleet and its amazing cargo had preceded them so that, when the caravan reached the city, its streets and parks and market squares had been jammed with thousands of people eager to see and greet it. Affonso, with Lopes riding beside him in a litter—de Mello had remained in Santo Antonio to begin his survey of the Kongo's riches—had directed the caravan to pass through every precinct, before crossing the Luezi bridges into the royal district, in order to satisfy their excited curiosity. Gil and Henriqué, however, had dropped out along the circuitous route and gone straight home. For the news that Henriqué had returned with the fleet had also preceded the caravan, and he was anxiously awaited there by his mother, sister and grandmother.

"You're not sick, are you, Henriqué?" his mother asked now. She had been closely scrutinizing her son's every weary gesture and soulful expression since he had stepped into the house. "We heard about the terrible sickness aboard the ships and how it killed so many of the white men. You didn't catch it from them, did you?"

"No, I'm just tired, Mother. It was a long, hard voyage. And now Bishop de Sousa wants me to assist him at the Thanksgiving Mass he will celebrate this evening. Maybe I should get some rest first. Would you mind?"

"Of course not. Go and get some rest. Tereza, show your brother to his room. He probably doesn't remember where it is."

The little girl jumped up and clutched Henriqué's hand.

"Oh, I remember where it is," Henriqué said with his sad smile. "But I cannot stay there anymore. I am a priest now and must stay with the other priests, in the cloister."

"I know where the cloister is too," Tereza said. "I will show you."

"What is wrong with him, Gil?" Beatriz asked after brother and sister, hand in hand, had left the house. "He *is* sick, isn't he? He caught the black death and you're not telling me."

"No, Nimi, he is healthy, I promise you."

"Then why is he so melancholy?"

"I don't know. He hasn't said. It may be a secret, something he is under a priestly vow not to reveal."

"What could it be?"

Gil shook his head and a moment of pensive silence fell on the room.

Leonor broke the silence. "Do you find this a good thing, Senhor Eenezh?" she asked.

"What, my lady?"

"This, all this. The coming of all these white men to the kingdom. Do you find it a good thing?"

"I am surprised you ask that, my lady. You of all people, you who played such an important role in bringing the white men to the kingdom in the first place."

"I do not regret the role I played in bringing the white men to the kingdom in the first place, *senhor.*"

"Because it put your son on the throne."

"Yes, because it put my son on the throne. I am not ashamed to admit it. It is what I wanted and we have all benefited by it, you no less than I. But that is all I wanted, nothing more. This, what is happening now, this talk of Bishop de Sousa's crusade . . . this is too much. White soldiers in every part of the kingdom, white priests in every village and town. I am not sure I find that a good thing at all."

"No, Mother, you are wrong," Beatriz said. "It *is* a good thing. It is God's will that the Faith be brought to all our people and that their souls be saved from eternal damnation. But the best thing is that Affonso will not have to marry Mfidi now after all."

"Who says that?" Gil asked.

"I say it. And so does Bishop de Sousa. There is no need for such a sinful marriage anymore. Because once the Nsundi are baptized in the crusade, along with everyone else, the trouble with them will be put to rest without Affonso ever having to take a wife and queen from among them."

"Does he also say this?"

"I have not spoken to him about it."

"Perhaps I should," Gil said and got up and started out of the house.

"You did not answer my question, Senhor Eenezh," Leonor called after him.

"What question was that, my lady?"

"Whether you find the coming of all these white men a good thing."

"No, my lady, I do not find it a good thing. But it is too late to complain of it now. For once the white men were allowed to come in the first place, it was only a matter of time before other white men would come after them. Mpanzu understood that. The Mbanda Vunda understood that. The NgangaKongo understood that. It was your mistake, my lady, that you did not understand it as well, that you did not understand it would be the price you would have to pay for putting your son on the throne."

Nuno and Gonçalo were waiting for Gil in the garden of the house and fell into step beside him when he came down from the veranda and headed for the São Salvador cathedral.

Forty Portuguese soldiers, armed with halberds, crossbows and arquebuses and wearing plumed helmets, chainmail and shoulder armor, were mustered in the plaza in front of the cathedral. Two lombard cannon, mounted on caissons, and two wagons of provisions and gunpowder were drawn up in their train. In addition, one hundred Kongo warriors in war paint and feathers, twenty armed with arquebuses, the rest with lances and shields, were assembled in a second squadron. A Dominican friar stood at the head of the combined column holding a tall wooden cross; a band of Kongo drummers and trumpeters brought up the rear. Rodrigues, also helmeted and armored, paced up and down in front of them, slapping his cutlass impatiently against his leg.

"What is this?" Gil asked the brothers as they entered the plaza.

Nuno looked at Gonçalo and, when Gonçalo shook his head, Nuno also shook his.

It was early afternoon and the caravan from the coast, with which Gil and Henriqué had traveled, had dispersed some time before; its loads of goods had been taken to the storehouses in the Portuguese quarter and the newly arrived settlers were making the acquaintance of the old-timers there. Even so, crowds of people still milled around the plaza, eager not to miss out on anything. The column of Portuguese soldiers and Kongo warriors must have seemed

to them just another entertainment brought about by the arrival of
the plague fleet.

"What's going on here, sir marshal? What's this fighting force
you've assembled?"

"A hunting party, *senhor.* We're off to hunt down Mpanzu."

"What? Whose idea was that? The bishop's?"

"No, the king's."

"I don't believe that. Where is he?"

"In the vicarage, with the bishop and Lopes."

Gil started up the cathedral steps.

"A moment, *senhor.* Where are you going?"

"Where do you think? To the king."

"He has not sent for you."

"Since when do I have to wait for him to send for me?"

"Since we have a new governor." Rodrigues pronounced Lopes's
title with ill-concealed sourness; evidently, he was as annoyed as de
Sousa had been that this newcomer now held the senior rank in the
Portuguese colony. "He has issued orders that no one is to come into
the king's presence unless specifically sent for."

"I don't give a damn what orders he has issued."

Rodrigues shrugged. Clearly, he had no intention of trying to
prevent Gil from entering the cathedral; to the contrary, he was
happy to see the new governor's orders flouted.

But Gil didn't enter the cathedral. Something else occurred to
him and he came back down the steps and asked, "Have you heard
that a new world has been discovered, sir marshal?"

"What new world is that?"

"Brasil."

Rodrigues shook his head.

"No one has mentioned it to you? Not Bishop de Sousa? Not our
new governor?"

"You're the first to mention anything about a new world to me,
senhor. Is it part of the Indies? I've heard the way to the Indies has
been discovered."

"Aye, I think it's part of the Indies."

Maybe it was a secret. Maybe de Mello and Lopes were keeping
it a secret even from Bishop de Sousa. For surely, if they had mentioned it to de Sousa, he would have mentioned it to Rodrigues.

Maybe it was a secret Henriqué had somehow come upon and been sworn to keep.

"His Majesty," Rodrigues barked and the soldiers and warriors in the plaza snapped to attention.

Affonso came out of the cathedral looking angry. Lopes and de Sousa followed him out looking severe.

"Where have you been, Gil? One moment you are by my side and when I next look for you, you have vanished."

"I took Kimpasi home to his mother. And then when I came here, I was prevented from going to you on Dom Alvaro's orders."

"You must understand, Senhor Eanes, that under the rules of the *regimento*—" Lopes started.

But Gil cut him off. "And, besides, what's going on here anyway, Mbemba? I'm told you've given permission to have Mpanzu hunted down. Is that true?"

Affonso glanced at the column of warriors and soldiers, then strode across the plaza down to the Luezi. He was still dressed in ceremonial European clothes and, when he got to the river's bank, he squatted on his heels in the reeds there, pulled his rapier from his belt and began poking it into the mud of the river's bottom. Gil glanced at Lopes and de Sousa. They remained on the cathedral steps with Rodrigues. Would Rodrigues now ask the bishop about Brasil? And if the bishop had heard nothing of it, would he ask Lopes? And what would Lopes say? Or had Lopes also heard nothing of it? Maybe de Mello had kept it secret even from him. Gil went after Affonso.

"It is true, isn't it? You have given permission for Mpanzu to be captured."

Affonso went on stabbing at the river.

"Why?"

"You know why." Affonso looked back at the three Portuguese on the cathedral steps.

"You said to me you didn't want Mpanzu harmed, Mbemba. You said to me he had been harmed enough. Those people will harm him. They'll kill him."

"No, they won't." Affonso stood up, leaving his rapier stuck in the river bottom. "They have my permission to capture him only in order to baptize him."

"Baptize him? They'll never baptize him. He'll never accept the sacrament. They offered it to him once when, if he had accepted it, he could have remained king. But he didn't. And he won't now."

Very deliberately, Affonso pulled his rapier from the river, wiped the mud from its blade and slipped it back into his belt.

"I don't understand this, Mbemba. Why did you agree to this? Why are you throwing Mpanzu to these dogs?"

"Because of King Manoel's ships."

"What have they to do with it?"

"Dom Alvaro says King Manoel sent these ships only because the Kongo, like Portugal, is a Catholic kingdom, only because I, like Manoel, am a Catholic king. He says Manoel would never have gone to such expense for a heathen king, would never have considered entering into this sort of alliance with a heathen kingdom."

"But you are not a heathen king. You are Catholic and this is a Catholic kingdom."

"Not if I marry Mfidi. Bishop de Sousa says he will excommunicate me if I take a second wife and queen. And then these will be the last ships I will ever see from the land on the other shore of the sea."

"But what about the annulment?"

"Bishop de Sousa is no longer willing to go ahead with it. He says it is no longer necessary. He says that, with the coming of so many more priests, he will be able to launch a great crusade of baptisms throughout the kingdom and especially among the Nsundi and by that insure their loyalty to my throne."

"Yes, Nimi told me that is what he intends."

"But he knows he will never succeed in baptizing the Nsundi until he baptizes Mpanzu. The Nsundi will only receive the sacrament if their ManiNsundi does."

"So for the sake of King Manoel's friendship, for the sake of the treasure of his ships, you are willing to throw your brother to these dogs."

"Why shouldn't I? Why should I go on protecting him? Did you not yourself tell me he is my enemy? Did you not yourself tell me he is raising an army against me? Why then should I let him stand in the way of my dream to make my kingdom part of the wider world? If all that is required of me to hold fast to that dream is to give my permission for Mpanzu to be captured and baptized, yes, I do it willingly."

Gil shook his head.

"Do not oppose me in this, Gil. I need you by my side now more than ever before."

"Oh, I remain by your side, Mbemba. Although I believe what you do is wrong, I am your friend and faithful servant and remain by your side."

"Ntondesi."

Gil watched Affonso walk back to the three white men on the cathedral steps and talk with them for a few moments. Then Lopes and Rodrigues came down into the plaza and took their places at the head of the column of soldiers and warriors beside the friar carrying the tall wooden cross. The Kongo trumpeters in the rear emitted a series of short, harsh blasts, the drummers started up a steady marching beat and the soldiers and warriors, wagons and cannon moved out of the plaza toward the Luezi's middle bridge. They made an impressive fighting force but, in this terrain, also a clumsy one. The soldiers in their heavy armor, the guns and wagons on their wooden wheels would find the going increasingly hard once they left the royal roads and struck off into the rugged hills of the Nsundi grassland where they'd have to go to hunt Mpanzu down.

Gil called Nuno and Gonçalo over. "Follow them," he said. "Follow the captain Rodrigues and the new Portuguese man Lopes. I wish to know how well they succeed in their hunt for the Mani-Nsundi."

V

I N THE FIRST WEEKS after the arrival of the plague fleet, a flurry of construction, much like that of the first years of Affonso's reign, got under way in São Salvador to accommodate the hundreds of new settlers and the wares they had brought. Additional dwellings and storehouses, shops and taverns were built along the narrow alleyways of the Portuguese quarter; the barracks and cloister were expanded; the bridges across the Luezi were shored up to handle the heavier traffic of carts and caissons; orchards and plantations of the imported fruit trees and food plants were put in in the outlying fields in anticipation of the next rainy season; and the foundation for a second church in the city, dedicated to Our Lady of the Victories, was laid on the other side of the Luezi to serve the plebeian districts. And construction on the kingdom's fourth church (counting Santo Antonio do Zaire) also got under way, this one in Mpangala, honoring the Holy Cross (the town was to change its name to that, Santa Cruz, once it was completed) in order to bolster the crusade for souls among the troublesome Nsundi.

Henriqué was going to serve in that church. Bishop de Sousa had acceded to his many petitions to be relieved of his duties as secretary at the vicarage so he could take up missionary work (for which, because of his Kongo blood, he considered himself far better suited), and he was departing for Mpangala this morning, the end of Easter week. Gil and Beatriz, accompanied by their old serving woman Nimi, went to the cloister to see him off.

He was at matins when they entered the cloister's interior courtyard, and since women weren't permitted in the chapel, they waited
for him there. It was a pretty place, graveled, a stone fountain at its
center with a shrine to the Holy Mother encircled by flowering trees.
Gil sat down on the fountain's lip. The cells of the priests and friars
in residence looked out onto it.

"Have they found him yet?" Beatriz asked.

Gil knew who she was asking about. She was asking about
Mpanzu. She had been asking about him intermittently ever since
learning of the fighting force that had been sent to hunt him down.
Gil shook his head. The chanting of the morning office in the chapel
harmonized pleasantly with the singing of the birds in the courtyard's trees.

"I hope they find him soon. And kill him."

"How cruel you are, Nimi."

"He was cruel enough to me, and to you as well, when matters
were the other way around. And he would be just as cruel now, if he
had the chance."

"I suppose that is so."

"Then why do you care what happens to him?"

"I don't."

"You behave as if you do. You behave as if you hope they never
find him. Bishop de Sousa says—"

"Oh, for pity's sake, Nimi, why do you always repeat what
Bishop de Sousa says? Why don't you once think for yourself?"

"About what?"

The other Nimi, the old serving woman, moved away, embarrassed to overhear a quarrel.

"About why all these ships have come. About what all these Portuguese want here."

"What do they want here?"

Gil didn't reply.

Beatriz went over to him at the fountain. "Tell me, Gil," she said
more quietly. "What do they want here?"

"I don't know, Nimi. I just don't know."

"But you believe with my mother that it is not a good thing that
they have come."

"Yes."

"But Affonso believes it is a good thing."

"He is mistaken."

"Have you told him that?"

"I have tried but he will not listen to me. He does not want to hear any ill of the Portuguese. He dare not. After all that has passed, he must believe their coming is a good thing."

"Yes," Beatriz said. "And so must I."

The chanting in the chapel ceased and for several moments there was only the singing of the birds in the trees. Then the sanctus bell rang and the priests and friars began filing out of the chapel. With his eyes cast down, counting the beads of his rosary, Henriqué hurried ahead of the others. He was dressed for the road in sandals and a hooded cassock, his blond hair, like his father's, tied in a queue, the string of bloodstones around his neck.

"How sad he seems," Beatriz said. "He always seems so sad."

It was true. Even when he smiled—as he did now, seeing his mother and father and Nimi waiting for him by the fountain—his light blue eyes seemed filled with all the sadness of the world.

"Are you ready for your journey, Kimpasi?"

"I just have a few more things to pack."

"You won't change your mind? Is there nothing I can say to change your mind?"

"No."

"I don't see why you have to go," Beatriz said petulantly. "There are already two priests in Mpangala, Father Duarte and Father José. That ought to be enough for a crusade even among the Nsundi."

"I don't like how they conduct their crusade. They are far too zealous, especially Father Duarte."

"What do you mean?" Gil asked.

"He is a man of the Inquisition, *pai,* and thinks its methods can be used here. I have heard he has taken to interfering in all the local ceremonies and customs, declaring them heathen rituals, sinful in the eyes of our Lord. The marriage and burial ceremonies. The birth feasts. The coming-of-age tests and trials. The courting dances. He regards all of it as the work of Satan and is having the *nsaku* who perform them and anyone who participates in them flogged and the fetishes used in them destroyed. I have heard that he has even set soldiers to ransacking the dwellings and holy places and gathering up the fetishes they find and burning them in bonfires in the market squares. It is madness. He is mad."

"You must not speak of him like that, Henriqué," Beatriz said in a mild panic. "He is your superior, the second priest in the kingdom after the bishop, and has power over you. He can cause you harm."

"It doesn't matter what harm he can cause me, Mother. What matters is the harm he is causing the Church. He will never bring the Nsundi to the Church with his methods. He will only drive them further away. That is why I must go to Mpangala. To show him that there are better methods by which to convert the Nsundi than his burnings and floggings."

"But can you show him?" Gil said. "I don't think you can."

"I must try, *pai.* And if I fail, then I must at least show the Nsundi that not all Catholic priests are like him."

Gil nodded. "Come, I will help you pack your things."

Neither Beatriz nor Nimi accompanied them to Henriqué's cell; women were also not permitted in the priests' cells. It was morning of another warm and sunny day, but the cell was windowless and cool and dark and austerely furnished: a hard palette on the stone floor, a stool and table against the stone wall, a jug and washbasin on the table, a crucifix above it. A rough woolen blanket was spread out on the palette. Henriqué squatted beside it and began packing his belongings into it. Gil sat down on the stool.

"Why is Nimi here, *pai?*"

"Your mother asked her to go to Mpangala with you, and she agreed."

"To keep watch over me?"

"Yes," Gil answered with a smile.

"She still thinks of me as a boy who cannot care for himself."

"No, Kimpasi, she knows you are a man. She sees you are a man, a strong man with strong ideas. Even so, every man, even a strong man, even a priest, is entitled to have a woman keep watch over him."

Henriqué had very few belongings to pack: a freshly laundered soutane, a change of underclothes, a shaving knife and soap, his breviary and vestments, little else. Gil watched him roll these into the blanket, then tie it with a rope so it could be slung over his shoulder.

"There is something about which I wish to speak to you, Kimpasi."

"What is that?"

"If you are under a vow not to speak of it, I will understand."

Finished with his packing, Henriqué turned to his father and sat back on his heels.

"This new world of Brasil. When you first told me of it, you also started to tell me who was being taken there to build its settlements. But then the *donatário* came and interrupted us and you have not spoken of it since. Are you not permitted to speak of it?"

The young priest looked out into the courtyard as if to see who might be there to overhear him. Then he said, "I will speak of it to you, *pai.*"

"I will keep it secret if you wish."

"Perhaps you should not. Perhaps it would be better if it were known. I will leave it to you to decide."

Gil leaned forward on the stool, resting his elbows on his knees.

"There is a great need for men in the new world, *pai*, thousands, even tens of thousands, to build the settlements that will make it either Portugal's or the Spains' according to the Treaty of Tordesillas. But the men who live there, the *indianos* as they are called, since many still believe this new world is part of the Indies, these *indianos* are of no use. They die when they are put to such work. So men must be taken there to do the work in their place."

"Yes, you told me that."

"But the men who are taken there to do the work are taken there against their will. They are taken there by force."

"Who are they?"

"At first they were felons and convicts and outlaws of all kinds. They were taken from prisons everywhere in Portugal and given their freedom if they agreed to go. And then they were taken from the prisons whether or not they agreed to go. But this need for men is greater than all the prisons in Portugal can provide. So other men had to be found. Serfs and indentured servants and vassals were given over by their lords for a price. The poorhouses were cleared out. Peasants were sold off the farms. Vagabonds and adventurers and disreputable characters of every stripe were arrested and sentenced to transportation to Brasil for their crimes. White men and Christians, even women and girls. The Infante Affonso, João's son and the rightful heir to the throne, was against this and that is why he was pushed aside in favor of Manoel, who is fierce in his desire to win the race for the new world against the monarchs of the Spains. But he too has not been able to find men enough to settle it as he would wish . . ."

Gil waited for his son to go on. But the youth fell into a momentary reverie as if distracted by a memory of men and women being rounded up in Lisbon for transportation against their will to the new world a thousand leagues across the Ocean Sea. Perhaps he himself had seen such a roundup and that was what had given him his mournful aspect.

"And?" Gil prompted him after a few moments of silence. "What has Manoel done to find men enough to settle the new world as he would wish?"

Henriqué started from his reverie. But he did not answer the question directly. He seemed to take up an entirely different train of thought.

"On our voyage out from Lisbon, *pai*," he said quietly, "we called at São Jorgé da Mina to revictual and take on fresh water and also to fetch the *donatário*, Dom Fernão, and bring him with us to the Kongo."

"Yes."

"There was a ship in the harbor when we dropped anchor there. She was bound for Brasil under the Portuguese flag. There were Negroes aboard her."

"Negroes? Ashanti?"

"They weren't Ashanti. They came from upcountry. Mandingo people. There were about one hundred men and as many women and children. The Ashanti had taken them captive in a war and brought them down to São Jorgé da Mina and the Ashanti chief there had sold them to the *donatário* for firearms and he, in turn, had sold them to the ship's captain for transportation to Brasil."

Again Gil waited for Henriqué to continue.

"Don't you see what this can mean, *pai?*"

Gil shook his head.

"It may mean Manoel is now turning to Africa to find the men he needs to build the settlements of Brasil."

• • •

THE RAINS WERE DRAWING NEAR; their iron scent was on the wind. At nightfall, clouds blew in on the iron-scented wind, streaking the sky in pastel shades, obscuring the moon and stars and letting fall a heavy dew. By daybreak, the clouds had scattered but soon were gathering again in leaden galleons, their underbellies streaked with gray. And Mpanzu still had not been found. On the morning of Holy Thursday, a light drizzle swept across the royal plateau but the wind blew away the clouds before the sun rose.

Beatriz was getting ready for the Ascension Day Mass, giving orders to her serving women, supervising the preparations for a feast, seeing that Tereza was properly dressed. Gil waited outside on the veranda. He was expecting Nuno and Gonçalo. In the preceding weeks, he had received regular reports from them on the movements of Rodrigues and Lopes and their expeditionary force. Apparently, at the outset, they had gotten hold of some good information on Mpanzu's whereabouts and had made the hard trek eastward along the Lelunda River to the Nsundi fishing village where Mpanzu had last been seen. But Mpanzu was no longer there, leaving them in a quandary about where or even in which direction next to pursue him. In their most recent report, the brothers had said that they had decided to next pursue him still farther eastward up the river into the endlessly rolling hills of that grassland wilderness—and that was the wrong direction. According to the intelligence Nuno and Gonçalo themselves had gathered, Mpanzu and his band of followers had, in fact, crossed the Lelunda and were moving south. So Gil had sent word to them to return to São Salvador. With any luck, they'd be back this morning before the start of the Ascension Day Mass.

And sure enough, while he was waiting for Beatriz and Tereza on the veranda, there was a stir in the gardens below. The warriors of his household guard were challenging someone entering the royal compound. He went down from the veranda, wondering why only one of the brothers had returned. What had happened to the other? He would never forgive himself if either of them had been hurt or killed. But it was neither of the brothers. It was Nimi. Just as he recognized her, Beatriz and Tereza came out on the veranda with their serving women, ready to go to the cathedral.

"Nimi," Beatriz cried and dashed down from the veranda. "Why are you here, *mchento?* It is Henriqué, isn't it? Something has happened to Henriqué."

"No, my lady, nothing has happened to Henriqué."

"Then why are you here?"

"I bring a message from him for his father."

"What is the message?"

The old woman looked at Gil.

"Go along to the cathedral with Tereza, Nimi. You mustn't keep Bishop de Sousa waiting."

"I am not a child, Gil. Don't send me off like a child. I want to hear what message my son has sent to his father. Bishop de Sousa can wait."

Gil didn't argue with her. "What is Kimpasi's message, *mchento?*"

"He says to tell you that the priest Duarte has conducted the *auto-da-fé.*"

Gil blanched at the phrase. A shiver of horror ran up his spine. He repeated it in disbelief. *"Auto-da-fé?"*

"He says you will understand the *auto-da-fé.*"

Gil replied with a suddenly dry mouth. "Yes, I understand it."

Beatriz looked at him. "But I do not understand it," she said, made suddenly apprehensive by Gil's strong reaction. "What is the *auto-da-fé?*"

Gil didn't get a chance to answer. The old serving woman answered in his place—with the vehemence of someone who knew personally of what she spoke, of someone who had witnessed what she now described, of someone who was not Catholic. *"Auto-da-fé,* my lady, it is the burning to death of people in a fire."

"What? What are you saying? That is an insanity. Why would anyone burn people to death in a fire? Why would Father Duarte? Who says such a terrible thing?"

"I told you, my lady. Your son says this terrible thing."

Beatriz's mouth was open; her big, luminous brown eyes were wide with confusion. There was a moment of hesitation. Then, suddenly, wildly, unthinkingly, she slapped the old serving woman across the face.

Gil grabbed her hand. She pulled away and, in a fury, was about to strike the old woman again but then realized that her daughter had run down from the veranda and was standing beside her, seeing everything, hearing everything.

"Go away from here, Tereza. Go along to the cathedral. You women, why are you standing there? Take the girl to the cathedral."

"I don't want to go to the cathedral," Tereza squealed and dodged deftly out of the way of the serving women who came hurrying down from the veranda. "I want to go to where the people are burning in the fire. Where are they, Nimi? Take me to the people burning in the fire."

"Come here, you naughty girl. Come here at once." Beatriz caught the scampering child and shook her angrily, venting her own disordered emotions on her. "There are no burning people, you silly goat. What an awful thing to say. You are going to the cathedral. You are already late." And as if fleeing the dreadful news she had heard, as if not wanting to hear so much more of it that she might have to accept it as true, she herself dragged Tereza off, the servants scurrying after them.

But then she stopped and turned back, letting the servants go on to the cathedral with Tereza. "Please forgive me, Nimi," she said. "I didn't mean to hurt you. It was only that what you said frightened me so. It is a terrible thing to hear."

"It is a more terrible thing to see, my lady."

"You saw it yourself?"

"I did."

"Who was it?" Gil asked.

"An old *nsaku* of the Nsundi. The priest Duarte had had him flogged many times for performing forbidden ceremonies. But he continued to perform them. Children were born and needed to be brought into the world properly. Youths came of age, maidens needed to be given husbands, people died. He would not allow these events to pass without the proper feasts and ceremonies. So even when all the other *nsaku* were too fearful to do so, this old one performed the dances and celebrations, no matter how many times the priest Duarte had him flogged. The devil was in him, the priest Duarte said, and the floggings were meant to drive the devil out of him. But when the floggings did not drive the devil out of him, the priest Duarte said fire would. So a stick was put into the ground in the main market square and the old *nsaku* was tied to the stick and bundles of firewood were piled up around him—"

"I don't want to hear any more." Beatriz clamped her hands over her ears. "I don't want to hear how it was done. Please, *mchento*. Don't go on."

The old woman shut her mouth into a hard, thin line, obviously glad not to have to go on.

"What about Kimpasi?" Gil asked. "What did he do? Did he try to stop it?"

"Yes."

"And?"

"He could not stop it."

"I know he could not stop it. But what happened when he *tried* to stop it? That is what I ask, *mchento*. Did he get into a fight with Father Duarte?"

"I did not see a fight," Nimi answered curtly, bristling at Gil's harsh tone.

"Well, that is something anyway."

"He refused to watch the *auto-da-fé*. He went down to the Lelunda River and, all the time the *nsaku* was burning in the fire, he stayed on his knees by the river, listening to the screams. He did not eat all that day. I brought food to him but he refused to eat. He told me to go to you and tell you what had happened. And to tell you to go to Bishop de Sousa and tell him what had happened. For all I know, he has not eaten since I left him."

Gil looked around, his mind racing, full of horrors.

"Now that I have brought his message to you, I will go back to him and see if he has eaten."

"Oh, yes, do that," Beatriz said. "Go back to him and make sure that he eats."

"And what shall I tell him his father will do with the message he has sent?" the old serving woman asked, still annoyed with Gil's brusque behavior.

"Tell him his father will do what he asks," Beatriz said. "He will go to Bishop de Sousa and tell him what has happened."

"What good would that do?" Gil snapped. "It would do no good."

"But His Grace must be told," Beatriz said.

"He doesn't need to be told," Gil said. "He already knows. Do you think Father Duarte would ever dare do such a thing without his permission?"

Beatriz didn't say anything.

"No, it is not Bishop de Sousa who must be told. It is Mbemba. He is the king."

His queen and children had already left for the cathedral but Affonso was waiting on his palace's front veranda when Gil came hurrying to him through the royal gardens. The scar across his cheek was livid; his face was twisted in anger.

"Have you already heard of it, Mbemba?" Gil asked, feeling out of breath from his own anger.

"How would I not already have heard of it? News of such terrible cruelty travels swiftly."

"And must as swiftly be punished."

"Yes, and must as swiftly be punished . . . if it is true."

"You do not believe it is true?"

"No. It is false news, put about by my enemies. To spread hatred against the Portuguese. To spread hatred against the Catholic faith. To spread hatred against me, who welcomed the Portuguese and their Faith to the kingdom."

"Who told you that? Did Bishop de Sousa tell you that?"

"Bishop de Sousa did not need to tell me that. I am Christian. I have studied Scripture. I have read the Gospel. I know the Faith and what it teaches. It teaches of a kind and loving God. It teaches of a compassionate and forgiving Savior. Nowhere does it teach of such terrible cruelty as this *auto-da-fé*. Such terrible cruelty is abhorrent to Christ. No Christian, and certainly no Christian priest, would throw an old man into a fire. This news that Father Duarte did so is a slander put about by my enemies, put about by Mpanzu, my worst enemy, in order to incite my people against me. Go to Mpangala and see for yourself if this is not so."

"And if I see that it is so?"

"Then I am its cause."

"Why?"

"Because it is I and no other who let loose these Portuguese in the kingdom."

"But you could not know that this is what would come of it."

"No, Gil, I could know. The NgangaKongo long ago foretold it. He long ago foretold that the Portuguese would bring evil to the kingdom."

VI

PORTUGUESE SOLDIERS—and not Nsundi warriors—stood guard at
Mpangala's river gate. They came sharply alert when Gil's big canoe
ran up through the reeds of the Lelunda embankment. It was late in
the afternoon of a partially overcast day, shafts of sunlight breaking
through the billowing, gray-streaked clouds. Besides his serving
woman Nimi, Gil had twenty men of his household guard with him,
five armed with arquebuses; he himself wore a cutlass in his belt, as
well as his usual ivory-handled knife, and a vest of chainmail. The soldiers, watching him keenly, fingering the wheel-locks of their guns,
made no move to open the river gate when he jumped from the canoe. A scurvy lot, mostly newcomers, survivors of the plague, they
blocked this south entrance to Mpangala with an insolent assurance,
as if they had commandeered the Nsundi town. Had they? Had the
auto-da-fé led to that? Gil hesitated only a moment; he hadn't come
looking for a fight, but he wouldn't shy away from one either, his
anger strong, and he ordered two of his warriors forward.

"Hold on there, you," one of the soldiers started to intervene.

And Gil drew his cutlass. "Stand aside, *soldato*. Stand aside and
let those men open the gate or open it yourself. One or the other.
Make up your mind quickly."

"Do as he says." This was the corporal of the guard, an old-timer,
hurrying over anxiously. "He speaks in the name of the Kongo king.
Open the gate for him."

The gate swung open.

Gil cast a hard look around, slipped the cutlass back in his belt and stepped through the gate. There were Portuguese soldiers on that side too, and they watched him with the same alert wariness as those outside. And like those outside, they too were mostly new-comers. Nearly half the soldiers landed from King Manoel's ships were being garrisoned in Mpangala. Indeed, along with the church of Santa Cruz, barracks for one hundred soldiers were being built at the town's main market square. Gil headed there.

And there was the pyre.

It caught him unaware and shocked him. He hadn't expected it. He wasn't thinking about it. He was thinking about something else. Approaching the market square, he was looking at the construction going on on the church and barracks on its east side, where Father José's house had stood, opposite the palisaded compound of the Mpangala chief. At this time of day, work was in full swing: Men were up on scaffoldings, laying tiles for the church's roof and campanile; women were bringing water from the well at the center of the square for the mortar being mixed on the barracks' walls. And he was thinking that all these men and women were Nsundi, that only Nsundi were doing the heavy work, that the Portuguese had assumed the roles of overseers and were standing aside and giving orders and that this was a new division of labor, very different from what had prevailed when the cathedral of São Salvador was built.

But then he saw the pyre and the shock of it diverted this train of thought. He knew it would be around here somewhere but he hadn't expected the sight of it to so unnerve him. A conical pile of cold gray ashes in front of the portal of the half-built church. A dozen bamboo posts staked in a circle around it. A twenty-foot-high wooden cross towering over it. As he approached it, squinting as if unwilling to see it too clearly, work on the church and barracks stopped and a pall of silence, as gloomy and glum as the overcast sky, fell upon the place.

"Where is Kimpasi, *mchento?* Go to him and tell him I am here."

Nimi went to the compound of the Mpangala chief. Gil's war-riors formed a phalanx across the market square. Gil took a deep breath, then walked straight into the pile of ashes and kicked at it with the toe of his boot, destroying its perfect conical shape. A moan rose up from the Nsundi on the construction site. He looked at them, then again kicked through the ashes. What was he looking for? What did he hope to find? What could remain of a man consumed by fire? But then his boot struck something more substantial than the powdery ash and he dropped to one knee. It was the lower half of a shattered skull, exploded by the fire's heat: the jawbone with a partial row of teeth. He lifted it out of the ash gingerly, but it crumbled in his hand.

"Senhor Eanes."

He looked up. Father Duarte had come out of the half-built church. Two halberdiers in full armor accompanied him. Still in the church, looking out, looking scared, was Father José.

"On whose authority did you do this, padre?" Gil asked quietly and stood up.

"Excuse me, *senhor?*"

"I ask you in the name of the Kongo king, padre," Gil repeated, raising his voice. "On whose authority did you have the *nsaku* killed in this cruel fashion?" He held out the crumbled bone and shattered teeth.

"On a higher authority than the Kongo king's, *senhor,*" the deacon answered defiantly. "On God's authority. To put an end to that sorcerer's devil worship. To put an end to his interference with God's crusade for lost souls."

"And have you, padre? Have you put an end to it? Do these lost souls now come flocking to you, padre, begging to receive the sacrament?"

"We make progress, *senhor.*"

"Progress?" Gil spat the word out with contempt. "You are a fool if you believe these people have given up the worship of their god because you have burned one of their ju-ju men at the stake. Of course they haven't. Why should they, when the god you hold out to them permits such terrible cruelty as this? Of course they go on worshiping their own god, only now they have the good sense to worship him in secret."

"That may be, *senhor.* But we are vigilant and quick to spy out such heresy."

"And when you spy it out, padre, what do you do? Do you burn that heretic at the stake too? How many in the end do you think you will have to burn before you will convince these people to accept the Faith of a kind and loving Christ?"

Father Duarte didn't reply to this.

Gil shook his head in disgust. "You have angered the king, padre. You have angered him greatly with this cruelty."

"Why should he be angered? I act on his behalf in what I do. These heathens, the Nsundi, are his enemies. By bringing them to the Faith . . . what does it matter to him how? By bringing them to the Church, I make of them loyal subjects of his crown."

"You will tell him that, padre. He will be interested to hear it. He does not understand that you performed the *auto-da-fé* on his behalf. In fact, he does not believe you performed it at all. That is why I have come. To take you to São Salvador so you yourself can explain to the king the reason for a cruelty he neither understands nor believes a Catholic priest would perform."

"I will be happy to do so, *senhor,* but, if you please, not until after Sunday's Mass. It will be a special Mass that I would be sorry to miss."

"What will be special about it?"

"I said just now that we make progress with the Nsundi, *senhor.* This is an example of the progress we make. At Sunday's Mass, we will celebrate the baptism of a Nsundi princess, Mfidi, daughter of Mpanzu. *Gloria in excelsis Deo.*"

"Her instruction has been completed?"

"Very much thanks to your son, Senhor Eanes. I myself had no end of difficulty with her, I will admit. She was stupid and obtuse and recalcitrant with me. But once I let Father Henriqué take over her instruction, as he requested, she caught on wonderfully quickly. It is a great triumph. It will make a powerful impression on all the heathens here, seeing the daughter of their banished prince receive the sacrament, don't you think?"

Gil took a moment to consider this. He would have dearly liked to spoil this zealous priest's pleasure in presiding over such a signal accomplishment as Mfidi's baptism by refusing to delay the departure to São Salvador. But he realized it would be no favor to Affonso to do so. Duarte was right: The baptism of Mpanzu's daughter would make a powerful impression on the Nsundi. Indeed, it might make almost as powerful an impression as the baptism of Mpanzu himself.

"Very well, padre. It will be as you wish. We will leave for São Salvador after Sunday's Mass."

The deacon smiled with smug satisfaction and went back into the half-built church. The two halberdiers, however, remained in the square, facing Gil's warriors.

"Where is His Grace, *pai?*"

Gil looked around. The gate in the palisade of the Mpangala chief's compound had swung open and Henriqué and Nimi came hurrying out.

"Isn't he with you? I thought you would bring him with you. You did speak to him, didn't you?"

"No, I didn't speak to him," Gil said. "I spoke to Mbemba."

"But why didn't you speak to His Grace? He must be told what is happening here."

"He doesn't need to be told. He already knows. You don't suppose Father Duarte does anything Bishop de Sousa doesn't already know?"

"No, I don't suppose he does."

Gil looked at the palisade gate. A crowd of people were peering through it with a tremulous curiosity. But no one came out. Everyone remained inside. That much anyway Father Duarte had accomplished with his *auto-da-fé:* instilled an uncomprehending fear in all those who had witnessed its incomprehensible horror.

"And what did Mbemba say when you spoke to him?"

"He didn't want to believe that a Catholic priest could commit such a cruelty."

"I cannot blame him," Henriqué said quietly. He looked awful, haggard and forlorn, as if he hadn't slept in days. "I didn't want to believe it either."

"But he will believe it now. I am taking Father Duarte to São Salvador so that Mbemba can hear it straight from this fanatic priest's own lips. And that will be the last any of us will ever hear of it again. Mbemba will not permit such cruelty in his kingdom."

"When do you take Father Duarte to him?"

"After the Mass on Sunday."

"Why wait until then?"

"Because of Mfidi's baptism. Mbemba would not want me to interfere with that."

At the mention of Mfidi's name, Henriqué glanced around to the chief's compound. Gil followed his glance. Maybe Mfidi was in the crowd at the compound's gate.

"Father Duarte tells me you were responsible for her instruction. He says you succeeded where he failed."

"Do you know her?"

"No."

"Come and meet her," Henriqué said and started back to the chief's compound.

"*Keba bota,* Gil Eenezh."

"Dom Bernardo. *Keba bota.*"

As Gil passed through the compound gate, the crowd there drew back and the Mpangala chief stepped forward. He was a stocky man with exceptionally big arms and chest, several years older than Gil, probably in his late forties. Unlike Affonso and the court in São Salvador and the ManiSoyo and the court in Santo Antonio do Zaire, he and his courtiers had not adopted Portuguese fashions. He wore a kanga in the old colors and design of the Nsundi house (sky blue bordered with white lightning bolts), and the warriors of his bodyguard were armed with lances and shields, not a single firearm among them.

"You are welcome in my house, Gil Eenezh," he said and grasped Gil's shoulders in the traditional form of greeting. "I am only sorry that my welcome is no more ceremonious than this. But these are uncertain times."

"I understand, Dom Bernardo. There is no need to trouble yourself about it."

"I thank you for your understanding. Nonetheless, be assured that, despite this lack of ceremony, I am no less ready to serve you and he whom we both serve, the ManiKongo. Come into my house and tell me why you are here and what service is wanted of me."

Gil took a quick look around for Henriqué and Nimi, who had preceded him into the compound, did not see them in the milling crowd and followed Bernardo to the veranda of the chief's big house. And he saw them there. A young girl stood between them, her eyes downcast: Mfidi a Mpanzu, NtinuNsundi, no more than fifteen or sixteen, small and pretty with close-cropped hair, her slim, shapely figure wrapped in a kanga of the Nsundi house, a string of river pearls around her slender throat.

"This is my father, Mfidi," Henriqué said, touching the girl's elbow.

"Gil Eenezh," she said and looked up from her feet.

And the expression in her eyes startled Gil. He had expected to see shyness in them, timidity, perhaps even a flash of girlish fright. But he saw none of these. What he saw was hate.

"I understand you are to be baptized this Sunday, *Ntinu*," he said, trying to soften her expression with a show of interest in her. "May I ask what Christian name has been chosen for you?"

But the girl's expression did not soften; her hard gaze held for a moment longer, then she lowered her eyes again without answering.

"No Christian name has yet been chosen, *pai*," Henriqué put in quickly to cover the girl's rudeness.

"Well, there still is time, I suppose. It is still three days until Sunday."

"Am I free to go now, Kimpasi?" the girl asked, still looking down.

"Go? Yes, you are free to go if you wish." There was a measure of annoyance in Henriqué's tone. "You are free to do whatever you wish."

Ignoring Henriqué's annoyance, the girl scooted into the chief's house, making no effort to conceal her desire to get away from Gil. Gil looked at Henriqué, expecting him to offer an explanation for the girl's behavior—clearly something peculiar was afoot here—but the youth said nothing, simply looked embarrassed. By this time, quite a number of people had gathered on the chief's veranda. The afternoon was lengthening into dusk, and although no ceremonies had been planned, preparations had begun for the evening meal, a meal that, if not exactly a feast, would nonetheless have to be one befitting a visitor from the court of the ManiKongo. Bernardo had gone into the house to arrange it and

came back out just as Mfidi went inside. He too looked at her with
some irritation, but also said nothing.

"It is my hope, Dom Bernardo, that you are going to no special
trouble on my account," Gil said. "A simple bowl of posho will be sufficient for my evening meal."

"A simple bowl of posho would be no trouble at all, Gil Eenezh.
You must allow me to go to a bit more trouble than that. And while
we eat, I will have the occasion to learn why you have come to
Mpangala and in what way I may be of service to you."

"I have come to Mpangala to escort Father Duarte to São Salvador. The ManiKongo has summoned him."

Bernardo cocked his head.

"It had been my intention to depart with him at once, this very
day in fact, and ask no service of you at all. But when I heard that the
NtinuNsundi was to be baptized this Sunday, I agreed to put off our
departure until then. So now I must ask a service of you, after all. Allow me to stay as a guest in your house."

"Of course. It will be an honor to my house."

"I would not ask you to put yourself to even this much trouble
on my account in such uncertain times as these, Dom Bernardo, but
I see that my son stays here with you, and as we are so little together
these days, this would be a rare chance for me to spend some time
with him."

"It is no trouble at all. It is even less trouble than a simple bowl
of posho. You will have the room directly next to his."

"Come, *pai*." Henriqué started into the chief's house, apparently
as eager now to get away as Mfidi had been.

Gil, however, did not immediately follow him. "You did not ask
me why the ManiKongo has summoned Father Duarte to São Salvador, Dom Bernardo," he said. "Do you not care to know?"

"I thought I did know. Is it not because of the killing of the
nsaku in the fire?"

"It is."

Bernardo nodded with apparent satisfaction and said nothing
further.

"Tell me, Dom Bernardo, as chief of Mpangala, did you approve
of this killing? Did you give your permission for it?"

"I neither approved of it nor gave my permission for it. It was done without any consultation with me."

"Did you oppose it, then?"

Bernardo did not answer right away. Then he said with a certain dryness of tone, "There are many soldiers of the Porta Geeze in Mpangala now, Gil Eenezh. Many with guns. Perhaps you have seen them yourself."

Nimi had preceded Gil and Henriqué into the house so the room where Gil was to stay for the next three days was already prepared when they got there; clean cloths, sponges, soapstone, a basin and a jar of hot water were waiting. Gil stripped out of his clothes, got down on his knees and, while Nimi poured out the hot water for him, began washing off the dust of the journey from São Salvador. Henriqué went over to the room's window and looked out.

"Mfidi will not be baptized on Sunday, *pai*," he said after a moment, staring out into the garden behind the chief's house.

Gil stopped washing and squinted up at him.

"Not this Sunday, *pai*. Not ever." Henriqué turned back into the room. "Her father forbids it and she is a faithful daughter and will not disobey him."

"Let me have that, *mchento*." Gil took a dry cloth from Nimi and wiped his eyes, then sat back on his heels. "How long have you known this?"

"All along. From the day I began her instruction. She told me Mpanzu had forbidden her ever becoming Catholic, ever marrying Mbemba, ever allowing herself to be used in any way to win the Nsundi over to the *false* ManiKongo."

"I am not surprised."

"I am afraid for her."

"Why?"

"Because of Father Duarte. Because of what he will do when she refuses to receive the sacrament on Sunday."

"I see."

"Do you, *pai*? Do you really see? Do you understand how important Mfidi's baptism is for Father Duarte? He believes it is crucial to his crusade here, that as a result of it he will succeed in converting all the Nsundi. So when Mfidi refuses to receive the sacrament from him on Sunday, in front of all the people here, he will fly into a rage. He will say the devil has taken hold of her soul, as he said of the poor old *nsaku*. He will say she is possessed of the Evil One and must be freed of him, as he said of the poor old *nsaku*. Freed by flogging and, if that does not free her, freed by fire. He will threaten her with the *auto-da-fé, pai,* in order to compel her to receive the sacrament. But she still will not receive it, out of loyalty to her father. So she will be flogged and then burned at the stake."

"Don't talk nonsense, Kimpasi. Father Duarte will do nothing of the sort. He wouldn't dare. Mfidi is under the protection of the ManiKongo. She is the king's betrothed."

"No longer, *pai.* Father Duarte knows that. Everyone knows that the king no longer intends to take a Nsundi princess for his wife and queen."

Gil looked at the cloth in his hand, used it to further dry himself, then wrapped it around his waist and stood up.

"So I want to get her away from here before Sunday. Will you help me, *pai?* Please help me. Help me get her away to Mpanzu where she will be safe from this fanatic priest."

"To Mpanzu? No, Kimpasi. I will help you get her away from Father Duarte but not to Mpanzu. To do that would be to act against Mbemba. And I will not act against him. Nor will I allow you to. He is your family and my friend."

Henriqué looked out the window into the chief's garden again. The last of the day's light was flickering out; the long blue shadows of dusk were gathering.

"If she refuses to be baptized by Father Duarte, well and good. I will take her to São Salvador where Bishop de Sousa can baptize her."

"But she also will refuse to be baptized by him." Henriqué looked around in anger. "Don't you understand, *pai?* Bishop de Sousa is as much her father's enemy as is Father Duarte."

"And you, Kimpasi? Are you also her father's enemy? Would she also refuse to be baptized by you?"

This caught the youth by surprise.

"You are a priest. You have instructed her in the Faith. And you care for her. It is plain to me that you care for her. Don't you care for her enough to want to save her soul?"

"Yes, I care for her enough for that."

"Then baptize her. Convince her to accept the sacrament from you. It's your duty, not only out of loyalty to Mbemba but also in fulfillment of your priestly vow to lead the heathen out of darkness into the light of the Faith. To shun your duty, to help her get away to Mpanzu, would be heresy in the eyes of your Church and rebellion in the eyes of your king."

Henriqué nodded slowly.

"Send for her. Fetch her here. We will both speak to her. I will help you convince her."

"No, *pai,* I will speak to her by myself. I do not want her to know that I told you she will refuse the sacrament on Sunday, that she wishes to flee to her father. I promised her I would not tell you."

"Why?"

"Because you also are her father's enemy," Henriqué said and walked out of the room.

Gil looked at Nimi.

"Do not trust him," she said.

"How can I not trust him? He is my son."

"Even so, you must not trust him. The *auto-da-fé* has changed him. He is no longer the boy you knew."

"What will he do?"

"Help her get to Mpanzu."

"Does he know where Mpanzu is?"

"She does. They would have tried to get to him before this, but the boy did not believe they could succeed without your help. But now that he knows he will not have your help, he will yield to her wishes and try it on his own."

"Tonight?"

"If not tonight, before Sunday anyway."

"And Bernardo? Where does he stand in this? Will he allow it?"

"He will neither allow it nor prevent it. The *auto-da-fé* has also affected him greatly. So he will look the other way."

"But we will not look the other way, Nimi. I am sorry for them both, but for Mbemba's sake and for the boy's sake too, we cannot allow this. We must keep close watch on them."

. . .

GIL'S SLEEP was shallow and restless that night, full of strange and violent dreams of people burning and screaming in the flames of the
auto-da-fé. And he awoke in a sweat, Nimi hissing in his ear.

"What is it?"

"The brothers are here."

Gil had expected her to say something about Henriqué and
Mfidi. "The brothers? Nuno and Gonçalo?"

"Yes."

"Why are they here? Send them to me. No, I will go to them.
Where are they?"

"They wait at the well in the market square."

"Yes, I will go to them. It is best that they do not come into the
chief's compound." He stood up and pulled on his leather trousers,
his body shimmering with a sheen of sweat, the dream of the *auto-
da-fé* still vivid in his mind.

"Are you ill, Gil Eenezh? You look as if you have fever."

"It is nothing, *mchento,* just a bad dream. What about Kimpasi
and Mfidi?"

"They sleep, no doubt also dreaming badly."

Barefoot and shirtless, Gil stepped out of his room and looked
into Henriqué's. It was still night, some hours yet until daybreak,
moonless and overcast, and he could only see a dim outline of his son
stretched out on the palliasse in there. If the youth was dreaming
badly, it did not show; he was lying very still. Perhaps he was only
feigning sleep in order to avoid answering Gil about whether Mfidi
had agreed to receive the sacrament from him. Gil went out of the
house, leaving Nimi behind to keep watch on them.

Despite the early hour, an unusual number of people were up
and about in the chief's compound, and there also was something unusual in the way they looked at him and fell silent as he passed out
the compound gate and hurried to the market square where Nuno
and Gonçalo were squatting under the baobab tree by the well, leaning on their guns.

"What is it, Nuno? Why have you come here? What news do you
bring me?"

The brothers jumped up and came forward quickly. Gil's warriors, who had spent the night camped in the square, also jumped up.

"There has been a fight, my lord," Nuno said breathlessly. "A great
fight. Between Mpanzu and the captain Rodrigues. Many have been
hurt and killed."

"Between Mpanzu and the captain Rodrigues? The captain Rodrigues found Mpanzu? But you sent word to me that he did not
know where Mpanzu was."

"He did not know, my lord. It was Mpanzu who found the captain Rodrigues."

"And attacked him?"

"Yes, my lord. Attacked and defeated him."

"Jesus."

"My lord?"

Gil looked across the square to the half-built church and barracks. Work on their construction had not yet resumed for the day. No
Portuguese, neither craftsmen nor soldiers, nor Father Duarte or Father José, were about. Evidently they were still asleep; evidently this
astonishing news had not yet reached them. But it had reached many
if not most of the Nsundi in Mpangala. More and more people were
popping out of their houses and rushing around.

"Tell me what happened, Nuno. Tell me everything. Tell me
quickly."

Unnerved by Gil's urgent tone, Nuno looked to his younger
brother for help.

"It was a great fight, my lord, as Nuno says," Gonçalo chimed in
eagerly. "But it was a short fight. It did not go on for more than half a
day. From sunrise to noon. Mpanzu set a trap the night before, when
the captain Rodrigues went into camp. The camp was in the valley of
the Lelunda and the warriors of Mpanzu were in the hills around it."

"How many warriors?" Gil interrupted, knowing that Rodrigues's force consisted of less than two hundred.

"Five times the number with the captain Rodrigues."

"Ten times," Nuno put in.

"Yes, maybe ten times," Gonçalo agreed.

"With firearms?"

"Yes, many had firearms," Gonçalo answered and went on. "At

first light, they came down from the hills into the camp and the surprise was complete, and by the time the sun stood directly overhead, the warriors and soldiers of the captain Rodrigues were running away. Mpanzu did not chase them. If he had chased them, he would have killed them all."

"Were you there? Did you see this yourself?"

"Yes, my lord." Nuno took over from his brother. "We were there," he said proudly. "We saw it ourselves."

"When was this? Where was it?"

"Four days ago. Four days' march to the east and north along the Lelunda. We came swiftly here after Mpanzu broke off the fight, always staying ahead of the captain Rodrigues."

"The captain Rodrigues is coming here?"

"Yes, my lord. He will be here before daybreak."

"But why did Mpanzu attack him?"

The question clearly stumped Nuno and again he turned to Gonçalo.

"Was he defending himself?" Gil pressed. "Did he fear that the captain Rodrigues would capture him?"

"No, my lord," Gonçalo answered. "The captain Rodrigues did not know he was there. As we sent word to you, he did not know where Mpanzu was. He had even given up the hunt for him altogether and was coming to Mpangala for food and rest when Mpanzu attacked him."

"Jesus," Gil said again, his mind racing.

Was this the beginning of an insurrection? Had Mpanzu gathered enough Nsundi around him—and firearms and gunpowder—to consider attempting to take back the throne from Affonso? Or at least to consider attempting to abduct his daughter from Mpangala? Or had he attacked Rodrigues in retribution for the *auto-da-fé,* to punish the Portuguese for killing one of his faithful ju-ju men? But whatever his reason, he had played straight into the hands of the Portuguese. For this was just what they needed to finally convince Affonso that Mpanzu was a threat to his throne. What would it matter now that Gil could prove to Affonso, by bringing Father Duarte to São Salvador, that it was the Portuguese and not Mpanzu who were responsible for the *auto-da-fé?* In light of Mpanzu's unprovoked attack, it would not matter at all. It would pale in comparison. Affonso preferred not to believe ill of the Portuguese. He would rather believe the worst of his brother. And now he had good reason to do so.

"Is Mpanzu following the captain Rodrigues? Is he also coming here?"

"We do not know, my lord. After he broke off the attack, he vanished into the hills again."

Gil looked around. The Portuguese in the town, the priests and soldiers and craftsmen, were still asleep, still blissfully unaware what had transpired, but by now all the Nsundi were awake, gathering excitedly in the streets and market squares and on the verandas of their houses. And in the chief's compound as well. Bernardo had come out of his house, surrounded by his courtiers and warriors, engaged in anxious, whispering conversations. What were they saying? What were they thinking? What emotions did they feel? Pride and pleasure, Gil supposed, but also fear. They could not help but take pride and pleasure in this audacious blow struck by their banished prince against those who had usurped his throne and committed the *auto-da-fé*. But also fear because they must know that this blow would be seen as an act of rebellion, not only against the Portuguese but also against the ManiKongo, and would surely bring a swift and terrible response.

As Nuno and Gonçalo had predicted, Rodrigues and his expeditionary force reached Mpangala just as dawn was breaking, the overcast sky partially clearing to reveal the last of the stars and patches of pale blue. They entered the town through the north gate, and the spectacle they presented confirmed the brothers' report of the suddenness and thoroughness of their defeat. Of the forty Portuguese soldiers who had set out, not more than twenty-five were still on their feet; of the one hundred Kongo warriors, nearly half were missing. And one of the lombard cannon was also missing, abandoned on the field of battle, and the two wheeled carts were filled with the worst of the wounded and the bodies of the dead. As they straggled through the gate in a disordered, shuffling column with the friar (without his cross) and Rodrigues (without his helmet) at its head and with Lopes nowhere to be seen, the Nsundi drew away from them and the Portuguese in the town at last awakened to what had happened. Fathers Duarte and José bolted out of the half-built church; soldiers and artisans rushed over from the half-built barracks.

"Fetch me some water," Rodrigues said hoarsely to no one in particular.

Two soldiers from the Mpangala garrison and Father José simultaneously dashed to the well. But Gil, already there with the brothers and his own warriors, cranked up the goatskin and brought it to the master-at-arms himself.

"Where is Dom Alvaro, sir marshal?" he asked.

Rodrigues took the goatskin, showing no surprise at seeing Gil, showing no expression at all in his profound exhaustion—although he was filthy, covered with caked mud, and had lost his helmet, he seemed unhurt—and looked around. "In there," he said, indicating one of the carts of bodies.

"Is he dead?"

"Dead or dying," Rodrigues said and took a long pull on the goatskin.

"He must be given the last rites," Father Duarte said. "Go to him, Father José. See if you can save him. But if you cannot, save his soul."

The fat young priest dashed away again.

"They had guns," Rodrigues said, lowering the goatskin and letting it hang in his hand by his side. "Did you know that, Senhor Eanes? The savages have guns." He wasn't looking at Gil when he said this. He was looking around the town, at the Nsundi in the market square and on the verandas of their houses and behind the palisade of the chief's compound. It was a rhetorical question. He didn't expect Gil to answer it. "Where did they get them?" he went on absently. "How did they get them? That's what I'd like to know."

"What happened, Dom Tomé?" Father Duarte demanded. "For the love of Mary, tell us what happened. We do not know what happened."

"Ask Senhor Eanes, padre. He knows everything that happens in this cursed kingdom. Don't you, *senhor?*" Rodrigues fixed Gil with a baleful look out of his one good eye, and when Gil took this also to be a rhetorical question and did not answer, he said, "The Nsundi have rebelled, padre. Mpanzu is leading them in a rebellion against the king."

"Oh, holy Mother of Christ."

"Do not be so quick to call it rebellion, sir marshal," Gil put in sharply. "You cannot be sure it is that."

"I cannot? Why not? He attacked me unprovoked. He fell on me with a thousand screaming savages armed with guns."

"Oh, holy Mother of Christ," Duarte cried out again.

"I was sent by the king to find him and he attacked me for no good reason. While my back was turned. While my men were asleep. A thousand savages fell on them and slaughtered them in their sleep. What am I to make of that, *senhor?* What am I to call it, if not rebellion?"

"If it is rebellion," Gil said, trying somehow to refute Rodrigues's logic, "why weren't you killed? Why weren't you all killed? Mpanzu could have slaughtered you all in your sleep. But he didn't. He let you go."

"That was his mistake. He should have killed me. Because now I am going to kill him. I should have killed him long ago. Bishop de Sousa was right. He always said Mpanzu should be killed. But His Majesty would not allow it. But now he will allow it. Oh, yes, you can be sure, now he will allow it."

"Who knows of this, Dom Tomé?" Father Duarte asked, clasping his hands as if in prayer. "Do the people here know?"

"Of course they know. They are Nsundi, aren't they? Look at them. Look at the expression on their faces. They are probably in it themselves. They probably also have guns. Where is their chief? Where is Dom Bernardo?"

"He is dead." This was Father José, rushing back from the cart of bodies. "He was shot through the head."

"What?" Rodrigues whirled to him. "Dom Bernardo was shot through the head?"

"Oh, no, Dom Tomé. Not Dom Bernardo. Dom Alvaro."

"Aye, that's so. He was shot through the head."

"Were you in time to hear his confession, Father José?" Father Duarte asked.

The fat priest shrugged helplessly.

"The poor soul." Father Duarte made the sign of the cross. "Arrange for the funeral, Father José."

"It's no great loss," Rodrigues muttered hoarsely with a grim sort of satisfaction. "He didn't belong here. He wasn't needed. He should have stayed on his ship."

"Who will be governor now?" Father Duarte asked.

"The *donatário,* I suppose. Fernão de Mello. But until he gets here from Santo Antonio, I will act in his place. Fetch the Mpangala chief to me."

But Rodrigues did not wait for Bernardo to be fetched; he set off for the chief's compound himself. Gil followed him. Father Duarte fell in step beside Gil.

"This is terrible, Senhor Eanes," he said, again clasping his hands in prayer. "It will have a terrible effect on the people here. It will destroy all the good work I have done among them. They will be more recalcitrant than ever. They will resist the Word of God even more. We must do something to counter it. We must not let them believe their heathen prince has gained the upper hand over us."

Gil walked away from him, looking for Henriqué and Mfidi. In all this commotion, they couldn't still be asleep. They didn't seem to have come out of the chief's house yet, however.

"Mpanzu's attack on me and my men, Dom Bernardo, was an attack on His Majesty as well," Rodrigues was saying. "It was an act of rebellion not only against the Portuguese, not only against the Catholic Faith, but also against the Kongo king who was baptized in the Faith and is the protector of the Portuguese in the kingdom."

Bernardo listened to this expressionlessly.

"And as you have sworn allegiance to the Kongo king and have been baptized in the Faith yourself, you can consider this rebellion to be an attack on you as well."

"What would you have me do?"

"Fight Mpanzu. In defense of your king, in defense of your Faith, in defense of your own person and position, join me in the war I will make against Mpanzu."

"It is not your place to ask that, sir marshal," Gil said. "If there is to be war with Mpanzu, it is for the ManiKongo to declare it, not you. We must send word to him first."

"Send word to him, Senhor Eanes. By all means, send word to him. I have no doubt how he will respond to it. And in the meantime we will prepare ourselves. Do you trust your people, Dom Bernardo? Do you trust them to fight Mpanzu?"

Bernardo did not reply.

"Of course you do not. Nor do I. Perhaps the Christians among them can be trusted to fight. But I am sure there are many here who are Mpanzu's men, whose loyalty is to him and not to you, who have been waiting all these years to rally to his banner in rebellion against the king and who also may have guns. So that is your task, Dom Bernardo. Root out those who cannot be trusted, disarm them and put them under guard."

"There is one more thing we should do, Dom Tomé," Father Duarte said.

"What is that, padre?"

"Baptize Mfidi. It will cool the ardor of any who might be tempted to go over to Mpanzu, seeing his daughter convert to the Faith."

"Is she ready to receive the sacrament?"

"We were going to baptize her at Sunday's Mass. But there is no reason we cannot do it at the Mass this morning. I will fetch her. Where is she, Dom Bernardo? Is she still in your house with Father Henriqué?"

As Father Duarte started into the chief's compound, Nimi emerged from the crowd milling around in there, and from the severe expression on her face, Gil knew instantly what she was coming to tell him. He turned and walked away from Rodrigues so as to be out of earshot when she reached him.

"Are they gone?"

"Yes."

"To Mpanzu?"

"Yes."

"How did they get out? I did not see them go."

"Bernardo showed them a way."

"I thought you said he would neither help nor hinder them. I thought you said he would only look the other way."

"News of Mpanzu's victory has influenced him even more than the *auto-da-fé*."

Gil looked up at the sky. The sun had risen but the breaks in the clouds were closing in again. It would be another overcast day. "I will tell Rodrigues that we are going back to São Salvador to bring Mbemba the news of Mpanzu's attack. But only you will go, *mchento*. I will go after Kimpasi. I cannot let him destroy himself in the kingdom of his birth and in the Church of his faith."

VII

N‍ear day's end, it began raining lightly, a misty drizzle blowing across the rolling, yellow hills of the Nsundi grassland, ten days' march (perhaps a hundred leagues) to the east of Mpangala along the valley of the Lelunda. Gil was crouched in the tall, wet grass on a hillside above the river, looking down at a small fishing village on its north bank. Mpanzu was in that village. Gil had sent Nuno and Gonçalo, unarmed, down to him to request an audience. That was two hours ago and Gil was waiting for them to return. The twenty warriors of his household guard, five with guns, were posted in a wide circle around the hilltop to make sure he wasn't taken by surprise by Mpanzu's men before the brothers got back.

Gil was fairly certain Mpanzu would grant the audience. He had instructed the brothers to say that he had come only to speak to his son, that no one knew he had come, that no one but a handful of his warriors had come with him and that he was willing to come into the village alone and unarmed and have his warriors placed under guard and disarmed as well. Under those circumstances, Mpanzu was likely to agree, if only out of curiosity. What was far less certain was whether Gil would be able to convince Henriqué to leave the village. But even if he couldn't, he had decided, he still had to go to Mpanzu. At the very least, he had to judge for himself how great a threat and what sort of threat Mpanzu posed for Affonso in order to better advise him. He knew only too well how Rodrigues and Bishop de Sousa would judge it and advise him.

The sun had set behind the cloud-wreathed hills, the rain had passed on into the west and cooking fires were being lighted in the village below when Gil at last spotted Nuno and Gonçalo climbing back up the hill from the river. He stood up.

"Has he agreed, *mbakala?*"

"He has, my lord."

"Are Kimpasi and Mfidi with him?"

"They are."

"And what conditions does he impose?"

"He imposes none, my lord. He says that, as a father himself, he understands a father's wish to speak to a disobedient son and so offers you safe conduct into his camp for that purpose."

Gil smiled at this. Mpanzu's simple decency and lack of guile reminded him of his long-lingering sympathy for the stolid, straightforward Nsundi prince. "Even so," he said and unbuckled his cutlass and removed his chainmail, "I will go to him alone and unarmed."

The fishing village was a good hideout for a rebel chieftain, a remote, nameless collection of fewer than twenty mud-and-grass huts clustered at a point on the Lelunda embankment where the river made a sharp bend, narrowed, then ran for a stretch white with rapids. Fishing pirogues were drawn up on the bank, hung about with circular fishing nets, and also with the baskets and traps the fishermen set in the rapids. But no one was fishing when Gil got there. What must have been the village's entire population of two hundred or so was gathered around a large bonfire in its one market square. And seated on an hourglass-shaped stool in front of the fire was Mpanzu.

Gil recognized him instantly, even at a distance, even after ten years. The Nsundi prince had grown as grotesquely fat as his father had been at that age. But unlike the old ManiKongo at that age, Mpanzu seemed healthy and strong, sitting alertly erect on the stool, his big hands planted firmly on his big knees, a cloak of lion fur thrown over his massive shoulders, a pillbox hat of basketweave set squarely on the gray curls of his head, a short crimson skirt embroidered with yellow sunbursts wrapped around the huge barrel of his stomach—the ancient dress of Kongo kings. The mutilation of the left side of his face, the missing ear, although ugly and still shocking to see, had softened somewhat with the years into the folds of his scarred and sagging flesh, and his bulging, goiterous eyes shone brightly in the firelight, watching Gil approach. Gil halted his approach a few paces away to look around for Mpanzu's gun-bearing warriors. He saw none. Where could they be out of sight in a small village like this?

"You are safe, Gil Eenezh," Mpanzu said in that husky growl of a voice that Gil well remembered, misunderstanding Gil's momentary hesitation. "You are under my protection here."

"I know that, MtuKongo, and thank you for it," Gil said and continued toward the bonfire, still puzzled about where the rebel Nsundi army could be hidden among these few poor huts.

"Not MtuKongo, Gil Eenezh. Do not address me as MtuKongo. I am no longer a prince of the Kongo."

"As ManiNsundi then?"

"Yes, as ManiNsundi. I am still lord of the Nsundi."

"That is evident to all. By your attack and defeat of the soldiers of the Portuguese and the warriors of the Kongo king, you have made that evident to all."

Mpanzu cocked his head in acknowledgment of Gil's salute, then raised a hand and, out of the crowd of villagers around the bonfire, two women came forward, one bringing another hourglass-shaped stool, the other cups of *malafu*. Gil took a cup and sat down on the stool and once more took a quick look around. The villagers were at his back, in the deepening shadows of the gathering dusk. He and Mpanzu sat side by side, facing the fire and, across it, the Lelunda River, no longer clearly seen in the twilight but pleasantly heard, running fast and lively around the bend and over the rapids.

"I was wondering, ManiNsundi. Where are the men who attacked and defeated the soldiers of the captain Rodrigues and the warriors of your brother? There must be many to have won such a victory."

"There are many. But as you have had the confidence to come to me without your bodyguard, I have sent mine away to show you an equal trust."

"*Ntondesi.*"

Mpanzu took a sip of his palm wine. Gil followed suit, not sure whether the absence of Nsundi warriors was truly a gallant gesture or simply a shrewd move to keep him from seeing too much. He had hoped to get an idea of not only the size of Mpanzu's army but also the quantity and quality of their firearms.

"I was also wondering why you made that attack, ManiNsundi. Was it to avenge the killing of the old *nsaku?* Or do you mean it to signal a war against your brother?"

Mpanzu's genial expression soured at this. "I was told you came here to speak to your son, Gil Eenezh, and for no other purpose. Was I mistaken? Do you have another purpose? Have you come here as a spy for my brother?"

"No, ManiNsundi, I have come here only to speak to my son. I wish to try to persuade him to come home with me and not destroy himself in a rash act of rebellion."

Mpanzu nodded in his thoughtful, ponderous way. "It is your right as his father to try to persuade him of that. I am grateful to him for the help he gave my daughter, but he is free to leave with you if he wishes. Kimpasi."

Gil looked around, startled. He hadn't realized Henriqué was standing just a few steps away in the first rank of villagers crowded around the fire. Partly this was because of the darkness in which he stood. But mainly it was because the youth was not dressed as Gil had expected him to be.

He was dressed as a villager, not a priest. He was barefoot and wore a kanga, not his cassock and sandals. His rosary and crucifix, along with the string of bloodstones, hung down from his neck onto his bare chest like a fetish, like a sorcerer's charm or amulet. And his long blond hair had been close-cropped. Mfidi stood behind him, peering over his shoulder at Gil with eyes full of hate.

"Forgive me, *pai,*" Henriqué said and stepped into the light of the bonfire. "Forgive me for what I did, but I could not have done otherwise. Her life was in danger."

"No, Kimpasi, you could have done otherwise." Gil's tone was sharp, that of a father scolding his son. "You could have baptized her and allowed me to take her to São Salvador, and you would have saved her life just as surely."

"But there was no time. Not after Father Duarte heard the news of Dom Tomé's defeat. He was in a panic to baptize her that very day.

He believed it was the only way to counter the impression Dom Tomé's defeat had made on the Nsundi. There is no saying what he would have done when she refused to receive the sacrament then. I had to help her get away."

"I don't want to argue with you, Kimpasi. I didn't come here to argue with you. What you did is done and cannot be undone. You have put the girl out of Mbemba's reach and he will not thank you for it. What concerns me now is that you do not make matters any worse for yourself. You must return at once to São Salvador and present yourself to Mbemba and ask for his understanding and forgiveness. And if your place in the Church and your vocation as a priest mean anything to you, you will also present yourself to Bishop de Sousa and ask for his understanding and forgiveness."

"No, *pai.*" Henriqué shook his head. "I will not do that. I do not require their understanding or forgiveness. I only require yours."

Gil glanced at Mpanzu. Mpanzu was looking at Henriqué with a pensive expression. There was no gloating in it. He obviously took no pleasure in the son's defiance of his father.

"Will you give me your understanding? Will you give me your forgiveness?"

"I do not know what you want me to understand and forgive. Are you telling me you intend to stay here with the ManiNsundi?"

"Yes."

"Have you lost all reason? Is it because of the girl? Have you so lost your reason over her that you are willing to throw away all the life you have ever known and turn against your family and faith and make yourself an outcast in the kingdom of your birth?"

"No, *pai,* not because of her."

"Because of what then?"

"Because I know now that the Portuguese bring evil to the Kongo and must be opposed, as the ManiNsundi opposes them."

"What evil? The *auto-da-fé?*"

"An evil more horrible than the *auto-da-fé.*"

"What evil is that?"

"You know what evil, *pai.* You have always known. You knew from the beginning and that is why you kept yourself apart from the Portuguese and lost your faith."

"Do not presume to tell me why I lost my faith or if I have lost my faith. Just answer what I ask you. What evil do you suppose the Portuguese bring to the Kongo that you must throw your life away to oppose?"

"First the theft of our souls, *pai*. Then the theft of our bodies."

It had been a long time, a very long time, since Gil had heard those words, that ominous prophecy. It had been ten years, and it sent a shiver down his spine hearing it now from the mouth of his son. "Where did you hear that? Who told you that? Did you tell him that, ManiNsundi?"

"No, Gil Eenezh, I did not tell him that," Mpanzu answered in his quiet, husky voice. "The NgangaKongo told him that."

"The NgangaKongo? Which NgangaKongo? That is the prophecy of Lukeni a Wene, and Lukeni a Wene is dead. I learned of his death years ago."

"Nonetheless, he is the one who told your son of the evil the Porta Geeze bring to our kingdom."

"What sorcery is this?"

"The sorcery of Lukeni a Wene," Mpanzu said and raised his big hand and pointed across the fire toward the river. "The sorcery of the high priest of my father."

The villagers who were crowded around that side of the fire moved aside to let Gil see what Mpanzu was pointing at: a small hut at the river's edge. And Gil remembered what Nuno and Gonçalo had told him, that Mpanzu had a great and important fetish with him, a fetish that lived in its own house. Was that small hut the house of this fetish?

"Lukeni a Wene is there, Gil Eenezh. Go to him. He will speak to you as he spoke to your son."

"Come, *pai*."

Gil glanced about uncertainly, then stood up and followed Henriqué. No one else did. Mpanzu remained seated on his stool. Mfidi went to stand by him. The villagers remained by the bonfire. When they reached the hut, Henriqué got down on his knees at the hut's low entryway and pulled aside the woven-grass hanging that covered it. Gil kneeled beside him and looked in.

It was so. Lukeni a Wene was in there. A small oil lamp was burning inside and, by its flickering orange glow, Gil saw the wizened hunchback dwarf seated against the hut's far wall. He was naked. His knees were drawn up. His chin rested on his knees. His thin arms were folded across his chest. A black leather amulet hung around his neck as the crucifix hung around Henriqué's. His body was painted white, unmoving except for the flickering shadows cast by the flickering flame of the oil lamp. And his eyes were closed. Gil waited for him to open them, to acknowledge the presence of visitors. But, of course, he did not open them. He was a corpse. A fetish, an icon, a relic that Mpanzu kept close, no different from the relic of a saint that a Portuguese prince might keep close and carry into war.

"Go inside, *pai*."

"He is dead, Kimpasi."

"I know, but please, go inside."

Gil looked back to the bonfire, to Mpanzu and Mfidi and the villagers watching him, then at Henriqué. The youth's light blue eyes were wide with an anxious urgency. He was anxious to be alone with his father; it was urgent that he speak to his father alone. So Gil crawled into the small hut, as if crawling into a tomb. Henriqué crawled in after him and let the woven-grass hanging drop behind them.

"What has happened, *mbakala?* You can tell me now. We are alone."

"I have heard the prophecy of the NgangaKongo, *pai,* the prophecy he made when the Portuguese first came to the kingdom, the prophecy you were the first to hear when you first came to the kingdom, before I was born. It is well known among the followers of Mpanzu and much repeated by them to explain why they rebel. But I had never heard it before I came here. And I know what it means."

They were on their knees, crouched under the low roof of the small hut, the corpse of the hunchback dwarf not an arm's length away. The air was close and damp but there was no smell of putrefaction. The corpse was well preserved.

"Listen, *pai*," Henriqué said in a hushed voice.

Gil listened but there was nothing to hear except the sound of the flame sputtering in the lamp and the sound of the river rushing over the rapids outside and the sound of cicadas whirring in the wet grass all around. Gil looked at the dead NgangaKongo, half-expecting, in the tomblike silence, the corpse to speak.

"First, they come to steal our souls."

This was, of course, not the corpse. It was Henriqué. His eyes were closed, like the corpse's, his brows furrowed in deep concentration.

"That is the simple part of the prophecy, the easiest to understand. From the very first, the Portuguese have come to the Kongo seeking souls. On every ship, priests have come on that quest, as I, a priest myself now, have come. We say we seek these souls in order to save them from the darkness of eternal damnation, to bring them into the light of eternal salvation. But for the NgangaKongo, it is theft. Because the NgangaKongo possesses those souls. Ever since there was a Kongo, the NgangaKongo has possessed the souls of the kingdom's people, so in seeking them, we seek to steal them from him."

Gil watched Henriqué intently. Beads of sweat had broken out on the youth's furrowed forehead, and he had taken his crucifix in one hand and was gripping it tightly.

"But the theft of our bodies? What did the NgangaKongo mean when he foretold that? That was the mystery in the prophecy. That was what no one could understand since, in all these years, no Portuguese have ever come seeking to steal our bodies."

"But you understand it?"

Henriqué opened his eyes. "Yes, *pai,* I understand it."

"What do you understand?"

"That the NgangaKongo foretold the discovery of Brasil."

"Kimpasi . . ."

"*Pai,* listen to me. Until now, the Portuguese had no need for bodies and so did not come here seeking to steal them. But with the discovery of Brasil, a great need for them arose. We have spoken of King Manoel's need for men to build the settlements there. We have spoken of the possibility that that is why he has sent his ships here now, to fill the holds not with gold or any other treasure, but with Kongo men to transport there."

"Yes, we have spoken of that, Kimpasi, but we cannot be certain it is so."

"I could not be certain until I heard the NgangaKongo's

prophecy. Just as you could not be certain what the prophecy meant until you heard of the discovery of Brasil. But now that I have heard the prophecy and you have heard of the discovery of Brasil, we can be certain."

Gil pondered this for a moment. Then he asked, "Have you spoken of this to Mpanzu?"

"No. He knows nothing of Brasil."

"Then that is not what incited him to start this war now?"

"He started this war before I ever got here to speak to him of anything."

"Then why did he start it now?"

"Because it was now or never. Because he saw that, if the Portuguese were ever to be driven out of the kingdom, they would have to be driven out now before any more came. He always trusted in the NgangaKongo's prophecy even though he did not fully understand it. He always believed the Portuguese would bring evil to the kingdom even though he did not know what the evil would be. So all these years, since they first came, he has watched and waited. And when he saw the five ships of King Manoel's fleet come, more than had ever come before, he saw that he must start the war now or never start it because soon there would be too many Portuguese in the kingdom to ever drive out again."

"I see."

"And he is right. Soon there will be too many Portuguese in the kingdom to ever drive out again. And they will take our people as slaves and transport them to this new world of Brasil. We know that now, you and I."

"No, Kimpasi, I know no such thing. I would need to know much more than this dead sorcerer's prophecy before I could know such an awful thing."

"Well, I know it. This war Mpanzu has started is a war to save our people from enslavement by the Portuguese. And, by this, he has become the true king of the Kongo, while Mbemba has become the Portuguese's fool."

Gil shook his head at the harshness of Henriqué's words. "And you will join in this war he makes against your mother's brother."

"Yes."

With a sigh, Gil sat back on his heels and, for several minutes, neither father nor son spoke, each thinking his own thoughts. The flame of the oil lamp hissed, the river ran by outside and the steady, metallic hum of the cicadas heightened the quiet in the Nganga-Kongo's sepulcher.

Then Gil asked, "Will you take Mfidi for your wife, Kimpasi? Is that your plan?"

"I cannot have a wife, *pai*. I am a priest."

"Your bishop will not consider you a priest after this, *mbakala*. He will not even consider you a Catholic."

"I am a better priest and Catholic than he. I believe in the grace of God and the mercy of our Lord Jesus Christ. I do not believe in burning men at the stake in order to steal their souls and enslave them."

"Where is he? He isn't with you? He stayed with Mpanzu?"

"Yes."

Beatriz did not want to believe this. She rushed down from the veranda to search for her son in the ranks of the twenty warriors of Gil's bodyguard standing with Nuno and Gonçalo under the flowering trees of the royal garden. They had been on the march with little rest for sixteen days, returning to São Salvador from Mpanzu's camp through intermittent rain squalls, and it was well past midnight and raining again. They backed away in surprise when Beatriz came hurrying woefully among them. It pained Gil to see her like this. She knew everything. The serving woman Nimi, who had gotten back to São Salvador three weeks before, had told her (as well as Affonso) everything that had happened in Mpangala, and now her hope of ever seeing her son again was being dashed. After a moment, Gil went to her and took her hand.

She pulled it away angrily. "How could you leave him with Mpanzu?"

"I did everything I could, Nimi. Believe me."

"But this will be the end of him," she cried out in anguish and began to weep. "Oh, Gil, this will be the end of him."

He put his arms around her and let her weep against his chest. The warriors watched this uneasily. Nimi, the other Nimi, came out on the veranda with Tereza and also watched in the light but steadily falling rain.

"Nuno," Gil called over Beatriz's head, still holding her tight. "Send the men home. They have served me well and I thank them for their service."

As the warriors trooped wearily out of the garden, Nimi and Tereza came down from the veranda.

"Why are you crying, Mother?" the little girl asked, tugging at the skirt of Beatriz's kanga. "Why does Mother cry, *pai?*"

"You shouldn't be up, Tereza. It is very late. You should be asleep. Mother will be all right. Take her inside, *mchento.*"

Beatriz raised her head from Gil's chest and watched her daughter and the serving woman go back into the house. Then she said, "His life is at an end, Gil. He is so young and his life has already come to its end."

"No, Nimi, it hasn't. Of course it hasn't."

"Yes it has. Bishop de Sousa says he will be defrocked and excommunicated and his soul damned to burn in the fires of hell for all eternity."

Gil shook his head angrily, his dislike of de Sousa welling up in his throat into a foul curse, and he would have cursed him, but he did not want to upset Beatriz any further.

"And Affonso has disowned him. I pleaded with him. I begged him to wait until the poor boy had a chance to explain himself. But he wouldn't wait, his fury is so great. I have never seen him in such a fury, Gil. He says there is no explanation for what Henriqué has done. He says he is a traitor, a Judas, and will be punished for his treachery. And you are under suspicion as well."

"I am? Why?"

"Bishop de Sousa says Father Duarte says you helped Henriqué get away with the girl. You didn't, did you?"

"Of course I didn't. Does Mbemba believe I did?"

"He might. His fury has robbed him of all reason."

"Do you?"

Beatriz did not answer right away.

"Look at me, Nimi. He is my son too. You cannot believe I had any part in this."

"I don't. But why did he do it? How could he go over to our worst enemy?"

"The boy had his reasons," Gil answered vaguely. "For one thing, he doesn't regard Mpanzu as our worst enemy."

"But he is our worst enemy. He is the Antichrist. That's what Bishop de Sousa calls him. He denies our Lord and wishes to keep the people in heathen darkness. And if he succeeds in his rebellion, he will drive us all into exile again." Beatriz began weeping again and again buried her face against Gil's chest. "But he won't succeed," she suddenly said in a muffled rage. "All the power of the kingdom and all the power of our Lord will be thrown against him."

"So, it has been decided. Mbemba will make war on Mpanzu." Gil had of course expected as much and said this more to himself than to her.

But she pushed away from him. "Of course he will. You didn't suppose he would let Mpanzu take his throne? You didn't suppose he would let us all be driven into exile again? He has already given the order. The soldiers of the São Salvador garrison will soon be marching to Mpangala along with thousands of Kongo warriors to reinforce Dom Tomé there. And they will hunt Mpanzu down and kill him and kill all those with him."

"Including Kimpasi?"

"Oh, Gil, we must think of a way to get him away from Mpanzu. We must think of a way to get him home again."

"We will, Nimi. Don't worry, we will think of something. But come now, let us go inside and get out of this infernal rain. I am wet and tired and want to sleep."

"Is she beautiful?" Beatriz asked as they went up the veranda steps into the house.

"Who?"

"Mfidi. Nimi says Henriqué has fallen under her spell."

"She is just a girl, a pretty girl." Gil unbuckled his cutlass and removed his chainmail and went to their sleeping chamber. "It wasn't her."

"Then what was it? I can't understand it. Henriqué never liked Mpanzu. He never forgot it was Mpanzu who made his life a misery when he was a little boy."

Gil sat down on his palliasse and began pulling off his boots.

"Was it the *auto-da-fé?* Is that what it was?"

"Partly, yes, it was the *auto-da-fé.*" Gil set his boots aside and lay back on the palliasse, his hands clasped beneath his head.

"It must have been a terrible thing for him to see. I think, if I had seen it, I too might have turned against the Faith."

"Come here, Nimi. Lie down beside me."

"Don't you want to wash first? I will send a serving woman to fetch hot water for you."

"No, just lie beside me. I will wash later. And we will talk about all this later."

She undid her kanga and let it fall to the floor and went to him. Her body, like his, was still wet with rain, and he ran his hand along its full and lovely and familiar curves, gently wiping her dry. She shivered under his touch and pressed her face into the corner between his chin and shoulder and began weeping again in despair for her son.

"Oh, Gil . . ."

"Ssh, Nimi, ssh. I will get him back, I promise. I will find a way to bring him home again."

"Soldiers of the Porta Geeze come, Gil Eenezh." This was the other Nimi. She stuck her head into the room, then quickly withdrew it when she saw what was going on in there. "They ask for you."

"Tell them I'm not here."

"They know you are here. They saw you return. They have been keeping close watch on the house for that purpose, to spy you out when you returned."

Gil sat up. So did Beatriz, wide-eyed, her hands around his neck.

"They say the bishop de Sooza summons you. They say it was he who had them keep close watch on the house so as to fetch you to him as soon as they had spied out that you had returned."

Gil wrapped on a kanga and went out on the front veranda. Beatriz also dressed hurriedly and followed him. Four halberdiers were standing in the garden below.

"His Grace summons you, Senhor Eanes," one of them started.

But Gil cut him off sharply. "It is late, *cabo,* and I have just returned from a long journey. Tell His Grace I will come to him after I have had some sleep."

"The king also awaits you, *senhor*."

"Who summons me, *cabo?* First you say the bishop. Now you say the king. Which is it? Speak clearly."

"It is the bishop who has summoned you, *senhor*," the soldier answered. "But I thought you would wish to know that the king also awaits you at the vicarage. As does the dowager queen Leonor."

Gil didn't like the sound of this.

"You must go, Gil," Beatriz said, standing at his shoulder. "Not to go would only draw more suspicion on yourself. I will go with you."

Lighted candles in silver candelabra on the large oak table that served as a desk, as well as in brass sconces on the stone walls, illuminated the vicarage's sitting room in a sinister light. Bishop de Sousa sat in his high-backed chair behind the table, dressed in a black cassock, wearing a black skullcap, his complexion a waxy, sickly pallor in the candlelight, his expression grim. Off to the side, a few paces away from the table, were two other high-backed chairs. Affonso sat in one, Leonor in the other, both dressed in the fashion of Portuguese royalty. A fourth chair stood in front of the table, facing the bishop. It was empty.

The four halberdiers followed Gil into the room. Two took up positions on either side of the empty chair; the other two stood guard at the door, their heavy axe-headed pikes held out at a sharp angle from their feet, barring it. Beatriz, however, pushed her way past them, glancing around half-worriedly, half-defiantly. Her presence surprised Bishop de Sousa.

"There is no need for you to be here, Dona Beatriz," he said, rising from his chair.

"My son is in danger and my husband is under suspicion, Your Grace. Where else would you have me be?"

Bishop de Sousa sat back down with a sigh and clasped his hands on the table. "Very well, but I ask you, please do not interfere in these proceedings."

"Come over here, Beatriz," Leonor said, beckoning her daughter to her side.

"What proceedings are these, Bishop?" Gil asked. "Have you brought the Inquisition here from Mpangala? Am I to fear that one of Father Duarte's pyres has been prepared for me too?"

"There is no need to take a pessimistic view, Senhor Eanes,"

Bishop de Sousa replied with a thin smile. "As long as you can answer our questions satisfactorily, you have nothing to fear. Won't you sit down?" He indicated the empty chair in front of him.

Gil ignored the invitation and turned to Affonso. "Is this your wish, Mbemba? Have you agreed to this trial?"

"It is not a trial, Gil," Affonso said very quietly. With an elbow on the armrest of his chair, he held his head in his hand and did not look at Gil. "His Grace has some questions for you. I would like to hear your answers to them."

"Questions or accusations?"

Affonso did not reply, nor look up.

"Do you doubt my loyalty to you, Mbemba? After all these years, do you require me to answer the accusations of this priest in order to be sure of it?"

Now Affonso did look up, and the fury in his face was terrible to see, the scar across his cheek on fire. "You went to Mpanzu, Gil, and while you were with him, he attacked Mpangala."

"What?"

"In the dead of night, his warriors fell on Mpangala and put it to the torch. They destroyed the church and barracks and killed many of the Portuguese soldiers there and took many of the Nsundi captive, their chief, Bernardo, among them."

"Jesus," Gil muttered, realizing now why he had not seen any warriors in Mpanzu's camp. "When was this?"

"I told you when it was. When you were with Mpanzu."

"But I was with him less than a day."

"Are you saying you did not know of the attack, Senhor Eanes?" Bishop de Sousa asked.

Gil turned to him. "Of course I did not know of it. Do you dare suggest that I was party to it?"

"Whatever I dare suggest, *senhor,* you must admit that it is an odd coincidence that you went to Mpanzu just at that time."

"You know very well why I went to him just at that time. I went to him in hope of persuading my son to come home with me."

"So you knew your son would be there. You knew that, after he fled Mpangala together with Mfidi, that was where he would go. To Mpanzu."

"Yes."

"And how did you come to know that, Senhor Eanes?"

"I am not interested in how he came to know it," Affonso broke in harshly and stood up, banging his chair away.

"But Your Majesty—"

"My only interest now is to know to whom he owes his allegiance. To me. Or to Mpanzu."

"You needn't ask me that, Mbemba. I have already answered that."

"Then you will show me where Mpanzu is."

"But you know where he is. Isn't he in Mpangala? You said he captured Mpangala."

"I said he attacked Mpangala. But he is too clever a warrior to have remained there and waited for my army to come against him. After the attack, he retreated again to his camp in the Nsundi hills. I don't know where that is. But you do. You were there."

"I doubt that the village where I was is Mpanzu's camp any longer. As you yourself say, he is a clever warrior. Surely, by now, he has a new camp."

"But you can find it, *senhor*," Bishop de Sousa said. "All you have to do is find your son, the renegade priest, and you will also find Mpanzu's new camp."

Gil looked at him, then back at Affonso. Then he sat down in the empty chair. "Have you told His Majesty about Brasil, Bishop?"

"Brasil?"

"You have not heard of it?"

De Sousa shook his head.

"What is Brasil?" Affonso asked.

"A new world that the Portuguese have discovered, Mbemba. A new world for which they need many slaves."

VIII

HUNKERED ON HIS HEELS among the mossy boulders and nests of
driftwood at the river's edge, Gil untangled the fishing lines he had
trailing out in the eddies and millrace of the fast-running stream, then
squinted downriver through the misty drizzle of low-lying clouds. He
couldn't see anyone down there. Nuno and Gonçalo were keeping
well out of sight back in the thick brush of the Lelunda's south bank.
Above, at the mouth of a small cave in the face of the escarpment
that reared up from the south bank (and which he had fixed up as a
shelter), a smoky fire was burning. Beatriz kneeled behind it, roasting
the dressed-out carcass of a wild pig Gil had killed earlier that morning. Mfidi stood beside her, looking upriver. Gil twisted on his heels
and also looked upriver but couldn't see anyone in that direction either and returned to adjusting his lines.

They were waiting for Henriqué. For three days now, they had
been waiting for him at this wilderness camp, some 120 leagues eastward up the valley of the Lelunda from Mpangala, in the hope he
would lead them to Mpanzu.

Although his suspicions about the Portuguese had hardened by
now into an ugly certainty, Gil had nonetheless agreed to try to find
Mpanzu for Affonso. There was going to be a war between the brothers, there was no avoiding it anymore, and Gil had decided he was
duty bound, out of a loyalty born of twenty years of friendship, to
help Affonso win that war. But, as he had argued in the vicarage that

night, finding Mpanzu wasn't going to be as simple as Bishop de
Sousa made it seem, because Gil wasn't at all sure he could find Henriqué again.

But Beatriz was sure she could. Even if Henriqué refused to respond to news that Gil had come looking for him, he wasn't likely to
ignore news that his mother had. So, avid to see Mpanzu's rebellion
crushed and anxious to rescue her son from it, she had offered herself as the bait with which to lure Henriqué out of hiding.

They had left at daybreak that next morning with only Nuno
and Gonçalo for an escort—the army of thousands that Affonso was
going to lead against Mpanzu once he was found was assembling in
the parks and squares of São Salvador as they left, war fever in the
city high—and had made straight for the fishing village on the
Lelunda that had been Mpanzu's last camp. Gil had no expectation
that it still was. After his raid on Mpangala, Mpanzu would certainly
have decamped, smart and wary enough to keep constantly on the
move. But Gil was gambling that the people of the fishing village
would know where he had gone and could be induced to get word
to him that Henriqué's mother, distraught to learn that her son had
quit home and family, begged for a chance to speak with him. The father who had allowed Gil to speak to the son would surely do no less
for the mother.

After a five-day wait in the fishing village, Mfidi had come for
them and, while (unknown to her) Nuno and Gonçalo followed, she
had brought them to this spot in the wilderness, another thirty
leagues farther upriver, for the rendezvous with their son.

Gil looked back up to the mouth of the cave. Turning the pig's
carcass absently over the smoky fire, Beatriz was trying to make conversation with Mfidi, anxious to hear something about Henriqué. But
the girl, rude and sullen, her eyes full of hate, kept her mouth resolutely shut, her face resolutely turned away. Feeling the tug of a fish
on one of his lines, Gil looked back to the river—and caught a
glimpse of someone on the opposite bank. Whoever it was had
ducked down in the tall yellow grass over there and was watching
him. Gil reeled in his line, unhooked a fair-sized carp and tossed it on
a flat stone with the six others he had caught so far that morning,
then rebaited the line and cast it back out into the stream, trying to

appear nonchalant, not wanting to scare whoever was watching away.

It probably was Henriqué. He probably had been over there keeping watch since long before Gil and Beatriz and Mfidi had gotten there, needing to make sure Mfidi hadn't been tricked, needing to satisfy himself that Gil and Beatriz had come alone. But had *he* come alone, Gil wondered, or had he been accompanied by Nsundi warriors from Mpanzu's camp? It couldn't be ruled out. Gil again squinted back downriver to where he believed Nuno and Gonçalo had concealed themselves. He hadn't seen hide nor hair of them since leaving the fishing village and hoped that was because of their skill as trackers. But what if they hadn't succeeded in following him here? That too couldn't be ruled out.

Henriqué revealed himself about an hour later. Mfidi was the first to see him and bolted down the escarpment, calling his name. Beatriz immediately went after her, forgetting the pig on the fire. He came out of the grass hesitantly and stopped at the water's edge on the opposite bank. His appearance must have given his mother a shock, because he was dressed as Gil had last seen him, like a Nsundi villager, not a Portuguese priest, except for his crucifix (like a Nsundi priest, then), his blond hair cut short. Mfidi dashed across the stream to him, skipping deftly from rock to rock, but Beatriz stayed where she was, momentarily at a loss. Then she began calling across to him in a rush of emotion.

Gil didn't go to them. He also remained where he was, sitting back on his heels and fooling with his fishing lines. He could guess easily enough what Beatriz was saying and could as easily guess what Henriqué's response would be. No matter how harshly she scolded him for what he had done, no matter how poignantly she pleaded with him to return home with her, he would adamantly refuse. But it didn't matter. All that mattered was that he had been lured out of hiding. Now, as long as Nuno and Gonçalo had managed to follow them here and Henriqué hadn't brought Nsundi warriors with him . . .

"*Pai.*"

Gil stood up.

"Why did you allow her to come here, *pai?*" Henriqué called to him angrily.

"Because I thought you would want to say goodbye to her," Gil replied.

This embarrassed the youth, and he looked away.

"You will never see her again. Because of this course you have chosen, you will never see any of your family again. I had my chance to say goodbye to you. I thought your mother should also have the chance. I even considered bringing Tereza with us so she could say goodbye to you as well."

Henriqué looked back, a glaze of tears blurring his light blue eyes.

"Well? Are you just going to go on standing there? Or are you going to come across and say goodbye to your mother properly and embrace her?"

"Are you alone, *pai?* Have you come here alone?"

Gil had known all along, of course, that in order to carry out his plan he would have to lie to his son. Even so, the lie caught in his throat and it took him a moment to spit it out. "Yes, Kimpasi, we have come here alone. And you?"

"I am also alone," the youth answered and then, picking his way from stone to stone, crossed the river.

"Oh, *mbakala.*" Beatriz rushed into his arms and began sobbing woefully. "Why do you do this?"

"Ask Fernão de Mello."

Beatriz stepped back. "Fernão de Mello?"

"You do not believe what I have told you about the Nganga-Kongo's prophecy."

"It is a thing too terrible to believe, *mbakala.*"

"Ask Fernão de Mello then. Ask him if he believes it. He is the one who can say for certain if it is so."

"Fernão de Mello is in Santo Antonio, Kimpasi," Gil said.

"No longer. He has gone to Mpangala to join in the war against Mpanzu."

"He has? You are well informed."

"It is Mpanzu who is well informed. He has spies everywhere. There are men everywhere in the kingdom who consider him the true ManiKongo and are willing to spy for him." Henriqué embraced his mother a final time, then went quickly back across the river.

While Beatriz remained at the river's edge looking across at her son with teary eyes, Gil climbed up the escarpment to the cave, fetched the pig from its spit, kicked out the fire, came back down, gathered up the fish he had caught and put them into the small dugout in which Mfidi had brought them here. Then he called to Beatriz. He expected her to make a fuss at the last moment but she understood the plan, and with reddened eyes and a muffled sob, she turned her back on her son and got into the dugout as Gil started paddling downriver. They both looked back once. Henriqué and Mfidi remained standing on the riverbank, watching to make sure Gil and Beatriz departed. Then the river made a sharp bend and they vanished from each other's view.

Gil paddled downriver for two hours. It was late in the afternoon and the misty drizzle had turned into a steadily falling rain when he put into a small cove of the river's north bank. He jumped out and immediately shoved the dugout back into the stream. Again he expected Beatriz to protest. She didn't.

"Shall I go to Fernão de Mello?" she asked. "Shall I go to him and ask if the NgangaKongo's prophecy is true?"

Gil shook his head. "There is no need. I know it is true."

"And still you are willing to do this?"

"I do it for Mbemba. And, besides, it is too late to do anything else. The war has started and the most we can hope to do now is rescue our son from it."

"Rescue him, Gil," Beatriz said and, picking up the dugout's paddle, resumed the trip downriver. "Bring him safely home."

Gil remained in the cove until night fell. There was an abandoned fisherman's hut on the grassy bluff overlooking the cove and he sheltered from the rain in it, cutting up the roasted pig for his supper. After that, he allowed himself to doze off for a little while, thinking to husband his strength. When he awoke, it was pitch dark and the rain had slackened again. He waited another hour, then made his way back up along the river's north bank to where he had left Henriqué.

Gonçalo was waiting for him.

"*Deo gratias,*" he muttered to himself, having worried whether he'd find either of the brothers there. "Where is Nuno? Is he following the trail?"

"He is, my lord. It is an easy trail to follow. Your son has been too long away among the white men to remember how to cover his trail."

The trail led away from the river, northeast into the rolling hills of the grassland. It was indeed easy to follow—Henriqué, trustingly, was doing nothing to conceal it—but, in addition, Nuno, a few hours in advance, having started to track Henriqué and Mfidi as soon as they had set off back to Mpanzu's camp, was marking it, slashing the bark of tree trunks, breaking the branches of shrubs, leaving behind little pyramids of stone. These led steadily to the northeast throughout that night and into the next morning, then turned due north and continued in that direction for the rest of the day. At dusk, the markers veered to the northwest. Gil and Gonçalo took a break to eat and sleep there before continuing throughout the remainder of that night. When the sun came up, they were climbing a long, steep rise, still traveling to the northwest, to the crest of a high hill. Nuno was lying in the tall grass of the hilltop, peering down the hill's other side. He glanced around as Gil and Gonçalo came up behind him and signaled them to keep quiet and lie down beside him. And Gil saw at once that they had reached their destination: Mpanzu's new camp.

It was a small stockaded village on the crest of another hill about a half-league away. A wide, deep, sluggish river, overflowing its marshy banks from the steady rainfall, ran through the valley between the two hills from north to south, probably emptying into the Lelunda. A grand profusion of flowering trees grew along its banks, and its lakelike surface (Gil at first mistook it for a lake because of its width) was colored white and pink by the feathers of the myriad heron and flamingo and ibis that flocked upon it. Behind the village on the hill was a small forest, also in full leaf and flower and also filled with birds.

"Where are we, Nuno?" Gil asked.

"The village is called Mbouila, my lord. To the north by west no more than twenty leagues, no more than two days' march, is Mpangala."

"And Mpanzu is in this village?"

"He is, my lord."

"Good. Now go to Mpangala and tell the ManiKongo that we have found his brother."

"And you, my lord?"

"I will remain here."

Nuno and Gonçalo looked at each other in some consternation. Then Gonçalo said, "I will remain here with you, my lord."

"No, both of you must go. And each of you must go by a different path so as to improve the chance that at least one of you will reach Mpangala to tell the ManiKongo where the ManiNsundi makes his new camp."

Again the brothers glanced at each other uneasily, clearly puzzled by this arrangement. It hadn't been part of the original plan.

"Two days' march there, you say, Nuno?"

"Yes, my lord."

"And what do you think? Another four days for the ManiKongo to march his army back?"

"No more than four, my lord, maybe only three."

"Then I will expect the attack on Mbouila in less than a week."

Gil gave Nuno and Gonçalo all that morning and until late into the afternoon to get well clear of Mbouila, to be well on their way to Mpangala. Then he climbed down the hillside and started toward the near shore of the lakelike river lying beneath Mbouila, a light but steady rain again falling from the thickly overcast sky.

Canoes were drawn up in the reeds of the flooded shore and about fifty men stood near them, Mpanzu's men, Nsundi warriors, rebels against the throne. Painted in camwood and lime, feathers in their hair, most were armed either with lances and shields or with long bows and arrows. But even while he was still some distance away, Gil could see that a few held arquebuses. If they were homemade and not taken from the Portuguese, they were truly astounding pieces of work. What marvelous craftsmen these people were. The woodwork and metalwork of the weapons seemed perfect, every detail of the mechanisms skillfully copied. But the arquebus (as were all firearms of the time) was a notoriously fickle weapon. If one spring or wheel-lock or hammerhead wasn't just right, if the barrel was slightly out of line, the damn thing could blow up in your face. Even those of Portuguese manufacture regularly did.

It took an exceptionally long time for the warriors to notice Gil walking toward them, even though he did nothing to conceal himself. Barefoot and wearing a kanga, clean-shaven, with a knife on his hip and a bow and quiver of arrows over his shoulders, obscured by the curtain of falling rain, he must have seemed to them just a lone hunter returning to his village from a hunt in the grassland.

But then they realized who he was. They saw his blond hair and light eyes and fair skin. And they seized him. He didn't resist. And the birds on the river, the heron and ibis and flamingo, raised a spectacular storm of pink and white feathers as they burst into flight.

"No, MANINSUNDI, my son did not betray you. I betrayed my son."

"Kill him," Mfidi hissed.

Mpanzu glanced at his daughter, then raised his big hand, and Henriqué, standing beside the girl, pushed her away in anger and confusion, aghast to have discovered his father had played him false.

"He did not know I would follow him," Gil went on. "I told him I would not and he trusted me. But I lied to him."

"Oh, *pai*," Henriqué groaned.

"And are you the only one to have followed him?"

"No. Two warriors of my household guard followed him with me."

"Where are they?"

"On their way to your brother in Mpangala to tell him where you can be found."

"And you did not go with them? Why? Why did you instead give yourself up to me?"

"To warn you."

"To warn me?" Mpanzu repeated incredulously.

"Yes, ManiNsundi, to warn you that Mbemba now knows where you are and will attack you in less than a week."

"What further lie is this?"

"It is no lie."

"First you act for Mbemba by tricking your son into leading you here. Then you act against Mbemba by revealing to me that you have done this. And you expect me to believe this isn't another of your lies?"

"I acted for Mbemba as his loyal liege man, ManiNsundi. Our friendship is very old and I owed him that loyalty. But in warning you of what I have done, I act against the Portuguese."

"Why should I believe you would act against the Porta Geeze, Gil Eenezh? They are your own people."

"Because I know now what evil they bring to this land."

They were standing at the main gate, the west gate, in the stockade that enclosed Mbouila. Two lombard cannon—these clearly of Portuguese manufacture, doubtless captured in the ambush of Rodrigues or the raid on Mpangala, pointing down the hillside toward the river—guarded the gate. The warriors who had seized Gil and had brought him across the river in their canoes and then up the steep hillside to this gate were clustered closely around him. Warriors were also clustered closely around Mpanzu; from the headdresses and war paint and regalia they wore, Gil judged that a few of them were Nsundi princes and chiefs who had joined Mpanzu in his rebellion against Affonso and were now members of his rebel court. Indeed, he recognized one of them: Bernardo, chief of Mpangala. Obviously, he hadn't been taken prisoner in the raid on his town but had gone over to Mpanzu willingly, impressed by the ferocity of that raid, impressed too by the success of the ambush of Rodrigues, appalled by the *auto-da-fé*. Henriqué and Mfidi stood beside him. Behind them, the gate was open, so that Gil could see into the village. With dusk now swiftly gathering and the rain still steadily falling, he couldn't see much. But he could see that there was a gate at the other end of the village, an east gate, which opened onto the forest behind the village.

How large an army did Mpanzu have in the village? Located on top of a high hill with a river in front and a forest behind, the village seemed reasonably defensible. But considering its modest size and discounting the women and children who lived there, it couldn't contain much more than fifteen hundred, perhaps two thousand men of fighting age. Did Mpanzu have more, scattered in other villages and camps like this across the grassland? He must have. Because if he didn't, the war against him would be a massacre. Affonso would make short work of the Nsundi rebellion if these were all the army Mpanzu had to put into the field against his brother's.

"What difference does it make why he has given himself up to you, ManiNsundi?" Bernardo interrupted with some impatience. "All that matters is that, since he has done so, whatever his reason, we know we are no longer safe here and must move on."

Mpanzu nodded thoughtfully at that but kept his bulging, goiterous eyes fixed on Gil, and they reflected his utter inability to grasp the contrary motive Gil gave for what he had done. Gil wasn't all that sure he grasped it himself.

"And move on quickly," Bernardo continued. "He says Mbemba will be here in less than a week. But if there is reason to doubt what he says, let us doubt this. If there is reason to believe he is playing us a trick, let us believe this is the trick. That his two warriors reached Mpangala long before he says and Mbemba is already on the march against us."

"Is he?"

"No, ManiNsundi, I have spoken the truth. But there would be no harm in heeding Bernardo's advice and departing this place as quickly as you can."

"And you, Gil Eenezh? What should I do with you?"

Gil shrugged.

"Kill him," Mfidi said again, pulling away from Henriqué. "If you do not kill him, he will follow us again. He will follow us wherever we go and send his warriors back to tell Mbemba wherever we are."

"I have no more warriors to send back, Mfidi. Now I am truly alone."

"What did you think when you gave yourself up to me?" Mpanzu asked, ignoring his daughter. "Did you not think I would kill you?"

"You had other chances to kill me, ManiNsundi, and you did not. During the first war with the Portuguese, you had many chances to kill me, but you did not."

Mpanzu shook his head, his skepticism clearly unabated.

"We could take him with us, ManiNsundi," Henriqué ventured. "If we have him with us, we would be sure he could not send back word where we are."

"And if I killed him, we would also be sure. I will decide which it is to be when I have puzzled out what trick he and my brother have planned for me. Until then, you are my prisoner, Gil Eenezh."

Gil was put into a small house in the village headman's com-

pound near the forest gate, which turned out to be Henriqué's house.
He discovered this in the middle of his first night there. Restless and
anxious anyway and only fitfully sleeping, he was easily awakened
that night by any sound and awoke with a start to the muffled
sounds, the little cries and sighs, of lovemaking in a nearby room. He
listened for a few moments, and thinking it was Henriqué's voice he
heard whispering urgently, he went to see, walking softly, and saw
Mfidi on her hands and knees, her kanga thrown up on her back, and
Henriqué kneeling behind her, his kanga folded away from his loins.
Mfidi glanced up and smiled defiantly, but Henriqué's eyes were
squeezed shut and he didn't see his father. Gil hurried away in embarrassment.

The next day dawned with a brilliant flash of lightning, a deafening crack of thunder and a terrific downpour that quickly turned
the village's market square into a muddy swamp. Gil went out on the
house's veranda, thinking he'd see Mpanzu making preparations to
move his rebel army on to another camp. But he saw nothing of the
sort. What he saw was the village awaken to its usual activities as if no
threat hung over it, while Mpanzu's warriors—Gil estimated there
were two thousand at most with no more than 250 firearms among
them—stood idly by. There was no sign that Mpanzu was breaking
camp, no sign that he was in any hurry to depart. Why did he delay?
Didn't he believe Gil? Did he still think it was some kind of trick? Or
had his spies spied out some new information about the army Gil
had warned was coming against him here?

Later that day, a group of women and children came to the
house to hear Henriqué preach the Gospel. Wearing a white soutane
instead of his kanga, he sat cross-legged on a mat in the front room, a
Bible open on his lap, a sort of altar set up behind him consisting of
a wooden crucifix and two palm-oil lamps. Once the women and
children were seated on mats of their own in a half-circle in front of
him, he began telling the story of the miracle of the loaves and fishes.
He told it with a gracious simplicity and the women and children listened to it with rapt attention. The shore of the lake where the miracle had occurred, as he told it, might have been the shore of the
lakelike river down the hill from the village, and the people gathered
there to be fed by the miracle might have been the people of this vil-

lage, and the miracle itself was no more incomprehensible to them than the miracles performed by their own ju-ju men. Gil looked at the crucifix. It was the work of a local carver. The features of the Christ, rounded and full, were those of these people, and the darkly stained wood of the bleeding body was the color of their skin, a Kongo Jesus of whom Bishop de Sousa would no doubt disapprove.

Suddenly Mfidi came dashing up onto the veranda. Heedless of intruding on his lesson, she went to Henriqué and whispered excitedly in his ear. He looked up at Gil standing in the doorway, quickly finished the story and dismissed the class. As they came out, discussing with some pleasure the story they had heard, Gil went in.

"Mbemba is on the march, *pai*," Henriqué said, standing up. "His army has left Mpangala."

Gil made a quick calculation. It was almost two full days since Nuno and Gonçalo had started for Mpangala. They very well could have reached there by now.

"But he does not march this way."

"Which way does he march?"

"Toward Mpanzu's old camp. Toward the fishing village on the Lelunda where Mpanzu made his last camp. He seems to think that it still is."

How could that be? That could only be if neither Nuno nor Gonçalo had succeeded in getting to Mpangala. Maybe, so deep in Nsundi country, with Mpanzu's spies everywhere, they had been captured on the way to Mpangala and killed. And maybe that was why Mpanzu had been in no great hurry to move on. Gil hurried back out on the house's veranda.

The rebel warriors in the village were no longer standing idly by. They were gathering around Mpanzu in the muddy, rain-drenched market square. And a contingent of about two hundred was marching out through the west gate with Bernardo in the lead.

"Where do they go, ManiNsundi?" Gil asked, dashing down from the veranda. "Where does Bernardo take them?"

"To make trouble for my brother."

"But they are so few. Mbemba has thousands with him."

"It will only take those few to make the trouble I wish."

"What trouble is that?"

"Mbemba seems to be mistaken about the location of my camp, Gil Eenezh. He seems to believe that I am still to be found in the fishing village on the Lelunda. I don't want to disappoint him. I want him to go on believing it."

"How do you propose to do that?"

"It will take him at least five, maybe six days to march his army to that fishing village. But it will take Bernardo and those warriors only two. So they will be waiting for him when he gets there. And they will attack him when he does, and he will think it is my army that is attacking him. And then, when Bernardo breaks off the fight and retreats because his warriors are too few to defeat Mbemba's thousands, Mbemba will chase him, thinking he is chasing me. And he will chase him to the south, away from here, because Bernardo will retreat to the south. And while Mbemba is chasing Bernardo to the south, I will move the rest of my army to another camp."

It seemed a good plan. But Gil couldn't help feeling there was something wrong with it. He couldn't help feeling Affonso wasn't to be outwitted quite so easily. He couldn't help feeling that Affonso might be outwitting Mpanzu. For, if Nuno and Gonçalo hadn't been captured and killed, if they had in fact reached Mpangala, Affonso's march toward the fishing village might be a diversion, a feint, a means of lulling Mpanzu into just this false sense of security.

And that night, as the rain fell and lightning flashed and thunder cracked, Gil counted the days, the days he had been in Mbouila, the days Nuno and Gonçalo needed to get to Mpangala, the days Affonso needed to get here. And he concluded that if neither Nuno nor Gonçalo had been captured and killed, then it would be three days at most before he would learn which of the Kongo kings, Mpanzu or Affonso, had succeeded in outwitting the other.

IX

H<small>E WAS WRONG.</small> He learned it the next night. He woke up thinking that what had awakened him was thunder. But it was not the thunder of the heavens. It was the thunder of Affonso's guns.

His first thought was for his son. He dashed into the next room. Henriqué wasn't there. Mfidi was, naked, clutching a cloth to her small breasts, cowering at the sound of the cannonade.

"You are the cause of this, Gil Eenezh," she hissed.

"Where is Kimpasi?"

"You betrayed him. You betrayed my father and you betrayed your son." The girl ran out of the house, dropping the cloth.

Gil ran out after her, into a pelting downpour. And just then cannon fired again. Their ball and shot smashed against the stockade on the southwest side of the village, splintering a large section of it. Gil ducked away from the flying debris, throwing up his hands. The attack was coming from down at the river. For the cannon to be in range of the stockade meant that the attacking soldiers and warriors had already crossed the river. How had they gotten there so fast? Maybe they were only part of Affonso's army. Maybe the main part was still marching toward the fishing village on the Lelunda in a diversionary maneuver. Gil started running after Mfidi again, thinking she must be running to Henriqué. He was desperate to get to Henriqué. He had promised Beatriz he would rescue their son from this war.

There was another volley of cannon fire. This time the ball and shot and scraps of iron and lengths of chain lofted over the stockade wall and crashed onto the roofs of the houses alongside it. People came rushing out of the houses. Goats and pigs and other livestock got loose. Children screamed. A fire started. Despite the rain, flames burst through the thatch of one roof and, because of the rain, turned into mushrooming plumes of black smoke. And in the chaos and confusion, rain and smoke, Gil lost sight of Mfidi. He stopped to look around. Warriors, armed with lances and shields, bows and arrows, arquebuses, axes and clubs, were running toward the main gate. Women and children, loaded down with baskets and bundles, were running toward the forest gate. Other fires started. But it wasn't only the bombardment that was starting the fires. The women were setting fire to their homes, destroying the village behind them as they fled with their belongings and children and livestock out the east gate into the forest behind the village while the warriors rushed to the village's defense at the main gate.

How many warriors did Mpanzu still have in Mbouila? Subtracting those who had made up Bernardo's raiding party, he probably had about fifteen hundred. Did Affonso have more than that? Did that part of his army which was now attacking Mbouila number more than fifteen hundred?

It did, at least three times more. Gil saw that as soon as he reached the main gate. The wooded near shore of the river below was swarming with Kongo warriors and Portuguese soldiers, and still more were coming across from the far shore. Four cannon had been hauled about a quarter of the way up from the river and emplaced as a front line across the path that climbed the hillside from the river to the village's main gate and were firing—and, occasionally, misfiring, because of their rain-soaked gunpowder—in as rapid succession as the torrential downpour permitted. The warriors and soldiers, running up out of the trees along the riverbank, gathered behind this line of guns in a restless multitude, drums beating, trumpets blaring, pennants flying, obviously waiting for the guns' bombardment to sufficiently reduce the village's defenses before launching their assault up the grassy hill.

And the village's defenses? Mpanzu's warriors were massing behind a front line of cannon of their own. There were four of them, two more than Gil realized Mpanzu had, also probably captured from the Portuguese at Mpangala. They were emplaced a hundred yards beyond the main gate, in the tall grass at the crest of the hill. When Gil reached the gate, they had not yet been fired. They were still being loaded and charged. Mpanzu, huge and imposing in his headdress of war feathers, his mutilated face drawn into a fierce grimace, was supervising the loading and charging with an amazing calm. Neither Henriqué nor Mfidi was anywhere to be seen in the billowing smoke and slashing sheets of rain.

Gil dashed out of the gate. "Where is Kimpasi?"

His words were drowned out by a thunderous roar. The first of Mpanzu's cannon had fired. The second and third misfired. Then the fourth fired and its recoil knocked the men firing it off their feet. Gil looked down the hill. Mpanzu's men weren't skilled cannoneers; they had only too recently learned how to use these weapons and were firing too hastily. Their volleys were far off the mark. One fell short while the other sailed harmlessly to the right. They were no match for Rodrigues's gunners. Gil saw the master-at-arms down the hill, racing back and forth behind the line of his guns. And then he saw Fernão de Mello down there too, in his long, hooded cloak, taller than all the others. And Affonso? Where was he? That might be him back in the trees at the riverbank, commanding the warriors still coming across the river. Before Gil could make certain, he was forced to fling himself to the ground. Rodrigues was returning Mpanzu's fire with a deadly, practiced accuracy.

The gate behind Gil was hit and torn from its hinges. The earth in front of him erupted in a shower of mud and stones. One of Mpanzu's cannon was blown over on its side, trapping two gunners beneath it. Shards of whistling metal sliced into the bodies of two others. Flames licked across the village's rooftops; flames sizzled in the wet grass. And then there was a piercing, bone-shivering cry, a wild, warbling ululation. Gil scrambled to his feet, sure that Affonso's men were about to launch their attack. But it wasn't Affonso's men who were going on the attack. It was Mpanzu's.

Two hundred of Mpanzu's warriors, brandishing lances and shields, axes and clubs, surged ahead of the line of their cannon and, screaming, charged down the hillside into the mouths of Rodrigues's guns. They were upon them before Rodrigues could reload and fire again, and passed them, throwing themselves bodily into the mass of startled Kongo warriors and Portuguese soldiers waiting behind the guns. Rodrigues went down; Gil saw him go down, trampled underfoot in the mud, and also saw de Mello running away, the skirts of his cloak flapping madly behind him.

But it was a suicide attack. Outnumbered ten to one, twenty to one, those two hundred Nsundi didn't have a chance. They were swallowed up in the opposing multitude, pounced upon, stabbed and axed, hammered and shot in a sudden, ferocious bloodletting of hand-to-hand fighting. And that it was a suicide attack was underscored by the fact that, in the midst of this close combat, Mpanzu calmly ordered his cannon to fire again, heedless of whether his own or Affonso's men would be killed in the cannonade. Three of the cannon misfired this time but the fourth was better aimed than before and scored a deadly hit into the violent disorder, cutting down as many Nsundi as Kongo and Portuguese. Gil turned to Mpanzu in horrified astonishment. What was he doing? Why had he sent those men to a certain death?

And then Gil saw why. The attack and cannonades were a diversion. Under the cover of their noise and smoke and raging fury, while the enemy was momentarily thrown into astounded disarray, Mpanzu's forces were beating a retreat. In squads of thirty and forty and then by the hundreds, the Nsundi warriors were breaking from their ranks behind their cannon and scrambling down from their posts on the stockade and escaping after their women and children back through the village and out the east gate into the forest. Affonso's ruse had worked. Mpanzu had been caught unprepared and was withdrawing in haste, not so foolish as to stand and fight his brother's superior numbers. With the suicide attack, with his heedless cannonades, he was sacrificing the few to save the many to fight again on another day in some other place.

"It is time, ManiNsundi."

Gil recognized the voice and spun around.

Henriqué had appeared on the run out of the smoke and rain, smeared with soot and mud, carrying a firearm. "You cannot delay any longer, ManiNsundi."

Gil looked back down the hill. The wild, sacrificial charge of the two hundred Nsundi was fast coming to its predictable end. More than half were already dead or dying, and the rest were being driven into the river and cut to pieces there, bloodying the rain-spattered waters. Soon the Kongo warriors and Portuguese soldiers would be able to turn their vehemence on Mbouila again. If Mpanzu himself was also to escape, he had little time left. But he didn't seem to be thinking of that at the moment. He was preoccupied with ordering yet another cannonade. He ignored Henriqué's warning.

And so Gil intervened. "Go, ManiNsundi," he shouted and ran to Mpanzu, grabbed his arm. "Go now and save yourself."

Mpanzu turned to him in astonished disbelief.

"Get him away from here, Kimpasi. Go with Kimpasi, Mani-Nsundi. You must not be captured."

The Kongo and Portuguese were regrouping. Rodrigues was back on his feet. And there was Affonso, in war feathers and paint, armed with a shield and a lance, a warrior king, pushing his way to the forefront of his multitudes, taking the commander's place in the lead of his army. The attack up the hill was but moments away.

"Go quickly, ManiNsundi," Gil shouted again. "There is no time to lose. I will fire the cannon for you. I will fire the cannon to hold them off while you get away."

Gil ran to the cannon.

But it was too hastily charged and its powder was wet. It blew up in his face.

RAINWATER WAS DRIPPING on his face. He tried to move his face away but the pain was unbearable and he plunged again into the black hole of unconsciousness where there was a measure of relief. Orange flames licked at the edges of the hole's blackness and he could smell the acrid smoke of the fire, but as long as he remained still, he was numb to the excruciating pain. So he tolerated the dripping rainwater, imagining it quenching the fire of his pain. What caused the pain? It radiated from a point between his eyes through every limb and tendon and muscle and bone of his body, but he had no memory of the injury that had caused it. He remembered only a sudden blow to that point between his eyes. Had his nose been broken? His skull fractured? His eyes gouged out?

He must have moved or have been moved because the rainwater was no longer dripping on his face. Or maybe it had stopped raining. He decided he had to make an effort to rouse himself from his stupor, despite the pain, because he did not want to be lying here when the rain started again. So with his eyes still closed, clinging to the anesthesia of unconsciousness, he made an effort. He moved his toes. He clenched the fingers of one hand and then the other. He raised one hand and rested it on his chest, and then the other. Then slowly, gingerly, he moved one hand up to his face and touched that point of pain between his eyes. It was caked with mud. He ran his fingers across his forehead, then down the bridge of his nose, then around his heavily bearded cheeks. The pain came from deep inside the cavern of his head, not its surface. The surface simply throbbed, hugely swollen, a warm, sticky fluid trickling down it. The fluid was blood. He was bleeding from the nose, the mouth, the ears. He was sensible enough to realize that these slight movements of his hand, this exploration of his injury, caused the bleeding.

His skull had been fractured. It was possible, considering the swelling, that his nose and cheekbones also had been shattered but he recognized the bleeding from his nose and ears and mouth as a sign that he had suffered a fractured skull when the cannon exploded in his face. And now he remembered that: Affonso leading the charge up the hill, Mpanzu and Henriqué racing after the retreating Nsundi into the sanctuary of the forest, his firing the cannon to slow Affonso's charge and give Mpanzu and Henriqué time to get away, the cannon exploding in his face. He lowered his hand to his chest and opened his eyes.

It was day, a leaden gray day but with occasional beams of sunlight striking through breaks in the clouds. Was it the same day the cannon exploded or days later? He rolled his head to the side and looked over the edge of the veranda. A Portuguese soldier was standing in his line of sight, taking off his helmet, wiping sweat from his face. The soldier moved on and then a procession of women and old men and children went by, carrying brush and firewood. Two soldiers followed them, shouting harshly in Portuguese, and then also passed from view. From what he could see, without raising his head and looking around and starting the bleeding again, he judged that the veranda on which he lay belonged to one of the burned-out houses at the west end of Mbouila's market square, not far from the main gate. He tried to push up on an elbow to look toward the market square.

"You must not do that, my lord. You will start the bleeding again."

Gil recognized the voice. Nuno and also Gonçalo were on the veranda with him. They must have returned with Affonso's conquering army and had found him lying among the dead and dying. One of them mopped away the blood trickling from his nose with a damp cloth.

"Help me," Gil croaked and sucked in his breath and bit his lip and, with Nuno's arm around him, managed to sit up.

Hordes of people were huddled in the muddy market square, some squatting on their heels, some kneeling, some restlessly squirming, some sprawled face down in the rain puddles. Portuguese soldiers and Kongo warriors stood guard over them. The buildings around the square were in ruins; smoke from the fires that had ruined them still swirled from them like a gray fog or low-lying clouds, but the rainy season was drawing to a close. The shafts of bright sunlight that struck through the overcast glittered in the smoke, mocking the misery of the people huddled in the square. They were captives, of course, the rebel warriors and their women and children who had not managed to get away. How many were they? Five or six, perhaps seven hundred, of which about half were warriors, the rest women and children. So almost a thousand fighting men had gotten away, to fight again in some other place, on another day. He tried to see if Henriqué and Mpanzu were among them or were among the lucky ones who had gotten away. He couldn't. His head throbbed dreadfully from the effort of sitting up, his sight was clouded, he was near swooning with pain. A twenty-foot-tall wooden cross loomed over the square—as an emblem of Christianity's triumph over the heathen Nsundi? Bishop de Sousa was standing by the cross while that procession of women and old men and children he had seen piled the brush and firewood they carried at its base.

"The bleeding has started again, my lord," Nuno said and again wiped Gil's face with a damp cloth. "You must lie down."

Gil pushed the cloth away and squinted hard at the brush and firewood piled up at the base of the cross. What was it for? It looked vaguely familiar. But then he saw Fernão de Mello and forgot about it.

With the hood of his cloak pulled over his head, eternally cold, and his hands tucked into the cloak's sleeves, the tall, gaunt, spectral man, now governor of the Kongo, was threading his way, seemingly aimlessly, through captives in the square. Rodrigues, his cutlass drawn, swinging it viciously to clear a path through the close-packed bodies, walked a step in front of him. And a step behind, no longer wearing his fighting headdress or his war paint but still barefoot and clad only in a kanga, came Affonso, unhurt but looking utterly done in. He glanced over toward Gil, but his gaze was unfocused and he didn't notice that Gil had regained consciousness and was sitting up. He stopped when de Mello stopped and went on when de Mello went on, as if in a trance.

As Gil watched, straining forward in Nuno's arms, de Mello stopped to consider a group of forlorn captives huddled on their knees in the shadow of the cross. They cringed away from him, their eyes downcast, their naked flesh shivering with fright. Withdrawing his hands from the sleeves of his cloak, de Mello pulled one of them to his feet, a young warrior, and ran his long, bony fingers over the warrior's shivering flesh, testing its firmness and the tone of the muscle underneath. Then he glanced back at Affonso. Wearily, grimly, his scar flaring, Affonso nodded. Rodrigues called over a halberdier.

And a woman screamed and jumped up. A little girl hiding between her legs was knocked over into the mud by the sudden movement and let out a pitiful cry. Rodrigues grabbed the woman and flung her back down beside the child. The child clutched at her, and together, lying in the mud, they screamed and cried. They were the woman and child of the warrior who had been selected and he looked back at them with unbearable sorrow when the halberdier led him away.

He led him out through the village's main gate. A score of other young warriors were already out there, crouched in the burned grass near the exploded cannon. They were chained together by iron collars around their necks. A fire was burning near them with an anvil beside it and a Portuguese blacksmith was relentlessly hammering out chains and iron collars on the anvil. And although it must have still been hot, the smith fastened a newly made collar around the neck of this latest warrior to be selected and brought out to him, and added him to the coffle crouched in the burned grass.

Gil looked back at de Mello. He now had the warrior's woman on her feet and was feeling her naked body with no special relish, indeed with a certain disgust. And then, again with Affonso's assent, she too was led away by a Portuguese soldier. The coffle to which she was added, consisting of young women, was located inside the main gate, from where she could see her husband but not touch him, from where she could call to him but not hear his response. The blacksmith who made the chains and collars for the men also made them for the women. The little girl, left behind in the mud, wailed and screamed for her parents until an old woman who was not selected picked her up. De Mello moved on.

Gil slumped back into Nuno's arms and closed his eyes. His nose was bleeding again, blood trickled from his ears, he tasted blood in his mouth, his head felt as if it must split in two. He was badly hurt, perhaps fatally, but nonetheless he understood what was going on. Affonso was selling those poor devils into slavery, selling them to de Mello to fill the holds of King Manoel's ships, selling them as payment for the treasure of those ships. But he was making sure he was selling only those he was entitled to sell: captives taken in a war. Had Henriqué been taken captive in this war? Had Mpanzu? Gil opened his eyes again.

And saw Beatriz. Like Nuno and Gonçalo, she must have come from Mpangala with Affonso's army and was now standing out there in the mud of the square among the captives. Gil immediately saw why she was there. Henriqué *had* been taken captive. He was squatting on his heels, his face turned away from his mother, who was bending down to him, her hand gripping his shoulder, talking to him with a fierce urgency. Not far from them was Mpanzu. And also Mfidi. They all had been taken captive. And now de Mello, his hands again tucked into his cloak sleeves, Affonso behind him, Rodrigues clearing a path for him with his cutlass, was making his way toward them.

Beatriz spun around and ran to Affonso, threw herself against him and began pounding his chest with her fists. He grabbed her wrists and held her away while watching, with his dazed, exhausted expression, de Mello and Rodrigues continue toward Henriqué. Beatriz screamed into her brother's face, twisted her hands from his grasp and dashed back to her son, putting herself between him and de Mello. She was trying to protect Henriqué, Gil realized; she was trying to shield him from the selection.

"Mbemba," Gil shouted.

But it really wasn't a shout; it was only a strangled cry choked off by his own blood and no one, except Nuno and Gonçalo, heard it. So he struggled to stand up, struggled to go to Affonso. And although they were against this and muttered warnings that he would only injure himself further by this, Nuno and Gonçalo helped him. But once he was on his feet, his knees gave way, and going forward to the veranda steps, he stumbled and fell down the steps. The commotion this caused attracted the attention his feeble cries couldn't, and Affonso turned to him and Beatriz came rushing over. Nuno lifted him into a sitting position on the bottom veranda step.

"Save our son," Beatriz pleaded, dropping to her knees in front of Gil. "Get him away from these slavers."

"Mbemba."

And although this too was an inaudible croak, Affonso saw the look in Gil's eyes and also came over.

"You owe me this, Mbemba."

Affonso squatted on his heels beside Beatriz. "What do you say?"

De Mello had stopped the selection and, with Rodrigues at his side, impatiently slapping his cutlass against his thigh, had turned toward Gil. Bishop de Sousa, standing at the pyre at the base of the cross, also turned to him.

"I cannot hear what you say, Gil."

"Have I not proved my loyalty to you? Did I not find Mpanzu for you?"

"You did."

"Then you owe me the freedom of my son in return."

"He has his freedom. I have forgiven him his treachery and given him his freedom in thanks to you. But he refuses it."

"Refuses it?"

"You must not let him," Beatriz broke in. "You must get him away from them. You must not let him go with them."

"Go with them? Go with who? Where?"

"He says he is their priest," Beatriz went on in a panic. "He says he is the priest of these rebels and must go with them wherever they go. He will even go with them into slavery in Brasil."

Gil looked toward Henriqué. The youth had only just now real-ized that his father was still alive and he looked back at him and smiled his awful melancholy smile.

"We must not let him do this, Gil. We must save him from it. He will not listen to me. He has closed his ears to me. But maybe he will listen to you. Go to him. Speak to him."

Beatriz clutched at Gil's hands, trying to get him to stand. But it was clear he couldn't. Blood was gushing from his nose and ears, his eyes had rolled up in his head.

"I will bring him to you," she said and started to dash away.

"No, Nimi."

She looked back.

"It would do no good. He will not listen to me either. He has made his choice." Gil again looked at the sad smile on his son's face. "He has chosen with Mpanzu against the Portuguese as you and I have chosen with Mbemba for them."

"I never chose for them."

"You did, Nimi. You chose for them when you let them make you a princess in your own land again. And this is the price you must pay for it, the enslavement of your son. Just as the enslavement of all these people is the price Mbemba must pay to make his kingdom part of their wider world."

Affonso stood up and turned his back on Gil.

"The NgangaKongo foretold it," Gil said to him.

And just then a terrible groan arose from the market square as if the people there had heard again their old sorcerer's prophecy.

But it wasn't that. It was that Affonso had raised his hand as a sig-nal to de Mello to resume his selection. And de Mello had gone over to select Mpanzu, their lord and prince.

The huge man, stripped of his fighting regalia and half-naked in a breechclout, did not have to be pulled to his feet. He stood up as soon as de Mello came for him, his mutilated face set in a grimace of defiance. His daughter, Mfidi a Mpanzu, as naked as when Gil had last seen her running away from the cannonades, also stood up and took her father's hand. Although de Mello had walked by him, Henriqué got to his feet as well. Beatriz started to run to him but Affonso stopped her.

"No, *mbakala*," she wailed, struggling in her brother's grip.

Henriqué glanced at her, smiling wanly, then started toward Mpanzu. But apparently he wasn't to go in the same slave coffle as the Nsundi prince. A soldier shoved him back. Mfidi wasn't to be part of Mpanzu's coffle either. But she couldn't be separated from her father so easily; she clung to his hand fiercely. So Rodrigues separated them. He slashed at her hand with his cutlass until he drew blood, and Mpanzu, speaking to her gently, peeled her fingers from his so as to save her from further injury. Even then, she tried to remain at his side, crying pitifully. Henriqué pulled her away and gathered her into his arms and held her as Mpanzu was led away.

But he wasn't led out the main gate to the coffle of his young warriors. He was led to Bishop de Sousa, standing at the pyre at the base of the cross with a breviary in his hands.

"They make the ManiNsundi Catholic, my lord," Nuno whispered in Gil's ear.

And Gil finally remembered what a pyre at the base of a cross was for. "You will allow this cruelty, Mbemba?" he said in his strangled voice. "You will also pay this price to the Portuguese?"

Affonso didn't hear him. He started walking toward Mpanzu. De Mello, his hands again tucked comfortably in the sleeves of his cloak, fell back. Rodrigues signaled to his soldiers and two hurried forward, one carrying a coil of rope, the other a flaming torch. Bishop de Sousa opened his breviary and began to pray.

"They make the lord of the Nsundi Catholic so that no Nsundi will ever again rebel against the Catholic king of the Kongo," Nuno said, holding Gil in his arms.

The soldier with the coil of rope pulled Mpanzu into the pyre and tied him to the cross. Affonso took the torch from the other soldier and Gil closed his eyes when Affonso touched the torch to the pyre and the pyre burst into flames.

EPILOGUE

WITHIN A WEEK of their capture, the 248 Nsundi warriors, their renegade priest, Henriqué Eanes, the 233 Nsundi women and children and the daughter of their prince, Mfidi a Mpanzu, were driven down from the upland savanna through the forest of the Mbata to the five Portuguese ships of King Manoel's plague fleet anchored in the cove in front of Santo Antonio do Zaire. They were driven down under the guard of nearly one thousand Kongo warriors and a hundred Portuguese soldiers because there was then still a real concern that the rebels who had escaped the battle of Mbouila might, under Bernardo's leadership, try to free them somewhere in the rugged terrain along the way. It proved an unnecessary precaution. Evidently, the horror of Mpanzu's death by fire had taken the heart out of the Nsundi rebellion and the 483 slaves, chained together in five separate coffles, reached the coast unmolested on the Feast of the Birth of the Virgin (September 8, 1502), a little more than twenty years after the first Portuguese ship, Diogo Cão's *Leonor,* sailed up the estuary of the Zaire.

What became of those slaves—the first to be taken from the Kongo for transportation across the Atlantic to the new world—no one can say exactly. According to the log of the plague fleet, one of the ships was lost at sea with all hands and cargo during the forty-two days of the rough and terrifying Middle Passage, and more than one hundred Nsundi died between decks on the other ships for lack

of fresh water. But whether Henriqué and Mfidi were among those
lost at sea or among those eventually landed in Brasil is unknown.
The records of the slave auctions in the Portuguese settlement at the
mouth of Brasil's January River contain no names.

Gil Eanes died in Mbouila. For a time, it seemed he might recover from his injuries, but the first attempt to carry him back to São
Salvador caused massive hemorrhaging and he breathed his last without regaining consciousness. Beatriz brought the body home and had
it buried in the floor of the São Salvador cathedral. The death of her
husband and the loss of her son had made her more devout. She refused to acknowledge any illogic in this; in her grief and confusion,
she refused to recognize that the death and loss she mourned were a
consequence of the Faith in which she now sought solace.

With Mpanzu's *auto-da-fé,* the peace he had disrupted was
restored and the kingdom's evangelization and modernization,
promised in King Manoel's *regimento* and the lodestar of Affonso's
reign, could proceed. The price that would have to be paid for it was
now unmistakable, but it was a price that Affonso, dreaming his
dreams of the wider world, was willing to pay so long as the number
of slaves taken in payment remained within reasonable bounds.

But it didn't remain within reasonable bounds. It couldn't. The
rapid settlement and development of the West Indies and Brasil, the
furious competition there between Portugal and the Spains and then
all the rest of Europe, created, in tragically short order, a boundless demand for slaves. And the traffic in them quickly became the main
business of Europe in Africa, generating unheard-of profits, producing
unimaginable fortunes. Virtually every ship that sailed to the Kongo
was a slave ship; virtually every man aboard those ships was a slaver.
Even the masons and carpenters, shopkeepers and soldiers who
came to advance the modernization of the kingdom, even the priests
who came to promote its evangelization, were unable to resist the
huge profits and got into the bloody business. As did the Kongo
themselves. Chiefs and headmen, lords and princes became the in-
dispensable middlemen of the trade, outfitting slaving gangs, organiz-
ing slave markets, selling their own servants and subjects for the
firearms with which to acquire more. And because prisoners of war
could be enslaved, they fomented wars, and because criminals could

be enslaved, they encouraged crime, and soon the few hundred taken at first became thousands and the thousands tens of thousands and, ultimately, millions in the years, in the centuries to come.

"Most powerful and most high prince and king, my brother, how excessive is the freedom given by your officials to the merchants who are allowed to come to this kingdom. We cannot reckon how great is the damage they do. The above-mentioned merchants daily seize our subjects, sons of the land and sons of our noblemen and vassals and relatives. Thieves and men of evil conscience, they grab our people and cause them to be sold; and so great, sir, is their corruption and licentiousness that our country is being utterly depopulated by them."

This is an excerpt from one of what is thought to have been more than a hundred letters—of which twenty-two have survived and can be read in the old royal archives in Lisbon—that Affonso wrote to the Portuguese king to protest the frighteningly swift and, from his standpoint, altogether unexpected and unacceptable escalation of slaving in the Kongo. He started writing directly to Manoel (and then to his successor João III) only after his repeated complaints to Fernão de Mello were repeatedly ignored. But the Portuguese king also repeatedly ignored him. And just how cold-bloodedly can be seen in another of Affonso's surviving letters. It accompanied six youths going to Lisbon to study at the College of Santo Eloi:

"We beg Your Highness to give them shelter and boarding and to treat them in accordance with their rank, as relatives of ours with the same blood. We remind you of this and beg your attention to it because we sent, from this kingdom to yours, ten youngsters who were most gifted to learn the service of God but about whom we do not know so far whether they are alive or dead, nor what happened to them, so that we have nothing to say to their fathers and mothers." Subsequent records show what happened to those ten youngsters. The ship on which they sailed never reached Lisbon. Once clear of the port of Santo Antonio do Zaire, she had made for Rio de Janeiro and the ten youngsters were sold into slavery there.

Cruelly and repeatedly rebuffed in this way—his twenty-two surviving letters form a heartbreaking litany of such rejected requests and disregarded appeals—Affonso made a heroic attempt to reclaim the rule of his kingdom from the slavers. He issued a royal decree banning the slave trade within the borders of his realm, threatening the severest punishment for all those caught participating in it. It was a desperate and ultimately vain command. Not only were the Portuguese slavers prepared to defy it, so were the Kongo slavers.

A conspiracy was hatched. It was acted on on Easter Day. While Affonso was attending Mass, eight Portuguese soldiers armed with arquebuses burst into the São Salvador cathedral. The dowager queen Leonor immediately sensed why they had come and flung herself in front of her son. Two of the shots struck her in the breast and she was killed on the spot. A third shot wounded the queen Inez and a fourth the princess Beatriz. The other four went astray, one blowing off the head of the Christ on the crucifix in the ambulatory. No one ever discovered who the assassins were. They fled the cathedral and were never caught. But the event ended all pretense of an alliance of brothers between the ManiKongo and the king of the Portuguese, and ended as well the last glimmer of Affonso's dream.

It is not known how much longer after this Affonso lived. The date of his death is given in the chronicles variously as ten years later, fifteen, twenty. If he lived that long, he lived long enough to witness the complete destruction of his kingdom. For, by then, slavers both black and white had overrun the Kongo, ravaging its forests, brutalizing its upland savannas, inciting wars between provinces and towns and villages, setting every chief and headman against every other, setting every lord and prince against the king. It wouldn't be until the late nineteenth century that Portugal would impose direct rule over the Kongo, and between then and Affonso's death, the chronicles list the names of fifty successor ManiKongos. But they were mere puppet kings, and their kingdom, mercilessly pillaged and plundered down through the centuries, was a mere ghost of the kingdom that Diogo Cão had chanced upon four hundred years before.